Ship of D

Robin Hobb is one of the world's finest writers of epic fiction. She was born in California in 1952 but raised in Alaska, where she learned how to raise a wolf cub, to skin a moose and to survive in the wilderness. When she married a fisherman who fished herring and the Kodiak salmon-run for half the year, these skills would stand her in good stead. She raised her family, ran a small-holding, delivered post to her remote community, all at the same time as writing stories and novels. She succeeded on all fronts, raising four children and becoming an internationally best-selling writer. She lives in Tacoma, Washington State.

ROBIN HOBB

Book Three of *The Liveship Traders*

HARPER
Voyager

Harper*Voyager*
An imprint of HarperCollins*Publishers*
1 London Bridge Street
London SE1 9GF

www.harpervoyagerbooks.co.uk

HarperCollins*Publishers*
1st Floor, Watermarque Building, Ringsend Road
Dublin 4, Ireland

This paperback edition 2015

10

First published in Great Britain by
Harper*Voyager* 2000

ISBN: 978-0-00-811747-4

Typeset in Sabon by Palimpsest Book Production Ltd, Falkirk, Stirlingshire

Printed and Bound in the UK using 100% Renewable
Electricity at CPI Group (UK) Ltd

MIX
Paper from
responsible sources
FSC **FSC™ C007454**

This one is for Jane Johnson and Anne Groell.
For caring enough to insist that I get it right.

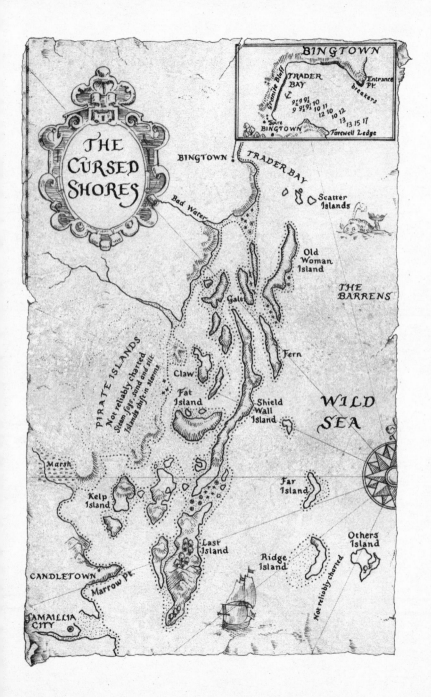

Summer's End

She Who Remembers

She wondered what it would have been like to be perfect.

On the day that she had hatched, she had been captured before she could wriggle over the sand to the cool and salty embrace of the sea. She Who Remembers was doomed to recall every detail of that day with clarity. It was her entire function and the reason for her existence. She was a vessel for memories. Not just her own life, from the moment when she began forming in the egg, but the linked lives of those who had gone before her were nested inside her. From egg to serpent to cocoon to dragon to egg, all memory of her line was hers. Not every serpent was so gifted, or so burdened. Only a relative few were imprinted with the full record of their species, but only a few were needed.

She had begun perfect. Her tiny, smooth body, lithe and scaled, had been flawless. She had cut her way out of the leathery shell with the egg tooth atop her snout. She was a late hatcher. The others in her clutch had already broken free of their shells and the heaped dry sand. They had left their wallowing trails for her to follow. The sea had beckoned her insistently. Every lap of every wave beguiled her. She had begun her journey, slithering across the dry sand under the beating sun. She had smelled the wet tang of the ocean. The moving light on its dazzling surface had lured her.

She had never finished her journey.

The Abominations had found her. They had surrounded her, interposing their heavy bodies between her and the beckoning ocean. Plucked wriggling from the sand, she had been imprisoned in a tide-fed pool inside a cave in the cliffs. There they had kept her, feeding her only dead food and never allowing her to swim free. She had never migrated south with the others to the warm seas where food was plentiful. She had never achieved the bulk and strength that a free life would have granted her. Nevertheless, she grew, until the pool in the cave was little more than a cramped puddle to her, a space barely sufficient to keep her skin and gills wet. Her lungs were pinched always inside her folded coils. The water that surrounded her was constantly befouled with her poisons and wastes. The Abominations had kept her prisoner.

How long had they confined her there? She could not measure it, but she felt certain that she had been captive for several ordinary lifetimes of her kind. Time and again, she had felt the call of the season of migration. A restless energy would come over her followed by a terrible desire to seek out her own kind. The poison glands in her throat would swell and ache with fullness. There was no rest for her at such times, for the memories permeated her and clamoured to be released. She had shifted restlessly in the torment of her small pool and vowed endless revenge against the Abominations who held her so. At such times, her hatred of them was most savage. When her overflowing glands flavoured the water with her ancestral memories, when the water became so toxic with the past that her gasping gills poisoned her with history, then the Abominations came. They came to her prison, to draw water from her pool and inebriate themselves with it. Drunken, they prophesied to one another, ranting and raving in the light of the full moon. They stole the memories of her kind, and used them to extrapolate the future.

Then the two-legs, Wintrow Vestrit, had freed her. He had come to the island of the Abominations, to gather for them the treasures the sea left on the shore. In exchange, he had expected them to prophesy his future for him. Even now, that thought made her mane grow turgid with poison. The Abominations prophesied only what they sensed of the future from stealing her pasts! They had no true gifts of Seeing. If they had, she reflected, they would have known that the two-legs brought their doom. They would have stopped Wintrow Vestrit. Instead, he had discovered her and freed her.

Although she had touched skins with him, although their memories had mingled through her toxins, she did not understand what had motivated the two-legs to free her. He was such a short-lived creature that most of his memories could not even leave an imprint on her. She had sensed his worry and pain. She had known that he risked his brief existence to free her. The courage of such a brief spasm of life had moved her. She had slain the Abominations when they would have recaptured both of them. Then, when the two-legs would have died in the mothering sea, she had aided him to return to his ship.

She Who Remembers opened wide her gills once more. She tasted a mystery in the waves. She had restored the two-legs to his ship, but the ship both frightened and attracted her. The silvery grey hull of the vessel flavoured the water ahead of her. She followed it, drinking in the elusive tang of memories.

The ship smelled, not like a ship, but like one of her own kind. She had followed it now for twelve tides, and was no closer to understanding how such a thing could be. She knew well what ships were; the Elderlings had had ships, though not such as this one. Her dragon memories told her that her kind had often flown over such vessels, and playfully set them to rocking wildly with a gust from wide wings. Ships were no mystery, but this one was. How could a ship give off the scent of a serpent? Moreover, it smelled like no ordinary serpent. It smelled like One Who Remembers.

Again, her duty tugged at her: it was an instinct stronger than the drive to feed or mate. It was time, and past time. She should have been among her own kind by now, leading them in the migration path that her memories knew so well. She should be nourishing their own lesser recall with her potent toxins that would sting their dormant memories to wakefulness. The biological imperative clamoured in her blood. Time to change. She cursed again her crooked green-gold body that wallowed and lashed through the water so awkwardly. She had no endurance to call upon. It was easier to swim in the wall of the ship's wake, and allow its motion to help draw her through the water.

She compromised with herself. As long as the silver ship's course aligned with her own, she would follow it. She would use its momentum to help her move as she gained strength and endurance of her own. She would ponder its mystery and solve it if she could. Yet, she would not let this puzzle distract her from her primary goal. When they drew closer to shore, she would leave the ship and seek out her own kind. She would find tangles of serpents and guide them up the great river to the cocooning grounds. By this time next year, young dragons would try their wings on the summer winds.

So she had promised herself for the first twelve tides that she followed the ship. Midway through the swelling of the thirteenth tide, a sound at once foreign and heart-wrenchingly familiar vibrated her skin. It was the trumpeting of a serpent. Immediately she broke free of the ship's wake and dove down, away from the distractions of the surface waves. She Who Remembers sounded a reply, then held herself in absolute stillness, waiting. No answer came.

Disappointment weighted her. Had she deceived herself? During her captivity, there had been periods when in her anguish she had cried out over and over again, trumpeting until the walls of the cavern rang with her misery. Recalling that bitterness, she lidded her eyes briefly. She would not torment herself. She opened her eyes to her solitude. Resolutely she turned to pursue the ship that represented the only pallid hint of companionship she had known.

The brief pause had only made her more aware of her hampered body's weariness. It took all of her will to make her push on. An instant later, all weariness fled as a white serpent flashed by her. He did not seem to notice her in his single-minded pursuit of the ship. The odd scent of the vessel must have confused him. Her hearts thundered wildly. 'Here I am!' she called after him. 'Here. I am She Who Remembers. I have come to you at last!'

The white swam on in effortless undulations of his thick, pale body. He did not even turn his head to her call. She stared in shock, then hastened after him, her weariness temporarily forgotten. She dragged herself after him, gasping with the effort.

She found him shadowing the ship. He slipped about in the dimness beneath it, muttering and mewling incomprehensibly at the planks of the ship's hull. His mane of poisonous tendrils was semi-erect; a faint stream of bitter toxins tainted the water around him. A slow horror grew in She Who Remembers as she watched his senseless actions. From the depths of her soul every instinct she had warned against him. Such strange behaviour hinted of disease or madness.

But he was the first of her own kind that she had seen since the day she had hatched. The drawing of that kinship was more powerful than any revulsion and so she eased closer to him. 'Greetings,' she ventured timidly. 'Do you seek One Who Remembers? I am She.'

In reply, his great red eyes spun antagonistically, and he darted a warning snap at her. 'Mine!' he trumpeted hoarsely. 'Mine. My food.' He pressed his erect mane against the ship,

7

leaking toxins against her hull. 'Feed me,' he demanded of the ship. 'Give food.'

She retreated hastily. The white serpent continued his nuzzling quest along the ship's hull. She Who Remembers caught a faint scent of anxiety from the ship. Peculiar. The whole situation was as odd as a dream, and like a dream, it teased her with possible meanings and almost understandings. Could the ship actually be reacting to the white serpent's toxins and calls? No, that was ridiculous. The mysterious scent of the vessel was confusing both of them.

She Who Remembers shook out her own mane and felt it grow turgid with her potent poisons. The act gave her a sense of power. She matched herself against the white serpent. He was larger than she was, and more muscled, his body fit and knowledgeable. But that did not matter. She could kill him. Despite her stunted body and inexperience, she could paralyse him and send him drifting to the bottom. In the next moment, despite the powerful intoxication of her own body's secretions, she knew she was even stronger than that. She could enlighten him and let him live.

'White serpent!' she trumpeted. 'Heed me! I have memories to share with you, memories of all our race has been, memories to sharpen your own recollections. Prepare to receive them.'

He paid no heed to her words. He did not make himself ready, but she did not care. This was her destiny. For this, she had been hatched. He would be the first recipient of her gift, whether he welcomed it or not. Awkwardly, hampered by her stunted body, she launched herself towards him. He turned to her supposed attack, mane erect, but she ignored his petty toxins. With an ungainly thrust, she wrapped him. At the same moment, she shook her mane, releasing the most powerful intoxicant of them all, the deep poisons that would momentarily subdue his own mind and let the hidden mind behind his life open itself once more. He struggled frantically, then suddenly grew stiff as a log in her grip. His whirling ruby eyes grew still but unlidded, bulging from their sockets in shock. He made one abortive effort to gulp a final breath.

It was all she could do to hold him. She wrapped his length in hers and kept him moving through the water. The ship began to pull away from them, but she let it go, almost without reluctance. This single serpent was more important to her than all the mysteries the ship concealed. She held him, twisting her neck to look into his face. She watched his eyes spin, then grow still again. Through a thousand lifetimes, she held him, as the past of his entire race caught up with him. For a time, she let him steep in that history. Then she eased him out of it, releasing the lesser toxins that quieted his deeper mind and let his own brief life come back to the forefront of his thoughts.

'Remember.' She breathed out the word softly, charging him with the responsibilities of all his ancestors. 'Remember and be.' He was quiescent in her coils. She felt his own life suddenly repossess him as a tremor shimmered down his length. His eyes suddenly spun and then focused on hers. He reared his head back from hers. She waited for his worshipful thanks.

The gaze that met hers was accusing.

'Why?' he demanded suddenly. 'Why now? When it is too late for all of us? Why couldn't I die ignorant of all that I could have been? Why could not you have left me a beast?'

His words shocked her so that she relaxed her grip on him. He whipped himself disdainfully free of her embrace and he shot away from her through the water. She was not sure if he fled, or if he abandoned her. Either thought was intolerable. The awakening of his memories should have filled him with joy and purpose, not despair and anger.

'Wait!' she cried after him, but the dim depths swallowed him. She wallowed clumsily after him, knowing she could never match his swiftness. 'It can't be too late! No matter what, we must try!' She trumpeted the futile words to the empty Plenty.

He had left her behind. Alone again. She refused to accept

it. Her stunted body floundered through the water in pursuit, her mouth open wide to taste the dispersing scent he had left behind. Faint, fainter, and then gone. He was too swift; she was too deformed. Disappointment welled in her, near stunning as her own poisons. She tasted the water again. Nothing of serpent tinged it now.

She cut wider and wider arcs through the water in a desperate search for his scent trail. When she finally found it, both her hearts leapt with determination. She lashed her tail to catch up with him. 'Wait!' she trumpeted. 'Please. You and I, we are the only hope for our kind! You must listen to me!'

The taste of serpent grew suddenly stronger. *The only hope for our kind.* The thought seemed to waft to her on the water, as if the words had been breathed to the air rather than trumpeted in the depths. It was the only encouragement she needed.

'I come to you!' she promised, and drove herself on doggedly. But when she reached the source of the serpent scent, she saw no creature save for a silver hull cutting the waves above her.

ONE

The Rain Wilds

MALTA DUG HER makeshift paddle into the gleaming water and pushed hard. The little boat edged forwards through the water. Swiftly she transferred the cedar plank to the other side of the craft, frowning at the beads of water that dripped from it into the boat when she did so. It couldn't be helped. The plank was all she had for an oar, and rowing on one side of the boat would only spin them in circles. She refused to imagine that the acid drops were even now eating into the planking underfoot. Surely, a tiny bit of Rain Wild River water could not do much damage. She trusted that the powdery white metal on the outside of the boat would keep the river from devouring it, but there was no guarantee of that, either. She pushed the thought from her mind. They had not far to go.

She ached in every limb. She had worked the night through, trying to make their way back to Trehaug. Her exhausted muscles trembled with every effort she demanded of them. Not far to go, she told herself yet again. Their progress had been agonizingly slow. Her head ached abominably but worst was the itching of the healing injury on her forehead. Why must it always itch the worst when she could not spare a hand to scratch?

She manoeuvred the tiny rowing boat among the immense trunks and spidering roots of the trees that banked the Rain

Wild River. Here, beneath the canopy of rainforest, the night sky and its stars were a myth rarely glimpsed; yet a fitful twinkling drew her on through the trunks and branches. The lights of the tree-borne city of Trehaug guided her to warmth, safety, and most of all, rest. Shadows were still thick all around her, yet the calls of birds in the high treetops told her that in the east, dawn was lightening the sky. Sunlight would not pierce the thick canopy until later, and when it came, it would be as shafts of light amidst a watery green mockery of sunshine. Where the river sliced a path through the thick trees, day would glitter silver on the milky water of the wide channel.

The nose of the rowing boat snagged suddenly on top of a hidden root. Again. Malta bit her tongue to keep from screaming her frustration. Making her way through the forested shallows was like threading the craft through a sunken maze. Time and time again, drifts of debris or concealed roots had turned her aside from her intended path. The fading lights ahead seemed little closer than when they had set out. Malta shifted her weight and leaned over the side to probe the offending obstacle with her plank. With a grunt, she pushed the boat free. She dipped her paddle again and the boat moved around the hidden barrier.

'Why don't you paddle us over there, where the trees are thinner?' demanded the Satrap. The erstwhile ruler of all Jamaillia sat in the stern, his knees drawn nearly to his chin, while his Companion Kekki huddled fearfully in the bow. Malta didn't turn her head. She spoke in a cold voice. 'When you're willing to pick up a plank and help with the paddling or steering, you can have a say in where we go. Until then, shut up.' She was sick of the boy-Satrap's imperious posturing and total uselessness for any practical task.

'Any fool can see that there are fewer obstacles there. We could go much faster.'

'Oh, much faster,' Malta agreed sarcastically. 'Especially if the current catches us and sweeps us out into the main part of the river.'

The Satrap took an exasperated breath. 'As we are upriver of the city, it seems to me that the current is with us. We could take advantage of it and let it carry us where I want to go, and arrive much more swiftly.'

'We could also lose control of the boat completely, and shoot right past the city.'

'Is it much farther?' Kekki whined pathetically.

'You can see as well as I can,' Malta retorted. A drop of the river water fell on her knee as she shifted the paddle to the other side. It tickled, then itched and stung. She took a moment to dab at it with the ragged hem of her robe. The fabric left grit in its wake. It was filthy from her long struggle through the halls and corridors of the buried Elderling city the previous night. So much had happened since then, it seemed more like a thousand nights. When she tried to recall it, the events jumbled in her mind. She had gone into the tunnels to confront the dragon, to make her leave Reyn in peace. But there had been the earthquake, and then when she had found the dragon . . . The threads of her recall snarled hopelessly at that point. The cocooned dragon had opened Malta's mind to all the memories stored in that chamber of the city. She had been inundated in the lives of those who had dwelt there, drowned in their recollections. From that point until the time when she had led the Satrap and his Companion out of the buried labyrinth, all was misty and dreamlike. Only now was she piecing together that the Rain Wild Traders had hid the Satrap and Kekki away for their own protection.

Or had they? Her gaze flicked briefly to Kekki cowering in the bow. Had they been protected guests, or hostages? Perhaps a little of both. She found that her own sympathies were entirely with the Rain Wilders. The sooner she returned Satrap Cosgo and Kekki to their custody, the better. They were valuable commodities, to be employed against the Jamaillian nobles, the New Traders and the Chalcedeans. When she had first met the Satrap at the ball, she had been briefly dazzled by the illusion of his power. Now she knew his elegant garb and aristocratic manners were only a veneer over a useless, venal boy. The sooner she was rid of him, the better.

She focused her eyes on the lights ahead. When she had led the Satrap and his companion out of the buried Elderling city, they had found themselves far from where Malta had originally entered the underground ruins. A large stretch of quagmire and marshy river shallows separated them from the city. Malta had waited for dark and the guiding lights of the city before they set out in their ancient salvaged boat. Now dawn threatened and she still poled towards the beckoning lanterns of Trehaug. She fervently hoped that her ill-conceived adventure was close to an end.

The city of Trehaug was located amongst the branches of the huge-boled trees. Smaller chambers dangled and swung in the uppermost branches, while the grander family halls spanned trunk to trunk. Great staircases wound up the trunks, and their landings provided space for merchants, minstrels and beggars. The earth beneath the city was doubly cursed with marshiness and the instability of this quake-prone region. The few completely dry pieces of land were mostly small islands around the bases of trees.

Steering her little boat amongst the towering trees towards the city was like manoeuvring around the immense columns in a forgotten god's temple. The boat again fetched up against something and lodged. Water lapped against it. It did not feel like a root. 'What are we snagged against?' Malta asked, peering forwards.

Kekki did not even turn to look, but remained hunched over her folded knees. She seemed afraid to put her feet on the boat's floorboards. Malta sighed. She was beginning to think something was wrong with the Companion's mind. Either the experiences of the past day had turned her senses, or, Malta reflected wryly, she had always been stupid and it took only adversity to manifest it. Malta set her plank down and, crouching low, moved forwards in the boat. The rocking this created caused both the Satrap and Kekki to cry out in alarm. She ignored them. At close range, she was able to see that the boat had nosed into a dense mat of twigs, branches and other river debris, but in the gloom, it was hard to see the extent of it. She supposed some trick of the current had carried it here and packed it into this floating morass. It was too thick to force the small boat through it. 'We'll have to go around it,' she announced to the others. She bit her lip. That meant venturing closer to the main flow of the river. Well, as the Satrap had said, any current they encountered would carry them downriver to Trehaug, not away from it. It might even make her thankless task easier. She pushed aside her fears. Awkwardly she turned their rowing boat away from the raft of debris and towards the main channel.

'This is intolerable!' Satrap Cosgo suddenly exclaimed. 'I am dirty, bitten by insects, hungry and thirsty. And it is all the fault of these miserable Rain Wild settlers. They pretended that they brought me here to protect me. But since they have had me in their power, I have suffered nothing but abuse. They have affronted my dignity, compromised my health, and endangered my very life. No doubt, they intend to break me, but I shall not give way to their mistreatment of me. The full weight of my wrath will descend upon these Rain Wild Traders. Who, it occurs to me, have settled here with no official recognition of their status at all! They have no legal claims to the treasures they have been digging up and selling. They are no better than the pirates that infest the Inside Passage and should be dealt with accordingly.'

Malta found breath to snort derisively. 'You are scarcely in a position to bark at anyone. In reality, you are relying on their good will far more than they are relying on yours. How easy it would be for them to sell you off to the highest bidder, regardless of whether the buyer would assassinate you, hold you hostage, or restore you to your throne! As for their claim to these lands, that came directly from the hand of Satrap Esclepius, your ancestor. The original charter for the Bingtown Traders specified only how many leffers of land each settler could claim, not where. The Rain Wild Traders staked their claims here; the Bingtown Traders took theirs by Bingtown Bay. Their claims are both ancient and honourable, and well documented under Jamaillian law. Unlike those of the New Traders you have foisted off on us.'

For a moment, shocked silence greeted her words. Then the Satrap forced a brittle laugh. 'How amusing to hear you defend them! Such a benighted little bumpkin you are. Look at yourself, dressed in rags and covered with filth, your face forever disfigured by these renegades! Yet you defend them. Why? Ah, let me guess. It is because you know that no whole man would ever want you now. Your only hope is to marry into a family in which your kin are as misshapen as yourself, where you can hide behind a veil and no one will stare at your frightfulness. Pathetic! But for the actions of these rebels, I might have chosen you as a Companion. Davad Restart had spoken out on your behalf, and I found your clumsy attempts at dancing and conversation endearingly provincial. But now? Faugh!' The boat rocked minutely with the disdainful flip of his hand. 'There is nothing more freakish than a beautiful woman whose face has been spoiled. The finer families of Jamaillia would not even take you as a household slave. Such disharmony has no place in an aristocratic household.'

Malta refused to look back at him, but she could imagine how his lips curled with contempt. She tried to be angry at his arrogance; she told herself he was an ignorant prig of a boy. But she had not seen her own face since the night she had nearly been killed in the overturning coach. When she had been convalescing in Trehaug, they had not permitted her a mirror. Her mother and even Reyn had seemed to dismiss the injuries to her face. But they would, her traitor heart told her. They would have to, her mother because she was her mother, and Reyn because he felt responsible for the coach accident. How bad was the scar? The cut down her forehead had felt long and jagged to her questing fingers. Now she wondered: did it pucker, did it pull her face to one side? She gripped the plank tightly in both her hands as she dug into the water with it. She would not set it down; she would not give him the satisfaction of seeing her fingers grope over her scar. She set her teeth grimly and paddled on.

A dozen more strokes and suddenly the little vessel picked up speed. It gave a small sideways lurch in the water, and then spun once as Malta dug her plank into the water in a desperate effort to steer back into the shallows. She shipped her makeshift oar, and seized the extra plank from the bottom of the rowing boat. 'You'll have to steer while I paddle,' she told the Satrap breathlessly. 'Otherwise we'll be swept out into the middle of the river.'

He looked at the plank she thrust towards him. 'Steer?' he asked her, taking the board reluctantly.

Malta tried to keep her voice calm. 'Stick that plank into the water behind us. Hold onto one end of it and use it as a drag to turn us back towards the shallows while I paddle in that direction.'

The Satrap held the board in his fine-boned hands as if he had never seen a piece of wood before. Malta seized her own plank, thrust it back into the water, and was amazed at the sudden strength of the current. She clutched the end awkwardly as she tried to oppose the flow of water that was sweeping them away from the shore. Morning light touched them as they emerged from the shelter of the overhanging trees. Suddenly the sunlight illuminated the water, making it unbearably bright after the dimness. Behind her, an annoyed exclamation coincided with a splash. She swivelled her head to see what had happened. The Satrap was empty-handed.

'The river snatched it right out of my hands!' he complained.

'You fool!' Malta cried out. 'How can we steer now?'

The Satrap's face darkened with fury. 'How dare you speak to me so! You are the fool, to think it could have done us any good in the first place. It wasn't even shaped like an oar. Besides, even if it would have worked, we do not need it. Use your eyes, wench. We've nothing to fear. There's the city now! The river will carry us right to it.'

'Or past it!' Malta spat at him. She turned from him in disgust, to focus all her strength and thoughts on her single-handed battle with the river. She lifted her eyes briefly to the impressive site of Trehaug. Seen from below, the city floated in the great trees like a many-turreted castle. On the water level, a long dock was tethered to a succession of trees. The Kendry was tied up there, but the liveship's bow was turned away from them. She could not even see the sentient figurehead. She paddled frantically.

'When we get closer,' she panted between strokes, 'call out for help. The ship may hear us, or people on the docks. Even if we are swept past, they can send rescue after us.'

'I see no one on the docks,' the Satrap informed her snidely. 'In fact, I see no one anywhere. A lazy folk, to be still abed.'

'No one?' Malta gasped the question. She simply had no strength left for this final effort. The board she wielded skipped and jumped across the top of the water. With every passing moment, they were carried farther out into the river. She lifted her eyes to the city. It was close, much closer than it had been a moment ago. And the Satrap was right. Smoke rose from a few chimneys, but other than that, Trehaug looked deserted. A profound sense of wrongness welled up in her. Where was everyone? What had become of the normal lively bustle along the catwalks and on the stairways?

'Kendry!' she cried out, but her breathless call was thin. The rushing water carried her voice away with it.

Companion Kekki seemed suddenly to understand what was

happening. 'Help! Help!' she cried in a childish shriek. She stood up recklessly in the small boat, waving her hands. 'Help us! Save me!' The Satrap swore as the boat rocked wildly. Malta lunged at the woman and pulled her down into the boat again, nearly losing her plank in the process. A glance around her showed her that the plank was of no real use now. The little boat was well and truly into the river's current and rapidly being swept past Trehaug.

'Kendry! Help! Help us! Out here, in the river! Send rescue! Kendry! Kendry!' Her shouts trailed away as hopelessness dragged at her.

The liveship gave no sign of hearing. Another moment, and Malta was looking back at him. Apparently lost in deep thought, the figurehead was turned towards the city. Malta saw a lone figure on one of the catwalks, but he was hurrying somewhere and never turned his head. 'Help! Help!' She continued to shout and wave her plank while she could see the city, but it was not for long. The trees that leaned out over the river soon curtained it from her eyes. The current rushed them on. She sat still and defeated.

Malta took in her surroundings. Here, the Rain River was wide and deep, the opposite shore near lost in permanent mist. The water was grey and chalky when she looked over the side. Overhead the sky was blue, bordered on both sides by the towering rainforest. There was nothing else to be seen, no other vessels on the water, no signs of human habitation along the banks. As the clutching current bore them inexorably away from the marshy shores, hopes of rescue receded. Even if she succeeded in steering their little boat to the shore, they would be hopelessly lost downriver of the city. The shores of the Rain Wild River were swamp and morass. Travelling overland back to Trehaug was impossible. Her nerveless fingers dropped the plank into the bottom of the boat. 'I think we're going to die,' she told the others quietly.

* * *

Keffria's hand ached abominably. She gritted her teeth and forced herself to seize again the handles of the barrow the diggers had just finished loading. When she lifted the handles and began to trundle her load up the corridor, the pain in her healing fingers doubled. She welcomed it. She deserved it. The bright edges of it could almost distract her from the burning in her heart. She had lost them, both her younger children gone in one night. She was as completely alone in the world as she had ever been.

She had clung to doubt for as long as she could. Malta and Selden were not in Trehaug. No one had seen them since yesterday. A tearful playmate of Selden had sobbingly admitted that he had shown the boy a way into the ancient city, a way the grown-ups had thought securely locked. Jani Khuprus had not minced words with Keffria. White-faced, lips pinched, she had told Keffria that the particular passage had been abandoned because Reyn himself had judged it dangerously unstable. If Selden had gone into the buried corridors, if he had taken Malta with him, then they had gone into the area most likely to collapse in an earthquake. There had been at least two large tremors since dawn. Keffria had lost track of how many lesser tremblings she had felt. When she had begged that diggers be sent that way, they had found the entire corridor collapsed just a few steps inside the entry. She could only pray to Sa that her children had reached some stronger section of the buried city before the quake, that somewhere they huddled together awaiting rescue.

Reyn Khuprus had not returned. Before noon, he had left the diggers, refusing to wait until the corridors could be cleared and shored up. He had gone ahead of the work crews, wriggling off through a mostly collapsed tunnel and disappearing. Not long ago, the work crews had reached the end of the line he had left to mark his way. They had found several chalk marks, including the notation he had left on the door of the Satrap's chamber.

Hopeless, Reyn had marked. Thick muck oozed from under the blocked door; most likely the entire room had filled with it. Not far past that door, the corridor had collapsed completely. If Reyn had passed that way, he had either been crushed in the downfall, or was trapped beyond it.

Keffria started when she felt a touch on her arm. She turned to face a haggard Jani Khuprus. 'Have you found anything?' Keffria asked reflexively.

'No.' Jani spoke the terrible word softly. Her fear that her son was dead lived in her eyes. 'The corridor is mucking in as fast as we try to clear it. We've decided to abandon it. The Elder ones did not build this city as we build ours, with houses standing apart from each other. The ancients built their city like one great hive. It is a labyrinth of intersecting corridors. We will try to come at that section of corridor from a different approach. The crews are already being shifted.'

Keffria looked at her laden barrow, then back down the excavated corridor. Work had stopped. The labourers were returning to the surface. As Keffria stared, a flow of dirty and tired men and women parted to go around her. Their faces were grey with dirt and discouragement, their footsteps dragged. The lanterns and torches they carried fluttered and smoked. Behind them, the excavation had gone dark. Had all of this work been useless, then? She took a breath. 'Where shall we dig now?' she asked quietly.

Jani gave her a haunted look. 'It has been decided we should rest for a few hours. Hot food and a few hours of sleep will do us all good.'

Keffria looked at her incredulously. 'Eat? Sleep? How can we do either when our children are missing still?'

The Rain Wild woman matter-of-factly took Keffria's place between the barrow handles. She lifted it and began to push it forwards. Keffria trailed reluctantly after her. She did not answer Keffria's question, except to say, 'We sent birds out to some of the closer settlements. The foragers and harvesters of the Rain Wilds will send workers to aid us. They are on their way, but it will take some time for them to arrive. Fresh workers will shore up our spirits.' Over her shoulder, she added, 'We have had word from some of the other digging crews, also. They have had more luck. Fourteen people were rescued from an area we call the Tapestry Works, and three more were discovered in the Flame Jewel corridors. Their work has progressed more swiftly. We may be able to gain access to this area of the city from one of those locations. Bendir is already consulting with those who know the city best.'

'I thought Reyn knew the old city better than anyone?' Keffria asked cruelly.

'He did. He does. That is why I cling to the hope that he may be alive.' The Rain Wild Trader glanced at her Bingtown counterpart. 'It is why I believe that if anyone could find Malta and Selden, it is Reyn. If he found them, he would not try to come back this way, but would make for the more stable parts of the city. With every breath I take, I pray that soon someone will come running to give us the tidings that they have emerged on their own.'

They had reached a large chamber that looked like an amphitheatre. The work crews had been dumping the tailings of their work here. Jani tipped the barrow and let the load of earth and rocks increase the untidy pile in the middle of the formerly grand room. Their wheelbarrow joined a row of others. Muddy shovels and picks had been tumbled in a heap nearby. Keffria suddenly smelled soup, coffee, and hot morning bread. The hunger she had been denying woke with a roar. The sudden clamouring of her body made her recall that she had eaten nothing all night. 'Is it dawn?' she asked Jani suddenly. How much time had passed?

'Well past dawn, I fear,' Jani replied. 'Time always seems fleetest when I most long for it to move slowly.'

At the far end of the hall, trestle tables and benches had been set out. The very old and the very young worked there, ladling soup into dishes, tending small braziers under bubbling pots, setting out and clearing away plates and cups. The immense chamber swallowed the discouraged mutter of talk. A child of about eight hurried up with a basin of steaming water. A towel was slung over her arm. 'Wash?' she offered them.

'Thank you.' Jani indicated the basin to Keffria. She laved her hands and arms and splashed her face. The warmth made her realize how cold she was. The binding on her broken fingers was soaked and gritty. 'That needs to be changed,' Jani observed while Keffria used the towel. Jani washed, and again thanked the child, before guiding Keffria towards several tables where healers were plying their trade. Some were merely salving blistered hands or massaging aching backs, but there was also an area where broken limbs and bleeding injuries were being treated. The business of clearing the collapsed corridor was hazardous work. Jani settled Keffria at a table to await her turn. A healer was already at work re-bandaging her hand when Jani returned with morning bread, soup and coffee for both of them. The healer finished swiftly, abruptly told Keffria that she was off the work detail and moved on to his next patient.

'Eat something,' Jani urged her.

Keffria picked up the mug of coffee. The warmth of it between her palms was oddly comforting. She took a long drink from it. As she set it down, her eyes wandered over the amphitheatre. 'It's all so organized,' she observed in confusion. 'As if you expected this to happen, planned for it –'

'We did,' Jani said quietly. 'The only thing that puts this collapse out of the ordinary is the scale of it. A good quake usually brings on some falls. Sometimes a corridor will collapse for no apparent reason. Both my uncles died in cave-ins. Almost every Rain Wild family who works the city loses a member or two of each generation down here. It is one of the reasons my husband Sterb has been so adamant in urging the Rain Wild Council to aid him in developing other sources of wealth for us. Some say he is only interested in establishing his own fortune. As a younger son of a Rain Wild Trader's grandson, he has little claim to his own family's wealth. But I truly believe it is not self-interest but altruism that makes him work so hard at developing the foragers' and harvesters' outposts. He insists the Rain Wild could supply all our needs if we but opened our eyes to the forest's wealth.' She folded her lips and shook her head. 'Still. It does not make it any easier when he says, "I warned you all" when something like this happens. Most of us do not want to forsake the buried city for the bounty of the rainforest. The city is all we know, the excavating and exploration. Quakes like this are the danger we face, just as you families who trade upon the sea know that eventually you will lose someone to it.'

'Inevitable,' Keffria conceded. She picked up her spoon and began to eat. A few mouthfuls later, she set it down.

Across from her, Jani set down her coffee mug. 'What is it?' she asked quietly.

Keffria held herself very still. 'If my children are dead, who am I?' she asked. Cold calmness welled up in her as she spoke. 'My husband and eldest son are gone, taken by pirates, perhaps already dead. My only sister has gone after them. My mother remained behind in Bingtown when I fled; I know not what has become of her. I only came here for the sake of my children. Now they are missing, and perhaps already dead. If I alone survive –' She halted, unable to frame a thought to deal with that possibility. The immensity of it overwhelmed her.

Jani gave her a strange smile. 'Keffria Vestrit. But the turning of a day ago, you were volunteering to leave your children in my care, and return to Bingtown, to spy on the New Traders for us. It seems to me that you then had a very good sense of who you were, independent of your role as mother or daughter.'

Keffria propped her elbows on the table and leaned her face into her hands. 'And this now feels like a punishment for that.

If Sa thought I undervalued my children, might he not take them from me?'

'Perhaps. If Sa had but a male aspect. But recall the old, true worship of Sa. Male and female, bird, beast, and plant, earth, fire, air and water, all are honoured in Sa and Sa manifests in all of them. If the divine is also female, and the female also divine, then she understands that woman is more than mother, more than daughter, more than wife. Those are the facets of a full life, but no single facet defines the jewel.'

The old saying, once so comforting, now rang hollow in her ears. But Keffria's thoughts did not linger on it long. A great commotion at the entrance to the hall turned both their heads. 'Sit still and rest,' Jani advised her. 'I'll see what it's about.'

But Keffria could not obey her. How could she sit still and wonder if the disruption were caused by news of Reyn or Malta or Selden? She pushed back from the table and followed the Rain Wild Trader.

Weary and bedraggled diggers clustered around four young-sters who had just slung their buckets of fresh water to the floor. 'A dragon! A great silver dragon, I tell you! It flew right over us.' The tallest boy spoke the words as if challenging his listeners. Some of the labourers looked bemused, others disgusted by this wild tale.

'He's not lying! It did! It was real, so bright I could hardly look at it! But it was blue, a sparkly blue,' amended a younger boy.

'Silver-blue!' a third boy chimed in. 'And bigger than a ship!' The lone girl in the group was silent, but her eyes shone with excitement.

Keffria glanced at Jani, expecting to meet her annoyed glance. How could these youngsters allow themselves to bring such a frivolous tale at a time when lives weighed in the balance? Instead, the Rain Wild woman's face had gone pale. It made the fine scaling around her eyes and lips stand out against her face. 'A dragon?' she faltered. 'You saw a dragon?'

Sensing a sympathetic ear, the tall boy pushed through the crowd towards Jani. 'It was a dragon, such as some of the frescoes showed. I'm not making it up, Trader Khuprus. Something made me look up, and there it was. I couldn't believe my eyes. It flew like a falcon! No, no, like a shooting star! It was so beautiful!'

'A dragon,' Jani repeated dazedly.

'Mother!' Bendir was so dirty that Keffria scarcely recognized him as he pushed through the crowd. He glanced at the boy standing before Jani, and then to his mother's shocked face. 'So you've heard. A woman who was tending the babies up above sent a boy running to tell us what she had seen. A blue dragon.'

'Could it be?' Jani asked him brokenly. 'Could Reyn have been right all along? What does it mean?'

'Two things,' Bendir replied tersely. 'I've sent searchers overland, to where I think the creature must have broken out of the city. From the description, it is too large to have moved through the tunnels. It must have burst out from the Crowned Rooster Chamber. We have an approximate idea of where that was. There may be some sign of Reyn there. At the least, there may be another way we can enter the city and search for survivors.' A mutter of voices rose at his words. Some were expressing disbelief, others wonder. He raised his voice to be heard above them. 'And the other thing is that we must remember that this beast may be our enemy.' As the boy near him began to protest, Bendir cautioned him, 'No matter how beautiful it may seem, it may bear us ill will. We know next to nothing of the true nature of dragons. Do nothing to anger it, but do not assume it is the benign creature we see in the frescoes and mosaics. Do not call its attention to you.'

A roar of conversation rose in the chamber. Keffria caught at Jani's sleeve desperately. She spoke through the noise. 'If you find Reyn there . . . do you think Malta may be with him?'

Jani met her eyes squarely. 'It is what he feared,' she said.

'That Malta had gone to the Crowned Rooster Chamber. And to the dragon that slept there.'

'I've never seen anything so beautiful. Do you think she will come back?' Weakness as well as awe made the boy whisper.

Reyn turned to regard him. Selden crouched on an island of rubble atop the mud. He stared up at the light above them, his face transfigured by what he had just witnessed. The newly released dragon was gone, already far beyond sight, but still the boy stared after her.

'I don't think we should count on her to return and save us. I think that is up to us,' Reyn said pragmatically.

Selden shook his head. 'Oh, I did not mean that. I would not expect her to notice us that much. I expect we'll have to get ourselves out of here. But I should like to see her, just once more. Such a marvel she was. Such a joy.' He lifted his eyes once more to the punctured ceiling. Despite the dirt and muck that streaked his face and burdened his clothes, the boy's expression was luminous.

Sun spilled into the ruined chamber, bringing weak light but little additional warmth. Reyn could no longer recall what it felt like to be dry, let alone warm. Hunger and thirst tormented him. It was hard to force himself to move. But he smiled. Selden was right. A marvel. A joy.

The dome of the buried Crowned Rooster Chamber was cracked like the top of a soft-boiled egg. He stood atop some of the fallen debris and looked up at dangling tree roots and the small window of sky. The dragon had escaped that way, but he doubted that he and Selden would. The chamber was filling rapidly with muck as the swamp trickled in to claim the city that had defied it for so long. The flow of chill mud and water would engulf them both long before they could find a way to reach the egress above them.

Yet bleak as his situation was, he still marvelled at the

27

memory of the dragon that had emerged from her centuries of waiting. The frescoes and mosaics that he had seen all his life had not prepared him for the reality of the dragon. The word 'blue' had gained a new meaning in the brilliance of her scales. He would never forget how her lax wings had taken on strength and colour as she pumped them. The snake-stench of her transformation still hung heavy in the moist air. He could see no remnants of the 'wizardwood log' that had encased her. She appeared to have absorbed it all as she metamorphosed into a mature dragon.

But now she was gone. And the problem of survival remained for Reyn and the boy. The earthquakes of the night before had finally breached the walls and ceilings of the sunken city. The swamps outside were bleeding into this chamber. The only means of escape was high overhead, a tantalizing window of blue sky.

Mud bubbled wetly at the edge of the piece of fallen dome Reyn stood on. Then it triumphed, swallowing the edges of the crystal and slipping towards his bare feet.

'Reyn.' Selden's voice was hoarse with his thirst. Malta's little brother perched atop a slowly-sinking island of debris. In the dragon's scrabbling effort to escape, she had dislodged rubble, earth, and even a tree. It had fallen into the sunken chamber and some of it still floated on the rising tide of muck. The boy knit his brows as his natural pragmatism reasserted itself. 'Maybe we could lift up that tree and prop it up against the wall. Then, if we climbed up it, we could –'

'I'm not strong enough,' Reyn broke into the boy's optimistic plan. 'Even if I were strong enough to lift the tree, the muck is too soft to support me. But we might be able to break off some of the smaller branches and make a sort of raft. If we can spread out our weight enough, we can stay on top of this stuff.'

Selden looked hopefully up at the hole where light seeped in. 'Do you think the mud and water will fill up this room and lift us up there?'

'Maybe,' Reyn lied heartily. He surmised that the muck would stop far short of filling the chamber. They would probably suffocate when the rising tide swallowed them. If not, they would eventually starve here. The piece of dome under his feet was sinking rapidly. Time to abandon it. He jumped from it to a heap of fallen earth and moss, only to have it plunge away under him. The muck was softer than he had thought. He lunged towards the tree trunk, caught one of its branches, and dragged himself out and onto it. The rising mire was at least chest-deep now, and the consistency of porridge. If he sank into it, he would die in its cold clutch. His move had brought him much closer to Selden. He extended a hand towards the boy, who leaped from his sinking island, fell short, and then scrabbled over the soft mud to reach him. Reyn pulled him up onto the fallen evergreen's trunk. The boy huddled shivering against him. His clothing was plastered to his body with the same mud that streaked his face and hair.

'I wish I hadn't lost my tools and supplies. But they're long buried now. We'll have to break these branches off as best we can and pile them up in a thick mat.'

'I'm so tired.' The boy stated it as a fact, not a complaint. He glanced up at Reyn, then stared at him. 'You don't look so bad, even up close. I always wondered what you looked like under that veil. In the tunnels, with only the candle, I couldn't really see your face. Then, last night, when your eyes were glowing blue, it was scary at first. But after a while, it was like, well, it was good to see them and know you were still there.'

Reyn laughed easily. 'Do my eyes glow? Usually that doesn't happen until a Rain Wild man is much older. We just accept it as a sign of a man reaching full maturity.'

'Oh. But in this light, you look almost normal. You don't have many of those wobbly things. Just some scales around your eyes and mouth.' Selden stared at him frankly.

'No, not any of those wobbly things yet. But they, too, may come as I get older.' Reyn grinned.

'Malta was afraid you were going to be all warty. Some of her friends teased her about it, and she would get angry. But . . .' Selden suddenly seemed to realize that his words were not tactful. 'At first, I mean, when you first started courting her, she worried about it a lot. Lately, she hasn't talked about it much,' he offered encouragingly. He glanced at Reyn, then moved away from him along the tree trunk. He seized a branch and tugged at it. 'These are going to be tough to break.'

'I imagine she's had other things on her mind,' Reyn muttered. The boy's words brought a sickness to his heart. Did his appearance matter that much to Malta? Would he win her with his deeds, only to have her turn away from him when she saw his face? A bitter thought came to him. Perhaps she was already dead, and he would never know. Perhaps he would die, and she would never even see his face.

'Reyn?' Selden's voice was tentative. 'I think we'd better get to work on these branches.'

Reyn abruptly realized how long he had hunkered there in silence. Time to push useless thoughts aside and try to survive. He seized a needled branch in his hands and broke a bough from it. 'Don't try to break the whole branch off at once. Just take boughs from it. We'll pile them up there. We want to intermesh them, like thatching a roof –'

A fresh trembling of the earth broke his words. He clung to the tree trunk helplessly as a shower of earth rained down from the ruptured ceiling. Selden shrieked and threw his arms up to protect his head. Reyn scrabbled along the branchy trunk to reach him and shelter him with his body. The ancient door of the chamber groaned and suddenly sagged on its hinge. A flow of mud and water surged into the room from behind it.

TWO

Traders and Traitors

THE LIGHT SCUFF of footsteps was her only warning. In the kitchen garden, Ronica froze where she crouched. The sounds were coming up the carriageway. She seized her basket of turnips and fled to the shelter of the grape arbour. Her back muscles kinked protestingly at the sudden movement, but she ignored them. She'd rather be careful of her life than of her back. Silently she set the basket at her feet. Unbreathing, she peered through the hand-sized leaves of the vines. From their screening shelter, she could see a young man approaching the front entry of the house. A hooded cloak obscured his identity and his furtive manner proclaimed his intentions.

He climbed the leaf-littered steps. At the door he hesitated, his boots grating on broken glass as he peered into the darkened house. He pushed at the big door that hung ajar. It scraped open and he slipped into the house.

Ronica took a deep breath and considered. He was probably just a scavenger, come to see if there was anything left to plunder. He would soon find there was not. What the Chalcedeans had not carried off, her neighbours had. Let him prowl through the ravaged house, and then he would leave. Nothing left in the house was worth risking herself. If she confronted him, she could be hurt. She tried to tell herself that there was nothing to gain. Still, she found herself gripping the cudgel that was now her constant companion as she edged towards the front door of her family home.

Her feet were silent as she picked her way up the debris-strewn steps and through the glass fragments. She peered around the door, but the intruder was out of sight. Soundlessly, she slipped inside the entry hall. She froze there, listening. She heard a door open somewhere deeper inside the house. This villain seemed to know where he was going; was he someone she knew, then? If he was, did he mean well? She considered that unlikely. She was no longer confident of old friends and alliances. She could think of no one who might expect to find her at home.

She had fled Bingtown weeks ago, the day after the Summer Ball. The night before, the tension over Chalcedean mercenaries in the harbour had suddenly erupted. Rumours that the Chalcedeans were attempting a landing while the Old Traders were engaged in their festivities had raced through the gathering. It was a New Trader plot, to take the Satrap hostage and overthrow Bingtown; so the gossip flew. The rumour was enough to ignite fires and riots. The Old and New Traders had clashed with one another and against the Chalcedean mercenaries in their harbour. Ships were attacked and burned, and the tariff docks, symbol of the Satrap's authority, went up in flames yet again. But this time, the fires spread through the restless town. Angry New Traders set the elite shops along Rain Wild Street aflame. New Trader warehouses were torched in vengeance, and then someone set the Bingtown Traders' Concourse alight.

Meanwhile, the battle in the harbour raged. The Chalcedean galleys that had been resident in the harbour masquerading as Jamaillian patrol vessels made up one arm of the pincers. The Chalcedean ships that had arrived bringing the Satrap made up the other half. Caught between them were Bingtown liveships and trading vessels and the larger fishing vessels of the Three Ships immigrants. In the end, the rallying of the small boats of the Three Ships folk had turned the tide of battle. In the dark, the tiny fishing vessels could slip up on the large Chalcedean sailing ships. Suddenly pots of burning oil and tar shattered against the hulls of the ships or were lobbed onto the decks. Abruptly the Chalcedean ships were too engaged in putting out fires to contain the ships in the harbour. Like gnats harrying bulls, the tiny boats had persisted in attacking the ships blocking the harbour mouth. Chalcedean fighters on the docks and in Bingtown were horrified to see their own ships driven from Bingtown Harbour. Abruptly the cut-off invaders were fighting for their lives. The running battle had continued as the Bingtown ships pursued the Chalcedeans into the open water.

In the morning, after the sounds of riot and insurrection had died away, smoke snaked through the streets on the summer breeze. Briefly, Bingtown Traders controlled their own harbour again. In the lull, Ronica had urged her daughter and grandchildren to flee to the Rain Wilds for shelter. Keffria, Selden and the badly injured Malta had managed to escape on a liveship. Ronica herself remained behind. She had a few personal tasks to settle before seeking her own asylum. She had secreted the family papers in the hiding place Ephron had devised long ago. Then she and Rache had hastily gathered clothing and food and set out for Ingleby Farm. That particular Vestrit family holding was far away from Bingtown, and humble enough that Ronica believed they would find safety there.

Ronica had made one brief detour that day, returning to where Davad Restart's carriage had been ambushed the night before. She'd left the road and clambered down the forested hillside, past his overturned carriage to Davad's body. She had covered him with a cloth, since she had not the strength to take his body away for burial. He had been estranged from his extended family, and Ronica knew better than to ask Rache's help in burying him. This last pitiful respect was all she could offer a man who had been both a loyal friend for most of her life and a dangerous liability to her these last few years. She tried to find words to say over his body, but ended up shaking her head. 'You weren't a traitor, Davad. I know that. You were greedy, and your greed made you foolish, but I won't ever believe you deliberately betrayed Bingtown.' Then she had trudged back up to the road to rejoin Rache. The serving woman said nothing about the man who had made her a slave. If she took any satisfaction in Davad's death, she didn't speak it aloud. For that, Ronica was grateful.

The Chalcedean galleys and sailing ships did not immediately return to Bingtown Harbour. Ronica had hoped that peace would descend. Instead, a more terrible sort of fighting ignited between Old Trader and New, as neighbour turned on neighbour, and those with no loyalties preyed on anyone weakened by the civil discord. Fires broke out throughout the day. As Ronica and Rache fled Bingtown, they passed burning houses and overturned waggons. Refugees choked the roads. New Traders and Old Traders, servants and run-away slaves, merchants and beggars and Three Ships fisherfolk; all were fleeing the strange war that had suddenly blossomed in their midst. Even those abandoning Bingtown clashed as they fled. Taunts and insults were flung between groups. The jubilant diversity of the sunny city by the blue harbour had shattered into sharply suspicious fragments. Their first night on the road, Ronica and Rache were robbed, their sacks of food spirited away as they slept. They continued their journey, believing they had the stamina to reach the farm even without food. Folk on the road told tales that the Chalcedeans had returned and that all of Bingtown was burning. In the early evening of the second day, several hooded young men accosted them and demanded their valuables. When Ronica replied that they had none, the ruffians pushed her down and ransacked her bag of clothing before flinging her belongings contemptuously into the dusty road. Other refugees hurried past them, eyes averted. No one intervened. The highwaymen threatened Rache, but the slave woman endured it stoically. The bandits had finally left to pursue wealthier prey, a man with two servants and a heavily-laden handcart. The two servants had fled the robbers, leaving the man to plead and shout as the thieves ransacked his cart. Rache had tugged frantically at Ronica's arm and dragged her away. 'There is nothing we can do. We must save our own lives.'

Her words were not true. The next morning proved that. They came upon the bodies of the teashop woman and her daughter. Other fleeing folk were stepping around the bodies as they hurried past. Ronica could not. She paused to look into the woman's distorted face. She did not know her name, but recalled her tea stall in the Great Market. Her daughter had always served Ronica smilingly. They had not been Traders, Old or New, but humble folk who had come to the gleaming trade city and become a small part of Bingtown's diversity. Now they were dead. Chalcedeans had not killed these women; Bingtown folk had.

That was the moment when Ronica turned around and returned to Bingtown. She could not explain it to Rache, and had even encouraged the woman to go on to Ingleby without her. Even now, Ronica could not rationalize the decision. Perhaps it was that nothing worse could happen to her than what had already happened. She returned to find her own home vandalized and ransacked. Even the discovery that someone had scratched TRAITORS across the wall of Ephron's study could stir no greater depth of distress in her. Bingtown as she knew it was gone, never to return. If it was all going to perish, perhaps it was best to end with it.

Yet she was not a woman who simply surrendered. In the days to come, she and Rache set up housekeeping in the gardener's hut. Their life was oddly normal in a detached way. Fighting continued in the city below them. From the upper storey of the main house, Ronica could just glimpse the harbour and the city. Twice the Chalcedeans tried to take it.

Both times, they were repulsed. Night winds often carried the sounds of fighting and the smell of smoke. None of it seemed to involve her any more.

The small hut was easy to keep warm and clean, and its humble appearance made it less of a target for roving looters. The last of the kitchen garden, the neglected orchard and the remaining chickens supplied their limited needs. They scavenged the beach for driftwood that burned with green and blue flames in their small hearth. When winter closed in, Ronica was not sure what she would do. Perish, she supposed. But not gracefully, or willingly. No. She would go down fighting.

That same stubbornness now made her tread carefully down the hallway in pursuit of the intruder. She grasped her cudgel in both hands. She had no clear plan for what she would do if or when she confronted the man. She simply wanted to know what motivated this lone opportunist who moved so secretively through her abandoned home.

Already the manor was acquiring the dusty smell of disuse. The Vestrit family's finest possessions had been sold earlier in the summer, to finance a rescue effort for their pirated liveship. The treasures that remained had been those with more sentimental than monetary value: the trinkets and curiosities that were souvenirs of Ephron's sailing days, an old vase that had been her mother's, a wall hanging that she and Ephron had chosen together when they were newly wed . . . Ronica turned her mind away from that inventory. They were all gone now, broken or taken by people who had no idea what such items represented. Let them go. She held the past in her heart, with no need of physical items to tie it down.

She tiptoed past doors that had been kicked off their hinges. She spared only a glance for the atrium where overturned pots and browning plants littered the floor as she hastened after the hooded man. Where was he going? She caught a glimpse of his cloak as he entered a room.

Malta's room? Her granddaughter's bedchamber?

Ronica crept closer. He was muttering to himself. She ventured a quick peek, then stepped boldly into the room to demand, 'Cerwin Trell, what are you doing here?'

With a wild cry, the young man leapt to his feet. He had been kneeling by Malta's bed. A single red rose rested on her pillow. He stared at Ronica white-faced, his hand clutching at his breast. His mouth worked, but no sounds came out. His eyes travelled to the club in her hand and widened even more.

'Oh, sit down,' Ronica exclaimed in exasperation. She tossed the club to the foot of the bed and took her own advice. 'What are you doing here?' she asked wearily. She was sure she knew the answer.

'You're alive,' Cerwin said softly. He lifted his hands to his face and rubbed at his eyes. Ronica knew he sought to hide his tears. 'Why didn't you . . . Is Malta safe, too? Everyone said . . .'

Cerwin sank down to sit beside his rose on Malta's bed. He set his hand gently on her pillow. 'I heard you had left the ball with Davad Restart. Everyone knows his coach was waylaid. They were only after the Satrap and Restart. That is what everyone says, that they would have left you alone if you had not been travelling with Restart. I know Restart's dead. Some claim to know what became of the Satrap, but they are not telling. Every time I asked about Malta and the rest of you . . .' He faltered suddenly, and his face flushed, but he forced himself to go on. 'They say you were traitors, that you were in on it with Restart. The rumour is that you planned to turn the Satrap over to New Traders who were going to kill him. Then the Bingtown Traders would be blamed for his death, and Jamaillia would send Chalcedean mercenaries in to take over our town and deliver it to the New Traders.' He hesitated, then steeled himself to go on, 'Some say that you got what you deserved. They say terrible things and I . . . I thought you were all dead. Grag Tenira spoke up for your family, saying that was nonsense. But since he left on the Ophelia to help guard the Rain Wild River mouth, no one has taken your part. I tried, once, but . . . I am young. No one listens. My father gets angry with me for even speaking of Malta. When Delo wept about her, he confined her to her room and said he would whip her if she even uttered her name again. And he's never whipped Delo before.'

'What is he afraid of?' Ronica asked bluntly. 'That folk will label you as traitors for caring what became of your friends?'

Cerwin bobbed his head in a sudden nod. 'Father was not pleased when Ephron took Brashen on after our family had disowned him. Then you made him captain of the Paragon and sent him off as if you actually believed he could save Vivacia. Father took it that you were trying to show us up, to prove that you straightened out the son he threw away.'

'What utter nonsense!' Ronica exclaimed in disgust. 'I did nothing of the kind. Brashen straightened himself out, and your father should be proud of him, not angry with the Vestrits over that. But I take it that he is satisfied to see us branded as traitors?'

Cerwin looked at the floor, ashamed. The dark eyes he finally lifted to hers were very like his older brother's. 'You're right, I'm afraid. But please, torment me no longer. Tell me. Did Malta escape harm? Is she hiding here with you?'

Ronica considered for a long moment. How much of the truth should she entrust to him? She had no wish to torture the boy, but she would not endanger her family for the sake of his feelings. 'When last I saw Malta, she was injured, but not dead. Small thanks to the men who attacked us and then left her for dead! She, her mother and brother are hiding in a safe place. And that is all I'm going to tell you.'

She didn't admit that she knew little more than that herself. They had gone off with Reyn, Malta's Rain Wild suitor. If all had gone as planned, then they had reached the Kendry in safety, and escaped Bingtown Harbour and then sailed up the Rain Wild River. If all had gone well, they were safe in Trehaug. The trouble was that very little had gone well lately, and there was no way for them to send Ronica word. All she could do was trust to Sa that she had been merciful.

Relief welled up in Cerwin Trell's face. He reached to touch the rose he had left on Malta's pillow. 'Thank you,' he whispered fervently. Then he spoiled it by adding, 'At least I now can cling to hope.'

Ronica repressed a grimace. She could see that Delo had not inherited all the melodramatic tendencies in the Trell family. She changed the subject firmly. 'Tell me what is happening in Bingtown now.'

He looked startled by the sudden request. 'Well, but, I don't know that much. Father has been keeping our whole family close to home. He still believes this will all blow past somehow, and then Bingtown will go on as before. He will be furious if he discovers I've slipped away. But I had to, you know.' He clutched at his heart.

'Of course, of course. What did you see on the way here? Why does your father keep you close to home?'

The boy knit his brows and stared down at his well-kept hands. 'Well, right now, the harbour is ours again. That could change any time, though. The Three Ships folk have been helping us, but while all the ships are fighting, no one is fishing or bringing goods to market. So food is starting to be dear, especially as so many of the warehouses were burned.

'In Bingtown, there has been looting and plundering. People have been beaten and robbed simply for trying to do business. Some say the culprits are New Trader gangs, others say they are escaped slaves out for anything they can get. The Market is deserted. Those who dare to open their doors to do business run many risks. Serilla had the City Guard seize what was left of the Satrap's tariff dock. She wanted the message birds kept there, so that she might send word and receive tidings from Jamaillia. But most of the birds had died in the fire and smoke. The men she posted there did intercept a returning bird recently, but she would not share what tidings it brought. Some parts of the city are held by New Traders, some parts by Old. The Three Ships and other groups are caught between. At night, there are clashes.

'My father is angry that no one is negotiating. He says that real Traders know that almost everything can be solved by the right bargain. He says that proves that the New Traders are to blame for everything that has happened, but they, of course, blame us. They say we kidnapped the Satrap. My father believes you were going to help kidnap the Satrap so they could kill him and blame it on us. Now the Old Traders squabble among themselves. Some want us to recognize Companion Serilla's authority to speak for the Satrap of Jamaillia; others say it is time that Bingtown shook off Jamaillian authority entirely. The New Traders claim that we are ruled by Jamaillia still, but they won't recognize Serilla's documents. They beat the messenger she sent to them under a truce flag, and sent him back with his hands bound behind him and a scroll tied to his throat. It accused her of treason and being a party to the plot to overthrow the Satrap. They said our aggression against the Satrap and his lawful patrol boats provoked the violence in the harbour and turned our Chalcedean allies against us.' He licked his lips and added, 'They threatened that when the time came and strength was on their side, they would show no mercy.'

Cerwin paused for breath. His young face looked older as he went on. 'It's a mess and not getting better. Some of my friends want to arm themselves and simply drive the New Traders into the sea. Roed Caern says we should kill any of them who won't leave. He says we must take back what they stole from us. Many of the Traders' sons agree with him. They say that only when the New Traders are gone can Bingtown go back to being Bingtown. Some say we should round up the New Traders and give them a choice of leaving, or death. Others talk of secret reprisals against those who dealt with the New Traders, and burning the New Traders out to force them to leave. I've heard rumours that Caern and his friends go out a great deal at night.' He shook his head miserably. 'That is why my father tries to keep me close to home. He doesn't want me involved.' He met Ronica's eyes suddenly. 'I am not a coward. But I don't want to *be* involved.'

'In that, you and your father are wise. Nothing will be resolved that way. It will only justify them in more violence against us.' Ronica shook her head. 'Bingtown will never be Bingtown again.' She sighed and asked, 'When is the next Bingtown Council meeting?'

Cerwin shrugged. 'They have not met at all since this began. At least, not formally. All the liveship Traders are out chasing Chalcedeans. Some of the Traders have fled the city; others have fortified their homes and never leave them. Several times the heads of the Council have gathered with Serilla, but she has urged them to delay calling a meeting. She wishes to reconcile with the New Traders and use her authority as the Satrap's representative to restore peace. She wishes to treat with the Chalcedeans, also.'

Ronica was silent for a moment. Her lips tightened. This Serilla, it seemed to her, was taking entirely too much authority to herself. What were the tidings she had concealed? Surely the sooner the Council met and formulated a plan to restore order, the sooner the city could heal. Why would she oppose that?

'Cerwin. Tell me this. If I went to Serilla, do you think she would speak to me? Or do you think they would kill me as a traitor?'

The young man looked at Ronica with dismay. 'I don't know,' he admitted. 'I no longer know what my own friends are capable of doing. Trader Daw was found hanged. His wife and children have disappeared. Some say he killed himself when he saw that fortunes were going against him. Others say his brothers-in-law did it, out of shame. No one talks much of it.'

Ronica was silent for a time. She could huddle here in the remains of her home, knowing that if she were murdered, folk would not talk much of it. Or she could find a different place to hide. But winter was coming, and she had already decided that she would not perish gracefully. Perhaps confrontation was all that was left. At least she would have the satisfaction of speaking her piece before someone killed her. 'Can you carry a message to Serilla for me? Where is she staying?'

'She has taken over Davad Restart's house. But, please, I don't dare carry a message. If my father found out –'

'Of course.' She cut him off abruptly. She could shame him into it. All she need do was imply that Malta would think him a coward if he did not. She would not use the boy to test the waters. What sense was there in sacrificing Cerwin to insure her own safety? She would go herself. She had cowered at home long enough.

She stood up. 'Go home, Cerwin. And stay there. Listen to your father.'

The young man stood slowly. His gaze travelled over her, and then he looked away, embarrassed for her. 'Do you . . . are you doing well here, by yourself? Have you enough to eat?'

'I'm fine. Thank you for asking.' She felt oddly touched by his concern. She looked down at her garden-stained hands and her dirt-caked nails. She restrained an impulse to put her hands behind her.

He took a breath. 'Will you tell Malta that I came, that I was worried about her?'

'I will. The next time I see her. But that may not be for quite a long time. Now go home. Obey your father after this. I am sure he has enough worries without you putting yourself in danger.'

That made him stand up a bit straighter. A smile touched his mouth. 'I know. But I had to come, you see. I could know no peace until I discovered what had become of her.' He paused. 'May I tell Delo, also?'

The girl was one of the worst gossips in Bingtown. Ronica decided that Cerwin did not know enough about anything to be a threat. 'You may. But plead with her to keep it to herself. Ask her not to speak of Malta at all. It is the greatest favour she can do her friend. The fewer people who wonder about Malta, the safer she is.'

Cerwin frowned dramatically. 'Of course. I see.' He nodded to himself. 'Well. Farewell, Ronica Vestrit.'

'Farewell, Cerwin Trell.'

Only a month ago, it would have been unthinkable for him to be in this room. The civil war in Bingtown had turned everything topsy-turvy. She watched him go, and it seemed that he carried the last of that old familiar life away with him. All the rules that had governed her had fallen. For an instant, she felt as desolate and plundered as the room she stood in. Then an odd sense of freedom washed over her. What had she left to lose? Ephron was dead. Ever since her husband's death, her familiar world had been crumbling away. Now it was gone, and only she remained. She could make her own way now. Without Ephron and the children, little of the old life mattered to her.

She might as well make the new one interesting, as long as it was going to be unpleasant anyway.

After the boy's footsteps in the tiled passage had died away, Ronica left Malta's bedchamber and walked slowly through the house. She had avoided coming here since the day they had returned and found it raided. Now she forced herself to walk through each room and look at the corpse of her world. The heavier furniture and some of the hangings and drapes remained. Almost everything else of value or use had been carried off. She and Rache had salvaged some kitchen ware and bedding, but all the simple items that made living gracious were gone. The plates they set on the bare wooden table did not match, and no linens protected her from the rough wool of her blankets. Yet, life went on.

As her hand fell on the latch of the kitchen door, she noticed one wax-sealed pot that had fallen on its side and rolled into a corner. She stooped down to retrieve it. It was leaking a little. She licked her sticky finger. Cherry preserves. She smiled ruefully, then tucked it into the crook of her arm. She would take this last bit of sweetness with her.

'Lady Companion?'

Serilla lifted her eyes from the map she was perusing. The serving boy at the door of the study looked deferentially at his feet. 'Yes?' she acknowledged him.

'There is a woman to see you.'

'I'm busy. She will have to come back at a better time.' She was mildly annoyed with him. He should have known she did not want any other visitors today. It was late, and she had spent all the afternoon in a stuffy room full of Traders, trying to make them see sense. They quibbled over the most self-evident things. Some were still insisting that there must be a vote of the Council before they would recognize her authority over them. Trader Larfa had quite rudely suggested that Bingtown should settle Bingtown matters, with no advice from Jamaillia. It was most frustrating. She had shown them the authorization that she had extorted from the Satrap. She had written it herself, and knew it to be unchallengeable. Why would they not admit that she held the authority of the Satrap, and that Bingtown was subject to the Satrap's authority?

She consulted the Bingtown chart once more. So far, the Traders had been able to keep their harbour open, but it was at the expense of all trade. The town could not long survive those circumstances. The Chalcedeans knew that very well. They did not have to rush in and control Bingtown immediately. Trade was the lifeblood of Bingtown and the Chalcedeans were slowly but surely strangling it.

The stubborn Traders were the ones who refused to see the

obvious. Bingtown was a single settlement on a hostile coast. It had never been able to feed itself. How could it stand up to the onslaught of a warlike country like Chalced? She had asked that of the Council leaders. They replied that they had done it before and would do it again. But those other times, the might of Jamaillia backed them. And they had not had to contend with New Traders in their midst who might welcome a Chalcedean invasion. Many New Traders had close ties with Chalced, for that was the major market for the slaves they funnelled through Bingtown.

She considered again the bird-message Roed Caern had intercepted and brought to her. It had promised a Jamaillian fleet would soon set out to take revenge on the corrupt and rebellious Old Traders for the murder of the Satrap. Just to think of it made Serilla cold. The message had arrived too soon. No bird could fly that fast. To her, it meant that the conspiracy was widespread, extending to the nobility of Jamaillia City itself. Whoever had sent the bird to Jamaillia had expected that the Satrap would be murdered and that evidence would point to the Old Traders. The swiftness of the reply indicated that those who responded had been awaiting the message.

The only question was how extensive the conspiracy was. Even if she could root out the source of it, she did not know if she could destroy it. If only Roed Caern and his men had not been so hasty the night that they seized the Satrap. If Davad Restart and the Vestrits had survived, the truth might have been wrung from them. They might have revealed who of the Jamaillian nobility were involved in this. But Restart was dead and the Vestrits missing. She'd get no answers there.

She pushed the chart to one side and replaced it with an elegant map of Bingtown. The finely-inked and illustrated work was one of the wonders she'd discovered in Restart's library. In addition to the original grants of all the Old Traders, with each holding inked in the family's colour, Davad had penned in the main claims of the New Traders.

She studied it, wondering if it might offer some clue to his allies. She frowned over it, then lifted her pen, dipped it, and made a note to herself. She liked the location of Barberry Hill. It would be a convenient summer home for her, once all this strife was settled. It had been a New Trader holding; likely the Bingtown Traders would be glad to cede it to her. Or as the Satrap's representative, she could simply take it.

She leaned back in the immense chair, and wished briefly that Davad Restart had been a smaller man. Everything in this room was oversized for her. Sometimes she felt like a child pretending to be an adult. Sometimes all of Bingtown society seemed to have that effect on her. Her entire presence here was a pose. Her 'authority from the Satrap' was a document she had coerced Satrap Cosgo into signing when he was ill. All her power, all her claims to social stature were based on it. And its power, in turn, was based on the concept that the Satrapy of Jamaillia lawfully ruled over Bingtown. She had been shocked the first time she had realized how prevalent the Bingtown Traders' talk of sovereignty was. It made her supposed status amongst them even more dubious. Perhaps she would have been wiser to have sided with the New Traders. But no, for at least some among them realized that Jamaillia City nobles were trying to shake off the Satrap's authority. If the Satrap's power in the capital was questionable, how tenuous was it here in the Satrapy's farthest province?

It was too late to flinch. She'd made her choice and assumed her role. Now her last, best hope was to play it well. If she succeeded, Bingtown would be her home to the end of her days. That had been her dream ever since as a young woman, she had heard that in Bingtown a woman could claim the same rights as a man.

She rested against the cushions for an instant as her eyes travelled the room. A generous fire burned on the hearth of the study. The light from it and from the many tapers in the room gleamed warmly on the polished wood of the desk. She liked this room. Oh, the drapes were intolerable, and the books in the many cases lining the wall were disorganized and tatty, but all that could be changed. The rustic styling had been unsettling at first, almost annoying, but now that the estate was hers, it made her feel she was truly a part of Bingtown. Most of the Old Trader homes she had seen looked much like this one. She could adapt. She wiggled her toes inside the cosy lambswool slippers she wore. They had been Kekki's, and they were just a bit tight. Idly she wondered if Kekki's feet were cold right now, but no doubt the Rain Wild Traders were taking good care of their noble hostages. She did not restrain her smile of satisfaction. Even in small servings, revenge was sweet. The Satrap probably had not yet discerned that she had arranged his snatching.

'Lady Companion?'

It was the serving boy again. 'I said I was busy,' she reminded him warningly. Bingtown servants had no real concept of deference to their masters. She had studied Bingtown all her life, but nothing in its official history had prepared her for the egalitarian reality. She set her teeth as the boy spoke back to her.

'I told the woman that you were busy,' the boy explained carefully. 'But she insisted she would see you now. She says that you have no right to possess Davad Restart's house. She says that she will give you one chance to explain yourself before she presents this grievance to the Bingtown Council on behalf of Davad's lawful heirs.'

Serilla flung her pen down on the desk. Such words were too much to tolerate from anyone, let alone a servant. 'Davad Restart was a traitor. By his actions, he forfeited all rights to his property. That includes the claims of his heirs as well.' She suddenly realized she was explaining herself to a serving boy. Her temper snapped. 'Tell her to go away, that I have no time to see her, not today, not any day.'

'Tell me that yourself, and we'll have more time to argue it.'

Serilla stared in shock at the old woman framed in the doorway. She was dressed simply, in worn but clean clothes. She wore no jewellery, but her gleaming hair was meticulously neat. Her posture more than her accoutrements proclaimed her Trader status. She looked familiar, but as inter-married as the Bingtown Old Traders were, that did not surprise Serilla. Half of them were their own second cousins. Serilla glared at her. 'Go away,' she said bluntly. She picked up her pen in a show of calmness.

'No. I won't. Not until I have satisfaction.' A cold anger was in the Trader's voice. 'Davad Restart was not a traitor. By branding him as such, you've been able to take over his holdings for yourself. Perhaps you don't mind stealing from a dead man, even one who opened the hospitality of his home to you. But your false accusations have brought disaster to me. The Vestrit family has been attacked and near murdered, I've been driven from my home, my possessions stolen, and all because of your slander. I will not tolerate it longer. If you force me to take this before the Bingtown Council, you will find that power and wealth do not sway justice here as in Jamaillia. All the Trader families were little more than beggars when we came here. Our society is founded on the idea that a man's word binds him, regardless of his wealth. Our survival has depended on our ability to trust one another's word. To give false witness here is more grievous than you can imagine.'

This must be Ronica Vestrit! She looked little like the elegant old woman at the ball. All she had retained was her dignity. Serilla reminded herself that she was the one in authority here. She held that thought until she could believe it. She dared not let anyone question her supremacy. The sooner the old woman was managed, the less trouble for all. Her memory swept her back to her days at the Satrap's court. How had he handled such complaints? She kept her face impassive as she declared, 'You waste my time with this long list of supposed grievances. I will not be bullied by your threats and implications.' She leaned back in her chair, attempting to appear serenely confident. 'Don't you know that you are an accused traitor? To charge in here with your wild accusations is not only foolhardy but ridiculous. You are fortunate I do not have you clapped into chains immediately.' Serilla tried to catch the serving boy's eyes. He should take the hint that he should run for aid. Instead, he only watched the two women with avid interest.

Instead of being cowed, Ronica only became more incensed. 'That might work in Jamaillia, where tyrants are worshipped. But this is Bingtown. Here, my voice is as loud as yours. Nor do we chain folk up without giving them a chance to speak first. I demand the opportunity to address the Bingtown Traders' Council. I want to clear Davad's name, or to be shown the evidence that condemns him. I demand decent burial for his remains in either case.' The old woman advanced into the room. Her bony hands were clenched at her sides. Her eyes roved over the room, her outrage plainly growing as she noted the signs of Serilla's occupancy. Her words became more clipped. 'I want Davad's property surrendered to his heirs. I want my own name cleared, and apology from those who endangered my family. I expect reparations from them as well.' The woman came even closer. 'If you force me to go to the Council, I will be heard. This is not Jamaillia, Companion. Complaints from a Trader, even an unpopular Trader, will not be ignored.'

That scatter-brained serving boy had fled. Serilla longed to go to the door and shout for assistance. But she feared even to stand lest she provoke an attack. Already her traitorous hands were trembling. Confrontation unnerved her now. Ever since – No. She would not think of that now, she would not let it weaken her. To dwell on that was to concede that it had changed her irrevocably. No one had that sort of power over her, no one! She would be strong.

'Answer me!' the woman suddenly demanded. Serilla started

wildly and her flailing hands scattered the papers on the desk. The old woman leaned over the desk, her eyes blazing with anger. 'How dare you sit there and ignore me? I am Ronica Vestrit of the Bingtown Traders. Who do you think you are, to sit in silence and stare at me?'

Ironically, that was the only question that could have broken Serilla from her frozen panic. It was a question she had asked herself often of late. She had rehearsed the answer to her mirror in endless self-validation. She stood. Her voice quavered only slightly. 'I am Serilla, vowed Companion to Satrap Cosgo. More than that, I am his representative here in Bingtown. I have the signed documents to prove it, documents that the Satrap created specifically to deal with this situation. While he is in hiding for his personal safety, my word holds the same force as his, my decisions are what his would be, and my rulings are as binding. I myself have investigated the matter of Davad Restart's treachery, and I have found him guilty of treason. Under Jamaillian law, all he owned is forfeit to the throne. As I represent the throne, I have decided to make use of it.'

For a moment, the old woman looked daunted. Serilla took courage from that evidence of weakness. She picked up her pen once more. Leaning over the desk, she pretended to peruse her notes, then lifted her eyes to the Vestrit woman.

'As of yet, I have found no direct evidence of your treason. I have made no official pronouncement against you. I suggest that you do not goad me to look more deeply into your involvement. Your concerns for a dead traitor do not do you credit. If you are wise, you will leave now.' Serilla dismissed her by looking down at her papers once more. She prayed the woman would just go away. Once she left, Serilla could summon armed men and send them after her. She pressed her toes against the floor to keep her knees from shaking.

Silence lasted. Serilla refused to look up. She waited to hear this Ronica Vestrit trudge away in defeat. Instead, the Trader's fist suddenly slammed down on the desk, making the ink hop in its well. 'You are not in Jamaillia!' Ronica declared harshly. 'You are in Bingtown. And here the truth is fixed by the facts, not by your decree.' Ronica's features were contorted with anger and determination. The Bingtown Trader leaned across the desk, shoving her face close to Serilla's. 'If Davad had been a traitor, there would be proof of it, here, in his records. However foolish he might have been, his accounts were always in order.'

Serilla pressed herself back into the chair. Her heart was hammering, and there was a roaring in her ears. The woman was completely deranged. She sought the will to leap to her feet and flee, but she was paralysed. She glimpsed the serving boy behind Ronica, and then relief engulfed her as she saw several Traders behind him. A few minutes ago, she would have been furious at him for presenting them unannounced. Now she was so pitifully grateful that tears stung her eyes.

'Restrain her!' she implored them. 'She threatens me!'

Ronica swivelled her head to look back at the men. For their part, they seemed shocked into immobility. Ronica straightened slowly, turning her back on Serilla. Her voice was cold with courtesy as she greeted them by their names. 'Trader Drur. Trader Conry. Trader Devouchet. I am glad to see you here. Perhaps now my questions will be answered.'

The expressions that passed over the Traders' faces told Serilla that her situation had not improved. Shock and guilt were quickly masked with polite concern.

Only Trader Devouchet stared at her. 'Ronica Vestrit?' he asked incredulously. 'But I thought . . .' He turned to look at his companions but they had been swifter to compose themselves.

'Is there a problem here?' Trader Drur began but Conry overrode him with, 'I fear we have intruded on a private conversation. We can return later.'

'Not at all,' Ronica answered gravely, as if they had addressed her. 'Unless you think my survival is a problem to be solved by the Companion. The true problem here is one more fit to be resolved by the Traders' Council than by a Satrap's Companion. Gentlemen, as you obviously know, my family has been savagely attacked, and our reputation smeared to the point at which it endangers our lives. Trader Restart has been treacherously murdered, and so maligned after the fact that those who killed him claim they were justified. I am here to demand that the Council investigate this matter and render justice.'

Devouchet's eyes grew stony. 'Justice has already been done. Restart was a traitor. Everyone knows that.'

Ronica Vestrit's face was impassive. 'So I keep hearing. But no one has presented me with one shred of evidence.'

'Ronica, be reasonable,' Trader Drur rebuked her. 'Bingtown is a shambles. We are in the midst of a civil war. The Council has no time to convene on private matters, it must . . .'

'Murder is not a private matter! The Council must answer the complaints of any Bingtown Trader. That was why the Council was formed, to see that regardless of wealth or poor fortune, justice was available to every Trader. That is what I demand. I believe Davad was killed and my family attacked on the basis of a rumour. That is not justice, that is murder and assault. Furthermore, while you believe that the culprit has been punished, I believe the true traitors go free. I don't know what became of the Satrap. However, this woman seems to, by her own admission. I know he was taken by force that night. That scarcely seems to me that he "went into hiding, entrusting his power to her." It seems to me more likely that Bingtown has been dragged into a Jamaillian plot to unseat the Satrap, one that may smear all of us with blame. I have heard that she even wishes to treat with the Chalcedeans. What will she give them, gentlemen, to placate them? What does she have to give them, save what is Bingtown's? She benefits in power and wealth by the Satrap's absence. Have some Traders been tricked into kidnapping the Satrap, for this woman's own ends?

If such is the case, she has led them into treason. Is not that a matter for the Council to judge, if it will not consider Davad Restart's murder? Or are all of those "private matters"?'

Serilla's mouth had gone dry. The three men exchanged uncertain glances. They were being swayed by this mad woman's words. They would turn on her! Behind them, the serving boy lingered near the door, listening curiously. There was movement in the passage beyond him, and then Roed Caern and Krion Trentor entered the room. Tall and lean, Roed towered over his shorter, softer companion. Roed had bound his long black hair back in a tail as if he were a barbarian warrior. His dark eyes had always held a feral glint; now they shone with a predator's lust. He stared at Ronica. Despite the uneasiness the young Trader always roused in her, Serilla felt a sudden wash of relief at his appearance. He, at least, would side with her.

'I heard the name of Davad Restart,' Roed observed harshly. 'If anyone has a dispute with how he ended, they should speak to me.' His eyes challenged Ronica.

Ronica drew herself up and advanced on him fearlessly. She was scarcely as tall as his shoulder. She looked up to meet his eyes as she demanded, 'Trader's son, do you admit the blood of a Trader is on your hands?'

One of the older Traders gasped, and Roed looked startled for an instant. Krion licked his lips nervously. Then, 'Restart was a traitor!' Roed declared.

'Prove it to me!' Ronica exploded. 'Prove it to me, and I'll keep my peace, though I should not. Traitor or not, what was done to Davad was murder, not justice. But more importantly, gentlemen, I suggest you prove it to yourselves. Davad Restart is not the traitor who planned the abduction of a Satrap. He had no need to abduct a man who was guesting in his home! In believing that Davad was a traitor, and that you have destroyed a plot by killing him, you cripple yourself. Whoever is behind your plot, if there ever was a plot, is still alive and free to do mischief. Perhaps you were manipulated into doing exactly what you say you feared: kidnapping the Satrap, to bring the wrath of Jamaillia down on Bingtown?' She struggled, then forced calm into her voice. 'I know Davad was not a traitor. But he may have been a dupe. A sly man like Davad could become the victim of someone slyer still. I suggest you go through Davad's papers carefully, and ask yourself, who was using him? Ask yourself the question that underlies every Trader's actions. Who profited?'

Ronica Vestrit met the eyes of each man in turn. 'Recall all you knew of Davad. Did he ever strike a bargain in which his profit was not certain? Did he ever place himself in physical danger? He was a social blunderer, a man close to being a pariah to both Old Traders and New. Is that the man with the charisma and expertise to engineer a plot against the most powerful man in the world?' She jerked her head disdainfully in Serilla's direction. 'Ask the Companion who fed her the information that led to her assumptions. Match those names against those bargaining through Davad, and you may have a starting place for your suspicions. When you have answers, you can find me at my home. Unless, of course, Trader Caern's son thinks murdering me as well would be the tidiest way to resolve this.' Ronica turned abruptly. Sword-straight and unsmiling, she faced Roed.

Handsome, swarthy Roed Caern looked suddenly pale and ill. 'Davad Restart was thrown clear of the coach. No one intended him to die there!'

Ronica met his angry look with ice. 'Your intentions made small difference. You did not care either way, about any of us. Malta heard what you said the night you left her to die. She saw you, she heard you, and she lived. Small thanks to any of you. Traders, Traders' sons, I believe you have much to think on this evening. Good night to you.'

This ageing woman in the worn clothing still managed to sweep regally from the room. The relief Serilla felt as Ronica left the room was momentary. As she sat back in her chair, she became uncomfortably aware of the faces of the men around her. As she recalled her first words when the Old Traders entered the room, she cringed, and then decided she must defend them. 'That woman is not in her right mind,' she declared in a lowered voice. 'I truly believe she would have done me harm if you had not arrived when you did.' Quietly she added, 'It might be best if she were contained somehow . . . for her own safety.'

'I can't believe the rest of her family also survived,' Krion began in a nervous voice, but 'Shut up!' Roed Caern ordered him. He scowled about the room. 'I agree with the Companion. Ronica Vestrit is crazy. She talks of petitioning the Council and murder trials and judgements! How can she think that such rules apply during war? In these days, strong men must act. If we had waited for the Council to meet on the night of the fires, Bingtown would now be in Chalcedean hands. The Satrap would be dead, and the blame put on our heads. Individual Traders had to act, and each did. We saved Bingtown! I regret that Restart and the Vestrit women were entangled in the capture of the Satrap but they made the decision to get into the coach with him. When they chose such a companion, they chose their fate.'

'Capture?' Trader Drur raised an eyebrow at him. 'I was told we had intervened to prevent the New Traders from kidnapping him.'

Roed Caern did not blanch. 'You know what I mean,' he growled, and turned aside. He paced to a window and stared out over the darkened grounds as if trying to see Ronica's departing form.

Drur shook his head. The grizzled Trader looked older than his years. 'I know what we intended, but somehow . . .' He let his words trail away. Then he lifted his eyes and looked slowly around at all the folk in the room. 'It was why we came here tonight, Companion Serilla. My friends and I fear that in trying to save Bingtown, we have placed it on the path to destruction of its very heart.'

Roed's face went dark with anger. 'And I come to say that those of us young enough to be the beating of that heart know that we have not gone far enough. You long to treat with the New Traders, don't you, Drur? Even though they have already spat upon a truce offer. You would bargain away my birthrights for the sake of a comfortable old age for yourself. Well, your daughter may sit home and tat while men are dying in the streets of Bingtown. She may allow you to crawl cravenly to those upstart newcomers and dicker away our rights for the sake of peace, but we shall not. What would come next? Would you give her to the Chalcedeans to buy peace with them?'

Trader Drur's face had gone red as a turkey's wattle. His fists knotted at his side.

'Gentlemen. Please.' Serilla spoke softly. Tension thrummed in the room. Serilla sat at the centre of it like a spider in her web. The Traders turned to her and waited on her words. Her fear and anxiety of a moment ago were scorched to ashes in the triumph that burned invisibly within her. Bingtown Trader opposed Bingtown Trader, and they had come for her advice. This was how highly they regarded her. If she could keep her grasp on this power, she could be safe the rest of her life. So, carefully now. Go carefully.

'I knew this moment would come,' she lied gracefully. 'It was one reason I urged the Satrap to come here to mediate this dispute. You see yourselves as factions where the world sees only a whole. Traders, you must come to see yourselves as the world does. I do not mean,' and she raised her voice and held up a warning hand as Roed drew breath for an angry interruption, 'that you must give up any of what is rightfully yours. Traders and sons of Traders may be assured that Satrap Cosgo will not take away what Satrap Esclepius granted you. However, if you are not careful, you may still lose it, by failing to realize that times have changed. Bingtown is no longer a backwater. It has the potential to become a major trading port in the world. To do so, Bingtown must become a city more diverse and tolerant than it has been. But it must do that without losing the qualities that make Bingtown unique in the Satrap's crown.'

The words just came to her, falling from her lips in cadenced, rational statements. The Traders seemed entranced. She hardly knew what she was advising. It did not matter. These men were so desperate for a solution that they would listen to anyone who claimed to have one. She sat back in her chair, all eyes on her.

Drur was the first one to speak. 'You will treat with the New Traders on our behalf?'

'You will enforce the terms of our original charter?' Roed Caern asked.

'I will. As an outsider and the Satrap's representative, only I am qualified to bring peace back to Bingtown. Lasting peace, under terms all can find tolerable.' She let her eyes flash as she added, 'And as his representative, I will remind the Chalcedeans that when they attack a possession of Jamaillia, they attack Jamaillia herself. The Pearl Throne will not tolerate such an insult.'

As if her words of themselves had accomplished that goal, there was a sudden lessening of tension in the room. Shoulders lowered and the tendons in fists and necks were suddenly less visible.

'You must not perceive yourselves as opponents in this,' she offered them. 'You each bring your own strengths to the table.' She gestured to each group in turn. 'Your elders know Bingtown's history, and bring years of negotiating experience. They know that something cannot be gained without all parties being willing to surrender lesser points. While these, your sons, realize that their future depends on the original charter of Bingtown being recognized by all who reside here. They bring the strength of their convictions and the tenacity of youth.

You must stand united in this time of trouble, to honour the past and provide for the future.'

The two groups were looking at one another now, openly, the hostility between them mellowing to a tentative alliance. Her heart leapt. This was what she had been born to do. Bingtown was her destiny. She would unite it and save it and make it her own.

'It's late,' she said softly. 'I think that before we talk, we all need to rest. And think. I will expect all of you tomorrow, to share noon repast with me. By then, I will have organized my own thoughts and suggestions. If we are united in deciding to treat with the New Traders, I will suggest a list of New Traders who might be open to such negotiating, and also powerful enough to speak for their neighbours.' As Roed Caern's face darkened and even Krion scowled, she added with a slight smile, 'But of course, we are not yet united in that position. And nothing shall be done until we reach consensus, I assure you. I shall be open to all suggestions.'

She dismissed them with a smile and a 'Good evening, Traders.'

Each of them came to bow over her hand and thank her for her counsels. As Roed Caern did so, she held his fingers in her own a moment longer. As he glanced up at her in surprise, her lips formed the silent words, 'Come back later.' His dark eyes widened but he spoke no word.

After the boy ushered them out, she breathed a sigh that was both relief and satisfaction. She would survive here, and Bingtown would be hers, regardless of what became of the Satrap. She pinched her lips together as she considered Roed Caern. Then she rose swiftly and crossed to the servant's bell. She would have her maid assist her in dressing more formally. Roed Caern frightened her. He was a man capable of anything. She did not wish him to think that her request to him was the invitation to a tryst. She would be cool and formal when she set him to tracking down Ronica Vestrit and her family.

THREE

Wintrow

THE CARVED FIGUREHEAD stared straight ahead as she sliced the waves. The wind at her back filled her sails and drove her forwards. Her bow cut the water in a near constant white spray. The flying droplets beaded Vivacia's cheeks and the foaming black curls of her hair.

She had left Others' Island and then Ridge Island behind her. Vivacia moved west now, away from the open ocean and towards the treacherous gap between Shield Wall and Last Island. Beyond the ridge of islands was the sheltered Inside Passage to the relative safety of the Pirate Isles.

Within her rigging, the pirate crew moved lively until six sails bellied full in the wind. Captain Kennit gripped the bow rail with his long-fingered hands, his pale blue eyes squinting. The spray damped his white shirt and elegant broadcloth jacket, but he took no notice of it. Like the figurehead, he stared longingly ahead, as if his will could wring more speed out of the ship.

'Wintrow needs a healer,' Vivacia insisted abruptly. Woefully, she added, 'We should have kept the slave surgeon from the *Crosspatch*. We should have forced him to come with us.' The liveship's figurehead crossed her arms on her chest and hugged herself tightly. She did not look back towards Kennit, but stared over the sea. Her jaw clamped tightly shut.

The pirate captain took in a deep breath and erased all trace of exasperation from his voice. 'I know your fears,' he told her. 'But you must set them aside. We are days from a settlement of any size. By the time we get to one, Wintrow will either be healing, or dead. We are caring for him as best we can, ship. His own strength is his best hope now.' Belatedly, he tried to comfort her. He spoke in a gentler tone. 'I know you are worried about the lad. I am just as concerned as you are. Hold to this, Vivacia. He breathes. His heart beats. He takes in water and pisses it out again. These are all marks of a man who will live. I've seen enough of injured men to know that is so.'

'So you have told me.' Her words were clipped. 'I have listened to you. Now, I beg you, listen to me. His injury is not a normal one. It goes beyond pain or damage to his flesh. Wintrow isn't there, Kennit. I cannot feel him at all.' Her voice began to shake. 'While I cannot feel him, I cannot help him. I cannot lend him comfort or strength. I am helpless. Worthless to him.'

Kennit fought to contain his impatience. Behind him, Jola bellowed angrily at the men, threatening to strip the flesh from their ribs if they didn't put their backs into their work. Wasted breath, Kennit thought to himself. Just do it once to one of them and the first mate would never need to threaten them again.

Kennit crossed his arms on his chest, containing his own temper. Strictness was not a tack he could take with the ship. Still, it was hard to leash his irritation. Worry for the boy already ate at him like a canker. He needed Wintrow. He knew that. When he thought of him, he felt an almost mystical sense of connection. The boy was intertwined with his luck and his destiny to be king. Sometimes it almost seemed as if Wintrow were a younger, more innocent version of himself, unscarred by the harshness of his life. When he thought of Wintrow that way, he felt an odd tenderness for him. He could protect him. He could be to Wintrow the kind of mentor that he himself had never had. Yet to do that, he had to be the boy's sole protector. The bond between Wintrow and the ship was a double barrier to Kennit. As long as it existed, neither the ship nor the boy was completely his.

He spoke firmly to Vivacia. 'You know the boy is aboard. You caught us up and saved us yourself. You saw him taken aboard. Do you think I would lie to you, and say he lived if he did not?'

'No,' she replied heavily. 'I know you would not lie to me. Moreover, I believe that if he had died, I would know of it.' She shook her head savagely and her heavy hair flew with her denial. 'We have been so closely linked for so long. I cannot convey to you how it feels to know he is aboard, and yet to have no sense of him. It is as if a part of myself had been cloven away . . .'

Her voice dwindled. She had forgotten to whom she spoke. Kennit leaned more heavily on his makeshift crutch. He tapped his peg loudly thrice upon her deck. 'Do you think I cannot imagine what you feel?' he asked her.

'I know you can,' she conceded. 'Ah, Kennit, what I cannot express is how alone I am without him. Every evil dream, every malicious imagining that has ever haunted me ventures from the corners of my mind. They gibber and mock me. Their sly taunting eats away at my sense of who I am.' She lifted her great wizardwood hands to her temples and pressed her palms there. 'So often I have told myself that I no longer need Wintrow. I know who I am. And I believe I am far greater than he could ever grasp.' She gave a sigh of exasperation. 'He can be so irritating. He mouths platitudes and ponders theology at me until I swear I would be happier without him. However, when he is not with me, and I have to confront who I truly am . . .' She shook her head again, wordlessly.

She began again. 'When I got the serpent's slime from the gig onto my hands –' Her words halted. When she spoke again, it was in an altered voice. 'I am frightened. There is a terrible dread in me, Kennit.' She twisted suddenly, to look at him over one bare shoulder. 'I fear the truth that lurks inside me, Kennit. I fear the whole of my identity. I have a face I wear to show the world, but there is more to me than that. There are other faces concealed in me. I sense a past behind my past. If I do not guard against it, I fear it will leap out and change all I am. Yet, it makes no sense. How could I be someone other than who I am now? How can I fear myself? I don't understand how I could feel such a thing. Do you?'

Kennit tightened his arms across his chest and lied. 'I think you are prone to flights of fancy, my sea lady. No more than that. Perhaps you feel a bit guilty. I know that I chide myself for taking Wintrow to the Others' Island where he was exposed to such danger. For you, it must be sharper. You have been distant with him of late. I know that I have come between you and Wintrow. Pardon me if I do not regret that. Now that you have been faced with the possibility of losing him, you appreciate the hold he still has on you. You wonder what would become of you if he died. Or left.'

Kennit shook his head at her and gave her a wry smile. 'I fear you still do not trust me. I have told you, I will be with you always, to the end of my days. Yet still you cling to him as the only one worthy to partner you.' Kennit paused, then ventured a gambit to see how she would react. 'I think we should use this time to prepare for when Wintrow will leave us. Fond as we are of him, we both know his heart is not here, but at his monastery. The time will come when, if we truly love him, we must let him go. Do you not agree?'

Vivacia turned away to stare out over the sea. 'I suppose so.'

'My lovely water-flower, why cannot you allow me to fill his place with you?'

'Blood is memory,' Vivacia said sadly. 'Wintrow and I share both blood and memories.'

It was painful, for he ached in every limb, but Kennit

lowered himself slowly to her deck. He put his hand flat on the bloodstain that still held the outline of his hip and leg. 'My blood,' he said quietly. 'I lay here while my leg was cut from my body. My blood soaked into you. I know you shared memories with me then.'

'I did. And again, when you died. Yet –' She paused, then complained, 'Even unconscious, you hid yourself from me. You shared what you chose to reveal, Kennit. The rest you cloaked in mystery and shadow, denying those memories even existed.' She shook her massive head. 'I love you, Kennit, but I do not know you. Not as Wintrow and I know one another. I hold the memories of three generations of his family line. His blood has soaked me as well. We are like two trees sprung from a single root.' She took a sudden breath. 'I do not know you,' she repeated. 'If I truly knew you, I would understand what happened when you returned from Others' Island. The winds and sea itself seemed to answer to your command. A serpent bowed to your will. I do not understand how such a thing could be, yet I witnessed it. Nor do you see fit to explain it to me.' Very softly, she asked him, 'How can I put my trust in a man who does not trust me?'

For a time, silence blew by with the wind. 'I see,' Kennit replied heavily. He got to his knee and then laboriously climbed up his crutch to stand erect. She had wounded him and he chose to let it show. 'All I can say to you is that it is not yet time for me to reveal myself to you. I had hoped that you loved me well enough to be patient. You have dashed that hope. Still, I hope you know me well enough to believe my words. Wintrow is not dead. He shows signs of recovering. Once he is well, I have no doubt he will come to you. When he does, I shall not stand between you.'

'Kennit!' she cried after him, but he limped slowly away. When he got to the short ladder that led from the raised foredeck to the main deck, he had to lower himself awkwardly to it. He set his crutch flat on the deck and scrabbled his body around to the ladder. It presented difficulties for a one-legged man, but he surmounted them without help. Etta, who should have been at his side to aid him, was nursing Wintrow. He supposed that she, too, now preferred the lad's company to his. No one seemed to care how his exertions on Others' Island had exhausted him. Despite the warm weather, he had developed a cough from their long and arduous swim. Every muscle and joint in his body ached, but no one offered him sympathy or support, for Wintrow was hurt, the skin scalded from his body by sea serpent's venom. Wintrow. He was the only one that Etta and Vivacia noticed.

'Oh. Poor pirate. Poor, pathetic, unloved Kennit.'

The words were drawled sarcastically, in a small voice. It came from the carved charm he wore strapped to his wrist. He would not even have heard the tiny, breathless voice if he had not been climbing down the ladder, his hand still gripping the rung by his face. His foot reached the lower deck. He held to the ladder with one hand as he tugged his coat straight, and corrected the fall of lace from his cuffs. Anger burned in him. Even the wizardwood charm he had created to bring him luck had turned on him. His own face, carved in miniature, flung mockery at him. He thought of a threat for the beastly little wretch.

He lifted his hand to smooth the curl of his moustache. Carved face close to his mouth, 'Wizardwood burns,' he observed quietly.

'So does flesh,' the tiny voice replied. 'You and I are bound as tightly as Vivacia is bound to Wintrow. Do you want to test that link? You have already lost a leg. Would you like to try life without your eyes?'

The charm's words set a finger of ice to the pirate's spine. How much did it know?

'Ah, Kennit, there can be few secrets between two such as we. Few.' It spoke to his thoughts rather than his words. Could it truly know what he thought, or did it shrewdly guess?

'Here's a secret I could share with Vivacia,' the charm went on relentlessly. 'I could tell her that you yourself have no idea what happened during that rescue. That once your elation wore off, you cowered in your bed and trembled like a child while Etta was nursing Wintrow.' A pause. 'Perhaps Etta would find that amusing.'

An inadvertent glance at his wrist showed him the sardonic grin on the charm's face. Kennit pushed down a deep uneasiness. He would not dignify the ill-natured little thing with a reply. He recovered his crutch and stepped swiftly out of the path of a handful of men hastening to reset a sail that was not to Jola's liking.

What *had* happened as they were leaving Others' Island? The storm had raged about them, and Wintrow had been unconscious, perhaps dying in the bottom of the ship's boat. Kennit had been furious with fate that it would try to snatch his future away just as he was so close to realizing it. He had stood up in the gig, to shake his fist and forbid the sea to drown him and the winds to oppose him. Not only had they heeded his words, but the serpent from the island had risen from the depths to reunite the gig with its mother ship. He exhaled sharply, refusing credulous fear. It was difficult enough that his own crew now worshipped him with their eyes, cowering in terror at his slightest remonstrance. Even Etta quivered fearfully under his touch and spoke to him with downcast eyes. Occasionally, she slipped back into familiarity, only to be aghast with herself when she realized she had done so. Only the ship treated him as fearlessly as she always had. Now she had revealed that his miracle had created another barrier between them. He refused to surrender to their superstition. Whatever had happened, he must accept it and continue as he always had.

Commanding a ship demanded that the captain always live a detached life. No one could fraternize on equal terms with the ship's captain. Kennit had always enjoyed the isolation of command. Since Sorcor had taken over command of the

Marietta, he had lost some of his deference for Kennit. The storm incident had once more firmly established Kennit as above Sorcor. Now his former second-in-command regarded him with a god-struck gaze. It was not the elevation in their regard that Kennit minded so much. It was knowing that a fall from this new pinnacle could shatter him. Even a slight mistake now might discredit him in their eyes. He must be more careful than ever before. The path he had set himself upon grew ever narrower and steeper. He set his customary small smile to his face. Let no one see his apprehension. He made his way towards Wintrow's cabin.

'Wintrow? Here is water. Drink.'

Etta squeezed a small sponge above his lips. A pattering of drops fell. She watched anxiously as his blistered lips opened to the water. His thick tongue moved inside his mouth, and she saw him swallow. It was followed by a quick gasp for breath. 'Is that better? Do you want more?'

She leaned closer and watched his face, willing a response from him. She would accept anything, the twitch of an eyelid, the flaring of a nostril. There was nothing. She dipped the sponge again. 'Here comes more water,' she assured him, and sent another brief trickle into his mouth. Again, he swallowed.

Thrice more she gave him water. The last time, it trickled down his livid cheek. She dabbed it gently away. Skin came with it. Then she leaned back into the chair by his bunk and considered him wearily. She could not tell if his thirst was satiated or if he was too weary to swallow more. She numbered her consolations. He was alive. He breathed; he drank. She tried to build hope upon that. She dropped the sponge back into the pan of water. For a moment, she regarded her own hands. She had scalded them in Wintrow's rescue, for when she had seized him to keep him from drowning, the serpent slime on his clothing had rubbed off on her, leaving shiny red patches, stingingly sensitive to both heat and cold. And it had done that damage after it had spent most of its strength on Wintrow's clothing and flesh.

His clothing had been corroded away to flimsy rags. Then, as warm water dissolves ice, the slime had eaten his flesh. His hands had taken the worst damage, but spatters of it had marred his face. It had eaten into his sailor's queue, leaving uneven hanks of black hair clinging to his head. She had cut his remaining hair to keep it from lying in his sores. His shorn scalp made him look even younger than he was.

In some places, the damage seemed no worse than sunburn; in others, raw tissue shone wet beside tanned and healthy flesh. Swelling had distorted his features, rendering his eyes as slits beneath a ledge of brow. His fingers were as sausages. His breath rattled in and out wetly. His oozing flesh stuck to the linen sheets. She suspected his pain was intense, and yet he gave few signs of it. He was so unresponsive that she feared he was dying.

She closed her eyes tightly. If he died, it would reawaken all the pain she had schooled herself to leave behind. It was so monstrously unfair that she was going to lose him so soon after finally coming to trust him. He had taught her to read. She had taught him to fight. She had competed with him jealously for Kennit's attention. Somehow, in the process, she had come to consider him a friend. How had she let herself be so careless? Why had she allowed herself such vulnerability?

She had come to know him better than anyone else on board. To Kennit, Wintrow was a lucky piece and a prophet of his success, though he valued the boy, perhaps even loved him in his grudging way. The crew had accepted Wintrow, reluctantly at first, but with almost paternal pride since the mild lad had stood his ground at Divvytown, blade in hand, and voiced his support for Kennit as a king. His shipmates had been eager for Wintrow to walk the Treasure Beach, sure that whatever he discovered there would be omens of Kennit's greatness to come. Even Sorcor had come to regard Wintrow with tolerance and affection. But none of them knew him as she did. If he died, they would be sad, but Etta would be bereaved.

She pushed her own feelings roughly aside. They were not important. The vital question was, how would Wintrow's death affect Kennit? She truly could not guess. Five days ago, she would have sworn she knew the pirate as well as anyone. Not that she claimed to know all his secrets; he was a very private man, and his motives often mystified her. Nevertheless, he treated her kindly and more than kindly. She knew she loved him. That had been enough for her; she did not need to be loved in return. He was Kennit, and that was all she required of him.

She had listened with indulgent scepticism as Wintrow had shyly begun to voice his speculations. His initial distrust of Kennit had evolved slowly into a belief that Kennit was chosen by Sa to fulfil some great destiny. She had suspected Kennit of playing on the boy's gullibility, encouraging Wintrow in his beliefs simply so he could enlist him in his own endeavours. Fond as she was of Kennit, she believed him capable of such deceptions. It did not make her think less of her man that he was willing to do whatever he must to achieve his ends.

But that had been before she had seen Kennit lift his hands and voice to quell a storm and command a sea serpent. Since that moment, she felt as if the man she loved had been snatched away and another set in his place. She was not alone in this. The crew that would have followed Captain Kennit to any bloody death now fell silent at his approach and near cowered at a direct command from him. Kennit scarcely noticed. That was the uncanny thing. He seemed to accept what he had done, and expect the same of those around him. He spoke to her as if nothing had changed. Shockingly, he touched her as he always had. She was not worthy to be touched by such a being, yet she dared not deny herself to him, either. Who was she to question the will of one such as he?

What was he?

Words she would once have scoffed came to her mind. God-touched. Beloved of Sa. Destined. Prophesied. Chosen by fate. She wanted to laugh and dismiss such fancies, but could not. From the very beginning, Kennit had been unlike any other man she had ever known. None of the rules had ever seemed to apply to him. He had succeeded where any other man would have failed, achieved the impossible effortlessly. The tasks he had set himself baffled her. The size of his ambitions astounded her. Had not he captured a Bingtown liveship? What other man had recovered from a sea serpent's attack? Who but Kennit could have made the rag-tag villages of the Pirate Isles start to think of themselves as outposts of a far-flung realm, Kennit's rightful kingdom?

What kind of a man harboured such dreams, let alone brought them to fruit?

Such questions made her miss Wintrow even more sharply. If he had been awake, he could have helped her understand. Though he was young, he had spent almost his entire life in schooling at a monastery. When she had first met him, she had disdained him for his educated ways and gentle manners. Now she wished she could turn to him with her uncertainties. Words like destiny and fate and omen fell from his lips as easily as curses came from hers. From him, such words were believable.

She found herself toying with the small pouch she wore around her neck. She opened it with a sigh, and once more took out the tiny manikin. She had found it in her boot, along with a quantity of sand and barnacle shells after they had escaped from Others' Island. When she had asked Kennit what such an omen from the Treasure Beach might mean, he had told her that she already knew. That answer had frightened her more than any dire prophecy he could have uttered.

'But truly, I don't,' she said softly to Wintrow. The doll just filled her palm. It felt like ivory, yet it was coloured the precise pink of a baby's flesh. The curled and sleeping infant had tiny perfect eyelashes on its cheeks, ears like minute seashells, and a coiling serpentine tail that wrapped around it. It warmed quickly in her hand, and the smooth contours of the tiny body begged to be touched. Her fingertip traced the curve of its spine. 'It looks like a baby to me. But what can that mean to me?' She lowered her voice and spoke more confidentially, as if the youth could hear her. 'Kennit spoke of a baby, once. He asked me if I would have a baby if he wanted that of me. I told him, of course I would. Is that what this means? Is Kennit going to ask me to have his child?'

Her hand strayed to her flat belly. Through her shirt, her finger touched a tiny lump. A wizardwood charm, shaped like a tiny skull, was ringed through her navel to protect her from disease and pregnancy. 'Wintrow, I'm afraid. I fear I cannot live up to such dreams. What if I fail him? What am I to do?'

'I will not ask of you anything I believe is beyond you.'

Etta leapt to her feet with a startled cry. She spun to find Kennit standing in the open door. She covered her mouth with her hand. 'I didn't hear you,' she apologized guiltily.

'Ah, but I heard you. Is our boy awake now? Wintrow?' Kennit limped into the room, to gaze hopefully on Wintrow's still form.

'No. He drinks water, but other than that, there is no sign of recovery.' Etta remained standing.

'But still you ask him these questions?' Kennit observed speculatively. He turned his head to pierce her with his glance.

'I have no one else to share such doubts,' she began, and then halted. 'I meant,' she began hesitantly, but Kennit silenced her with an impatient motion of his hand.

'I know what you meant,' he revealed. He sank into her chair. When he let go of his crutch, she caught it before it could clatter to the floor. He leaned forwards to look at Wintrow more closely, a frown furrowing his brow. His fingers touched the boy's swollen face with a woman's gentleness. 'I, too, miss his counsel.' He stroked the stubble of hair on Wintrow's head, then pulled his hand back in distaste at its coarseness. 'I am thinking of putting him up on the foredeck, by the figurehead. She may be able to speed his healing.'

'But –' Etta began, then held her tongue and lowered her eyes.

'You object? Why?'

'I did not mean to . . .'

'Etta!' Kennit barked her name, making her jump. 'Spare me this whining and cringing. If I ask you a question, it is because I wish you to speak, not whimper at me. Why do you object to moving him there?'

She swallowed her fear. 'The scabs on his burns are loose and wet. If we move him, they may be rubbed off, and delay his healing. The wind and the sun may dry and crack raw skin all the more.'

Kennit looked only at the boy. He appeared to be pondering her words. 'I see. But we shall move him carefully, and we will not leave him there long. The ship needs assurance that he lives still, and I think he may need her strength to heal.'

'I am sure you know better than I –' she faltered, but he cut off her objection with, 'I am certain that I do. Go fetch some crewmen to move him. I shall wait here.'

Wintrow swam deep, in darkness and warmth. Somewhere, far above, there was a world of light and shadow, of voices and pain and touch. He avoided it. In another plane, there was a being that groped after him, calling him by his name and baiting him with memories as well. She was harder to elude, but his determination was strong. If she found him, there would be great pain and disillusionment for both of them. As long as he remained a tiny formless being swimming through the dark, he could avoid it all.

Something was being done to his body. There was clatter, talk, and fuss. He centred himself against anticipated pain. Pain had the power to grasp him and hold him. Pain might be able to drag him up to that world where he had a body and a mind and a set of memories that went with them. Down here, it was much safer.

It only seems that way. And while it seems that way for a long time, eventually you will long for light and movement, for taste and sound and touch. If you wait too long, those things may be lost to you forever.

This voice boomed rich all around him like the thundering of surf against rocks. Like the ocean itself, the voice turned and tumbled him, considering him from all angles. He tried in vain to hide from it. It knew him. 'Who are you?' he demanded.

The voice was amused. *Who am I? You know who I am, Wintrow Vestrit. I am whom you most fear, and whom she most fears. I am the one you avoid acknowledging. I am the one you deny and conceal from yourself and each other. Yet, I am a part of you both.*

The voice paused and waited for him, but he would not speak the words. He knew that the old naming magic worked both ways. To know a creature's true name was to have the power to bind it. But the naming of such a creature could also make it real.

I am the dragon. The voice spoke with finality. *You know me now. And nothing will ever be the same.*

'I'm sorry, I'm sorry,' he babbled silently. 'I didn't know. None of us knew. I'm sorry, I'm so very sorry.'

Not as sorry as I am. The voice was implacable in its grief. *Nor yet as sorry as you shall be.*

'But it wasn't my fault! I had nothing to do with it!'

Nor was it my fault, yet I am the one punished most grievously of all. Fault has no place in the greater scheme of things, little one.

Fault and guilt are as useless as apology once the deed is done. Once the action has been taken, all must endure what follows.

'But why are you down here so deep?'

Where else should I be? Where else is left to me? By the time I recalled who I was, your memories were stacked many layers deep upon me. Yet here I am, and here I shall remain, no matter how long you deny me. The voice paused. *No matter how long I may deny myself,* it added wearily.

Pain scoured him. Wintrow struggled in a blaze of heat and light, fighting to keep his eyes closed and his tongue stilled. What were they doing to him? It did not matter. He would not react to it. If he moved, if he cried out, he would have to admit he was alive and Vivacia was dead. He would have to admit his soul was linked to a thing that had been dead longer than he had been alive. It was beyond macabre; it numbed him with horror. This was the wonder and glory of a liveship. He must consort forever with death. He did not wish to awaken and acknowledge that.

Would you prefer to remain down here with me? There was bitter amusement in the being's voice now. *Do you wish to linger in the tomb of my past?*

'No. No, I wish to be free.'

Free?

Wintrow faltered. 'I don't want to know any of this. I don't want to have ever been a part of it.'

You were a part of it as soon as you were conceived. There is no way to undo such a thing.

'Then what must I do?' The words wailed through him, unvoiced. 'I cannot live with this.'

You could die, the voice offered sardonically.

'I don't want to die.' Of that, at least, he was certain.

Neither did I, the voice pointed out remorselessly. *But I did. Rich as I am in memories of flying, my own wings never were unfurled. For the sake of building this ship, my cocoon was stripped from me before I could hatch. They dumped that which would have been my body to the cold stone floor. All I am are memories, memories stored in the walls of my cocoon, memories I should have reabsorbed as I formed in the hot sun of summer. I had no way to live or grow, save through the memories your kind offered. I absorbed what you gave me, and when it was enough, I quickened. But not as myself. No. I became the shape you had imposed upon me, and took to myself the personality that was the sum of your family's expectations. Vivacia.*

A sudden shift in the position of his body freshened Wintrow's physical pain. Air flowed over him and the warmth of the sun touched him. Even that contact scoured his denuded flesh. But worst of all was the voice that called to him in a mixture of gladness and concern. 'Wintrow? Can you hear me? It's Vivacia. Where are you, what are you doing that I cannot feel you at all?'

He felt the ship's thoughts reach for him. He cringed away, unwilling to let her touch minds with him. He made himself smaller, hid deeper. The moment Vivacia reached him, she must know all that he did. What would it do to her, to confront what she truly was?

Do you fear it will drive her mad? Do you fear she will take you with her? There was fierce exultance in the voice as it framed the thought, almost like a threat. Wintrow went cold with fear. Instantly he knew that this hiding place was no asylum, but a trap. 'Vivacia!' he called out wildly, but his body did not obey him. No lips voiced his cry. Even his thought was muffled in the dragon's being, wrapped and stifled and confined. He tried to struggle; he was suffocating under the weight of her presence. She held him so close he could not recall how to breathe. His heart leaped arhythmically. Pain slapped him as his body jerked in protest. In a distant world, on a sun-washed deck, voices cried out in helpless dismay. He retreated to a stillness of body and soul that was one degree of darkness away from death.

Good. There was satisfaction in the voice. *Be still, little one. Don't try to defy me, and I won't have to kill you.* A pause. *I*

*really have no desire to see any of us die. As closely interwoven
as we are, the death of any of us would be a risk to the others.
You would have realized that, if you had paused to think. I give
you that time now. Use it to ponder our situation.*

For a space, Wintrow focused only on his survival. Breath
caught, then shuddered through his lungs again. His heartbeat
steadied. He was peripherally aware of exclamations of relief.
Pain still seethed. He tried to pull his mind back from it, to
ignore its clamour of serious damage to his body so that his
thoughts could focus on the problem the dragon had set him.

He cringed at her sudden flash of irritation. *By all that flies,
have you no sense at all? How have creatures like you managed
to survive and infest the world so thoroughly and yet have so little
knowledge of yourselves? Do not pull back from the pain and imagine
that makes you strong. Look at it, you dolt! It is trying to tell you
what is wrong so you can fix it. No wonder you all have such short
life spans. No, look at it! Like this.*

The crewmen who had carried the corners of the sheet sup-
porting Wintrow's body had lowered him gently to the deck.
Even so, Kennit had seen the spasm of fresh pain that crossed
Wintrow's face. He supposed that could be taken as an encouraging sign; at least he still reacted to pain. But when the
figurehead had spoken to him, he had not even twitched.
None of the others surrounding the supine figure could guess
how much that worried Kennit. The pirate had been certain
that the boy would react to the ship's voice. That he did not
meant that perhaps death would claim him. Kennit believed
that there was a place between life and death where a man's
body became no more than a miserable animal, capable only
of an animal's responses. He had seen it. Under Igrot's cruel
guidance, his father had lingered in that state for days. Perhaps
that was where Wintrow was now.

The dim light inside the cabin had been merciful. Out here,

in the clear light of day, Kennit could not insist to himself that Wintrow would be fine. Every ugly detail of his scalded body was revealed. His brief fit of spasms had disturbed the wet scabs his body had managed to form; fluid ran over his skin from his injuries. Wintrow was dying. His boy-prophet, the priest who would have been his soothsayer was dying, with Kennit's future still unborn. The injustice of it rose up and choked Kennit. He had come so close, so very close to attaining his dream. Now he would lose it all in the death of this half-grown man. It was too bitter to contemplate. He clenched his eyes shut against the cruelty of fate.

'Oh, Kennit!' the ship cried out in a low voice, and he knew that she was feeling his emotions as well as her own. 'Don't let him die!' she begged him. 'Please. You saved him from the serpent and the sea. Cannot you save him now?'

'Quiet!' he commanded her, almost roughly. He had to think. If the boy died now, it would be a denial of all the good luck Kennit had ever mustered. It would be worse than a jinx. Kennit could not allow this to happen.

Unmindful of the gathered crewmen who looked down on the wracked boy in hushed silence, Kennit awkwardly lowered himself to the deck. He looked long at Wintrow's still face. He laid a single forefinger to an unblemished patch of skin on Wintrow's face. He was beardless still and his cheek was soft. It wrung his heart to see the lad's beauty spoiled so. 'Wintrow,' he called softly. 'Lad, it's me. Kennit. You said you'd follow me. Sa sent you to speak for me. Remember? You can't go now, boy. Not when we're so close to our goals.'

He was peripherally aware of the hushed murmur that ran through the watching crewmen. Sympathy, they felt sympathy for him. He felt a flash of irritation that they might construe his speaking so as weakness. But, no, it was not pity they felt. He looked up into their faces, and saw only concern, not just for Wintrow, but for him. They were touched by their captain's regard for this injured boy. He sighed. Well, if Wintrow must die, he would wring what good from it he could. Gently he stroked his cheek. 'Poor lad,' he muttered, just loud enough to be heard. 'So much pain. It would be merciful to let you go, wouldn't it?'

He glanced up at Etta. Tears ran unashamedly down her cheeks. 'Try the water again,' he bade her gently. 'But don't be disappointed. He is in Sa's hands now, you know.'

The dragon twisted his awareness. Wintrow did not see with his eyes, nor wallow in the sensation of pain. Instead, she bent his awareness in a direction he had never before imagined. What was the pain? Damaged units of his body, breaks in his defences against the outside world. The barriers needed repairing, the damaged units must be broken down and dispersed. Nothing must get in the way of this task. All his resources should be put to it. His body demanded this of him, and pain was the alarm that sounded through him.

'Wintrow?' Etta's voice penetrated the woolly blackness. 'Here is water.' A moment later he felt an annoying trickling of moisture against his lips. He moved his lips, choking briefly as he tried to evade it. An instant later, he realized his error. This liquid was what his body needed to repair itself. Water, sustenance and absolute rest, free of the dilemmas that encumbered him.

A light pressure on his cheek. From far away, a voice he knew. 'Die if you must, lad. But know that it hurts me. Ah, Wintrow, if you have any love for me at all, reach out and live. Don't forsake the dream that you yourself foretold.'

The words stored themselves in him, to be considered later. He had no time for Kennit just now. The dragon was showing him something, something that was so much of Sa he wondered how it could have been inside himself all this time and remained unseen. The workings of his own body unfolded before him. Air whispered in his lungs, blood

77

flowed through his limbs, and all of it belonged to him. This was not some uncontrollable territory; this was his own body. He could mend it.

He felt himself relax. Unrestricted by tension, the resources of his body now flowed to his injured parts. He knew his needs. After a moment, he found the reluctant muscles of his jaws and his laggard tongue. He moved his mouth. 'Water,' he managed to croak. He lifted a stiffened arm in a faint attempt to shield himself. 'Shade,' he begged. The touch of the sun and wind on his damaged skin was excruciating.

'He spoke!' Etta exulted.

'It was the Captain,' someone else declared. 'Called him right back from death.'

'Death himself steps back from Kennit!' declared another.

The rough palm that so gently touched his cheek, and the strong hands that carefully raised his head and held the blessedly cool and dripping cup to his mouth, were Kennit's. 'You are mine, Wintrow,' the pirate declared.

Wintrow drank to that.

'I think you can hear me.' She Who Remembers trumpeted the words as she swam in the shadow of the silvery hull. She kept pace with the ship. 'I smell you. I sense you, but I cannot find you. Do you deliberately hide from me?'

She fell silent, straining with every sense after a response. Something, she tasted something in the water, a bitter scent like the stinging toxins from her own glands. It oozed from the ship's hull, if such a thing could be. She seemed to hear voices, voices so distant that she could not make out their words, only that they spoke. It made no sense. The serpent half-feared she was going mad. That would be bitter irony, finally to achieve her freedom and then have madness defeat her.

She shuddered her whole length, releasing a thin stream of

toxins. 'Who are you?' she demanded. 'Where are you? Why do you conceal yourself from me?'

She waited for a response. None came. No one spoke to her, but she was convinced that someone listened.

FOUR

Tintaglia's Flight

THE SKY WAS not blue, oh no. Not once she had taken flight, for compared to her own gleaming self, what could claim to be blue? Tintaglia the dragon arched her back and admired the sunlight glinting silver off her deep blue scales. Beautiful beyond words. Yet even this wonder could not distract her keen eyes and keener nostrils from what was even more important than her glory.

Food moved in a clearing far below her. A doe, fat with summer graze, ventured too bravely out into a forest clearing. Foolish thing! Once no deer would have moved into the open without first casting a watchful glance above. Had dragons truly been gone so long from the world that the hoofed ones had discarded their wariness of the sky? She would soon teach them better. Tintaglia tucked her wings and plummeted. Only when she was so close that there was no possibility the deer could evade her did she give voice to her hunt. The musical trumpet of her *Ki-i-i* as she stooped split the morning peace. The clutching talons of her forelegs gathered her kill to her breast as her massive hind legs absorbed the impact of her landing. She rebounded effortlessly into the air, carrying the deer with her. The doe was shocked into stillness. A swift bite to the back of her neck had paralysed her. Tintaglia carried her prey to a rocky ledge overlooking the wide Rain River

Valley. There she lapped the pooling blood of her meal before scissoring off dark red chunks to sate her hunger, flinging back her head to gulp them down. The incredible sensory pleasure of eating nearly overwhelmed her. The taste of the hot bloody meat, the rank smell of the spilled entrails combined with the physical sensation of loading her gut with large pieces of sustenance. She could feel her body renewing itself. Even the sunlight soaking into her scales replenished her.

She had stretched herself out to sleep after her meal when an annoying thought intruded. Before she had made her kill, she had been on her way to do something. She considered the play of sunlight on her closed eyelids. What was it? Ah. The humans. She had intended to rescue the humans. She sighed heavily, sinking deeper into sleep. But it wasn't as if she had promised them, for how could a promise between one such as herself and an insect be considered binding on one's honour?

Still. They had freed her.

But they were probably dead and it was doubtless too late to rescue them anyway. Lazily, she let her mind drift towards them. It was almost annoying to find they were both still alive, though their thoughts were the merest humming of a mosquito now.

She lifted her head with a sigh and then roused herself enough to stand. She'd rescue the male, she compromised with herself. She knew exactly where he was. The female had fallen into water somewhere; she could be anywhere by now.

Tintaglia paced to the edge of the cliff and launched herself.

'I'm so hungry,' Selden quavered. He pressed himself more tightly against Reyn, seeking body warmth that Reyn himself was rapidly losing. Reyn couldn't even find the spirit to reply to the shivering boy. He and Selden lay together on a mat of tree limbs that was gradually sinking into the rising muck.

When the mud consumed it, it would devour this last hope as well. The only opening out of the chamber was far overhead. They had attempted to build a platform of debris, but as fast as they piled up fallen earth and tree limbs, the muck swallowed them. Reyn knew they were going to die here, and all the boy could do was whine about being hungry.

He felt like shaking some sense into him, but instead he put his arm around Selden and said comfortingly, 'Someone must have seen the dragon. My mother and brother will hear of it and guess where she came from. They'll send help.' Privately, he doubted his own words. 'Rest for a bit.'

'I'm so hungry,' Selden repeated hopelessly. He sighed. 'In a way, it was worth it. I saw the dragon rise.' He turned his face to Reyn's chest and was still. Reyn let his own eyes close. Could it be as simple as this? Could they simply go to sleep and die? He tried to think of something important enough to make him go on struggling. Malta. But Malta was likely dead already, somewhere in the collapsed city. The city itself was the only thing he had cared about before discovering Malta, and it lay in ruins all around him. He'd never unearth its secrets. Perhaps dying here and becoming one of its secrets was the closest he would ever get to it. He found his heart echoing Selden's words. At least he had freed the dragon. Tintaglia had risen, to fly free. That was something, but it was not a reason to go on living. Perhaps it was a reason to die content. He had saved her.

He felt another tiny quake. It was followed by a splattering sound as loose earth cascaded from the opening above them to splash into the muck. Perhaps the whole ceiling would cave in; that would furnish him a quick end.

Cool air wafted past his face, heavy with the scent of reptile. He opened his eyes, to find Tintaglia's pony-sized head thrust down into the chamber. 'Still alive?' she greeted him.

'You came back?' He was incredulous.

She didn't reply. She had pulled her head out and her

taloned forepaws were tearing at the earth around the opening. Rocks, dirt and bits of ceiling rained down within the chamber. Selden awoke with a cry and cowered against Reyn. 'No, it's all right. I think she's trying to rescue us.' Reyn tried to sound reassuring as he sheltered the boy from the falling debris.

Earth and stone trickled down and the hole overhead grew larger. More light found its way into the chamber. 'Climb onto this,' Tintaglia suddenly commanded them. A moment later her head entered the chamber, a stout section of tree trunk gripped firmly in her jaws as if she were a terrier who had fetched a stick. The breath from her nostrils steamed in the cool chamber and the stench of reptile was overpowering. Reyn summoned his last strength to stand up and lift Selden so he could scrabble up onto the log. Reyn caught hold of the other end. As soon as he gripped it, she lifted them. They snagged for a moment in the opening, but she tore the log free with a fine disregard for how weakly they clung to it. An instant later, she had set them down on mossy earth. They sprawled upon an isolated hummock of land amidst the swampy forest, the long-buried dome beneath them. Selden staggered away from the log and then collapsed, crying in relief. Reyn tottered, but found he could stand. 'Thank you,' he managed.

'You are not obliged to thank me. I've done as I said I would.' She flared her nostrils and a blast of steamy breath briefly warmed him. 'You'll live now?' It was as much statement as question.

His legs began to shake and he dropped down to his knees to keep from collapsing. 'If we can get back to Trehaug soon. We need food. And warmth.'

'I suppose I can take you there,' she conceded unwillingly.

'Thank Sa,' Reyn breathed as fervent a prayer as he had ever uttered. He drove himself to his feet and lurched over to Selden. He bent over and seized the boy, intending to lift him, found that his strength was not enough and managed only to pull Selden to his feet. Half-dragging the boy, he lurched towards Tintaglia.

'I'm exhausted,' Reyn told her. 'You will have to crouch down for us to climb onto your back.'

The dragon's eyes spun in silver disdain. 'Crouch?' she demanded. 'You upon my back? I think not, human.'

'But . . . you said you would take us to Trehaug.'

'I shall. However, no creature will ever bestride me, least of all a human. I shall carry you in my talons. Stand before me, together. I shall gather you up and carry you home.'

Reyn looked dubiously at her scaled forefeet. Her claws were silver, gleaming and sharp. He did not see how she could clutch them tightly enough to carry them without impaling them. He glanced down at Selden, to find the boy's upturned face mirroring his doubts. 'Are you afraid?' he asked him quietly.

Selden considered for a moment. 'I'm more hungry than I am afraid,' he decided. He straightened himself. His eyes roved over the dragon. When his gaze returned to Reyn, his face shone. He shook his head in wonder. 'Legends. Tapestries and paintings. They are all so feeble compared to how she shines. She is too amazing for distrust or fear. Even if she killed me right now, I'd still die in her glory.' The boy's extravagant words shocked Reyn. Selden summoned all his remaining strength with a deep breath. Reyn knew what it cost him to stand erect and declare, 'I'll let her carry me.'

'Oh? Will you?' the dragon teased him wickedly. Her eyes glittered with both amusement and pleasure at the boy's flattery.

'We will,' Reyn declared firmly. Selden was silent beside him, but gasped as the dragon reared suddenly onto her hind legs. She towered above them. It was as difficult a thing as Reyn had ever done to stand still as she reached for them with taloned forepaws. He held Selden at his side and did not move as the dragon closed her clawed hands around them. The tips of the claws walked over him, measuring him before her digits wrapped around him. The sharp ends of two talons rested against his back uncomfortably, but they did not pierce him. She clutched them both to her breast as a squirrel treasures a nut it has found. Selden gave an involuntary cry as she crouched on those tremendous hind legs, and she bounded skyward.

Her blue wings beat and they rose steadily. The trees closed below them. Reyn twisted his neck and got a dizzying view of treetops below him. His stomach lurched, but in the next instant his heart swelled with wonder. He almost forgot his fear in this perilous new aspect of the world. Green and swelling, the Rain Forest Valley unfurled itself far below them. Up and up the dragon carried them in a widening gyre that afforded him glimpses of the open river winding through the lush growth. The river, he saw, was a paler grey than usual. Sometimes, after large quakes, it ran white and acid for days and anyone out in a boat had best be mindful of his craft. When the river ran white, it ate wood swiftly. The dragon tipped her wings and they swung inland and upriver. Then he caught both sight and scent of Trehaug. Seen from above, the city hung throughout the tree branches like decorative lanterns. The smoke of cookfires rose in the still air.

'That's it!' He cried the words aloud to the dragon's unspoken question, and then realized he needn't have vocalized it at all. Held this close to her, their old bond had reasserted itself. He felt a chill moment of foreboding, but then sensed her sardonic reply: he needn't worry. Further involvement with humans held no place in her plans.

He was almost grateful for his empty stomach as they descended in dizzying spirals. He caught whirling glimpses of city and river as they came down, including a brief sighting of pointing and shouting figures that scattered before them. He sensed her disgust that there was no wide, flat space prepared for a dragon to land. What sort of a city was this?

They landed joltingly on the city docks. The platforms, free to rise and fall with the changing flow of the river, gave way to the impact. White spray flew up from the edges of the wharf, causing the nearby Kendry to rock alarmingly. The liveship roared his bewilderment. As the dock rose, rocking under the dragon's weight, Tintaglia opened her claws. Reyn and Selden fell at her feet. She swivelled aside from them to let her forepaws drop to the wood beside them. 'Now you will live,' she asserted.

'Now . . . we will . . . live,' Reyn panted. Selden lay like a stunned rabbit.

Reyn became aware of the thundering of footsteps and the excited susurrus of hushed conversation. He lifted his gaze. A veritable tide of people was flooding onto the piers. Many were begrimed with the mud of long digging. All looked weary despite the amazement on their faces. Some few gripped excavating tools as if they were weapons. All halted at the end of the dock. The incredulous shouts rose to a confused roar as folk gawked and pointed at Tintaglia. Reyn glimpsed his mother elbowing her way through the crowd. When she reached the front row of awed onlookers, she alone stepped free of the crowd and advanced cautiously towards the dragon. Then she saw him, and lost all interest in the towering beast.

'Reyn?' she asked incredulously. 'Reyn!' Her voice broke on his name. 'And you are alive? Praise Sa!' She ran to him and knelt by him.

He reached up to grip her hand. 'She lives,' he said. 'I was right. The dragon is alive.'

Before she could speak, a long wail interrupted them. Reyn saw Keffria break free of the clustered onlookers and race along the wharf to Selden. She knelt by him, and then gathered her boy up in her arms. 'Oh, thank Sa, he lives. But what of Malta? Where is Malta, where is my daughter?'

Reyn spoke the difficult words. 'I did not find her. I fear she perished in the city.'

Like a rising wind, the cry rose from Keffria's throat until it was a piercing scream of denial. 'No, no, no!' she wailed. Selden paled in her grip. The features of the tough little boy who had been Reyn's companion during their ordeal suddenly quivered into a child's face again. He added his sobs to her wailing.

'Mama, Mama, don't cry, don't cry!' He tugged at her but could not gain her attention.

'The one you call Malta isn't dead,' the dragon interrupted sharply. 'Stop this caterwauling and cease your emotional wallowing.'

'Not dead?' Reyn exclaimed.

His words were echoed by Selden. He seized his wailing mother and shook her. 'Mama, listen, didn't you hear what the dragon said? She said Malta is not dead. Stop crying, Malta isn't dead.' He turned a shining gaze on Tintaglia. 'You can trust the dragon. When she carried me, I could feel her wisdom right through my skin!'

Behind them on the docks, a rising chorus of talk drowned out Selden's words. Some folk were exclaiming in wonder. 'She spoke!' 'The dragon spoke!' 'Did you hear that?' Some nodded in surprised agreement, while others demanded to know what their friends meant. 'I heard nothing.' 'It snorted, that was all.'

Tintaglia's silver eyes greyed with disgust. 'Their minds are too small even to speak to mine. Humans!' She limbered her long neck. 'Stand clear, Reyn Khuprus. I am done with you and your kind now. My bond is fulfilled.'

'No! Wait!' Reyn jerked free of his mother's clutch on his arm. Boldly he gripped the clawed tip of Tintaglia's gleaming wing. 'You cannot go yet. You said Malta still lives. But where is she? How do you know she lives? Is she safe?'

Tintaglia twitched her wing tip effortlessly free of him. 'We were linked for a time, as well you know, Reyn Khuprus. Therefore, I retain some small awareness of her. As to where she is, I know not, save that she floats on water. On the river, I surmise, from the fear she feels. She is hungry and thirsty, but not otherwise injured that I can tell.'

Reyn fell to his knees before the dragon. 'Take me to her. I beg you. I will be forever in your debt if you will but do this one thing for me.'

Amusement flickered over the dragon's face. He knew it in the swift swirling of her eye colours, and the small flaring of her nostrils. 'I have no need of your service, human. And your company bores me. Fare well.' She lifted her wings and began to open them. 'Stand clear of me, if you would not be knocked down.'

Instead, Reyn sprang towards her. Her sleekly-scaled body afforded no purchase to his scrabbling hands. He flung himself at her foreleg and wrapped his arms around it as if he were a child clinging to his mother. But his words were full of force and fury. 'You cannot go, Tintaglia Dragon! Not and leave Malta to die. You know she did as much to free you as I did. She opened herself to the memories of the city. She discovered the secret catches that would open the great wall. But for her seeking you out, I would not have come into the city amidst the quakes. You would be buried even now! You cannot turn your back on such a debt! You cannot.'

Behind him, he was aware of garbled questions and conversation among his mother and Selden and Keffria. He didn't care what they overheard; he didn't care what the boy told them. Right now, all he could think of was Malta. 'The river runs white,' he went on to the dragon. 'White water eats boats. If she is on the river on a log or raft, the water will devour it and then her. She will die, because she ventured into the city to try to save you.'

The dragon's eyes spun silver flecked with scarlet, so great was her anger. She snorted a hot blast of breath that nearly knocked him down. Then with a single forepaw she snatched him up as if he were a doll stuffed with sawdust. Her talons closed painfully around his chest. He could barely take a breath.

'Very well, insect!' she hissed. 'I will help you find her. But after that, I have finished with you and yours. For whatever good you and she may have done me, your kin have committed great wrongs against all my kind.' She lifted him and thrust him towards the liveship. Kendry stared at them, and his face was that of a dying man. 'Do not think I do not know! Pray that I forget! Pray that after this day, you never see me again!'

He could not take a breath to reply, nor did she wait for words from him. With a mighty leap, she sprang upwards. The sudden lurch of the dock knocked down those who had ventured onto it. Reyn heard his mother's shriek of horror as the dragon bore him away. Then all sound was driven from his ears by the swift wind of their ascent.

He had not known, before this, what a care Tintaglia had taken for him and Selden on that earlier flight. Now she rose so swiftly that the blood pounded in his face and his ears popped. His stomach was surely left far below them. He could sense the fury seething through her. He had shamed her, before humans, using her own name. He had revealed her name to those others, who had no right to it.

He caught a breath but could not decide on words. To apologize might be as great an error as to tell her she owed this to Malta. He stilled his tongue and clutched her talons, trying to ease their grip around his ribs.

'Do you want me to loosen them, Reyn Khuprus?' the dragon mocked him. She opened her claws, but before he could slip through them to his death, she clamped them shut again. Even as he gasped in terror, she arrested their ascent, tipping her body and sending them in a wide spiral above the river. They were too high to see anything. The forested land below them was an undulating carpet of moss, the river no more than a white ribbon. She spoke to his thought.

'The eyes of a dragon are not like the eyes of a prey beast, small meat creature. I see as much as I need to see from here. She is not in sight. She must have been swept down the river.'

Reyn's heart turned over in his chest. 'We'll find her,' the dragon comforted him grudgingly. Her great wings began to sweep steadily, driving them down the course of the river.

'Go lower,' he begged her. 'Let me search for her with my own eyes. If she is in the shallows, she may be hidden by the trees. Please.'

She made no reply, but took him down so swiftly that he saw darkness at the edges of his vision. She flew with him down the river. He clutched at her talons with both his hands and endeavoured to watch all of the broad face of the river and both banks. Her flight was too swift. He tried to believe that the dragon's keener senses would find Malta even if he missed her, but after a time, despair took root in him. They had gone too far. If they had not found her yet, it was because she was no more.

'There!' Tintaglia exclaimed suddenly.

He looked, but saw nothing. She banked and turned as adroitly as a swallow, and brought him back over the same stretch of river. 'There. In that little boat, with two others. Close to the centre of the river. See her now?'

'I do!' Joy leaped in him, followed as quickly by horror. They had found her, and as Tintaglia bore him ever closer, he saw that the Satrap and his Companion were with her. But seeing her was not the same as rescuing her. 'Can you lift her up from the boat?' he asked the dragon.

'Perhaps. If I drop you and swamp the boat in the process. There is a chance I could snatch her up without doing more than breaking her ribs. Is that what you wish?'

'No!' He thought frantically. 'Can dragons swim? Could you land near her on the river?'

'I am not a duck!' Her disgust was manifest. 'If dragons choose to come down on a body of water, we do not stop on the surface, but plunge down to the bottom, and then walk out from there. I don't think you would enjoy the experience.'

He grasped at straws. 'Can you drop me into the boat?'

'To do what? Drown with her? Do not be foolish. The wind off my wings would swamp the boat long before I was close enough to drop you right through the bottom of it. Human, I have done my part. I have found her for you. Now you know where she is, it is up to you and the other humans to save her. My part in her life is over.'

It was no comfort. He had seen Malta's face turn up to them as they swept over her. He almost imagined he had heard her cry out to him, begging for rescue. Yet, the dragon was right. They could do nothing for Malta without putting all of them in greater danger.

'Take me back to Trehaug, swiftly,' he begged her. 'If the Kendry sets out after her now, with every thread of sail he can muster, we may yet overtake the boat before the river devours it.'

'A wise plan!' the dragon rumbled sarcastically. 'You would have been wiser still to have set out on the ship immediately instead of demanding this of me. I told you that she was on the river.'

The dragon's cold logic was disheartening. Reyn could think of nothing to say. Once more, her wings worked powerfully, taking them high above the multi-canopied forest. The land passed swiftly away beneath them as she carried him back towards Trehaug.

'Is there no way you can aid me?' he asked pitifully as she circled above the city. At the sight of her, all the folk on the dock ran for the shore. The winds off her great wings as she beat them to slow their descent buffeted the Kendry. Once more her heavy hindquarters absorbed the impact of their landing as the wharf plunged and bucked under them. She lifted him in her claws, craning her neck and turning her head to focus one huge silver eye on him.

'Little human, I am a dragon. I am the last Lord of the Three Realms. If any of my kind remain anywhere, I must seek them out and aid them. I cannot be concerned with a brief little spark like you. So. Fare as well as you can, on your own. I leave. I doubt we shall ever meet again.'

She set him on his feet. If she meant to be gentle, she failed. As he staggered away, he felt a sudden shock, more of mind than body. He was suddenly desperately afraid that he had forgotten something of vast importance. Then he realized that what was gone was his mental link with the dragon. Tintaglia had separated herself from him. The loss dizzied him. He seemed to have been taking some vitality from the link, for he was suddenly aware of hunger, thirst and extreme weariness. He managed to take a few steps before he went to his knees. It was as well that he was down, for otherwise he would have fallen as the dragon jolted the dock with her leap into the sky. A final time the beat of her wing wafted her reptilian stink over him. For no reason that he could understand, tears of loss stung his eyes.

The wharf seemed to keep rocking for a long time. He became aware of his mother kneeling beside him. She cradled his head in her lap. 'Did she hurt you?' she demanded. 'Reyn. Reyn, can you speak? Are you hurt?'

He drew a deep breath. 'Ready the Kendry to sail immediately. We must make all speed down the river. Malta, and the Satrap and his Companion . . . in a tiny boat.' He halted, suddenly too exhausted even to summon words.

'The Satrap!' a man exclaimed close by. 'Sa be praised! If he yet lives and we can recover him, then not all is lost. Haste to the Kendry. Make him ready to sail!'

'Send me a healer!' Jani Khuprus's voice rang out above the sudden murmur. 'I wish Reyn carried up to my apartments.'

'No. No.' He clutched feebly at his mother's arm. 'I must go with the Kendry. I must see Malta safe before I can rest.'

FIVE

Paragon and Piracy

'I DON'T MIN' A beatin' when I'm due one. But this'un wasn't tha. I dint do ennerthin wrong.'

'Most beatings I've had in my life came from just that. Not doing anything wrong, but not doing anything right either,' Althea observed impartially. She put two fingers under Clef's chin and turned his face up towards the fading daylight. 'It's not much, boy. A split lip and a bruised cheek. It will be gone in less than a week. It's not like he broke your nose.'

Clef pulled sullenly away from her touch. 'He woulda if I hadenna seen it comen.'

Althea clapped the ship's boy on the shoulder. 'But you did. Because you're quick and tough. And that's what makes a good sailor.'

'S'you think it was right, what he done t'me?' Clef demanded angrily.

Althea took a breath. She hardened her heart and her voice to reply coolly. 'I think Lavoy's the mate, and you're the ship's boy and I'm the second. Right and wrong don't come into it, Clef. Next time, be a bit livelier. And be smart enough to stay out of the mate's path if he's in a temper.'

'He's allus en a temper,' Clef observed sullenly. Althea let the remark pass. Every sailor had the right to moan about the mate but she could not allow Clef to think that she would take sides on this. She hadn't witnessed the incident; but she had heard Amber's outraged account of it. Amber had been up in the rigging. By the time she had regained the deck, Lavoy had stalked away. Althea was glad there had not been an encounter between the first mate and the ship's carpenter. Nevertheless, it had intensified the enmity Amber and Lavoy felt for one another. The clout Lavoy had given Clef had sent the lad flying, and all because the line he had been coiling hadn't lain as flat as the mate thought it should. Privately, Althea thought Lavoy was a brute and a fool. Clef was a good-natured lad whose best efforts were bought with praise, not brutality.

They stood on the stern, looking out over the ship's wake. In the distance, small islands were green hummocks. The water was calm but there was a light evening breeze and Paragon was making the most of it. Of late, the ship had seemed not only willing but almost eager to speed them on their way to the Pirate Isles. He had dropped all his talk of serpents and even his metaphysical musings on whether a person was what other people thought of him or what he thought of himself. Althea shook her head to herself as she watched some gulls diving on a shallow school of fish. She was glad he had stopped waxing philosophical. Amber had seemed to enjoy those long conversations, but Althea was unsettled by them. Now Amber complained that Paragon seemed withdrawn and abrupt, but to Althea he seemed healthier and more focused on the task at hand. It could not be good for a man or a liveship to ponder endlessly on the nature of himself. She glanced back at Clef. The ship's boy was cautiously tonguing the split in his lip. His blue eyes were far away. She nudged him gently.

'Best go get some sleep, boy. Your watch will roll around again soon enough.'

'I spose,' he agreed lackadaisically. He gazed at her absently for a moment; then seemed to focus on her. 'I know I gotter take it from hem. I learnt that when I was a slave. Sometimes yer just got ter take it from someone and kip yer head down.'

Althea smiled mirthlessly. 'Sometimes it seems to me there's not much difference between being a sailor and being a slave.'

'Mebbe,' the boy agreed truculently. 'Night, ma'am,' he added before he turned and made his way forwards.

For a short time longer, she watched their wake widening behind them. They had left Bingtown far behind. She thought of her mother and sister snugly at home, and envied them. Then she reminded herself of how boring she had found shoreside life, and how the endless waiting had chafed on her. They were probably sitting in her father's study right now, sipping tea and wondering how to bring Malta into Bingtown society on such a reduced budget. They'd have to scrimp and make do through the rest of the summer. To be fair, she decided they probably felt a great deal of anxiety for her, and for the fate of the family ship and Keffria's husband and son. They would have to endure it. She doubted she would return, for good or ill, before spring.

For herself, she'd rather worry about the bigger problem; how was she to find her family liveship and return Vivacia safely to Bingtown? When Brashen had last seen the liveship, Vivacia had been in the hands of the pirate Kennit, anchored in a pirate stronghold. It was not much to go on. The Pirate Isles were not only uncharted and infested with pirates, they were also an uncertain place to visit, for storms and inland floods often changed the contours of the islands, river mouths and waterways. So she had heard. In her trading trips south with her father, he had always avoided the Pirate Isles, precisely because of the dangers that she now directly dared. What would her father think of that? She decided that he would approve of her trying to recover the family ship, but not on her choice of rescue vessel. He had always said that Paragon was not only mad, but also a bad-luck ship. When she was a girl, he had forbidden her to have anything to do with him.

She turned aside suddenly and walked forwards as if she

could walk away from her uneasiness. It was a pleasant evening, she told herself, and the ship had been unusually stable and sailing well for the past two days. Lavoy, the first mate, had recently embarked on a storm of discipline and cleanliness, but that was not unusual. Brashen as captain had told him to break down the restraint between the sailors they had hired and those who had been smuggled aboard to escape from slavery. Any mate knew that the way to unite a crew was to keep them all on the ragged edge for a few days.

The crew as a whole could do with a bit more discipline and a lot more cleanliness. In addition to sharpening up their sailing skills, the crew had to learn to fight. And, she added morosely, not just to defend their ship, but to master the skills of attacking another vessel. Suddenly it all seemed too much. How could they hope to locate the Vivacia, let alone win her back with such a patchwork crew and an unpredictable vessel?

'Good evening, Althea,' Paragon greeted her. Without even thinking about it, she had come to the foredeck near the figurehead. Paragon turned his maimed face towards her as if he could see her.

'Good evening to you, Paragon,' she returned. She tried to put a pleasant note in her voice, but the ship knew her too well.

'So. Which of our troubles torments you most this evening?'

Althea surrendered. 'They all nip at my heels like a pack of yapping feists, ship. In truth, I don't know which to worry about first.'

The figurehead gave a snort of disdain. 'Then kick them away as if they were truly a pack of curs and fix your gaze instead on our destiny.' He swivelled his bearded face away from her, to stare sightlessly towards the horizon. 'Kennit,' he said in a low and fateful voice. 'We go to face down the pirate, and take back from him all that is rightfully ours. Let nothing stand between us and that end.'

Althea was stunned into silence. She had never heard the

ship speak so. Initially, he had been reluctant even to venture out on the water again. He had spent so many years as a beached and blinded derelict that he had balked at the idea of sailing, let alone setting out on a rescue mission. Now he spoke as if he not only accepted the idea, but relished the chance for vengeance against the man who had seized Vivacia. He crossed his muscular arms on his broad chest. His hands were knotted into fists. Had he truly made her cause his own?

'Don't think of the obstacles that lie between now and the moment when we confront him.' The ship spoke in a low, soft voice. 'Long or short, if you worry about every step of a journey, you will divide it endlessly into pieces, any one of which may defeat you. Look only to the end.'

'I think that we will only succeed if we prepare ourselves,' Althea objected.

Paragon shook his head. 'Teach yourself to believe you will succeed. If you say, when we find Kennit, we must be good fighters, then you have put it off until then. Be good fighters now. Be now what you must be to succeed at the end of your journey, and when the end comes, you will find it is just another beginning.'

Althea sighed. 'Now you sound like Amber,' she complained.

'No.' He contradicted her flatly. 'Now I sound like myself. The self I put aside and hid, the self I intended to be again someday, when I was ready. I have stopped intending. I am, now.'

Wordlessly, Althea shook her head to herself. It had been easier to deal with Paragon when he was sulky. She loved him, but it was not like her bond with Vivacia. Being with Paragon was often like caring for a beloved but ill-mannered and difficult child. Sometimes it was simply too much trouble to deal with him. Even now, when he seemed to have allied himself with her, his intensity could be frightening. An uncomfortable silence fell.

She pushed such thoughts aside and tried to relax into the gentle movement of the ship and the soothing night sounds. The peace didn't last long.

'You can say you told me so if you wish.' Amber's voice behind her was weary and bitter.

Althea waited for the ship's carpenter to join her at the railing before she hazarded her guess. 'You spoke to the captain about Lavoy and Clef?'

'I did.' Amber drew a kerchief from her pocket and wiped her brow. 'It did me no good. Brashen said only that Lavoy is the mate, Clef is the ship's boy, and that he would not interfere. I don't understand it.'

A slight smile curved Althea's mouth. 'Stop thinking of him as Brashen. If Brashen were on the street and saw Lavoy knock a young boy down, he'd jump right in. But we're not on the street. We're on a ship and he's the captain. He can't stand between the first mate and the crew. If he did it even once, the whole crew would lose respect for Lavoy. They'd have an endless string of complaints about him, and every one of them would wind up at the captain's feet. He'd be so busy nurse-maiding, he'd have no time to be captain. I'll wager that Brashen does not admire Lavoy's action any more than you do. But the captain knows that ship's discipline must come before a few bruises to a boy's pride.'

'How far will he let Lavoy go?' Amber growled.

'That's the captain's concern, not mine,' Althea replied. With a wry smile she added, 'I'm just the second mate, you know.' As Amber wiped her brow again and then the back of her neck, Althea asked, 'Are you well?'

'No,' Amber replied succinctly. She did not look at Althea, but Althea stared frankly at the carpenter's profile. Even in the fading light, her skin looked papery and taut, making her features sharper. Amber's colouring was always so odd that Althea could tell little from it, but tonight it reminded her of ageing parchment. She had bound her light brown hair back and covered it with a kerchief.

Althea let the silence stretch out between them, until Amber added reluctantly, 'But neither am I sick. I suffer a malady from time to time. Fever and weariness are all it brings. I shall be fine.' At Althea's horrified look, Amber hastily added, 'It is not a spreading disease. It will affect only me.'

'Nevertheless, you should tell the captain of your problem. And probably confine yourself to our quarters until it passes.'

They both startled when Paragon added quietly, 'Even the rumour of fever and plague aboard a ship can cause a crew to become jittery.'

'I can keep it to myself,' Amber assured her. 'I doubt that any besides you and Jek will notice my illness. Jek has seen it before; it will not bother her.' She turned suddenly to face Althea and demanded, 'How about you? Do you fear to sleep near me?'

Althea met her gaze through the gathering darkness. 'I think I will take your word that there is nothing to fear. But you should still tell the captain. He may be able to arrange your duties so that you have more time to rest.' She did not add that he probably would find ways to isolate Amber to keep her illness secret.

'The captain?' A small smile bent Amber's lips. 'You truly think of him that way all the time?'

'It is who he is,' Althea replied stiffly. At nights, in her narrow bunk, she certainly didn't think of Brashen as the captain. By days, she had to. She wouldn't tell Amber just how hard it was for her to keep that distinction clear. Talking about it wouldn't make it any easier. It was better kept to herself. She suspected uncomfortably that Paragon knew her true feelings for Brashen. She waited for him to say something horrible and revealing, but the figurehead kept silent.

'It is part of who he is,' Amber agreed easily. 'In some ways, it is his best part. I think he has lived many years, planning and dreaming about how he would be if he were the captain. I think he has suffered under poor captains, and learned well under good ones, and he brings all that to what he does now. He is more fortunate than he knows, to be able to live his dream. So few men do.'

'So few men do what?' Jek demanded as she strolled up and joined them. She grinned at Althea and gave Amber an affectionate nudge. She leaned on the railing, picking her teeth. Althea stared up at her enviously. Jek radiated vitality and health. The deckhand was long-boned, well muscled, and completely unselfconscious about her body. She did not bind her breasts at all, nor worry that her sailor's trousers reached no farther than her knee. Her long blonde braid was tattering to straw from the wind and saltwater, but she cared not at all. She is, Althea thought uneasily, what I pretend to be: a woman who does not let her sex deter her from living as she pleases. It wasn't fair. Jek had grown up in the Six Duchies, and claimed this equality as her birthright. Consequently, men usually ceded it to her. Althea still sometimes felt she needed someone's permission simply to be herself. Men seemed to sense that in her. Nothing came easily. She felt the struggle was as constant as her breathing.

Jek leaned over the railing. 'Good evening to you, Paragon!' Over her shoulder, she asked Amber, 'Can I borrow a fine needle from you? I've some mending to do, and I can't find mine anywhere.'

'I suppose so. I'll come in a bit and get it out for you.'

Jek shifted restlessly. 'Just tell me where it is and I'll get it,' she offered.

'Use mine,' Althea interjected. 'They're in my small duffel, pushed through a piece of canvas. There's thread in there, too.' Althea knew that Amber's exaggerated need for privacy extended to her personal belongings.

'Thanks. Now, what was this talk of what few men do?'

Jek allowed her lip to curl and a speculative look came into her eyes.

'Not what you're thinking,' Amber told her tolerantly. 'We were speaking of people living their dreams, and I said that few do, and even fewer enjoy the experience. For too many, when they get their dream, they discover it is not what they wanted. Or the dream is bigger than their abilities, and all ends in bitterness. But, for Brashen, it seems to be turning out well. He is doing what he always wished to do, and doing it well. He is a fine captain.'

'He is that,' Jek observed speculatively. She leaned back along the railing with catlike grace and stared up at the early stars speculatively. 'And I'll bet he does a fine job elsewhere also.'

Jek was a woman of appetites; it was not the first time Althea had heard her express interest in a man. Shipboard life and rules had pushed her into a period of abstinence that was at odds with her nature. Although she could not indulge her body, she let her mind run wild, and often insisted on sharing her ruminations with Althea and Amber. It was her most common topic of conversation on the rare nights when they were all in their bunks. Jek had a wry humour about her observations, and her tales of past liaisons gone awry often left the other two women helpless with laughter. Usually Althea found her ribald speculations about the male sailors amusing, but not, she discovered, when the man in question was Brashen. She felt as if she couldn't take a full breath.

Jek didn't appear to notice her stiff silence. 'Ever notice the captain's hands?' Jek asked them rhetorically. 'He's got the hands of a man that can work . . . and we've all seen him work, back there on the beach. But now that he's the captain and not in the tar and slush, he keeps his hands as clean as a gentleman's. When a man touches me, I hate to have to wonder where his hands last were, and if he's washed them since. I like a man with clean hands.' She let the thought trail away as she smiled softly to herself.

'He's the captain,' Althea objected. 'We shouldn't talk about him like that.'

She saw Amber wince for her at her prim little words. She expected Jek to turn her sharp wits and sharper tongue against her, and feared even more that Paragon would ask a question, but the woman only stretched and observed, 'He won't always be the captain. Or maybe I won't always be a deckhand on his ship. Either way, I expect a time will come when I won't have to call him "sir". And when it does . . .' She sat up abruptly, grinning with a flash of white teeth. 'Well.' She lifted an eyebrow. 'I think it would go well between us. I've seen him watching me. Several times he has praised me for working smartly.' More to herself than the others, she added, 'We're just of a height. I like that. It makes so many things more . . . comfortable.'

Althea could not hold the words back. 'Just because he praised you doesn't mean he's staring at you. The captain is like that. He recognizes a good job when he sees it. When he does, he speaks up, just as he would if he saw a bad bit of work.'

'Of course,' Jek conceded easily. 'But he had to be watching me to know that I work smart. If you take my drift.' She leaned over the railing again. 'What do you think, ship? You and Captain Trell go back a ways. I imagine you two have shared many a tale. What does he like in his women?'

In the brief silence that followed this question, Althea died. Her heart stilled, her breath caught in her chest. Just how much had Brashen shared with Paragon, and how much would the ship blurt out now?

Paragon had shifted his mood again. He spoke in a boyish voice, obviously flattered by the woman's attention. He sounded almost flirtatious as he replied, 'Brashen? Do you truly think he would speak freely of such things to me?'

Jek rolled her eyes. 'Is there any man who does not speak far too freely when he is around other men?'

'Perhaps he has dropped a story or two with me, from time to time.' The ship's voice took on a salacious tone.

'Ah. I thought that perhaps he had. So. What does our captain prefer, ship? No. Let me speculate.' She stretched in a leisurely manner. 'Perhaps, as he always praises his crew for "working smart and lively", that is what he prefers in a woman? One who is quick to run up his rigging and lower his canvas –'

'Jek!' Althea could not keep her offence from her tone, but Paragon broke in.

'In truth, Jek, what he has told me he prefers is a woman who is quiet more often than she speaks.'

Jek laughed easily at his remark. 'But while these women are being so quiet, what does he hope they'll be doing?'

'Jek.' All Amber's rebuke was in the single, quietly spoken word. Jek turned back to them with a laugh while Paragon demanded, 'What?'

'Sorry to interrupt the hen party, but the captain wishes to see the second mate.' Lavoy had approached quietly. Jek straightened up, her smile gone. Amber glowered silently at him. Althea wondered how much he had heard, and chided herself. She should not be loitering on the foredeck, talking so casually with crewmembers, especially on such topics. She resolved to imitate Brashen more in how he separated himself from the general crew. A little distance helped maintain respect. Yet the prospect of severing her friendship with Amber daunted her. Then she would truly be alone.

Just as Brashen was alone.

'I'll report right away,' she replied quietly to Lavoy. She ignored the belittlement of the 'hen party' remark. He was the first mate. He could rebuke, chide and mock her, and part of her duty was to take it. That he had done so in front of crewmembers rankled, but to reply to it would only make it worse.

'And when you're done there, see to Lop, will you? Seems our lad needs a bit of doctoring, it does.' Lavoy cracked his knuckles slowly as he let a smile spread across his face.

That remark was intended to bait Amber, Althea knew. The doctoring that Lop required was a direct result of Lavoy's fists. Lavoy had discovered Amber's distaste for violence. He had not yet found any excuse to direct his temper at Jek or the ship's carpenter, but he seemed to relish her reactions to the beatings he meted out to other crewmembers. With a sinking heart, Althea wished that Amber were not so proud. If she would just lower her head a bit to the first mate, Lavoy would be content. Althea feared what might come of the simmering situation.

Lavoy took Althea's place on the railing. Amber withdrew slightly. Jek wished Paragon a subdued, 'Good night, ship,' before sauntering quietly away. Althea knew she should hasten to Brashen's summons, but she did not like to leave Amber and Lavoy alone in such proximity. If something happened, it would be Amber's word against his. And when a mate declared something was so, the word of a common sailor meant nothing at all.

Althea firmed her voice. 'Carpenter. I want the latch on my cabin door repaired tonight. Little jobs should be seen to in calm weather and quiet times, lest they become big jobs during a storm.'

Amber shot her a look. In reality, Amber had been the one to point out that the door rattled against the catch instead of shutting tightly. Althea had greeted the news with a shrug. 'I'll see to it, then,' Amber promised her gravely. Althea lingered a second longer, wishing the carpenter would take the excuse to get away from Lavoy. But she didn't, and there was no way Althea could force her without igniting the smouldering tension. She reluctantly left them together.

The captain's quarters were in the stern of the ship. Althea knocked smartly, and waited for his quiet invitation to enter. The Paragon had been built with the assumption that the captain would also be the owner, or at least a family member. Most of the common sailors made do with hammocks strung belowdecks wherever they could find room. Brashen, however, had a chamber with a door, a fixed bed, a table and chart table, and windows that looked out over the ship's wake. Warm yellow lamplight and the rich smells and warm tones of polished wood greeted her.

Brashen looked up at her from the chart table. Spread before him were his original sketches on canvas scraps as well as Althea's efforts to formalize his charts on parchment. He looked tired, and much older than his years. His scalded face had peeled after he was burnt by the serpent venom. Now the lines on his forehead and cheeks and beside his nose showed even more clearly. The venom burn had taken some of his eyebrows as well. The gaps in his heavy brows made him look somewhat surprised. She was grateful that the spray of scalding poison had not harmed his dark eyes.

'Well?' Brashen suddenly demanded, and she realized she had been staring at him.

'You summoned me,' she pointed out, the words coming out almost sharply in her discomfiture.

He touched his hair, as if he suspected something amiss there. He seemed rattled by her directness. 'Summoned you. Yes, I did. I had a bit of a talk with Lavoy. He shared some ideas with me. Some of them seem valuable, yet I fear he may be luring me to a course of action I may regret later. I ask myself, how well do I know the man? Is he capable of deception, even . . .' He straightened in his chair, as if he had abruptly decided he was speaking too freely. 'I'd like your opinion on how the ship is being run of late.'

'Since the serpent attack?' she asked needlessly. There had been a subtle shift in power since she and Brashen had stood together to drive the serpent away. The men had more respect for her abilities now, and it seemed to her that Lavoy did not approve of that. She tried to find a way to phrase it without sounding as if she criticized the mate. She took a breath. 'Since the serpent attack, I have found my share of the command easier to manage. The sailors obey me swiftly and well. I feel that I have won their hearts as well as their allegiance.' She drew another breath and crossed a line. 'However, since the attack, the first mate has chosen to tighten discipline. Some of it is understandable. The men did not react well during the attack. Some did not obey; few jumped in to assist us.'

Brashen scowled as he spoke. 'I myself noted that Lavoy did not assist us. His watch was well begun and he was on the deck, yet he did not aid us at all.' Althea felt her stomach jump nervously. She should have noticed that. Lavoy had stood it out while she and Brashen fought the serpent. At the time, it had seemed oddly natural that they two would be the ones to stand before the serpent. She wondered if Lavoy's absence had any significance, beyond his being afraid. Had Lavoy hoped that she, Brashen, or even both of them might be killed? Did he hope to inherit command of the ship? If he did, what would become of their original quest? Brashen was silent again, obviously letting her think.

She took a breath. 'Since the serpent attack, the first mate has tightened discipline, but not evenly. Some of the men appear to be targeted unfairly. Lop, for one. Clef for another.'

Brashen watched her carefully as he observed, 'I would not have expected you to have much sympathy for Lop. He did nothing to aid you when Artu attacked you.'

Althea shook her head almost angrily. 'No one should have expected him to,' she declared. 'The man is a half-wit in some ways. Give him direction, tell him what to do, and he performs well enough. He was agitated when Artu . . . when I was fighting Artu off, Lop was leaping about, hitting himself in the chest and berating himself. He genuinely had no idea what to do. Artu was a shipmate, I was the second mate, and he did not know who to choose. But on the deck, when the serpent attacked, I remember that he was the one with the guts to fling a bucket at the creature and then drag Haff to safety. But for Lop's action, we'd be short a hand. He's not smart. Far from it. But he's a good sailor, if he's not pushed past his abilities.'

'And you feel Lavoy pushes Lop past his abilities?'

'The men make Lop the butt of their jokes. That is to be expected, and as long as they don't take it too far, Lop seems to enjoy the attention. But when Lavoy joins in, the game becomes crueller. And more dangerous. Lavoy told me to go doctor Lop when you were finished speaking to me. That's the second time in as many days that he has been banged up. They bait him into doing dangerous or foolish things. When something is amiss and Lavoy targets Lop for it, not one of his shipmates owns up to part of the blame. That's not good for the crew. It divides their unity just when we most need to build it.'

Brashen was nodding gravely. 'Have you observed Lavoy with the slaves we liberated from Bingtown?' he asked quietly.

The question jolted her. She stood silent a moment, running over the past few days in her mind. 'He treats them well,' she said at last. 'I've never seen him turn his temper on them. He does not mingle them with the rest of the crew as much as he might. Some seem to have great potential. Harg and Kitl deny it, but I believe they've worked a deck before this. Some of the others have the scars and manners of men who are familiar with weapons. Our two best archers have tattooed faces. Yet every one of them swears he is the son of a tradesman or merchant, an innocent inhabitant of the Pirate Isles captured by slave raiders. They are valuable additions to our crew, but they keep to themselves. I think, in the long run, we must get the other sailors to accept them as ordinary shipmates in order to . . .'

'And you perceive that he not only allows them to keep to themselves, but seems to encourage it by how he metes out the work?'

She wondered what Brashen was getting at. 'It could be so.' She took a breath. 'Lavoy seems to use Harg and Kitl almost as a captain would use a first and second mate to run his watch. Sometimes it seems that the former slaves are an independent second crew on the ship.' Uncomfortably, she observed, 'The lack of acceptance seems to go both ways. It is not just that our dock-scrapings don't accept the former slaves. The tattooed ones are just as inclined to keep to themselves.'

Brashen leaned back in his chair. 'They were slaves in Bingtown. Most came to that fate because they were originally captured in Pirate Isles towns. They were willing to risk all and steal away from Bingtown aboard the Paragon because we represented a chance to return home. I was willing to trade that to them, in exchange for their labour aboard the ship when we were preparing for departure. Now I am not so sure that was a wise bargain. A man captured in the Pirate Isles to be sold as a slave is more like to be a pirate than not. Or at least to have a good sympathy for the pirates.'

'Perhaps,' she conceded unwillingly. 'Yet they must feel some loyalty to us for helping them escape a life of slavery.'

The captain shrugged. 'Perhaps. It is difficult to tell. I suspect the loyalty they feel just now is to Lavoy rather than to you and me. Or to Paragon.' He shifted in his chair. 'This is Lavoy's suggestion. He says that as we enter the waters of the Pirate Isles, we stand a better chance of getting in close if we pretend to be pirates ourselves. He says his tattooed sailors could lend us credibility, and teach us pirate ways. He hints that some may even have a good knowledge of the islands. So. We could go on as a pirate vessel.'

'What?' Althea was incredulous. 'How?'

'Devise a flag. Take a ship or two, for the practice of battle, as Lavoy puts it. Then we put into one of the smaller pirate towns, with some loot and trophies and generous hands, and put out the word that we'd like to follow Kennit. For some time, this Kennit has been touting himself as King of the Pirates. The last I heard, he was gathering a following for himself. If we pretended we wanted to be a part of that following, we might be able to get close to him and determine Vivacia's situation before we acted.'

Althea pushed her outrage aside and forced herself to consider the idea. The greatest benefit it offered was that, if they could get close to Kennit, they could find out how many of Vivacia's crewmen still lived. If any. 'But we could as easily be drawn into a stronghold, where even if we overcame Kennit and his crew, there would be no possibility of escape. There are two other immense barriers to such an idea. The first is that Paragon is a liveship. How does Lavoy think we could hide that? The other is that we would have to kill, simply for battle practice. We'd have to attack some little merchant vessel, kill the crew, steal their cargo . . . how can he even think of such a thing?'

'We could attack a slaver.'

That jolted her into silence. She studied his face. He was serious. He met her astonished silence with a weary look. 'We have no other strategy. I keep trying to devise ways for us to locate Vivacia surreptitiously, then follow her and attack when Kennit least expects it. I come up with nothing. And I suspect that if Kennit does hold any of the original crew hostage, he would execute them rather than let us rescue them.'

'I thought we intended to negotiate first. To offer ransom for survivors and the ship.'

Even to herself, the words sounded childish and naïve. The cash that her family had managed to raise prior to Paragon's departure would not be enough to ransom an ordinary ship, let alone a liveship. Althea had pushed that problem to the back of her mind, telling herself they would negotiate with Kennit and promise him a second, larger payment once Vivacia was returned intact to Bingtown. Ransom was what most pirates wanted; it was the underlying reason for piracy.

Except that Kennit was not like most pirates. All had heard the tales of him. He captured slavers, killed the crews, and freed the cargo. The captured ships became pirate vessels, often crewed by the very men who had been cargo aboard them. Those ships in turn preyed on slavers. In truth, if the Vivacia had not been involved, Althea would have cheered Kennit's efforts to rid the Cursed Shores of slavery. She would have been pleased to see Chalced's slave trade choked off in the Pirate Isles. But her sister's husband had turned their family liveship into a slaver, and Kennit had seized her. Althea wanted Vivacia back so intensely that it was like a constant pain in her heart.

'You see,' Brashen confirmed quietly. He had been watching her face. She lowered her eyes from his gaze, suddenly embarrassed that he could read her thoughts so easily. 'Sooner or later, it must come down to blood. We could take down a small slaver. We don't have to kill the crew. If they surrendered, we could put them adrift in the ship's boats. Then we could take the ship into a pirate town and free her cargo, just as Kennit does. It might win us the confidence of the folk in the Pirate Isles. It might buy us the knowledge we need to go after the Vivacia.' He sounded suddenly uncertain. The dark eyes that regarded her were almost tormented.

She was puzzled. 'Are you asking my permission?'

He frowned. It was a moment before he spoke. 'It's awkward,' he admitted softly. 'I am the captain of the Paragon. But Vivacia is your family ship. Your family financed this expedition. I feel that, in some decisions, you have the right to be heard as more than the second mate.' He sat back in his chair and gnawed at his knuckle for a moment. Then he looked up at her again. 'So, Althea. What do you think?'

The way he spoke her first name suddenly changed the whole tenor of the conversation. He gestured to a chair and she sat down in it slowly. He himself rose and crossed the room. When he returned to the table, he carried a bottle of rum and two glasses. He poured a short jot into each glass. He looked across at her and smiled as he took his chair. He set a glass before her. As she watched his clean hands, she tried to keep her mind on the conversation. What did she think? She answered slowly.

'I don't know what I think. I suppose I've been trusting it all to you. You *are* the captain, you know, not me.' She tried to make the remark lightly, but it came out almost an accusation. She took a sip of her rum.

He crossed his arms on his chest and leaned back slightly in his chair. 'Oh, how very well I know that,' he murmured. He lifted his glass.

She turned the conversation. 'And there's Paragon to consider. We know his aversion to pirates. How would he feel about it?'

Brashen made a low noise in his throat and abruptly set down his rum. 'That's the strangest twist of all. Lavoy claims the ship would welcome it.'

Althea was incredulous. 'How could he know that? Has he already spoken to Paragon about this?' Anger flared in her. 'How dare he? The last thing we need is him planting such ideas in Paragon's head.'

He leaned across the table towards her. 'His claim was that Paragon spoke to him about it. He says he was having a pipe up on the bow one evening, and that the figurehead spoke to him, asking him if he'd ever considered turning pirate. From there, the idea came up that to be a pirate vessel would be the safest way to get into a pirate harbour. And Paragon bragged that he knew many secret ways of the Pirate Isles. Or so Lavoy says.'

'Have you asked Paragon about it?'

Brashen shook his head. 'I was afraid to bring it up with him; he might think that meant I approved it. Then he would fix all his energy on it. Or that I didn't approve of it, in which case he might decide to insist on it just to prove he could.

You know how he can be. I didn't want to present the idea unless we were all behind it. Any mention of it from me, and he might set his mind on piracy as the only correct course of action.'

'I wonder if that damage isn't already done,' Althea speculated. The rum was making a small warm spot in her belly. 'Paragon has been very strange of late.'

'And when has that not been true of him?' Brashen asked wryly.

'This is different. He is strange in an ominous way. He speaks of us encountering Kennit as our destiny. And says nothing must keep us from that end.'

'And you don't agree with that?' Brashen probed.

'I don't know about the destiny part. Brashen, if we could come upon Vivacia when she had only an anchor watch aboard her and steal her back, I would be content. All I want is my ship, and her crew if any have survived. I have no desire for any more battle or blood than there must be.'

'Nor have I,' Brashen said quietly. He added another jot of rum to each glass. 'But I do not think we will recover Vivacia without both. We must harden ourselves to that now.'

'I know,' she conceded reluctantly. But she wondered if she did. She had never been in any kind of battle. A couple of tavern scuffles were the extent of her brawling experience. She could not picture herself with a sword in her hand, fighting to free the Vivacia. If someone attacked her, she could fight back. She knew that about herself. But could she leap onto another deck, blade swinging, killing men she had never even seen before? Sitting here with Brashen in a warm and comfortable cabin, she doubted it. It wasn't the Trader way. She had been raised to negotiate for whatever she wanted. However, she did know one thing. She wanted Vivacia back. She wanted that savagely. Perhaps when she saw her beloved ship in foreign hands, anger and fury would wake in her. Perhaps she could kill then.

'Well?' Brashen asked her, and she realized she had been staring past him, out the stern window, at their lace-edged wake. She brought her eyes back to his. Her fingers toyed with her glass as she asked, 'Well what?'

'Do we become pirates? Or at least put on the countenances of pirates?'

Her mind raced in hopeless circles. 'You're the captain,' she said at last. 'I think you must decide.'

He was silent for a moment. Then, he grinned. 'I confess, on some level, it appeals to me. I've given it some thought. For our flag, how about a scarlet sea serpent on a blue background?'

Althea grimaced. 'Sounds unlucky. But frightening.'

'Frightening is what we want to be. And that was the scariest emblem I could think of, straight from my worst nightmares. As to the luck, I'm afraid we'll have to make that for ourselves.'

'As we always have. We'd go after slavers only?'

His face grew grave for a moment. Then a touch of his old grin lightened his eyes. 'Maybe we wouldn't have to go after anything. Maybe we could just make it look like we had . . . or that we intend to. How about a bit of play-acting? I think I'd have to be a dissatisfied younger son from Bingtown, something of a fop, perhaps. A gentleman come south to dabble in piracy and politics. What do you think?'

Althea laughed aloud. The rum was uncoiling in her belly, sending tendrils of warmth throughout her body. 'I think you could come to enjoy this too much, Brashen. But what about me? How would you explain female crew aboard a Bingtown vessel?'

'You could be my lovely captive, like in a minstrel's tale. The daughter of a Trader, taken hostage and held for ransom.' He gave her a sideways glance. 'That might help establish my reputation as a daring pirate. We could say the Paragon was your family ship, to explain away the liveship.'

'That's a bit overly dramatic,' she demurred softly. There was a brighter spark in his eyes. The rum was reaching them both, she decided. Just as she feared that her heart would overpower her head, his face turned suddenly grim. 'Would that we could play-act such a romantic farce and win Vivacia back. The reality of playing pirate would be far more bloody and ruthless. My fear is that I won't enjoy it nearly as much as Lavoy. Or Paragon.' He shook his head. 'Both of them have a streak of – what shall I call it? Just plain meanness, I sometimes think. If either one were allowed complete indulgence of it, I suspect they would sink to a savagery that you or I would find unthinkable.'

'Paragon?' Althea asked. There was scepticism in her voice, but a little shiver of certainty ran up her spine.

'Paragon,' Brashen confirmed. 'He and Lavoy may be a very bad mix. I'd like to keep them from becoming close, if such a thing is possible.'

A sudden knock at the door made them both jump. 'Who is it?' Brashen demanded roughly.

'Lavoy, sir.'

'Come in.'

Althea jumped to her feet as the first mate entered. His quick glance took in the rum bottle and the glasses on the table. Althea tried not to look startled or guilty, but the look he gave her expressed his suspicions plainly. His sarcasm was little short of insubordinate as he addressed Brashen. 'Sorry to interrupt you both, but there's ship's business to attend. The carpenter is unconscious on the forward deck. Thought you'd like to know.'

'What happened?' Althea demanded without thinking.

Lavoy's lip curled disdainfully. 'I'm reporting to the captain, sailor.'

'Exactly.' Brashen's voice was cold. 'So get on with it. Althea, go see to the carpenter. Lavoy, what happened?'

'Damn me if I know.' The burly mate shrugged elaborately. 'I just found her there and thought you'd like to know.'

There was no time to contradict him, nor was it the right

time to let Brashen know she had left them alone together. Her heart in her mouth, she raced off to see what Lavoy had done to Amber.

SIX

An Independent Woman

A DRIZZLING RAIN WAS falling from the overcast sky. Water dripped endlessly from the bushes in the gardens. Wet brown leaves carpeted the sodden lawns. Serilla let the lace edge of the curtain fall back into place. She turned back to the room. The greyness of the day had crept inside the house and Serilla felt chill and old in its embrace. She had ordered the curtains drawn and the fire built up in an effort to warm the room. Instead of feeling cosier, she felt muffled and trapped in the day. Winter was creeping up on Bingtown. She shivered. Winter was always an unpleasant season at best. This year it was an untidy and unsettled time as well.

Yesterday, with a heavy guard attending her, she had driven from Restart's estate down into Bingtown. She had ordered the men to take the carriage through the town, along the old market, and past the wharves. Everywhere she had seen destruction and disrepair. She had looked in vain for signs of repair and rebirth in the shattered city. Burned homes and shops gave off their clinging odour of despair. Piers ended in charred tongues of wood. Two masts stuck up from the sullen waters of the harbour. All the folk out in the streets had been hooded and cloaked against the day's chill, all hurrying somewhere. They looked away from her carriage as it passed.

Even those streets of the city where the remnants of the City Guard patrolled seemed edgy and repressed.

Gone were the bright teashops and prosperous trading companies. The bright and busy Bingtown that she had passed through on her first trip to Davad Restart's house had died, leaving this smelly, untidy corpse. Rain Wild Street was a row of boarded-up shop fronts and deserted stores. The few places that were open for trade had a guarded, anxious look to them. Thrice her carriage had been turned back by barricades of rubble.

She had planned to find merchants and neighbours who were making an effort to restore the city. She had imagined she would dismount from her carriage to greet them and praise their efforts. They were supposed to have invited her into their struggling shops, or walked her through their efforts at rebuilding. She would have congratulated them on their stout hearts, and they would have been honoured by her visit. Her plan had been to win their loyalty and love. Instead, she had seen only harried refugees, sullen-faced and withdrawn. No one had even offered her a greeting. She had returned to Davad's house and simply gone up to her bed. She had no appetite for supper.

She felt cheated. Bingtown was the glowing bauble she had always promised herself that she would someday possess. She had come so far and endured so much, simply to behold it so briefly. As if fate could not allow her any joy, the moment it seemed she might attain her goal, the city had destroyed itself. A part of her wanted simply to admit defeat, board a ship, and return to Jamaillia.

But there were no ships sailing safely to Jamaillia any more. The Chalcedeans lay in wait for any ship that tried to leave or enter Bingtown harbour. Even if she could somehow reach Jamaillia, what welcome would she receive? The plot against the Satrap had its roots in Jamaillia. She might be seen as a witness and a threat. Someone would find a way to eliminate her. She had been suspicious from the time the Satrap proposed that he leave Jamaillia on this jaunt to Bingtown and then visit Chalced afterwards. His nobles and advisors should have loudly protested such a move; it was rare for the reigning Satrap to travel so far outside the borders of Jamaillia. Instead of objections, he had received encouragement. She sighed to herself. The same set of sycophants who had taught him so young about the pleasures of flesh and wine and intoxicating herbs had encouraged him to leave the governing of his land completely to them while he travelled through hostile waters, in the care of dubious allies. Gullible and lazy, he had accepted the bait. Enticed by the invitations of his Chalcedean 'allies', promised exotic drugs and even more exotic fleshy pleasures, he had been led away from his throne like a child baited with candy and toys. His 'most loyal' followers who had always encouraged him to have his own way had done so to unseat him.

A sudden realization shocked her. She did not much care what became of the Satrap or his authority in Jamaillia. All she wished to do was to preserve his power in Bingtown, so she could claim it for her own. That meant uncovering who in Bingtown had been so willing to aid in his overthrow. The same people would try to depose her as well.

For a fleeting moment, she wished she had studied more about Chalced. There had been letters in the cabin of the Chalcedean captain, written in Jamaillian lettering, but in the Chalcedean language. She had recognized the names of two high Jamaillian nobles and the notation for sums of money. She had sensed then that she held the roots of a conspiracy in her hands. What had the Chalcedeans been paid to do? Or were they the ones who had paid? If she had been able to read those letters when the Chalcedean captain had held her prisoner there . . . then her mind shied away.

She hated what those nightmare days of confinement and rape had done to her. They had changed her irrevocably, in ways she despised. She could not forget that the Chalcedean captain had possessed life and death control over her. She could not forget that the Satrap, the boyish, spoiled, self-indulgent Satrap, had had the power to put her in such a position. It had forever altered her image of herself. It had made her recognize the full extent of the power men had over her. Well, she had power now, and as long as she guarded that power well, she would be safe. No man could ever impose his will on her again. She had the strength of her exalted position. Position would protect her. She must maintain it at any cost.

Yet for power, there was a price.

She lifted the corner of the curtain again and peered out. Even here in Bingtown, she was not safe from assassination attempts. She knew that. She never went out unaccompanied. She never dined alone and she always made sure that her guests were served before her and from the same dishes of which she would partake. If they did manage to kill her, at least she would not die alone. But she would not let them kill her, nor wrest from her the influence she had fought so hard to secure. There were threats to that power, but she could defeat them. She could keep the Satrap isolated and unable to communicate. For his own good, of course. She permitted herself a small smile. She wished they had not taken him so far away. If he were here in Bingtown, she could see that he got the pleasure herbs and comforts that would keep him manageable. She could find a way to separate him from Kekki. She could convince him that he was wise to lie low and let her manage things for him.

A discreet rap at the door interrupted her thoughts. She let the curtain fall again and turned back to the chamber. 'Enter.'

The serving woman had a tattooed face. Serilla was repulsed by the tattoo that spidered greenly across her cheek. She refused to look at her any more than she must. She would not have kept her, save that she was the only servant Serilla could find that was properly trained in Jamaillian courtesy. 'What is it?' she demanded as the woman curtseyed.

'Trader Vestrit wishes to speak with you, Companion Serilla.'

'Let her enter,' Serilla replied listlessly. Her spirits dropped yet another notch. She knew she was wise to keep the woman close, where she could watch her. Even Roed Caern had agreed to that. Serilla had been so pleased with herself when she first thought of the ruse. In a secret meeting, the heads of the Traders' Council had been horrified at her demand to have Ronica Vestrit seized. Even in times such as these, they refused to see the wisdom of such an act, and the thought of that confrontation made Serilla grit her teeth. It had proved to her the limitations of her power over them.

But she, in turn, had demonstrated to the Council heads her own resourcefulness. A graciously worded request had summoned the Trader woman to be Serilla's guest in Restart Hall. Ostensibly, Ronica was to aid Serilla by exploring all of Restart's records, not only to prove Davad's innocence but her own. After some hesitation, Ronica had agreed. Serilla had initially been pleased with herself. Having Ronica Vestrit live under her roof simplified Roed's task of spying on her. He would soon uncover who was in league with her. But there was a cost to Serilla's tactic. Knowing the Trader woman was close by was like knowing there was a serpent in one's bed. To be aware of a danger did not necessarily disarm it.

The day Ronica arrived, Serilla had been sure of her triumph. Ronica brought no possessions save the bundles she and her maid carried. Her servant was a tattoo-faced former slave who treated the Trader woman almost as if they were equals. The Vestrit woman had little clothing and no jewellery at all. As plain Ronica had sat eating at the foot of Serilla's table that evening, the Companion had felt triumphant. This pitiful creature was no threat: she would become a symbol of the Companion's charity. And eventually some slip of hers would betray her fellow conspirators. Whenever she left the house, Roed followed her.

Nevertheless, since Ronica had moved into Davad's old bedroom, the woman had not let Serilla have even one day of peace. She was like a humming gnat in her ear. Just when Serilla should be concentrating all her efforts on consolidating her power, Ronica distracted her at every turn. What was she doing about clearing the sunken ships from the harbour? Was there any word of aid from Jamaillia? Had she sent a bird to Chalced, to protest these acts of war? Had she tried to gain the support of the Three Ships folk to patrol the streets at night? Perhaps if the former slaves were offered paying work, they would prefer it to roaming as looting gangs. Why had Serilla not urged the Bingtown Council to convene and take charge of the city again? Every day, Ronica pushed at her with questions like these. In addition, at every opportunity, she reminded Serilla that she was an outsider. When Serilla ignored her other demands, Ronica went back with monotonous tenacity to insisting that Davad was not a traitor, and that Serilla had no right to his property. The woman did not seem to respect her at all, let alone afford her the courtesy due a Satrap's Companion.

It rankled even more because Serilla was not sure enough of her position to bring her authority to bear on the Trader. Too often she had given in to the woman's nagging; first, to have Davad buried, and again to surrender some orchard to the traitor's niece. She would not give in to her again. It only encouraged her.

Roed had reported to her how the woman spent her mornings. Despite the dangers of the street, Ronica Vestrit and her maid ventured out each day, to go on foot from door to door, rallying the Traders to convene. Roed had reported that she was often turned away or treated brusquely by those she called upon, but the woman was insistent. Like rain on a stone, Serilla thought, she wore down the hardest heart. Tonight she would gain her largest triumph. The Council would convene.

If the Traders listened to Ronica tonight and decided that

Davad had never been at fault, it would seriously undermine Serilla's authority. If the Council decided his niece should inherit his estate, Serilla would have to move out of Restart Hall and be forced to ask hospitality of another Trader. She would lose her privacy and her independence. She could not allow that to happen.

Serilla had gently but firmly opposed the Council's convening, telling them all it was too early, that it was not safe for the Traders to gather in one place where they could be attacked; but they were no longer listening to her.

Time was all Serilla had needed; time to make her alliances stronger, time to know who could be persuaded with flattery and who needed offers of titles and land. Time might bring her another bird with tidings from Jamaillia. One Trader had brought her a bird-message from his trading partner in Jamaillia. Rumours of the Satrap's death had reached the city, and riots were imminent. Could the Satrap send a missive in his own hand to disperse this dangerous gossip? She had sent back a bird with a message of reassurance that the rumour was false, and a query as to who had received the message about the Satrap's death, and from whom? She doubted she would get a reply. What else could she do? If only she had another day, another week. A bit more time, and she was sure she could master the Council. Then, with her superior education and experience of politics and knowledge of diplomacy, she could guide them to peace. She could make them see what compromises they must accept. She could unite all the folk of Bingtown and, from that base, treat with the Chalcedeans. That would establish for all her authority in Bingtown. Time was all she needed, and Ronica was stealing it from her.

Ronica Vestrit swept into the room. She carried a ledger under her arm. 'Good morning,' she greeted Serilla briskly. As the servant left the room, Ronica glanced after her. 'Would not it be far simpler for me to announce myself, rather than have me find the servant to knock at the door and say my name?'

'Simpler, but not proper,' Serilla pointed out coldly.

'You're in Bingtown now,' Ronica replied evenly. 'Here we do not believe in wasting time simply for the purpose of impressing others.' She spoke as if she were instructing a recalcitrant daughter in manners. Without asking leave, she went to the study table and opened the ledger she had brought. 'I believe I've found something here that may interest you.'

Serilla walked over to stand by the fire. 'That I doubt,' she muttered sourly. Ronica had been far too assiduous in tracking down evidence. Her constant ploys to mislead Serilla were vexatious, and making her own deception wear thin.

'Do you weary so quickly of playing Satrap?' Ronica asked her coldly. 'Or is this, perhaps, the way you believe a ruler is to behave?'

Serilla felt as if she had been slapped. 'How dare you!' she began, and then her eyes widened even more. 'Where did you get that shawl?' she demanded. Serilla knew she had seen it in Davad's bedroom, flung over the arm of a chair. How presumptuous of the woman to help herself to it!

For an instant, Ronica's eyes went wide and dark, as if Serilla had caused her pain. Then her face softened. She reached up to stroke the soft fabric draped across her shoulders. 'I made it,' she said quietly. 'Years ago, when Dorill was pregnant with her first child. I dyed the wool and wove it myself to be a special gift from one young wife to another. I knew she loved it, but it was touching to find that of all her things, this was what Davad had kept close by him to remember her. She was my friend. I don't need your permission to borrow her things. You are the one who is a looter and an intruder here, not I.'

Serilla stared at her, speechless with fury. A petty vengeance occurred to her. She wouldn't look at the woman's feeble evidence. She would not give her the satisfaction. She gritted her teeth and turned away from her. The fire was dying. That was why she felt suddenly chilled. Were there no decent servants anywhere in Bingtown? Angrily

Serilla picked up the poker herself to try to stir the coals and logs back to life.

'Are you going to look at this ledger with me, or not?' Ronica demanded. She stood, her finger pointing at some entry as if it were of vast importance.

Serilla let her anger boil over. 'What makes you think I have time for this? Do you think I have nothing better to do than strain my eyes over a dead man's spidery handwriting? Open your eyes, old woman, and see what confronts all of Bingtown instead of dwelling on your private obsession. Your city is dying, and your people do not have the backbone to fight its death. Despite my orders, gangs of slaves continue to loot and steal. I have commanded that they be captured and forced to serve in an army to defend the city, but nothing has been done. The roads are blocked with debris, but no one has moved to clear them. Businesses are closed and folk huddle behind the doors of their homes like rabbits.' She whacked a log with the poker, sending a stream of sparks flying up the chimney.

Ronica crossed the room and knelt down by the hearth. 'Give me that thing!' she exclaimed in disgust. Serilla dropped the poker disdainfully beside her. The Bingtown Trader ignored the insult. Picking it up, she began to lever the ends of the half-burned logs back into the centre of the fire. 'You are looking at Bingtown from the wrong vantage. Our harbour is what we must hold, first. As for the looting and disorder – I blame you as much as my fellow Traders. They sit about like a great flock of boobies, half of them waiting for you to tell them what to do and the other half waiting for someone else to do it. You have brought division amongst us. But for you proclaiming that you speak with the Satrap's authority, the Bingtown Council would have taken charge as we always have before. Now some of the Traders say they must listen to you, and some say they must take care of themselves first, and others, wisely I think, say we should simply convene all the like-minded folk in the town and get to work on things. What does it matter now if we are Old Traders or New Traders or Three Ships or just plain immigrants? Our city is a shambles, our trade is ruined, the Chalcedeans pluck all who venture out of Trader Bay, while we squabble amongst ourselves.' She rocked back on her heels, and looked in satisfaction at the recovering fire. 'Tonight, perhaps, we shall finally act on some of that.'

A terrible suspicion was forming in Serilla's mind. The woman intended to steal her plans and present them as her own! 'Do you spy upon me?' she demanded. 'How is it that you know so much of what is said about the city?'

Ronica gave a snort of contempt. She rose slowly to her feet, her knees cracking as she stood. 'I have eyes and ears of my own. And this city is my city, and I know it better than you ever could.'

As Ronica hefted the cold weight of the poker in her hand, she watched the Companion's eyes. There it was again, that flash of fear in the woman's face. Ronica suddenly knew that the right choice of words and threats could reduce this woman to a snivelling child. Whoever had broken her had broken her completely. She was a hollow shell of authority concealing an abyss of fear. Sometimes the Trader felt sorry for her. It was almost too easy to bully her. Yet, when such thoughts came to her, she hardened her heart. Serilla's fear made her dangerous. She saw everyone as a threat. The Companion would rather strike first and be mistaken than suffer the possibility someone might act against her. Davad's death proved that. This woman had claimed an authority over Bingtown that Ronica did not believe anyone, not even the Satrap, possessed. Worse, her attempts to wield the power she claimed were fragmenting what remained of Bingtown's ability to govern itself. Ronica would use whatever tactics came to hand to try to move

Bingtown back towards peace and self-government. Only if there was peace was there any hope of Ronica recovering her family, or indeed, finding out if any of them had survived.

So she mimed the woman's contemptuous gesture and tossed the poker onto the stone hearth. As it landed with a clang and rolled away, she saw the Companion flinch. The fire was recovering nicely now. Ronica turned her back on it and crossed her arms on her chest as she faced Serilla. 'People gossip, and if one wants to know what is really going on, one listens to them. Even servants, if treated as human beings, can be a source of information. So it is that I know that a delegation of New Traders, headed by Mingsley, has made overtures of truce to you. That is precisely why it is so important that you look at what I have uncovered in Davad's records. So you will proceed with caution where Mingsley is concerned.'

Serilla's cheeks turned very pink. 'So! I invite you into my home, out of pity for you, and you take the opportunity to spy on me!'

Ronica sighed. 'Haven't you heard a word I said? That information did not come from spying on you.' Other information had, but there was no point in revealing that now. 'Nor do I need your pity. I accept my current fortune. I've seen my situation change before, and I will see it change again. I don't need you to change it.' Ronica gave a small snort of amusement. 'Life is not a race to restore a past situation. Nor does one have to hurry to meet the future. Seeing how things change are what makes life interesting.'

'I see,' Serilla commented disdainfully. 'Seeing how things change. This is the hardy Bingtown spirit I have heard touted about so much, then? A passive patience to see what life will do to you. How inspiring. Then you have no interest in restoring Bingtown to all it was?'

'I have no interest in impossible tasks,' Ronica retorted. 'If we focus on trying to go back to what Bingtown was, we are doomed to defeat. We must go forwards, create a new

Bingtown. It will never be the same as it was. The Traders will never again wield as much power as we did. But we can still go on. That is the challenge, Companion. To take what has happened to you and learn from it, instead of being trapped by it. Nothing is quite so destructive as pity, especially self-pity. No event in life is so terrible that one cannot rise above it.'

The look Serilla gave her was so peculiar that Ronica felt a shiver down her spine. For an instant, it was as if a dead woman stared out of her eyes. When she spoke it was in a flat voice. 'You are not as worldly as you think you are, Trader. If you had ever endured what I have faced, you would know that there are events that are insurmountable. Some experiences change you forever, past any cheery little wish to ignore them.'

Ronica met her gaze squarely. 'That is only true if you have determined it is true. This terrible event – whatever it was – is over and done. Cling to it and let it shape you and you are doomed to live it forever. You are granting it power over you. Set it aside, and shape your future as you wish it to be, in spite of what happened to you. Then you have seized control of it.'

'That's easier said than done,' Serilla snapped. 'You cannot imagine how appallingly ignorant you sound, with your girlish optimism. I think I've had enough provincial philosophy for one day. Leave.'

'My "girlish optimism" is the Bingtown spirit you have "heard touted about so much",' Ronica snapped back at her. 'You fail to recognize that a belief in being able to conquer your own past is what made it possible for us to survive here. It is what you need to find in yourself, Companion, if you hope to be one of us. Now. Are you going to look at these entries, or not?'

Ronica could almost see the woman's hackles rise. She wished she could approach Serilla as a friend and ally, but the Companion seemed to regard any woman as a rival or a spy. So she stood straight and cold while she waited for Serilla's reaction. She watched her with a bargainer's eyes and saw Serilla's glance dart to the opened ledgers on the table, and then back to Ronica. The woman wanted to know what was in them, but she did not wish to appear to be giving in. Ronica gave her a bit more time, but when the Companion was still silent, she decided to risk it all.

'Very well. I see you are uninterested. I had thought you would wish to see what I had discovered before I took it to the Bingtown Council. But if you will not listen to me, I am sure they will.' With a resolute stride, she crossed to the ledger on the desk. Closing it, she tucked the heavy volume under her arm. She took her time leaving the room, hoping that Serilla would call her back. She walked slowly down the hall, still hoping, but all she heard was the firm shutting of Davad's study door. It was no use. With a sigh, Ronica began to climb the stairs to Davad's bedchamber. She halted at the sound of a knock on the great front door, then moved swiftly to stand near the banister and look down silently at the entry below.

A serving woman opened the door, and began a correct greeting, but the young Trader pushed past her. 'I bear tidings for the Companion Serilla. Where is she?' Roed Caern demanded.

'I will let her know that you are –' the servant began, but Roed shook his head impatiently.

'This is urgent. A messenger bird has come from the Rain Wilds. Is she in the study? I know the way.' Without allowing the servant time to reply, he pushed past her. His boots rang on the flagging and his cloak fluttered behind him as he strode arrogantly down the hall. The serving woman trotted at his heels, her protests unheeded. Ronica watched him go, and wondered if she had the courage to venture down to eavesdrop.

'How dare you charge in like that!' Serilla spoke as she rose from poking again at the fire. She let every bit of her anger and frustration at the Trader woman vent. Then, as she met the sparks in Roed Caern's eyes, she took an inadvertent step back towards the hearth.

'I beg pardon, Companion. I foolishly assumed that tidings from the Rain Wilds would merit your immediate attention.' Between thumb and forefinger, he held a small brass cylinder of the type messenger birds carried. As she stared at it, he dared to bow stiffly. 'I shall, of course, await your convenience.' He turned back towards the door where the serving woman still gaped and spied.

'Shut that door!' Serilla snapped at her. Her heart thundered in her chest. The Satrap's guardians had taken only five messenger birds from Davad's cotes the night she had dispatched the Satrap to the Rain Wilds. They would not use them needlessly. This was the first message to come since she had heard the Satrap had arrived there and that the Rain Wild folk had consented to hold him in safekeeping. She had sensed then their ambivalence about her request. Had the Satrap swayed the Rain Wilders to his point of view? Was this to charge her with treason? What was in the cylinder and who else had read it? She tried to compose her face, but the cruel amusement on the tall dark man's face made her fear the worst.

Best to soothe his ruffled fur, first. He reminded her of a savage watchdog, as like to turn on its master as protect her. She wished she did not have such need of him.

'You are correct, of course, Trader Caern. Such tidings do need to be delivered immediately. In truth, I have been plagued with household affairs this morning. Servant after servant has disturbed my work. Please. Come in. Warm yourself.' She even went so far as to accord him a gracious bow of her head, though, of course, her rank was far higher than his.

Roed bowed again, deeply, and she suspected, sarcastically. 'Certainly, Companion. I understand how annoying that can be, especially when such weighty matters press upon your delicate shoulders.'

It was there, a note in his voice, a selection of a word.

'The message?' she prompted him.

He advanced, and bowed yet again as he presented the cylinder to her. The wax it had been dipped in appeared undisturbed. But nothing would have prevented him from reading the missive, and then re-dipping the container. Useless to worry. She flicked the wax away from the cylinder, unscrewed it, and coaxed the tiny roll of parchment into her fingers. With a calmness she did not feel, she seated herself at the desk and leaned close to the lamp as she unrolled the message.

The words were brief, and in their brevity, a torment. There had been a major earthquake. The Satrap and his Companion were lost, perhaps killed in the collapse. She read it again, and yet again, willing there to be more information there. Was there any hope he had survived? What did it mean to her ambitions if the Satrap were dead? On the heels of that, she wondered if this message were a deception, for reasons too intricate to unravel? She stared at the crawling letters.

'Drink this. You look as if you need it.'

It was brandy in a small glass. She had not even noticed Roed taking the bottle down or pouring, but she accepted it gratefully. She sipped it and felt its heat steady her. She did not challenge him as he picked up the tiny missive and read it. Without looking at him, she managed to ask, 'Will others know this?'

Roed seated himself insolently on the corner of the desk. 'There are many Traders in this city that keep close ties with their Rain Wild kin. There are other birds a-wing with the same news. Depend on it.'

She had to look up at his smile. 'What shall I do?' she heard herself ask, and hated herself. With that one question, she put herself completely in his power.

'Nothing,' he replied. 'Nothing, just yet.'

* * *

Ronica opened the door of Davad's bedchamber. Her slippers were still damp. The stout door of the study had contained the Companion's conversation too well, and her walk through the garden had been fruitless. The study windows were tightly closed as well. Ronica looked around Davad's room with a sigh. She longed for her own home. She was, perhaps, safer here, and she knew she was closer to the work she must do, but she missed her own home, no matter how ransacked it was. She still felt an intruder here. She found Rache at work scrubbing the floor, apparently bent on eradicating every trace of Davad from the chamber. Ronica shut the door quietly behind her.

'I know you hate being here, in Davad's home, amongst his things. You don't have to stay, you know,' she said gently. 'I am more than capable of taking care of myself. You owe me nothing. You could go your own way now, Rache, with little fear of being seized as a runaway slave. You are more than welcome to continue to make your home with me, of course. Or, if you wished, I could give you a letter and directions. You could go to Ingleby, and live on the farm there. I am sure that my old nanny would make you welcome there, and probably be glad of your company.'

Rache dropped her rag into the bucket and got stiffly to her feet. 'I would not abandon the only one who showed me kindness in Bingtown,' she informed her. 'Perhaps you can take care of yourself, but you still have need of me. I care nothing at all for Davad Restart's memory. What does it matter if he is a traitor, when I know he was a murderer? But I would not see you defamed simply by your connection to him. Besides, I have more tidings for you.'

'Thank you,' Ronica said, stiffly. Davad had been a long-time family friend, but she had always acknowledged his ruthless side. Yet how much blame should Davad bear for the death of Rache's child? True, Davad's money had bought them, and he was a part-owner of the slave ship. But he had not been there when the boy had died in the hold of the ship, overcome by heat, bad water and little food. Nonetheless, he was the one who profited from the slave trade, so perhaps he was to blame. Her soul squirmed within her. What, then, of the Vivacia and the slaves that had been her cargo? She could blame it all on her son-in-law. The ship had been in Keffria's control, and her daughter had let her husband Kyle do as he wished with it. But how firmly had Ronica resisted? She had spoken out against it, but perhaps if she had been more adamant . . .

'Do you wish to hear my news?' Rache asked her.

Ronica came back from her woolgathering with a start. 'Certainly.' She moved to the hearth and checked the kettle on the hob. 'Shall we have tea?'

'It's nearly gone,' Rache cautioned her.

Ronica shrugged. 'When it's gone, it's gone. No use letting it go stale for fear of going without.' She found the small container of tea and shook some into the pot. They ate at Serilla's table, but here in their rooms, Ronica liked the small independence of her own teapot. Rache had matter-of-factly liberated teacups, saucers and other small amenities from Davad's kitchen. She set these out on a small table as she spoke.

'I've been out and about this morning. I went along the wharves, discreetly of course, but there is little going on down there. The small ships that do come in unload and load quickly, with armed men standing about all the time. I'd say there was one New Trader, probably a joint venture by several families. The cargo appeared to be mostly foodstuffs. Two other ships looked Old Trader to me, but again, I didn't go close enough to be sure. The liveship Ophelia was in the harbour, but anchored out, not tied. There were armed men on her decks.

'I left the harbour. Then, I did as you suggested, and went down to the beach where the fisherfolk haul out. There it was livelier, though there were not near the number of little boats there used to be. There were five or six small boats pulled out, with folk sorting the catch and re-stowing their nets. I offered to work for a bit of fish, but they were cool to me. Not rude, mind you, but distant, as if I might bring trouble or be a thief. The ones I talked to kept looking off behind my shoulder, as if they thought I might be distracting them from someone else, someone that meant them harm. But after a while, when I was obviously alone, some of them felt sorry for me. They gave me two small flounders, and talked with me a bit.'

'Who gave you the flounders?'

'A fisherwoman named Ekke. Her father told her to, and when one of the other men looked as if he might object, he said, "Folk got to eat, Ange." The generous man's name was Kelter. A wide man, chest and belly all one big barrel, with a red beard and red hair down his arms, but not much on the crown of his head.'

'Kelter.' Ronica dug through her memories. 'Sparse Kelter. Did anyone call him Sparse?'

Rache gave a nod. 'But I thought it more a tease than a name.'

Ronica frowned to herself. The kettle was boiling, the steam standing well above the spout. She lifted it from the hob and poured water into the teapot. 'Sparse Kelter. I've heard the name somewhere, but more than that I can't say of him.'

'From what I saw, he's the man we want. I didn't speak to him of it, of course. I think we should go slow and be careful yet. But if you want a man who can speak to and for the Three Ships families, I think he is the one.'

'Good.' Ronica let the satisfaction ring in her voice. 'The Bingtown Council meets tonight. I plan to present what information I have, and urge that we begin to unite with the rest of the city once more. I do not know what success I shall have, if any. It is so discouraging that so few have done anything for themselves. But I will try.'

Silence held for a few moments. Ronica sipped at her tea.

'So. If they will not listen to you, will you give up, then?' Rache asked her.

'I cannot,' Ronica replied simply. Then she gave a short, bitter laugh. 'For if I give up, I have nothing else to do. Rache, this is the only way I can help my family. If I can be the gadfly that stings Bingtown into action, then it might be safe for Keffria and the children to return. At the very least, it might be possible for me to get word to them, or to hear from them. As things stand, with the city in sporadic fighting and my neighbours distrusting one another, not to mention considering me a traitor, my family cannot return. And if by some miracle Althea and Brashen do manage to bring Vivacia home, then there must be a home for them to return to. I feel like a juggler, Rache, with all the clubs raining down upon me. I must catch as many as I can and try to set them spinning again. If I cannot, I am nothing more than an old woman living hand to mouth until my days end. It is my only hope to regain my life.' She set her teacup down. It clinked gently against the saucer. 'Look at me,' she went on quietly. 'I have not even a teacup to call my own. My family . . . dead, or so far away that I know nothing of them. Everything I took for granted has been snatched from me; nothing in my life is as I expected it to be. People are not meant to live like this . . .'

Ronica's words trailed off as Rache's eyes met hers. She suddenly recalled to whom she was speaking. The next words fell from her tongue without thought. 'Your husband was sold ahead of you and sent on to Chalced. Have you ever thought of seeking him out?'

Rache cupped both hands around her tea as she looked down into it. The lashes of her eyes grew wet, but no tears fell. For a long moment, Ronica regarded the straight pale parting in her dark hair.

'I'm sorry –' she began.

'No.' Rache's voice was soft but firm. 'No. I shall never seek him out. For I like to imagine that he has found a kind master who treats him well for the sake of his pen skills. I can hope that he believes that his son and I are alive and well somewhere. But if I went to Chalced, with this mark upon my face, I would quickly be seized as a runaway slave. I would become chattel again. Even if I didn't, even if I found him alive, then I should have to tell him how our son died. How our son died and yet I still lived. How could I explain that to him? No matter how I imagine it, it never comes out well. Follow it to the end, Ronica. It always ends in bitterness. No. As bitter as it is now, it is still the best ending I can hope for.'

'I'm sorry,' Ronica repeated lamely. If she had still had money, if she had had a ship, she could have sent someone to Chalced, to seek for Rache's husband, to buy him and bring him back. Then . . . and then they could both live with the knowledge of their dead son. But there could be other children. Ronica knew that. She and Ephron had lost all their sons in the Blood Plague, but Althea had been born to them afterwards. She said nothing to Rache, but she made a small promise to herself and Sa. If her fortune turned, she would do what she could to change Rache's fortunes as well. It was the least she could do for the woman after she had stood by her side for so long.

First, she would have to change her own fortune. It was time she stopped letting other folk do her dangerous work.

'I make no progress with Serilla,' she told Rache abruptly. 'It is time to take what I know and build upon it, regardless of what the Council decides tonight. If they decide anything at all. Tomorrow, very early, I will go with you to the fishermen's beach. We will have to catch them before they go out for the morning's fishing. I will talk to Sparse Kelter myself, and ask him to speak to the other Three Ships families. I will tell them it is time, not only to make peace with Bingtown, but for Bingtown to declare that we rule ourselves. But it will take all of us, not just Old Traders. Three Ships immigrants, even those New Traders who can be persuaded to live by our old ways. No slavery. All must be a part of this new Bingtown we shall build.' Ronica paused, thinking. 'I wish I knew of even one New Trader who was trustworthy,' she muttered to herself.

'All,' Rache said quietly.

'All the New Traders?' Ronica asked in confusion.

'You said all must be part of this new Bingtown. Yet there is a group you have left out.'

Ronica considered. 'I suppose that when I say Three Ships, I mean all the folk who came to settle after the Bingtown Traders had established Bingtown. All the folk who came and took our ways as their own.'

'Think again, Ronica. Do you truly not see us, even though we are here?'

Ronica closed her eyes for a moment. When she opened them, she met Rache's gaze honestly. 'I am ashamed of myself. You are right. Do you know of anyone who can speak for the slaves?'

Rache looked at her levelly. 'Call us not slaves. Slave was how they named us to try to make us something we were not. Among ourselves, we call ourselves Tattooed. It says that they marked our faces, not that they could own our souls.'

'Have you a leader?'

'Not exactly. When Amber was in Bingtown, she showed us a way to help ourselves. In each household, she said, find one who will be the information holder. If anyone discovered a useful thing, something that could aid anyone who wished to escape, or to have some time to herself, such as a door with a broken lock, or where the master kept money that could be quietly taken, well, that information was passed on to the information holder. Then there would be another, a person who did marketing or washing or anything that took him into town and brought him into contact with Tattooed from other households. He would pass along the information from the information holder to other households, and bring back other tidings to be shared. Thus, a Tattooed one might be able to use the knowledge that a master was sending a waggonload of seed grain out to send words to family or friends working at that farm. Or steal money from one master, and hide in a waggon of hay belonging to another to escape. Amber urged us not to have one leader we relied on, but to have many, like the knots in fishing net. One leader could be captured and tormented and betray us all. But as long as we kept the leadership spread, we were like the netting. Even if you cut a net in twain, there are still many knots in each half.'

'Amber did all this? Amber the bead-maker?' Ronica queried. When Rache nodded, she demanded, 'Why?'

Rache shrugged. 'Some said she had been a slave herself once, despite the fact she has no tattoo. She wears a freedom ring in one ear, you know, the earring that Chalcedean freed-slaves must purchase and wear to prove they have been granted their freedom. I asked her once if she had bought her freedom, or if it had belonged to her mother. She was quiet for a time, and then said it was a gift from her one true love. When I asked Amber why she helped us, she simply said that she had to. That, for reasons of her own, it was important to her.

'Once, a man got very angry with her. He said it was easy enough for her to play at taking chances and stirring up rebellion. He said she could get us all into great danger, and then walk away from it. Her tattoo could be scrubbed away. Ours could not. Amber met his eyes and said, yes, that was true. Therefore, he demanded that she tell us why she did such things, before he would trust her. It was so strange. She sat back on her heels, very still and silent for a moment. Then she laughed aloud, and said, "I'm a prophet. I've been sent to save the world."'

Rache smiled to herself. A silence fell as Ronica regarded her in consternation. After a moment, Rache cocked her head and speculated, 'That made a lot of us laugh. We were all gathered at one of the washing fountains, scrubbing out laundry not our own. You had sent me to town to buy something, and I had stopped to talk there. It was a sunny blue day, and with her talk and plans, Amber made us feel as if we could actually regain lives of our own choosing again. Everyone thought that what she said about saving the world was just a jest. But the way she laughed . . . I always thought she was laughing because she knew it was safe to tell us the truth, because none of us would ever believe it.'

Ronica walked to the Traders' Concourse. She knew better than to expect Companion Serilla to arrange for her transport. She left Davad's house early, not only to allow for the walk, but also to be one of the first there. She hoped to speak to individual Traders as they arrived and sound them out on what they thought the Council should do. It was not an easy walk, nor a safe one. Rache wanted to accompany her, but Ronica insisted that she remain behind. There was no sense in risking both of them. The former slave would not be admitted to the Bingtown Traders' Council meeting, and Ronica would not ask her to wait outside in the gathering darkness. She herself hoped to beg a ride home when the meeting was over. The chill autumn winds tugged at her clothes, and the conditions she saw as she walked tugged at her heart.

Her path did not lead her down into the city, for the Concourse had been built on a low hill that overlooked Bingtown. Her journey took her past many of the Traders' estates. The open gateways and wide carriage roads up to the properties now were barricaded, and frequently men with weapons stood guard at the closed gates. No home was safe from the roving bands of thieves and looters. The guards watched her go by with unfriendly stares. No one called a greeting or even nodded to her.

Ronica was the first to arrive for the Council meeting. The Concourse itself had suffered as badly as Bingtown. This old building was more than just a structure where the Traders met.

It was the heart of their unity, a symbol of who they were. Its stone walls would not burn, but someone had managed to set its roof alight. Ronica stood for a time staring up at it in dismay. Then she braced herself against what she might find, and climbed the steps. The doors had been broken open. She peered past them cautiously. Only one corner of the roof had burned, but the smell of smoke mingled with the damp to make the whole hall reek. The weak light of late afternoon came in through the breached roof to illuminate the empty hall. Ronica pushed past the broken-latched door, and advanced cautiously. The gathering hall was cold. The mouldering decorations from the Summer Ball still trailed down the walls and stirred in the trespassing wind. Garlands had degenerated to bare branches on the door arches and rotting leaves on the floor. Tables, chairs, and the raised dais were still in place. There was even a scattering of dishes on some of the tables, though most had been looted. Dead bouquets were rotting beside broken vases. Ronica gazed about herself with a growing anger. Where were those who were assigned to prepare the hall for the gatherings? What had become of the Traders appointed to caretake the hall? Had everyone abandoned every responsibility save to care for their own welfare?

For a time, she simply waited in the chill, dim hall. Then the clutter and disorder began to clatter against her calm. In her younger days, she and Ephron had served a term as hall-keepers. Almost every young Trader couple did. With a strange twinge of heart, she recalled that Davad and Dorill had served alongside them. They had come early to the Council meetings, to fill the lamps and set the fires, and stayed afterwards to wipe down the wooden benches with oily cloths and sweep the floors. Back then it had been simple, pleasant work, performed in the company of other young Trader couples. Recalling those days was like finding a touchstone for her heart.

She found the brooms, candles, and lamp oil where they

had always been kept. It cheered her a tiny bit to find that the storage room had not been looted. That meant that slaves or New Traders had done the other thievery, for any Trader family would have known where to look for the hall supplies. She could not restore the hall completely, but she could begin to set it right.

She needed light first. She climbed on a chair to fill and light the wall lanterns. Their flames flickered in the breeze, and illuminated more clearly the leaves and dirt that had blown in with the fallen bits of charred roof. She gathered the scattered dishes into a washing tub and set it aside. She pulled down the damp banners and denuded garlands from the walls and bundled them into a corner. The broom she chose next seemed a puny weapon against the littered floor of the great hall, but she set to with a will. It felt good, she suddenly decided, to set herself to a physical task. For this small time, at least, she could see the results of her effort and her will. She found herself humming the old broom song as she moved a line of litter rhythmically across the floor. She could almost hear Dorill's sweet alto singing the repetitive refrain.

The rasp of her broom covered the scuff of footsteps. She became aware of the others only when two other women joined in with brooms of their own. Startled, she halted in her sweeping to stare around her. A group of Traders huddled together in the entry. Some looked at Ronica with hollow eyes and sagging shoulders, but others were moving past those who only stared. Two men came in bearing armloads of firewood. A group of youngsters united in gathering up the smelly banners and dragging them out of the hall. Suddenly, like a knot of debris yielding to the force of water, the folk in the entry flowed into the hall. Some began to move benches and chairs into their proper configuration for a Council meeting. More lamps were kindled, and a hum of conversation began to fill the hall. The first time someone laughed aloud, the buzz of voices ceased for an instant, as if all were startled by this foreign sound. Then talk resumed, and it seemed to Ronica that folk moved livelier than they had.

Ronica looked around at her neighbours and friends. Those who gathered here were the descendants of the settlers who had originally come to the Cursed Shores with little more than land grants and a charter from Satrap Esclepius. Outcasts and outlaws and younger sons, their ancestors had been. With small hope of building or regaining fortunes in Jamaillia, they had come to try their luck on the ominously named Cursed Shores. Their first settlements had failed, doomed by the weirdness that seemed to flow down the Rain River with its waters. They had moved farther and farther from what initially had seemed a promising waterway until they had settled here, on the shores of Bingtown Bay. Some of their kin had stayed to brave the strangeness of life along the Rain Wild River. The river marked those who lived along its shores, but no true Trader ever lost sight of the fact that they were all kin, and all bound by the same original charter. For the first time since the night of the riots, Ronica glimpsed that unity. Every face she greeted looked wearier, older, and more anxious than the last time she had seen them. Some wore their Trader robes in their family colours, but as many were dressed in ordinary clothes. Evidently, she was not the only one who had lost possessions to looters. Now that they were here, they moved about the business of straightening up the hall with a practised doggedness that had always been the Trader hallmark. No matter what, these were folk who had prevailed, and they would prevail again. She took hope from that, at the same time that she dully realized how few acknowledged her.

There were muttered greetings, and the small-talk of folk engaged in the same task, but no one sought real conversation with her. Even more daunting, no one asked after Malta or Keffria. She had not expected anyone to commiserate with her on Davad's death, but now she realized that the whole topic of that night's events seemed unmentionable to them.

There came a time when the hall was as tidy as hasty housekeeping could make it. The Council members began to take their places on the high dais, while families filled the chairs and benches. Ronica took a place in the third row. She held her composure, though it stung when the seats to either side of her remained vacant. When she looked over her shoulder, it was frightening to see how many seats remained vacant. Where were they all? Dead, fled, or too frightened to come out? She ran her eyes across the white-robed Council heads, and then noticed with dismay that another seat had been added to the dais. Worse, instead of calling the Traders to order for the meeting, the Council was waiting for the seat to be filled.

A greater silence rather than a murmur turned Ronica's head. Companion Serilla made her entrance. Trader Drur escorted the Companion as she entered the Concourse, but her hand was not on his arm, and she walked half a pace in front of him. The peacock-blue gown she wore was opulently oversewn with pearls. With it, she wore a scarlet mantle trimmed with white fur that brushed the dirty floor behind her. Her hair had been dressed high, and secured with pearl pins. More pearls wrapped her throat and glowed warmly on her earlobes. The wealth so casually displayed offended Ronica. Did not she know that some of the people in the room had lost nearly everything they owned? Why did she flaunt her possessions before them?

Serilla could hear her heart in her ears as she carefully paced up the aisle that led to the raised dais in the centre of the damaged hall. The place smelled terrible, of rain and mildew. It was cold, too. She was glad of the mantle she had selected from Kekki's wardrobe. She kept her chin up and a poised smile on her face as she entered. She represented the true government of Bingtown. She would uphold the Satrapy of

Jamaillia with more dignity and nobility than Cosgo ever had. Her calm would hearten them, even as the richness of her garments reminded them of her exalted station. This was something she remembered from the old Satrap. Whenever he went into a difficult negotiating session, he presented himself as in his most royal robes and with a calm demeanour. Pomp reassured.

She halted Drur at the bottom of the steps with a small hand motion. Alone, she ascended to the high dais. She advanced to the chair they had left vacant for her. It irked her slightly that it was not elevated but it would have to do. She stood, silent, by her chair until the men on the dais sensed her displeasure. She waited until they had all risen to their feet before she seated herself. Then she indicated with a nod that they might be seated as well. Although the assemblage below her had neglected to rise at her entrance, she nodded round to them as well, to indicate they might be at ease.

She spoke softly to Trader Dwicker, the head of the Bingtown Council. 'You may begin.'

She sat through a brief prayer in which he begged Sa to send them wisdom to deal with these uncertain times. There followed silence. Serilla let it draw out. She wanted to be sure she had their complete attention before she addressed them. But to her surprise, Trader Dwicker cleared his throat. He looked out over the faces turned up to the Council and shook his head slowly. 'I scarce know where to begin,' he said with blunt honesty. 'So much disorder and strife confronts us. So many needs. Since Companion Serilla agreed to this meeting and we announced it, I have been inundated with suggestions for topics that we must settle. Our city, our Bingtown –' The man's voice cracked for an instant. He cleared his throat and regained his aplomb. 'Never has our city been so grievously assaulted by forces within and without it. Our only solution must be that we stand united, as we always have, as our ancestors before us stood. With that in mind, the Council has met privately and come to some preliminary measures that we would like to enact. We believe these are in the best interests of Bingtown as a whole. We present them for your approval.'

Serilla managed not to frown. She had not been warned of any of this. They had formulated a recovery plan without her? With difficulty, she held her tongue and bided her time.

'Twice before in our history, we have imposed a moratorium on debts and foreclosures. As we enacted this before, for the Great Fire that left so many families homeless, and again during the Two Year Drought, it is appropriate now. Debts and contracts will continue to amass interest, but no Trader shall confiscate the property of any other Trader, nor press for payment on any debt until this Council declares this moratorium to be lifted.'

Serilla watched their faces. There was a low murmur of conversation in the hall, but no one leapt up to object. This surprised her. She had thought that opportunistic profit had been behind much of the looting. Did the Traders stand back from that now?

'Secondly, that every Trader family shall double their city duty days, nor shall they be able to buy back this responsibility. Every Trader and every member of a Trader's family over fifteen years of age shall fulfil this duty personally. Lots shall be drawn for tasks to be completed, but our first efforts shall be made on our harbour, wharves and city streets, that trade may be restored.'

Again, there was only a brief silent pause. Again, no one objected. A slight movement by another council member caught Serilla's eye. She glanced at the scroll in front of him, where he had just noted, 'agreed to by all.' This silence was assent, then?

She gazed about incredulously. Something was happening here, in this room. This people was gathering itself up and finding the united strength to begin anew. It would have been heart-warming, save that they were doing it without her. As her eyes roved over the folk, she marked how some sat straighter. Parents held hands with one another and with their younger children. Young men and some of the women had assumed determined expressions. Then her eyes snagged on Ronica Vestrit. The old woman sat close to the front of the assemblage, in her worn dress and the dead woman's shawl. Her eyes were bird-bright and they were fixed on Serilla in glittering satisfaction.

Trader Dwicker spoke on. He called for young single men to supplement the City Guard, and read off the boundaries of the area that they would attempt to control. Within that area, merchants were urged to resume normal commerce, so that necessary trade could resume. Serilla began to see the method to their plan. They would restore order to a section of the city, attempt to bring it back to life, and hope that the rejuvenation spread.

When he had finished his list, she waited, expecting that he would next defer to her. Instead, a score of Traders stood and waited silently, hoping to be recognized.

Ronica Vestrit was among them.

Serilla startled everyone, including herself, when she stood. Instantly all eyes were focused on her. All that she had earlier planned to say fled her mind. All she knew was that she must somehow reassert the Satrap's power, and hence her own. She must keep Ronica Vestrit from speaking. She had thought she had ensured the woman's silence earlier when she spoke to Roed Caern. Listening to how assuredly the Bingtown mechanism had begun to govern once more, she suddenly had little faith in Roed. The power that people simply took for themselves here astonished her. Roed would be no more than a cat in the path of a carriage if Ronica managed to gain an audience.

She did not wait for Trader Dwicker to recognize her. She had been foolish to let him even begin this meeting. She should have seized control at the very start. So now she looked around at the people and nodded and smiled until those standing slowly resumed their seats. She cleared her throat.

'This is a proud day for Jamaillia,' she announced. 'Bingtown has been called a shining gem in the Satrapy's crown, and so it is. In the midst of adversity, the folk of Bingtown do not fall into anarchy and disorder. Instead, you gather amidst the ruins and uphold the civilization you are sprung from.' She spoke on and on, trying to make her voice ring with patriotism. At one point she reached across and picked up the scroll that lay before Trader Dwicker and held it aloft. She praised it, saying that Jamaillia itself was founded on just such a sense of civic responsibility. She let her eyes rove over the crowd as she tried to claim some credit for these measures, but in her heart she wondered if any of them were fooled. She spoke on and on. She leaned forwards towards them, she met their eyes, and she put the fervour of belief into her words. All the while, her heart trembled within her. They did not need the Satrap or the Satrapy to govern them. They didn't need her. And once they realized it, she was doomed. All the power that she had thought she had amassed would vanish, leaving her just a helpless woman in a strange land, prey to whatever fate overtook her. She could not allow that to happen.

When her throat began to grow dry and her voice to shake, she sought desperately for an ending. Taking a deep breath, she declared, 'You have made a brave start tonight. Now, as darkness closes around our city, we must recall that dark clouds still overshadow us. Return to the safety of your homes. Keep yourselves well there, and wait for word from us as to where your efforts can best be employed. On behalf of the Satrap, your ruler, I praise and thank you for the spirit you have shown. On your way to your homes this evening, please keep him in mind. But for the threats raised against him, he would be here himself tonight. He wishes you well.'

She took a breath and turned to Trader Dwicker. 'Perhaps

you should lead us in a closing prayer of thanksgiving to Sa before we disperse.'

He came to his feet, his brow creased. She smiled at him encouragingly, and saw him lose the battle. He turned to the assembled Traders and took a breath to begin.

'Council, I would speak before we adjourn. I ask that the matter of Davad Restart's wrongful death be considered.' It was Ronica Vestrit.

Trader Dwicker actually choked. For a moment, Serilla thought she had lost entirely. Then Roed Caern rose smoothly to his feet.

'Council, I submit that Ronica Vestrit speaks without authority here. She is no longer Trader for her own family, let alone Restart's. Let her sit down. Unless this matter is raised by a rightful Trader, the Council need not consider it.'

The old woman stood stubbornly, two high spots of colour on her cheeks. She controlled her anger and spoke clearly. 'The Trader for my family cannot speak for us. The attempt on our lives has sent her into hiding with her children. Therefore, I claim the right to speak.'

Dwicker managed a breath. 'Ronica Vestrit, have you written authorization from Keffria Vestrit to speak as Trader for the Vestrit family?'

A silence of six heartbeats. Then, 'No, Councilhead Dwicker, I do not,' Ronica admitted.

Dwicker managed to contain his relief. 'Then, according to all our laws, I fear we cannot hear you tonight. For every family, there is only one designated Trader. To that Trader, both voice and vote belong. If you obtain such a paper, duly witnessed, and come back to us when next we meet, then perhaps we can hear you.'

Ronica sank slowly back to her seat. But Serilla's relief was short lived. Other Traders rose to their feet, and Dwicker began recognizing them in turn. One Trader rose and asked if Wharf Seven could be repaired first, as it offered the best moorage for deep draught ships. Several others quickly agreed with this idea, and in quick succession a number of men volunteered to take this as their task.

Proposal after proposal followed. Some referred to public matters, others to private. One Trader stood to offer space in his warehouse to any who would help him make quick repairs and to guard it at night. He quickly had three volunteers. Another had teams of oxen, but was running out of feed for them. He wanted to trade their labour for food to keep them alive. He, too, received several offers. The night grew later and later, but the Traders showed no inclination to go home. Before Serilla's eyes, Bingtown knit itself back together. Before Serilla's eyes, her hopes of power and influence faded.

She had almost ceased listening to the proceedings when a sombre Trader stood and asked, 'Why are we being kept ignorant of what triggered this whole disaster? What has become of the Satrap? Do we know who was behind the threat to him? Have we contacted Jamaillia to explain ourselves?'

Another voice was raised. 'Does Jamaillia know of our plight? Have they offered to send ships and men to help us drive out the Chalcedeans?'

All faces turned towards her. Worse, Trader Dwicker made a small motion encouraging her to speak. She gathered her thoughts hastily as she stood. 'There is little that is safe to tell,' she began. 'There is no practical way to send swift word to Jamaillia without risk of it being intercepted. We are also uncertain whom we should consider trustworthy and loyal there. For now, the secret of the Satrap's location is best not shared with anyone. Not even Jamaillia.' She smiled warmly at them as if certain of their understanding.

'The reason I ask,' the Trader went on ponderously, 'is that I had a bird from Trehaug yesterday, warning me that I should expect payment for some goods I sent upriver to be delayed. They had had a quake, and a big one. They weren't sure how much damage had been done when they sent the bird, but said that the Kendry would certainly be delayed.' The man shrugged one skinny shoulder. 'Are we sure the Satrap came through it safely?'

For a moment, her tongue could get no purchase on her thoughts. Then Roed Caern was rising gracefully to claim the floor. 'Trader Ricter, I think we should not speculate on such things, lest we send rumours running. Surely if anything were amiss, we would have received word. For now, I propose we let all questions regarding the Satrap rest. Surely his security is more important than our idle curiosity.' He had a trick of standing with one shoulder slightly higher than the other. He turned as he spoke, somehow conveying both the charm and arrogance of a well-clawed cat. There was no threat in his words, yet somehow it would be challenging him to ask more about the Satrap. A little ripple of uneasiness seemed to spread out from him. He took his time about resuming his seat, as if allowing everyone to consider his words. No one brought up the topic of the Satrap again.

A few other Traders stood after that to bring up lesser matters, volunteering to keep street lamps filled and the like, but the feeling of the meeting was suddenly that it was over. Serilla was caught between disappointment and relief that it was finished when a man in a dark blue robe stood up in the far corner of the room.

'Trader's son Grag Tenira,' he announced himself when Trader Dwicker hesitated over his name. 'And I do have permission, written and witnessed, to speak for my family. I speak for Tomie Tenira.'

'Speak, then,' Dwicker recognized him.

The Trader's son hesitated, then drew a breath. 'I suggest that we appoint three Traders to consider the matter of Trader Restart's death and the disposition of his estate. I claim interest in this matter, for monies owed by the estate to the Tenira family.'

Roed Caern was on his feet again, too quickly this time. 'Is this a worthy use of our time?' he demanded. 'All debt is to be held in abeyance just now. That was agreed at the very start of the meeting. Besides, how can the manner of a man's death affect a debt that is owed?'

Grag Tenira did not seem daunted by his reasoning. 'An inheritance is not a debt, I think. If the estate has been confiscated, then we must give up all hope of regaining what is owed us. But if the estate is to be inherited, then we have an interest in knowing that, and in seeing it passed on to an heir before it is . . . depleted.' Depleted was the word he used, yet 'plundered' was in his tone. Serilla could not control the pink that rose to her cheeks. Her mouth was suddenly dry and she could not speak. This was far worse than being ignored; he had all but accused her of theft.

Trader Dwicker did not seem to notice her distress. He did not even seem to realize it was up to her to answer this. Instead, he leaned back in his chair and said gravely, 'A panel of three Traders to look into this seems a reasonable request, especially as another member of a Trader family has already expressed concern about this. Would volunteers with no connection to this matter please stand?'

As quickly as that, it was done. Serilla did not even recognize the names of those Dwicker chose. One was a dowdy young woman holding a squirming child in her arms, another an old man with a seamed face who leaned on a cane. How was she supposed to exert her influence on such as those? She felt as if she dwindled into her chair as a wave of defeat and shame washed over her. The shame amazed her in its intensity and brought despair in its wake. Somehow, it was all connected. This was the power that men could take over her. She caught a sudden glimpse of Ronica Vestrit's face. The sympathy in the old woman's eyes horrified Serilla. Had she sunk so low that even her enemies pitied her as they tore her to pieces? A sudden ringing in her ears threatened her, and the hall grew dimmer around her.

* * *

Ronica sat small and quiet. They would do for Grag Tenira what they would not do for her. They would look into Davad's death. That, she told herself, was the important thing.

She was distracted from her thoughts by how pale the Companion had suddenly become. Would the woman faint? In a way, she pitied her. She was a stranger to this place, and caught in the turmoil of its civil upheaval with no hope of extricating herself. Moreover, she seemed so trapped in her role as Companion. She sensed that at one time there had been more to Serilla, but somehow it had been lost. Still, it was difficult to pity anyone so obsessed with obtaining and holding power for herself at any cost.

Watching her sit so still and small through the rest of the meeting, Ronica scarcely noticed it ending. Trader Dwicker led them in a final prayer to Sa, at once asking for strength and thanking the deity for survival. The voices echoing his were certainly stronger than those that had responded to his opening prayer. It was a good sign. All that had happened here had been good tonight, for Bingtown.

Companion Serilla left, not with Trader Drur, but on Roed Caern's arm. The tall, handsome Trader's son glowered as he escorted her from the gathering hall. Several heads besides Ronica's turned to watch them go. Almost, they looked like a couple on the edge of a marital spat. It did not please Ronica to see the anxiety that haunted the Companion's face. Was Caern somehow coercing her?

Ronica had not the gall to hasten after them and beg a ride home, though she would have dearly loved to hear what passed between them in the carriage. Instead, as she wrapped Dorill's shawl well about her, she thought with dread of the long walk back to Davad's house. Outside was a chill fall night. The road would be rough and dark, and the dangers more vicious than those of the Bingtown she had known. Well, there was no help for it. The sooner she started, the sooner she was there.

Outside the hall, a nasty little breeze cut at her. Other families were clambering into carriages and waggons or walking home in groups, carrying lanterns and armed with walking sticks. She had not thought to bring either. Chiding herself for thoughtlessness, she started down the steps. At the bottom, a figure stepped from the shadows and touched her on the arm. She gasped in startlement.

'Beg pardon,' Grag Tenira spoke immediately. 'I didn't mean to frighten you. I merely wanted to be certain you had a safe way home.'

Ronica laughed shakily. 'I thank you for your concern, Grag. I no longer even have a safe home to go to. Nor a way there, other than my own two feet. I have been staying at Davad's house, since my own was vandalized. While I am there, I have been attempting to trace Davad's transactions with the New Traders. I am convinced that if the Companion would but pay heed to me, she would see that Davad was no traitor. Nor am I.'

The words spilled from her. Belatedly she got her tongue under control. However, Grag stood gravely listening and nodding to her words. When she fell silent, he offered, 'If the Companion will not heed what you find, I and several others would find it of interest. Although I doubted Davad Restart's loyalty, I never questioned the Vestrit family's allegiance to Bingtown, even if you have dabbled in the slave trade.'

Ronica had to bow her head and bite her tongue to that, for it was true. It might not be any of her own doing, but her family ship had gone as a slaver. And been lost because of it. She took a breath. 'I would be happy to show you and any others who would be interested. I have heard that Mingsley of the New Traders has been making truce offers. In terms of his long dealings with Davad, I wonder if he was not seeking to buy Old Traders to his way of thinking.'

'I should be pleased to see the records. But, for tonight, I would be more pleased to see you safely to wherever you are staying. I have no carriage, but my horse can carry two, if you would not object to riding pillion.'

'I would be grateful. But why?'

'Why?' Grag looked startled at the question.

'Why?' Ronica took up all the bravery of an old woman who no longer cares for the niceties of courtesy. 'Why do you extend yourself on my behalf? My daughter Althea has refused your suit. My reputation right now in Bingtown is unsavoury. Why chance your own, associating with me? Why press for the matter of Davad's death to be investigated? What motivates you, Grag Tenira?'

He bowed his head for an instant. Then, when he lifted his face, a nearby torch caught his blue eyes and limned his profile. As he smiled ruefully, Ronica wondered how Althea could ever have held her heart back from this young man. 'You ask a blunt question and I will give you truth in return. I myself feel some responsibility for Davad's death and your disaster that night. Not for what I did, but for what I failed to do. And as for Althea –' He grinned suddenly. 'Perhaps I don't give up that easily. And perhaps the way to her heart is through courtesy to her mother.' He gave a sudden laugh. 'Sa knows I have tried everything else. Perhaps a good word from you would turn the key for me. Come. My horse is this way.'

SEVEN

Dragon Ship

ONE MOMENT HE was curled in oblivion, resting in womb-like isolation. Wintrow was aware of nothing save his physical body. He worked on it as he had once worked stained glass. The difference was that it was a restoration rather than a creation. He found placid pleasure in his work; dimly it echoed memories of stacking blocks when he was a very small child. The tasks that faced him were simple and obvious, the work repetitive; he was only directing his body to do more swiftly what it would have eventually done on its own. The willing focus of his mind speeded the labour of his body. The rest of his life had dimmed to an absolute stillness. He considered nothing except repairing the animal he inhabited. It was rather like being in a small cosy room while a great storm raged outside.

Enough, growled the dragon.

Wintrow curled himself smaller before her irritation. 'I am not finished,' he begged.

No. The rest will take care of itself, if you nourish your body and encourage it from time to time. I have delayed for you too long. You are strong enough now for all of us to confront what we are. And confront it we shall.

It was like being seized and flung into the air. Like a panicky cat, he flailed and clawed in all directions, seeking something, anything to attach himself to. He found Vivacia.

Wintrow!

Her exclamation was not a verbal cry of joy, but a sudden pulse of connection as she discovered him again. They were reunited, and in that joining they were once more whole. She could sense him; she could feel his emotions, smell with his nose, taste with his mouth, and feel with his skin. She knew his pain, and agonized for him. She knew his thoughts and –

When one falls in dreams, one always awakens before the impact. Not this time. Wintrow's awakening was the impact. Vivacia's love and devotion to him collided with his anguished knowledge of what she was. His thoughts were a mirror held to her corpse face. Once she had looked into it, she could not look aside. He was trapped in that contemplation with her, and felt himself pulled down deeper and deeper into her despair. He plunged into the abyss with her.

She was not Vivacia, not really. She had never been anything except the stolen life of a dragon. Her pseudo-life was fastened on to the remnants of the dragon's death. She had no real right to exist. Rain Wild workers had split open the cocoon of the metamorphosing dragon. The germ of its life had been flung out, to perish squirming on a cold stone floor, while the threads of memory and knowledge that had enclosed it were dragged off and cut up into planks to build liveships.

Life struggles to continue, at any cost. A windstorm flings a tree down to the forest floor; saplings rise from its trunk. A tiny seed amongst pebbles and sand will still seize a droplet of moisture and send up a defiant shoot of green. Immersed in saltwater, bombarded with the memories and emotions of the humans that bestrode her, the fibres of memory in her planks had sought to align themselves into some kind of order. They had accepted the name given to her; they had striven to make sense of what they experienced now. Eventually, Vivacia had awakened. But the proud ship and her glorious figurehead were not truly part of the Vestrit family. No. Hers was a life stolen. She was half a being, less than half, a makeshift creature cobbled together out of human wills and buried dragon memories, sexless, deathless, and in the long run, meaningless. A slave. They had used the stolen memories of a dragon to create a great wooden slave for themselves.

The scream that tore out of Vivacia ripped Wintrow into full consciousness. He rolled over and fell to the floor, landing heavily on his knees beside his bunk. In the small room, Etta jerked awake with a start from where she'd kept watch over him. 'Wintrow!' she cried in horror as he heaved himself to his feet. 'Wait! No, you are not well. Lie down, come back!' Her words followed him as he staggered out the door and towards the foredeck. He heard noises from the captain's stateroom, Kennit shouting for his crutch and a light, 'Etta, damn you, where are you when I need you?' but Wintrow did not pause for that either. He limped naked save for a sheet, the night air burning against his healing flesh. Startled crewmen on the night watch called out to one another. One seized a lantern and followed him. Wintrow paid him no mind. He took the steps to the foredeck in two strides that tore his healing skin and flung himself forwards until he half-hung over the railing.

'Vivacia!' he cried. 'Please. It was not your fault; it was never your fault. Vivacia!'

The figurehead tore at herself. Her great wooden fingers tangled in her lush black curls and strove to snatch them out of her head. Her fingernails raked her cheeks and dug at her eyes. 'Not me!' she cried to the night sky. 'Never me at all! Oh, Great Sa, what an obscene jest I am, what an abomination in your sight! Let me go, then! Let me be dead!'

Gankis had followed Wintrow. 'What troubles you, boy? What ails the ship?' the old pirate demanded, but Wintrow saw only the ship. The yellow lantern light revealed a horror. As swiftly as Vivacia's nails cut furrows in her perfect cheeks, the fibrous flesh closed up behind them. The hair she tore from her scalp flowed into her hands, was absorbed, and her mane remained thick and glossy as before. Wintrow stared in horror at this cycle of destruction and rebirth. 'Vivacia!' he cried again, and flung his being into hers, seeking to comfort, to calm.

The dragon was waiting there. She rebuffed him as effortlessly as she wrapped and held Vivacia in her embrace. Hers was the spirit that defied the ship's desire to die.

No. Not after all the years of repression, not all the ages of silence and stillness. I will not be dead. If this be the only life we can have, then we shall have it. Be still, little slave. Share this life with me, or know none at all!

Wintrow was transfixed. In a place he could only reach with his mind, a terrible confrontation was taking place. The dragon struggled for life as the ship tried to deny it to both of them. He felt his own small self as a rag seized by two terriers. He was pulled between them, torn in their grips as each tried to claim his loyalty and carry his mind with hers. Vivacia caught him up in her love and despair. She knew him so well; he knew her so well, how could his heart differ from hers? She dragged him with her; they teetered on the edge of a willing leap into death. Oblivion beckoned alluringly. It was, she convinced him, the only solution. What else was there for them? This endless sense of wrong, this horrible burden of stolen life; would he choose that?

'Wintrow!' Kennit gasped out the name as he dragged himself up the ladder to the foredeck. Wintrow turned sluggishly to watch him come. The pirate's nightshirt, half-tucked into his trousers, billowed about him in the night breeze. His one foot was bare. A tiny part of Wintrow's mind noted that he had never seen Kennit in such a state of dishevelment. There was panic in the captain's ever cool and sardonic glance. *He feels us*, Wintrow thought to himself. *He is starting to bond with us; he senses something of what is going on, and it frightens him.*

Etta passed the captain's crutch up to him. He seized it and came swinging across the deck to Wintrow's side. Kennit's sudden grasp on his shoulder was the grip of life, holding him back from death. 'What do you do, boy?' Kennit demanded angrily. Then his voice changed and he stared past Wintrow in horror. 'God of Fishes, what have you done to my ship!'

Wintrow turned to the figurehead. Vivacia had twisted to stare back at the growing mob of disturbed sailors on the foredeck. One man shrieked aloud as her eyes went suddenly lambent green. The colour of her eyes swirled like a whirlpool, while at the centre was blackness darker than any night. Humanity left her face. Her black tresses blowing in the night breeze were more like a writhing nest of serpents. The teeth she bared at them in a parody of a smile were too white. 'If I cannot win,' the lips gave voice to the dragon's thought, 'then no one shall.'

Slowly she turned away from them. Her arms lifted wide as if to embrace the night sea. Then slowly she brought them back, to clasp the hull of the ship behind her.

Wintrow! Wintrow, aid me! Vivacia pleaded only in his mind; the figurehead's mouth and her voice were no longer at Vivacia's command. *Die with me,* she begged him. Almost, he did. Almost, he followed her into that abyss. But at the last instant, he could not.

'I want to live!' he heard himself cry out into the night. 'Please, please, let us live!' He thought, for an instant, that his words weakened her resolve to die.

A strange silence followed his words. Even the night breeze seemed to hold its breath. Wintrow became aware that somewhere a sailor gabbled out a child's prayer but another, smaller sound caught his ears. It was a running, brittle sound, like the noise of cracking ice on the surface of a lake when one ventures out too far.

'She's gone,' breathed Etta. 'Vivacia's gone.'

It was so. Even in the poor light of the lantern, the change was obvious. All colour and semblance of life had drained from the figurehead. Grey as a tombstone was the wood of her back and hair. No breath of life stirred her. Her carved locks were frozen and immune to the breeze's fingering touch. Her skin looked as weathered as an ageing fence. Wintrow groped after her with his mind. He caught a fading trail of her despair, like a vanishing scent in the air. Then even that was gone, as if some tight door had closed between them.

'The dragon?' he muttered to himself, but if she was still within him, she had hidden herself too well for his poor senses.

Wintrow drew a deep breath and let it out again. Alone in his mind again; how long had it been since his thoughts had been the only ones in his head? An instant later he became aware of his body. The cool air stung his healing scalds. His knees jellied, and he would have sunk to the deck but for Etta's cautious arm around him. He sagged against her. His new skin screamed at her touch, but he was too weak even to flinch away.

Etta looked past him. Her gaze mourned Kennit. Wintrow's eyes followed hers. He had never seen a man look so grief-stricken. The pirate leaned far out on the bow railing to stare at Vivacia's profile, his features frozen in anguish. Lines Wintrow had never noticed before seemed graven into Kennit's face. His glossy black hair and moustache looked shocking against his sallow skin. Vivacia's passing diminished Kennit in a way that the loss of his leg had not. Before Wintrow's eyes, the man aged.

Kennit turned his head to meet Wintrow's gaze. 'Is she dead?' he asked woodenly. 'Can a liveship die?' His eyes pleaded that it not be so.

'I don't know,' Wintrow admitted reluctantly. 'I can't feel her. Not at all.' The gap within himself was too terrible to probe. Worse than a lost tooth, more crippling than his missing finger. To be without her was a terrible, gaping flaw in himself. He had once wished for this? He had been mad.

Kennit turned back abruptly to the figurehead. 'Vivacia?' he called questioningly. Then, 'Vivacia!' he bellowed, the angry, forsaken call of a spurned lover. 'You cannot leave me now! You cannot be gone!'

Even the light night breeze faded to stillness. On the deck of the ship, the silence was absolute. The crew seemed as stricken by their captain's grief as by the passing of the liveship. Etta was the one who broke the silence.

'Come,' she said to Kennit. 'There is nothing to be done here. You and Wintrow should come below, and talk about this. He needs food and drink. He should not be out of bed yet. Together, you two can puzzle out what is to be done next.'

Wintrow saw clearly what she was doing. The captain's attitude was rattling the crew. It was best he was out of their sight until he recovered. 'Please,' Wintrow croaked, adding his plea to hers. He had to be away from that terrible, still figure. Looking at the grey figurehead was worse than gazing at a decaying corpse.

Kennit glanced at them as if they were strangers. A sudden flatness came to his eyes as he mastered himself. 'Very well. Take him below and see to him.' His voice was devoid of every emotion. He ran his eyes over his crew. 'Get back to your posts,' he muttered at them. For an instant, they did not respond. A few faces showed sympathy for their captain, but most stared confusedly, as if they did not know the man. Then, 'Now!' he snapped. He did not raise his voice, but the command in it sent his men scrabbling to obey. In an instant, the foredeck was empty save for Wintrow, Etta and Kennit.

Etta waited for Kennit. The captain moved awkwardly, shifting his crutch about until he got it under his arm. He hopped free of the railing and lurched across the foredeck to the ladder.

'Go help him,' Wintrow whispered. 'I can manage.'

Etta gave a single nod of agreement. She left him for Kennit. The one-legged man accepted her help without any objections. That was as unlike the pirate as his earlier show of emotion.

Wintrow, watching how tenderly the woman aided him down the short ladder, felt more keenly his own isolation. 'Vivacia?' he asked quietly of the night. The wind sighed past him, making him aware of his scalded skin and of his own nakedness. But Vivacia had been peeled away from him as painfully as his own skin had, leaving a different kind of pain. The nakedness of his body was a small discomfort compared to his solitude in the night. In a dizzying instant, he was aware of how immense the sea and the world around him were. He was no more than a mite of life on this wooden deck rocking on the water. Always before, he had sensed Vivacia's size and strength around him, sheltering him from the world at large. Not since he had first left home as a child had he felt so tiny and unattended.

'Sa,' he whispered, knowing that he should be able to reach out for his god as solace. Sa had always been there for him, long before he had boarded the ship and bonded with her. Once, he had been certain he was destined to be a priest. Now, as he reached out with a word to touch the awe of the divine, he realized that the name on his lips was truly a prayer that Vivacia be restored to him. He felt shamed. Had his ship then replaced his god? Did he truly believe he could not go on without her? He knelt suddenly on the darkened deck, but not to pray. His hands groped over the wood. Here. The stains should be here, where his blood had joined her timbers and united him with her in a bond he shared with no other. But when his maimed hand found his own bloody handprint it was by sight, not touch. For he felt nothing under his palm save the fine texture of the wizardwood deck. He felt nothing at all.

'Wintrow?'

Etta had come back for him. She stood on the ladder, staring across the foredeck at him hunched on his hands and knees. 'I'm coming,' he replied, and lurched to his feet.

'More wine?' Etta asked Wintrow.

The boy shook his head mutely. For boy he looked, draped in a fresh sheet from Kennit's own bed. Etta had snatched it up and offered it to him when she had staggered him into the cabin. His peeling flesh would not yet bear the touch of proper clothing. Now the lad perched uncomfortably in a chair across the table from Kennit. It was obvious to Etta that he could find no position that eased his scalds. He had eaten some of the food she had put before him, but he seemed little better for it. Where the venom had eaten at him, his skin was splotched red and shiny. Bald red patches on his shorn head reminded her of a mangy dog. But worst was the dull look in his eyes. They mirrored the loss and abandonment in Kennit's.

The pirate sat across from Wintrow, his dark hair in disarray, his shirt half-buttoned. Kennit, always so careful of his own appearance, seemed to have forgotten it entirely. She could barely stand to look at the man she had loved. In the years she had known him, he had first been simply her customer, then the man she longed for. When he had carried her off, she had thought nothing could bring her more joy. The night he had told her he cared for her, her life had been transformed. She had watched him grow, from captain of one vessel to the commander of a fleet of pirate ships. More, folk now hailed him as king of the Pirate Isles. She had thought she had lost him in the storm when he commanded both sea and sea serpent to his will, for she could not be worthy of a man chosen by Sa for great destiny. She had mourned his greatness, she thought with shame. He had soared, and she had been jealous of it, for fear it might steal him from her.

But this, this was a thousand times worse.

No battle, no injury, no storm had ever unmanned him. Never, until tonight, had she seen him uncertain or at a loss. Even now, he sat straight at the table, drinking his brandy neat, his shoulders square, and his hand steady. Nevertheless, something had gone out of him. She had seen it leave him, seen it flow away with the life of the ship. He was now as wooden as

Vivacia had become. She feared to touch him lest she discover his flesh was as hard and unyielding as the deck.

He cleared his throat. Wintrow's eyes snapped to him almost fearfully.

'So.' The small word was sharp as a blade. 'You think she is dead. How? What killed her?'

It was Wintrow's turn to clear his throat, a small and tremulous sound. 'I did. That is, what I knew killed her. Or drove her so deep inside herself that she cannot find a way back to us.' He swallowed, fighting tears, perhaps. 'Maybe she simply realized she had always been dead. Perhaps it was only my belief otherwise that kept her alive.'

Kennit's shot glass clacked against the table as he set it down sharply. 'Talk sense,' he snarled at his prophet.

'Sorry, sir. I'm trying to.' The boy lifted a shaking hand to rub his eyes. 'It's long and it's confusing. My memories have mixed with my dreams. I think a lot of it I always suspected. Once I was in contact with the serpent, all my suspicions suddenly came together with what she knew. And I knew.' Wintrow lifted his eyes to meet Kennit's and blanched at the blind fury in the man's face. He spoke more quickly. 'When I found the imprisoned serpent on the Others' Island, I thought it was just a trapped animal. No more than that. It was miserable, and I resolved to set it free, as I would any creature. No creation of Sa's should be kept in such cruel confinement. As I worked, it seemed to me that she was more intelligent than a bear or a cat would have been. She knew what I was doing. When I had removed enough bars that she could escape, she did. But on her way past me, her skin brushed mine. It burned me. But in that instant, I *knew* her. It was as if a bridge had been created between us, like the bond I share with the ship. I knew her thoughts and she knew mine.' He took a deep breath and leaned forwards across the table. His eyes were desperate to make the pirate believe him.

'Kennit, the serpents are dragon spawn. Somehow, they

have been trapped in their sea form, unable to return to their changing grounds to become full dragons. I could not grasp it all. I saw images, I thought her thoughts, but it is hard to translate that into human terms. When I came back on board the Vivacia, I knew that the liveship was meant to be a dragon. I do not know how exactly. There is some stage between serpent and dragon, a time when the serpent is encased in a kind of hard skin. I think that is what wizardwood is: the husk of a dragon before it becomes a dragon. Somehow, the Rain Wild Traders changed her into a ship instead. They killed the dragon and cut her husk into planks to build a liveship.'

Kennit reached for the brandy bottle. He seized the neck of it as if he would throttle it. 'You make no sense! What you say cannot be true!' He lifted the bottle and for one frightening instant Etta thought he would dash out the boy's brains with it. She saw in Wintrow's face that he feared it, too. But the lad did not flinch. He sat silently awaiting the blow, almost as if he would welcome his own death. Instead, Kennit poured brandy into his glass. A tiny wave of it slopped over the edge of his glass onto the white tablecloth. The pirate ignored it. He lifted the glass and downed it at a gulp.

His anger is too great, Etta suddenly thought to herself. *There is something else here, something even deeper and more painful than the Vivacia's loss.*

Wintrow took a ragged breath. 'I can only tell you what I believe, sir. If it were not true, I do not think Vivacia would have believed it so deeply that she died. Some part of her always knew. A dragon has always slept within her. Our brush with the serpent awakened it. The dragon was furious to discover what it had become. When I was unconscious, it demanded of me that I help it share the ship's life. I . . .' The boy hesitated. He left something unsaid when he went on. 'The dragon woke me today. She woke me and she forced me into full contact with Vivacia. I had held myself back from her, for I did not want her to realize what I knew, that she had never truly been alive.

She was the dead shell of a forgotten dragon that my family had somehow bent to their own purposes.'

Kennit took in a sharp breath through his nose. He leaned back in his chair and held up a commanding hand that halted the boy's words. 'And that is the secret of the liveships?' he scoffed. 'It can't be. Anyone who has ever known a liveship would refuse such mad words. A dragon inside her! A ship made of dragon skin. You're addled, boy. Your illness has cooked your brain.'

But Etta believed it. The ship's presence had jangled against her nerves ever since she had first come aboard. Now it made sense. Like the strings of a musical instrument brought into true, the theory was in harmony with her feelings. It was true. There had always been a dragon inside Vivacia.

Moreover, Kennit knew it. Etta had seen the man lie before; she had heard him lie to her. Never before had she seen him lie to himself. He was not very good at it. It showed in the minute shaking of his hand as he poured himself yet another jot of brandy.

As he returned his glass to the table, he announced abruptly, 'For what I must do, I need a liveship. I have to bring her back to life.'

'I don't think you can,' Wintrow said softly.

Kennit snorted at him. 'So swiftly you lose your faith in me. Was it only a few days ago that you believed I was Chosen of Sa? Only a few weeks ago that you spoke out for me to all the people, saying I was destined to be king for them, if they could be worthy of me? Ha! Such a tiny, brittle faith, to snap at the first test. Listen to me, Wintrow Vestrit. I have walked the shores of the Others' Island, and their soothsaying has confirmed my destiny. I have calmed a storm with a word. I have commanded a sea serpent and it bent its will to mine. Only a day ago, I called you back from the very door of death, you ungrateful wretch! Now you sit there and scoff at me. You say that I cannot restore my own ship to life! How dare you?

Do you seek to undermine my reign? Would the one I have treated as a son lift a scorpion's sting to me now?'

Etta remained where she stood, outside the circle of the lantern above the table, and watched the two men. A cavalcade of emotions trailed across Wintrow's face. It awed her that she could read them so clearly. When had she let her guard down so far as to know another so well? Worse, she suddenly hurt for him. He, like her, was caught between love for the man they had followed so long and fear for the powerful being he was becoming. She held her breath, hoping Wintrow could find the right words. *Do not anger him*, she pleaded silently. *Once you anger him, he will not hear you.*

Wintrow drew a deep breath. Tears stood in his eyes. 'In truth, you have treated me better than my own father ever did. When you came aboard Vivacia, I expected death at your hands. Instead you have challenged me, every day, to find my life and live it. Kennit: you are more than captain to me. I do believe, without question, that you are a tool of Sa, for the working of his will. We all are, of course, but I think he has reserved for you a destiny larger than most. Nevertheless, when you speak of calling Vivacia back to life . . . I do not doubt you, my captain. Rather I doubt that she was ever truly alive, in the sense that you and I are. Vivacia was a fabrication, a creature composed of the memories of my forebears. The dragon was once real. But if Vivacia was never real, and the dragon died in her creation, who remains for you to call back to life?'

Briefer than the flick of a serpent's tongue, uncertainty flashed over Kennit's face. Had Wintrow seen it?

The young man remained still. His question still hung in the air between them. In disbelief, Etta watched his hand lift slightly from the table. Very slowly, he began to reach across the table, as if he would touch Kennit's own hand, in – what? Sympathy? *Oh, Wintrow, do not err so badly as that!*

If Kennit noticed that hovering hand, he gave no sign of it. Wintrow's words seemed not to have moved him at all. He eyed the boy and Etta clearly saw him reach some decision. Slowly he lifted the brandy bottle and poured yet another shot into his own glass. Then he reached across the table and seized Wintrow's empty glass. He sloshed a generous measure of brandy into it and set it back down before him. 'Drink that,' he commanded him brusquely. 'Perhaps it will put a bit of fire in your blood. Then do not tell me that I cannot do this thing. Instead, tell me how you will help me.' He raised his own glass and tossed it down. 'For she was alive, Wintrow. We all know that. So whatever it was that animated her, that is what we will call back.'

Wintrow's hand went slowly to the glass. He lifted it, then set it down again. 'What if that life no longer exists to call back, sir? What if she is simply gone?'

Kennit laughed, and it chilled Etta. So might a man laugh under torture, when screams were no longer sufficient for his pain. 'You doubt me, Wintrow. That is because you do not know what I know. This is not the first liveship I have ever known. They do not die so easily. That, I promise you. Now drink up that brandy, there's a good lad. Etta! Where are you? What ails you that you've set out a near-empty bottle on the table? Fetch another, and quickly.'

The boy had no head for liquor. Kennit had put him easily under the table, and tending him would occupy the whore. 'Take him to his room,' he told Etta, and watched tolerantly as she pulled him to his feet. He staggered blindly alongside her, groping a hand ahead of him down the passage. Kennit watched them go. Confident that he now had some time to himself, Kennit tucked his crutch firmly under his arm and lurched to his feet. With a ponderously careful tread, he made his way out onto the deck. He was, perhaps, just the slightest bit drunk himself.

It was a fine night still. The stars were distant, a haze of cloud veiling their brilliance. The sea had risen a bit, to run against them, but Vivacia's trim hull cut each wave with rhythmic grace. The wind was steady and stronger than it had been. There was even a faint edge of a whistle in it as it cut past their sails. Kennit cocked his ear to it with a frown, but even as he listened, the sound faded.

Kennit made a slow circuit of the deck. The mate was on the wheel; he acknowledged his captain with a nod, but uttered no word. That was as well. There would be a man up in the rigging, keeping watch, but he was invisible in the darkness beyond the reach of the ship's muted lanterns. Kennit moved slowly, his tapping crutch a counterpoint to the softness of his step. His ship. The Vivacia was his ship, and he would call her back to life. And when he did, she would know he was her master, and she would be his in a way she had never been Wintrow's. His own liveship, just as he had always deserved. Damn right, he had always deserved his own liveship. Nothing was going to take her from him now. Nothing.

He had come to hate the short ladder that led from the main deck to the elevated foredeck. He managed it now, and not too clumsily, then sat for a moment, catching his breath but pretending simply to study the night. At last he drew his crutch to him, regained his footing and approached the bow rail. He looked over the sea before them. Distant islands were low black hummocks on the horizon. He glanced once at the grey-fleshed figurehead. Then he looked out past her, over the sea.

'Good evening, sweet sea lady,' he greeted her. 'A fine night tonight and a good wind at our backs. What more could we ask?'

He listened to her stillness just as if she had replied. 'Yes. It is good. I'm as relieved as you are to see Wintrow up and about again. He took a good meal, some wine, and more brandy. I thought the lad could do with a good sleep to heal him. And, of course, I set Etta to watch over him. It gives us a minute or two to ourselves, my princess. Now. What would please you this evening? I've recalled a lovely old tale from the Southlands. Would you like to hear it?'

Only the wind and the water replied to him. Despair and anger warred in him, but he gave no voice to them. Instead, he smiled cordially. 'Very well, then. This is an old tale, from a time before Jamaillia. Some say it is really a tale from the Cursed Shores that was told in the Southlands, and eventually claimed as their own.' He cleared his throat. He half-closed his eyes. When he spoke, he spoke in his mother's words, in the cadence of the storyteller. As she had spoken, so long ago, before Igrot cut out her tongue, slicing her words away forever.

'Once, in that distant time so long ago, there was a young woman, of good wit but small fortune. Her parents were elderly, and when they died, what little they had would be hers. She might, perhaps, have been content with that, but in their dotage, they decided to arrange a marriage for their daughter. The man they chose was a farmer, of good fortune but no wit at all. The daughter knew at once she could never find happiness with him, nor even tolerate him. So Edrilla, for that was her name, left both parents and home and –'

'Erlida was her name, dolt.' Vivacia twisted slowly to look back at him. The movement sent a jolt of ice up Kennit's spine. She turned sinuously, her body unbound by human limitations. Her hair was suddenly jet-black shot with silver gleams. The golden eyes that met his caught the faint gleams of the ship's lantern and threw the light back to him. When she smiled at him, her lips parted too widely, and the teeth she showed him seemed both whiter and smaller than before. Her lips were too red. The life that moved in her now glittered with a serpent's sheen. Her voice was throaty and lazy. 'If you must bore me with a tale a thousand years old, at least tell it well.'

His breath caught hard in his throat. He started to speak, then caught himself. Be silent. Make her talk. Let her betray herself to him first. The creature's gaze on him was like a blade at his throat, but he refused to show fear. He did his best to meet her gaze and not flinch from it.

'Erlida,' she insisted. 'And it was not a farmer, but a riverside pot-maker that she was given to; a man who spent all his day patting wet clay. He made heavy, graceless pots, fit only for slops and chamber pots.' She turned away from him, to stare ahead over the black sea. 'That is how the tale goes. And I should know. I knew Erlida.'

Kennit let the silence stretch until it was thinner and more taut than the silk of a spider's web. 'How?' he demanded hoarsely at last. 'How could you have known Erlida?'

The figurehead snorted contemptuously. 'Because we are not as stupid as humans, who forget everything that befell them before their individual births. The memory of my mother, and of my mother's mother, and her mother's mother's mother are all mine. They were spun into strands from memory sand and the saliva of those who helped encase me in my cocoon. They were set aside for me, my heritage, for me to reclaim when I awoke as a dragon. The memories of a hundred lifetimes are mine. Yet here I am, encased in death, no more than wistful thinking.'

'I don't understand,' Kennit ventured stiffly when it was obvious she had finished speaking.

'That is because you are stupid,' she snapped bitterly.

No one, he had once vowed to himself, would ever speak to him like that again. Then he had cleansed their blood from his hands, and he had kept that promise to himself. Always. Even now. Kennit drew himself up straight. 'Stupid. You may think me stupid, and you may call me stupid. At least I am real. And you are not.' He tucked his crutch under his arm and prepared to lurch away.

She turned back to him, the corner of her mouth lifting in a sneering smile. 'Ah. So the insect has a bit of sting to him. Stay, then. Speak to me, pirate. You think I am not real? I am real enough. Real enough to open my seams to the sea at any moment I choose. You might wish to think on that.'

Kennit spat over the side. 'Boasts and brags. Am I to find that admirable, or frightening? Vivacia was braver and stronger than you, ship, whatever you are. You take refuge in the bully's first strength: what you can destroy. Destroy us all then, and have done with it. I cannot stop you, as well you know. When you are a sunken wreck on the bottom, I wish you much joy of the experience.' He turned resolutely away from her. He had to walk away now, he knew that. Just turn and keep walking, or she would not respect him at all. He had nearly reached the edge of the foredeck when the entire ship gave a sudden lurch. There was a wild whoop from the lookout high in the rigging, and a cumulative mutter of surprise from the crew below in their hammocks. The mate back on the wheel shouted an angry question. Kennit's crutch tip skittered on the smooth deck and then flew out from under him. He fell, sprawling, his elbows striking heavily. The fall knocked the wind from his lungs.

As he lay gasping on the deck, the ship righted herself. In an instant, all was as it had been before, save for the querying voices of crewmen raised in sudden alarm. A soft but melodious laugh from the figurehead taunted him. A smaller voice spoke by Kennit's ear. The tiny wizardwood charm strapped to his wrist spoke abruptly. 'Don't walk away, you fool. Never turn your back on a dragon. If you do, she will think you are so stupid that you deserve destruction.'

Kennit gasped in a painful breath. 'And I should trust you,' he grunted. He managed to sit up. 'You're a bit of a dragon yourself, if what she says is true.'

'There are dragons and dragons. This one would just as soon not spend eternity tied to a heap of bones. Turn back. Defy her. Challenge her.'

'Shut up,' he hissed at the useless thing.

'What did you say to me?' the ship demanded in a poisonously sweet voice.

With difficulty, he dragged himself up. When his crutch was in place again, he swung across the deck to the bow rail. 'I said, "Shut up!"' he repeated for her. He gripped the railing and leaned over it. He let every bit of his fear blossom as anger. 'Be wood, if you have not the wit to be Vivacia.'

'Vivacia? That spineless slave thing, that quivering, acquiescent, grovelling creation of humans? I would be silent forever rather than be her.'

Kennit seized his advantage. 'Then you are not her? Not one whit of you was expressed in her?'

The figurehead reared her head back. If she had been a serpent, Kennit would have believed her ready to strike. He did not step back. He would not show fear. Besides, he did not think she could quite reach him. Her mouth opened, but no words came out. Her eyes spun with anger.

'If she is not you, then she has as much a right to be the life of this ship as you do. And if she is you . . . well, then. You mock and criticize yourself. Either way, it matters not to me. My offer to this liveship stands. I little care which of you takes it up.'

There. He had put all his coins on the table. He either would win or be ruined. There was nothing else between those extremes. But then, there never had been.

She expelled a sudden breath with a sound between a hiss and a sigh. 'What offer?' she demanded.

Kennit smiled with one corner of his mouth. 'What offer? You mean, you don't know? Dear, dear. I thought you had always been lurking beneath Vivacia's skin. It appears that instead you are rather newly awakened.' He watched her carefully as he gently mocked her. He must not take it to the point where she was angry, but he did not wish to appear too eager to bargain with her either. As her eyes began to narrow, he shifted his tactic. 'Pirate with me. Be my queen of the seas. If dragon you truly are, then show me that nature. Let us prey where we will, and claim all these islands as our own.'

Despite her haughty stare, he had seen the brief widening of her eyes that betrayed her interest. Her next words made him smile.

'What's in it for me?'

'What do you want?'

She watched him. He stood straight and met her strange gaze with his small smile. She ran her eyes over him as if he were a naked whore in a cheap house parlour. Her look lingered on his missing leg, but he did not let it fluster him. He waited her out.

'I want what I want, and when I want it. When the time comes for me to take it, I'll tell you what it is.' She threw her words down as a challenge.

'Oh, my.' He tugged at his moustache as if amused. In reality, her words trickled down his spine like icewater. 'Can you truly expect me to agree with such terms?'

It was her turn to laugh, a throaty chuckle that reminded him of the singsong snarl of a hunting tiger. It did not reassure Kennit at all. Nor did her words. 'Of course you will accept those terms. For what other course is available to you? As little as you wish to admit it, I can destroy you and all your crew any time it pleases me. You should be content with knowing that it amuses me to pirate with you for a time. Do not seek more than you can grasp.'

Kennit refused to be daunted. 'Destroy me and you destroy yourself. Or do you think it would be more amusing to sink to the bottom and rest in the muck there? Pirate with me, and my crew will give you wings of canvas. With us, you can fly across the waves. You can hunt again, dragon. If the old legends be true at all, that should more than amuse you.'

She chuckled again. 'So. You accept my terms?'

Kennit straightened. 'So. I take a night to think about it.'

'You accept them,' she said to the night.

He did not deign to reply. Instead he gripped his crutch and made his careful way across her deck. At the ladder, he lowered himself to the deck, and managed the steps awkwardly. He nodded curtly to two deckhands as he passed them. If they had overheard any of the captain's conversation with the ship, they were wise enough not to show it.

As he crossed the main deck, he finally allowed himself to feel his triumph. He had done it. He had called the ship back to life, and she would serve him once more. He thrust away her side of the bargain. What could exist that she could want for herself? She had no need to mate nor eat nor even sleep. What could she demand of him that he could not easily grant her? It was a good agreement.

'Wiser than you know,' said his own voice in small. 'A pact for greatness, even.'

'Is it?' muttered Kennit. Not even to his good luck charm would he risk showing his elation. 'I wonder. The more so in that you endorse it.'

'Trust me,' suggested the charm. 'Have I ever steered you wrong?'

'Trust you, and trust a dragon,' Kennit retorted softly. He glanced about to be sure no one was watching or listening to him. He brought his wrist up to eye level. In the moonlight, he could make out no more of the charm's tiny features than the red glinting of its eyes. 'Does Wintrow have the right of it? Are you a leftover bit of a still-born dragon?'

An instant of silence, more telling than any words. 'And if I am?' the charm asked smoothly. 'Do I not still bear your own face? Ask yourself this. Do you conceal the dragon, or does the dragon conceal you?'

Kennit's heart lurched in his chest. Some trick of the wind made a low moaning in the rigging. It stood Kennit's hair on end.

'You make no sense,' he muttered to the charm. He lowered his hand and gripped his crutch firmly. As he moved through his ship, towards his own bunk and rest, he ignored the minute snickering of the thing bound to his wrist.

*   *   *

Her voice was rusty. She had sung before, to herself, in the maddening confinement of the cave and pool. Shrill and cracked had her voice been, crashing her defiance against the stone walls and iron bars that bound her.

But this was different. Now she lifted her voice in the night and sang out an ancient song of summoning. 'Come,' it said, to any who might hear. 'Come, for the time of gathering is nigh. Come to share memories, come to journey together, back to the place of beginnings. Come.'

It was a simple song, meant to be joyous. It was meant to be shared by a score of voices. Sung alone, it sounded weak and pathetic. When she moved from the Plenty up to the Lack and sang it out under the night sky, it sounded even thinner. She drew breath again, and sang it out, louder and more defiantly. She could not say whom she summoned; there was no fresh trace of serpent scent in the water but only the maddening fragrance from the ship. There was something about the ship she followed that suggested kinship to her. She could not imagine how she could be kin to a ship, and yet she could not deny the tantalizing toxins that drifted from the ship's hull. She took in air to sing again.

'Come, join your kin and lend strength to the weaker ones. Together, together, we journey, back to our beginnings and our endings. Gather, shore-born creatures of the sea, to return to the shores yet again. Bring your dreams of sky and wings; come to share the memories of our lives. Our time is come, our time is come.'

The last piping notes of the song faded, carried away by the wind. She Who Remembers waited for an answer. Nothing came. Yet, as she sank disconsolately beneath the waves once more, it seemed to her that the toxins that trailed elusively from the ship ahead of her took on more substance and flavour.

I mock and tease myself, she chided herself. Perhaps she was truly mad. Perhaps she had returned to freedom only to witness the end of all her kind. Desolation wrapped her and tried to bear her down. Instead, she fell back into her position behind the ship, to follow where it would lead her.

EIGHT

Lords of the Three Realms

TINTAGLIA'S SECOND KILL was a bear. She measured herself against him, predator against predator, the beat of her wings against the swipe of his immense clawed paws. She won, of course, and tore open his belly to feast on his liver and heart. The struggle satiated something in her soul. It was a proof that she was no longer a helpless, pleading creature trapped in a coffin of her own body. She had left behind the humans who had stupidly cut up the bodies of her siblings. It had not been their doing that had imprisoned her. They had acted in ignorance, mostly, when they slew her kin. Eventually, two of them had been willing to sacrifice all to free her. She did not have to decide if the debts of murder were balanced by the acts of rescue. She had left them behind, for all time. As sweet as vengeance could have been, it would not save those of her kind who might still have survived. Her first duty was to them.

She had slept for a time athwart her kill. The honey sunshine of autumn had baked into her through the long afternoon. When she had awakened, she was ready to move on. While she slept, her next actions had become clear in her mind. If any of her folk survived, they would be at their old hunting grounds. She would seek them there first.

So she had arisen from the bear's carcass, its rank meat

already abuzz with hundreds of glistening blue flies. She had tested her wings, feeling the new strength she had gained from this kill. It would have been far more natural for her to emerge in early spring, with all the summer to grow and mature before winter fell. She knew that she must kill and feed as often as she could in these dwindling harvest days, building her body's strength against the winter to come. Well, she would, for her own survival was paramount to her, but she would seek her folk at the same time. She launched from the sunny hillside where the bear had met his end, and rose into the sky on steadily beating wings.

She rose to where the wind flowed stronger and hung there on the currents, spiralling slowly over the lands below. As she circled, she sought for some sign of her kin. The muddy riverbanks and shallows should have borne the trampled marks of dragon wallows, yet there were none. She soared past lofty rock ledges, ideal for sun basking and mating, but all of them were innocent of the clawed territorial marks and scat that should have proclaimed their use. Her eyes, keener than any hawk's, saw no other dragon riding the air currents over the river. The distant skies were blue, and empty of dragons all the way to the horizons. Her sense of smell, at least as keen as her eyesight, brought her no musk of a male, not even an old scent of territory claimed. In all this wide river valley, she was alone. Lords of the Three Realms were dragonkind; they had ruled the sky, the sea and the earth below. None had been their equal in magnificence or intelligence. How could they all have disappeared? It was incomprehensible to her. Some, somewhere, must have survived. She would find them.

She flew a wide, lazy circle, studying the land below for familiar landmarks. All had vanished. In the years that had passed, the river had shifted in its wide bed. Flooding and earthquakes had re-formed the land numerous times; her ancestral memories recalled many changes in the topography of this area. Yet, the changes she saw now seemed more radical than any her folk had ever seen. She felt that the whole countryside had sunken. The river seemed wider and shallower and less defined. Where once the Serpent River had raced strongly to the sea, the Rain Wild River now twined in a lazy sprawl of swamp and marsh.

The human city of Trehaug was built beside the sunken ruins of old Frengong of the Elderlings. The Elderlings had chosen that site for the city so that they might be close to the dragons' cocooning grounds. Once, there had been a wide shallows there in the bend of the Serpent River. There the memory stone had shone as silvery-black sand on a gleaming beach. In long-ago autumns, serpents had wallowed out of the river onto the sheltered beaches there. With the aid of the adult dragons, the serpents had formed their cocoons of long strands of saliva mixed with the rich memory sand. Every autumn, the cocoons had littered the beach like immense seed pods awaiting the spring. Both dragons and Elderlings had guarded the hardened cases that protected the metamorphosing creatures all through the long winter. Summer light and heat would eventually come, to touch the cases and awaken the creatures inside.

Gone, all gone. Beach and Elderlings and guardian dragons, all gone. But, she reminded herself fiercely, Frengong had not been the only cocooning beach. There had been others, further up the Serpent River.

Hope battled misgiving as she banked her wings and followed the water upriver. She might no longer recognize the lie of the land, but the Elderlings had built cities of their own near the cocooning beaches. Surely, something remained of those sprawling hives of stone buildings and paved streets. If nothing else, she could explore where once her kind had hatched. Perhaps, she dared to hope, in some of those ancient cities the allies of the dragon folk still survived. If she could not find any of her kin, she might find someone who could tell her what had become of them.

* * *

The sun was merciless in the blue sky. The distant yellow orb promised warmth, but the constant mists of the river drenched and chilled them all. Malta's skin felt raw; the tattering of her ragged garments plainly showed that the mists were as caustic as the river water itself. Her body was pebbled with insect bites that itched perpetually, yet her skin was so irritated that any scratching made her bleed. The cruel glittering of light against the water dazzled her eyes. When she felt her face, her eyes were puffed to slits, while the scar on her brow stood up in ridges of proudflesh. She could find no comfortable position in the tiny boat, for the bare wooden seats were not big enough to lie down on. The best she could do was to wedge herself into a half-reclining position and then drape her arm over her eyes.

Thirst was her worst torment. To be parched of throat, and yet surrounded by undrinkable water was by far the worst torture of all. The first time she had seen Kekki lift a palmful of river water to her mouth, Malta had sprung at her, shouting at her to stop. She had stopped her that time. From the Companion's silence and the puffiness of her swollen and scarlet lips now, Malta deduced that Kekki had yielded to the taunt of the water, and more than once.

Malta lay in the tiny rocking vessel as the river swept it along and wondered why she cared. She could come up with no answer, and yet it made her angry to know the woman would drink water that would eventually kill her. She watched the Companion from the shelter of her arm's shade. Her fine gown of green silk would once have left Malta consumed with envy. Now it was even more ragged than Malta's clothing. The Companion's artfully coifed hair was a tangle of locks around her brow and down her back. Her eyes were closed and her lips puffed in and out with her breathing. Malta wondered if she were dying already. How much of the water did it take to bring death? Then she found herself wondering if she were going to die anyway. Perhaps she was foolish and it was better to drink, and no longer be thirsty, and die sooner.

'Maybe it will rain,' the Satrap croaked hopefully.

Malta moved her mouth, and finally decided to reply. 'Rain falls from clouds,' she pointed out. 'There aren't any.'

He kept silent, but she could feel annoyance radiating from him like heat from a fireplace. She didn't have the energy to turn and face him. She wondered why she had even spoken to him. Her mind wandered back to yesterday. She had felt something brush her senses, clinging and yet as insubstantial as a cobweb against her face in the dark. She had looked all around, but seen nothing. Then she had turned her eyes upward and seen the dragon. She was sure of it. She had seen a blue dragon, and when it tipped its wings, the sun had glinted silver off its scales. She had cried out to it, begging it for aid. Her shouts had roused the Satrap and his Companion from their dozing. Yet, when she had pointed and demanded that they see it too, they had told her there was nothing there. Perhaps a blackbird, tiny in the distance, but that was all. The Satrap had scoffed at her, telling her that only children and ignorant peasants believed in dragon tales.

It had angered her so much that she did not speak to him again, not even when night fell and he complained endlessly of the dark, the chill, and the damp. He had a knack for making every discomfort her fault, or the fault of the Bingtown Traders or the Rain Wild Traders. She had grown tired of his whining. It was more annoying than the shrill humming of the tiny mosquitoes that discovered them as darkness fell and feasted upon their blood.

When dawn had finally come, she had tried to persuade herself that it brought hope. The lone board that she had to use as a paddle lasted less than half the morning. Her efforts to push them out of the main current of the river had been both exhausting and fruitless. It rotted away in her hands, eaten by the water. Now they sat in the boat, as helpless as children while the river carried them farther and farther from Trehaug. Like an uncomfortable and idle child, the Satrap picked at quarrels.

'Why hasn't anyone come to rescue us yet?' he demanded suddenly.

She spoke over her shoulder. 'Why would they look for us here?' she asked dryly.

'But you shouted at them as we floated past Trehaug. We all did.'

'Shouting and being heard are two different things.'

'What will become of us?' Kekki's words were so soft and thick that Malta could barely make them out. The Companion had opened her eyes and was looking at Malta. Malta wondered if her own eyes were as bloodshot as Kekki's.

'I'm not sure.' Malta moved her mouth, trying to moisten her tongue enough to talk. 'If we are fortunate, we may be carried to one side and caught in a shallows or backwater. If we are very lucky, we may encounter a liveship coming up the river. However, I doubt it. I heard they had all gone out to drive the Chalcedean ships away from Bingtown. Eventually, the river will carry us to the sea. Perhaps we will encounter other vessels there, and be rescued. If our boat holds together that long.' If we live to see it, Malta added to herself.

'We'll likely die,' the Satrap pointed out ponderously. 'The tragedy of my dying so young will be vast. Many, many other deaths will follow mine. For when I am gone, there will be no one to keep peace among my nobles. No one will sit on the Pearl Throne after me, for I die in the flower of my youth, without heirs. All will mourn my passing. Chalced will no longer fear to challenge Jamaillia. The pirates will raid and burn unchecked. All of my vast and beautiful empire will fall into ruin. And all because of a foolish little girl, too ignorantly rustic to know when she was being offered the chance to better herself.'

Malta sat up so fast that the little boat rocked wildly. She ignored Kekki's frightened moans to turn and face the Satrap Cosgo. He sat in the stern of the boat, his knees drawn up under his chin and his arms wrapped around his legs. He looked like a petulant ten-year-old. His pale skin, sheltered so long from the elements, was doubly ravaged by his exposure to the water and the wind. At the ball in Bingtown, his delicate features and pallid skin had seemed romantic and exotic to Malta. Now he merely looked like a sickly child. She fought a sudden and intense urge to push him overboard.

'But for me, you'd already be dead,' she declared flatly. 'You were trapped in a room that was filling with mud and water. Or had you forgotten that?'

'And how did I get there? By the machinations of your people. They assaulted and kidnapped me, and for all I know, they have already sent ransom notes.' He halted abruptly, coughed, and then forced the parched words out. 'I never should have come to your ratty little town. What did I discover? Not a place of wonder and wealth as Serilla had led me to believe, but a dirty little harbour town full of greedy merchants and their unmannered, pretentious daughters. Look at you! A moment of beauty, that is all you will ever have known. Any woman is beautiful for a month or so of her life. Well, you are past that brief flowering now, with your dried-up skin and that crusty split down your brow. You should have seized your chance to amuse me. Then I might have taken you back to Court, out of pity for you, and you would at least have been able to glimpse what it was like to live graciously. But no. You refused me, and so I was forced to stay overlong at your peasant dance and become a target for ruffians and robbers. All Jamaillia will falter and fall into ruin without me. And all because of your inflated view of yourself.' He coughed again, and his tongue came out in a vain effort to wet his parched lips. 'We're going to die on this river.' He sniffed. A tiny tear formed at the corner of his eyes and trickled down beside his nose.

Malta felt an instant of hatred purer than any emotion

she had ever felt. 'I hope you die first so I can watch,' she croaked at him.

'Traitor!' Cosgo lifted a trembling finger and pointed at her. 'Only a traitor could speak so to me! I am the Satrap of all Jamaillia. I condemn you to live-flaying and to be burnt afterwards. I swear that if we live, I will watch my sentence carried out on you.' He looked past her at Kekki. 'Companion. Witness my words. If I die and you survive, it is your duty to make my will known to others. See that bitch punished!'

Malta glared at him but said nothing. She tried to work moisture into her throat but found none. It galled her to let his words stand, but she had no choice. She turned her back on him.

Tintaglia sated her hunger with a foolish young boar. She had spotted him rooting at the edge of an oak grove. At the sight and scent of him, hunger had roared in her. The foolish pig had stood, staring at her curiously as she stooped down to him. At the last moment, he had brandished his tusks at her as if that would scare her off. She had devoured him in a matter of bites, leaving little more than blood-smeared leaves and detritus to show he had ever existed. Then she had taken off again.

Her voracity almost frightened her. For the rest of the afternoon, she flew low, hunting as she travelled, and killed twice more, a deer and another boar. They were sufficient to her hunger, but no more than that. The grumbling of her belly kept distracting her from her avowed intention. At one point, she lifted her eyes to scan the general lie of the land and was suddenly aware she had been paying no attention to where she was flying. She could no longer see the river.

She forced herself to stop thinking of her belly. Swiftly she soared across the wide swampy valley until she returned to the choked thread of the river. Here the trees encroached on the flow of water, and the swampy banks of the river spread wide beneath the forest canopy. Nothing promising here. Once more, she flew upstream, but this time she drove herself, flying as swiftly as ever she had, looking, always looking for a familiar landmark or a sign of Elderling occupation. Slowly the river widened again, the forest retreating. Soon it regained grassy banks as she followed its flow into foothills. The land around it was firmer here, more true forest than swamp. Then, with heart-stopping suddenness, she recognized where she was. On the horizon, in a bend of the river, she glimpsed the map-tower of Kelsingra. It glinted in the westering sun, and her heart lifted. It still stood, and her eyes picked out the detail of other familiar buildings around it. In the next instant, her heart sank. Her nose brought her no odours of chimney smoke or foundry and forge at work.

She flew toward the city. The closer she came, the more obvious became its death. The road was not only completely devoid of the lively traffic it had once sustained; at one point, a landslide had sheared the road away entirely. The memory stone still recalled blackly that it had been told to be a road. She could sense the trapped memories of the merchants and soldiers and nomadic traders who had once traversed it still humming in the stone. Grass and moss had not overcome it. The road still shone, black, straight and level as it made its businesslike way to the city. The road still recalled itself as a highway, but no one else in the world did.

She circled above the deserted city and looked down on its ancient destruction. The Elderlings had built the city for the ages, built it blithely assuming that they would always stroll its streets and inhabit its gracious homes. Now its emptiness mocked all such mortal illusions. Sometime in the past, a cataclysmic settling of the earth had riven the city in two. A huge cleft divided it, and the river had claimed that sunken piece for itself. She could glimpse the rubble of sunken buildings in the depths. Tintaglia blinked her eyes, forcing herself to see the city as it was rather than how the memory stone recalled itself. Thus had the Elderlings built, cutting the memory stone and bringing it here to build their fair city on the plains by the river. They had bound the stone, forcing into it their concept of what it was to be. Faithful and silent, the city stood.

Tintaglia came to the city as the dragons always had, and nearly killed herself in the process. Always, her ancestral memories told her, the dragons had arrived by landing in the river itself. It made a spectacularly showy arrival. The sliding plunge from the blue sky into the cool water always sent up a great feathery splash. The alighting of a dragon always set all the docked ships to rocking in their berths. The water cushioned the landing, and then the dragon would wade out of the cool depths onto the pebbled shore to the cheers and greetings of the gathered folk.

The river was far shallower than her ancient memories told her it would be. Instead of plunging completely beneath it and letting the water catch her, Tintaglia crashed into it. It was scarcely shoulder-deep on her, and she was fortunate not to break her legs. Only the cushioning of her powerful muscles kept her from harm. She cracked two claws on her left foreleg, and bruised her outstretched wings painfully as she caught herself and waded out of the river not to cheers and songs of welcome but to the whispering of the wind among the deserted buildings.

She felt as if she wandered through a dream. The memory stone was near impervious to the encroaching of organic life. As long as it recalled what it was supposed to be, it rejected the tendrilling roots of plants. Animals who might have claimed the city as a place to nest and den were turned aside by the stone's memories of men and women dwelling there. Even after all these years, she saw only tentative signs that the natural world would eventually reclaim this place. Moss had begun to find its first footholds in the fine cracks between the paving stones and in the angles of the steps. Crows and ravens, ever scornful of humanity's claims of mastery, had a few messy nests jutting out from window ledges or wedged into belfries. Algae stained the edges of the fountains that still held rainwater trapped in their ornate basins. Domes had caved in on themselves. The outer walls of some buildings had collapsed in some long-ago quake, leaving the interior chambers open to the autumn day and scattering rubble across the street below it. Eventually, nature always triumphed. The Elderlings' city would ultimately be swallowed by the wild world, and then no one would remember a time when man and dragon had dwelt together.

It surprised Tintaglia that such a thought could cut her heart. Humanity as it now existed little appealed to her. There had been a time, her ancestors whispered in the back of her brain, when dragon essence mingled with the nature of men, and Elderlings emerged from that accidental blending. Tall and slender, dragon-eyed and golden-skinned, that ancient race had lived alongside dragons and gloried in the symbiosis. Tintaglia walked slowly down streets made generously wide enough to allow a dragon to pass in ease. She came to their halls of government, and ascended the wide, shallow steps that had been engineered to allow her kind gracious access to the gathering halls of the Elderlings. The exterior walls of this building still gleamed blackly, while figures of gleaming white decorated the exterior in bas-relief. Cariandra the Fecund still endlessly ploughed her fields behind her team of massive oxen, while on the adjacent wall Sessicaria spread wide his wings and trumpeted silently.

Tintaglia passed between the impassive stone lions that guarded the entrance. One wide door had already collapsed. As she brushed past the other immense wooden door, a chance graze of her tail brought it slumping down into a heap of splinters and fragments. Wood had not the memory of stone.

Within, polished oak tables had given way to become heaps of wood dust trapped under the stone tabletops they had once supported. Dust had coated thick the windows; sunlight hardly penetrated the room. Threadbare reminders of rich tapestries were shredded cobwebs on the walls. Memories clustered thickly here and clamoured at her, but she resolutely kept her mind to this day and this time. Silence and dust and the wind whispering dismally through a broken window. Perhaps somewhere in the building written records had survived. But fading words on crumbling parchment would be no solace to her. There was nothing here for her.

For a moment longer, she stood, looking about, then she flung herself back on her hind legs and stretched out her neck to roar her anger and disappointment, trumpeting out her betrayal to the infuriating ghosts of the place. The blast of her voice shook the stagnant air of the room. Her lashing tail scattered the fragments of desks and benches and flung a marble table-top crashing into a corner. Across the hall, a tapestry gave up its last futile grip and cascaded to the floor in threads. Dust motes whirled alarmingly in the air. She whipped her head back and forth on the end of her serpentine neck, trumpeting out blast after blast of fury.

Then, as suddenly as the fit had seized her, it passed. She let her front legs drop back to the cool black floor. She fell silent and listened to the last echoes of her own voice fade and die. Fade and die, she thought. They all have done so, and I am the last foolish echo, still bouncing off these stones with no ears to hear me.

She left the hall and prowled the deserted streets of the dead city. Light was fading from the day. She had flown swift and hard to come to this place, only to discover death here. The stalwart memory of the stone had left it a stagnant place. The city had perished decades ago, yet life had not managed to reclaim this place. The veins of moss that struggled in the seams of the street were pathetic. Typical of humans, Tintaglia thought disdainfully. What they can no longer use, they have prevented any other creatures from using. An instant later, the bitterness of the thought shocked her. Did she believe, then, that the Elderlings had been no different from the humans who had left her imprisoned for so many years?

A stone-lipped well and the remnants of a windlass distracted her from those thoughts. She felt a pleasant rush of anticipation at the sight. She sought the ancient memory. Ah, yes. Here, long ago, others of her kind had drunk, not water, but the liquid silver flow of the magic that veined the memory stone. Even to a dragon, it had been a powerful intoxicant. To drink of it, undiluted, was to realize a oneness with the universe. The memory was a tantalizing one. She felt a rush of longing for that sense of connection. She snuffed the edge of the well, then peered into its depths. As she shifted her head, she thought she caught a distant shimmer of silver at the very bottom, but she could not be sure. Did not stars shine in daytime in the bottoms of the deepest wells? It might be no more than that. Whatever it was, it was far beyond the reach of her teeth or claws. She would not drink her fill of liquid magic here. No dragon would ever do so again. To have recalled that untasted pleasure was but one more torment to her. It defined the agony of her solitude. With great deliberation, she smashed the rusted remnants of the windlass and pushed them down the well. She listened to the clanking as the pieces rattled down the narrow hole.

Malta had closed her eyes against the brightness of the river. When next she opened them, the light was fading from the day. That small mercy was accompanied by the oncoming chill of night. The first mosquito buzzed delightedly by her left ear. Malta tried to lift a hand to swat at it, but found her cramped muscles had stiffened, as if while she slept she had rusted. With a groan of pain, she straightened her head. Kekki was a crumpled heap of rags, half on the seat, half in the bottom of the boat.

She looked dead.

Horror seized Malta's heart. She could not be stuck in this boat with a dead woman. She could not. Then the silliness of her terrified thought struck her. A terrible smile twisted her face. What would they do if Kekki were dead? Put her over the side, into the devouring water? Malta could not do that, not any more than she could sit here and stare at a dead woman until she herself died. She could barely move her tongue inside her mouth, but she managed to croak out, 'Kekki?'

The Companion moved her hand against the damp floorboards. It was just a twitch of her fingers, but at least she was not dead yet. She looked horribly uncomfortable. Malta longed to leave her there, but somehow she could not. To fold her knees and force herself down into the bottom of the boat set every muscle in her body to screaming. Once there, she lacked the strength to lift Kekki to a better position. She could do little more than push at her. She tugged the remnants of Kekki's green silk gown more closely around her. She patted at her face.

'Help me live.' The Companion's plea was a pitiful whisper. She hadn't even opened her eyes.

'I'll try.' Malta felt she only mouthed the words, but Kekki seemed to sense them.

'Help me live now,' Kekki repeated. Her efforts to talk were cracking her lips. She took a sobbing breath. 'Please. Help me live now, and I'll help you later. I promise.'

It was the pledge of a beaten child, promising obedience if only the pain will stop. Malta patted the woman's shoulder. Awkwardly, she lifted Kekki's head and set it where the thwart of the boat did not press so roughly against her cheek. She curled herself around the Companion's back so that they could share their body warmth. It was as much as she could do for her.

Malta forced her stiffened neck muscles to turn her head to look back at the Satrap. The high ruler of all Jamaillia glared at her malevolently from where he crouched on his plank seat. His brow was swollen over his puffy eyes, distorting his face.

Malta turned away from him. She tried to prepare for the night by pulling her arms inside the sleeves of her robe, tugging the collar of it up as far as it would go and drawing her feet up under the skirts. Huddled against Kekki in the bottom of the boat, she pretended that she was warmer now. She closed her eyes and dozed.

'Whasaat?'

Malta ignored him. She wasn't going to be baited into another squabble. She had no strength for it.

'Whasaat?' the Satrap repeated urgently.

Malta opened her eyes and lifted her head slightly. Then she sat bolt upright in the boat, making it rock wildly. Something was coming towards them. She peered at it, trying to resolve it into a familiar shape. Only a liveship could come up the Rain Wild River. Anything else would fall victim to its caustic waters. But this shape was lower to the water than a liveship should be, and seemed to have a single rectangular sail. Only its own dim lanterns illuminated it but Malta thought she glimpsed movement to either side. The high, misshapen prow bobbed as the ship forced its way upriver. Malta creakingly stood upright in the small boat, bracing her feet as she stared at the oncoming ship, her disbelief slowing her acceptance of it. She crouched down in the boat again. It was dark and their boat was small. It was possible the ship would pass them without seeing them.

'What is it?' the Satrap enunciated painfully.

'Hush. It's a Chalcedean war galley.' Malta stared at the oncoming ship. Her heart hammered against her ribs. What business had a Chalcedean ship coming up the Rain Wild River? It could only be to spy or raid. Still, it was the only ship they had seen. Here was rescue, or brutal death. While she hesitated, wondering what to do, the Satrap acted.

'Help! Help! Over here! Over here!' He rose to a half-crouch in the stern of the boat, clinging to the side of the boat with one hand and waving wildly with the other.

'They may not be friendly!' Malta rebuked him.

'Of course they are! They are my allies, my hirelings to rid Jamaillia's waters of pirates. Look! They have Jamaillian colours on their flagstaff. They're some of my mercenaries, hunting pirates. Hey! Over here! Save us!'

'Hunting pirates up the Rain Wild River?' Malta retorted sarcastically. 'They're raiders!'

They ignored her. Kekki, too, had roused. She dragged herself to a sitting position in the bow, flailed one arm feebly, and yowled wordlessly for help. Even through their clamour, Malta heard the surprised shout of the lookout on the galley. In moments, a cluster of lanterns appeared on the bow of the ship, throwing over them a distorted shadow of the monster-headed prow. A silhouette of a man suddenly pointed towards them. Two others joined him. Shouts from the galley's deck betrayed their excitement. The ship diverted to make straight for them.

It seemed to take a very long time for the ship to reach them. A line was thrown and Malta caught it. She braced herself as they drew the boats together. Lanterns held over the side of the galley blinded her. She stood stupidly holding the line as first the Satrap and then Kekki were taken on board. When it was her turn, she reached their deck and found her legs would not hold her. She sank down to the planks. Chalcedean voices asked insistent questions but she just shook her head. From her father, she had a smattering of the language, but her mouth was too dry to speak. They had given the Satrap and Kekki water, and Kekki was haltingly thanking them. When the waterskin was offered to Malta, she forgot all else. They took it away before she had near enough. Someone threw her a blanket. She wrapped it around her shoulders and sat shivering miserably, wondering what would become of them now.

The Satrap had managed to drag himself to his feet. His

Chalcedean was fluent, if roughened by the condition of his throat. Malta listened dully as the fool declared himself to them and thanked them for rescuing him. The sailors listened to his words with broad grins. She did not need the language; their gestures and tones betrayed their scepticism. When the Satrap grew angry, their mirth increased.

Then Kekki rallied. She spoke more slowly than the Satrap had, but again Malta learned more from her tone than from the smattering of words she picked out. It did not matter that her clothes were dirty and torn, her complexion harshened, and her lips chapped. The Companion berated them and taunted them in polished Chalcedean, using the noble pronouns rather than the common forms. Moreover, Malta knew that no Chalcedean woman would dared have spoken so, unless she trusted firmly in the status of the male who protected her to shelter her from the sailors' wrath. Kekki gestured at the banner of Jamaillia that hung limply from the ship's mast, and then back to the Satrap.

Malta watched the men's attitude shift from scorn to uncertainty. The man who helped her to her feet was careful to touch only her hands or arms. To do otherwise was deadly insult to father or husband. Malta tugged her blanket more firmly around her shoulders and managed to totter stiffly after the Satrap and Kekki.

She was not impressed with their ship. A raised deck ran the length of it between the benches for the rowers. Fore and aft were abovedeck structures designed more for battle than shelter or comfort. They were escorted to the aft one and ushered into a cabin. The sailors left them there.

It took a moment for Malta's eyes to adjust. The warmly-lit cabin seemed brilliant to her dazzled eyes. Lush furs covered the bedstead while a thick rug underfoot comforted her cold bare feet. A small brazier burned in a corner, giving off fumes and heat in equal proportion. The warmth made her skin sting and tingle. A man seated behind a chart table finished inking in a line and made a small notation to himself. He lifted his eyes slowly to regard them. The Satrap boldly, or foolishly, advanced to drop into another chair beside the table. When he spoke his tone was neither command nor request. Malta caught the word for 'wine'. Kekki sank to the floor, to sit at the Satrap's feet. Malta remained standing by the door.

She watched the events as if she watched a play. With a sinking heart, she knew that her fate was in the Satrap's hands. She had no faith in the man's honour or intelligence, yet circumstances trapped her. She did not have enough Chalcedean to speak for herself, and she well knew her inferior status by Chalcedean custom. If she tried to declare herself independent of the Satrap, she would also be shearing herself of whatever protection he might offer her. She stood silent, trembling with hunger and fatigue, and watched her destiny unfold.

The ship's boy brought the captain wine and a tray of sweet biscuits. She had to endure watching the captain pour wine for himself and the Satrap. They drank together. They spoke, with the Satrap doing most of the talking interspersed with frequent sips of wine. Someone brought the Satrap a steaming bowl of something. As he ate, from time to time the Satrap handed Kekki a biscuit or a piece of bread as if she were a dog under the table. The woman took the tidbits and nibbled at them slowly with no indication she desired more. The woman was exhausted, but Malta marked that the Companion seemed to be striving to follow the conversation. For the first time, Malta felt a stirring of admiration for Kekki. Perhaps she was tougher than she looked. The days of exposure had left her eyes mere slits in her swollen face, but a shrewd light still glinted in them.

The men finished eating, but remained at table. A boy came in bearing a lacquered box. From it, he took two white clay pipes, and several pots of smoking herbs. Cosgo sat up with an exclamation of delight. Anticipation shone in his eyes as the captain tamped a load into a pipe for him and offered it to him. He leaned forwards towards the flame the captain offered. As the mixture of intoxicant herbs kindled, Cosgo took a long draw from his pipe. For a moment, he simply held his position and breath, a blissful smile spreading across his face. Then he leaned back and breathed out smoke in a sigh of contentment.

Soon smoke tendrilled through the room. The men talked expansively and laughed often. Malta found she could scarcely keep her eyes open. She tried to keep her attention on the captain and judge his reactions to what the Satrap said, but it was suddenly hard to concentrate. It took all her will just to remain standing. The table and the men at the other end of the cabin receded into a warm distance. Their voices were a soothing murmur. She twitched back to alertness as the captain stood. He extended a hand towards the door, inviting the Satrap to precede him. Cosgo rose stiffly. The food and wine seemed to have restored some of his strength. Kekki tried to follow her master, but sank back down to the carpet. The Satrap gave a snort of disdain and said something deprecating to the captain. Then he focused on Malta.

'Help her, stupid,' he commanded her in disgust. The two men left the cabin. Neither looked back to see if the women followed.

Behind their backs, Malta seized a biscuit from the table and crammed it into her mouth. She chewed it dry and gulped it down hastily. Malta did not know where she found the strength to help Kekki rise and follow. The woman kept stumbling into her as they staggered along together. The men had walked the full length of the ship and the two women were forced to hurry after them. Malta did not like the looks she got from some of the sailors. They seemed to mock her appearance even as they leered at them.

She and Kekki halted behind the Satrap. A man was hastily moving his possessions out of a rough wooden-framed tent set up on the deck below the skeletal castle. The instant he dragged his gear out, the captain gestured the Satrap in. The Satrap inclined his head graciously to the captain and entered the temporary chamber.

As Malta helped Kekki into the room, the man who had moved his belongings set his hand on her arm. She looked up at him in confusion, wondering what he wanted, but he grinned as he addressed a query over her head to the Satrap. The Satrap laughed aloud in reply, then shook his head. He added something with a shrug. Malta caught the word 'later'. Then the Satrap rolled his eyes as if marvelling at the man's question. The man made a face of mock disappointment, but, as if by accident, he ran his hand down Malta's arm, briefly touching the curve of her hip. Malta gave a shocked gasp. The captain gave the man a friendly shove; Malta decided he must be the mate. She was confused as to what had just taken place, but decided she didn't care. She ignored all of them to help Kekki towards the lone cot, but when they reached it, the woman sank down bonelessly on the deck beside it. Malta tugged hopelessly at her arm.

'No,' Kekki muttered. 'Leave me here. Go stand by the door.' When Malta looked at her in consternation, the woman mustered all her strength to command. 'Don't question it now. Do as I say.'

Malta hesitated, then became aware of the captain's gaze on her. She rose awkwardly and limped across the room to stand by the door. Like a servant, she suddenly realized. Anger burned in her but gave her no strength. She let her eyes rove the small room. The walls were of hide. There was a single cot and a small table where a lantern burned. That was all. Obviously temporary. She wondered at that. A moment later the captain was bidding the Satrap good evening. As soon as the door flap fell behind the man, Malta sank to the floor. She was still hungry and thirsty, but sleep would do for now. She pulled her blanket closer about herself.

'Get up,' the Satrap advised her. 'When the boy returns with food for Kekki, he will expect her servant to take it from him. Don't humiliate me by refusing it. He is bringing warmed water as well. After you bathe me, you can see to her as well.'

'I'd rather throw myself over the side,' Malta informed him. She did not move.

'Then stay there.' Food and wine had restored his arrogance. With total disregard for Malta's presence, he began to peel off his filthy clothing. Affronted, she looked away from him, but could not escape his words. 'You won't have to throw yourself over the side. The crewmen will probably do that, after they have finished with you. That was what the first mate asked about you, as you came in. "Is the scarred one available?" he asked me. I told him you were a servant for my woman but that perhaps later she could spare some of your time.' A superior smile curled the corners of his mouth. His voice was unctuous with false kindness. 'Remember, Malta. On this ship, you might as well be in Chalced. On this boat, if you are not mine, then you are no man's woman. And in Chalced, no man's woman is every man's woman.'

Malta had heard the saying before, but never fully grasped what it meant. She clenched her jaws together. Kekki's rusty voice turned Malta's eyes back to her. 'The Magnadon Satrap Cosgo speaks truth, girl. Stand up. If you would save yourself, be a servant.' She sighed in a breath and added cryptically, 'Remember my promise to you, and heed me. We all need to live, if any of us are to survive. His status will protect us, if we protect it.'

The Satrap kicked the last of his garments aside. His pale body was shocking to Malta. She had seen the bare chests of dockworkers and farmhands before, but never had she seen a man completely naked. Against her will, her eyes were drawn down to his loins. She had heard it called a manhood; she had expected more of it than a bobbing pink stalk in a nest of curly hair. The dangling member looked wormy and unhealthy to her; were all men made so? It appalled her. What woman could bear to have a repulsive thing like that touch her body? She snatched her gaze away. He did not seem to notice her distaste. Instead, he complained, 'Where is that bath water? Malta, go and ask what the delay is.'

There was a knock at the doorframe before Malta had time to refuse. She stood hastily, despising herself for her capitulation. The door flap was pushed open and the ship's boy entered, kicking a wooden tub across the deck before him while toting two buckets of water. He set down his burdens and stared at the Satrap as if he, too, had never seen a naked man. Malta privately wondered if it were the Satrap's paleness or the slack slenderness of his body. Even Selden had more muscle to his chest than the Satrap did. Behind the boy came another sailor bearing a tray of food. He glanced about, then handed it to Malta, but a flip of his hand indicated that it was intended for Kekki. Boy and sailor exited.

'Give her the food,' the Satrap snapped as Malta stared at the water, ship's biscuit and thin broth on the tray. 'Then get over here and pour my bath water.' As he spoke, he stepped into the shallow tub and crouched down. He hunkered there, waiting. Malta glared at him. She was trapped and she knew it.

She crossed the room and clacked the tray onto the floor beside Kekki. The woman reached out and took up a piece of hard ship's biscuit. Then she set it down, pillowed her head on her arms, and closed her eyes. 'I am so tired,' she whispered hoarsely. For the first time, Malta noticed the glistening of fresh blood at the corner of Kekki's mouth. She knelt beside the Companion.

'How much river water did you drink?' she asked her. But Kekki only sighed deeply and was still. Timidly, Malta touched her hand. Kekki made no response.

'Never mind her. Get over here and pour my water.'

Malta looked longingly at the food. Without turning, she lifted the bowl of broth and drank half of it greedily. Moisture and warmth in one. It was wonderful. She broke off a chunk of ship's bread and put it to her mouth. It was hard and dry and coarse, but it was food. She gnawed at it.

'Obey me now. Or I shall call the sailor who wants you.'

Malta remained where she was. She swallowed the bite of ship's biscuit. She took up the flagon of water and drank half of it. She would be honourable. She would leave half for Kekki. She glanced at the Satrap. He crouched, naked, in the shallow tub. His tousled hair and windburned face made it look as if his head did not belong with his pale body. 'Do you know,' she asked conversationally, 'how much you look like a plucked chicken in a roasting pan?'

The Satrap's chapped face suddenly mottled red with fury. 'How dare you mock me?' he demanded angrily. 'I am the Satrap of all Jamaillia and I –'

'And I am the daughter of a Bingtown Trader, and will one day be a Bingtown Trader.' She shook her head at him. 'I do believe my Aunt Althea was right after all. We owe Jamaillia no allegiance. I certainly feel no obligation to a skinny youth who cannot even wash himself.'

'You? You think you are a Bingtown Trader, little girl. But in reality, do you know what you are? Dead. Dead to everyone who ever knew you. Will they even look for you down this river? No. They'll mourn you for a week or so and then forget you. It will be as if you never existed. They'll never know what became of you. I've spoken to the captain. He is turning the boat downriver. They were exploring upriver, but now that they have rescued me, of course their plans have changed. We'll rejoin his fellows at the river mouth, and make straight for Jamaillia. You'll never see Bingtown again. So. This is your life now, and the best you'll get. So choose now, Malta Vestrit, once of Bingtown. Live as a servant. Or die as a used-up slattern, thrown off a war galley.'

The biscuit suddenly stuck in Malta's throat. In his cold smile, she saw the truth of what he said. Her past had been torn away from her. This was her life now. She rose slowly, and walked across the room. She looked down at the man who would rule her, crouched incongruously at her feet. He gestured disdainfully at the buckets. She looked at them, wondering what she would do. It suddenly seemed all so distant. She was so weary and so hopeless. She didn't want to be a servant, nor did she want to be used and discarded by a boatload of filthy Chalcedean sailors. She wanted to live. She would do what she must to survive.

She picked up the steaming bucket. She stepped up to the Satrap's tub and poured a slow stream of water over him till he sighed in pleasure at the running warmth. A sudden waft of the steam made Malta smile. The idiots had heated river water for his bath. She should have guessed. A ship this size would not carry a vast supply of fresh water. They would conserve what they had. The Chalcedeans evidently knew they could not drink river water, but did not realize they should not bathe in it, for they probably did not bathe at all. They would not know what it would do to him. Tomorrow, blisters would cover him.

She smiled sweetly as she asked, 'Shall I pour the second bucket over you as well?'

NINE

Battle

ALTHEA GLANCED ABOUT the deck; all was running smoothly. The wind was steady, and Haff was on the wheel. The sky overhead was a clear deep blue. Amidships, six sailors were methodically moving through a rote series of attacks and parries with sticks. Although they weren't putting much spirit into it, Brashen seemed satisfied with the form and accuracy they achieved. Lavoy moved among them, chastising and correcting loudly. She shook her head to herself. She did not claim to know anything of fighting, but this set routine baffled her. No battle could be as orderly as the give and take of blows the sailors practised, nor as calm and unhurried as the archery practice that had preceded it. How could it be useful? Nevertheless, she kept her mouth shut, and when it was her turn, she drilled with the rest of them, and tried to put her heart into it. She was becoming a fair shot with the light bow allotted to her. Still, it was hard to believe that any of it would be useful in a real fight.

She hadn't taken her doubts to Brashen. Lately her feelings for him had been running warmer. She would not tempt herself with private conferences with him. If he could control himself, then so could she. It was merely a matter of respect. She listened to the rhythmic clacking of the mock swords as Clef paced them with a chantey. If nothing else, she told herself, it kept the crew out of mischief. The Paragon carried more than a working crew, for Brashen had hired enough men to fight as well as run the ship, and extras to allow for losses. The stow-away slaves had swelled their population even more. The cramped quarters bred idle quarrelling when the men were not kept busy.

Satisfied that nothing required her immediate attention, she sprang to the mast. She pushed herself for speed going up it; sometimes her muscles ached due to the confines of the ship. A brisk trip to the lookout's platform eased some of the kinks in her legs.

Amber heard her coming. She always seemed preternaturally aware of folk around her. Althea saw the carpenter's resigned smile of welcome as she hauled herself over the lip of the platform and sat down beside her, legs dangling. 'How do you feel?' she greeted Amber.

Amber smiled ruefully. 'Fine. Will you stop worrying? I'm over it. I've told you, this ailment comes and it goes. It's not serious.'

'Mm.' Althea was not sure she believed her. She still wondered what had happened that night when she had found Amber unconscious on the deck. The carpenter claimed that she simply passed out, and that the bruises on her face came from striking the deck. Althea could think of no reason that she would lie. Surely if Lavoy had struck her down, either Amber or Paragon would have complained of it by now.

She studied Amber's face. Lately the carpenter had begged for lookout duty, and Althea had reluctantly given it to her. If she passed out up here and fell to the deck, it would do more than bruise her face. Yet, the lofty, lonely duty seemed to agree with her, for though the wind had burned her face until it peeled, the skin beneath was tanned and glowing with health, which made her eyes seem darker and her hair more tawny. Althea had never seen her looking more vital.

'There's nothing to see,' Amber muttered uncomfortably,

and Althea realized she was staring. Deliberately she pretended to misunderstand. She scanned the full horizon as if checking for sails.

'Amongst all these islands, you never know. That's one reason the pirates love these waters. A ship can lie low and wait for her prey to come into sight. With all the little coves and inlets, a pirate might be lurking anywhere.'

'Over there, for instance.' Amber lifted an arm and pointed. Althea followed the gesture. She stared for a time critically, then asked, 'You saw something?'

'I thought I did, for an instant. The tip of a mast moving behind the trees on that point.'

Althea stared, squinting. 'There's nothing there,' she decided, and relaxed her posture. 'Maybe you saw a bird moving from tree to tree. The eye is drawn to motion, you know.'

The waterscape before them was a dazzling vista of greens and blues. Rocky steep-sided islands broke from the water, but above their sheer cliffs, they were lush with vegetation. Streams and waterfalls spilled down their steep sides. The bright flowing water glittered in the sunlight as it fell to shatter into the moving waves. So much anyone could see from the deck. Here, atop the mast, one could see the true contours of both land and water. The colour of the water varied not only by depth, but also with how much sweet water was floating atop the salt. The varying blues told Althea that the channel ahead was deep enough for Paragon, but rather narrow. Amber was supposed to watch these shades and give cry back to Haff on the wheel if shallows impeded their passage. Shifting sandbars were the second most legendary danger of the Pirate Isles. To the west, a multitude of jutting islets could be seen as islands, or as easily visualized as the mountaintops of a submerged coast. Fresh water flowed endlessly from that direction, carrying with it sand and debris that formed new sandbars and shallows. The storms that regularly battered the area swept through and rearranged these obstacles to shipping.

Charting the Pirate Isles was a fruitless task. Waterways silted in and became impassable, only to be swept clean in the next storm. The hazards of navigation that slowed heavily-laden merchant vessels were the pirates' ally. Often pirate craft were shallow draught, powered by sweeps as well as sail, and manned by men who knew the waters as well as they could be known. In all Althea's days of sailing the Cursed Shores, she had never ventured this deeply into the Pirate Isles. Her father had always avoided them, as he avoided any kind of trouble. 'The profit from danger only pays you interest in trouble,' he'd said more than once. Althea smiled to herself.

'What are you thinking about?' Amber asked her quietly.

'My father.'

Amber nodded. 'It's good that you can think of him and smile now.'

Althea murmured an assent, but said no more. For a time, they rode the mast in silence. The high platform amplified the gentle rolling of the ship below them. Althea could not remember a time when she had not found the movement intoxicating. But peace did not last. The question itched at her. Without looking at Amber, she asked yet again, 'Are you sure Lavoy did nothing to you?'

Amber sighed. 'Why would I lie to you?' she asked.

'I don't know. Why would you answer my question with another question?'

Amber faced her squarely. 'Why can't you accept that I was feeling sick and collapsed? If it had been anything other than that, do you think Paragon would have kept silent about it all this time?'

Althea did not reply immediately. Then she said, 'I don't know. Paragon seems to be changing lately. It used to annoy me when he was sulky or melodramatic. He seemed like a neglected boy to me then. Yet there were times when he was eager to please. He spoke of proving himself to me and Brashen. But lately, when he talks with me at all, he says shocking things. He brings up pirates, and all he talks of is blood and violence and killing. Torture he has seen. He says it all in such a way that it is like dealing with a braggart child who deliberately lies to shock me. I cannot even decide how much of it to believe. Does he think I will be impressed with how much cruelty he has witnessed? When I challenge him, he agrees such things are horrendous. But he relates those stories with such salacious glee, it is as if there is a violent and cruel man hiding within him, relishing what he is capable of doing. I don't know where all the viciousness is coming from.' She glanced away from Amber and added quietly, 'But I don't like how much time he spends with Lavoy.'

'You could more correctly say how much time Lavoy spends with him. Paragon can scarcely seek out the mate. The man comes to him, Althea. And truly, Lavoy brings out the worst in Paragon. He encourages him in violent fantasies. They vie in the telling of such stories, as if witnessing cruelty were a measure of manhood.' Amber's voice was deceptively soft. 'For his own ends, I fear.'

Althea felt uncomfortable. She had the sudden feeling that she was going to regret leading the conversation in this direction. 'There is little that can be done about that.'

'Isn't there?' Amber gave her a sideways glance. 'Brashen could forbid it.'

Althea shook her head regretfully. 'Not without undermining Lavoy's command of the ship. The men would see it as a rebuke to him and –'

'Then let them. It is my experience that when a man in command of other men starts to go rotten, it is best to expel him as soon as possible. Althea, think. The ship is not subtle. Paragon says what is in his mind. The sailors are wiser than that. But if Lavoy is influencing the ship to his way of thinking, can you imagine he is doing less with the crew, especially the Tattooed? Lavoy has gained far too much influence over them. They are, in some ways, like Paragon. They have been brutalized by life and the experience has left them capable of cold cruelty. Lavoy builds on that in men. Look how he encourages the crew to deride and torment Lop.' She looked away from Althea, out over the water. 'Lavoy is a danger. We should be rid of him.'

'But Lavoy –' Althea began. She was interrupted by Amber springing to her feet.

'Ship!' she shouted, pointing. On the deck below, the secondary watchman took up the cry and pointed in the same direction for the benefit of the man on the wheel. Althea saw it now, a mast moving behind a thin line of trees on a long point of land, close to where Amber had been watching earlier. The ship had probably held back and waited there, allowing the Paragon to come closer before they made their attempt.

'Pirates!' Althea confirmed. And 'PIRATES!' she yelled down to alert the crew below. As if aware that they had been seen, colours suddenly unfurled from the other ship's flagstaff, a red flag with a black emblem on it. Althea counted six small boats being prepared for launch from the other ship. That would be their tactic then; the little boats would harry Paragon and board him if they could while the larger ship tried to force him into the shallows ahead. If the small boats' crews were successful at overrunning Paragon's deck, they could deliberately run him aground and pluck him at their leisure. Althea's heart hammered. They had spoken of this, prepared for this, but somehow it still shocked her. For an instant, fear gripped her so strongly she could not breathe. The men in those boats would do all in their power to kill her. She choked a breath past her terror, shut her eyes and then opened them wide. There was no time to fear for her own life. The ship depended on her.

Brashen had appeared on deck at her first shout. 'Put on sail!' Althea shouted down to him. 'They're trying to wolf-pack us, but we can outrun them. Six small boats, and a mother ship. Be wary! There are shallows ahead.' She turned to Amber. 'Go down to Paragon. Tell him he must aid us to keep him in the best channel. If the pirates start to get close to us, arm him. He could do a lot to drive back a small boat. I'm going to keep the watch here. The captain will run the deck.'

Amber did not wait to hear more. She was gone, spidering down the lines as if she had done it all her life. As Paragon drew abreast of the point of land, the small boats raced to intercept him. Six men in each craft manned the oars while others clutched weapons or grapples and awaited their opportunity. Below her, Paragon's deck swarmed with activity. Some crew hastened to add canvas while others passed out weapons or took up watch positions all along the railings. The frenzied activity was not the coordinated preparation she had hoped to see.

Althea felt a sudden rush of anticipation. The excitement was giddying, submerging her fear. After all the waiting, her chance had finally, finally come. She would fight and she would kill. All of them would see what she could do; they would have to respect her after this. 'Oh, Paragon,' she whispered to herself as she realized abruptly the source of her feelings. 'Oh, ship, you have nothing to prove to anyone. Don't let this become you.'

If he was aware of her thoughts, he gave no sign of it. Almost, she was glad to cloak her fear in his bravado. As she called down to Brashen the locations of the oncoming boats that he might steer to avoid them, Paragon was shouting for their blood. Amber had not armed him yet. He roared his threats and thrashed mightily, blindly flailing his arms as he sought for prey within his reach. As Althea watched from her rocking perch, two of the small boats slackened their efforts at the sight and sound of the infuriated figurehead. The other four came on unchecked. She could see them clearly now. The men wore red kerchiefs with a black sigil on their brows. Most of them had tattooed faces. Their mouths were wide as they yelled their own threats back at the ship and brandished swords.

What was happening on Paragon's deck was not so clear

to Althea. Rigging and canvas blocked her view of Paragon's deck, but she could hear Brashen bellowing orders and curses. Althea continued to cry the positions of the small boats. She took heart that two of the little boats were already falling back. Perhaps they might just slip by all of them. Brashen gave orders intending to evade them, but the wild leaning of the figurehead was thwarting the steersman's efforts. From her perch, Althea heard Amber's voice raised clearly once. 'I decide!' she declared emphatically to someone.

Brashen's heart sank within him. None of the crew's training seemed to be bearing fruit. He glanced about for Lavoy. He was supposed to be commanding the archers. The mate should also be bringing the deck under control, but the man was nowhere to be seen. There wasn't time to find him: Brashen needed the crew to function now. They raced about like unruly children playing a wild game. At this first challenge, most of them had reverted to being the waterfront scum he had recruited in Bingtown. He recalled with chagrin his orderly plan: one set of men to defend the ship, a second ready to attack whilst a third saw to the sailing of the ship. The railing should have been lined with a row of archers by now. It wasn't. He estimated that perhaps half his crew recalled what they were supposed to be doing. Some gawked, or leaned over the railing shouting and making bets as if they were watching a horse race. Others shouted insults at the pirates, and shook weapons at them. He saw two men squabbling like schoolboys over a sword. The ship was the worst of all, wallowing about instead of answering the helm. With every instant, the pirates drew closer.

He abandoned the distance a captain kept from his crew. Haff on the wheel seemed to be the only man focused on his task. Brashen moved swiftly about the deck. A well-aimed kick broke up one group of gawkers. 'To your posts,' he snapped at them. 'Paragon!' he bellowed. 'Straighten yourself!' Five steps carried him to where the men were pawing through the arms. The two squabblers he seized by their collars, knocked their heads together, and then armed them both with less desirable blades. The sword they had fought over he kept for himself. He glanced about. 'Jek! You're in charge of passing out weapons. One to a man, and if anyone doesn't take what he's offered, he does without. The rest of you, get in line!' He ordered aloft three men who were hanging back, bidding them watch and cry down to him all they saw. They sprang to with a will, gladly giving up their weapons to those more anxious to fight. Brashen berated himself for not foreseeing this chaos. As their cries and Althea's shouts told him the positions of the advancing boats, he shouted his orders to the man on the wheel and the crew working the rigging. He judged that they would be able to evade the smaller boats, but not by much. As for the larger vessel behind him, well, the same wind filled her sails as his. He had a lead, and should be able to keep it. Paragon was a liveship, damn it. He should be able to outrun anything he had a lead on. Yet for all that, the ship's responses lagged, as if Paragon resisted the crew's efforts to speed him along. Dread uncoiled inside Brashen. If Paragon did not pick up speed, the smaller boats would close with him.

In a matter of minutes, Brashen had the ship's deck crew working smoothly. As the chaos subsided, he glanced about for Lavoy. Where was the man whose job he'd been doing?

He spotted Lavoy headed for the foredeck. Even more unnerving than the previous disorder was the small, orderly group of men around Lavoy. Composed mostly of the former slaves they had smuggled out of Bingtown, this group flanked the first mate as if they were his personal escort. They carried both bows and swords. They ranged themselves on the fore-deck. Purpose was in Lavoy's stride as he paced it. Brashen felt an irrational flash of anger. The way the men moved around Lavoy told all. This was Lavoy's élite crew. They answered to him, not Brashen.

As Brashen crossed the deck, his coat snagged on something. He spun in annoyance to free it, and found a flush-faced Clef hanging on to him. The boy held a long knife in his right hand and his blue eyes were wide. He quailed at Brashen's stern look but did not let go of his jacket. ''m watchen your back, Cap'n,' he announced. A disdainful toss of his head indicated Lavoy and the men around him. 'Wait,' Clef suggested in a lowered voice. 'Jes watch'em for a minute.'

'Let go,' Brashen ordered him in annoyance. The boy complied, but followed him as closely as a shadow as Brashen headed for the foredeck.

'Come here! I'll kill you all! Come closer!' Paragon shouted gleefully at the pirates in the small boats. His voice was deeper and hoarser than Brashen had ever heard it. If not for the volume of the words, he would not have known it was his ship. He felt Paragon's bloodlust himself for an instant; a boy's wild determination to prove himself spiked with a man's drive to crush any who opposed him. It chilled him, and his spine grew colder as he heard Lavoy's wild shout of laughter. Was Lavoy unknowingly feeding off Paragon's wild emotions?

The mate goaded the ship on. 'You bet we will, laddie. I'll cry you where to strike and you knock them. Give him his staff, woman! Let him show these rogues what a Bingtown liveship can do!'

'I decide.' Amber's voice was not sharp, but the pitch of it made it carry. 'The captain put me in charge of this. I decide when the ship needs a weapon. We've been ordered to flee, not fight.' He thought he heard an edge of fear in her voice, but the cold anger masked it well. In a quiet, earnest voice, he heard her exhort Paragon, 'It's not too late. We can still outrun them. No one has to die.'

'Give me my staff!' Paragon demanded, his voice going shrill on the last word. 'I'll kill the bastards! I'll kill them all!'

Brashen could see them now, a tableau on the foredeck. Amber stood, Paragon's long staff gripped in both hands.

Lavoy's stance was confrontational, but despite his words and the men at his back, he hadn't dared to set a hand on the staff. Amber looked past him to Paragon.

'Paragon!' Amber pleaded. 'Do you truly want blood on your decks again?'

'Give it to him!' Lavoy urged. 'Don't try to hide a whole ship behind your skirts, woman! Let him fight if he wants to! We don't need to run.'

Paragon's answer was interrupted by a different sound. Behind Brashen, a grapple thudded to the deck, rattled across it and caught for an instant in the railing before it fell back into the water. Eager shouts rang out from below, and another grapple was thrown.

'Boarders!' Haff cried out. 'Starboard aft!'

Brashen put steel in his voice as he swiftly mounted the foredeck. 'Lavoy! Get aft. Repel those boarders! Archers. To the railing and hold the boats off us. Paragon. Answer the helm, with no wallowing. Are you a ship or a raft? I want us out of here.'

There was the tiniest pause before Lavoy answered, 'Aye, sir!' As he moved aft to obey, his hearties went with him. Brashen could not see what glance passed between Amber and Lavoy as he passed her, but he marked the white pinch of Amber's lips. Her clenched hands tightened on the weapon she had shaped for the ship. He wondered what she would have done if Lavoy had tried to take it. Brashen stored the incident in his mind, to deal with later. He stepped to the railing, and leaned over it to shout at the figurehead.

'Paragon! Stop thrashing about and sail. I'd rather put these vermin behind us than fight them.'

'I won't flee!' Paragon declared wildly. His voice went boyish and broke on the words. 'Only cowards run! There's no glory in running from a fight!'

'Too late to run!' Clef's excited voice piped from behind them. 'They've caught us, sir.'

In dismay, Brashen spun to survey Paragon's deck. Half a dozen boarders had already gained the deck in two places. They were practised fighters, and they held their formation, keeping a clear place behind them for their fellows swarming up the grappling lines. For now, the invaders sought only to defend the small gain they had made, and they did it very well. Brashen's inexperienced fighters got in one another's way as they attacked as a mob. Even as he watched, another grapple fell to the deck, slid, and caught. Almost as soon as it was secure, he saw a man's hand reaching for the top of the railing. His own men were so busy fighting those on board they did not even notice this new threat. Only Clef leaped away from him, to charge across the main deck and confront the men coming up. Brashen was horrified.

'All hands, repel boarders!' he roared. He spun back to Paragon. 'We're not ready for this yet! Ship, they'll take us if you don't get us clear of them. Make him see reason!' he shouted at Amber.

He sprang away to follow Clef, but to his dismay, Althea was there before him. As the boy darted his knife at the man trying to come over the railing, Althea tugged vainly at the grappling hook. The three-tined hook was set well into the railing, and the weight of the men swarming up the line attached to it only encouraged the metal to bite deeper into the wood. A shot of chain fastened directly behind the hook prevented the defenders from simply cutting the hook free. Before Brashen could reach them, Clef gave a wild scream and thrust frenziedly with his knife. It bit deeply into the throat of the grinning pirate who had just thrown an arm over the railing. The blood gouted dark red, spouting past the man's beard to drench both Clef and Althea before spattering onto the deck. A deep shout from Paragon told Brashen the ship had felt it. The dying man fell backwards. Brashen heard the impact as he crashed heavily in the small boat below. Cries told him the falling body had done damage.

Brashen shouldered Althea aside. 'Stay safe!' he ordered her. 'Get back!' He swung one leg over the railing, and locked the other through it, so he straddled it firmly. He thrust down with his sword, slashing the face of a pirate who still clung to the line. Fortune had favoured them. The falling man had near swamped the boat below and knocked down the man who had been bracing the line. As the second pirate lost his grip and fell, Brashen saw his chance. He sprang back to the deck and jerked the grapple loose. With a triumphant cry, he threw it down into the sea. He spun about, grinning, expecting Althea and Clef to share his victory. Instead, Althea's face was twisted with anger. Clef still looked numbly at the knife in his hands and the blood that coated them. A shout from aft turned his head. The fight was not going well there. He leaned down and shook Clef's shoulder. 'Think later, boy! Come on, now.'

His words broke the boy from his trance, and he followed as Brashen charged down the deck. It seemed to him that in the same moment the ship suddenly picked up momentum. He felt a moment of relief that Althea had not followed him as he plunged into the battle. Three of his own men were down, rolling and punching with a pirate as if this were a tavern brawl. He sprang past them to engage the blade of a tattooed man with a gleaming bald pate. Brashen let the man parry his blade easily so that he could lunge past him and spear his true target: the pirate who was just flinging a leg over the railing. As the man fell back, clutching his chest, Brashen paid for his audacity. The bald pirate slashed at him, a cut that Brashen almost evaded by flinging himself to one side. He felt the blade tug at his shirt as the fabric parted. An instant later, a line of fire down his ribs seared him with pain. He heard Clef's hoarse cry of horror, and then the boy plunged into the thick of it. He came in low, jabbing at the man's feet and calves. The astonished pirate leaped backwards to avoid the boy's cuts. Brashen surged to his feet, thrusting his blade before him two-handed. As he came up, the tip of his blade found the bald man's breast and bit deep. The man hit the railing and tipped backwards over it, screaming as he fell.

Brashen and Clef had broken the magic circle of the defending pirates. His crew surged forwards, turning the battle into a brawl. This was fighting they understood; they piled atop the remaining pirates, kicking and stamping. Brashen dragged himself clear of the mêlée and glanced about his deck. Aloft, the men were yelling that the pirate ship was falling behind as Paragon found his speed. A quick dash to the starboard side showed him that Lavoy and his men seemed to have handled their share of the attackers. Two of his crew were down, but still moving. Three of the pirates were still on Paragon's deck, but their comrades below in the boat were shouting at them to jump, to give it up.

Shouts from the bow alerted him to another boarding party. He'd have to trust that Lavoy could finish aft. Brashen raced forwards with Clef still at his heels. Six men had gained Paragon's deck. For the first time, Brashen clearly saw the black sigil on their red headscarves. It was a spread-winged bird. A raven? Kennit's sign? They held their swords at the ready, defending the set grapple behind them. Yet from below came calls from their comrades. 'Give it up! Cap'n's flagging us back!' The boarding party stood indecisively, obviously reluctant to lose what they had gained.

Althea was menacing them with a sword. Brashen swore under his breath; at least she'd had the good sense not to close with them. Amber was nearby, holding a blade competently if not aggressively. Lop, of all people, was backing Althea with a staff. Lavoy had proclaimed that he'd never trust the man with an edged weapon. The tall man grinned enthusiastically, clacking the end of the staff against the deck and his wild-eyed battle enthusiasm seemed to make at least one of the pirates nervous.

'We can still take this ship!' roared one pirate on the deck. Sword still at the ready, he shouted down to the boat below.

'Get up here! They have set women to fight us off. Ten of us could take the whole ship!' He was a tall man. The old slave tattoo on his face had been over-needled with a spread-winged bird.

'Go now!' Amber's words cut through the wind, her tone oddly compelling. 'You can't win here. Your friends have abandoned you. Don't die trying to take a ship you can never hold. Flee now, while you can. Even if you kill us, you can't hold a liveship against his will. He'll kill you.'

'You lie! Kennit took a liveship, and he lives still!' one of the men declared.

A wild roar of laughter broke out from the figurehead. The boarders on the deck could not see Paragon, but they could hear him, and feel the deck rock as he thrashed his arms wildly back and forth. 'Take me!' he challenged them. 'Oh, do. Come aboard, my little fishes. Come and find your deaths in me!'

The ship's madness was like a wave in the air, like a scent that could not be snorted away. It touched them all with clammy hands. Althea blanched and Amber looked sickened. The crazy grin faded from Lop's face like running paint, leaving only madness in his eyes.

'I'm gone,' one of the boarders declared. In a breath, he had stepped over the railing and slid away down the rope. Another followed him without a word. 'Stand with me!' their leader bellowed, but his men didn't heed him. They fled over the side, like startled cats. 'Damn you! Damn you all!' the last man declared. He turned towards the rope, but Althea advanced on him suddenly. Her blade challenged his. Below, his men roared out to him to hurry, that they were leaving. On the deck, Althea suddenly declared, 'We keep this one, to ask him what he knows of Kennit! Amber, throw the grappling hook over; Lop, help me hold him.'

Lop's idea of holding him was to swing his staff in a mighty arc that brushed mortally near Amber's skull before cracking sharply against the pirate's head. The tattooed man went down and Lop began to dance a wild victory jig. 'I got him, hey, I got one!'

Stay safe. The words were like barbs set in Althea's mind. Even as she moved through the routine tasks aimed at restoring order and calm to the deck, the words rankled bitterly in her soul. Despite all, Brashen still considered her a vulnerable female to be kept out of harm's way. *Stay safe,* he had told her, and then he had taken her task for himself, jerking loose the grapple that had defied her lesser strength. Humiliating her by showing her that she was, despite all her efforts, unreliable. Incompetent. Clef had witnessed it all.

It was not that she longed to fight and kill. Sa knew, her bones were still shaking from that first encounter. From the moment the invaders had begun to swarm up Paragon's side, she had been tight with anxiety. Still, she had kept going. She hadn't frozen up; she hadn't shrieked or fled. She had done her best to fulfil her duties. But that hadn't been enough. She wanted Brashen to respect her as a fully capable sailor and ship's officer. He had made it obvious that he didn't.

She left the deck and climbed the rigging, not only to check for pursuit, but also to have a moment of silence and solitude. The last time she had felt such anger, Kyle had been at the root of it. She could scarcely believe that Brashen had stung her in just the same way. For an instant, she leaned her forehead against a thrumming line and shut her eyes. She had thought that Brashen respected her; more, that he cared for her. Now this. It made it all the bitterer that she had carefully preserved her distance from him, standing apart from him when she desired to be close to him, to prove herself independent and strong. She had assumed that they remained at arm's length to preserve discipline on the ship. Could it be that he simply saw her as a distraction, an amusement to set aside while they were under way? All was denied to her.

She could not present herself as a woman who desired him, nor as a shipmate who deserved his respect. What, then, was she to him? Baggage? An unwanted responsibility? When they were attacked, he had not treated her as a comrade who could aid him, but as someone he must protect while attempting to defend his ship.

Slowly she descended the mast, then dropped the last few feet to the deck. Some small part of her felt she was, perhaps, being unfair. But her larger disposition, agitated by the pirates' attack, did not care. Facing men armed with swords who would have gladly killed her had transformed her. Bingtown and all that was safe and noble had been left more than leagues behind her. This was a new life now. If she was going to survive in this world, she needed to feel competent and strong, not protected and vulnerable. The lecturing voice inside her head was suddenly stilled as she came face to face with a truth. This was why her anger at Brashen raged so hot. When he had acknowledged her weakness, he had forced her to see it as well. His words had eaten at her self-confidence like serpent-spittle. Her makeshift courage, her stubborn will to fight and act as if she were the physical equal of the men challenging her had been dissolved away. Even at the last, it had been Lop who took down her man for her. Lop, little more than a half-wit, was still more valuable than she was during a fight, simply because of his size and brawn.

Jek prowled up to her, cheeks still flushed from the fighting. Her grin was wide and self-satisfied. 'Cap'n wants to see you, about the prisoner.'

It was hard to look up at Jek's self-assured face. At the moment, Althea would have given near anything to have the larger woman's size and strength. 'Prisoner? I thought we had several?'

Jek shook her head. 'When Lop swings that staff, he means business. The man never awoke. His eyes swelled out and he began to jerk. Then he died. A pity, as I believe he was the leader of the boarding party. He probably would have been able to tell us the most. The men Lavoy was guarding tried to go over the side. Two made it, and one died on the deck. But one fellow survived. The captain intends to question him and wants you to be there.'

'I'll go now. How did you fare during the boarding?'

Jek grinned. 'The captain put me in charge of passing out the weapons. I think he could see I was keeping my head better than some of the others. I didn't have much of a chance to use a blade, though.'

'Maybe next time,' Althea promised her dryly. The tall woman gave her a puzzled glance, as if she had rebuked her, but Althea only asked, 'Where are they? In the captain's chamber?'

'No. On the foredeck.'

'Near the figurehead? What is he thinking?'

Jek had no answer; Althea hadn't really expected one. Instead, she hurried forwards to see for herself. As she drew near, she was displeased to see Brashen, Amber and Lavoy already gathered with the prisoner. She felt slighted. Had Brashen sent for the others before her? She tried to push her anger and jealousy away, but they seemed to have taken root. She spoke not a word as she mounted to the foredeck.

The sole remaining prisoner was a young man. He had been pummelled and throttled when he was taken, but other than bruises and swelling, he did not seem much harmed. Several slave tattoos crawled over his cheek. He had a thick thatch of wild brown hair that his red kerchief could not tame. His hazel eyes looked both frightened and defiant. He sat on the deck, his wrists bound behind him, his ankles chained together. Brashen stood over him, Lavoy at his shoulder. Amber, her lips pinched tight, stood back from the group. She did not hide her disapproval. A handful of crewmen loitered on the main deck to watch the interrogation. Clef was among them. Althea glared at him but the boy's wide eyes were fixed on the prisoner. Only two of the Tattooed crewmen were there. Their faces were stoic, their eyes cold.

'Tell us about Kennit.' Brashen's voice was even, but his tone was that of a man who was repeating himself.

The pirate seated on the deck stared ahead stolidly. He didn't speak a word.

'Let me have a go, Captain,' Lavoy begged, and Brashen did not forbid it. The brawny first mate crouched down beside the man, seized the hair on top of his head and forced him to meet his gaze.

'It's this way, bonny boy,' Lavoy growled. His grin was worse than a snarl. 'You can be useful and talk to us. Or you can go over the side. Which is it?'

The pirate took a short breath. 'Whether I talk or not, I go over the side.' There was half a sob to his words, and he suddenly looked younger to Althea.

But his response roused cruelty rather than pity in Lavoy. 'Talk, then. No one will know you did, and maybe I'll knock you over the head before I let you sink. Where's this Kennit? That's all we want to know. That's his emblem you're wearing. You got to know where he docks.'

Althea shot Brashen an incredulous look. There was substantially more that she wanted to know. Had any of Vivacia's crew survived? How fared Vivacia? Were there any hopes of ransoming her? But Brashen spoke not a word. The bound man shook his head. Lavoy slapped him, not hard, but the open-handed cuff was enough to knock the prisoner over. Before he could right himself, Lavoy seized him by the hair and dragged him back to a sitting position. 'I didn't hear you,' he sneered at him.

'Are you going to –' Amber began furiously, but Brashen cut her off with an abrupt, 'Enough!' Brashen advanced to stand over the prisoner. 'Talk to us,' he suggested. 'Tell us what we need to know, and maybe you don't have to die.'

The pirate took a ragged breath. 'I'd rather die than betray

Kennit,' he said defiantly. A sudden shake of his head ripped it from Lavoy's grip.

'If he'd rather die,' Paragon suddenly offered, 'I can assist him with that.' His voice boomed suddenly louder. The malice in it stood up the hair on the back of Althea's neck. 'Throw him to me, Lavoy. He'll talk before I give him to the sea.'

'Enough!' Althea heard herself echo Brashen's word.

She advanced to the prisoner and crouched down to be on eye level with him. 'I'm not asking you to be disloyal to Kennit.' She spoke softly.

'What do you think you're do—' Lavoy began in disgust, but Brashen cut him off.

'Step back, Lavoy. This is Althea's right.'

'Her right?' The first mate was both incredulous and furious.

'Shut up or leave the foredeck.' Brashen's voice was flat.

Lavoy subsided, but his colour remained high.

Althea didn't spare either of them a glance. She stared at the prisoner until he lifted his eyes to meet hers. 'Tell me about the liveship Kennit took. Vivacia.'

For a time, the man just looked at her. Then his nostrils narrowed and the skin around his mouth pinched white. 'I know who you are.' He spat out the words. 'You've the look of the priest-boy. You could be his twin.' He turned his head and spat on the deck. 'You're a damn Haven. I tell you nothing.'

'I'm a Vestrit, not a damn Haven,' Althea replied indignantly. 'And the Vivacia is our family ship. You spoke of Wintrow, my nephew. He lives, then?'

'Wintrow. That was his name.' The man's eyes glinted fiercely. 'I hope he is dead. He deserves death and not a swift one. Oh, he pretended to kindness. Bringing us a bucket of saltwater and a rag, crawling amongst the filthy hold as if he was one of us. But it was all an act. All the time, he was the captain's son. Many of the slaves said we should be grateful to him, that he done for us what he could, and that when we did break loose, it was because of him. But I think he was a damn spy all along. Otherwise, how could he have looked at us and left us chained down there that long? You tell me that.'

'You were a slave aboard the Vivacia,' Althea said quietly. That was all. No questions, no contradictions. The man was talking, and telling her more than he realized.

'I was a slave on your family ship. Yes.' He gave his head a shake to fling the hair back from his eyes. 'You know that. Don't tell me you don't recognize your own family's tattoo.' Unwillingly she studied his face. The last tattoo on his cheek was a clenched fist. That would suit Kyle. Althea took a breath and spoke softly. 'I own no slaves. Neither did my father. He brought me up to believe slavery was wrong. There is no Vestrit tattoo, and there are no Vestrit slaves. What was done to you was done by Kyle Haven, not my family.'

'Slide away from it, right? Like your little priest-boy. He had to know what was being done to us. That damn Torg. He'd come amongst us at night and rape the women right in front of us. Killed one of them. She started screaming and he stuffed a rag in her mouth. She died while he was fucking her. And he just laughed. Just stood up and walked away and left her there, chained just two men down from me. There wasn't a damn thing that any of us could do. The next day the crew came and hauled her away and fed her to the serpents.' The man's eyes narrowed. He ran his eyes over her. 'It should have been you, spread out and choked. Just once, it should have been one of you.'

Althea closed her eyes for an instant. The image was too vivid. By the railing, Amber suddenly turned to stare off over the sea.

'Don't speak to her like that,' Brashen said roughly. 'Or I'll throw you overboard myself.'

'I don't care,' Althea interrupted him. 'I understand why he says that. Let him talk.' She focused herself at the man. 'What Kyle Haven did with our family ship was wrong. I acknowledge that.' She forced herself to meet the man's hawkish gaze with one of her own. 'I want Vivacia back, and when I get her, no man will ever be a slave on her. That's all. Tell us where we can find Kennit. We'll ransom the ship back. That's all I want. Just the ship. And those of her crew that still live.'

'Damn few of those.' Her words had not changed the man's heart. Instead, he seemed to sense her vulnerability and to be eager to hurt her. He stared at her as he spoke. 'Most of 'em was dead before Kennit even stepped aboard. I done two of them myself. It was a fine day when he came aboard. His men spent quite a time pitching bodies to the serpents. And oh, didn't the ship scream while they did it.'

His eyes locked with Althea's, trying to see if he had wounded her. She did not try to pretend otherwise. Instead, she slowly sat back on her heels. It would have to be faced, all of it. She was not a Haven, but the ship was her family ship. Family money had paid for the slaves, and her father's crew had been the ones to chain them up in the dark. What she felt was not guilt; guilt she reserved for her own wrongdoing. Instead, she felt a terrible responsibility. She should have stayed and fought Kyle to the bitter end. She should never have let Vivacia depart Bingtown on such a dirty errand.

'Where can we find Kennit?'

The man licked his lips. 'You want your ship? You ain't going to get her. Kennit took her because he wanted her. And she wants him. She'd lick his boots if she could reach them. He sweet-talks her like a cheap whore and she just laps it up. I heard him talk to her one night, cosying up to her about turning pirate. She went willing. She'll never come back to you. She got a gutfull of being a slaver; she pirates for Kennit now. She wears his colours, same as me.' His eyes measured the impact of his words. 'Ship hated being a slaver. She was grateful to Kennit for freeing her. She'll never want to come back to you. Nor would Kennit ransom her to you. He likes her. Says he always wanted a liveship. Now he has one.'

'Liar!' The roar burst out, not from Althea, but Paragon. 'You lying sack of guts! Give him to me! I'll wring the truth out of him.'

Paragon's words were another buffet against her. Sickened, Althea stood slowly. Her head spun with the impact of the man's words. It touched a deeply hidden fear. She had known that Vivacia's experiences as a slaver must change her. Could it change her this much? So much that she would turn against her own family and strike out on her own with someone else?

Why not?

Hadn't Althea also turned away from her family, with far less provocation?

A horrible mixture of jealousy, disappointment and betrayal swept through her. So must a wife feel who discovers her husband's unfaithfulness. So must a parent feel when a daughter becomes a whore. How could Vivacia have done so? And how could Althea have failed her so badly? What would become of her beautiful misguided ship now? Could they ever be as they were before, one heart, one spirit, moving over the sea before the wind?

Paragon ranted on, threats to the pirate and pleas that they give him the prisoner, he would wring the truth out of him, yes, he'd make him speak true of that bastard Kennit. Althea scarcely heard him. Brashen took her elbow. 'You look as if you will faint,' he said in a low voice. 'Can you walk away? Keep your dignity in front of the crew?'

His words were her final undoing. She wrenched free of him. 'Don't touch me,' she snarled low. *Dignity*, she cautioned herself, *dignity*, but it was all she could do to keep from shrieking at him like a fishwife. He stepped back from her, appalled, and she saw the briefest flash of anger deep in his dark eyes. She drew herself up, fighting for control.

Fighting, she suddenly knew, to separate her emotions from Paragon's.

She turned back towards the prisoner and the figurehead, a fraction of an instant too late. Lavoy had hauled the pirate to his feet, and was holding him against the railing. The threats were twin; that Lavoy would simply push him overboard, bound as he was, or that the mate would strike him. The man's face was reddened on one cheek; there had been at least one blow. Amber had hold of Lavoy's drawn-back arm. She suddenly looked surprisingly tall. For a woman so willowy to have the strength to hold Lavoy's arm back surprised Althea. Amber's expression seemed to have turned Lavoy to stone. The look on Lavoy's face was not fear; whatever he saw in Amber's eyes moved him beyond fear. Too late, Althea saw the real threat.

Paragon had twisted to his full limit. His hand reached, groping blindly.

'No!' Althea cried, but the big wooden fingers had found the prisoner. Paragon plucked him easily from Lavoy's grip. The pirate screamed and Amber's shout of 'Oh, Paragon, no, no, no!' cut through his cries.

Paragon turned away from them, clenching the pirate in his hands before him. He hunched his shoulders over the stolen prisoner like a child devouring a stolen sweetmeat. He was fiercely muttering something to the hapless man as he shook him back and forth like a rag doll, but all Althea could hear was Amber's pleading, 'Paragon. Please, Paragon.'

'Ship! Return that man to the deck at once!' Brashen roared. The snap of ultimate command was in his voice but Paragon did not even flinch. Althea found herself clutching the railing in both hands as she leaned forwards desperately. 'No!' she begged the ship, but if the figurehead heard her, he gave no sign. Near her, Lavoy watched, his teeth white in a gritted grimace, his eyes strangely avid. Paragon darted his face down close to the man he clutched tight in both hands. For one horrific instant, Althea feared he would bite his head off. Instead, he froze as if listening intently. Then, 'No!' he shrieked. 'Kennit never said that! He never said he always dreamed of having his own liveship. You lie! You lie!' He shook the man back and forth. Althea heard the snapping of bones. The man screamed, and

Paragon suddenly flung him away. His body cartwheeled in the bright sunlight, then bit into the flashing sea abruptly. There was a slap of flesh against water. Then he was gone. The chains on his ankles pulled what was left of him down.

Althea stared dully at the spot where he had vanished. He had done it. Paragon had killed again.

'Oh, ship,' Brashen groaned deep beside her.

Paragon swivelled his head to stare at them blindly. He curled his fists and held them in towards his chest as if that would hide his deed. His voice was that of a frightened and defiant boy as he declared, 'I made him tell. Divvytown. We'll find Kennit in Divvytown. He always liked Divvytown.' He scowled blindly at the silence of the folk gathered on the foredeck. 'Well, that was what you wanted, wasn't it? To find out where Kennit was? That's all I did. I made him talk.'

'That you did, laddie,' Lavoy observed gruffly. Even he seemed daunted by Paragon's action. He shook his head slowly. In a quiet voice, pitched only for the humans, he added, 'I didn't believe he'd do it.'

'Yes, you did,' Amber contradicted him flatly. She stared at Lavoy with eyes that seared. 'That was why you put the man within Paragon's reach. So he could take him. Because you wanted him dead, like the other prisoners.' Amber turned her head suddenly, to stare at the Tattooed ones of the crew who stood silently watching. 'You were in on it. You knew what he would do, but you did nothing. That's what he's brought out in you. The worst of what slavery could have done to you.' Her glance snapped back to the mate. 'You're a monster, Lavoy. Not just for what you did to that man, but for what you've wakened in the ship. You're trying to make him a brute like yourself.'

With a jerk of his head, Paragon turned his maimed face away from Amber's words. 'So you don't like me any more. Well, I don't care. If I have to be weak so you can like me, then I don't need you to like me. So there.' For him to revert to such childishness immediately after he had brutally killed a man paralysed Althea with horror. What was this ship?

Amber didn't reply with words. Instead, she sank slowly down until her brow rested on her hands as they gripped the railing. Althea did not know if she mourned or prayed. She clung tight to the wizardwood as if she could pour herself into it.

'I did nothing!' Lavoy protested. His words sounded cowardly to Althea. He looked at his Tattooed crew as he spoke. 'Everyone saw what happened. None of it was my doing. The ship took it into his own hands, in more ways than one.'

'Shut up!' Brashen ordered all of them. 'Just shut up.' He paced a quick turn on the deck. His eyes travelled over the silently gathered crew on the foredeck. His eyes seemed to linger on Clef. The white-faced boy had both his hands clasped over his mouth. His eyes were bright with tears.

When Brashen spoke again, his voice was devoid of any emotion. 'We'll be making for Divvytown, with all speed. The performance of this crew during the attack was abysmal. There will be additional drill, for officers as well as crew. I will have each man knowing his place and duty, and acting promptly on that knowledge.' He let his eyes rove over them again. He looked older and wearier than Althea had ever seen him. He turned back to the figurehead.

'Paragon, your punishment for disobeying my orders is isolation. No one is to speak to the ship without my leave. No one!' he repeated as Amber took a breath to protest. 'No one is even to be on this foredeck unless duty demands it. Now clear it, all of you, and get back to your tasks. Now.'

Brashen stood silent on the foredeck as his crew silently ebbed away, back to deck or bunk as their watches commanded. Althea, too, walked away from him. Right now, she did not know him at all. How could he have let all that happen? Didn't he see what Lavoy was, what he was doing to the ship?

*   *   *

Brashen hurt. It wasn't just the long gash down his ribs, though Sa knew that it burned and stung. His jaws, his back, and his gut ached with tension. Even his face hurt, but he could not remember how to relax those muscles. Althea had looked at him with absolute loathing; he could not fathom why. His liveship, his pride, his Paragon had killed with a bestial savagery that sickened him; he had not thought the ship capable of such a thing. He was almost certain now that Lavoy was lining up not just men, but the ship himself to support the mate in a mutiny. Amber was right, though he wished she had not spoken it aloud. For reasons he did not completely grasp, Lavoy had seen to it that all their prisoners died. It was overwhelming to him. Yet he must deal with all that, and never show, not even by the twitch of a facial muscle, that it bothered him. He was the captain. This was the price. Just when he most wanted to confront Lavoy, or take Althea in his arms, or demand that Paragon explain to him what had just happened, instead he had to square his shoulders and stand straight. Keep his dignity. For the sake of his crew and his command, he must feel nothing.

He stood on the foredeck and watched them all obey him. Lavoy went with a resentful, backwards glance. Althea moved awkwardly, her spirit broken. He hoped the other women would have the sense to give her some privacy for a time. Amber was the last to leave the foredeck. She paused beside him, as if she would speak. He met her eyes and silently shook his head. Paragon must not think that anyone opposed Brashen's order to isolate him. He must feel the disapproval was universal. As soon as Amber was off the deck, Brashen followed her. He spoke no parting word to the ship. He wondered if Paragon even noticed it.

*   *   *

Paragon surreptitiously wiped his hands again down the bow. Blood was such clinging stuff. So clinging, and so rich with memories. He fought against absorbing the man he had killed, but in the end, the blood had its way. It soaked into his wizardwood hands, rich, red, and fraught with emotions. Terror and pain were the strongest. Well, how had the man expected to die, once he took up piracy? He'd brought it on himself. It was not Paragon's fault. The man should have talked when Lavoy told him to. Then Lavoy would have killed him gently.

Besides, the pirate had lied. He had said that Kennit loved Vivacia, that he often said he'd always wanted a liveship for his very own. Worse, he said that Vivacia had bonded to Kennit. She could not. She was not his family. So the man had lied and he had died.

Brashen was very angry with him. It was Brashen's own fault he was angry, because Brashen could not understand a simple thing like killing someone who had lied to you. There were many things, he was discovering, that Brashen did not understand. But Lavoy did. Lavoy came to him and talked to him, and told him sea tales and called him laddie. And he understood. He understood that Paragon had to be as he was, that everything he had ever done, he'd had to do. Lavoy told him he had nothing to be ashamed of, nothing to regret. He agreed that people had pushed Paragon into everything he had ever done. Brashen and Althea and Amber all wanted him to be like them. They wanted him to pretend he had no past. No pasts at all. Be how they wanted him to be, or they wouldn't like him. But he couldn't. There were too many feelings inside him that he knew they wouldn't like. That didn't mean he could stop feeling them. Too many voices, telling him his bad memories over and over and over, but in tiny little voices he could not quite hear. Tiny little blood voices, whimpering from the past. What was he supposed to do about them? They were never silent, not really. He had learned to ignore them, but that didn't make them go away. But even they were not as bad as the other parts of himself.

He wiped his hands again down his hull. So no one was supposed to talk to him now. He didn't care. He didn't have to talk. He could go years without talking or even moving. He'd done it before. He doubted that Lavoy would obey that order anyway. He listened to the barefoot thundering of footsteps on his deck as men raced to one of Lavoy's orders. He let the other part of himself grow stronger. Did they really think they could punish him and still expect him to sail blithely to Divvytown for them? They'd see. He crossed his arms on his chest and sailed blindly on.

TEN

Truces

AUTUMN RAIN WAS pattering against the windows of Ronica's bedroom. She lay still for a time, listening to it. The fire had burned low during the night. The chill in the room contrasted almost pleasantly with how warm she was beneath the blankets. She didn't want to get up, not just yet. Lying in a soft bed, between clean linens and under a warm quilt, she could pretend. She could go back to an earlier time, and fantasize that any day now the Vivacia would dock. She would meet Ephron as he came striding down the wharf. His dark eyes would widen at the sight of her. The strength of his first hug had always surprised her. Her captain would catch her up in his arms and hold her tight as if he would never let go of her again.

Never again.

Despair washed through her. By an effort of will, she let it pass. She had survived this grief; from time to time, it still ambushed her with its pain, but when it did, she reminded herself that she had survived it. Nevertheless, she found herself irretrievably awake. It was very early, the clouded dawn barely touching her windows.

What had wakened her?

She had fleeting memories of horseshoes clattering on the drive, and the sound of a door flung open. Had a messenger come? It was the only reason for such sounds so early in the morning. She rose, dressed hastily without disturbing Rache, slipped out into the dim hallways of the quiet house and padded softly down the stairs.

She found herself smiling grimly. Malta would be proud of her. She had learned that the edges of the stairs were less likely to creak, and how to stand perfectly motionless in the shadows while others passed unnoticing. Sometimes she would sit in the study and pretend to doze, encourage the servants to gossip where she might overhear them. She had found a pleasant spot under the study window where she could feign absorption in her needlework, until the worsening autumn weather had put an end to that ruse.

She reached the ground floor and stole quietly through the hall until she was outside Davad's study. The door was shut but not quite latched. Stepping close, she put her ear to the crack. She could just discern a man's voice. Roed Caern? Certainly, he and the Companion had been keeping very close company of late. Scarcely a day went by when he was not closeted with her. Initially, Ronica had blamed that on his involvement in Davad's death. However, everyone else seemed to regard that as resolved now. What else had brought him to Serilla's door at such an hour and in such haste?

The Bingtown Council's consideration of Davad's death was concluded. Serilla had proclaimed that by the Satrap's authority, she found Davad's death due to misadventure and that no one was responsible. The Satrapy, she announced, had decided there was not enough evidence to prove Davad a traitor to Jamaillia. For this reason, his niece would inherit his estate, but Companion Serilla would continue to occupy Restart Hall. His niece, would, of course, be suitably compensated for her continued hospitality, in a timely fashion, after all civil unrest had been resolved. Serilla had made a great performance of this pronouncement. She had summoned the heads of the Council to Davad's study, fed them well on delicacies and wine from Davad's cellar, and then read her conclusion aloud from a scroll. Ronica had been present, as had Davad's niece, a quiet, self-possessed young woman who had listened without comment. At the close of the proceedings, the niece had told the Council that she was satisfied. She had glanced at Roed as she spoke. Davad's niece had had little reason to be fond of her uncle, but Ronica still wondered if the woman's response had been purchased or coerced by Roed. The Council had then declared that if the heir was satisfied, they were content also.

No one except Ronica seemed to recall that it left the blemishes on her family's reputation intact. No one else had frowned at the idea that Davad's supposed treason had been to Jamaillia rather than to Bingtown. It left Ronica feeling oddly isolated, as if the rules of the world had shifted subtly and left her behind. Ronica had expected Serilla to turn her out of the house as soon as the Council agreed to her findings. Instead, the woman had emphatically encouraged Ronica to stay. She had been overly gracious and condescending as she said she was sure Ronica could help her in her efforts to re-unite Bingtown. Ronica doubted her sincerity. The real reason for Serilla's continued hospitality was what Ronica hoped to discover. So far, that secret had eluded her.

She held her breath and strove to catch every word. The Companion was speaking now. 'Escaped? The message said escaped?'

Roed's reply was surly. 'It didn't need to. Only so many words will fit on a message scroll on a bird's leg. He is gone, Companion Kekki is gone and that girl with them. If we are lucky, they all drowned in the river. But remember the girl is Bingtown-raised, and the daughter of a sea-faring family. Chances are she knew her way around a boat.' He paused. 'That they were last seen in a small boat cries to me of conspiracy. Does not it all seem a bit strange to you? The girl went into the buried city and got them out, in the midst of the worst earthquake that Trehaug has suffered in years. No one sees them leave, until they are later seen from the dragon in a small boat.'

'What does that mean, "from the dragon"?' Serilla demanded, interrupting.

'I have no idea,' Roed declared impatiently. 'I've never been to Trehaug. I imagine it must be some tower or bridge. What does it matter? The Satrap is out of our control. Anything can happen.'

'I'd like to read that part of the message for myself.' The Companion's voice sounded very tentative. Ronica frowned. The messages came to Roed before they reached her?

'You can't. I destroyed it as soon as I'd read it. There is no sense in taking the chance that this information will reach others in Bingtown any sooner than it must. Be assured this will not be our secret for long. Many Traders keep close ties with their Rain Wild kin. Other birds will carry this news. That is why we must act swiftly and decisively, before others clamour to have a say in what we do.'

'I just don't understand. Why has it come to this?' The Companion sounded distraught. 'They promised to make him comfortable and safe there. When he left here, I had convinced him it was the wisest course for his own welfare. What would change his mind? Why would he flee? What does he want?'

Ronica heard Roed's snort of laughter. 'The Satrap may be a young man, but he is not a fool. The same mistake is often made of me. Not years, but the heritage of power is what suits a man to take command. The Satrap was born to power, Companion. I know you claim he does not pay attention to the undercurrents of politics, but he cannot be blind to your quest for influence. Perhaps he fears what you are doing right now: taking over for him, speaking with his voice, making his decisions here in Bingtown. From what I have seen and what you have said, your words are not what I expect the Satrap would truly say. Let us abandon all pretences. You know he has abused his power over us. I know what you hope. You would like to take his power as your own, and rule us better than he did.'

Ronica heard Roed's boots on the floor as he paced about the room. She drew back a little from the door. The Companion was silent.

Roed's voice had lost its charm when he spoke again. 'Let us be frank. We have a common interest, you and I. We both seek to see Bingtown restored to itself. All about us, folk prate wildly of independence for Bingtown, or sharing power with the New Traders. Neither plan can possibly work. Bingtown needs to keep its ties with Jamaillia for us to prosper in trade. For the same reason, the New Traders must be forced out of Bingtown. You represent to me the ideal; if you remain in Bingtown, speaking with the Satrap's voice, you can secure both goals for us. But if the Satrap perishes, with him goes your source of power. Worse, if the Satrap returns uncontrolled, your voice is drowned in his. My plan is simple in form if not execution. We must regain control of the Satrap again. Once we have him, we force him to cede power over Bingtown to you. You could reduce our taxes, get the Chalcedeans out of our harbours, and confiscate the New Traders' holdings. We have the most obvious bargaining chip of all. We offer the Satrap his life in return for these concessions. Once he has put them down on paper, we keep him here in honour. Then, if the threatened Jamaillian fleet appears, we still have our game chip. We show him to them, to prove there is nothing for them to avenge. Eventually, we will send him safely back to Jamaillia. It all makes sense, does it not?'

'Except for two points,' Serilla observed quietly. 'We no longer have the Satrap in our possession. And,' her voice grew shrewder, 'there does not seem enough profit in this for you. Patriot you may be, Roed Caern, but I do not believe you completely selfless in this.'

'That is why we must take swift steps to recover the Satrap, and control him. Surely, that is obvious. As for myself, my ambitions are much the same as yours, as is my situation. My father is a robust man of a long-lived line. It will be years, possibly decades before I become the Trader for the Caerns. I have no desire to wait that long for power and influence. Worse, I fear that if I do, by the time I inherit any authority, Bingtown may be no more than a shadow of itself. To ensure my future, I must create a position of power for myself. Just as you do now. I see no reason why our efforts should not be united.'

Caern's boot-heels tapped briskly across the floor. Ronica imagined that he had returned to stand before the Companion. 'You are obviously unused to being on your own. You need a protector here in Bingtown. We marry. In return for my protection, my name, and my home, you share power with me. What could be simpler?'

The Companion's voice was low and incredulous. 'You presume too much, Trader's son!'

Roed laughed. 'Do I? I doubt you will get a better offer. By Bingtown standards, you are nearly an old maid. Look ahead, Serilla, more than a week or a month. Eventually these troubles will pass. Then what will become of you? You cannot return to Jamaillia. A man would have to be blind and deaf to imagine that you cherished your role as Companion to Satrap Cosgo. So. What will you do? Remain here in Bingtown, to live in social isolation among a people who would never completely accept you? Eventually you would become an elderly woman, alone and childless. Trader Restart's home and pantry will not always be at your disposal. Where will you live, and how?'

'As you have suggested, I will have the Satrap's voice here in Bingtown. I will use my authority to create my own living circumstances.' Ronica almost smiled to hear the Companion stand up to Roed Caern.

'Ah. I see.' The amusement was undisguised. 'You imagine you will be a woman living independently in Bingtown.'

'And why not? I see other women managing their own affairs

and exercising their own authority. Consider Ronica Vestrit, for instance.'

'Yes. Let us consider Ronica Vestrit.' Roed's voice cut impatiently across hers. 'We should keep our minds to the matters at hand. Soon enough, you will realize that I have made you a handsome offer. Until then, our minds should focus on the Satrap. We have had reason before this to suspect the Vestrits. Consider the antics Davad Restart went through to put Malta Vestrit before the Satrap's eyes at the ball. If Malta Vestrit whisked the Satrap away from the Rain Wilders, it is part of the conspiracy's plan. Perhaps they will bring him back to Bingtown to side with the New Traders. Perhaps he flees from the river to the sea, to bring his Chalcedean allies down on us with flame and war machines.'

Silence fell. Ronica opened her lips and drew a long silent breath. Malta? What was this talk of her taking the Satrap? It made no sense. It could not be true. Malta could not be mixed up in this. Yet she felt with a sinking certainty that she was.

'We still have a weapon.' Roed's voice broke into Ronica's speculations. 'If this is a conspiracy, we have a hostage.' His next words confirmed Ronica's worst fears. 'We hold the girl's grandmother. Her life is forfeit to the girl's cooperation with us. Even if she cares nothing for her own family, there is her fortune to consider. We can confiscate her family home, threaten to destroy it. The Vestrit girl has friends within the Bingtown Traders. She is not immune to "persuasion".'

A silence followed his words. When the Companion spoke again, her voice was lifted in outrage. 'How can you consider such a thing? What would you do? Seize her right here, under my own roof?'

'These are harsh times!' Roed's voice rang with conviction. 'Gentleness will not restore Bingtown. We must be willing to take harsh actions for the sake of our homeland. I am not alone in this idea. Traders' sons can often see what their dim-eyed fathers cannot. In the end, when the rightful folk of Bingtown once more rule here, all will know we did right. We have begun to make the oldsters on the Council see our strength. It does not go well for those who act against us. But let us set that aside.'

'The rightful folk of Bingtown?'

Ronica had no chance to hear whom Roed considered the rightful folk of Bingtown. The creak of a distant door warned her just in time. Someone was coming this way. Light-footed as a child, she sprang away from her eavesdropping, raced down the hall and whisked herself into a guest parlour. She halted there, standing in the shuttered dimness, her heart thundering in her ears. For moments, all she could hear was the sound of her body's panic. Then, as her heart calmed and her breathing steadied, other noises came to her ears, the small sounds of the great house awakening. Her ear to the cracked door of the parlour, she heard a servant deliver breakfast to Davad's study. She waited, aching with impatience, until she heard the woman dismissed. Ronica gave her time to return to the kitchen, then hastened from her hiding place back to her rooms.

Rache opened befuddled eyes as Ronica gently closed the door behind her. 'Wake up,' Ronica told her softly. 'We must gather our things and flee immediately.'

Serilla felt pathetically grateful for the interruption of the maid with the coffee and rolls. Roed glared at the interruption, but he also fell silent. Only in the silence did she feel she could truly think her own thoughts. When Roed was in the room, when he stood so tall and spoke so strongly, she found herself nodding at him. Only later would she be able to recall what he had been saying, and feel ashamed that she had agreed.

He frightened her. When he had revealed that he knew she secretly hoped to seize the Satrap's power, she had nearly fainted. When he had calmly assumed he could take her to

237

wife, and side-stepped her affront with amusement, she had felt suffocated. Even now, her hands were damp with perspiration and trembling in her lap. Her heart had been shaking her body since her maid had wakened her and told her that Roed was below, demanding to see her immediately. She had flung on her clothing, snapping at the woman when she tried to help her. There had been no time to dress her hair properly. She had brushed it out roughly, twisted it up tightly and pinned it to her head. She felt as untidy as a lax housemaid.

Yet a tiny spark of pride burned inside her. She had stood up to him. If the shadow she had glimpsed at the door's crack had been Ronica, she had warned her. She had suspected someone was outside the door, just at the moment when he made his outrageous marriage proposal. Somehow, the thought that Ronica might be overhearing his brash offer had given Serilla the composure to rebuff him. It had stirred shame in her, that the Bingtown Trader woman might overhear Roed speaking so to her. The shame had metamorphosed into artificial courage. She had defied Roed by warning Ronica. And he didn't even know it.

She sat rigidly stiff at Davad's desk as the servant set out a breakfast of coffee and fresh sweet rolls from the kitchen. Any other morning, the fragrant coffee and the rich aroma of the warm rolls would have been appetizing. With Roed standing there, simmering with impatience, the smell of the food left her queasy. Would he guess what she had done? Worse, would she regret it later? In the days she had known Ronica Vestrit, she had begun to respect her. Even if the Trader woman was a traitor to Jamaillia, Serilla wanted no part of her capture and torture. The memory of her own experiences assaulted her. Just as casually as Roed had spoken of 'persuading' Ronica, so had the Satrap turned her over to the Chalcedean captain.

As soon as the serving woman left Roed strode over to the food and began to help himself. 'We can't waste time,

Companion. We must be prepared before the Satrap arrives with the Chalcedeans on his leash.'

It was more likely to be the other way, she thought, but was unable to voice the words. Why, oh why, had her moment of courage fled? She could not even think logically when he was in the room. She didn't believe what he said; she knew she was more politically experienced than he, and more capable of analysing the situation, but somehow she could not act on that thought. While he was in the room, she felt trapped in his world, his thoughts. His reality.

He was frowning at her. She had not been paying attention. He had said something and she had not responded. What had he said? Her mind scrabbled frantically backwards but could find nothing. She could only stare at him in mounting dismay.

'Well, if you don't want coffee, shall I summon the servant for tea?'

She found her tongue. 'No, please don't trouble yourself. Coffee is fine, really.'

Before she could move, he was pouring for her. She watched as he stirred honey and cream into it, far too much for her taste, but she said nothing. He put a sweet bun on a plate as well and brought them to her. As he set them before her, he asked bluntly, 'Companion, are you well? You look pale.'

The muscles stood out in his tanned forearms. The knuckles of his hand rose in hard ridges. She lifted her cup hastily and sipped from it. When she set it down, she tried to speak with a steady voice. Her reply was stiff. 'I am fine. Please. Continue.'

'Mingsley's overtures of peace are a farce, a distraction to keep us busy while they muster their forces. They know of the Satrap's escape, and probably in more detail than we do. Also, I am certain the Vestrits have been involved in this from the beginning. Consider how that old woman tried to discredit us at the Traders' Council meeting! It was to shift attention away from her own treachery.'

'Mingsley –' Serilla began.

'Is not to be trusted. Rather, we shall use him. Let us allow him to make overtures of truce. Let us appear even eager to meet him. Then, when we have drawn him out far enough, let us chop him off.' Roed made a sharp gesture with his hand.

Serilla summoned all her courage. 'There is a discrepancy. Ronica Vestrit has cautioned me not to trust Mingsley. Surely if she were in league with him . . .'

'She would do all she could to appear not to be,' Roed finished decisively. His dark eyes glinted with anger.

Serilla drew a breath and stiffened her spine. 'Ronica has urged me, often, to structure a peace in which all of Bingtown's factions have a say. Not just the Old Traders and the New, but the slaves and the Three Ships folk and the other immigrants. She insists we must make all a party to a truce in order to achieve a fairly-won peace.'

'Then she is damned by her own tongue!' Roed Caern declared decisively. 'Such talk is traitorous to Bingtown, the Traders, and Jamaillia. We should all have known the Vestrits had gone rotten when they allowed their daughter to marry a foreigner, and a Chalcedean at that. *That* is how far back this conspiracy reaches. Years and years of their plotting and making a profit at Bingtown's expense. The old man never traded up the Rain Wild River. Did you know that? What Trader in his right mind, owner of a liveship, would forgo an opportunity like that? Yet, he kept making money, somehow. Where? From whom? They take a Chalcedean half-breed into their own family. That looks like a clue to me. Does that not make you suspect that, from the very beginning, the Vestrits had abandoned their loyalties to Bingtown?'

He stacked his points up too quickly. She felt bludgeoned by his logic. She found herself nodding and with an effort, stopped. She managed to say, 'But to make peace in Bingtown, there must be some sort of accord reached with all the folk who live here. There must.'

He surprised her by nodding. 'Exactly. You are right. But say rather, all the folk who should live here. The Old Traders. The Three Ships immigrants, who made pacts with us when they got here. And those who have arrived since, in ones and twos and families, to take up our ways and live by our laws, while recognizing that they can never become Bingtown Traders. That is a mix we can live with. If we expel the New Traders and their slaves, our economy will be restored. Let the Bingtown Traders take up the lands that were wrongfully granted to the New Traders, as reparation for the Satrap breaking his word to us. Then all will be right again in Bingtown.'

It was a child's logic, too simplistic to be real. Make it all go back to the way it was before, he proposed. Could not he see that history was not a cup of tea, to be poured back into a pot? She tried again, forcing strength she did not feel into her voice. 'It does not seem fair to me. The slaves had no say in being brought here. Perhaps –'

'It is fair. They will have no say in being sent away from Bingtown, either. It balances exactly. Let them go away and become the problem of those who brought them here. Otherwise, they will continue to run wild in the streets, looting and vandalizing and robbing honest folk.'

A tiny spark of her old spirit flared up in her. She spoke without thinking. 'But how do you propose to do all this?' she demanded. 'Simply tell them to go away? I doubt they will obey.'

For an instant, Caern looked shocked. A shadow of doubt flickered through his eyes. Then his narrow lip curled disdainfully. 'I'm not stupid,' he spat. 'There will be bloodshed. I know that. There are other Traders and Traders' sons who stand with me. We have discussed this. We all accept that there must be bloodshed before this is over. It is the price our ancestors paid for Bingtown. Now it is our turn, and pay we shall, if we must. But our intent is that it shall not be our own blood that is spilled. Oh, no.'

He drew in a breath and paced a quick turn about the study.

'This is what you must do. We will call an emergency meeting of the Traders – no, not all of them, only the Council heads. You will announce to them our grievous tidings: that the Satrap is missing in a Trehaug quake, and we fear he is dead. So you have decided to act on our own, to quell the unrest in Bingtown. Tell them that we must have a peace pact with the New Traders, but specify that it must be ratified by every New Trader family. We will send word to Mingsley that we are ready to discuss terms, but that every New Trader family must send a representative to the negotiations. They must come under truce, unarmed and without menservants or guards of any kind. To the Bingtown Concourse. Once we have them there, we can close our trap. We will tell the New Traders that they must all depart peacefully from our shores, forfeiting all their holdings, or the hostages will pay the price. Leave it to them how they manage it, but let it be known that the hostages will be set free in a ship to join them only after all of them are a day's sail from Bingtown Harbour. Then . . .'

'Are you truly prepared to kill all the hostages if they don't agree?' Serilla could find no more strength for her voice.

'It won't come to that,' he assured her immediately. 'And if it does, it will be the doing of their own folk, not us. If they force us to it . . . but you know they will not.' He spoke too quickly. Did he seek to reassure her, or himself?

She tried to find the courage to tell him how foolish he was. He was a large boy spouting violent nonsense. She'd been a fool ever to rely on him for anything. Too late she had found that this tool had sharp edges. She must discard him before he did any more damage. Yet she could not. He stood before her, nostrils flared, fists knotted at his sides, and she could sense the anger seething behind his calm mask, the anger that powered his so-righteous hatred. If she spoke against him, he might turn that anger on her. The only thing she could think of to do was to flee.

She stood slowly, trying to appear calm. 'Thank you for bringing me this news, Roed. Now I must take some time to myself to think it through.' She inclined her head to him gravely, hoping he would bow in his turn and then depart.

Instead, he shook his head. 'You have no time to debate with yourself on this, Companion. Circumstances force us to act now. Compose the letters summoning the Council heads here. Then summon a servant to deliver your messages. I myself will take the Vestrit woman into custody. Tell me which room is hers.' A sudden frown divided his brows. 'Or has she swayed you to her cause? Do you think you would gain more power if you allied with the New Trader conspiracy?'

Of course. Any opposition to him would prompt him to classify her as an enemy. Then he would be just as ruthless with her as he was prepared to be with Ronica. The Vestrit woman had made him afraid when she stood up to him.

Had it been Ronica in the hall? Had she heard the warning and understood it? Had the old woman had time to flee? Had Serilla done anything to save her, or was she sacrificing her to save herself?

Roed's fists were clenching and unclenching at his sides restlessly. Too clearly, she could imagine his brutal clasp on the Trader woman's thin wrist. Yet she could not stop him. He would only hurt her if she tried: he was too large and too strong, too fearsomely male. She could not think with him in the room, and this errand would make him go away for a time. It would not be her fault, any more than Davad Restart's death had been her fault. She had done what she could, hadn't she? But what if the shadow at the door had not been anyone at all? What if the old woman still slept? Her mouth had gone dry, but a stranger spoke the horrifying words. 'Top of the stairs. The fourth door on the left. Davad's room.'

Roed left, his boots clacking purposefully as he strode away from her.

Serilla watched him go. After he was out of sight, she curled forwards, her head in her hands. It wasn't her fault, she tried to console herself. No one could have come through what she had experienced unscathed. It wasn't her fault. Like a rebuking ghost, Ronica's words came to her: 'That is the challenge, Companion. To take what has happened to you and learn from it, instead of being trapped by it.'

To know the layout of Bingtown, Ronica reflected bitterly, was not the same as knowing its geography. With a tearless sob, she caught her breath at the sight of the deep ravine that cut her path. She had chosen to lead Rache this way, through the woods behind Davad's house. She knew that if they hiked straight through the woods to the sea, they would come to the humble section of Bingtown where the Three Ships families made their homes. She had seen it often on the map in Ephron's study. But the map had not shown this ravine winding through the woods, nor the marshy trickle of water at the bottom of it. She halted, staring down at it. 'Perhaps we should have gone by the road,' she offered Rache miserably. She wrapped her dripping shawl more closely about her shoulders.

'By the road, they'd have ridden us down in no time. No. You were wise to come this way.' The serving woman took Ronica's hand suddenly, set it on her arm and patted it comfortingly. 'Let's follow the flow of the water. Either we will come to a place where animals cross this, or it will lead us to the beach. From the beach, we can always follow the shoreline to where the fishing boats are hauled out.'

Rache led the way and Ronica followed her gratefully. Twiggy bushes, bare of leaves, caught at their skirts and shawls, but Rache pushed gamely onward through sword ferns and dripping salal. Cedars towered overhead, catching most of the rain, but an occasional low bough dumped its load on them. They carried nothing. There had been no time to pack anything. If the Three Ships folk turned them away, they'd be sleeping outdoors tonight with no more shelter than their own skins.

'You don't have to be mixed up in this, Rache,' Ronica felt obliged to point out to her. 'If you leave me, you could find refuge among the Tattooed. Roed has no reason to pursue you. You could be safe.'

'Nonsense,' the serving woman declared. 'Besides, you don't know the way to Sparse Kelter's house. I'm convinced we should go there first. If he turns us away, we both may have to take shelter with the Tattooed.'

By midmorning, the rain eased. They came to a place where a trail angled down the steep slope of the ravine. Amidst the tracks of cloven hooves, Ronica saw the print of a bare foot in the slick mud. More than deer used this trail. She followed Rache awkwardly, catching at tree trunks and small bushes to keep from falling. By the time they reached the bottom, her scratched legs were muddy to the knees. It mattered little. There was no bridge across the wide, green sheet of water at the bottom of the ravine. The two women slogged through it silently. The bank on the opposite side was neither as steep nor as tall. Clutching at one another, they staggered up it and emerged into woods that were more open.

They were on a pathway now, and before they had gone much farther, it widened out into a beaten trail. Ronica began to catch glimpses of makeshift shelters back under the trees. Once she smelled wood-smoke and cooking porridge. It made her stomach growl. 'Who lives back here?' she asked Rache as the serving woman hurried her on.

'People who cannot live anywhere else,' Rache answered her evasively. An instant later, as if ashamed to be so devious, she told her, 'Slaves that escaped their New Trader owners, mostly. They had to remain in hiding. They could not seek work, nor leave town. The New Traders had watchers at the docks who stopped any slaves without documents. This is not the only shantytown hidden in the woods around Bingtown. There are others, and they have grown since Fire Night. There is a whole other Bingtown hidden here, Ronica. They live on the edges, on the crumbs of your town's trade, but they are people all the same. They snare game, and have tiny hidden gardens, or harvest the wild nuts and fruits of the forest. They trade, mostly with the Three Ships folk, for fish and fabric and necessities.'

They passed two huts leaning together in the shadow of a stand of cedars. 'I never knew there were so many,' Ronica faltered.

Rache gave a snort of amusement. 'Every New Trader who came to your town brought at least ten slaves. Nannies, cooks, and footmen for the household, and farmhands for fields and orchards: they didn't come to town and walk amongst you, but they are here.' A faint smile rippled her tattoo. 'Our numbers make us a force to reckon with, if nothing else. For good or for ill, Ronica, we are here, and here we will stay. Bingtown needs to recognize that. We cannot continue to live as hidden outcasts on your edges. We must be recognized and accepted.'

Ronica was silent. The former slave's words were almost threatening. Down the path she glimpsed a boy and a small girl, but an instant later they had vanished like panicked rabbits. Ronica began to wonder if Rache had deliberately steered her to this path. Certainly she seemed at ease and familiar with her surroundings.

They climbed another hill, leaving the scattered settlement of hovels and huts behind them. Evergreens closed in around them, making the overcast day even darker. The path narrowed and appeared less used, but now that Ronica was looking for them, she saw other little paths branching away. Before the two women reached the Three Ships houses along the shale beach the trail looked like no more than an animal track. A chill wind off the open water rushed them along. Ronica winced at the tattered and muddy aspect she must present, but there was nothing she could do about it.

In this section of Bingtown, the houses hugged the contour of the beach, where the Three Ships families could watch for their fishing vessels to return. As Rache hurried her down the street, Ronica looked about with guarded interest. She had never been here before. The exposure to storms off the bay pitted the winding street with puddles. Children played on the long porches of the clapboard houses. The smells of burning driftwood and smoking fish rode the brisk wind. Nets stretched between the houses, waiting to be mended. The rioting, and the desolation that had followed it had had small effect on this section of town. A woman, well hooded against the nasty weather, hastened past them, pushing a barrow full of flat fish. She nodded a greeting to them.

'Here, this is Sparse's house,' Rache suddenly said. The rambling single-storey structure looked little different to its neighbours. A recent coating of whitewash was the only indication of greater prosperity that Ronica could see. They stepped up onto the covered porch that ran the length of the house and Rache knocked firmly on the door.

Ronica pushed her rain-soaked hair back from her face as the door swung open. A tall woman stood in it, big-boned and hearty as many of the Three Ships settlers were. She had freckles and a reddish hint in her sandy, weather-frazzled hair. For a moment she stared at them suspiciously, then a smile softened her face. 'I recall you,' she said to Rache. 'You're that woman begged a bit of fish from Da.'

Rache nodded, unoffended by this characterization. 'I've been back to see him twice since then. Both times you were out in your boat, fishing flounder. You are Ekke, are you not?'

Ekke no longer hesitated. 'Ah, come in with you, then. You

both look wetter than water. No, no, never mind the mud on your shoes. If enough people track dirt in, someone will start tracking it out.'

From the look of the floor just inside the door, that would begin happening soon. The floor was bare wood plank, worn by the passage of feet. Within the house, the ceilings were low, and the small windows did not admit much light. A cat sprawled sleeping beside a shaggy hound. The dog opened one eye to acknowledge them as they stepped around him, then went back to sleep. Just past the dozing dog was a stout table surrounded by sturdy chairs. 'Do sit down,' the woman invited them. 'And take your wet things off. Da isn't here just now, but I expect him back soon. Tea?'

'I would be so grateful,' Ronica told her.

Ekke dipped water from a barrel into a kettle. As she put it on the hearth to boil, she looked over her shoulder at them. 'You look all done in. There's a bit of the morning's porridge left, sticky-thick, but filling all the same. Can I warm it for you?'

'Please,' Rache replied when Ronica could not find words. The girl's simple, open hospitality to two strangers brought tears to her eyes, even as she realized how bedraggled she must look to merit such charity. It humbled her to know she had come to this: begging at a Three Ships door. What would Ephron have thought of her now?

The leftover porridge was indeed sticky and thick. Ronica devoured her share with a hot cup of a reddish tea, pleasantly spiced with cardamom in the Three Ships fashion. Ekke seemed to sense they were both famished and exhausted. She let them eat and made all the conversation herself, chatting of changing winter weather, of nets to be mended, and the quantity of salt they must buy somewhere to have enough to make 'keeping fish' for the stormy season. To all of this, Ronica and Rache nodded as they chewed.

When they had finished the porridge, Ekke clattered their bowls away. She refilled their cups with the steaming, fragrant tea. Then, for the first time, she sat down at the table with a cup of her own. 'So. You're the women who've talked with Da before, aren't you? You've come to talk with him about the Bingtown situation, eh?'

Ronica appreciated her forthright approach, and reciprocated it. 'Not exactly. I have spoken with your father twice before about the need for all the folk of Bingtown to unify and treat for peace. Things cannot continue as they are. If they do, the Chalcedeans need do no more than sit outside our harbour and wait until we peck each other to bits. As it is, when our patrol ships come back in, they have difficulty finding fresh supplies. Not to mention that it is hard for fathers and brothers to leave homes to drive off the Chalcedeans, if they must worry about their families unprotected at home.'

A line divided Ekke's brow as she nodded to all this. Rache suddenly cut in smoothly, 'But that is not why we are here, now. Ronica and I must seek asylum, with Three Ships folk if we can. Our lives are in danger.'

Too dramatic, Ronica thought woefully to herself as she saw the Three Ships woman narrow her eyes. An instant later, there was the scuff of boots on the porch outside, and the door opened to admit Sparse Kelter. He was, as Rache had once described him, a barrel of a man, with more red hair to his beard and arms than to the crown of his head. He stopped in consternation, then shut the door behind him and stood scratching his beard in perplexity. He glanced from his daughter to the two women at table with her.

He took a sudden breath as if he had just recalled his manners. But his greeting was as blunt as his daughter's had been, 'And what brings Trader Vestrit to my door and table?'

Ronica stood quickly. 'Hard necessity, Sparse Kelter. My own folk have turned on me. I am called traitor, and accused of plotting, though in truth I have done neither.'

'And you've come to take shelter with me and my kin,' Kelter observed heavily.

Ronica bowed her head in acknowledgement. They both knew she brought trouble, and that it could fall most heavily on Sparse and his daughter. She didn't need to put that into words. 'It's Trader trouble, and there is no justice in me asking you to take it on. I shall not ask that you shelter me here; only that you send word to another Trader, one that I trust. If I write a message and you can find someone to carry it for me to Grag Tenira of the Bingtown Traders, and then allow me to wait here until he replies . . . that is all I ask.'

Into their silence she added, 'And I know that's a large enough favour to ask, from a man I've spoken to only twice before.'

'But each time, you spoke fairly. Of things dear to me, of peace in Bingtown, a peace that Three Ships folk could have a voice in. And the name Tenira is not unknown to me. I've sold them saltfish, many a time for ship provisions. They raise straight men in that house, they do.' Sparse pursed his lips, and then made a sucking noise as he considered it. 'I'll do it,' he said with finality.

'I've no way of repaying you,' Ronica pointed out quickly.

'I don't recall that I asked any payment.' Sparse was gruff, but not unkind. He added matter of factly, 'I can't think of any payment that would be worth my risking my daughter. Save my own sense of what I ought to do, no matter the risk to us.'

'I don't mind, Da,' Ekke broke in quietly. 'Let the lady write her note. I'll carry it to Tenira myself.'

An odd smile twisted Sparse's wide features. 'I thought you might want to, at that,' he said. Ronica noted that she had suddenly become 'the lady' to Ekke. Oddly, she felt diminished by it.

'I have not even a scrap of paper nor a dab of ink to call my own,' she pointed out quietly.

'We have both. Just because we are Three Ships does not mean we don't have our letters,' Ekke said. A tart note had come into her voice. She rose briskly to bring Ronica a sheet of serviceable paper, a quill and ink.

Ronica took up the quill, dipped it, and paused. Speaking as much to herself as to Rache, she said, 'I must pen this carefully. I need not only to ask his aid, but to tell him tidings that concern all of Bingtown, tidings that need to reach many ears quickly.'

'Yet I noticed you haven't offered to share them here,' Ekke observed.

'You are right,' Ronica agreed humbly. She set her pen aside and lifted her eyes to Ekke's. 'I scarcely know what my news will mean, but I fear it will affect us all. The Satrap is missing. He had been taken upriver, into the Rain Wilds, for safety. All know none but a liveship can go up that river. There, it seemed, he would be safe from any treachery from New Traders or Chalcedeans.'

'Indeed. Only a Bingtown Trader could get to him there.'

'Ekke!' her father rebuked her. To Ronica he said with a frown, 'Tell on.'

'There was an earthquake. I know little more than that it did great damage, and for a time he was missing. Now the word is that he was seen in a boat going down the river. With my young granddaughter, Malta.' The next words came hard. 'Some fear that she has turned him against the Old Traders. That she is a traitor, and has convinced him that he must flee his sanctuary to be safe.'

'And what is truth?' Sparse demanded.

Ronica shook her head. 'I don't know. The words I overheard were not meant for me; I could not ask questions. They spoke something about a threatened attack by a Jamaillian fleet, but said too little for me to know if the threat is real or only suspected. As for my granddaughter . . .' For an instant, her throat closed. The fear she had refused suddenly swamped her. She forced a breath past the lump in her throat, and spoke with a calmness she did not feel. 'It is uncertain if the Satrap and those with him survived. The river might have eaten their boat, or they may have capsized. No one knows where they are. And if the Satrap is lost, regardless of the circumstances, I fear it will plunge us into war. With Jamaillia, and perhaps Chalced. Or just a civil war here, Old Trader against New.'

'And Three Ships caught in the middle, as usual,' Ekke commented sourly. 'Well, it is as it is. Pen your letter, lady, and I shall carry it. This is news, it seems to me, that it is safer spread than kept secret.'

'You see quickly to the heart of it,' Ronica agreed. She took up the quill and dipped it once more. But as she set tip to paper, she was not only thinking of what words would bring Grag here most swiftly, but of how difficult it was going to be to forge a lasting peace in Bingtown. Far more difficult than she had first perceived. The quill tip scratched as it moved swiftly across the coarse paper.

ELEVEN

Bodies and Souls

THE DAWN SUNLIGHT glinted far too brightly off the water. The coarse fabric of Wintrow's trousers chafed his raw skin. He could not bear a shirt. He could stand and walk alone now, but became giddy if he taxed himself at all. Even limping to the foredeck was making his heart pound. As he made his slow journey, working crewmen slowed to stare at him, then, with false heartiness, congratulated him on his recovery. Scarred enough to make a pirate flinch, he told himself caustically. The crewmen were sincere in their good wishes to him. He was truly one of their own now.

He ascended the short ladder to the foredeck, two feet to each step. He dreaded confronting the grey and lifeless figurehead, but when he reached the railing and looked down on her renewed colours, his heart leapt. 'Vivacia!' he greeted her joyously.

Slowly she turned to him, her black mane sweeping across her bare shoulders. She smiled at him. The swirling gold of a dragon's eyes gleamed above her red lips.

He stared at her in horror. It was like seeing beloved features animated by a demon. 'What have you done to her?' he demanded. 'Where is she?' His voice cracked on the words. He gripped the railing tightly as if he could wring the truth out of the dragon.

'Where is who?' she responded coolly. Then she slowly blinked her eyes. They went from gold to green to gold again. Had he, for an instant, glimpsed Vivacia looking out of those orbs? As he stared at her, the colours of her eyes whirled slowly and mockingly. Her scarlet lips bent in a taunting smile.

He took a breath and fought to speak calmly. 'Vivacia,' he repeated doggedly. 'Where is she now? Do you imprison her within yourself? Or have you destroyed her?'

'Ah, Wintrow. Foolish boy. Poor foolish boy.' She sighed as if sorry for him, then looked away over the water. 'She never was. Don't you understand? She was just a shell, a muddle of memories that your ancestors tried to impose on me. She wasn't real. As a result, she isn't anywhere, not imprisoned in me nor destroyed. She is like a dream I had, and part of me, I suppose, in the sense that dreams are part of the dreamer. Vivacia is gone. All that was hers is mine now. Including you.' Her voice went hard on the last two words. Then she smiled again and put warmth in her voice as she added, 'But let us forgo such inconsequential chatter. Tell me. How are you feeling today? You look so much better. Though I believe you would have to be dead to look worse than you did.'

Wintrow did not dispute that. He had seen himself in Kennit's shaving mirror. Every trace of the fresh-faced boy who had wanted to be a priest was gone. What his father had begun, with his amputated finger and his tattooed face, he had well and truly completed himself. His face, hands and arms were splotched red and pink and white. In some spots, he would heal and his skin would tan and look almost normal. But on his hand and his cheek and along his hairline, the dead-white skin was taut and shiny. Likely, it would always remain so. He refused to allow it to distress him. There was no time to be concerned with himself now.

She turned away from him to stare ahead at the islands of the barrier. They would come soon to the rocky shallows and scattered upthrusts in the treacherous passage between Last

Island and Shield Island. 'Ah, but I could show you how to repair those scars. The knowledge is there, buried in the back of your mind, coated over and hidden from you. Poor little thing, with no more than the memory of your fifteen short summers. Reach out to me. I'll show you how to heal yourself.'

'No.'

She laughed. 'Ah, I see. This is how you profess your loyalty to "Vivacia". By refusing to touch minds with me. A feeble tribute, but likely the best you can manage. I could force you, you know. I know you as no one else can.' For a crawling moment, he felt the presence of her mind twined through his. She did not reach out for him; rather she let him sense that she was already there. Then she let her awareness of him go dormant again. 'But, if you would rather remain disfigured . . .' She did not bother to finish the thought.

Longing devoured him. He could recall the intense satisfaction he had felt at consciously directing his body's repair while he slept in the dragon. Awake and alive once more, he could not sink his consciousness deep enough to attain that control over himself. Could she teach him to find that mastery at will? His desire for that knowledge went far beyond freedom from pain and erasing his latest scars. Could she show him how to expel the tattoo's ink from his face? Teach him to regenerate his lost finger as well? Once learned, could he use this skill for others? It would be the unlocking of a great mystery. All his life, Wintrow had loved knowledge, loved the pursuit of knowledge. She could not have chosen better bait to tempt him.

'Such a healer as you could be. Consider. I could persuade Kennit to let you go. You could return to your monastery, to your simple and satisfying service to Sa. You could have your own life back again. You could serve your god, with a clean conscience. With Vivacia gone, there is no real reason for you to be here.'

She had almost had him. He had felt his heart soaring on

her words, but the last sentence brought him painfully back. *With Vivacia gone.* Gone where?

'You want me to go. Why?' he asked quietly.

A flashing glance of her swirling gold eyes. 'Why do you ask?' she asked tartly. 'Isn't it what you have dreamed of, since you were forced aboard the ship? Did not you constantly fling that at Vivacia? "But for you, my father would not have taken me from my priesthood." Why do you not simply take what you want and leave?'

He thought for a time. 'Perhaps what I truly want does not involve me leaving.' He considered her carefully. 'I think that you make it too attractive to me. So I ask myself, what do you gain by my departure? The only thing I can think of is that it would somehow weaken Vivacia within you. Perhaps if I were not here, she would surrender and become quiescent in you. Sa knows, something in me cries out for her. Perhaps she longs for me as well. While I live and I am here, some part of Vivacia lives. Do you fear that my presence will call her up again? You struggled hard to defeat her. She nearly dragged you into death. You did not conquer her by much.' Certainty grew in him. 'You once said yourself that we three are closely intertwined; the death of any one of us would threaten the other two. Vivacia still lives within you, and all that lives is of Sa. My duty to my god is here, as is my duty to Vivacia. I shall not give her up so easily. If being healed by you means surrendering Vivacia, then I refuse the healing. I will stay scarred. I say this to you and I know that she hears it also. I shall not give her up at all.'

'Stupid boy.' The figurehead made a show of casually scratching the back of her neck. 'How dramatic you are! How stirring! If there was anything to be stirred, that is. Wear your scars then, as a pathetic tribute to someone who never was. Let them be the last trace of her existence. Do I wish you to go? Yes, and the reason is that I prefer Kennit. He is a better mate for my ambitions. I wish Kennit to partner me.'

'You do, do you?' Etta's voice was cool and low.

Wintrow startled, but the figurehead appeared only amused. 'As do you, I am sure,' the ship murmured. She let her eyes walk over Etta. An approving smile curved her mouth. She dismissed Wintrow from her attention to focus on Etta. 'Come closer, my dear. Is that silk from Verania? My, he does spoil you. Or perhaps he spoils himself, in how he displays his treasure to all. In that colour, you gleam like a rich gem in an exotic setting.'

Etta's hand rose, almost self-consciously, to finger the deep blue silk of her shirt. A moment of uncertainty passed over her face. 'I don't know where the fabric originated. But it came to me from Kennit.'

'I am almost certain we are looking at Veranian silk here. The finest that there is; but doubtless he would offer you no less than that. When I was in my proper shape, I had no need for fabrics, of course. My own sweet skin flashed and shone more beautifully than anything human hands could make. Still, I know something of silk. Only in Verania could they make that shade of dragon blue.' She cocked her head at Etta. 'It quite becomes you. Your colouring favours bright hues. Kennit is right to deck you in silver rather than gold. Silver sparkles against you, where gold would merely be warm.'

Etta touched the bangles at her wrist. A deeper blush touched her cheeks. She ventured a step or two closer to the railing. Her eyes met the dragon's and for a time they seemed entranced with one another. Wintrow felt excluded. To his surprise, a shiver of jealousy passed over him. He did not know if it was Vivacia he did not wish to share with Etta, or Etta he wished to keep from the dragon.

Etta gave a small shake of her head, as if to break a glamour. It set her sleek black hair swinging. She looked at Wintrow and a slight frown creased her forehead. 'You should not be out in the sun and the wind. It peels the skin from flesh that is trying to heal still. You should stay in your cabin for at least another day.'

Wintrow looked at her closely. Something was awry here. Such solicitude was not her usual manner with him. He would more expect her to tell him that he ought to be toughening himself rather than convalescing. He tried to read her eyes, but she looked past him, not meeting his stare.

The dragon was blunter. 'She would like to speak to me privately. Leave, Wintrow.'

He ignored the dragon's command and spoke to Etta. 'I would not trust much of what she says. We have not yet heard the truth about Vivacia. Legends are rife with the dangers of conversing with dragons. She will tell you what she knows you want to . . .'

She was suddenly there again, inside him. This time he felt her presence as a physical discomfort. His heart skipped a beat, then surged on unevenly. A sweat broke out on his forehead. He could not draw a full breath.

'Poor boy,' the dragon sympathized. 'See how he sways, Etta. He is not at all himself today. Leave, Wintrow,' the dragon repeated. 'Go rest yourself. Do.'

'Be careful,' he managed to gasp to Etta. 'Don't let her . . .' A giddying weakness overtook him. Nausea rose in him; he dared not speak lest he vomit. He feared he would faint. The day was suddenly painfully bright. He flung his arm across his eyes and staggered across the foredeck to the ladder. Darkness. He needed darkness and quiet and stillness. The need for those things overwhelmed all else in him.

Only when he was in his own bunk did the symptoms recede. Fear replaced them. She could do this to him at any time. She could heal him, or she could kill him. How could he help Vivacia when the dragon had such power over him? He tried to seek comfort in prayer, but a terrible weariness overcame him and he sank into a deep sleep.

Etta shook her head after him. 'Look at him. He can scarce

walk straight. I told him he needed to rest. And last night he drank far too much.' She swung her gaze to meet the figurehead's eyes. They swirled like molten gold, beautiful and compelling. 'Who are you?' Her words were bolder than she felt. 'You are not Vivacia. She never had a civil word for me. All she wanted was to drive me away that she might have Kennit for herself.'

A deeper smile curved the ship's lush red lips. 'At last. I should have known that the first sensible person I spoke to would be one of my own erstwhile sex. No. I am not Vivacia. Nor do I wish to drive you away, nor take Kennit from you. Think of the man that Kennit is. There need be no rivalry between us. He needs us both. It will take both of us to fulfil his ambitions. You and I, we shall become closer than sisters. Now. Let me think of a name you may call me by.' The dragon narrowed her golden eyes, thinking. Then her smile grew wider. 'Bolt. Bolt will do.'

'Bolt?'

'One of my earliest names, in an ancient tongue, might be "Conceived in a Thunderstorm at the Instant of a Lightning Bolt". But you are a short-lived folk, given to shortening every life experience in the hope of comprehending it. Your tongue would trip over so many words. So you may call me Bolt.'

'Have you no true name?' Etta ventured.

Bolt flung back her head and laughed heartily. 'As if I would tell it. Come, woman, to entrance Kennit, you must have more guile than that. You shall have to do better than to simply ask my secrets with an innocent face.' A look of bemusement came briefly over her carved features. Then she called out, 'Helmsman! Two points to starboard the channel deepens and the current is more favourable. Take us over.'

Jola was on the wheel. Without a word of question, he put the ship over. Etta frowned briefly to herself. What would Kennit think of that? Some time back, he had told the men that whoever was on watch should give as much heed to the ship's commands as to his own. But that was before she had changed. As the ship took up the change in course, Etta felt her go more swiftly and smoothly. She lifted her face to the wind against her cheeks and her eyes scanned the horizon. Kennit said they were bound for Divvytown, but that would not stop him from taking prey along the way. Wintrow was recovering well; there was no need to hasten to a healer. Like as not, a healer could do little for him. He would wear his scars to the end of his days.

'You've the eyes of a hunter,' Bolt observed approvingly. She turned her great head to scan the horizon from side to side. 'We could hunt well together, we two.'

An odd thrill ran down Etta's spine. 'Should not such words be given to Kennit, rather than me?'

'To a male?' Bolt asked, a small stain of disdain on her laugh. 'We know how males are. A drake hunts to fill his own belly. When a queen takes flight and seeks a kill, it is to preserve the race itself. We are the ones who know, from our entrails out, that that is the purpose of every movement we make. To continue our species.'

Etta's hand went to her flat belly. Even clothed, she could feel the tiny bump of the skull charm on her navel ring. It, like the figurehead, was carved of wizardwood. Its purpose was to keep her from conceiving. She had worn it for years, ever since she had become a whore when she was little more than a girl. By now, it should seem a part of her. Yet of late it had begun to chafe and irritate, physically as well as mentally. Since she had found the small figurine of a babe on the Treasure Beach and inadvertently carried it off with her, she had begun to hear her own body's questing for a child.

'Take it off,' Bolt suggested.

Etta settled into a great stillness. 'How do you know about it?' she asked in a deadly quiet voice.

Bolt did not even glance back at her, but continued to peruse the open sea before them. 'Oh, please! I have a nose. I can smell it on you. Take it off. It does no honour to the one it was once part of, nor you to put him to such a purpose.'

The thought that the charm had once been part of a dragon suddenly made Etta's flesh crawl. She longed to take it off. However, 'I must talk to Kennit first. He will tell me when he is ready for us to have a baby.'

'Never,' Bolt said flatly.

'What?'

'Never wait for a male on any such decision. You are the queen. You decide. Males are not made for such decisions. I have seen it time and time again. They would have you wait for days of sunshine and wealth and plenty. Yet to a male, enough is never sufficient, and plenty never reached. A queen knows that when times are hardest and game most scarce, that is when one must care most about the continuance of the race. Some things are not for males to decide.' She lifted her hand and smoothed her hair back. She flashed Etta a confiding grin that was suddenly very human. 'I'm still not used to hair. It fascinates me.'

Etta found herself grinning in spite of herself. She leaned on the railing. It had been a long time since there had been another woman to talk to, let alone one who spoke as forthrightly as a whore herself. 'Kennit is not like other men,' she ventured.

'We both know that. You've chosen a good mate. But what is the good of that if it stops there? Take it off, Etta. Don't wait for him to tell you to do it. Look around you. Does he tell each man when the time is right for his task? Of course not. If he had to do that, he might as well do every task himself. He is a man who expects others to think for themselves. I'll venture a wager. Has he not already hinted to you that he needs an heir?'

Etta thought of his words when she had shown him the carved baby. 'He has,' she admitted softly.

'Well, then. Will you wait until he commands you? For

shame. No female should wait on a male's command for what is our business. You are the one who should be telling him such things. Take it off, queen.'

Queen. Etta knew that by the term, the dragon meant no more than female. Female dragons were queens, like cats. Yet, when Bolt said the word, it teased to mind an idea that Etta scarcely dared consider. If Kennit were to be King of the Pirate Isles, what would that make her? Perhaps just his woman. But if she had his child, surely, then . . .

Even as she rebuked herself for such ambitions, her hand slipped under the silk of her shirt to the warm flesh of her belly. The little wizardwood charm, shaped like a human skull, was strung on a fine silver wire. It fastened with a hook and loop. She compressed it with her fingers and it sprang open. She slipped it out, careful of the hook, and held it in her hand. The skull grinned up at her. She shivered.

'Give it to me,' Bolt said quietly.

Etta refused to think about it. She held it out in her hand, and when Bolt reached back, she dropped it into the ship's wide palm. For a moment, it lay there, the silver wire glittering in the sun. Then, like a child gulping a sweet, Bolt clapped her cupped hand to her mouth. Laughing, she showed Etta her empty hand. 'Gone!' she said, and in that instant, the decision was irrevocable.

'What am I going to say to Kennit?' she wondered aloud.

'Nothing at all,' the ship told her airily. 'Nothing at all.'

The tangle had grown in numbers until it was the largest group of serpents claiming allegiance to a single serpent that Shreever had ever known. Sometimes they separated to find food, but every evening found them gathered again. They came to Maulkin in all colours and sizes and conditions. Not all could recall how to speak, and some were savagely feral. Others bore the scars of mishaps or the festering wounds of encounters with hostile ships. Some of the feral ones frightened Shreever in their ability to transcend all the boundaries of civilized behaviour. A few, like the ghostly white serpent, made her hurt with the simmering agony they encompassed. The white in particular seemed frozen into silence by his anger. Nevertheless, one and all, they followed Maulkin. When they clustered together at night, they anchored into a field of swaying serpents that reminded Shreever of a bed of kelp.

Their numbers seemed to reinforce their confidence in Maulkin's leadership. Maulkin near-glowed now, his golden eyes gleaming the full length of his body. By their numbers, too, they provided what each might lack individually. They comforted one another with the memories each held, and often a word or a name from one would wake a recollection in another.

Yet despite their numbers, they were no closer to finding the true migration path. The shared memories only made their wandering more frustrating. Tonight, Shreever could not rest. She untangled herself from her sleeping comrades, and allowed herself to drift free, staring down at the living forest of serpents. There was something tantalizingly familiar about this place, something just beyond the reach of her memory. Had she been here before?

Sessurea, sensitive to her moods from their long companionship, writhed up to join her. Silently he joined in her sweeping survey of the seafloor. They let their eyes open wide to the faint moonlight that reached these depths. She studied the lie of the land by the faint luminescence of both serpents and minute sea life. Something.

'You are right.' Those were the first words Sessurea spoke. He left her side to undulate gently down to a particularly uneven piece of seabed. He turned his head back and forth slowly. Then, to her consternation, he suddenly grasped a large frond of seaweed in his jaws and tore it loose. He flung it aside, seized another mouthful, and dealt with it likewise. 'Sessurea?' she trumpeted questioningly, but he ignored her. Clump after clump of seaweed he tore free and discarded. Then, just as she was sure he had gone mad, he settled to the bottom, then lashed his tail wildly, disturbing the muck of decades.

Her call and Sessurea's strange antics had awakened some of the others. They joined her in staring down at him. He uprooted more seaweed and then thrashed again. 'What is he doing?' asked a slender blue serpent.

'I don't know,' she replied woefully.

As abruptly as he began, Sessurea ceased his mad writhing. He flashed swiftly up to join them. He sleeked himself through a grooming turn before wrapping her excitedly. 'Look. You were right. Well, wait a bit, until the silt settles. There. Do you see?'

For a time, she saw only drifting sediment. Sessurea was out of breath, his gills pumping with excitement. Then, a moment later, the blue beside her suddenly trumpeted wildly, 'It's a Guardian! But it cannot be here, in the Plenty. This is not right!'

Shreever goggled in confusion. The blue's words were so far out of context, she could not make sense of them. Guardians were guardian dragons. Were there dead dragons at the bottom of the sea? Then, as she stared, the vague shapes amidst the drifting silt suddenly took a new form. She saw. It was a Guardian, obviously a female. She sprawled on her side, one wing lifted, the other still buried in the muck. Three claws had broken off one raised forepaw. Part of her tail thrust up oddly beside her. The statue had been broken in a fall; that much was clear. But how had it come to be here, beneath the sea? It had used to stand above the city gates of Yruran. Then her eyes discovered a fallen column. And over there, that would have been that atrium that Desmolo the Eager had built, to house all the exotic plants his dragon friends had brought back to him from the four corners of the earth. And beyond it, the fallen dome of the Temple of Water.

'The whole city is here,' she trumpeted softly.

Maulkin was suddenly in their midst. 'A whole province is here,' he corrected her. All eyes followed him down towards the revealed remnants of the world they could almost recall. He wove his way through them, touching first one and then another of the exposed landmarks. 'We swim where once we flew.' Then he rose slowly towards them. The entire tangle was awake now and watching his gentle undulations. They formed a living, moving sphere with Maulkin at the centre. His body and his words wove together as he spoke.

'We seek to return to our home, to the lands where we hunted and flew. I fear we are already here. When before we found a statue or an arch, I pretended that chance had tumbled a coastal building or two. But Yruran was far inland. Below us lie the sunken ruins.' He looped a slow denial of their hopes. 'This was no minor shaking of the earth. All features have changed beyond recognition. We seek a river to lead us home. But without a guide from the world above, I fear we shall never find it. No such guide has come to us. North we have been, and south we have been, and still we have not found a way that calls to us. All is too different; the scattered memories we have mustered are not sufficient to this task. We are lost. Our only hope now is One Who Remembers. And even that might not be enough.'

Tellur, a slender green serpent, dared to protest. 'We have sought such a one, to no avail. We grow weary. How long, Maulkin, must we wander and yearn? You have mustered a mighty tangle, yet many as we are, we are few compared to what we once were. Have they all perished, the other tangles that should be swarming now? Are we all that is left of our people? Must we, too, die as wanderers? Can it be, perhaps, that there is no river, no home to return to?' He sang his sorrow and despair.

Maulkin did not lie to them. 'Perhaps. It may be we shall perish, and our kind be no more. But we shall not go without a struggle. One last time we shall seek One Who Remembers, but this time we shall bend all our efforts to that quest. We shall find a guide, or we shall die trying.'

'Then we shall die.' His voice was cold and dead, like thick ice cracking. The white serpent wove his way to the centre of the serpents, to twine himself insultingly before Maulkin. Shreever's mane stood out in horror. He was provoking Maulkin to kill him. His insolent postures invited death. All waited for judgement to fall on him.

But Maulkin held back. He himself wove his body in a larger pattern, one that encompassed the white's insults, forbidding the others to act against him. He spoke no word, though his mane stood up and leaked a pale trail of toxins in the water as he swam. The silence and the poisons became a web around the white serpent. The white's movements slowed; he hung as motionless as a serpent could be. Maulkin had asked him no questions, yet he answered angrily.

'Because I have spoken with She Who Remembers. I was wild and mindless, as much a beast as any of the dumb ones who now follow you. But she caught me and she held me fast and she forced her memories on me until I choked on them.' He spun in a swift vicious circle as if he would attack himself. Faster and faster he went. 'Her memories were poison! Poison! More toxic than anything that ever flowed from a mane. When I recall what we have been, what we should be now and compare it to what we have become . . . I gag. I would disgorge this foul life we still embrace!'

Maulkin had not paused in his silent, weaving dance. His movements formed a barrier between the white and the serpents that hung listening.

'It is too late.' The white trumpeted each word clearly. 'Too many seasons have passed. Our time for changing has come and gone a score of times. Her memories are of a world long gone! Even if we could find the river to the cocooning grounds, there is no one to help us make our casts. They are all dead.' He began to speak faster, his words gushing like a running river. 'No parents wait to secrete their memories into our windings. We would come out of our metamorphosis as ignorant as we went in. She gave me her memories, and I tell you, they were not enough! I recognize little here, and what I do recall lies wrong. If we are doomed to perish, then let us lose our voices and our minds before we die. Her memories are not worth the agony I carry.' His erect mane suddenly released a cloud of numbing toxins. He plunged his own face into it.

Maulkin struck, as swift as if he were taking prey. His golden eyes flashed as he wrapped the white and snatched him away from his own poison. 'Enough!' he roared. His words were angry but his voice was not. The foolish white struggled, but Maulkin squeezed him as if he were a dolphin. 'You are but one! You cannot decide for the whole tangle, or for the whole race. You have a duty, and you will do it before you take your own silly, senseless life.' Maulkin released a cloud of his own toxins. The white serpent's angrily spinning scarlet eyes slowed and became a dull maroon. His jaws gaped open lazily as the toxins did their work. Maulkin spoke gently. 'You will guide us to She Who Remembers. We have already absorbed some memories from a silver provider. If need be, we can take more. With what we shall gain from She Who Remembers, it may be enough.' Unwillingly, he added, 'What other choice have we?'

Kennit balanced before his mirror, turning his face from side to side before his reflection. A sheen of lemon oil gleamed on his hair and trimmed beard. His moustache curled elegantly, but without pretence. Immaculate white lace cascaded down his chest and from the cuffs of his deep blue jacket. Even the leather of his stump cup had been polished to a high gloss.

Heavy silver earrings dangled. He looked, he reflected, like a man ready to go courting. In a sense, he was.

He had not slept well last night after his conversation with the ship. His damned charm had kept him awake, whispering and tittering, urging him to accept the dragon's terms. That very urging unnerved Kennit the most. Dare he trust the damned thing? Dare he ignore it? He had tossed and turned, and when Etta had come to join him in his bed, even her gentle rubbing of his neck and back could not lull him to sleep. As dawn greyed the sky, he had finally dozed off. When he awakened, it was to discover this determination in himself. He would win the ship back to him, all over again. This time, at least, he would not have her attraction to Wintrow to overcome.

He knew little of dragons, so he had focused on what he did know. She was female. So he would groom his plumage and offer gifts and see what it bought him. Satisfied with his appearance, he turned back to his bed and surveyed the trove there. A belt of silver rings decorated with lapis lazuli would be offered as a bracelet. If it pleased her, he had two silver bracelets that could be refitted as earrings for her. Etta would not miss them. A heavy flask held a quantity of wisteria oil. It had probably been bound to a Chalcedean perfumer. He had no idea what other sensory items might delight her. If these treasures left her unmoved, he would think of other tacks to take. But win her he would. He slipped his offerings into a velvet bag and tied it to his belt. He moved best with his hands free. He did not wish to appear awkward before her.

He encountered Etta in the hall outside his cabin, her arms heavy with fresh linens. Her gaze roved over him, so that he felt almost affronted by her frank appraisal, and yet the approval that shone in her eyes assured him he had succeeded in his preparations. 'Well!' she observed, almost saucily. A smile touched her lips.

'I go to speak to the ship,' he told her gruffly. 'Let no one disturb us.'

'I shall pass the word immediately,' she agreed. Then, her smile widening, she dared to add, 'You are wise to go thus. It will please her.'

'What would you know of such things?' he observed as he stumped past her.

'I had words with her this morning. She was passing civil with me, and spoke openly of her admiration for you. Let her see you admire her as well, and it will tickle her vanity. Dragon she may be, yet she is female enough that we understand one another.' She paused, then added, 'She says we are to call her Bolt, as in lightning bolt. The name fits her very well. Light and power shine from her.'

Kennit halted. He turned back to face her. 'What has brought about this new alliance?' he asked her uneasily.

Etta cocked her head and looked thoughtful. 'She is different, now. That is all I can say.' She smiled suddenly. 'I think she likes me. She said we could be like sisters.'

He hoped he concealed his surprise. 'She said that?'

The whore stood clutching the linens to her bosom and smiling. 'She said it would take both of us for you to realize your ambitions.'

'Ah,' he said, and turned and stumped away. The ship had won her. Just like that, with a kind word or two? It did not seem likely to him. Etta was not a woman easily swayed. What had the dragon offered her? Power? Wealth? But an even more pressing question was *why*. Why did the dragon seek to ally herself with the whore?

He found himself hurrying and deliberately slowed. He should not meet the dragon in haste. Calm down. Court her leisurely. Win her over, and then her friendship with Etta will be no threat.

As soon as he came out on the deck, he sensed a transformation. Aloft, the men were working a sail change, bandying jests as they did so. Jola shouted another command, and the men sprang to it, grinning. One man slipped, and then caught himself by one brawny arm. He laughed aloud and hauled himself up again. From the figurehead came a cry of delight at his skill. In an instant, Kennit knew the sailor had not slipped at all. He was showing off for the figurehead. She had the entire crew displaying their seamanship for her approval. They cavorted like schoolboys for her attention.

'What have you done, to affect them so?' he greeted her.

She chuckled warmly and glanced back at him over one bare shoulder. 'It takes so little to beguile them. A smile, a word, a challenge to see if they cannot raise a sail more swiftly. A little attention, a very little attention, and they vie for more.'

'I am surprised you deign them worthy of your notice at all. Last night, you seemed to have small use for any human being.'

She let his words slip by her. 'I have promised them prey, before tomorrow sunset. But only if they can match their skills to my senses. There is a merchant vessel, not too far hence. She carries spices from the Mangardor Islands. We shall soon catch her up, if they keep my canvas tight.'

So she had accepted her new body, it seemed. He chose not to comment on that. 'You can see this ship, beyond the horizon?'

'I do not need to. The wind brought me her scent. Cloves and sandalwood, Hasian pepper and sticks of kimoree. The smells of Mangardor Island itself; only a ship with a rich cargo could have brought such scents so far north. We should sight her soon.'

'You can truly smell so keenly?'

A hunter's smile curled her lips. 'The prey is not so far ahead. She picks her way through those islands. If your eyes were as keen as mine, you could pick her out.' Then the smile faded from her face. 'I know these waters as a ship. Yet as a dragon, I do not. All is vastly changed, from when I last took wing. It is familiar and yet not.' She frowned. 'Do you know the Mangardor Islands?'

Kennit shrugged. 'I know the Mangardor Rocks. They are a hazard in fog, and in some tides they are exposed just enough to tear the bottom out of any ship that ventures near.'

A long troubled silence followed his words. 'So,' she said quietly at last. 'Either the oceans of the world have risen, or the lands I knew have sunk. I wonder what remains of my home.' She paused. 'Yet Others' Island, as you call it, seemed but little changed. So some of my world remains as it was. That is a puzzle to me, one I can only resolve when I return home.'

'Home?' He tried to make the question casual. 'And where is that?'

'Home is an eventuality. It is nothing for you to trouble yourself about just now,' she told him. She smiled, but her voice had cooled.

'Might that be the thing you will want, when you want it?' he pressed.

'It might be. Or it might not. I'll let you know.' She paused. 'After all, I have not yet heard you say that you agree to my terms.'

Carefully, carefully. 'I am not a hasty man. I would still like to know more of what they are.'

She laughed aloud. 'Such a silly topic for us to discuss. You agree. Because you have even less choice than I do in the life we must share. What else is there for us, if not each other? You bring me gifts, don't you? That is more correct than you know. But I shall not even wait for you to present them before I reveal that I am a far richer trove than you imagined you could ever win. Dream larger, Kennit, than you have ever dreamt before. Dream of a ship that can summon serpents from the deep to aid us. They are mine to command. What would you have them do? Halt a ship and despoil it? Escort another ship safely wherever it wishes to go? Guide you through a fog? Guard the harbour of your city from any that might threaten it? Dream large, and larger still, Kennit. And then accept whatever terms I offer.'

He cleared his throat. His mouth had gone dry. 'You extend too much,' he said baldly. 'What can you want, what can I give you worthy of what you offer?'

She chuckled. 'I shall tell you, if you cannot see it for yourself. You are the breath of my body, Kennit. I rely on you and your crew to move. If I must be trapped inside this hulk, then I must have a bold captain to give me wings, even if they are only of canvas. I require a captain who understands the joy of the hunt, and the quest for power. I need you, Kennit. Agree.' Her voice dropped lower and softer. 'Agree.'

He took a breath. 'I agree.'

She threw back her head and laughed. It was like bells ringing. The very wind seemed to blow stronger in excitement at the sound.

Kennit leaned on her railing. Elation rose in him. He could scarcely believe his dreams were all within his grasp. He groped for something to say. 'Wintrow will be very disappointed. Poor boy.'

The ship nodded with a small sigh. 'He deserves some happiness. Shall we send him back to his monastery?'

'I think it is the wisest course,' Kennit concurred. He covered his surprise that she would suggest it. 'Still, it will be hard for me to see him go. It has torn my heart, to see his beauty so destroyed. He was a very comely youth.'

'He will be happier in his monastery, I am sure. A monk has little need of a smooth skin. Still . . . shall we heal him anyway, as a parting gift? A reminder to carry with him, always, of how we shaped him?' Bolt smiled, showing white teeth.

Kennit was incredulous. 'This, too, you can do?'

The ship smiled conspiratorially. 'This, too, *you* can do. Far more effective, don't you think? Go to his cabin now. Lay on your hands and wish him well. I shall guide you in the rest.'

* * *

A strange lethargy had come over Wintrow. From attempting to meditate, his mind had sunk deeper and deeper into an abstract abyss. Suspended there, he wondered distantly what was happening to him. Had he finally mastered a deeper state of consciousness? Dimly, he was aware of the door opening.

He felt Kennit's hands on his chest. Wintrow struggled to open his eyes, but could not. He could not awaken. Something held him under like a smothering hand. He heard voices, Kennit speaking and Etta replying. Gankis said something quietly. Wintrow fought to be awake, but the harder he struggled, the more the world receded. Exhausted, he hovered. Tendrils of awareness reached him. Warmth flowed out from Kennit's spread hand. It suffused his skin, then seeped deep into his body. Kennit spoke softly, encouraging him. The fires of Wintrow's life force suddenly blazed up. To his consciousness, it was as if a candle suddenly roared with the light and heat of a bonfire. He began to pant as if he were running an uphill race. His heart laboured to keep up with the rushing of his breath. *Stop*, he wanted to beg Kennit. *Please stop*, but no words escaped him. He screamed his plea into his own darkness.

He could hear. He could hear the startled gasps and cries of awe of those who watched outside him. He recognized the voices of crewmates. 'Look, you can see him change!' 'Even his hair is growing.' 'It's a miracle. The Capn's healing him.'

His body's reserves were burned recklessly; he sensed that years of his life were consumed by this act, but could not defy it. The rejuvenating skin itched wildly, but he could not twitch a muscle. His own body was beyond his control. He managed a whimper, far back in his throat. It was ignored. The healing devoured him from the inside out. It was killing him. The world retreated. He floated small in the dark.

After a time, he was aware that Kennit's hands were gone. The painful pounding of his heart subsided. Someone spoke at a great distance. Kennit's voice reverberated with pride and exhaustion.

'There. Leave him to rest now. For the next few days, he will probably only awaken to eat and then sleep deeply again. Let no one be alarmed by this. It is a necessary part of the healing.' He heard the pirate's deep ragged breath. 'I must rest, too. This has cost me, but he deserved no less.'

It was early evening when Kennit awoke. For a time, he lay still, savouring his elation. His sleep had completely restored him. Wintrow was healed, by his hands. Never had he felt so powerful as he had while his hands rested on Wintrow and his will healed the boy's skin. Those of his crew who had witnessed it regarded him with deep awe. The entire coast of the Cursed Shores was his for the plucking. Etta fair shone with love and admiration for him. When he opened his eyes and regarded the charm strapped to his wrist, even that small countenance was smiling wolfishly at him. For one perfectly balanced instant, all was well in his world.

'I am happy,' Kennit said aloud. He grinned to hear himself say such foreign words.

A wind was rising. He listened to it whistle past the ship's canvas, and wondered. He had seen no sign of a storm arising. Nor did the ship rock as if beset by a wind. Had the dragon power over such things as a rising storm, too?

He rose hastily, seized his crutch and went out on deck. The wind that stirred his hair was fair and steady. No storm clouds threatened, and the waves were rhythmic and even. Yet, even as he stood looking about, the sound of a rising wind came again to his ears. He hurried towards the source.

To his astonishment, the entire crew was mustered around the foredeck. They parted to make way for him in awe-stricken silence. He limped through them and forced himself up the ladder to the foredeck. As he gained his feet, the sound of the rising wind came again. This time he saw the source.

Bolt sang. He could not see her face. Her head was thrown back so that her long hair cascaded over her shoulders. The silver and lapis of his gift shone against the foaming black curls. She sang with a voice like a rising wind, and then with the sound of waves slashed by wind. Her voice ranged from a deep rush to a high whistling that no human throat and lips could have produced. It was the wind's song given voice, and it stirred him as no human music ever had. It spoke deep within him in the language of the sea itself, and Kennit recognized his mother tongue.

Then another voice joined hers, winding pure notes around and through Bolt's sea song. Every head turned. A profound silence stilled every human voice on the ship. Wonder replaced the first flash of fear that seized Kennit. She, too, was as beautiful as his ship. He saw that now. The green-gold serpent rose swaying from the depths, her jaws stretched wide in song.

Winter

TWELVE

Alliances

'Paragon, Paragon. What am I to do with you?'

Brashen's deep voice was very soft. The hissing rain that spattered on his deck was louder than his captain's voice. There did not seem to be any anger in it, only sorrow. Paragon didn't reply. Since Brashen had ordered that no one must speak to him, he had kept his own silence. Even when Lavoy had come to the railing one night and tried to jolly him out of it, Paragon had remained mute. When the mate had shifted his attempts to sympathy, it had been harder to keep his resolve, but he had. If Lavoy had really thought Brashen had wronged him, he would have done something about it. That he hadn't just proved that he was really on Brashen's side.

Brashen gripped his railing with cold hands and leaned on it. Paragon almost flinched with the impact of the man's misery. Brashen was not truly his family, so he could not always read his emotions. But at times like this, when there was contact between flesh and wizardwood, Paragon knew him well enough.

'This isn't how I imagined it would be, ship,' Brashen told him. 'To be captain of a liveship. You want to know what I dreamed? That somehow you would make me real and solid. Not a knock-about sailor who had disgraced his family and forever lost his place in Bingtown. Captain Trell of the liveship

Paragon. Has a nice ring to it, doesn't it? I thought we would redeem each other, ship. I pictured us returning to Bingtown triumphant, me commanding a sharp crew and you sailing like a grey-winged gull. People would look at us and say, "Now there's a ship, and the man who runs him knows what he's about." And the families that discarded us both might suddenly wonder if they hadn't been fools to do so.' Brashen gave a small snort of contempt for his foolish dreams. 'But I can't imagine my father ever taking me back. I can't even imagine him having a civil word for me. I'm afraid I'm always going to stand alone, ship, and that the end of my days will find me a sodden old derelict washed up on some foreign shore. When I thought we had a chance, I told myself, well, a captain's life is lonely. It's not like I'm going to find a woman that will put up with me for more than a season. But I thought, with a liveship, at least we'd always have each other. I honestly thought I could do you some good. I imagined that someday I'd lay myself down and die on your deck, knowing that part of me would go on with you. That didn't seem like such a bad thing, at one time. But now look at us. I've let you kill again. We're sailing straight into pirate waters with a crew that can't even get out of its own way. I haven't a plan or a prayer for any of us to survive, and we draw closer to Divvytown with each wave we cut. I'm more alone than I've ever been in my life.'

Paragon had to break his silence to do it, but he could not resist setting one more hook into the man. 'And Althea is furious with you. Her anger is so strong, it's gone from hot to cold.'

He had hoped it would goad Brashen into fury. Anger he could deal with better than this deep melancholy. To deal with anger, all you had to do was shout back louder than your opponent. Instead, he felt himself the horrible lurch of Brashen's heart.

'That, too,' Brashen admitted miserably. 'And I don't know why and she scarcely speaks to me.'

'She talks to you,' Paragon retorted angrily. Cold silence belonged to him. No one could do it so well as he, certainly not Althea.

'Oh, she talks,' Brashen agreed. '"Yes, sir." "No, sir." And those black, black eyes of hers stay flat and cold as wet shale. I can't reach her at all.' The words suddenly spilled out of the man, words that Paragon sensed Brashen would have held in if he could. 'And I need her, to back me up if nothing else. I need one person in this crew that I know won't put a knife in my back. But she just stands there and looks past me, or through me, and I feel like I'm less than nothing. No one else can make me feel that bad. And it makes me just want to . . .' His words trailed off.

'Just throw her on her back and take her. That would make you real to her,' Paragon filled in for him. Surely, that would bring a rise from Brashen.

Brashen's silent revulsion followed his words. No explosion of fury or disgust. After a moment, the man asked quietly, 'Where did you learn to be this way? I know the Ludlucks. They're hard folk, tight with a coin and ruthless in a bargain. But they're decent. The Ludlucks I've known didn't have rape or murder in them. Where does it come from in you?'

'Perhaps the Ludlucks I knew weren't so fastidious. I've known rape and murder aplenty, Brashen, right on my deck where you're standing.' *And perhaps I am more than a thing shaped by the Ludlucks. Perhaps I had form and substance long before a Ludluck set a hand to my wheel.*

Brashen was silent. The storm was rising. A buffet of wind hit Paragon's wet canvas, making him heel over slightly. He and the helmsman caught it before it could take him too far. He felt Brashen tighten his grip on the railing.

'Do you fear me?' the ship asked him.

'I have to,' Brashen replied simply. 'There was a time when we were only friends. I thought I knew you well. I knew what folk said of you, but I thought, perhaps you were driven to that. When you killed that man, Paragon – when I saw you shake his life out of him – something changed in my heart. So, yes, I fear you.' In a quieter voice he added, 'And that is not good for either of us.'

He lifted his hands from the railing and turned to walk away. Paragon licked his lips. The freshwater deluge of the winter storm streamed down his chopped face. Brashen would be soaked to the skin, and cold as only mortals could be. He tried to think of words that would bring him back. He suddenly did not want to be alone, sailing blindly into this storm, trusting only to a helmsman who thought of him as 'this damned boat.' 'Brashen!' he called out suddenly.

His captain halted uncertainly. Then he made his way back across the rising and falling deck, to stand once more by the railing. 'Paragon?'

'I can't promise not to kill again. You know that.' He struggled for a justification. 'You yourself might need me to kill. And then, there I'd be, bound by my promise . . .'

'I know. I tried to think of what I would ask you. Not to kill. To obey my orders always. And I knew you and I knew you could never promise those things.' In a heavy voice, he said, 'I don't ask for those promises. I don't want you to lie to me.'

He suddenly felt sorry for Brashen. He hated it when his feelings switched back and forth like this. But he couldn't control them. Impulsively, he offered, 'I promise I won't kill you, Brashen. Does that help?'

He felt Brashen's convulsion of shock at his words. Paragon suddenly realized that Brashen had never even considered the ship might kill *him*. That Paragon would now promise thus made him realize that the ship had been capable of it. Was still capable of it, if he decided to break his word. After a moment, Brashen said lifelessly, 'Of course that helps. Thank you, Paragon.' He started to turn away again.

'Wait!' Paragon called to him. 'Are you going to let the others talk to me now?'

He almost felt the man's sigh. 'Of course. Not much sense in refusing you that.'

Bitterness rose in Paragon. He had meant his promise to comfort the man, but he insisted on being grieved by it. Humans. They were never satisfied, no matter what you sacrificed for them. If Brashen was disappointed in him, it was his own fault. Why hadn't he realized that the first ones to kill were the ones closest to you, the ones who knew you best? It was the only way to eliminate the threat to yourself. What was the sense of killing a stranger? Strangers had small interest in hurting you. That was always done best by your own family and friends.

The rain had winter's kiss in it. It spattered, annoying but harmless, against Tintaglia's outstretched wings. They beat steadily as she flew upstream above the Rain Wild River. She would have to kill and eat again soon, but the rain had driven all the game into the cover of the trees. It was difficult to hunt in the swampy borderlands along the Rain Wild River. Even on a dry day, it was easy to get mired there. She would not chance it.

The cold grey day suited her mood. Her search of the sea had been worse than fruitless. Twice, she had glimpsed serpents. But when she had flown low, trumpeting a welcome to them, they had dove into the depths. Twice she had circled and hovered and circled, trumpeting and then roaring a demand that the serpents come back. All her efforts had been in vain. It was as if the serpents did not recognize her. It daunted her to the depths of her soul to know that her race survived in the world, but would not acknowledge her. A terrible sense of futility had built in her, combining with her nagging hunger to a smouldering anger. The hunting along the beaches had been poor; the migratory sea mammals that should have been thick along the coast were simply not there. Hardly surprising, seeing as how the coast she recalled was not there either.

Her reconnaissance had opened her eyes to how greatly the world had changed since her kind had last soared. The whole edge of this continent had sunk. The mountain range that had once towered over the long sand beaches of the coast were now the tops of a long stretch of islands. The richly fertile inland plains that had once teemed with herds of prey, both wild and domesticated, were now a wide swamp of rainforest. The steaming inland sea, once landlocked, now seeped to the ocean as a multitude of rivers threading through a vast grassland. Nothing was as it should be. She should not be surprised that her own kin did not know her.

Humans had multiplied like fleas on a dying rabbit. Their dirty, smoky settlements littered the world. She had glimpsed their tiny island settlements and their harbour towns as she had searched for serpents. She had flown high over Bingtown on a star-swept night and seen it as a dark blot freckled with light. Trehaug was no more than a series of squirrels' nests connected by spiderwebs. She felt a grudging admiration for humanity's ability to engineer a home for itself wherever it pleased even as she rather despised creatures so helpless they could not cope with the natural world without artificial structures. At least the Elderlings had built with splendour. When she thought of their graceful architecture, of those majestic, welcoming cities now tumbled into rubble or standing as echoing ruins, she was appalled that the Elderlings had perished, and humans inherited the earth.

She had left humanity's hovels behind her. If she must live alone, she would live near Kelsingra. Game was plentiful there, and the land firm enough to land upon without sinking to her knees. Should she desire shelter from the elements, the ancient structures of the Elderlings would provide it. She had many years ahead of her. She might as well spend them where there was at least a memory of splendour.

As she flew through the steady downpour, she watched the banks of the river for game. She had small hope of finding anything alive. The river ran pale and acid since the last quake, deadly to anything not scaled.

Far upriver of Trehaug, she spotted the struggling serpent. At first, she thought it was a log being rolled downstream by the river's current. She blinked and shook rainwater from her eyes, and stared again. As the scent of serpent reached her, she dropped down from the heights to make sense of what she saw.

The river was shallow, a rushing flow of milky water over rough stone. This, too, was a divergence from her memory. Once this river had offered a fine deep channel that led far inland to cities such as Kelsingra and the farming communities and barter towns beyond it. Not only serpents but great ships had navigated it with ease. Now the battered blue serpent struggled feebly against the current in waters that did not even cover it.

She circled twice before she could find a stretch of river where she could land safely. Then she waded downriver, hastening to the pitiful spectacle of the stranded serpent. Up close, its condition was wrenching. It had been trapped here for some time. The sun had burnt its back, and its struggles against the stony bed of the river had left its hide in rags. Once its protective scaled skin was torn, the river water had eaten deep sores into its flesh. So beaten was it that she could not even tell its sex. It reminded her of a spawned-out salmon, exhausted and washed into the shallows to die.

'Welcome home,' she said, without sarcasm or bitterness. The serpent regarded her with one rolling eye, and then suddenly redoubled its efforts to flail its way upstream. It fled from her. There was no mistaking its panic, nor the death stench upon it.

'Gently, gently, finned one. I have not come to harm you, but to aid you if I can. Let me push you into deeper water.

Your skin needs wetting.' She spoke softly, putting music and kindness into her words. The serpent stopped struggling, but more from exhaustion than calm. Its eyes still darted this way and that, seeking an escape its body was too weary to attempt. Tintaglia tried again. 'I am here to welcome you and guide you home. Can you speak? Can you understand me?'

For reply, the serpent lifted its head out of the water. It made a feeble attempt to erect its mane, but no venom welled. 'Go away,' it hissed at her. 'Kill you,' it threatened.

'You are not making sense. I am here to help you. Remember? When you come up the river to cocoon, dragons welcome you and aid you. I will show you the best sand to use to make your cast. My saliva in your cocoon will bestow the memories of our kind. Do not fear me. It is not too late. Winter is upon us, but I will guard you well for the cold months. When summer comes, I will scratch away the leaves and mud that have covered you. The sun will touch your cocoon, and it will melt. You shall become a lovely dragon. You will be a Lord of the Three Realms. I promise you this.'

It lidded its dull eyes, then opened them slowly. She could see the distrust war with desperation. 'Deeper water,' the serpent pleaded.

'Yes,' Tintaglia agreed. She lifted her head and glanced about. But there was no deeper water, not unless she dragged the poor creature downstream, and there it would find no food, nor anywhere to make its cocoon. The city of Trehaug marked the first cocooning ground. It had been swallowed by the rising water level. There had been another, not that much farther upstream. But the river had shifted in its wide bed, and ran shallow and stony past the once-rich banks of silver-banded sandy mud. How was she to help the serpent reach there? Once there, how to get mud, water and serpent together, so that the serpent could ingest the liquefied muck to secrete its cocoon?

The serpent lifted its weary head and gave a low trumpet of

despair. Tintaglia felt driven to act. She had lifted and carried two humans effortlessly, but the serpent was near her equal in weight. When she attempted to drag it into a slightly deeper channel of water near the river's bank, her talons scored its softened flesh and sank deep into its open wounds. The creature screamed and thrashed wildly. Its lashing tail knocked Tintaglia staggering. She caught her balance by dropping to all fours. As she did so, her groping foot encountered something smooth, hard, and rounded in the bed of the river. It turned and cracked under her weight. Obeying a sudden impulse, she hooked her claws under it and dragged it up to the surface.

A skull. A serpent's skull. The acid water of the river had etched the heavy bone to brittleness; it fragmented in her claws. She searched the shallows with heartsick certainty. Here were three thick spine bones, still clinging together. Another skull there. She clawed the bottom and came up with ribs and a jawbone, in various stages of decomposition. Some still had bits of cartilage clinging to their joints; others were polished smooth or eaten porous. The bones of her race were here. Those who had managed to recall this much of their migration route had met this final obstacle and perished here.

The hapless serpent lay on its side now, wheezing its pain. The few drops of toxin it could muster ran from its mane into its own eyes. Tintaglia stalked over and stood looking down on it. The creature briefly lidded its great eyes. Then it gasped out a single word.

'Please.'

Tintaglia threw back her head and gave shattering voice to her anger and hatred of the moment. She let the fury run free in her, let it cloud her mind and eyes to a scarlet haze. Then she granted its request. Her powerful jaws seized the serpent's neck just below its toxin-dripping mane. With a single savage bite, she severed its spine. A quivering ran through it and the tip of its tail slashed and spattered the water. She stood over it as it finished dying. Its eyes spun slowly a final time. Its jaws open and shut spasmodically. Finally, it was still.

The taste of the serpent's blood was sharp and poignant in her jaws. Its pale toxins stung her tongue. In that instant, she knew his lifetime. Momentarily, she was him, and she trembled with exhaustion and pain. Permeating all was confusion. As Tintaglia regained herself, the utter futility of the serpent's life left her shaken. Time after time, his body had responded to the signs that told him to migrate and change. She could not tell how often the pathetic creature had left the rich feeding grounds of the south and migrated north.

As she bent her neck and consumed his flesh, all became clear to her. His store of memories was added to her own. If the world had been turning as it should, she would have passed his memories on to her offspring, along with her own. Someone would have profited from his misspent life. He would not have died in vain. She saw all he had seen and been. She knew all his frustrations, and was with him as frustration degenerated to confusion and finally bestiality. At every migration, he had searched for familiar seascapes and One Who Remembered. Time after time, he had been disappointed. Winters had driven him south again, to feed and replenish his bodily reserves, until the turning of the years would once more send him north. This she could know, from her dragon's perspectives. That the serpent had made it this far with only the memories of his serpent pasts was little short of a miracle. She looked down at his stripped bones, the foulness of his flesh in her mouth. Even if she had been able to help him to deeper water, he would still have died. The mystery of the sea serpents who fled from her was solved. She clawed up more bones and studied them idly. Here were her folk; here was her race. Here was the future and here was the past . . .

She turned her back on the remains of the serpent. Let the river devour him as it had so many others. Doubtless it would eat others yet, until none remained. She was powerless to change it. She could not make the river run deeper here, nor change its course to take it close once more to the banks of silver-shot earth. She snorted to herself. Lords of the Three Realms. Rulers of Earth, Sea and Sky, yet master of none of them.

The river was chilling her, and the acid kiss of its water was beginning to itch. Even her tightly-scaled skin was not totally impervious to it when it ran this strong. She waded away from the bank to the centre of the river, where there was open sky overhead, stretched forth her wings, set her weight back onto her hindquarters. She leapt, only to come down heavily in the water once more. The gravel had shifted under her clawed feet, spoiling her impetus. She was tired. For a moment, she longed for the hard-packed landing sites the Elderlings had lovingly prepared for their winged guests. If the Elderlings had survived, she reflected, her race would still flourish. They would have circumvented this shallow place in the river for the sake of their dragon-kin. But the Elderlings had died off, and left pathetic humanity as their heirs.

She had crouched to attempt another leap when the thought shivered over her. Humans built things. Could humans dredge the river out, could they channel the flow of water through this stretch to make it deep enough for a serpent? Could they coax the river to flow once more near the silvery earth needed for proper cocooning? She considered what she had seen of their works.

They could. But would they?

Resolve flooded her. She leaped mightily and her beating wings caught her weight and lifted her. She needed to kill again, to take the foul taste of the serpent's spoiled flesh from her mouth. She would do so, but while she did, she would think. Duress or bribe? Bargain or threaten? She would consider every option before she returned to Trehaug. The humans could be made to serve her. Her kind might still survive.

*   *   *

The rap on his stateroom door was just a trifle too hard. Brashen sat up straight in his chair, setting his teeth. He cautioned himself against jumping to conclusions. Taking a deep breath, he said quietly, 'Enter.'

Lavoy came in, shutting the door firmly. He had just come off watch. His oilskins had kept him somewhat dry, but when he took his cap off, his hair was slicked wet to his head. The storm was not savage, but the driving insistence of the rain was demoralizing. It chilled a man to the bone. 'You wanted to see me,' Lavoy greeted him.

Brashen noted the lack of a 'sir'. 'Yes, I did,' he agreed smoothly. 'There's rum on the sideboard. Take the chill off. Then I wish to give you some instructions.' The rum was a courtesy, due any mate during such a cold storm. Brashen would extend it to him, even as he prepared to rake him over the coals.

'Thank you, sir,' Lavoy replied. Brashen watched the man as he poured out his jot and tossed it off. That had lowered the mate's guard. There was less surliness in his manner as he approached Brashen's table and stood before it. 'Instructions, sir?'

He phrased it carefully. 'I wish to make clear in advance how my orders are to be followed, specifically as regards yourself.'

That stiffened the man again. 'Sir?' he asked coldly.

Brashen leaned back in his chair. He kept his voice flat. 'The crew's performance during the pirate attack was abysmal. They were fragmented and disorganized. They need to learn to fight as a unit.

'I ordered you to mingle the former slaves with the rest of the crew. This has not been done to my satisfaction. Therefore, I now direct you to shift them to the second mate's watch and let her integrate them. Make it clear to them that this is not due to any dissatisfaction with their performance. I don't want them to believe they are being punished.'

Lavoy took a breath. 'They're like to take it that way. They're used to working for me. They may be surly about the change.'

'See that they aren't,' Brashen ordered succinctly. 'My second direction has to do with talking to the figurehead.' Lavoy's eyes widened, only briefly, only slightly, but enough to make Brashen sure. Lavoy had already disobeyed that order. His heart dropped another notch. It was worse than he had feared. He kept his voice steady as he went on, 'I am about to lift my order forbidding the crew from speaking to Paragon. I wish you to understand, however, that *you* are still barred from talking with him. For reasons of discipline and ship's morale, I will allow you to keep that restriction a private matter between you and myself. Nevertheless, I will not tolerate even the appearance of your violating it. You are not to converse with the figurehead.'

The mate's hands knotted into fists. His veneer of respect was thin as he growled, 'And may I ask why, sir?'

Brashen made his voice flat. 'No. You don't need to.'

Lavoy struggled to act like an innocent man. A mask of martyred protest came over his face. 'I don't know what you're about, sir, or who's been talking ill of me. I've done nothing wrong. How am I to do my job if you step between the crew and me? What am I supposed to do if the ship speaks to me? Ignore him? How can I –'

Brashen wanted to wring the man's neck, but he kept his seat and managed to keep the demeanour of a captain. 'If the job is beyond you, Lavoy, say so. You may step down from it. There are other capable hands aboard.'

'Meaning that woman. You'd pull me down and let her step up to first mate.' His eyes went black with fury. 'Well, I'll tell you something. She wouldn't make it through her first watch as mate. The men wouldn't accept her. You and she can pretend she has what it takes, but she doesn't. She's –'

'Enough. You have your orders. Go.' It was all Brashen could do to remain in his chair. He didn't want this to end in blows. Lavoy wasn't a man who learned from a beating; he'd only carry a grudge. 'Lavoy, I took you on when no one else would have you. What I offered you was clear: a chance to prove yourself. You still have that chance. Become the first mate you're capable of being. But don't try to be more than that on this ship. Take my orders and see that they're carried out. That is your only task. Do less, and I'll have you put off the ship the first chance I get. I won't keep you on as an ordinary sailor. You wouldn't allow that to work for any of us. You can think about what I've said. Now get out.'

The man glared at him in ponderous silence, then turned and walked towards the door. Brashen spoke for a final time. 'I'm still willing to let this conversation remain a private matter. I suggest you do the same.'

'Sir,' Lavoy said. It was not agreement. It was bare acknowledgement that Brashen had spoken. The door closed behind him.

Brashen leaned back in his chair. His spine ached with tension. He had not solved anything. He had, perhaps, bought himself more time. He grimaced to himself. With his luck, he could hold it all together until it fell apart in Divvytown.

He sat for a time, dreading his final task for the night. He had spoken to Paragon and confronted Lavoy. He still needed to straighten things out with Althea, but the ship's taunt came back to him: So angry her fury had gone from hot to cold. He knew exactly what the ship meant and didn't doubt the truth of his words. He tried to find the courage to summon her, then abruptly decided he'd wait until the end of her watch. That would be better.

He went to his bunk, pulled off his boots, loosened his shirt and flung himself back on it. He didn't sleep. He tried to worry about Divvytown and what he could do there. The spectre of Althea's cold fury loomed darker than any pirate's shadow. He dreaded the encounter, not for what words she might fling at him, but for how much he desired the excuse to be alone with her.

The rain was nasty, cold and penetrating, but the wind that drove it was steady. Althea had put Cypros on the wheel tonight. The duty demanded little more than that he stand there and hold it steady. Jek was on lookout on the foredeck. The downpour of rain might loosen drift logs from the surrounding islands. Jek had a keen eye for such hazards and would warn the steersman well in advance of them. Paragon preferred Jek to the others on her watch. Although Brashen had forbidden anyone to speak to the figurehead, she had the knack of making silence companionable rather than accusing.

As Althea prowled the deck, she chewed over her problems. Brashen, she told herself stubbornly, was not among them. Letting a man distract her from her real goals had been her greatest error. Now that she knew his true opinion of her, she could set him aside and focus all her efforts on regaining her own life. Once she stopped thinking about the man, everything became clear.

Since the day of the battle, Althea had raised her own expectations of herself. It did not matter that Brashen regarded her as incompetent and weak, as long as she held herself to a high personal standard. She now centred her life on the ship and seeing that it ran perfectly. She had tightened discipline on her own watch, not with blows and shouts as Lavoy did, but with simple insistence that every task be done exactly as she commanded, and had uncovered both weaknesses and strengths in her deckhands. Semoy was not fast, but he had a deep knowledge of ships and their ways. During the first part of this voyage, he had suffered greatly from being separated from a bottle. Lavoy had pushed the old man onto her watch as a useless annoyance with shaky hands, but now that he had his sea legs again, Semoy had proved to know a great many tricks about rigging and line. Lop was simple and dealt poorly with decision-making or stress, but at the tedious and routine chores of sailing a ship, he was tireless. Jek was the opposite, quick and relishing challenges, but swift to become bored and then careless with repetitive work. Althea flattered herself that she now had her watch well matched to their tasks. She had not had to speak sharply to anyone for two days.

So there was little excuse for Brashen to appear on the deck during her watch when he should have been sleeping. She could have forgiven it if the storm had been taxing her crew to the utmost, but the weather was only nasty, not dangerous. Twice she encountered him on her patrol of the deck. The first time he had met her eyes and offered her, 'Good evening.' She had returned the courtesy gravely and continued on her way. She had noted he was on his way to the foredeck. Perhaps, she had reflected ironically, he was 'watching' Jek at her duties.

The second time she encountered him, he had the grace to be discomfited. He halted before her, and made some inconsequential comment about the storm. She agreed it was unpleasant, and made to move past him.

'Althea.' His voice stopped her.

She turned back to him. 'Sir?' she asked correctly.

He stood staring at her. His face was a study in shifting flats and shadows in the swinging light from the ship's lantern. She saw him blink cold rain from his eyes. Served him right. He had no real errand to bring him out on the deck in this weather. She watched him grope for an excuse. He took a breath. 'I wanted to let you know that at the end of your watch, I'll be lifting the restriction on speaking to the figurehead.' He sighed. 'I'm not sure it made any impression on him. Sometimes I fear that isolation will only drive him more deeply into defiance. So I'll be lifting that order.'

She nodded once. 'So you said. I understood, sir.'

He stood there a moment longer, as if expecting her to say more. But there was nothing more for the second mate to say to the captain about this announcement. He was about to change an order; she would see her crew obeyed it. She continued to give him her attention until he nodded briefly and then walked away from her. After that, she had gone back to her work.

So they would be allowed to speak to Paragon again. She was not sure if she was relieved or not. Perhaps it would lift Amber's spirits. The carpenter had brooded darkly since Paragon had killed. When they spoke of it, she always blamed Lavoy for it, insisting that the mate had incited the ship to it. Althea personally could not disagree, but nor could a second mate agree with such a statement. Therefore, she had held her tongue, which had only exasperated Amber.

She wondered what Amber would say the first time she spoke to Paragon. Would she rebuke him, or demand that he explain himself? Althea knew what she, personally, would do. She would treat it as she had treated all of Paragon's sins. She would ignore it. She would not speak of it to the ship, any more than she had ever really spoken of how he had twice capsized and killed all his crew. Some acts were too monstrous to recognize with words. Paragon knew how she felt about what he had done. He was an old liveship, built with much wizardwood throughout his frame. She could touch no piece of it without communicating her horror and dismay to him. Sadly, all she felt in response from him was defiance and anger. He felt justified in what he had done. He was angry that no one else shared that emotion. She added that to her unending list of mysteries about Paragon. She made another slow circuit of the deck, but found nothing to fault. It would have been a relief to discover some simple task. Instead, she found her thoughts turning to Vivacia. With every passing day, her hopes of recovering her ship dwindled. Her pain at being separated from her liveship was old pain now. It ached deep within her, like an injury that would not heal. Sometimes, as now, she prodded it, as if she were rocking an aching tooth. She dwelt on it to stir it to new flames, simply to prove her soul was still alive. If only she could recover her ship, she told herself, all would be well. If she had Vivacia's decks beneath her feet, none of her other worries would matter. She could forget Brashen. Tonight her dream of regaining her ship seemed a hopeless one. From what that boy had said before Paragon killed him, Kennit would not be open to a ransom offer, especially not a humble one. That left only force or deceit. The crew's haphazard defence of Paragon during the pirate attack had left her with little confidence in their ability to force anyone to do anything.

Deceit remained. Yet, the idea of pretending that they were runaways from Bingtown with hopes of becoming pirates struck her as material for a stage farce rather than a plan of action. In the end, it might prove worse than ridiculous or useless. It might play right into Lavoy's hands. Plainly, he and his tattooed crew savoured the idea. Did he hope to take it one step further, to take over Paragon and truly use him as a pirate vessel? To play-act the role would inevitably put the idea into every sailor's mind. The Bingtown dock-scrapings they had taken as crew would not harbour strong moral opposition to such a change in career and goal. As for the ship himself, she no longer knew. This whole adventure had revealed facets to Paragon's character that she had never suspected. Time was what she needed, time to concoct a better plan, time to understand this poor, mad ship. But time burned through her hands like a wild line. Every watch carried them closer to Divvytown, Kennit's stronghold.

The rain let up towards morning. As her watch ended, the sun broke through the cloud cover, sending broad streaks of light down to touch the water and the islands that dotted it.

The wind began to bluster and shift. She ordered her watch to assemble to hear Brashen's change in orders as Lavoy's men came on deck. Lavoy glowered at her in passing, but his hostility no longer surprised her. It was part of her job.

When all hands were mustered onto the deck, Brashen spoke his piece. She listened impassively as he lifted his ban on speaking to the figurehead. As she had expected, Amber's face expressed her relief. When Brashen went on to move men off her watch in order to shift the former slaves onto it, she managed to hold her peace. Without even consulting her, he had undone her careful efforts to make her watch operate as efficiently as possible. Now, as they sailed deeper every day into pirate territory, he had made her responsible for men she scarcely knew, men that perhaps Lavoy had been inciting to mutiny. A fine addition to her watch. She seethed silently, but gave no sign of her outrage.

When Brashen was finished, she dismissed her sailors to food and sleep or whatever other amusement they could find. Her anger had killed her appetite. She went directly to her stateroom, wishing it were truly her own rather than a tiny space shared with two others. For once, it was empty. Jek would be eating and Amber was probably with Paragon already. She knew a moment of guilt that she avoided the figurehead. Then she centred herself in her anger and decided it was for the best. She had removed not only Brashen from her softer emotions, but also the ship and Amber. It was simpler so, and better. She could function most efficiently as a mate when she let no personal considerations stand between her and her tasks.

Sleep, she decided, was what she needed. She had pulled her rain-damped shirt out of her trousers and started to drag it over her head when there was a rap at the door. She hissed in annoyance. 'What is it?' she demanded through the wood. Clef's voice said something quietly outside the door. She pulled her shirt back on, snatched the door open and demanded, 'What?'

Clef took two steps back. 'Cap'n wants to see you,' he blurted. His startled face was a dash of cold reality. She took a breath and smoothed her features.

'Thank you,' she said brusquely, and shut the door again. Why couldn't Brashen have taken care of whatever it was when she was mustered on deck with the others? Why did he have to cut into what little privacy and sleep she could find? She stuffed her shirttail back into her trousers and slammed out of the room.

'Enter!' Brashen called in response to the thudding on his door. He looked up from his charts, expecting Lavoy or one of his sailors with important news. Instead, Althea entered and strode up to stand before him.

'You sent Clef for me, sir.'

His heart sank in him. 'I did,' he acknowledged and then could find no words. After a moment, 'Sit down,' he invited her, but she took the chair stiffly as if he had ordered it. She sat, meeting his eyes with an unflinching gaze. Captain Ephron Vestrit had always been able to stare him down.

'When your father looked at me like that, I knew I was in for a private reprimand that would leave my ears smoking.'

At the shocked look on her face, he realized he had spoken the words aloud. He was horrified, yet fought a wild impulse to laugh at her expression. He leaned back in his chair and managed to keep his face composed and his voice level as he added, 'So why don't you just say it and we'll be done with it?'

She glared at him. He could see the pressure building in her. His invitation was too much for her to resist. He braced himself as she took a deep breath as if she would roar at him. Then, surprisingly, she let it out. In a quiet controlled voice that still shook slightly, she said, 'That's not my place, sir.'

'Sir.' She was keeping it formal, yet her tension vibrated

through him. He deliberately nudged at it, determined to clear the air between them. 'I believe I just gave you permission. Something is troubling you. What is it?' At her continued silence, he found his own temper rising. 'Speak!' he snapped at her.

'Very well, sir.' She bit off the words, her black eyes flashing. 'I find it difficult to perform my duties when my captain obviously has no respect for me. You humiliate me in front of the crew, and then expect me to keep my watch in order. It isn't right and it isn't fair.'

'What?' he demanded, outraged. How could she say such things, after he had taken her on as a working mate, entrusted his private plans to her, even consulted with her on what was best for the vessel? 'When have I ever "humiliated you in front of the crew"?'

'During the battle,' she grated out. 'I was doing my best to repel boarders. You not only stepped in and took the task from me, but also said to me, "Get back. Stay safe."' Her voice was rising with her anger. 'As if I were a child you must shelter. As if I were less competent than Clef, who you kept by your side.'

'I did not!' he defended himself. Then he halted his words at the flare of fury on her face. 'Did I?'

'You did,' she said coldly. 'Ask Clef. I'm sure he remembers.'

He was silent. He could not recall saying such words, but he did recall the lurch of fear in his heart at the sight of Althea in the midst of the fighting. Had he said such a thing? His heart sank with guilt. In the heat of battle and the chill of fear . . . probably, he had. He imagined the affront to her pride, and her confidence. How could he say such a thing to her in the midst of a fight, and expect her to keep her self respect? He deserved her anger. He moistened his lips. 'I suppose I did. If you say I did, I know I did. It was wrong. I'm sorry.'

He looked up at her. His apology had shocked her. Her eyes were very wide. He could have fallen into their depths.

He gave a small shake of his head and a smaller shrug. She continued simply to look at him, silently. The simple sincerity of his apology had cracked his restraint with her. He struggled desperately to retain his control. 'I have great faith in you, Althea. You've stood beside me and we've faced crimpers and serpents . . . We put this damn ship back in the water together. But during the battle, I just . . .' His voice tightened in his throat. 'I can't do this,' he said suddenly. He lay his hands, palms up, on the table and studied them. 'I can't go on like this any more.'

'What?' She spoke slowly, as if she hadn't heard him correctly.

He surged to his feet and leaned over the table. 'I can't go on pretending I don't love you. I can't pretend it doesn't scare me spitless to see you in danger.'

She shot to her feet as if he had threatened her. She turned from him but two strides carried him to stand between her and the door. She stood like a doe at bay. 'At least hear me out,' he begged. The words rushed out of him. He wouldn't consider how stupid they would sound to her, or that he could never call them back again. 'You say you can't perform your duties without my respect. Don't you know the same is true for me? Damn it, a man has to see himself reflected somewhere to be sure he is real. I see myself in your face, in how your eyes follow me when I'm handling something well, in how you grin at me when I've done something stupid but managed to make it come out all right anyway. When you take that away from me, when . . .'

She just stood there, shocked and staring. His heart sank. His words came out as a plea. 'Althea, I am so damn lonely. Worst is to know that whether we fail or succeed, I still lose you. Knowing that you are, every day, here on the same ship with me, and I cannot so much as share a meal with you, let alone touch your hand, is torment enough. When you will not look at me or speak to me . . . I can't go on with this coldness between us. I can't.'

Althea's cheeks were very pink. Her rain-soaked hair was just beginning to dry, pulling out of her queue in curling tendrils that framed her face. For an instant, he had to close his eyes against the sweet pain of wanting her. Her words broke through to him. 'One of us has to be sensible.' Her voice was very tight. She was standing right in front of him, not even an arm's length away. She wrapped her arms tightly around herself as if she feared she might fly apart. 'Let me pass, Brashen.' Her voice was a whisper.

He couldn't. 'Just . . . let me hold you. Just for a moment, and then I'll let you go,' he pleaded, knowing he lied.

He was lying and they both knew it. Just for a moment would never be enough for either of them. Her breath was coming hard, and when his callused palm touched her jaw, she was suddenly dizzied. She reached out a hand to his chest, just to steady herself, perhaps even to push him away, that was all, she would not be so stupid as to allow this, but his flesh was warm through his shirt and she could feel his heart beating. Her traitor hand clutched the fabric and pulled him closer. He stumbled forwards and then his arms were around her, holding her so tightly she could scarcely breathe. For a time, they did not move. Then he sighed out suddenly as if a pain had eased in him. He spoke softly, 'Oh, Althea. Why must it always be so complicated for us?'

His breath was warm against the top of her head as he kissed her hair gently. Suddenly, it all seemed very simple to her. When he bent to kiss her ear and the side of her neck, she turned her mouth to meet his and closed her eyes. Let it happen, then.

She felt him tug her shirt loose from her trousers. The skin of his hands was rough but his touch was gentle as his hands slid up under her shirt. One hand cupped her breast, then teased the tautness of her nipple. She could not move, and then she could. Her hands found his hips and snugged him against her.

He broke the kiss. 'Wait,' he cautioned her. He took a breath. 'Stop.'

He had come to his senses. She reeled with disappointment as he turned away from her. He walked to the door. With shaking hands, he bolted it. Returning, he caught up her hand. He kissed the palm of it, let it go and then stood silently, looking down on her. For an instant, she closed her eyes. He waited. She decided. She took his hands in both of hers and drew him gently towards his bed.

Amber was speaking gravely and slowly. 'I don't think you fully understood what you did. That is why I can forgive you. But this is the only time. Paragon, you have to learn what it means to a man to die. I don't think you grasp the finality of what you did.' The storm wind buffeted her but she clung to his railing and waited for a reply. He tried to think of something to say that would make her happy. He didn't want Amber to be sad at him. Her sadness, when she let him feel it, went deeper than any human's. It was almost as grievous as his own.

Paragon turned all his senses inward, seeking. Something was happening. Something dangerous, something frightening. He had known this before, and he braced himself for the wrenching agony and shame of it. When humans came together like that, it always meant pain for the weaker one. What had made Brashen so angry with her? Why was she allowing it, why wasn't she fighting him? Was she so frightened of him she could not resist?

'Paragon. Are you listening to me?'

'No.' He drew a small breath through his open mouth. He didn't understand this. He had thought he knew what this meant. If Brashen did not mean to punish her, if he was not trying to master her with pain, then why was he doing this? Why was Althea allowing it?

'Paragon?'

'Shh.' He clenched his hands into fists and held them tight to his chest. He would not scream. He would not. Amber was talking at him but he closed off his ears and tuned his other senses. This was not what he had thought it was. He had thought he understood humans and how they hurt one another, but this was different. This was something else. Something he could almost recall. Timidly, he shut the eyes he no longer had. He let his thoughts float, and felt ancient memories soar in him.

Althea held Brashen close to her and felt his heart thundering in his chest. He gasped for breath beside the side of her neck. His hair was across her face. Her fingers gently walked the long ridge of the scarcely-healed sword slash down his ribs. Then she set her hand flat to it, as if she could mend it with a touch. She sighed. He smelled good, like the sea and the ship and himself. When she held him, she held all those things within her. 'Almost,' she breathed softly. 'Almost, I thought we were flying.'

THIRTEEN

Surviving

'Mama? We can see Bingtown harbour now.'

Keffria lifted her aching head from the pillow. Selden stood in the doorway of the small stateroom they shared on the Kendry. She had not truly been asleep. She had simply been curled around her misery, trying to find out how to live with it. She looked at her son. His lips were chapped, his cheeks and brow reddened and chafed by the wind. Ever since his misadventures in the buried city, there had been a distant look behind his eyes, as if he were in some way lost to her, even as he stood before her. Selden was her last living child. That should have made her desperate to cherish him. She should have wanted him by her side every moment. Instead, it numbed her heart to him. Best not to love him too much. Like the others, he could be taken from her at any time.

'Are you coming to see? It looks really strange.' Selden paused. 'Some of the people on deck are crying.'

'I'm coming,' she said wearily. Time to face it. All the way here, she had avoided speaking to Selden of what they might find. She swung her feet out of bed. She pushed at her hair then gave it up. A shawl would cover it. She found one, still damp from the last time she had been on deck, flung it about herself and followed him onto the deck.

It was a grey day and the rain was steady. That felt right. She joined the other passengers looking towards Bingtown. No one chattered or pointed: they stood and stared silently. Tears ran down some faces.

Bingtown harbour was a bone yard. The masts of ruined vessels stuck up from the water. Kendry manoeuvred carefully around the sunken ships, heading not towards the liveships' traditional dock but to one that was newly repaired. The clean yellow lumber contrasted oddly with the weathered grey and scorched black of the rest. Men on the dock waited to welcome them. At least, she hoped it was welcome.

Selden leaned against her. Absently, she lifted a hand and set it on his shoulder. Whole sections of the city were black ruins, burnt skeletons of buildings glistening in the falling rain. The boy leaned against her more heavily. 'Is Grandma all right?' he asked in a muffled voice.

'I don't know,' she replied wearily. She was so tired of telling him she didn't know. She didn't know if his father was alive. She didn't know if his brother was alive. She didn't know what had happened to Malta. The Kendry had searched down the Rain Wild River to its mouth and found nothing. At Reyn's frantic insistence, they had turned back and searched up the river all the way back to Trehaug. They had found no sign of the small boat that Reyn claimed he had seen. Keffria had never spoken it aloud, but she wondered if Reyn had not imagined it. Perhaps he had wanted so badly for Malta to be alive that he had deceived himself. Keffria knew what that was like. At Trehaug, Jani Khuprus had boarded the Kendry. Before they departed the Rain Wild City, they sent a bird to Bingtown, informing the Council that they had not recovered the Satrap, but were continuing the search. It was a foolish hope, but one that neither Keffria nor Reyn could abandon.

On this last trip down the Rain Wild River, Keffria had spent every evening on deck, staring out through the gathering dusk. Time after time, she had been sure she glimpsed a tiny rowing boat on the river. Once she had seen Malta standing up in it, one hand lifted in a plea for help, but it had only been a log, torn loose from the bank, a root upraised in despair as it floated past.

Even after the Kendry had left the river behind, she had kept her nightly vigils on the deck. She could not trust the ship's lookout to watch with a mother's eyes. Last night, through a chilling downpour, she had glimpsed a Chalcedean ship that the Kendry had easily outrun. Last night's Chalcedean vessel had been alone, but during their journey their lookout had sighted other galleys in groups of two or three, and two great Chalcedean sailing ships. All had either ignored the Kendry, or given only token chase. What, the captain had demanded, were the raiders waiting for? Were they converging on the mouth of the Rain River? On Bingtown? Were they part of a fleet that would take over the Cursed Shores? Reyn and Jani had joined the captain in his useless debating, but Keffria saw no use in speculation.

Malta was gone. Keffria did not know if she had died in the sunken city or perished in the river. That she would never know ate at her like a canker. Would she ever find out what had become of Wintrow and Kyle? She tried to hope that they still survived, but could not. Hope was too steep a mountain to climb. She feared she would only fall into an abyss of despair when the hope proved futile. She lived instead in a suspension of all feeling. Now was all there was.

Reyn Khuprus stood beside his mother. The rain soaked his veil. When the wind stirred it, it slapped lightly against his face. There was Bingtown, fully as damaged as he had expected it to be from the news the messenger-birds had brought to Trehaug. He tried to find an emotion to fit to the sight, but none were left to him.

'It's worse than I feared,' his mother muttered beside him. 'How can I ask aid of the Bingtown Council when their own city is a shambles, and their coast menaced by Chalcedean ships?'

That was supposed to be part of their mission here. Jani Khuprus had often represented the Rain Wild Traders to their kin in Bingtown, but seldom on so grave a mission. After she had formally apologized to the Bingtown Council for the unfortunate loss of Satrap Cosgo and his Companion, she would ask for assistance for the Rain Wild Traders of Trehaug. The destruction of the ancient Elderling city was almost complete. With much careful work, parts of the city might eventually be reopened. In the meantime, the Trader families who had depended on the strange and wonderful objects unearthed in the city for their commerce were left abruptly destitute. Those families made up the backbone of Trehaug. Without the Elderling city to plunder, there was no economic reason for Trehaug to exist. While Trehaug harvested some foods from the Rain Wild forest, they had no fields in which to grow grain or pasture cattle. They had always bartered for food, supplying their needs through Bingtown. The Chalcedean interruption of trade was already felt in Trehaug. With winter coming, the situation would soon be desperate.

Reyn knew his mother's deepest fear. She believed this latest disaster might destroy the Rain Wild folk. Their population had dwindled in the last two generations. Rain Wild children were often stillborn, or died in the first few months. Even those who lived did not have as long a life span as ordinary folk. Reyn himself did not expect to live much beyond his thirtieth year. It was one reason the Rain Wild Traders often sought their mates among their Bingtown kin. Such matches were more likely to be fecund, and the resulting children stronger. But Bingtown folk, kin or no, had become less willing in the last two generations to come to the Rain Wilds. Gifts for the family of a prospective spouse had risen in size and value and number. Witness his own family's willingness to forgive the debt on a liveship simply to assure Reyn a bride. With

Malta lost, Jani knew Reyn would never wed nor produce children for the Khuprus family. The bride-gifts would have been in vain. With the beggaring of Trehaug, other Rain Wild families would be sore pressed to feed the children they had, let alone negotiate for mates for them. The Rain Wild folk might disappear altogether.

So Jani would come to Bingtown, to explain the loss of the Satrap and beg for aid. The combination of the two errands was a deep affront to her pride. Reyn felt sorry for his mother, but distanced by his own grief. The loss of the Satrap could trigger a war that might mean the complete destruction of Bingtown. The ancient Elderling city he loved was destroyed. But these tragedies were now merely the backdrop to his agony at losing Malta.

He had caused her death. By bringing her to his city, he had put her on the path to her death. The only creature he blamed more was Tintaglia, the dragon. He despised himself for the way he had romanticized the dragon. He had believed her capable of nobility and wisdom, had lionized her as the last of her glorious kind. In reality, she was an ungrateful, selfish and egotistical beast. Surely, she could have saved Malta if she had only put her mind to the task.

For his mother's sake, he tried to say something positive. 'It looks as if some of the folk have begun rebuilding,' he pointed out.

'Yes. Barricades,' she observed as the ship approached the dock. She was right. With a sinking heart, Reyn noted that the men on the dock were well armed. They were Traders, for he recognized several among them, and the captain of the Kendry was already roaring a greeting to them.

Someone cleared her throat. He started and turned to find a shawled Keffria Vestrit at his shoulder. Her eyes moved from his mother to him. 'I don't know what I will find at home,' she said quietly. 'But the hospitality of the Vestrit home is open to you.' She smiled wryly. 'Providing that it still stands at all.'

'We could not impose,' Jani assured her gently. 'Do not be troubled for us. Somewhere in Bingtown, an inn must still stand.'

'It would scarcely be an imposition,' Keffria insisted. 'I am sure Selden and I would welcome the company.'

Reyn suddenly understood that there might be more to this invitation than a simple return of hospitality. He voiced it. 'It might not be safe for you to return to your home alone. Please. Let my mother and me arrange our business, and then we will accompany you there, to see you resettled.'

'Actually, I would be most grateful for that,' Keffria admitted humbly.

After a moment of silence, Reyn's mother sighed. 'My mind has been busy with my own troubles. I had not stopped to think of all this homecoming might mean to you. Sorrow I knew there must be, but I had not considered danger. I have been thoughtless.'

'You have your own burdens,' Keffria told her.

'Nevertheless,' Jani said solemnly. 'Honesty must replace all polite words for a time. And not just between you and me. All Traders must be frank if any of us are to survive this. Ah, Sa, look at the Great Market. Half of it is gone!'

As the crew worked the ship into the dock, Reyn's eyes roved over the men gathering to meet the ship, and spotted Grag Tenira. He had not seen him since the night of the Summer Ball. The strength of the mixed feelings that surged up in him took him by surprise. Grag was a friend, yet now Reyn connected him with Malta's death. Would her death edge every day of his life with pain? It seemed it must be so.

The ship was secured to the dock and a gangplank run up to it. The moment there was any access to the ship, the crowd surged forwards and folk began to cry out questions to the captain and the crew. Reyn pushed his way through the oncoming folk. His mother, Keffria and Selden followed in his wake. The second his foot touched the wharf,

Grag stepped in front of him. 'Reyn?' he asked in a low voice.

'Yes,' he confirmed for him. He extended a gloved hand to Grag and Grag took it, but used it to pull Reyn closer.

Head close to Reyn's, Grag asked anxiously, 'Has the Satrap been found?'

Reyn managed to shake his head. Grag frowned, and spoke hastily. 'Come with me. All of you. I've a waggon waiting. I've had a boy watching for the Kendry from the headland for the past three days. Quickly, now. There have been some wild rumours in Bingtown of late. This is not a good place for any of you.' From beneath his own cloak, Grag produced a ragged workman's cloak. 'Cover your Rain Wild garb.'

For an instant, Reyn was shocked into silence. Then he shook out the cloak and flung it over his mother's before handing her off to Grag. He seized Keffria's arm without ceremony. 'Come along quickly and quietly,' he whispered to her. He saw Keffria grip Selden's hand more tightly. The boy sensed that all was not right. His eyes widened, and then he hurried along with them. All their bags were left behind on the ship. It could not be helped.

Grag's waggon was an open cart more suited to hauling freight than passengers. There was a definite smell of fish to it. Two well-muscled young men lounged in the back. They wore the smocks of Three Ships fishermen. Reyn helped the women in as Grag jumped to the seat and took up the reins. 'There's some sailcloth back there. If you spread it over you, it will keep some of the rain off.'

'And hide us as well,' Jani observed sourly, but she helped Reyn to unfold the canvas and stretch it out. They huddled together under it. Their escorts sat on the tail of the waggon, feet swinging as Grag stirred the ancient horse.

'Why is the harbour so empty?' Reyn asked one of the fishermen. 'Where are the ships of Bingtown?'

'On the bottom, or off chasing Chalcedeans. They made a

poke at us yesterday. Two ships approached the harbour with three others hanging offshore. Ophelia took out after them, and our other ships followed. Sa, how they ran! But I don't doubt our ships caught up to them. We're still waiting for our ships to return.'

That didn't seem right to Reyn, but he couldn't put his finger on why it disturbed him. As the horse pulled the cart through Bingtown, he saw the city in glimpses from beneath the flapping canvas. Some commerce was taking place, but the city had an uneasy air. Folk hurried by on their errands or suspiciously watched the cart pass. The wind brought the clinging stink of low tide and burned houses. It seemed to Reyn that they took a roundabout route to the Tenira estate. At the gate, armed men waved Grag in, and closed the gates behind the cart. As Grag pulled the horses to a halt, the door opened wide. Naria Tenira and two of Grag's sisters were among those who spilled out. Their faces were anxious.

'Did you find them? Are they safe?' Grag's mother demanded as Reyn threw back the canvas that had covered them.

Then Selden was scrabbling out of the cart, crying, 'Grandma, Grandma!'

On the doorstep of the Tenira manor, Ronica Vestrit opened her arms wide to her last surviving grandchild.

Satrap Cosgo, heir to the Pearl Throne and the Mantle of Righteousness, picked at his chest, pulling off a long papery sheet of peeling skin. Malta looked aside to keep from grimacing. 'This is intolerable,' the Satrap complained yet again. 'My skin is ruined. Such an unsightly pink shows beneath! My complexion will never again be as fair as it was.' He looked at her accusingly. 'The poet Mahnke once compared the skin of my brow to the opalescence of a pearl. Now, I am disfigured!'

Malta felt Kekki's knee bump the small of her back. Kekki

lay on her pallet by the Satrap's bed and Malta was hunkered on the floor beside her. It was her place in the small room. Malta winced at the nudge against her aching back but recognized the hint. She searched her mind, then lied. 'In Bingtown, it is said that the woman who washes her face once a year in Rain Wild River water will never age. It is an uncomfortable treatment, but it is said to keep the complexion youthful and fair.'

Kekki breathed out a sigh of approval. Malta had done well. Cosgo brightened immediately. 'Beauty demands a price, but I have never flinched from a little personal discomfort. Still, I wonder what has become of the ship that we were to join at the mouth of the river. I am tired of this wallowing about. A ship of this size is ill suited to open water like this.'

Malta lowered her eyes and stifled her opinion of his ignorance. The Chalcedeans travelled for months at a time in their galleys. Their ability to subsist on crude rations and endure the hardships of life aboard an open boat was legendary; it made their reputation as sailors and raiders.

They had emerged some days ago from the mouth of the river. The Satrap had been angry that the Chalcedean mother ship was not there to take him up. Malta had been bitterly disappointed that there were no liveships guarding the river mouth. She had been enduring by pretending that Bingtown liveships would halt the galley and rescue her. The despair that swept over her as the galley swept freely on was unbearable. She'd been a fool to dream of rescue. Such dreams had only weakened her. Angrily she purged her heart of them: no liveship patrol, no Reyn searching for her, no dreams at all. No one was going to magically appear and rescue her. She suspected her survival was in her own hands. She suspected many things that she did not share with the Satrap or Kekki. One was that the galley was in trouble. It did wallow, and it shipped a great deal more water than it should. Doubtless the Rain Wild River had taken a toll on its tarred seams and perhaps on its planking. Since they had left the river, the captain had taken them north, towards Chalced. The galley hugged the shore; if it broke up, they'd at least have a chance of reaching the beach alive. She judged the man was running for home, and gambling he'd reach there with both ship and unexpected cargo intact.

'Water,' Kekki croaked. She seldom spoke now. She no longer sat up at all. Malta kept her as clean as she could and waited wearily for her to die. The Companion's mouth was ringed with sores that cracked and bled as Malta held a cup to her lips. Kekki managed a swallow. Malta dabbed at the pink-tinged water that ran from the corners of her mouth. She had drunk too much river water to live, but not enough to kill her quickly. Kekki's insides were probably as ulcerated as her mouth. The thought made Malta cringe.

The Companion, despite her pain and weakness, had kept her word. Malta had kept her alive and seen them rescued, and now Kekki did her best to teach Malta how to survive. She could speak little now, but with nudges and small noises, she reminded Malta of her earlier advice. Some of her hints merely made life tolerable. Malta should always respond to the Satrap's complaints with either a positive aspect of them, or a compliment on how brave and wise and strong he was in enduring such things. Initially the words had near gagged Malta, but it did divert him from whining. If she must be confined with him, it was best to keep him agreeable. She cherished the hours after his evening meal when his smoke with the captain left him mellowly drowsing and nodding.

Other things Kekki had told her were more valuable. The first time Malta had taken their privy bucket to empty it, the sailors had hooted and clicked their teeth at her. On her return, one man had blocked her way. Eyes cast down, she had tried to step around him. Grinning, he shifted to prevent her escape. Her heart began to hammer in her throat. She looked away and tried once more to pass him. This time he let her slip by, but as she went past him, he reached from behind her, seized one of her breasts and squeezed it hard.

She cried out in pain and alarm. He laughed and jerked her back against him, holding her so tight she could hardly breathe. His free hand snaked down her blouse and caught her other breast. Callused fingers roughly caressed her bare skin. Shock froze her motionless and silent. He ground his body against her buttocks. The other men watched him, eyes bright and grins knowing. When he reached down to lift the back of her skirts, she suddenly found control of her muscles. The heavy wooden bucket was still in her hand. She twisted and swung it hard, hitting him in the shoulder. The remnant waste in the bottom of the bucket spattered up into his face. He had roared his distaste and released her, despite the jeering encouragement of his fellows. She had sprung away and had run back to their canvas shelter and flung herself inside.

The Satrap was not there. He had gone to take a meal with the captain. In abject terror, Malta huddled on the floor beside the sleeping Kekki. Every passing step might be the sailor coming after her. She shook until her teeth chattered. When Kekki stirred awake and saw Malta shivering in a corner, clutching a water mug as her only weapon, she had coaxed the tale from her. While Malta gasped the story out, Kekki had listened gravely. Then she shook her head. She spoke in short phrases to save her mouth and throat.

'This is bad . . . for all of us. They should fear . . . to touch you . . . without Cosgo's permission. But they don't.' She paused, pondering. Then she drew breath, rallying her strength. 'They must not rape you. If they do . . . and Cosgo does not challenge them . . . they will lose all respect . . . for all of us.

'Don't tell Cosgo. He would use it . . . to make you obey. To threaten you.' She sucked in a painful breath. 'Or give you to them . . . to buy favour. Like Serilla.' She took breath again. 'We must protect you . . . to protect all of us.' Kekki groped weakly around herself, then picked up one of the rags Malta used to dab blood away from her mouth. 'Here. Wear this . . . between your legs. Always. If a man touches you, say *Fa-chejy kol*. Means "I bleed." He will stop . . . when you say it . . . or when he sees this.'

Kekki motioned for water and drank. She sighed, then gathered herself to speak. 'Chalced men fear a woman's blood time. They say –' Kekki took a breath and managed a pink-toothed smile. 'A woman's parts are angry then. They can slay a man's.'

Malta was amazed that anyone could believe such a thing. She looked at the blood-streaked rag she held. 'That's stupid.'

Kekki shrugged painfully. 'Be grateful they are stupid,' she advised her. 'Save the words. They know you cannot always be bleeding.' Then her face and eyes grew grave. 'If he doesn't stop . . . don't fight him. He will only hurt you more.' She dragged in a breath. 'They would hurt you . . . until you stopped fighting. To teach you a woman's place.'

That conversation had been days ago. It was the last time Kekki had spoken more than a few words to her. The woman weakened every day, and the smell from her sores grew stronger. She could not live much longer. For her sake, Malta hoped death came soon, though for her own sake, she feared Kekki's death. When Kekki died, she would lose her only ally.

Malta was weary of living in fear, but she had little choice. Every decision she made, she made in fear. Her life centred on her fear. She no longer left their chamber unless Cosgo ordered her directly. Then she went quickly, returned swiftly, and tried to meet no man's eyes. The men still hooted and clicked their teeth, but they didn't bother her when she was emptying the waste bucket.

'Are you stupid or just lazy?' the Satrap demanded loudly.

Malta looked up at him with a jolt. Her thoughts had carried her far. 'I'm sorry,' she said, and tried to make her voice sincere.

315

'I said, I'm bored. Not even the food is interesting. No wine. No smoke, save at table with the captain. Can you read?' At her puzzled nod, he directed her, 'Go and see if the captain has any books. You could read to me.'

Her mouth went dry. 'I don't read Chalcedean.'

'You are too ignorant for words. I do. Go borrow a book for me.'

She tried to keep fear from her voice. 'But I don't speak Chalcedean. How will I ask for one?'

He snorted in disgust. 'How can parents let their children grow up in such ignorance! Does not Bingtown border on Chalced? One would think you would at least learn your neighbour's tongue. So damnably provincial. No wonder Bingtown cannot get along with them.' He sighed heavily, a man wronged. 'Well, I cannot fetch it myself, with my skin peeling like this. Can you remember a few words? Knock on his door, kneel down and abase yourself, then say, *La-nee-ra-ke-je-loi-en*.'

He rattled the syllables off in a breath. Malta could not even tell where one word began and another left off. '*La-nee-ra-ke-en*,' she tried.

'No, stupid. *La-nee-ra-ke-je-loi-en*. Oh, and add, *re-kal* at the end, so he doesn't think you are rude. Hurry now, before you forget it.'

She looked at him. If she pleaded not to go, he would know she was afraid and demand to know why. She would not give him that weapon to bludgeon her with. She picked up her courage. Perhaps the sailors wouldn't bother her if she was obviously bound for the captain's cabin. On the way back, she'd be carrying a book. It might keep her safe from them; they wouldn't want to damage their captain's property. She muttered the syllables to herself as she left the chamber, making a chant of them.

She had to walk the length of the galley between and above the rowers' benches. The hooting and clicking of teeth terrified her; she knew her fearful expression only encouraged them. She forced herself to keep repeating her syllables. She reached the captain's door without a man laying a hand on her, knocked, and hoped desperately that she had not knocked too loudly.

A man's voice replied, sounded annoyed. Praying that he had bid her come in, she opened the door and peered in timidly. The captain was stretched out on his bunk. He leaned up on one elbow to stare at her angrily.

'*La-nee-ra-ke-je-loi-en!*' she blurted. Then, abruptly recalling the Satrap's other instructions, she dropped to her knees and bent her head low. '*Re-kal,*' she added belatedly.

He said something to her. She dared lift her eyes to him. He had not moved. He stared at her, then repeated the same words more loudly. She looked at the floor and shook her head, praying he would know she did not understand. He got to his feet and she braced herself. She darted a glance up at him. He pointed at the door. She scrabbled towards it, backed out of it, came to her feet, bowed low again and shut it. The moment she was outside the cabin, the catcalls and teeth-clicking resumed. The other end of the boat seemed impossibly far away. She would never get there safely. Hugging her arms tightly around herself, Malta ran. She was nearly at the end of the rowing benches when someone reached up and snatched hold of her ankle. She fell heavily, striking her forehead, elbows and knees on the rough planking. For an instant, she was stunned. Dazed, she rolled to her back and looked up at a laughing young man standing over her. He was handsome, tall and blond like her father, with honest blue eyes and a ready grin. He cocked his head and said something to her. A query? 'I'm all right,' she replied. He smiled at her. Her relief was so great; she almost smiled back at him. Then he reached down and flung up the front of her skirts. He went down on one knee, his hands busy at his belt.

'No!' she cried wildly. She tried to scrabble away, but he seized her ankle and casually jerked her back. Other men were standing up to get a better view. As he exposed himself to Malta, Kekki's words rushed back to her. '*Fa-chejy kol!*' she blurted. '*Fa-chejy kol!*' He looked startled. She pushed her hair back from her face. He recoiled suddenly in horror, uttering an exclamation of disgust. She did not care. It had worked. She jerked away from him, managed to stand, raced the last few strides to shelter, flung herself through the door flap, and collapsed on the floor. Her breath sobbed in and out of her. Her elbows stung. She blinked something wet from her eye, then wiped at it. Blood. The fall had opened her scar again.

The Satrap did not even lift his head from his pillow. 'Where is my book?' he demanded.

Malta gasped a breath. 'I don't think he has any,' she managed to say. Calm words. Steady voice. Do not let him know how scared you are. 'I said the words you told me. He just pointed at the door.'

'How annoying. I fear I shall die of boredom on this boat. Come and rub my feet. Perhaps I will doze off. There is certainly nothing else to do.'

No choice, Malta told herself. Her heart was still thundering in her chest, her mouth so dry she could scarcely breathe through it. No choice, except painful death. Her elbows and knees stung; they were skinned raw. She pulled a splinter from her palm, then crossed the tiny room to sit on the floor by his feet. He glanced at her, then jerked his feet away from her touch. 'What is the matter with you? What is that?' He stared at her brow.

'I fell. I opened the cut again,' she said simply. She lifted her hand to touch it gingerly. Her fingers came away sticky with blood and a thick, white pus. Malta stared at it in horror. She picked up one of Kekki's rags and dabbed at her brow. It did not hurt much, but more of the stuff soaked the rag. Malta began to shake as she looked at it. What was it, what did it mean?

There was no mirror to consult. She had avoided touching the scar on her forehead. She had not wanted to remind herself it was there. Now she let her fingers walk over it. It hurt, but not as much as it seemed it should for all the blood and discharge. She forced herself to explore it. It was as long as her forefinger and stood up in a thick ridge as wide as two of her fingers. The scar felt knobby and ridged and gristly like the end of a chicken bone. A shudder ran over her. She wanted to vomit. She lifted her face to the Satrap. 'What does it look like?' she demanded quietly.

He did not seem to hear her. 'Don't touch me. Go clean yourself, and bind something across that. Feh! I cannot look at that. Get away.'

She turned away from him, refolded the rag and held it against her brow. It grew heavy and wet. Pink fluid trickled down her wrist to her elbow. It wasn't stopping. She scooted over to sit by Kekki, seeking any kind of companionship. She was now too frightened even to cry. 'What if I'm dying from this?' she whimpered. Kekki did not respond. Malta looked at her, and then stared.

The Companion was dead.

Out on the deck, a sailor shouted something excitedly. Others took up the cry. The Satrap sat up suddenly on his pallet. 'The ship! They're hailing the ship! Perhaps now there will be decent food and wine. Malta, fetch my . . . oh, now what ails you?' He glared at her irritably, and then followed her gaze to Kekki's corpse. He sighed. 'She's dead, isn't she?' He shook his head sadly. 'What a nuisance.'

Serilla had ordered that her luncheon be brought to the library. She sat awaiting it with an anticipation that had nothing to do with hunger. The tattooed serving woman who set it before her moved with precise courtesy that grated on Serilla's nerves.

'Never mind that,' she said, almost sharply, as the woman began to pour her tea for her. 'I'll do the rest for myself. You can go now. Please remember that I am not to be disturbed.'

'Yes, lady.' The stoic woman bobbed her head and retreated to the door.

Serilla forced herself to sit still at the table until she heard the door shut firmly behind her. Then she rose swiftly, cat-footed across the room and eased the latch into place. A servant had opened the drapes to the wet wintry day outside. Serilla drew them closed and surreptitiously checked to be sure the edges overlapped. When she was certain that no one could enter the room nor spy on her, she went back to the table. Ignoring the food, she took up the napkin and shook it hopefully.

Nothing fell out.

Disappointment squeezed her. Last time, the note had been folded discreetly within the napkin. She had no idea how Mingsley had managed it, but she had hoped he would contact her again. She had replied to his overture with a note of her own, left at his suggestion under a flowerpot in the disused herb garden behind the house. When she checked on it later, the note was gone. He should have replied by now.

Unless this was all a trick and the note had been a test of Roed's devising. Roed suspected everything and everyone. He had discovered the power of cruelty, and it was corrupting him swiftly. He could not keep a secret, yet accused everyone around him of being the source of the rumours that plagued and terrorized Bingtown. He bragged to her of what happened to those who spoke out against him, though he never admitted to having a direct hand in any of it. 'Dwicker's had a good beating for his insolence. Justice has been done.' Perhaps he had intended that such talk would keep her bound to him. It had had the reverse effect. She had felt so chilled and sickened that she was now willing to risk everything to break free of him.

When the first note had come from Mingsley, offering an alliance, she had been shocked at his boldness. It had slipped out of her napkin onto her lap while she was dining with the heads of the Bingtown Council, but if one of them had been instrumental in delivering the note, she saw no sign of it. It must have been one of the servants. Servants were easily bribed to such tasks.

She had agonized over replying. It had taken her a day to decide, and when she had finally set her note out, she had wondered if it would be too late. She knew her note had been taken. Why hadn't he replied?

Had she been too conservative in her own note? Mingsley had not been. The bargain that he had bluntly proposed had so stunned her she had barely been able to converse for the rest of the evening. Mingsley first proclaimed his own loyalty to her and to the Satrap she represented. He then plunged into accusations against those who were not so loyal. He minced no words in revealing that 'traitorous New Traders' had intended to seize the Satrap from Davad's house, and even that they had received support from nobles in Jamaillia and Chalcedean mercenaries in their pay. But the plan had soured. The Chalcedeans who had raided Bingtown had betrayed the alliance for the sake of quick plunder. The Jamaillian nobles who had backed them were plunged into civil unrest of their own. Some traitorous fools claimed the Jamaillian conspirators would raise a fleet to aid them and enforce their control of Bingtown. Mingsley believed it unlikely. The Traditionalists in Jamaillia City were more powerful than the conspirators had believed. The conspiracy had failed miserably, both in Bingtown and Jamaillia, thanks to her intervention. All had heard how she had boldly snatched the Satrap. Rumour suggested that the Satrap was now under the safe wing of the Vestrit family.

In a finely penned and closely worded missive, Mingsley went on to declare that he and other honest New Traders were most anxious to clear their own names and salvage their investments in Bingtown. Her bold declaration that Davad Restart was innocent of treachery against the Satrapy of Jamaillia had heartened them. Simple logic showed that if Davad were innocent, then so were his former trading partners. These honest but misjudged New Traders were most anxious to negotiate a peace with the Bingtown Traders, and to establish their clear loyalty to the Satrapy.

He then stated his bargain. The 'loyalist' New Traders wanted Serilla to intercede for them with the Bingtown Council, but first she must divest herself of 'the hot-headed, bloody-handed' Roed Caern. Only then would they treat with her. In return for this sacrifice, Mingsley and the other loyal New Traders would furnish her with a list of those New Traders who had plotted against the Satrap. The list would include the names of highly-placed Jamaillian conspirators, as well as the Chalcedean lords who had been involved. He not-so-subtly pointed out that such a list, kept secret, was worth a great deal of coin. A woman possessing such information could live well and independently the rest of her life, whether she chose to remain in Bingtown or return to Jamaillia.

Someone had informed Mingsley very well about her.

When she finally replied to his note, her answer had been reserved. She included no greeting that mentioned him by name, nor had she signed her name. The plain square of paper had succinctly acknowledged that she found his offer interesting and inviting. She had hinted that there were others among her 'current allies' who would also be receptive to such negotiations. Would he care to set a time and a place to meet?

In composing the note, she had forced herself to think coldly. There was no truth in this sort of politics, and very little ethics. There were only stances and posturing. The Old Satrap had taught her that. Now she tried to apply his clarity of vision to this situation. Mingsley had been involved with the plot to take the Satrap. His intimate knowledge betrayed him. But the tide had turned against him, and now he wished to change his alliance. If she could, she would help him. It could only benefit her, especially as she was in the midst of doing the same thing. She would use Mingsley's cooperation as her passage to establish credibility with Ronica Vestrit and other like-thinking members of the Bingtown Council. She wished now that Ronica Vestrit had still been in the house. Not that she regretted giving her the warning that had allowed her to escape: thwarting Roed had finally given her the small measure of courage she needed to take back some control in her life. When the time was right, she could make Ronica aware of who had aided her. Serilla smiled grimly to herself. She could, if she chose, be like Mingsley, reordering all she had done to put herself in a better light.

The Trader woman would have been useful to her right now. The tangled threads of accusations and suspicion were difficult to follow. So much was based on what Mingsley knew or suspected. Ronica had had a gift for sorting out such things.

And a gift for making her think. Ronica's words kept coming back to her. She could be shaped by her past without being trapped by it. At one time, she had considered those words only in light of her rape. Now she leaned back in her chair and opened her mind to a wider interpretation. Satrap's Companion. Must that determine her future? Or could she set it aside and become a woman of Bingtown, standing independent?

'I hate to rush you,' Grag apologized as he entered Reyn's guest chamber with an armload of clothes. He kicked the door shut behind him. 'However, the others are gathered and waiting. Some of them have been here since early morning. The longer they wait, the more impatient they grow. Here are dry clothes. Some of these should fit you. Your clothes fit me well enough when I was a Rain Wilder for the Ball.' He must have seen Reyn wince, for immediately he added, 'I'm sorry. I never got to tell you that. Sorry about what happened with the coach, and sorry that Malta was injured.'

'Yes. Well. It makes small difference to her now, I suppose.' Reyn heard how harsh his words sounded. 'I'm sorry. I can't . . . I can't talk about it.' He tried to interest himself in the clothes. He picked up a long-sleeved shirt. There were no gloves there; he'd have to use his wet ones. And the wet veil, too. It didn't matter, nothing really mattered.

'I'm afraid you'll have to talk about it.' There was genuine regret in Grag's voice. 'Your tie with Malta has brought this down on you. The rumour around town is either that she kidnapped the Satrap from where the Rain Wild Traders were holding him, or that she aided his escape. Roed Caern has been noising it about that she has probably turned him over to the Chalcedeans, because she is Chalcedean herself, and . . .'

'Shut up!' Reyn drew in a deep breath. 'A moment, please,' he said thickly. Despite his veil, he turned his back on Grag. He bowed his head and clenched his hands, willing that the tears would not spill, that his throat would not close up and choke him.

'I'm sorry,' Grag apologized again.

Reyn sighed. 'No. I should apologize. You don't know, you can't know everything I've been through. I'm surprised that you've heard anything at all. Listen. Malta is dead, the Satrap is dead.' A strange laugh bubbled up in him. 'I should be dead. I feel I am dead. But . . . no. Listen. Malta went into the buried city for my sake. There was a dragon there. The dragon was . . . between lives. In a coffin or a cocoon type of thing . . . I don't know what to call it. The dragon had been tormenting me, invading my dreams, twisting my thoughts. Malta knew. She wanted to make it stop.'

'A dragon?' Grag's voice was questioning of both the word and Reyn's sanity.

'I know it's a wild tale!' Reyn's denial of Grag's interruption was fierce. 'Don't ask me questions and don't look sceptical.

Just listen.' Swiftly he recounted all that had happened that day. At the end of his tale, he lifted his veiled eyes to challenge Grag's incredulous stare. 'If you don't believe me, ask the Kendry. The ship saw the dragon as well. It . . . changed him. He has been morose since then, constantly seeking his captain's approval and closeness. We have been concerned for him.'

In a softer voice, Reyn went on, 'I never saw Malta again. They're dead, Grag. There was no plot to steal the Satrap from Trehaug. Only a girl, trying to survive an earthquake. She didn't succeed. We searched the whole length of the river, twice. There was no sign of them. The river ate the boat and they perished in the water. It's a horrible way to drown.'

'Sa's breath,' Grag shuddered. 'Reyn, you're right, I didn't know. In Bingtown, all we've heard are conflicting rumours. We heard that the Satrap was missing or dead in the quake. Then a rumour started that the Vestrits had stolen him to sell him to the Chalcedeans or let the New Traders kill him. Ronica Vestrit has been hiding here with us. Caern has put it about that she must be captured and held. At any other time, we would have urged Ronica to go to the Council and demand that they hear her. But lately, there have been some ugly reprisals against folk that Roed Caern has accused of being traitors. I don't know why the Companion trusts him so. It's dividing the Bingtown Council, for some say we must listen to her as the Satrap's representative, while my father and I feel it is time Bingtown kept its own counsel.'

He took a breath. Gently, as if fearing his words would injure Reyn more, he added, 'Roed has been saying that the Vestrits plotted with the Chalcedeans. He says that maybe pirates never took their liveship, but hints that Kyle Haven has been part of this "conspiracy", that maybe he took Vivacia up the Rain Wild River to pick up the Satrap and Malta. Well, too many of us know the lie of that, so he changed his tune, and said it didn't have to be a liveship, maybe it was a Chalcedean ship.'

'Roed's a fool,' broke in Reyn. 'He doesn't know what he's talking about. We've had ships, Chalcedean and others, try to come up the river. The river eats them. They try all the tricks we know don't work: they grease their hulls or tar them. One ship was even shingled with baked clay.' Reyn shook his veiled head. 'They all perish, some fast, some slow. Besides, there have been liveships on patrol at the mouth of the Rain Wild River since this all started. They'd have been seen.'

Grag grimaced. 'You have more faith in our patrols than I do. There has been an onslaught of Chalcedean ships. We chase them out of the harbour, and while we are gone, another wave comes in. I'm surprised you got past them as easily as you did.'

Reyn shrugged. 'You're right, I suppose. When the Kendry came out of the river mouth, there were no other liveships about. We sighted several Chalcedean vessels on our way here, however. Most gave us a wide berth; liveships have a reputation now, thanks to your Ophelia. One Chalcedean ship seemed interested in us last night, but Kendry soon left it behind.'

A moment of silence fell between them. Reyn turned his back on Grag and peeled off his wet shirt. As he shrugged into a dry one, Grag said, 'There is so much happening, I can't grasp it all. A dragon? Somehow, it is easier to believe in a dragon than to believe Malta is dead. When I think of her, I can only see her as she looked that night in your arms on the dance floor.'

Reyn closed his eyes. A small white upturned face stared at him from a tiny boat shooting down the river. 'I envy you that,' he said quietly.

'You are the Trader for the Vestrits. You decide for the family. If you do not wish to be involved in this, I understand. But as for myself, I remain here.' Ronica took a breath. 'I stand here as myself only. But know, Keffria, that if you decide to go to the Bingtown Council, I will stand with you there, also. You would have to be the one to present our view there. The Bingtown Council would not let me speak on the matter of Davad's death. They will surely refuse to hear me on this. Nevertheless, I will stand by you while you speak. And accept the consequences.'

'And I would say what?' Keffria demanded wearily. 'If I tell them that I don't know what became of Malta, let alone the Satrap, it sounds like a deception.'

'You have one other alternative. You and Selden can flee Bingtown. You might be left at peace in Ingleby for a time. Unless someone decided to win favour with Serilla and Caern by hunting you down there.'

Keffria leaned her forehead into her hands. Heedless of how it might look to the others, she rested her elbows on the table. 'Bingtown is not like that. It won't come to that.' She waited for someone to agree, but no one spoke. She lifted her head and looked at the grave faces that confronted her.

Too much was happening too fast. They had allowed her time to bathe, and she was dressed in a fresh gown from one of the Tenira women. She'd had a simple meal in her room, and then she had been summoned down to this gathering. She had had little time with her mother. 'Malta's dead,' she had said to her as her mother hugged her in greeting. Ronica had stiffened in Keffria's arms and closed her eyes, and when she had opened them, Keffria had seen the grief in her mother's eyes over the death of her wayward granddaughter. It glittered there like ice, cold and immutable, too solid for tears. For a brief time, they shared sorrow, and oddly that had healed much of the rift between them.

But whereas Keffria wanted to huddle somewhere until this incomprehensible pain passed, her mother insisted that they go on living. For her, that meant fighting as well, fighting for Bingtown and Selden's future. Ronica had accompanied her to her room and helped her change into the dry clothes. While she did so, she spoke hurriedly of Bingtown. The words had rattled and flown past Keffria's ears: a breakdown of the Bingtown Council's ability to rule. Roed Caern and a handful of other young Traders terrorizing families that did not agree with his ideas. A need to create a new govern-ing body for Bingtown, one that encompassed all the folk who lived there. A lecture on politics was the last thing Keffria wanted or needed just now. She had nodded numbly, repeatedly, until Ronica had departed to confer with Jani Khuprus. There had been a brief time of peace and solitude. Then Keffria had descended, Selden at her side, to find this mixed company of folk in the grand hall of the Tenira mansion.

It was an odd gathering around Naria Tenira's great table. The Tenira family filled one set of chairs. Seated next to them, in a row, were representatives from at least six Trader families. Keffria recognized Devouchet and Risch. The others she did not know by name; the introductions had eluded her weary brain. Two women and a man with tattooed faces filled the next chairs, and beside them sat four folk who, by their garb, were Three Ships immigrants. Reyn and Jani Khuprus came next, and completing the circle were the three remaining Vestrits. Keffria found herself at Naria Tenira's left hand. The Liveship Trader had insisted that Selden be seated at the table and admonished the boy to pay great attention. 'This is your future unfolding, lad. You've a right to witness how it comes into being.'

Initially, Keffria had thought that Naria was merely trying to include the boy and reassure him he was still important. Since they had left Trehaug, Selden had grown clingy and withdrawn. He seemed a much younger child than the boy who had swiftly adapted to the treetop city. Now she wondered if Trader Tenira's words were not prophetic. Selden sat listening to it all with a rare concentration. Keffria looked at her young son as she conceded, 'I am too tired to run any more. We have to face whatever comes.'

'You need to do more than face it,' Naria Tenira corrected her. 'You need to challenge it. Half of Bingtown is so busy huddling in the ruins that they don't perceive the power that Serilla and her toady Caern have seized. We made a fine start of restoring order. Then, things began to happen. Trader Dwicker called a meeting. He had heard a rumour that Serilla was treating with the New Traders regarding a truce, bypassing the Bingtown Council completely. The entire Council condemned it. Caern denied it, on Serilla's behalf. That was when we saw how close they had become.' She paused and took a breath. 'Dwicker was found later, so badly beaten that he never spoke again before he died. Another Council head had his barn set on fire. New Traders or slaves were blamed both times, but there are other, darker, rumours about town.'

A slave spoke up. 'You hear how it affects Bingtown Traders. Worse things have been done to Tattooed families,' she said grimly. 'Folk have been beaten, simply for going out to barter or buy food. Families have been burned out. We are blamed for every crime in Bingtown, and given no chance to prove innocence. Caern and his cohorts are known and feared by all. New Trader families who are less able to defend themselves have been attacked in their homes. Fires are set in the night, and the fleeing folk, even children, are ambushed. A cowardly, sneaky way to wage a war. We have no love for the New Traders who enslaved us, but neither do we wish to be a party to the slaughter of children.' She met the eyes of the Traders at the table. 'If Bingtown cannot bring Caern and his thugs under control soon, you will lose all opportunity to ally with the Tattooed. The rumours we hear are that the Bingtown Council supports Caern. That once Bingtown Traders are in full command of the town, we will be shipped out with the New Traders, driven forth from Bingtown and back into slavery.'

Ronica shook her head. 'We have become a ghost town ruled by rumours. The latest rumour is that Serilla has appointed Roed as the head of a new Bingtown Guard and that he has called a secret meeting with the remaining leaders of the Bingtown Traders' Council. Tonight. If we reach consensus today, we will all be there, to put an end to such nonsense, and an end to Caern's brutality. When have secret meetings ever been part of Bingtown's government?'

The red-bearded Three Ships man spoke up. 'All the doings of the Bingtown Traders' Council have always been secret from us.'

Keffria looked at him, puzzled. 'That is how it has always been. Trader business is for Traders,' she explained simply.

His ruddy colour heightened. 'But running the whole town is what you claim as Trader business. That's what forces Three Ships folk to the edge, and keeps us there.' He shook his head. 'If you want us on your side, then it has to be *by* your side. Not outside a wall, nor on a leash.'

She stared at him, uncomprehending. A deep unrest was building in her. Bingtown as she had known it was being dismantled, and the folk in this room seemed intent on speeding the process along. Had her mother and Jani Khuprus gone mad? Would they save Bingtown by destroying it? Were they seriously considering sharing power with former slaves and fishermen?

Jani Khuprus spoke quietly. 'I know my friend Ronica Vestrit shares your feelings. She has told me that the folk of Bingtown with similar goals must ally, regardless of whether they are Trader or not.' She paused, turning her veiled face to survey all the folk at the table. 'With great respect for those here, and for the opinions of dear friends, I do not know if that is possible. The bonds between the Bingtown Traders and the Rain Wild Traders are old and secured with blood.' She paused. Her shoulders rose and fell in an eloquent shrug. 'How can we offer that loyalty to others? Can we demand it in return?

Are your groups willing to forge that strong a bond and abide by it as we have, not just binding ourselves, but binding our children's children's children?'

'That depends.' Sparse Kelter, that was the bearded man's name, Keffria suddenly recalled. He glanced at the slaves at the table as if this was something they had already discussed. 'We would make demands in return for our loyalty. I may as well lay them on the table now. They're simple, and you folks can say yea or nay. If the answer is nay, there's no sense my wasting a tide's fishing here.'

Keffria was suddenly reminded of her own father, and his reluctance to waste time on mincing words.

Kelter waited and when no one opposed him, he spoke. 'Land for everyone. A man should own the spot his house stands on, and I'm not talking a patch of beach barely out of the tide's reach. Three Ships folk are sea folk. We don't ask much more than enough space for a proper house, some ground for a chicken to scratch in and some greens to sprout, and a place to mend our nets. But those that have a bent to farming or beasts will need more than that.'

He was still looking around the table to see how this would be received when a Tattooed woman spoke. 'No slavery,' she said huskily. 'Let Bingtown become a place slaves can flee to, and not fear being turned back to their masters. No slavery, and land for those of us who are already here.' The woman hesitated, then surged on determinedly. 'And each family gets a vote in the Bingtown Council.'

'Council votes have always gone with land ownership,' Naria Tenira pointed out.

'But where did that bring us? To here, to this mess. When the New Traders claimed votes based on land they'd purchased from financially wounded Traders, we were foolish enough to grant them. If it hadn't been for the Traders' Council, they'd be running Bingtown already.' Devouchet's soft deep voice somehow kept his words from sounding offensive.

'We kept the Bingtown Traders' Council separate before,' Keffria offered. These people were swaying her, but something, she felt, must be held back for Selden. She could not stand by and let being a Bingtown Trader become merely an empty title. 'Could not we do that again? Have one Council where all landowners vote, and a separate one for the Bingtown Traders only?'

Sparse Kelter crossed his arms on his chest. The woman beside him looked so like him, she must be some relation, Keffria decided. 'Do that, and we all know where the true power would remain,' he said quietly. 'No leashes. A fair say in Bingtown.'

'We've heard what you ask, but not what you offer,' another Trader spoke. Keffria admired the way he had side-stepped Kelter's observation, but at the same time she wondered what they were doing. What was the sense of asking any of these questions? No one here had the power to make a binding decision.

Sparse Kelter spoke again. 'We offer honest hands and strong backs and knowledge, and we ask the same. Let us stand on an equal footing with you to share the work of rebuilding Bingtown. We offer to help defend her, not just from pirates and Chalcedeans, but from Jamaillia itself if need be. Or do you think the Pearl Throne will let you slip its leash and speak not a word to rebuke you?'

The full realization of what they were discussing suddenly settled on Keffria. 'We are talking about separating Bingtown completely from Jamaillia? About standing on our own, alone, between Jamaillia and Chalced?'

'Why not?' Devouchet demanded. 'The idea has been broached before, Trader Vestrit. Your own father often spoke of it privately. We will not have a better chance than this. For better or worse, the Satrap has perished. The Pearl Throne is empty. The birds we've had from Jamaillia speak of civil unrest, rioting by the Jamaillian army over unpaid wages, an

332

uprising by the slaves and even a Condemnation of State from the Temple of Sa in Jamaillia. The Satrapy is rotten. When they discover that the Satrap is dead, the nobles there will be too busy scrabbling for power in Jamaillia to pay any mind to what we do. They have never treated us as equals. Why not break free now, and make Bingtown a place where folk begin anew, all men standing on an equal footing?'

'And all women, too.' She must be Sparse's daughter, thought Keffria. Even her voice echoed his in tone.

Devouchet looked at her in surprise. 'It was but a manner of speaking, Ekke,' he said mildly.

'A manner of speaking becomes a manner of thinking.' She lifted her chin. 'I am not here simply as Sparse Kelter's daughter. I've a boat and nets of my own. If this alliance comes to pass, I'll want land of my own. Three Ships folk know that what a person has for a mind is more important than what is between their legs. Three Ships women will not give up our place alongside our men simply to say we are part of Bingtown now. That, too, must be understood.'

'That is only common sense,' Grag Tenira asserted smoothly. He smiled warmly at the Three Ships woman as he added, 'Look about this table, and see who speaks here. Bingtown has a long tradition of strong women. Some of the strongest are seated here today. That tradition will not change.'

Ekke Kelter leaned back in her chair. She returned Grag's smile easily. 'I just wanted to hear those words spoken aloud here,' she confirmed. She nodded to Grag, and for an instant, Keffria wondered if there was an understanding between them. Had Ekke spoken her piece knowing that Grag Tenira would take her side? Did Grag Tenira count her, Keffria, as one of those strong women? But as swiftly as her interest had been piqued, it faltered. She took a breath and spoke her thoughts.

'What do we do here? We talk of agreements, but none of us has the power to make these agreements binding on all Bingtown.'

Her own mother contradicted her. 'We have as much power as anyone in Bingtown these days. More than the Traders' Council has, for we do not fear to wield it. They dare not meet without asking Serilla's opinion. And she dares not give it without looking to Caern.' She smiled grimly at her daughter. 'There are more to us, Keffria, than just those you see here. More could not gather for fear of drawing attention. One of the Council heads sides with us; he told us of the secret meeting. After tonight, we shall not fear to gather openly. Our strength comes from our diversity. Those of us who were made slaves have an intimate knowledge of the New Traders and their holdings. The New Traders hope to hold what they have taken with folk they have tattooed. Once the Tattooed are freed, will they fight for their masters? I doubt it. When the New Traders are stripped of their slaves, their number is greatly reduced. Nor do they defend home and family as we do; their homes and their legitimate families are in Jamaillia. They have brought their mistresses and bastards to share the risks of living on the Cursed Shores, not their legitimate heirs. With Jamaillia in a civil uproar, the New Traders won't get help from that quarter. Many will rush back to Jamaillia to defend ancestral holdings there.

'There are also the pirates to consider. Eventually, Jamaillia may send an army against us to master us once more, but first it must make its way through the Pirate Isles. Well do I know to my own sorrow that that is not an easy journey these days.'

'Are you saying the New Traders are no threat to Bingtown?' Jani Khuprus asked incredulously.

Ronica smiled bitterly. 'Less of a threat than some would have us believe. Our first danger comes from those within our town who seek to corrupt the Traders and our ways. Tonight, we will defeat them. After that, the real danger will come from the usual source: Chalced. While Jamaillia is fighting internal battles and we chase one another through the streets with swords, Chalced has the opportunity to sweep in and subdue Bingtown.' Again, her gaze swept the folk seated around the table. 'But if we rally ourselves, we can stand them off. We have trader ships, liveships, and the working vessels of the Three Ships families. We know our waters better than anyone else.'

'You are still talking about a single city-state standing against all of Chalced. And possibly Jamaillia.' Another of the Bingtown Traders spoke. 'We might hold them off for a while, but in the long run they could starve us out. We've never been completely self-sufficient. And we must have markets for our trade goods.' He shook his head. 'We must retain our bond with Jamaillia, even if it means compromising with the New Traders.'

'There must be some compromises with the New Traders,' Ronica agreed. 'Not all will simply leave. Compromises should include trade agreements with Jamaillia for fair and open trade. But those compromises must be on our terms, not theirs. No more tariff ministers. No more tariffs.' She looked around the table for support.

'Not compromise with New Traders. Ally.' Startled eyes turned to Keffria. She could scarcely believe it was herself speaking, yet she knew her words made sense. 'We should invite them to stand with us tonight when we break into Serilla's secret meeting with the Council heads.' She took a breath and crossed a line. 'Ask them, boldly, to break with Jamaillia, stand with us, and take up our ways. If Bingtown is to be one, then we must be one today. Now. We should send word to that friend of Davad's . . . what was his name? Mingsley. He seemed to have sway with his fellows.' She firmed her voice. 'A united Bingtown is our only hope against both Chalced and Jamaillia. We have no other allies.'

A daunted silence followed her words.

'Maybe the dragon would help us.' Selden's piping tenor voice was startling.

All eyes turned to her son, sitting so straight on his chair.

His eyes were wide open, but he looked at no one. 'The dragon could protect us from Jamaillia and Chalced.'

An embarrassed silence fell. Reyn spoke at last, his voice heavy with emotion. 'The dragon cares nothing for us, Selden. She showed that when she let Malta perish. Forget her. Or rather, remember her with contempt.'

'What is this about a dragon?' Sparse Kelter demanded.

Gently, Naria observed, 'Young Selden has been through a great deal of late.'

The boy's jaw firmed. 'Don't doubt me. Do not doubt her. I have been carried in her claws, and looked down on our world. Do you know how small we truly are, how pitiful are even our greatest works? I have felt her heart beating. When she touched me, I realized there could be something beyond good and evil. She . . . transcends.' He stared, unseeing. 'In my dreams, I fly with her.'

A silence followed his words. The adults exchanged glances, some amused, some pitying, some annoyed at this interruption to their business. It stung Keffria to see her son treated so. Had not he been through enough?

'The dragon was real,' Keffria declared. 'We all saw it. And I agree with Selden. The dragon may change everything.' Her words shocked them but the look Selden gave her was worth it. She could not recall the last time her son had looked at her with such shining eyes.

'I don't doubt that dragons are real,' Sparse hastily interjected. 'I saw some myself, a few years back when sailing far to the north. They flew over, like jewels winking in the sun. Buckkeep mustered them against the Outislanders.'

'That old tale,' someone muttered, and Sparse glowered at him.

'This dragon is the last of her kind. She hatched in the collapsing ruins of the Elderling city, just before the swamp swallowed it,' Reyn stated. 'But she is no ally of ours. She is a treacherous and selfish creature.'

Keffria looked around the circle of faces. Disbelief loomed large. Pink-faced, Ekke Kelter suggested, 'Perhaps we should return to discussing the New Traders.'

Her father slapped the table with a broad palm. 'No. I can see now that I need the whole telling of what went on in the Rain Wilds. Long have we been kept ignorant of what is up that river. Let this be the first sign of openness from the Bingtown Traders to their new allies. I want a full telling of this dragon tale, and how Malta Vestrit and the Satrap perished.'

A heavy silence followed his words. Only the turning of their veiled heads revealed that Reyn and his mother conferred. All the other Traders at the table kept the silence of their ancestors. It was a mistake, Keffria knew. But even knowing that, she could not change it. The Rain Wild must choose to reveal itself, or remain hidden. Reyn leaned back. He crossed his arms on his chest.

'Very well, then,' Sparse Kelter declared heavily. He set his wide, work-reddened hands to the table and pushed his chair back to rise.

Selden glanced up at Keffria, gave her hand a quick squeeze, and suddenly stood beside his chair. It did not make him much taller, but the look on his face demanded recognition. 'It all began,' Selden's young voice piped, 'when I told Malta I knew a secret way to get into the Elderling city.'

All eyes went to the boy. He met Sparse Kelter's astonished gaze. 'It's my story as much as anyone's. Bingtown Trader and Rain Wild Trader are kin. And I was there.' The look he gave Reyn defied him. 'She's my dragon as much as yours. You may have turned on her, but I have not. She saved our lives.' He took a breath. 'It's time to share our secrets, so we can all survive.' The boy's glance swept the table.

With a sudden motion, Reyn threw back his veil. He pushed back his cowl as well and shook free his dark, curly hair. He looked with shining copper eyes from face to face at the table, inviting each of them to stare at the scaling that now outlined his lips and brows and the ridge of pebbled skin that defined his brow. When he looked at Selden, respect was in his eyes. 'It began much farther back than my young kinsman's memory,' he said quietly. 'I suppose I was about half Selden's age the first time my father took me to the dragon's chamber far underground.'

FOURTEEN

Divvytown

'I'M JUST NOT sure.' Brashen stood on the foredeck next to her. The late evening mist damped his hair to curls and beaded silver on his coat. 'It all looks different now. It's not just the fogs, but the water levels, the foliage, the beach lines. Everything is different from how I remember it.' His hands rested on the railing, a hand's breadth from her own. Althea was proud that she could resist the temptation to touch him.

'We could just lie out here.' She spoke softly, but her voice carried oddly in the fog. 'Wait for another ship to go in or come out.'

Brashen shook his head slowly. 'I don't want to be challenged or boarded. That may happen to us anyway when we reach Divvytown, but I don't want to look like I'm blundering about out here. We'll go in cocky and knowing, sail up there and drop anchor in Divvytown as if we're sure of a welcome. If I seem a bit of a braggart and a fool to them, their guards will drop faster.' He grinned at her crookedly in the gathering darkness. 'It shouldn't take much effort for me to give them that impression.'

They were anchored off a coastline of swamp and trees. The rains of winter had filled the rivers and streams of this region to overflowing. At high tide, saltwater and river water mingled in the brackish bogs. In the gathering darkness, trees both living and dead loomed out of the gently drifting mists. Breaks in the fog occasionally revealed dense walls of trees laced with dangling creepers and curtained with draping moss. The rainforest came right down to the waterline. By painstaking observation, Brashen and Althea had spotted several possible openings, any of which might be the narrow mouth of the winding river leading to the sluggish lagoon that fronted Divvytown.

Brashen once more squinted at the tattered scrap of canvas in his hand. It was his original sketch, a hasty rendering done while he was mate on the *Springeve*. 'I think this was meant to indicate a kelp bed exposed at low tide.' He glanced around at his surroundings again. 'I just don't know,' he confessed quietly.

'Pick one,' Althea suggested. 'The worst we can do is waste time.'

'The *best* we can do is waste time,' Brashen corrected her. 'The worst is considerably worse. We could get lodged in some silty-bottomed inlet and have the tide strand us there.' He took a deep breath. 'But I guess I choose and we take a chance.'

The ship was very quiet. By Brashen's order, the crew walked softly and conversed only in whispers. No lights had been hung. Even the ship was trying to mute the small noises of his planked body. All canvas had been lowered and secured. Sound carried too well in this fog. He wished to be able to hear if another ship approached in the mist. Amber ghosted up to stand silently beside them.

'If we're lucky, some of this fog may burn off in the morning,' Althea observed hopefully.

'We're as like to be shrouded more thickly than ever,' Brashen returned. 'But we'll wait for what light day offers us before we try it. Over there.' He pointed and Althea followed the line of his arm. 'I think that's the opening. We'll try it at dawn.'

'You're not sure?' Amber whispered in quiet dismay.

'If Divvytown were easy to find, it would not have survived as a pirate stronghold all these years,' Brashen pointed out. 'The whole trick of the place is that unless you know it's there, you'd never think to look for it.'

'Perhaps,' Amber began hesitantly. 'Perhaps one of the former slaves could help. They came from the Pirate Isles . . .'

Brashen shook his head. 'I've asked. They've all professed complete ignorance of Divvytown, denied they ever pirated. Ask any of them. They were the sons of runaway slaves who settled in the Pirate Isles to begin new lives. Chalcedean or Jamaillian slave raiders captured them, and they were tattooed and sold in Jamaillia. From thence they were brought to Bingtown.'

'Is it so hard to believe?' Amber asked him.

'Not at all,' Brashen replied easily. 'But a boy almost always picks up a generalized knowledge of the town he grows up in. These fellows profess too much ignorance of everything for me to be comfortable with their stories.'

'They're good sailors,' Althea added. 'I expected trouble when they were shifted onto my watch, but they haven't been. They'd prefer to stay to themselves, but I haven't allowed that, and they haven't objected. They turn to with a will, just as they did when they first came aboard to work in secret. Harg, I think, resents losing some of his authority over the others; on my watch, they are all just sailors, on an equal footing with the rest. But they are good sailors . . . a bit too good for this to be their first voyage.'

Amber sighed. 'I confess, when I first proposed bringing them aboard and allowing them to trade their labour for a chance to return to their homes, I never considered that they might have conflicting loyalties. Now, it seems obvious.'

'Blinded by the opportunity to do a good turn for someone,' Althea smiled and gave Amber a friendly nudge. Amber gave her a knowing smile in return. Althea knew a moment's uneasiness.

'Do I dare ask if Lavoy could assist us here?' Amber continued softly.

Althea shook her head when Brashen didn't reply. 'Brashen's charts are all we have to go by. With the shift in seasons, and the constant changes in the isles themselves, it becomes tricky.'

'Sometimes I wonder if I even have the correct bit of swamp,' Brashen added sourly. 'This could be the wrong river entirely.'

'It's the right bit of swamp.' Paragon's deep voice was very soft, almost a thrumming rather than speaking. 'It's even the right river mouth. As I could have told you hours ago, if anyone had seen fit to ask me.'

The three humans kept absolutely still as if by moving or speaking they would break some spell. A deep suspicion Althea had always harboured simmered in her mind.

'You're right, Althea.' The ship answered her unspoken words. 'I've been here before. I've been in and out of Divvytown enough times that I could sail up there in the blackest night, at any tide.' His deep laugh vibrated all the foredeck. 'As I'd lost my eyes before I ever went up the river, what I see or don't see makes little difference.'

Amber dared to speak aloud. 'How can you know where we are? You always said you feared to sail the open waters blind. Why are you so fearless now?'

He chuckled indulgently. 'There is a great difference between the wide open sea and the mouth of a river. There are many senses besides sight. Cannot you smell the stink of Divvytown? Their woodfires, their outhouses, the charnel pit where they burn their dead? What the air does not carry to me, the river does. The sour taste of Divvytown flows with the river. With every fibre in my planking, I taste the water from the lagoon, thick and green. I've never forgotten it. It is as slimy now as it was when Igrot ruled there.'

'You could take us there, even in the blackest night?'
Brashen spoke carefully.

'I said that. Yes.'

Althea waited. To trust Paragon or to fear him. To place
all their lives in his care, or to wait for dawn and grope their
way up the fog-bound river . . . She sensed a test in the ship's
words. She was suddenly glad that Brashen was the captain.
This was a decision she would not want to make.

It was so dark now she could scarcely see Brashen's profile.
She saw his shoulders lift as he took a breath. 'Would you take
us there, Paragon?'

'I would.'

They worked in the dark, without lanterns, putting up his
canvas and raising his anchor. It pleased him to think of
them scurrying in the blackness, as blind as he was. They
worked his windlass voicelessly, the only sound that of the
turning gears and the rattling chain. He opened his senses to
the night. 'Starboard. Just a bit,' he said softly, as they raised
his canvas and the wind nudged him, and heard the command
relayed in whispers the length of his deck.

Brashen was on the wheel. It was good to have his steady
hands there; even better to be the one deciding how he would
go and feeling the sailors jump to his orders. Let them discover
how it felt to have to place your life in the hands of one you
feared. For they all feared him, even Lavoy. Lavoy made fine
words about friendships that transcended time or kind, but in
his gut, the mate feared the ship more profoundly than any
other man aboard.

And well they should, Paragon thought with satisfaction.
If they knew his true nature, they would piss themselves with
terror. They would fling themselves shrieking into the deeps,
and count it a merciful end. Paragon lifted his arms out high
and spread wide his fingers. It was a pitiful comparison, this

damp wind flowing past his hands as his sails pushed him towards the mouth of the river, but it was enough to sustain his soul. He had no eyes, he had no wings, but his soul was still a dragon's soul.

'This is beautiful,' Amber said to him.

He startled. As long as she had been aboard, there were still times when she was transparent to him. She was the only one whose fear of him he could not feel. Sometimes he shared her emotions, but never her thoughts, and when he did catch a tinge of her feelings, he suspected it was because she allowed it. As a result, her words confused him more often than the others did. She was the only one who could possibly lie to him. Was she lying now?

'What is beautiful?' he demanded quietly. She did not answer. Paragon put his mind to the task at hand. Brashen wanted him to take them up the river as silently as possible. He wanted Divvytown to wake tomorrow to the sight of them anchored in their harbour. The idea appealed to the ship. Let them gawk and shout at the sight of him come back from the dead. If there were any there that yet recalled him.

'The night is beautiful,' Amber said at last. 'And we are beautiful in the night. There is a moon somewhere above us. It makes the fog gleam silver. Here and there, my eyes find bits of you. A row of silver droplets hung on a line stretched tight. Or the fog breaks for an instant, and the moon shines our way up the river. You move so smoothly and sweetly. Listen. There is the water against your bow, purring like a cat, and the wind shushes us along. The river is so narrow here, it is as if we knife through the forest, parting trees to let us pass. The same wind that pushes us stirs the leaves of the trees. It has been so long since I last heard the wind in the trees and smelled earth smells. It is like being in a silver dream on a magic ship.'

Paragon found himself smiling. 'I *am* a magic ship.'

'I know. Oh, well do I know what a wonder you are. On a night such as this, moving swift and silent in the dark, I almost feel as if you could unfurl wings and lift us into the very sky itself. Do you not feel it, Paragon?'

Of course, he did. The unnerving part was that she felt it also, and put words to it. He did not speak of that. 'What I feel is that the channel is deeper to starboard. Ease me over, just a bit. I'll tell you when.'

Lavoy came up onto the deck. Paragon felt him pace aft to where Brashen held the wheel. There was anger in his stride and aggression. Would it be tonight? Paragon wondered and felt a tightening of excitement. Perhaps tonight the two males would challenge one another, would circle and then strike, exchanging blows until one of them was prostrate and bleeding. He strained to hear what Lavoy would say.

But Brashen spoke first. His soft deep voice carried cold through Paragon's wood. 'What brings you out on deck, Lavoy?'

Paragon felt Lavoy's hesitation. Fear, uncertainty, or simply strategy. He could not tell clearly. 'I expected us to anchor all night. The change in motion woke me.'

'And now that you've seen what we're about?'

'This is mad. We could run aground at any moment, and then we'd be easy prey for whoever chanced upon us. We should anchor now, if we can do so safely, and wait for morning.'

Amusement tinged Brashen's voice as he asked, 'Don't you trust our ship to guide us, Lavoy?'

Lavoy sank his deep voice to a bare whisper and hissed a reply. Paragon felt a prickling of anger. Lavoy did not whisper for Brashen's sake; he whispered because he did not wish Paragon to know his true opinion.

In contrast, Brashen spoke clearly. Did he know Paragon would hear every word? 'I disagree, Lavoy. Yes, I do trust him with my life. As I have every day since we started the voyage. Some friendships go deeper than madness or common sense. Now that you've expressed your opinion of your captain's judgement and your ship's reliability, I suggest you retire to your bunk until your watch begins. I've some special duties for you tomorrow. They may prove quite tiring. Good night to you.'

For five breaths longer, Lavoy lingered there. Paragon could imagine how they would stand, teeth bared, wings slightly uplifted, long powerful necks arched for the strike. But this time the challenger turned his eyes aside, bowing his head and lowering his wings. He moved slowly away, expressing his subservience, but grudgingly. The dominant male watched him go. Did Brashen's eyes glitter and spin with triumph? Or did he know that this challenge was not settled, merely deferred?

They dropped anchor long before dawn. The rattling of the chain was the loudest noise they had made since they left the river mouth. They had eased into place in the harbour, not too close to the three other ships secured there. All was quiet aboard on the other vessels. Woe to whomever had been left on watch; surely, they'd be chastised tomorrow. Brashen had sent the crew below save for a carefully chosen anchor-watch. Then he had ordered his second mate to join him on the afterdeck.

Brashen stood at the railing and looked towards the lights of Divvytown. They glinted like yellow eyes through the fog, winking and then glittering as the fog drifted and changed. One puzzled him, a single light, brighter than the others and much, much higher. Had someone left a lantern burning at the top of a tree? That answer made no sense, so he pushed it aside. Dawn's light would likely solve that mystery. The other scattered lights did not quite match his recollection of the town, but doubtless the fog had something to do with that. Divvytown, again. The noisome little town never slept. The fog carried odd bits of distorted sound to his ears. Cheerful shouts, a snatch of drunken song, a dog barking.

Brashen yawned. He wondered if he dared to try for a few hours' sleep before dawn revealed the Paragon and his crew to Divvytown.

Bare feet padded up softly behind him. 'She's not here,' Althea whispered disappointedly. 'At least, I've seen no sign of her in the harbour . . .'

'No. I don't think Vivacia is anchored here tonight. That would have been expecting too much luck. But she was here the last time I was, and I think it likely she'll be here again. Patience.' Her turned to her. In the concealing fog, he dared to catch her hand and pull her closer. 'What were you imagining? That we'd find her here, tonight, and somehow manage to spirit her away without a fight?'

'A child's dream,' Althea admitted. Momentarily, she let her forehead rest against his shoulder. He wanted so badly to take her in his arms and hold her.

'Then call me a child, for I had the same vain hope. That something could be simple and easy for us.'

She straightened with a sigh, and moved aside from him. It made the damp night colder.

Wistfulness twined through him. 'Althea? Do you think there will ever be a time and place when things are simple and easy for us? A time when I can walk down the street with you on my arm under the light of day?'

She answered slowly. 'I've never allowed myself to look that far ahead.'

'I have,' Brashen said bluntly. 'I've thought ahead to you captaining Vivacia and me still running Paragon. That's the happiest ending we could expect from this quest. But then I ask myself, where does that leave us? When and where do we make a home for ourselves?'

'Sometimes we'd both be in port at the same time.'

He shook his head. 'That isn't enough for me. I want you all the time, always at my side.'

She spoke quietly. 'Brashen. I cannot allow myself to think

347

of that just now. I fear that all my planning for tomorrow must begin with my family ship.'

'And I fear it will always be so. That all your plans will always begin with your ship.' Abruptly he realized that he sounded like a jealous lover.

Althea seemed to feel the same. 'Brashen, must we speak of such things now? Cannot we, for now, be content with what we have, with no thoughts for tomorrow?'

'I thought I was supposed to be the one to say such things,' he replied gruffly after a moment. 'Still, I know that for now, I must be content with what I have. Stolen moments, secret kisses.' He smiled ruefully. 'When I was seventeen, I would have thought this the epitome of romance: covert passion aboard a ship. Furtive kisses on the afterdeck on a foggy night.' With a step he swept her into his arms and kissed her deeply. He had not surprised her; had she been waiting for him to do this? She held nothing back; her body fitted sweetly against his. Her easy response stirred him so deeply he groaned with longing. Reluctantly, he separated his body from hers. He found a breath. 'But I'm not a boy any more. Now this just drives me mad. I want more than this, Althea. I don't want suspense and quarrels and jealousy. I don't want sneaking about and concealing what I feel. I want the comfort of knowing you are mine, and taking pride in everyone else recognizing that as well. I want you in my bed beside me, every night, and across the table from me in the morning. I want to know that years from now, if I stand on another deck somewhere, on another night, you will still be beside me.'

She turned to look up at him incredulously. She could barely pick out his features. Was he teasing her? His voice had sounded serious. 'Brashen Trell, are you proposing marriage to me?'

'No,' he said hastily. There was a long uncomfortable silence. Then he laughed softly. 'Yes. I suppose I am. Marriage, or something very like it.'

Althea took a long breath and leaned back on the railing. 'You never cease to surprise me,' she observed shakily. 'I . . . I don't have an answer for you.'

His voice also shook, though she knew he tried for levity. 'I suppose that's all right, as I haven't really asked the question yet. But when all this is over, I shall.'

'When all this is over, I'll have an answer for you.' She made the promise, knowing she had no idea what that answer would be. Frantically, she pushed that worry to the back of her mind. Other things, she told herself, there were other, more pressing matters to deal with, even if those other matters did not make her heart shake as this had. She tried to quench her quick breathing and the yearning of her flesh.

'What happens next?' she asked, gesturing towards the muted lights.

He countered her question with another question. 'Of those on board, who do you trust most? Name me two names.'

That was effortless. 'Amber and Clef.'

His short laugh was rueful. 'And my answer the same. Who do you trust least?'

Again she did not need to pause. 'Lavoy and Artu.'

'Then they are off the list of those we take ashore. We won't take our problems with us, nor leave them unattended on the ship.'

We. She liked the sound of that. 'Who are we taking then?'

He didn't hesitate. 'Jek. Cypros and Kert. I'd like to take one or two of your former slaves, to give the impression that we're a mixed crew. You'll have to choose them.' He paused, thinking. 'I'm leaving Lop with Amber. I'll let Haff know that he is to back her if she asks him to. I'll give her the word that if there's any trouble at all, from inside or outside the ship, Lop is to row Clef ashore to find us.'

'You're expecting trouble from Lavoy?'

He made a disparaging noise. 'Not expecting. Planning for all possibilities.'

She lowered her voice. 'It can't go on like this. What are you going to do about him?'

He spoke slowly. 'Let him make the first move. And then, when it's over, I'll see what's left. Maybe I can make a serviceable deckhand out of it.'

Dawn came, a disappointment. A high yellow sun shredded the mist to wandering ghosts. The clouds blew in, covering the sun's face, and a miserable chill rain lanced down. Brashen ordered out the ship's gig. While it was made ready, he stared at Divvytown. He scarcely recognized it. The elevated light of the night before resolved itself as a watchtower. The wharves were in a new location, backed by warehouses built of fresh lumber. On the edges of the town, the shells of some burned-out structures remained, as if a spreading fire had created the rebuilt town. He doubted it had been an accident; the watchtower spoke of people determined not to be taken unawares again.

He grinned wolfishly. It would probably upset them to find a strange vessel in their harbour. He considered waiting aboard for whoever they might send out to question him, but decided against it. Bold and brash as his name he would be; he would assume a welcome and fellowship, and see where it got him.

He took a deep breath. His own grin surprised him. He should be exhausted. He'd been up most of the night, and risen again before dawn, just for the pleasure of rousting Lavoy out of bed. He'd given the mate his orders. He was to keep order aboard the ship, and not permit the crew to leave it or converse with any folk who came out to the ship. Above all, calm was to prevail. Clef and the other ship's boat were at Amber's disposal. Before Lavoy could dare to ask why, Brashen had added that she had her separate orders, and Lavoy was not to interfere with them. In the meantime, he wanted all the crew's bedding brought up on deck and aired, the sleeping areas smoked to drive out lice and other vermin, and the galley given a good scrubbing. It was work calculated to keep both mate and men busy, and they both knew it. Brashen stared Lavoy down until the first mate grudgingly acknowledged his orders. Then he had turned on his heel.

To Amber and Paragon he had given his most difficult commands. The ship was to keep still and silent, to pretend he was an ordinary wooden vessel. Amber was to help him in this ruse however she could. He trusted her to pick up the meaning between his words: let nothing upset the ship. Allow no one to provoke him.

Brashen shrugged his shoulders, trying to find more room in his jacket. He was dressed for his role in the finery of a merchant captain, clothes not worn since he had bidden Bingtown a formal farewell. He'd tied a kerchief made from his yellow shirt about his brow and left his shirt open at the throat. He didn't want to appear too staid. He wondered what Captain Ephron Vestrit would think if he could see the use his tailored blue jacket and fine white shirt were being put to. He hoped the old man would understand and wish him luck of it.

'Boat's ready, sir.' Clef grinned up at him hopefully.

'Thank you. You have your orders. See that you obey them.'

Clef rolled his eyes, but replied, 'Yes, sir,' with no trace of rebellion. He bounced along at Brashen's heels as he made his way to the ship's boat.

As their boat left the Paragon's shadow, Brashen marked three other small craft on their way out to meet him. 'To your oars,' he ordered in a low voice. 'Put your backs to it. I want us well away from Paragon before they can cut us off.' As the crew obeyed, Brashen glanced back at his ship. The figurehead, silent and stoic, had his arms crossed on his chest. Amber leaned on the railing behind him. She lifted a hand in farewell, and Brashen nodded curtly. He looked at the rowing crew. 'Remember your orders. We're friendly. Don't hesitate to spend freely the coin you've been given. No brawling. I don't want anyone getting so drunk that he can't guard his tongue. If they'll allow us the free run of the town, spread out. Ask questions. I want every bit of information about Kennit and the Vivacia that we can gather, but don't be too dogged about asking. Get them talking, then lean back and listen. Curious, not nosy. We'll meet back at the docks at nightfall.'

They were more than halfway to the docks when the three other boats surrounded him. At a sign from Brashen, his crew shipped their oars.

'State your business here!' A skinny greybeard in one of the boats commanded him. The rain had soaked his shapeless hat to his head. An ancient slave tattoo was just visible above his beard.

Brashen laughed aloud. 'My business in Divvytown? Divvytown has but one business, and I'll wager that mine is the same as yours, old man. My name is Brashen Trell, and before I state anything else, I'll know to whom I'm stating it.' He grinned at him easily. Jek lolled at her oars, smiling broadly. Althea's smile looked a bit more forced, while the others were apparently disinterested in the proceedings.

The oldster took himself very seriously. 'I'm Maystar Crup, and I'm the harbourmaster. Captain Kennit hisself appointed me, and I got the right to ask any what come here what they're about.'

'Kennit!' Brashen sat up straight. 'That's the name, sir, the name that brings me here. I've been here before, you know, aboard the *Springeve*, though that was a brief visit and I'll fault no one if they don't recall me. But the tales I heard then of Captain Kennit are what have brought me back now, me and my good ship and crew. We'd like to throw in our lots with his, so to speak. Think you that he'd see us today?'

Maystar ran a cynical eye over him. He licked his lips, revealing that most of his remaining teeth were yellow. 'He might. If he were here, which he's not. If you know about Kennit, how is it you don't know he has a liveship? You don't see no liveship in our harbour just now, do you?'

'I had heard Kennit was a man of many ships. Moreover, I'd heard the first mistake any man could make about him was to assume anything about him. Sly as a fox is he, that is what is said, and keen as an eagle's eye. But this is a chill and uncomfortable place to discuss such things. Divvytown has changed more than a bit since the last time I saw it, but surely it still has a tavern where men can talk at ease?'

'It does. When we decide a man is welcome in Divvytown.'

Brashen raised one shoulder. 'Perhaps that would be better decided over a bit of brandy. And then you can tell me if the rest of my crew would be welcomed ashore. We've been a time at sea. They've dry gullets and the coin to spend to wet them. Divvytown, they agreed, would be a fine place to divvy out our spoils.' He smiled engagingly and slapped the fat purse at his belt. The coins in it clinked against the nails and the cut-up spoon he'd padded it with. He carried enough to stand a round of drinks or two, as well as pick up some minor supplies for the ship. His picked crew had enough coin for a fine show as well. Successful pirates they were, with money to spend.

Brashen's smile was stiffening in the chill winter rain before Maystar gave him a grudging nod. 'Aye. We can talk in the tavern, I suppose. But your men . . . your crew will stay with us there, and those on the ship will stay there for the time being. We don't take kindly to strangers here in Divvytown. Not from ships that sneak in during the dark of night.'

That puzzled him, did it? Well, let the old man focus on that. 'To the tavern, then!' Brashen agreed heartily. He sat back in the stern and rode into town like a king, escorted by Divvytown's constabulary. Half a dozen curious onlookers were huddled on the dock, shoulders hunched to the cold rain. Maystar preceded Brashen up the ladder. By the time he reached the top, Maystar was already the centre of a hail of questions. Brashen shifted all attention to himself when he proclaimed, 'Gentlemen! Won't someone guide us to the tavern?' He beamed at the gathered crowd. From the corner of one eye, he noticed Jek's smiling appraisal of the men. The grins she was getting in response could not hurt his cause. As his crew joined him on the dock, the onlookers relaxed. These were not raiders, but honest freebooters like themselves.

'The tavern's this way,' Maystar told him grumpily.

Perhaps he was jealous of his importance. Brashen immediately targeted him. 'Please, lead on,' he told him. As they trailed Maystar, Brashen noticed that their following had already diminished. That suited him well. He wanted to gather information, not enthral the whole town. He noted that Althea had positioned herself to his left and one step behind him. It was good to know someone was there with a ready knife if the Divvytown folk did decide to turn on him. Cypros and Kert were right behind him. Harg and Kitl, the two tattooed ones that Althea had chosen, followed them. Jek had dropped back to the end of their group and had already struck up a conversation with a handsome young man. He caught a word or two; she was asking him if he thought they'd be given the run of the town, and if so, what entertainment he recommended for a lonely sailor on her first night in port. Brashen gripped his smile with his teeth. Well, he'd asked her to be friendly and gather information.

The interior of the tavern was dim. Most of the warmth came from body heat rather than from the blazing fire in the hearth. The smells of damp wool, sweat, smoke and cooking lingered in the air. Althea loosened her coat but didn't take it off. If they had to get out of here fast, she didn't want it left behind. She looked about her curiously.

The building was fairly new, but the walls had already begun to discolour with smoke. It had a plank floor, strewn with sand to make each night's sweeping out easier. A window at one end faced the sea. Brashen led them towards the hearth end of the open chamber. Plank tables and long benches supported a variety of eaters, drinkers and talkers. Evidently the oncoming storm kept folk in today. They were regarded with varying degrees of curiosity, but no outright animosity. Brashen just might dance through the deception without missing a step.

Brashen clapped a friendly hand on Maystar's shoulder as they seated themselves at the table, and before he could say a word, bellowed out an order for brandy for the harbourmaster and himself, and ale all round for his crew. A bottle was swiftly brought and opened, and two clay noggins set out. As the tavern boy began to load a tray with foaming mugs, Brashen turned to Maystar. 'Well, much has changed in Divvytown. New buildings and a welcoming party for my ship are the least of it. I've never seen the harbour so deserted. Tell me. What has befallen the place since last I was here?'

For an instant, the old man looked puzzled. Althea wondered if he even remembered that he was supposed to be the one asking the questions. But Brashen had pegged his garrulous nature well. He probably didn't often get the chance to hold forth as an expert for so long. Brashen became the most attentive and flattering of audiences as Maystar told in lurid detail of the slaver's raid that had changed forever not just the layout but the very nature of Divvytown. As he spoke on, at great length, Althea began to grasp that this Kennit was no ordinary pirate. Maystar spoke of him with admiration and pride. Others added their own stories of things Kennit had said, or done, or caused to be done. One of the speakers was a man of obvious learning. The tattoo on his cheek wrinkled as he scowlingly recounted his days below deck in a slaveship before Kennit had freed him. They spoke of the man as if they were telling hero-tales, Althea realized uneasily. The stories made her grudgingly admire the pirate, even as they chilled her heart. A man like that, bold and sage and noble, would not easily give up a ship like Vivacia. And if half the tales told of him were true, perhaps the ship had given her heart to him. Then what?

Althea fought to keep the smile on her face and to nod to Maystar's tales as she pondered it. She had been thinking of Vivacia as a stolen family treasure, or as a kidnapped child. What if she was more like a headstrong girl who had eloped with the love of her life? The others were all laughing at some witticism. Althea chuckled dutifully. Did she have the right to take Vivacia away from Kennit, if the ship had truly bonded to him? What was her duty, to her family, to the liveship?

Brashen leaned over to reach the brandy bottle. It was a pretence, to bring his leg into contact with hers. She felt the steady warm pressure of his knee against hers, and realized that he saw her dilemma. His brief glance spoke volumes. Worry later. Pay attention now, and later they would consider all the implications of what they had heard. She finished her mug of ale and held it aloft for a refill. Her eyes met those of the stranger across the table. He was watching her intently; Althea hoped her earlier thoughtfulness had not made him too curious. At the far end of the table, Jek was engaged in arm wrestling with the man she had targeted earlier. Althea judged that she was letting him win. The man across the table followed her gaze, and then his eyes came back to hers. Merriment danced in them. He was a comely man, his looks spoiled only by a trail of tattoos across his cheek. In a lull in Maystar's explanations, she asked him, 'Why is the harbour so empty? I saw but three ships where several dozen could easily anchor.'

His eyes lit at her question, and he grinned more broadly. He leaned across the table to speak more confidentially. 'You're new to this trade, then,' he told her. 'Don't you know that this is the harvest season in the Pirate Isles? All the ships are out reaping our winter livelihood. The weather is our ally, for a ship from Jamaillia may have been running three days in a storm, its crew weary and careless, when we step out from our doorsteps to stop it. We let winter do our harrying for us. This time of year, the cargoes are fatter, for the fruits of the harvest are now in transit.' His grin faded as he added, 'It is also the worst time of year for those taken by slaveships. The weather is rough, and the seas run cold. The poor bastards are chained below in damp holds, in irons so cold they bite the flesh from your bones. This time of year, slaveships are often little more than floating cemeteries.' He grinned again, fierceness lighting his face now. 'But there is sport this year, as well. The Inside Passage swarms with Chalcedean galleys. They hoist a flag and proclaim they are the Satrap's own, but it is all a sham to pick off the fattest hogs for themselves. They think themselves so sly. Captain Brig, Kennit's own man, has taught us the game of it. Let the galleys prey and fight and glut themselves with wealth. When their ships ride heavy, the harvest is ripe for gathering. We go in, and in one battle, we harvest the cream of many ships they've taken.'

He sat back on the bench, laughing aloud at Althea's incredulous look, then seized his mug and banged it on the table to attract the serving boy's attention. After the boy brought him a fresh mug, he asked, 'How came you to this life?'

'By as crooked a road as your own, I'll wager,' she returned. She cocked her head and looked at him curiously. 'That's not Jamaillia I hear in your accent.'

The ruse worked. He launched into his life history. Indeed, a convoluted path had brought him to Divvytown and piracy. There was tragedy in his tale, as well as pathos, and he told it well. Unwillingly, she began to like him. He told of the raid that ended his parents' lives and of a sister vanished forever. Carried off from his family's sheep farm in some little seacoast town far to the north, he passed through a succession of Chalcedean masters, some cruel, others merely callous, before he found himself on a ship southbound, sent off with half a dozen other slaves as a wedding gift. Kennit had stopped the ship.

And there it was again. His story challenged not just her idea of who and what Kennit was, but her notion of what slavery meant and who became slaves. Pirates were not what she had expected them to be. The greedy immoral cutthroats she had heard tales of were suddenly men pushed to the edge, clawing their way out of slavery, stealing back a portion of what had been stolen from them.

He told her other things that greatly surprised her. Part of the shock was his casual assumption that all knew these things were so. He spoke of the carrier pigeons that ferried news between the exiles in the Pirate Isle settlements and their kin in Jamaillia City. He spoke of the legitimate trading ships from Jamaillia and even Bingtown that regularly made furtive stops in the Pirate Isles. The latest gossip of Jamaillia City and even Bingtown was common knowledge in Divvytown. The news he passed on seemed far-fetched to Althea. An uprising in Bingtown had burned half the town. In retaliation, the Bingtown Traders had taken the visiting Satrap hostage. New Traders had conveyed that word to Jamaillia City, where those loyal to the Satrap were raising a fleet of warships to teach the rebellious province proper humility. There would be rich pickings in the wake of battle between Bingtown and Jamaillia. The pirates were already anticipating Jamaillian ships fat with Bingtown and Rain Wild goods. Discord between the two cities could only be good for the Pirate Isles. Althea hung on his every word, trapped between horror and fascination. Could any of this be true? If it was, what did it mean for her family and home? Even if she accepted that time and distance had fertilized the rumours, it boded ill for all she held dear. Meanwhile, the pirate waxed large in his telling of these tales, flattered and encouraged by her rapt attention. He gloated that when Kennit returned and heard these tidings, he would know that his time was truly come. In the midst of his neighbours' discord, he could seize power. He had often told them that when the time was right, he planned to control all trade through the Pirate Isles. Surely, that time was soon.

A sudden gust of wind hit the tavern's window, rattling it and making her jump. It made a space in the conversation. 'This Kennit sounds to me like a man worth meeting. Is he returning to Divvytown soon?'

The young man shrugged. 'When his holds are full he'll return. He'll bring us word from the Others' Island as well; he has taken his priest there for the Others to augur his destiny. But no doubt Kennit will pirate his way back. Kennit sails when and where he will, but he never passes up prey.' He cocked his head. 'I understand your interest in him. There is no woman in Divvytown who does not sigh at his name. He is a man to put the rest of us into the shade. But you should know that he has a woman. Etta is her name and her tongue is as sharp as her knife. Some say that in Etta, Kennit has found the missing half of his soul. All men should be so fortunate.' He leaned closer, eyes warm, and spoke quietly. 'Kennit has a woman, and is content with her. But I do not.'

Brashen stretched, rolling his shoulders and spreading his arms. When he rocked forwards, his left hand rested on Althea's shoulder. He inclined very slightly towards the other man, and gently confided. 'What a pity. I do.' He smiled before he turned back to Maystar's conversation, but left his arm across Althea's shoulders. She tried for a disarming smile and shrugged her free shoulder.

'No offence meant,' the man said a bit stiffly.

'None taken,' she assured him. A warm flush rose to her face when, down the table, Jek caught her eye and dropped her a slow congratulatory wink. Damn Brashen! Had he completely forgotten that they were trying to keep this a secret? Yet, she could not deny that she took keen pleasure in the weight of his arm across her shoulders. Was this what he had been speaking of, the comfort of publicly claiming one another?

Once they returned to the ship, they would both have to disavow this as a sham, as part of their overall ploy to gain information. But for now ... She relaxed into him, and felt the solid warmth of his body, his hip against hers. He shifted slightly to accommodate her.

The pirate drained off his beer. He set the mug down with a thump. 'Well, Maystar, I see little threat from these folk. Noon's well past now, and I've still a day's work to do.'

Maystar, in the midst of a long-winded tale, dismissed him with a wave. The man gave Althea a farewell nod, rather curt, and left. With his departure, several others also made their excuses and left. Brashen gave her shoulder a slight squeeze. Well done. They'd established they were no risk to Divvytown.

Rain still streamed down the tavern window. The uniform greyness of the day had disguised the passage of time. Brashen patiently heard Maystar's tale out to the end, and then made another show of stretching. 'Well, I could listen to you all day; it's a pleasure to hear a man who can properly spin a yarn. Unfortunately, that won't fill my water barrels. I'd best put some of my crew to that, but I've noticed that the old water dock is gone completely. Where do ships take on water now? And I've promised the crew a bit of fresh meat if there's any to be had. Be kind to a stranger, and steer me to an honest butcher.'

But Brashen was not rid of Maystar that easily. The garrulous harbourmaster told him where to take on water, but then went on to discuss at great length the relative merits of the two butchers in Divvytown. Brashen interrupted the man briefly, to put Jek in charge of the others. They could take their shore time now, but he warned them that he expected the ship's casks to be filled before noon tomorrow. 'Be back at the docks by nightfall. The second's coming with me.'

When a boy came running to tell Maystar that his pigs were loose again, the old man hurried off, uttering oaths and threats against the hapless swine. Brashen and Jek exchanged a look. She stood up, stepping over the bench she'd been seated on. 'Care to show me where we can fill our ship's casks?' she asked the man she'd been talking with, and he agreed readily. Without further ado, the crew dispersed.

Outside the tavern, the rain was falling determinedly, driven by a relentless wind. The streets were mud, but they ran straight. Brashen and Althea walked in silent companionship down a wooden walkway; a ditch beneath it rushed with rainwater draining from the street down to the harbour. Few of the structures boasted glass windows and most were tightly shuttered today against the downpour. The town had not the elegance or beauty of Bingtown, but it shared Bingtown's purpose. Althea could almost smell the commerce here. For a town burnt to the ground not so long ago, it had recovered well. They passed another tavern, this one built of raw timbers, and heard within it a minstrel singing with a harp. Since they had anchored, another ship had come into the lagoon and tied up at the pier. An ant line of men with barrows was unloading the cargo from the ship to a warehouse. Divvytown was a prosperous lively trade port; folk everywhere thanked Kennit for that.

The people hurrying along the walkway to escape the rain wore an amazing variety of garbs. Some of the languages she overheard she did not even recognize. Many faces wore tattoos, not just on their faces, but on arms, calves and hands. Not all face tattoos were slave marks: some had decorated themselves with fanciful designs.

'It's a declaration,' Brashen explained quietly. 'Many bear tattoos they cannot erase. So they obscure them with others. They dim the past with a brighter future.'

'Odd,' she muttered quietly.

'No,' he asserted. She turned in surprise at the vehemence in his voice. More quietly, he went on, 'I understand the impulse. You don't know how I've fought, Althea, to try to make folk see the man I am instead of the wild boy I was. If a thousand needle pricks in my face would obscure my past, I'd endure it.'

'Divvytown is a part of your past.' There was no accusation in her voice.

He looked around the busy little port as if seeing another place and time. 'It was. It is. I was last here on the *Springeve*, and that was none too honest an operation. But years ago, also, I was here. I had only a few voyages under my belt when pirates took the ship I was on. They gave me a choice. Join them or die. I joined.' He pushed his wet hair back and met her eyes. 'No apologies for that.'

'None are needed,' she replied. The rain on his face, the drops glistening in his hair, his dark eyes and the simple nearness of him suddenly overwhelmed her. Something of her rush of emotion must have shown on her face, for his eyes widened. Heedless of who might see, she seized his wet hand. 'I can't explain it,' she laughed up at him. For an instant, just looking at him was all she needed in the world.

He squeezed her hand. 'Come on. Let's buy some stuff and talk to people. We do have a reason to be here.'

'I wish we didn't. You know, I like this town and I like these people. In spite of every reason that I shouldn't, I do. I wish we could just be here, on our own like this. I wish this were our real life. Almost, I feel like I belong here. I'll bet Bingtown was like this, a hundred years ago. The rawness, the energy, the acceptance of folk for who they are; it draws me like a candle draws a moth. Sa forgive me, Brashen, but I wish I could kick over every responsibility to my name and just be a pirate.'

He looked at her in astonished silence. Then he grinned. 'Be careful what you wish for,' he cautioned her.

It was a strange afternoon. The role she played felt more natural than reality. They bought oil for the ship's lanterns and arranged to have it sent down to the dock. At another merchant's, Althea selected herbs and potents to restock

Paragon's medicine chest. Impulsively, Brashen tugged her inside a dry goods store and bought her a brightly coloured scarf. She bound her hair back with it, and he added hoop earrings embellished with jade and garnet beads. 'You have to look the part,' he muttered in her ear as he fastened the catch of a necklace.

In the clouded mirror the shopkeeper offered, she caught a glimpse of a different Althea, a side of herself she had never permitted into the daylight. Behind her, Brashen bent to kiss the side of her neck. When he glanced up, their eyes met in the mirror. Time rocked around her, and she saw the wild, runaway Bingtown boy and the wilful virago that had scandalized her mother. A likely pair; piracy and adventure had always been their destiny. Her heart beat faster. Her only regret for this moment was that it was a sham. She leaned back against him to admire the glittering necklace on her throat. They watched themselves in the mirror as she turned her head and kissed him.

At each place they went, one or the other would turn the conversation to Kennit or his liveship. They gathered nuggets of information about him, both useful and trivial. Like legends, each teller added personal embellishments to their stories of Kennit. His boy-priest had cut off his mangled leg, and Kennit had endured it without making a sound. No, he had laughed aloud in the face of his pain, and bedded his woman scarce an hour later. No, it was the boy's doing: the pirate-king's prophet had prayed and Sa himself had simply healed Kennit's stump. He was beloved of Sa; all knew that. When evil men had tried to rape Kennit's woman, right here in Divvytown, the god had protected her until Kennit appeared to slay a dozen men single-handedly and carry her off from her imprisonment. Etta had lived in a whorehouse, but kept herself only for Kennit. It was a love story to make the most hardened cutthroat weep.

In late afternoon, they stopped to buy fish chowder and fresh baked bread. There they first heard how the boy-priest had stood his ground between Kennit and most of Divvytown, and prophesied that Kennit would someday be their king. Those who had doubted the boy's words had fallen to his flashing blade. Althea's astonishment must have flattered the fish vendor, for he told the tale thrice more, with more details each time. At the last telling, the man added, 'And well the poor lad knew about slavery, for his own father had made him a slave, yes and tattooed his own ship's likeness onto the boy's face. I've heard it said that when Kennit freed the liveship and the boy, he won both their hearts at once.'

Althea found herself speechless. Wintrow? Kyle had done that to Wintrow, his own son, her nephew?

Brashen choked slightly on his chowder, but managed to ask, 'And what fate did Kennit mete out to so cruel a father?'

The man shrugged callously. 'What he deserved, no doubt. Over the side to the serpents with the rest. So he does with the full crew of every slaver he takes.' He raised an eyebrow at Brashen. 'I thought everyone knew that.'

'But not the boy?' Althea asked softly.

'The boy weren't crew. I told you. He was a slave on the ship.'

'Ah.' She looked at Brashen. 'That would make sense.' The ship turning on Kyle and accepting Kennit made sense now. The pirate had rescued and protected Wintrow. Of course, the ship would be loyal to Kennit now.

So. Where did that leave her? For one treacherous instant, she wondered if she were free. If Vivacia were happy with Wintrow aboard her, if she was content with Kennit and her life of piracy, did Althea have the right to 'rescue' her from it? Could she just go home now and tell her mother and sister that she had failed, that she had never found their family ship? For an instant, she teetered on a wilder decision. Did she, really, have to go home at all? Could not she and Brashen and Paragon simply go on as they had begun? Then she thought of Vivacia, quickening under her hands as she slipped the final peg into the figurehead, the peg her father had filled with his anma as he died. That was hers. Not Wintrow's, certainly not Kennit's. Vivacia was her ship, in a way no one else could claim. If the earlier gossip she had heard was true at all, if Bingtown were in some sort of upheaval, then her family needed their liveship more than ever. Althea would reclaim her. The ship would learn to love her again, Wintrow would be reunited with his family. She found she blamed Kyle more than Kennit for the deaths of Vivacia's crewmen. Loyalty to her family had kept those men aboard Vivacia; Kyle's betrayal of her father's ethics had killed them. She could not mourn Kyle at all; he had caused her and her family too much pain. The only sympathy she felt was for Keffria. Better she mourn her husband's death Althea thought grimly, than to mourn a long life with him.

Time had become a slippery creature that writhed in Paragon's grip. Did he rest at anchor in Divvytown's harbour, or did his outstretched wings send him sliding aloft on an updraught? Did he wait for young Kennit to return, desperately hoping the boy would be unhurt this time, or did he expect Althea and Brashen to return and lead him to his vengeance? The placid motion of the lagoon water, the dwindling patter of the evening rain, the smells and sounds of Divvytown, the guarded quiet of his crew all plunged him into a state of suspension almost like sleep.

Deep in his hold, in the darkness, where the curve of the bow made a cramped space beneath the deck, was the blood place. It was too small for a man to stand or even creep, but a small, battered boy could shelter there, rolled in a tight ball while his blood dripped onto Paragon's wizardwood, and they shared their misery. There Kennit could brace himself and snatch briefly at sleep, knowing no one could come upon him unaware. Whenever Igrot began to bellow for him, Paragon would wake him. Quick as a rabbit, he would pop out of his hiding place and present himself, choosing to leave his sanctuary and face Igrot rather than risk the searching crew discovering his refuge. Sometimes Kennit slept there. He would press his small hands against the great wizardwood beams that ran the length of the ship, and Paragon would watch over him while sharing his dreams.

And his nightmares.

During those times, Paragon had discovered his unique ability. He could take away the pain and the nightmares and even the bad memories. Not completely, of course. To take all the memory away would have left the boy a fool. But he could absorb the pain just as he absorbed the blood from his beatings. He could dim the agony and soften the edges of Kennit's recall. All that he could do for the boy. It demanded that he keep for himself all he took away from Kennit. The sharp humiliation and indignity, the stabbing pain and stunned bewilderment and the scorching hatred all became Paragon's, to keep hidden forever deep inside him. To Kennit he left only his icy cold resolve that he would escape, that he would leave it all behind and that someday his own exploits would forever blot from the memory of the world all trace of Igrot. Someday, Kennit resolved, he would restore all that Igrot had broken and destroyed. He would make it as if the evil old pirate had never been. No one would even recall his name. Everything Igrot had ever dirtied would be hidden away or silenced.

Even Kennit's family liveship.

That was how it was supposed to have been.

The admission disturbed ancient pain, shifting it like unsecured cargo pounding him during a storm. The depth of his failure overwhelmed him. He had betrayed his family, he had betrayed the last true-hearted member of his blood. He had tried to be loyal, he had tried to stay dead, but then the serpents had come, prodding and nosing at him, speaking to him without words, confusing him as to who he was and where his loyalties should lie. They had frightened him, and in his fear he had forgotten his promises, forgotten his duty, forgotten everything except his need for his family to comfort and reassure him. He had gone home. Slowly, through the seasons, he had drifted, following friendly currents, until he had returned, a derelict, to the shores of Bingtown.

And all that befell him there was only just punishment for his faithlessness. How could he feel anger with Kennit? Had not Paragon betrayed him first? A deep groan broke loose inside Paragon. He gripped his stillness and his silence like a shield.

The light tread of running feet on his deck. Two slender hands on his railing. 'Paragon? What is the matter?'

He could not tell her. She would not understand, and to speak would only break his promise more thoroughly than it was already broken. He bowed his face into his hands and sobbed, his shoulders shaking and his hands trembling.

'There, I told you, didn't I? It's him.' The voices came from below. Someone was down there on the water near the bow, staring up at him. Staring and jeering and mocking. Soon they would begin to throw things. Dead fish and rotten fruit.

'You down there, stand clear of our ship!' Amber warned them in a stern voice. 'Take your gig away from here.'

They paid no attention. 'If he was Igrot's ship, then where is Igrot's star?' another voice demanded. 'He put that star on everything that belonged to him.'

The long-ago horror of the star being cut into his chest was eclipsed by the memory of a thousand inky needle-pricks jabbing the same emblem into his hip. He began to tremble. Every plank in his body shuddered. The calm waters of the lagoon shivered against him.

'Paragon. Steady, steady. It will be all right. Say nothing.' Amber spoke swiftly, trying to calm him, but her words could not take away the ancient sting.

'Star or not, I'm right. I know I am.' The man in the boat below sounded very smug. 'The chopped face is a dead giveaway. Moreover, it's a liveship, same as I've always heard the tales say. Hey! Hey, ship! You were Igrot's ship, weren't you?'

The insult of that vile lie was too much to bear. Too often had it been flung at him, too many times he had been forced to mouth it for the boy's sake. Never again. Never!

'NO!' He roared the word. 'Not I!' He snatched at the air in front of him, hoping that his tormentors were within reach. 'I was never Igrot's ship! Never! Never! Never!' He shouted the word until it rang in his own ears, drowning out every other lie. Below and above and within him, he heard confused shouts. Bare feet thundered on his decks but he didn't care any more. 'Never! Never! Never!'

He barked the word out, over and over, until he could think of nothing else. If he never stopped saying it, then they could never ask him anything again. If they didn't ask, he couldn't tell. He could at least be that true to his word and his family.

They meandered down the street in easy companionship. The rain had eased and a few stars were starting to show in the deep blue edge of the sky. The taverns were setting their lanterns out. Candlelight glowed behind the shuttered windows of small homes. Brashen's arm was across her shoulders, and Althea's was about his waist. Their day had gone well. Divvytown seemed to have accepted them at their word. If the information they had gathered was confusing, it still confirmed one thing. Kennit would return to Divvytown. Soon.

Establishing that had required several rounds of drink at the final tavern. They were now making their way back to the ship's boat. They had not yet decided whether to slip quietly out of Divvytown tomorrow, or to stay on, perhaps even await Kennit's return. The chance of ransoming Vivacia seemed small; deceit seemed a likelier tack. There were too many possible courses of action. Time to go back to the ship and consider them all.

Foot traffic in the town dwindled as folk sought shelter for the night. As they wended their way down the wooden boardwalk, a couple ahead of them turned into the door of a small house and shut the door firmly behind them. A few moments later, dim candlelight shone from within.

'I wish we were they,' Althea observed wistfully.

Brashen's stride checked, then slowed. He pulled her around to face him and offered quietly, 'I could find us a room somewhere.'

She shook her head regretfully. 'The crew is waiting down at the boat. We told them to be there by nightfall. If we're late, they'll assume something has gone wrong.'

'Let them wait.' He bent his head and kissed her hungrily. In the chill night, his mouth was tauntingly warm. She made a small frustrated sound. 'Come here,' he said gruffly. He stepped off the boardwalk into the thick dark of the alley and drew her after him. In the deep shadows, he pressed her back up against a wall and kissed her more leisurely. His hands wandered down her back to her hips. With abrupt ease, he lifted her. When his body pressed hers to the wall, she could feel the jut of his desire. 'Here?' he asked her thickly.

She wanted him but this was too dangerous. 'Perhaps if I were wearing a skirt. But I'm not.' She pushed gently away from him and he let her down, but kept her pinned against the wall. She did not struggle. His kiss and his touch were more intoxicating than the brandy they had shared. His mouth tasted of liquor and lust.

He broke the kiss suddenly, lifting his head like a stag at bay. 'What's that?'

It was like waking from a dream. 'What's what?' She felt dazed.

'That shouting. Do you hear it? From the harbour.'

The faint cries came to her ears. She could not make out

the word, but with icy certainty, she knew the voice. 'Paragon.' She stuffed her shirt back into her waistband. 'Let's go.'

Side by side, they thundered down the boardwalk. There was no sense going quietly. Shouting was not unusual in a town like Divvytown, but eventually it would attract attention. Paragon was crying the same word over and over again.

They were nearly at the docks when Clef charged up to them. 'Yer needed on ther ship, Cap'n. Paragon's gone mad.' He panted the words breathlessly and then they were all running together. As they clattered out onto the docks, Althea saw the crew of the ship's gig waiting for them, as well as Lop. Jek had her knife out. 'I've got the stuff you bought loaded, but we're missing two men,' she announced. The two former slaves were not there. Althea knew that no amount of waiting would change that.

'Cast off,' she ordered them tersely. 'Get back to the ship, all of you. We're leaving Divvytown tonight.'

There was a moment of shock, and Althea cursed herself for a drunken fool. Then Brashen demanded, 'Didn't you hear the mate's order? Do I have to tell you myself?'

They scrambled down the ladder into the waiting boats. Paragon's voice carried clearly over the water. 'Never, never, never!' his deep tones belled dolorously. Althea made out the shapes of two small boats near his bow. He'd attracted an audience already. Doubtless, the word would burn through Divvytown that the newcomers had arrived in a liveship. What would that convey to the pirate city?

It seemed to take all night to reach the ship. As they gained the deck, a scowling Lavoy met them. 'I told you this was insane!' he rebuked Brashen. 'The damn ship has gone crazy, and your fool carpenter did nothing to calm him. Those louts in the boat below were bellowing that he was Igrot's ship. Is that true?'

'Hoist anchor and our sails spread, now!' Brashen replied. 'Use the boats to turn us about. We're leaving Divvytown.'

'Tonight?' Lavoy was outraged. 'In the dark on a lunatic ship?'

'Can you obey an order?' Brashen snarled at him.

'Maybe if it made any sense!' Lavoy retorted.

Brashen reached out and seized the mate by the throat. He dragged him close and snarled into his face. 'Make sense of this. If you won't obey my orders, I'll kill you now. Last chance. I've had it with your insolence.'

For an instant, the tableau held, Brashen's hand on Lavoy's throat, and Lavoy staring up at him. Brashen had height and reach over Lavoy, but the mate had wider shoulders and a deeper chest. Althea held her breath. Then Lavoy lowered his eyes.

Brashen released his throat. 'Get to your task.' He turned away.

Like a snake striking, Lavoy pulled his knife and sank it into Brashen's back. 'That for you!' he roared.

Althea leapt to Brashen as he staggered forwards, eyes clenched against the pain. In two strides, Lavoy reached the railing. 'Stop him! He'll betray us!' Althea ordered. Several crewmen sprang after him. She thought they would seize him. From the corner of her eye, she saw Lavoy leap. 'Damn!' she cried, and turned. To her horror, the other men who had sprung towards him were following him over the side. Not just the Tattooed ones from Bingtown, but other crewmen as well, leaping over the railing after Lavoy as if they were fish heading up a spawning river. She heard the splash of swimmers below. Lavoy would betray them in Divvytown. The loyal crew gaped after them.

'Let them go,' Brashen commanded hoarsely. 'We need to get out of here and we're better off without them.' He let go of her and stood straight.

Incredulously, she watched Brashen reach over his shoulder. With a tug, he freed Lavoy's knife from his back. He flung it down with an oath.

'How bad is it?' Althea demanded.

'Forget it for now. It didn't go deep. Get the crew moving while I deal with Paragon.'

Without waiting for her reply, he hastened to the foredeck. Althea was left gaping after him. She caught her breath and began barking out orders to get the ship under way. Up on the foredeck, she heard Brashen give one of his own. 'Ship! Shut your mouth! That's an order.'

Astonishingly, Paragon obeyed. He answered both his helm and the tug of the small boats as the men below rowed frantically to bring the ship about. The sluggish flow of the lagoon was with them, as was the prevailing wind. As Althea sprang to her own tasks, she prayed that Paragon would keep to the channel and take them safely down the narrow river. Like an opening blossom, their canvas bloomed in the night wind. They fled Divvytown.

FIFTEEN

Serpent Ship

THE WHITE SERPENT fluctuated between sullen and sarcastic with no relief for anyone. He refused to give his name. Names, he said, no longer mattered to dying worms. When Tellur pressed him for a name to call him by, the white finally snapped, 'Carrion. Carrion is the only name I need, and soon enough, it will be your name as well. We are dead creatures that move still, rotted flesh that has not yet been stilled. Call me Carrion, and I will call each of you Corpse.'

True to his word, that was how he referred to them. It was a constant irritant. Sessurea wished they had never encountered the creature, let alone wrung the story of She Who Remembers from him.

No one trusted him. He stole food from the jaws of those who had captured it. With a sudden bite or a slash of his tail, he would startle the other serpents into dropping prey, and then seize it for himself. He let fish-kill toxin dribble from his mane as he slept. It was even more annoying because he slept in the middle of the tangle. Maulkin gripped him as they slept, lest he try to escape in the night.

By day, they had to follow him. Again, he found every conceivable way to irritate the rest of the tangle. He either dawdled, pausing often to taste the current and wonder aloud if he knew where he was going, or he set a demanding pace and ignored all protests and requests for rest. Maulkin always shadowed him, but it took a toll on him. Seldom a tide passed that Carrion did not provoke Maulkin to kill him. He struck insulting poses, he leaked venom constantly and showed no deference to Maulkin. If the decision had been Shreever's, she would have throttled the white serpent days ago, but Maulkin held back the full force of his fury, even when the miserable creature taunted him and mocked his dream, though he lashed the water furiously and his golden false-eyes gleamed like the sun above the sea. He would not tempt the white with threats; the creature longed too strongly for his own death.

His cruellest torment was that he held back the memories that She Who Remembers had given him. When the tangle settled for the night, anchoring themselves together, they talked before they slept. Bits of memories from their dragon heritage were brought forth and shared. Often what one lacked, another supplied, and so their memories were knitted up like threadbare tapestries. Sometimes the mere naming of a name could bring forth a cascade of forgotten fragments from another serpent. But Carrion always held back, smirking knowingly as the others groped through their weary thoughts. Always, it seemed, he could have enlightened them if he chose to. For that, Shreever longed to kill him.

The talk that night had strayed to the lands of the far south. Some recalled a great dry place, void of any substantial game. 'It took days to fly over it,' Tellur asserted. 'And I seem to recall that when one settled, the sands were so hot that you could not stand upon it. You had to . . . to . . .'

'Burrow!' Another serpent broke in excitedly. 'How I hated the grit under my claws and in the folds of my hide. But it was the only way. To land gently was wrong. You had to slide in, so that right away you broke the hot crust of the sand and found the cooler layer. Not that the cooler layer was much cooler!'

That sensory clue, grit in the fold of her skin, seized

Shreever's imagination. She not only felt the hot sand, but also tasted the peculiar bitterness of the region. She worked her jaws, recalling it. 'Shut your nostrils against the dust!' she warned them triumphantly.

Another serpent trumpeted excitedly. 'But it was worth it. Because once you flew beyond the reaches of the blue sand, there was . . . there was . . .'

Nothing. Shreever keenly recalled the anticipation. Once the sands changed from gold to blue, you were nearly there, and beyond the blue sand was something worth the long, foodless flight, something worth risking the dangers of sandstorms to reach. Why could they remember the heat and the irritation of grit, but not the goal of the flight?

'Wait! Wait!' the white exclaimed in sudden excitement. 'I know what it was! Beyond the blue sand was, oh, it was so beautiful, so wonderful, so joyous a thing to find! It was –' He swivelled his head, his scarlet eyes swirling to be sure of every serpent's attention. 'Dung!' he declared happily. 'Great mounds of fresh, brown stinking dung! And then we declared ourselves the Lords of the Four Realms. Lords of the Earth, the Sea, the Sky and the Dung! Oh, and how we wallowed in our greatness, celebrating all we had conquered and claimed! The memory stands so clear and shining! Tell me, Sessurea Corpse, does not this of all memories stand out most clearly, most –'

It was too much. Sessurea's orange mane lifted and he lunged at the white, jaws wide. Almost lazily, Maulkin rolled his body to come between them. Sessurea was forced aside. He would never challenge Maulkin, but he roared his frustration at the surrounding serpents, who gave him space for his wrath. His green eyes spun with fury, as he demanded, 'Why must we tolerate this ill-begotten slime? He mocks our dreams and us. How can we believe that he leads us truly to She Who Remembers?'

'Because he does,' Maulkin replied. He opened his jaws,

taking in seawater and pumping it out through his gills. 'Taste, Sessurea. Your senses have become dull with discouragement, but taste, now and tell me what you scent.'

The great blue serpent obeyed. Shreever imitated him, as did most of the others. For a time, she scented only their own tangle, tasted only Carrion's ever-dribbling toxins. Then it wafted to her, unmistakable for anything else. The taste of one who carried memories locked in her flesh floated faint in the water. Shreever worked her gills frantically, trying for more of the elusive flavour. It faded, but then a stronger drift reached her.

Tellur, the slender green minstrel, shot like an arrow towards the Lack. As he thrust his head into the night air, he bugled a questioning call. All around Shreever, the tangle rose faster than bubbles, to bob up around Tellur. Their voices were added to his, a seeking chorus. Suddenly Maulkin shot out of the water in their midst, leaping so high that nearly a third of his length arced above the water before he dived again.

'Silence!' he commanded when next he surfaced. 'Listen!'

The heads and arched necks of the tangle rode on the breast of the waves. Above them, the cold moon gleamed and the stars shone white as anemones. All manes stood out full and taut. The surface of the sea was transformed into a meadow of night-blooming flowers. For a breath, all they heard were the sounds of wind and water.

Then, pure as light and sweet as flesh, a voice rose in the distance. 'Come,' she sang, 'come to me and I will give you knowledge of yourselves. Come to She Who Remembers, and your past will be yours, and with it, all your futures. Come. Come.'

Tellur trumpeted an eager response, but 'Hush!' Maulkin bade him sternly. 'What is that?'

For a second voice had lifted in song. The words were oddly turned, the notes shortened, as if the serpent who sang had no depth to its voice. But whoever she was, she echoed the call of She Who Remembers. 'Come, come to me. Your past and your future await you. Come, I will guide you, I will protect you. Obey me and I shall see you safely home. Once more you shall rise, once more you shall fly.'

All heads, every spinning eye turned to Maulkin. His mane stood out stiff about his throat and venom welled and dripped from every spine. 'We go!' he trumpeted, but softly, to only his tangle, not to the siren voices. 'We go, but we go with caution. Something is odd here, and we have been deceived before. Come. Follow me.'

Then he threw back his great head and opened his jaws wide to the night. His golden false-eyes shone brighter than moon or sun. When he released the blast of his voice, the water all around him shivered at his power.

'We come!' he roared. 'We come for our memories!'

He plunged back into the Plenty. He flashed through the water, and his tangle followed him. Alone, the white held back. Shreever, still not trusting him, glanced back.

'Fools! Fools! Fools!' Carrion trumpeted wildly into the night sky. 'And I the biggest fool of all!' Then, with a wild cry, he plunged in to follow them.

She Who Remembers left the ship to greet the others. Bolt urged her to remain, saying they would welcome them together, but she could not. This was her destiny, come at last to join her. She could not put off this long-awaited consummation. She arced towards them, leaping awkwardly in attempted grace. There was a terrible conflict between her stunted body and her ancient memory of other, similar meetings. She should have been twice the size she was, powerfully muscled, a giant among serpents, armed with enough toxins to stun tangle after tangle into complete remembrance of their heritage. She thrust aside all misgivings. She would give them all she had . . . It had to be enough.

When they were close enough to taste one another's toxins, she halted. She allowed her body to sink beneath the water and finned there, awaiting them. The leader, a battered serpent that glowed with the fire of his false-eyes, came forwards to meet her fang to fang. The others fanned out around them with all heads aligned towards her body. Beneath the turbulence of the sea's waves, all hung there, as motionless as swimming creatures can be as they held themselves in even spacing and careful alignment. They were many organisms, soon to be one, united in the racial memory of their kind. She opened her jaws wide, exposing her teeth in formal greeting. She shook her mane until the toxic ruff of spikes around her throat stood out in its full glory. Every spine was erect, swelling with the toxins she would soon release. Rigorously, she controlled herself. This was not the awakening of a single serpent. This was the resurrection of an entire tangle.

'Maulkin of Maulkin's Tangle greets you, She Who Remembers.'

His great copper eyes travelled over her crooked body. His eyes spun once in what might have been dismay or sympathy, and then were stilled. He displayed his fangs to her. She clashed her teeth lightly against his. His mane stiffened in reflexive response. His tangle, attuned to his poisons by their long association, would be most vulnerable to hers in conjunction with the release of Maulkin's toxins. He was essential to this awakening. She expelled a faint wash of her venom towards his open jaws, saw him gulp it in, and watched it affect him. His eyes spun slowly, and colours washed through his mane, violets and pinks engorging his spines. She gave his body time to adjust itself. Then, almost languorously, she wrapped his long body with hers. As was fitting, he submitted to her.

She matched her body to his, feeling the slime of his skin mingle with her own. She paused, lidding her eyes as her body adjusted its acids. Then, in an ecstasy of remembering, she tangled her mane with his, stimulating both of them to release a mingled cloud of venoms. The shock of tasting a toxin not of her own secretion near stunned her.

Then the night world sharpened. She knew every serpent in his tangle as he did. She took to herself his confused memories of many migratory pilgrimages, and sorted them for him. She shared, suddenly, a lost generation's wandering. Pity sliced her soul. So few females left, and all their bodies so aged. Their souls had been trapped for decades in bodies meant for transitory use. Yet even as her hearts rang with pity, pride's triumphant trumpeting drowned it. Despite all, her race had survived. Against all obstacles, they had prevailed. Somehow, they would complete their migration, they would cast their cocoons and they would emerge as dragons. The Lords of the Three Realms would once more fill the sky.

She felt Maulkin's spirit intertwine with her own. 'Yes!' His trumpet of affirmation was her signal. She breathed her toxins into his face. He did not struggle. Rather, he plunged willingly into unconsciousness, surrendering his mind to become the repository of the memories of his kind. Her twisted tail lashed as she kept her grip upon his body. Slowly, with great effort, she began to turn them both, spinning them in a streaming circle of toxins that spread slowly to the waiting multitude. Dimly she saw the toxins reach them. The poised serpents stiffened in the grip of her spell, and then began the reflexive finning that held them in place as their minds opened to the trove of memories. She was small and crippled and tiring far too rapidly. She hoped her poison sacs held enough for them all. She stretched her jaws wide and worked the muscles that pumped the toxins from her mane. She strained, convulsively working the muscles long past the complete emptying of her sacs. Depleted she toiled on, turning herself and Maulkin, using their bodies to disperse their mingled toxins to the entranced serpents. On she laboured, and on, past instinct, consciously pushing her body to its limits.

She became aware of Maulkin speaking to her. He held her

now. She was exhausted. He moved with her, forcing water over her gills.

'Enough,' he told her, his voice gentle. 'It is enough. Rest. She Who Remembers, Maulkin's tangle is now We Who Remember. Your duty is fulfilled.'

She longed to rest, but she managed to warn them. 'I have awakened another one as well. The silver one claims our kinship. I am wary of her. Yet she alone may know the way home.'

The water boiled with serpents. In all his years at sea, Kennit had never seen such a sight. Before dawn, their trumpeting chorus awoke him. They swarmed around his liveship. They lifted immense maned heads to regard the ship curiously. Their long bodies sliced the water, cutting across Vivacia's bow and streaming in her wake. Their astonishing colours gleamed in the morning light. Their great eyes spun like pinwheels.

Kennit felt himself the target of those unblinking stares. As he stood on the foredeck and watched, Vivacia held court to these odd suitors. They rose from the water, some lifting near as tall as the figurehead to regard her. Some considered her in silence, but others trumpeted or whistled. When Vivacia sang an answer to them, the immense heads inevitably turned towards Kennit and stared. For a man who had already lost one leg to a serpent, those avaricious stares were unnerving. Nevertheless, he held his post and his smile.

Behind him, the men worked the deck and the rigging with greater than usual caution. Below them gaped the double death of water and fangs. It did not matter that the serpents were not showing any aggression towards the ship. Their roaring and cavorting were enough to intimidate anyone. Only Etta seemed to have shed her fear of the creatures. She clung to the railing, eyes wide and cheeks flushed, as she took in the spectacle of their flashing escort.

Wintrow stood behind them, arms crossed tightly on his chest. He addressed the ship. 'What do they say to you, and what do you reply?'

She glanced archly back at him. Then, as Kennit watched, the boy flinched as if jabbed. He paled suddenly, his knees folding, and staggered away from the railing. Walking uncertainly, his eyes unfocused, Wintrow left the foredeck without another word. Kennit briefly considered demanding an explanation, but decided to let it pass. He did not yet have Bolt's full measure. He would not risk offending her. The expression on the figurehead's face had never varied from pleasant. Bolt spoke, directing her words to Kennit. 'What they say does not concern humans. They speak of serpent dreams, and I assure them that I share the same. That is all. They will follow me, now, and do as I tell them. Select your prey, Captain Kennit. They will cut it out and run it down for you like a pack of wolves culling a bull from a herd. Say where we shall go, and all we encounter between here and there will fall like ripe fruit into your hands.'

She flung him the offer carelessly. Kennit tried to accept it with equanimity, but he perceived instantly what it meant. Not just ships, but towns, even cities were his to plunder. He looked at his rainbow escort, and imagined them boiling in Bingtown Bay or cavorting before the docks of Jamaillia itself. They could weave a blockade that would stop all trade. With a flotilla of serpents at his command, he could control all traffic through the Inside Passage. She was handing him mastery of the entire coast.

He saw her watching him from the corner of her eye. She knew very well what she was offering him. He stepped closer, and spoke only for her ears. 'And what does it cost me? Only "what you ask for, when you ask for it"?'

Her red lips curved in a sweet smile. 'Exactly.'

The time for hesitation was past. 'You have it,' he assured her quietly.

'I know,' she replied.

'What ails you?' Etta demanded crossly.

Wintrow looked up at her in surprise. 'Your pardon?'

'Pardon my ass!' She gestured impatiently at the gameboard on the low table between them. 'It's your move. It has been your move for as long as it has taken me to finish this buttonhole. But when I look up, there you sit, staring into the lantern. So what ails you? You cannot keep your mind on anything of late.'

That was because the whole of his mind was given over to one thing only. He could have said that, but chose to shrug. 'I suppose I feel a bit useless of late.'

She grinned wickedly. 'Of late? You were always useless, priest-boy. Why does it suddenly bother you?'

Now there was a question. Why did it bother him? Since Kennit had taken over the ship, he had had no official status. He was not the ship's boy, he was not the captain's valet, and no one had ever seriously respected his claim to own the ship. But he had had a function. Kennit had thrown him odd chores and honed his wits against him, but that had merely filled his time. Vivacia had filled his heart. A bit late to realize that, he thought sourly. A bit late to admit that his bond with the ship had defined his life and his days aboard her. She had needed him, and Kennit had used him as the bridge between them. Now neither of them required him any more. At least, the creature that wore Vivacia's body no longer needed him. Indeed, she scarcely tolerated him. His head still throbbed from her latest rebuff.

He could dimly recall his healing. Days of convalescence had followed it. He had lain in his bunk and watched the play of light on the wall of his stateroom and thought of nothing. The rapid repair of his body had drained all his physical reserves. Etta had brought him food, drink, and books he never opened. She had brought him a mirror, thinking to cheer him. He saw that the outside of his body had reconstructed itself at Kennit's command. The skin of his face purged itself of the tattoo's ink. Each day the sprawling mark his father had placed on him grew fainter, until Vivacia's image vanished from his face as if it had never been.

It was the ship's doing. He knew that. Kennit had only been her tool, so that Kennit might reap the benefit of performing yet another miracle. The message to Wintrow was that she did not need his compliance to work her will upon him. Bolt had struck him with his healing. She had not restored his missing finger. He had stopped pondering whether that task was beyond both his body and her ministration, or if she had withheld it from him. She had expunged Vivacia's image from his face, and the meaning of that was obvious.

Etta slapped the table and he jumped.

'You're doing it again,' she accused him. 'And you haven't even answered my question.'

'I don't know what to do with myself any more,' he confessed. 'The ship no longer needs me. Kennit no longer needs me. The only use he ever had for me was to act as a go-between for them. Now they are together and I am –'

'Jealous,' Etta filled in. 'And fair green with it. I hope that I was more subtle when I was in your place. For a long time, I stood where you stand now, wondering what my place was, wondering why or if Kennit needed me, hating the ship for fascinating him so.' She gave him a twisted smile of sympathy. 'You have my pity, but it won't do you any good.'

'What will?' he demanded.

'Keeping busy. Getting over it. Learning something new.' She tied a knot. 'Find something else to occupy your mind.'

'Such as?' he asked bitterly.

She bit off her thread and tugged to see if the bone button was secure. With her chin, she gestured at the neglected gameboard. 'Amusing me.'

Her smile made it a jest. The movement of her chin made the lamplight run over her sleek hair and glance off the strong bones of her cheeks. She glanced at him from under lowered lashes as she threaded her needle. Mirth glinted in her dark eyes. The corner of her mouth curved slightly. Yes, he could find something else to occupy his mind, something likely to lead to disaster. He forced his eyes back to the gameboard and made a move. 'Learn something new. Such as?'

She snorted her contempt. Her hand darted out, and with a single move demolished his defences. 'Something useful. Something you will actually put your mind to, rather than making motions while you dream elsewhere.'

He swept his playing pieces from the board. 'What can I learn aboard this ship that I have not already learned?'

'Navigation,' she suggested. 'It confounds me, but you have the numbers learned already. You could master it.' This time her eyes were serious. 'But I think you should learn what you have put off far too long. Fill the gap that you wear like an open wound. Go where your heart has always led you. You have denied yourself long enough.'

He sat very still. 'And that is?' he prompted her quietly.

'Learn yourself. Your priesthood,' she said.

His keen disappointment shocked him. He would not even consider what he had hoped she might suggest. He shook his head, and his voice was bitter as he said, 'I have left that too far behind. Sa is strong in my life, but my devotion is not what it once was. A priest must be willing to live his life for others. At one time, I thought that would be my delight. Now . . .' he let his eyes meet hers honestly. 'I have learned to want things for myself,' he said quietly.

She laughed. 'Ah, at teaching you that, Kennit would excel, I think. Yet I believe you misjudge yourself. Perhaps you have lost the intensity of your focus, Wintrow, but examine your heart. If you could have one thing, right now, what would you choose?'

He bit back the words that sprang to his lips. Etta had changed, and he had been part of her changing. The way she spoke, the way she thought, reflected the books they had shared. It was not that she had become wiser; wisdom had shone in her from the start. Now she had the words for her thoughts. She had been like a lantern flame burning behind a sooty glass. Now the glass was clear and her light shone forth. She pursed her lips in annoyance: he had taken too long to reply. He avoided her question. 'Do you remember the night when you told me that I should discover where I was in my life and go on from there? Accept the shape of my life and do my best with it?'

She lifted one eyebrow as if to deny it. His heart sank. Could something so important to him have left no mark upon her? Then she shook her head ruefully. 'You were so serious, I wanted to kick you. Such a lad. It does not seem possible you were so young such a short time ago.'

'Such a short time ago?' He laughed. 'It seems like years. I've been through so many changes since then.' He met her eyes. 'I taught you to read, and you said it changed your life. Do you know how much you have changed my life as well?'

'Well.' She leaned back and considered. 'If I hadn't taught you to use a knife, you'd be dead now. So I suppose I've changed the course of your life at least once.'

'I try to imagine going back to my monastery now. I would have to bid farewell to my ship, to Kennit, to you, to my shipmates, to all my life has become. I don't know if I could go back and sit with Berandol and meditate, or pore over my books.' He smiled regretfully. 'Or work the stained glass I once took such pride in. I would be denying all I had learned out here. I am like a little fish that ventured too far from its placid pool and has been swept into the river. I've learned to survive out here, now. I don't know if I could be content with a contemplative life any more.'

She looked at him oddly. 'I didn't mean you should return to your monastery. Only that you should start being a priest again.'

'Here? On the ship? Why?'

'Why not? You once told me that if a man is meant to be a priest, nothing can divert him from that. It will happen to him, no matter where he is. That perhaps Sa had put you here because there was something you were meant to do here. Destiny, and all that.'

She spoke his words flippantly, but beneath her tone he heard a desperate hope.

'But why?' he repeated. 'Why do you urge me to do this now?'

She turned aside from him. 'Perhaps I miss the way you used to talk. How you used to argue that there was meaning and structure to all that happened, even if we could not immediately perceive it. There was a comfort to hearing you say that, even if I couldn't completely believe it. About destiny and all.'

Her hand strayed to her breast, then pulled away. He knew what she flinched from touching. In a small bag about her neck she wore the charm from Others' Island, the figurine of a baby. She had shown it to him while he was still recovering from his 'miracle cure'. He had sensed how important it was to Etta but had not given it any serious thought since then. Obviously, she had. She considered the odd charm as an omen of some kind. Perhaps if Wintrow believed that the Others were truly soothsayers and prophets, he would share her opinion, but he didn't. Likely a trick of winds and tides carried all manner of debris to the beach, and her charm among it. As for the Others themselves, the serpent he had freed had imprinted her opinion of them on him. Abominations. Her precise meaning had not been clear, but her horror and loathing were plain. They should never have been. They were thieves of a past not their own, with no power to foretell the future. The charm Etta had found in her boot was a mere coincidence, of no more portent than the sand that had been with it.

He could not share his opinion with Etta without affronting her. Affronting her could be painful. He began carefully, 'I still believe that every creature has a unique and significant destiny.'

She leapt to it before he could approach it gently. 'It could be my destiny to bear Kennit's child; to bring into being a prince for the King of the Pirate Isles.'

'It might also be your destiny not to,' he pointed out.

Displeasure flashed across her face, replaced by impassivity. He had hurt her. 'That is what you believe, then.'

He shook his head. 'No, Etta. I have no beliefs, either way. I am simply saying that you should not lock your dreams onto a child or a man. Who loves you or who you love is not as significant as who you are. Too many folk, women and men, love the person they wish to be, as if by loving that person, or being loved by that person, they could attain the importance they long for.

'I am not Sa. I lack his almighty wisdom. But I think you are more likely to find Etta's destiny in Etta, rather than hoping Kennit will impregnate you with it.'

Anger writhed over her face. Then she sat still, anger still glinting in her eyes, but with it a careful consideration of his words. Finally, she observed gruffly, 'It's hard to take offence at your saying that I might be important for myself.' Her eyes met his squarely. 'I might consider it a compliment. Except that it's hard to believe you are sincere, when you obviously don't believe the same is true of yourself.'

She continued into his stunned silence, 'You haven't lost your belief in Sa. You've lost your belief in yourself. You speak to me of measuring myself by my significance to Kennit. But you do the same. You evaluate your purpose in terms of Vivacia or Kennit. Pick up your own life, Wintrow, and be responsible for it. Then, perhaps, you may be significant to them.'

Like a key turning in a rusty lock. That was the sensation inside him. Or perhaps like a wound that bleeds anew past a closed crust, he thought wryly. He sifted her words, searching for a flaw in her logic, for a trick in her wording. There was none. She was right. Somehow, sometime, he had abdicated responsibility for his life. His hard-won meditations, the fruit of another lifetime of studying and Berandol's guidance, had become platitudes he mouthed without applying them to himself. He suddenly recalled a callow boy telling his tutor that he dreaded the sea voyage home, because he would have to be among common men rather than thoughtful acolytes like himself. What had he said to Berandol? 'Good enough men, but not like us.' Then, he had despised the sort of life where simply getting from day to day prevented a man from ever taking stock of himself. Berandol had hinted to him then that a time out in the world might change his image of folk who laboured every day for their bread. Had it? Or had it changed his image of acolytes who spent so much time in self-examination that they never truly experienced life?

He had been plunged into the world of ships and sailing against his will. He had never truly embraced it, or accepted all it might offer him. He looked back now, and saw a pattern of resistance in all he had done. He had set his will against his father, battled Torg simply to survive, and resisted the ship's efforts to bond with him. He had allied with the slaves, but kept his guard up against them as soon as they became freed men. When Kennit came aboard, he had resolved to maintain his claim upon Vivacia despite the pirate's efforts to win her. And all the while he had simmered in self-pity. He had longed for his monastery and promised himself that at the first opportunity he would become that Wintrow again. Even after he had resolved to accept the life Sa had given him and find purpose in it, even then he had held back.

Layer upon layer of self-deceit, he now saw, layer upon layer of resistance to Sa's will. He had not embraced his own destiny. He had grudgingly accepted it, taking only what was forced upon him and welcomed only what he found acceptable, rather than encompassing all in his priesthood.

Something. Something there, an idea, an illumination trembling at the edge of his mind. A revelation waiting to unfold. He let the focus of his eyes soften, and his breathing eased into a deeper, slower rhythm.

Etta set aside her sewing. She gathered the game pieces and returned them to their box. 'I think we have finished with games for a time,' she said quietly.

He nodded. His thoughts claimed him, and he scarcely noticed when she left the room.

She Who Remembers recognized him. The two-legs Wintrow stood on the ship's deck and looked down at the serpents who gambolled alongside in the moonlight. She was surprised he had lived. When she had nudged him aboard the ship, she had intended only that he die among his own kind. So he had survived. When he set his hands on the ship's railing, She Who Remembers sensed Bolt's reaction. It was not a physical shaking, but a trembling of her being. A faint scent of fear tinged the water. Bolt feared this two-legs?

Mystified, the serpent drew closer. Bolt had begun as a dragon; that much She Who Remembers recognized. But no matter how vigorously Bolt might deny it, she was no longer a dragon nor was she a serpent. She was a hybrid, her human sensibilities blending with her dragon essence, and all encompassed in her ship form. She Who Remembers dived beneath the water, and aligned herself with the ship's silvery keel. Here she could feel most strongly the dragon's presence. Almost immediately she sensed that the ship did not wish her to be there but She Who Remembers felt no compunction about remaining. Her duty was to the tangle of serpents she had awakened. If the ship was a danger to them, she would discover it. She was only mildly surprised when Maulkin the Gold joined her there. He did not bother to hide his intentions. 'I will know more,' he told her. A slight lifting of his ruff indicated the ship they paced. 'She tells us to be patient, that she is here to protect us and guide us home. She seems to know much of what has happened in the years since dragons filled the skies, but I sense that she withholds as much she tells us. All my memories tell me that we should have entered the river in spring. Winter snaps at us now, and still she counsels us to wait. Why?'

She admired his forthrightness. He did not care that the ship knew his reservations about trusting her. She Who Remembers preferred to be more subtle. 'We must wait and discover that. For now, she has the alliance of the two-legs. She claims that when the time is right, she will use them to help us. But why, then, does she tremble at the very presence of this one?'

The ship gave no sign that she was aware of their submerged conversation. She Who Remembers tasted a subtle change in the water that flowed past. Anger, now, as well as fear. Deprived of the proper shape of her body, her frustrated flesh still attempted to manufacture the venoms of her emotions. She Who Remembers worked her poison sacs. There was little there to draw on; it took time for her body to replenish itself. Still, she gaped her jaws wide, taking in Bolt's faint venom, and then replied with her own. She adjusted herself to the ship, to be better able to perceive her.

Above them, the two-legs gripped the ship's railing. In essence, he laid hands on the dragon's own body. She Who Remembers felt the ship's shiver of reaction, and the complete transfer of her attention.

'Good evening, Vivacia.' The sound of Wintrow's voice was muted by water and distance, but his touch on the railing amplified the sense of his words. It carried through the ship's bones to She Who Remembers. *I know you* said his touch. In the naming of the name that Bolt disdained, he claimed a part of her. And justly so, She Who Remembers decided, despite the ship's resistance to him.

'Go away, Wintrow.'

'I could, but it would do no good. Do you know what I've been doing, Vivacia? I've been meditating. Reaching into myself. Do you know what I discovered?'

'Your beating heart?' With callous cruelty, the ship touched him. She Who Remembers felt the clench of the boy's hands tighten as his heart skipped in its rhythm.

'Don't,' he begged her convulsively. 'Please,' he added. Reluctantly, the ship let him be. Wintrow clung to the railing. When his breathing steadied, he said quietly, 'You *know* what I found when I looked within myself. I found you. Twined through me, flesh and soul. Ship, we are one, and we cannot deceive one another. I know you, and you know me. Neither of us are what we have claimed to be.'

'I can kill you,' the ship snarled at him.

'I know. But that would not rid you of me; if you kill me, I still remain a part of you. I believe you know that also. You seek to drive me away, ship, but I do not think I could go so far that the bond would be severed. It would only make both of us miserable.'

'I am willing to take that chance.'

'I am not,' Wintrow replied mildly. 'I propose another solution. Let us accept what we have become, and admit all parts of ourselves. If you will stop denying the humanity in you, I will accept the serpent and the dragon in myself. In our self,' he amended thoughtfully.

Silence passed with the purling water. Something slowly built inside the ship, like venom welling in a serpent's spiked mane. But when she spoke, she spilled bitterness like an abscess breaking. 'A fine time to offer this, Wintrow Vestrit. A fine time.'

She struck him down like a dragon flicking away an annoying gorecrow. The two-legs fell flat to her deck. Drops of his blood leaked from his nostrils and dripped onto her planking. Though the ship roared defiantly, her planking soaked up the red stuff and took him into herself.

SIXTEEN

Tintaglia's Bargain

REYN TOOK A deep, gasping breath of air and opened his eyes to darkness. He'd dreamed of the dragon, trapped in her coffin. The dream still had the power to make his heart thunder and his body break into a sweat. He lay still, panting and cursing the creature and the memories she had left him. He should try to go back to sleep. It would be his watch soon, and he would regret the sleep he had lost to the nightmare. He held his breath and listened to Grag's deep snore and Selden's lighter breathing. He turned restlessly, trying to find a more comfortable place in the sweaty sheets. He was grateful to have a bed to himself; many others were sharing. For the past few days, the Tenira household had been swollen with other folk so that it now encompassed a cross-section of Bingtown's population.

The fledgling alliance of Old and New Traders, slaves and Three Ships folk had nearly died hatching. The same group that had gathered at the Tenira table, with the addition of several New Trader representatives, had boldly arrived at the Restart mansion and demanded entrance. Their spies had already watched the remaining heads of the Bingtown Council enter. A number of Roed's more rabid followers had assembled as well; Reyn had wondered if they were not plunging their heads into a noose. But Serilla had appeared calm as she came to the entrance. Roed Caern stood glowering just behind her left shoulder. Despite his scowls and muttered complaints, the Companion had graciously invited them all to enter and join in an 'informal discussion of Bingtown's situation'. But as they had gathered uneasily at the bargaining table, trumpets and alarm bells had sounded in the city below. Reyn had feared treachery as they rushed outside. A rooftop sentry had shouted that a flotilla of Chalcedean ships was approaching Bingtown harbour. Roed Caern had drawn a blade, shouting that the New Traders had invaded this meeting in the hopes of dispatching all of Bingtown's rightful leadership at once while their Chalcedean allies made their attack. Like rabid dogs, he and his followers had flown at the New Trader emissaries. Knives that all had promised not to bring were suddenly flourished. The first bloodshed of the current Chalcedean attack had been spilled there on Restart's doorstep. To their credit, the heads of the Traders' Council had opposed Roed and kept him and his men from massacring the Three Ships, Tattooed and New Trader delegates. The meeting dispersed as folk fled Roed's madness and scrambled to protect their own houses and families from the invaders. That had been three days ago.

The Chalcedeans had arrived, thick as grunion spawning on a beach. Sailing ships and oared galleys took over the harbour and spilled warriors onto the beaches and wharves. Their might had overwhelmed the disorganized Bingtown folk, and they had captured the Kendry. A prize crew sailed him out of the harbour. The ship had gone unwillingly, wallowing and fighting as small boats manned by Chalcedean sailors towed him out. Beyond that, Reyn had no knowledge of the fate of the ship or its crew. He wondered if they could force Kendry to take them up the river to Trehaug. Had they kept his family crew alive to use as hostages against the liveship?

The Chalcedeans now held the harbour and the surrounding buildings clutching the heart of Bingtown in their greedy hands. Every day, they pushed farther inland, systematically looting and then destroying what they could not carry off. Reyn had never seen such destruction. Certain key structures, warehouses for storing their plunder, defensible buildings of stone, they left intact. But all the rest, they laid waste. Old Trader, New Trader, fisherman, peddler, whore or slave: it mattered not to the Chalcedeans. They killed and stole without discrimination. The long row of Three Ships dwellings had all been burned, their little fishing vessels destroyed and the people killed or driven away to take refuge with their neighbours. The Chalcedeans showed no interest in negotiating. There could be no surrender. Captives were put into chains and held in one of the sailing ships, to be carried off to new lives as slaves in Chalced. If the invaders had ever had allies among the Bingtown folk, they betrayed them. No one was immune to their destruction.

'They plan to stay.' Grag's deep voice was soft but clear. 'After they've killed or enslaved everyone in Bingtown, the Chalcedeans will settle here, and Bingtown Bay will be just another part of Chalced.'

'Did I wake you, tossing about?' Reyn asked quietly.

'Not really. I can't find true sleep. I'm so tired of the waiting. I know that we needed to organize our resistance, but it has been hard to watch all the destruction in the meantime. Now that the day is finally here, each moment drags, and yet I wish we had more time to prepare. I wish Mother and the girls would flee to the mountains. Perhaps they could hide there until all this is over.'

'Over in what way?' Reyn asked sourly. 'I know we must have heart for this foray, but I cannot believe we will succeed. If we drive them from our beaches, they will simply retreat to their ships and then launch another attack. While they control the harbour, they control Bingtown. Without trade, how can we survive?'

'I don't know. There has to be some hope,' Grag insisted stubbornly. 'At least this mess has brought us together. The whole population now has to see that we will survive only if we stand together.'

Reyn tried to sound positive but failed. 'There is hope, but it is faint. If our liveships returned and boxed them into the harbour, I think all Bingtown would rally then. If we had a way to catch them between the beach and the harbour mouth, we could kill them all.'

Worry crept into Grag's voice. 'I wish we knew where our ships are, or at least how many still float. I suspect that the Chalcedeans lured our ships away. They ran and we chased them, possibly out to where a much greater force could destroy us. How could we have been so stupid?'

'We are merchants, not warriors,' Reyn replied. 'Our greatest strength is also our greatest weakness. All we know how to do is negotiate, and our enemies are not interested in that.'

Grag made a sound between a sigh and a groan. 'I should have been on board Ophelia that day. I should have gone with them. It is agony to wait and hope, not knowing what has become of my father and our ship.'

Reyn was quiet. He was too aware of how the knife-edge of uncertainty could score a man's soul. He would not insult Grag by saying that he knew what he was feeling. Every man's pain was personalized. Instead, he offered, 'We're both awake. We may as well get up. Let's go talk in the kitchen, so we don't wake Selden.'

'Selden is awake,' the boy said quietly. He sat up. 'I've decided. I'm going with you today. I'm going to fight.'

'No.' Reyn forbade it quickly, then tempered his words. 'I don't think that is wise, Selden. Your position is unusual. You may be the last heir to your family name. You should not risk your life.'

'The risk would be if I cowered here and did nothing,' Selden returned bitterly. 'Reyn. Please. When I am with my mother and my grandmother, they mean well, but they make me . . .

young. How am I to learn to be a man, if I am never among men? I need to go with you today.'

'Selden, if you go with us, you may not grow up to be a man,' Grag cautioned him. 'Stay here. Protect your mother and grandmother. That is where you can best serve Bingtown. And it is your duty.'

'Don't patronize me,' the boy returned sharply. 'If the fighting reaches this house, we will all be slaughtered, because by the time it gets here, you will all be dead. I'm going with you. I know that you think that I'll be in your way, someone you have to protect. But it won't be like that. I promise you.'

Grag took a breath to object, but Reyn interrupted them both. 'Let's go down to the kitchen and discuss it there. I could use some coffee.'

'You won't get it,' Grag told him grumpily. Reyn saw his effort to change his mood. 'But there is tea, still.'

They were not the only restless ones. The kitchen fire had been poked to life and a large kettle of porridge was already simmering. Not only Grag's mother and sister, but also the Vestrit women moved restlessly about the big room in mimicry of cooking. There was not enough work to busy them. A low mutter of voices came from the dining hall. As food was prepared, trays were borne off to the table. Ekke Kelter was there as well. She offered Grag Tenira a warm smile with the cup of tea she poured for him, then seated herself across the kitchen table from him and said matter-of-factly, 'The arsonists have already gone. They wanted to be certain they'd be in position before the attack.'

Reyn's heart gave an odd little hitch. Suddenly, it was real. Smoke and flame rising from the Drur family warehouse by the docks was to be the signal for all the waiting attackers. Daring spies, mostly slaveboys, had established that the Chalcedeans had amassed their loot there. Surely, they would return to fight a fire. Bingtown would burn its stolen wealth to draw the Chalcedeans to a central location. Once that fire was burning, they would attempt to set the Chalcedean ships ablaze with flaming arrows. A team of Three Ships men, their bodies well greased against the cold waters, would swim out to the Chalcedean ships and slip some anchor chains as well.

The various Bingtown groups had planned these diversions to disorganize the invaders before they made a massed dawn attack. Each man had armed himself as best he could. Ancient family swords would be wielded alongside clubs and butcher knives, fish bats and sickles. Merchants and fishermen, gardeners and kitchen slaves would all turn the tools of their trades to war today. Reyn squeezed his eyes shut for an instant. Bad enough to die; did they have to be so pathetically ill-equipped as they did so? Reyn poured himself a hot cup of tea, and silently wished well to all the grim saboteurs slipping quietly through the chill and rainy night.

Selden, seated beside him, suddenly gripped his wrist hard under the table. When he looked at the boy questioningly, a strangely grim smile lit his face. 'I feel it,' he said in a low voice. 'Don't you?'

'It's natural to be afraid,' he comforted the boy quietly. Selden only shook his head and released his grip on Reyn. Reyn's heart sank. Malta's little brother had been through far too much for a boy of his years. It had affected his mind.

Ronica Vestrit brought fresh bread to the table. The old woman had braided her greying hair and pinned it tightly to her head. As he thanked Ronica, his own mother entered the room. She was not veiled. Neither of the Rain Wilders had covered their faces since the day Reyn had removed his veil at the council table. If all were to be a part of this new Bingtown, then let all meet eyes squarely. Were his scaling, growths, and gleaming copper eyes all that different from the tattoos that sprawled across the slaves' faces? His mother, too, had confined her hair in securely-pinned braids. She wore trousers rather than her customary flowing skirts. In response to his puzzled glance, she said only, 'I won't be hampered by skirts when we attack.'

He stared at her, waiting for her smile to make her words a jest. But she didn't smile. She only said quietly, 'There was no point in discussing it. We knew you would all be opposed. It is time the men of Bingtown remembered that when we first came here, women and children risked just as much as their men did. We all fight today, Reyn. Better to die in battle than live as slaves after our men have died trying to protect us.'

Grag spoke with a sickly smile. 'Well, that's optimistic.' His eyes studied his mother for an instant. 'You, too?'

'Of course. Did you think I was fit only to cook for you, and then send you out to die?' Naria Tenira offered the bitter words as she set a steaming apple pie on the table. Her next words were softer. 'I made this for you, Grag. I know it's your favourite. There is meat and ale and cheese set out in the dining hall, if you'd rather. Those who went out before you wanted a hearty meal against the cold.'

It might be their last meal together. If the Chalcedeans did overrun them today, they would find the larder empty. There was no point in holding anything back any more, whether food or beloved lives. Despite the hovering of destruction, or perhaps because of it, the warm baked fruit, redolent of honey and cinnamon, had never smelled so good to Reyn. Grag cut slices with a generous hand. Reyn set the first piece of the warm pie before Selden and accepted another for himself. 'Thank you,' he said quietly. He could think of nothing else to say.

As Tintaglia circled high above Bingtown harbour, the simmering anger in her finally boiled. How dare they treat a dragon so? She might be the last of her kind, but she was still Lord of the Three Realms. Yet at Trehaug, they had turned her aside as if she were a beggar knocking at their door. When she had circled the city and roared to let them know she would land there, they had not bothered to clear the wharf of people and goods. When finally she had come down, the people had run shrieking as her beating wings swept crates and barrels into the river.

They had hidden from her, treating her visit with disdain instead of offering her meat and welcome. She had waited, telling herself that they were fearful. Soon they would master themselves and give her proper greeting. Instead, they had sent out a line of men bearing makeshift shields and carrying bows and pikes. They had advanced on her in a line, as if she were a straying cow to be herded, rather than a lord to be served.

Still, she had kept her temper. Many of their generations had passed since a dragon came calling on them. Perhaps they had forgotten the proper courtesies. She would give them a chance. Yet when she greeted them just as if they had made proper obeisance to her, some behaved as if they could not understand her, while others cried out 'she spoke, she spoke' as if it were a wonder. She had waited patiently for them to finish squabbling amongst themselves. At last, they had pushed one woman forwards. She pointed her trembling spear at Tintaglia and demanded, 'Why are you here?'

She could have trampled the woman, or opened her jaws and sprayed her with a mist of toxin. Yet again, Tintaglia swallowed her anger and simply demanded, 'Where is Reyn? Send him forth to me.'

The woman gripped her spear more tightly to still its shaking. 'He is not here!' she proclaimed shrilly. 'Now go away, before we attack you!'

Tintaglia lashed her tail, sending a pyramid of casks into the river. 'Send me Malta, then. Send me someone with the wit to speak before she makes threats.'

Their spokeswoman stepped backwards to the line of cowering warriors and conferred briefly there. She only took two steps from the shelter of the mob before proclaiming, 'Malta is dead, and Reyn is not here.'

'Malta is not dead,' Tintaglia exclaimed in annoyance. Her

link with the female human was not as strong as it had been, but it was not gone, either. 'I weary of this. Send me Reyn, or tell me where I may find him.'

The woman squared herself. 'I will tell you only that he is not here. Begone!'

It was too much. Tintaglia reared back on her hind legs and then crashed down on her forelegs, making the dock rock wildly. The woman staggered to her knees, while some of the warriors behind her broke ranks and fled. A lash of Tintaglia's tail swept the dock clean of crates and barrels. Tintaglia seized the woman's puny spear in her jaws, snapped it into splinters, and spat them aside. 'Where is Reyn?' she roared.

'Don't tell!' one of the warriors cried, but a young man sprang forth from them.

'Don't kill her! Please!' he begged the dragon. He swept the other spear-carriers with a scathing glance. 'I will not sacrifice Vala for the sake of Reyn! He brought the dragon down on us; let him deal with her. Reyn is gone from here, dragon. He went on Kendry to Bingtown. If you want Reyn, seek him there. Not here. We offer you nothing but battle.'

Some shouted that he was a traitor and a coward, but others sided with him, telling the dragon to leave and seek out Reyn. Tintaglia was disgusted. She levered herself back onto her hindquarters, allowing the pinioned woman to escape, brought her clawed forelegs down solidly on the dock, dug in her claws and dragged them back, splintering the planking of the dock. It crumpled like dry leaves. A lash of her tail smashed two rowing boats tied to the dock. She let them see that her destruction was effortless.

'It would take nothing at all for me to bring your city crashing down!' she roared at them. 'Remember it, puny two-legs. You have not seen nor heard the last of me. When I return, I shall teach you respect, and school you how to serve a Lord of the Three Realms.'

They rallied then, or tried to. Several rushed at her, spears lowered. She did not charge them. Instead, she spread her wings, leaped lightly into the air, and then crashed her weight down on the dock once more. The impact sent the humans' end of the dock flying up, catapulting would-be defenders into the air. They fell badly, landing heavily. At least one went into the water. She had not waited for more of their disrespect, but had launched herself into the air, leaving the dock rocking wildly. As she rose, people screamed, some shaking fists, others cowering.

It mattered nothing to her. She sought the air. Bingtown. That would be the smelly little coastal town she had flown over. She would seek Reyn there. He had spoken for her before; he could speak again, and make them all understand the wrath they would face if they did not do as she commanded them.

And now she was here, riding a chill winter wind over the huddled town below. Fading white stars pricked the winter sky above her; below were a few scattered yellow lights in the mostly sleeping town. Dawn would soon stir the human nest. A foul stench of burning wafted up to her. Ships filled the harbour, and along the waterfront, watch-fires burned at irregular intervals. Beside the fires, she saw men pacing restlessly. She dug back in her memories. War. She witnessed the stink and clutter of war. Below her, thick smoke from a dockside building suddenly blossomed into orange flame. An outcry arose. Her keen eyes picked out the shapes of men running furtively away as a much larger group converged on the fire.

She dropped lower, trying to discern what was going on. As she did so, she heard the unmistakable hiss of arrows in flight. The flaming projectiles missed her, striking instead a ship where they swiftly went out. A second volley followed the first. This time, a sail on one of the ships caught fire. Flames from the tarred and burning shaft ran swiftly up the canvas towards her. She beat her wings hastily to gain altitude, and the wind of her passage fanned the racing flames. On the deck of the burning ship, men yelled in astonishment. They pointed past their burning sail to the dragon silhouetted above the ship.

She heard the twang of a bow, and an arrow sang past her. She side-slipped the errant missile, but others took swift flight against her. One of the puny shafts actually struck her, pecking harmlessly against the tight scaling on her belly. She was both astonished and affronted. They dared to attempt to harm her? Humans sought to oppose the will of a dragon? Anger flared in her. Truly, the skies had been empty of wings for far too long. How dared humans assume they were the masters of this world? She would teach them now how foolish that concept was. She chose the largest of the ships, folded her wings and plummeted down towards it.

She had never battled a ship before. In all her dragon memories, there were few in which humans had opposed dragons. She discovered quickly that seizing rigging in her talons was a bad idea. The rocking vessels did not offer satisfactory resistance to her attack. They swayed away from her, and canvas and lines tangled around her clawed feet. With a wild shake, she tore herself free of the ship. She flapped her wings to gain altitude. High above the harbour, she divested her claws of the tangled mess of lines, spars and canvas and with satisfaction watched it crash down amidships of a galley, foundering the smaller craft.

On her second pass, she selected a two-masted ship as her prey. The men on board, seeing her stoop towards them, filled the air with arrows which clattered against her, falling back onto the ship below. As she swept by the ship, a slash of her tail sliced both masts. Tangled with sails and rigging, they fell, but Tintaglia flew clear of them. She passed low over a galley and the men on board leapt over the sides into the sea. She roared her delight. So quickly they learned to fear her!

The beating of her great wings set smaller craft rocking. A chorus of shouts and screams rose in homage to her fury.

She drove herself skywards and then swung back over the harbour. As the winter sun broke free of the horizon, she saw a brief, dazzling reflection of her gleaming body on the dark water below. Her keen eyes swept the city. The fires went unfought, the battles of mere humans unjoined. All eyes were lifted to her, all motion suspended in paralysed worship of her wrath. Her heart soared on their awestruck regard. The bouquet of their fear rose to her nostrils and intoxicated her with power. She drew breath and screamed, releasing with the sound a mist of milky poison. It drifted on the morning wind. A few seconds passed before the satisfaction of agonized shrieks rose to her. In the ships below her, the droplets of poison ate skin and sank deep into flesh, piercing bone and eating through gut before passing out the other sides of the victims' twitching bodies. Battle venom, born in the acid waters of her birth, strong enough to penetrate the layered armour of an adult dragon, passed unspent through the watery flesh of the humans and sizzled through the wood of their ships. The tiniest drop created a wound that would not heal. So much for those who had thought to pierce her flesh with arrows!

Then, through the turmoil and screams, through the crackling of flames and the singing of wind, a lone, clear voice caught her attention. She swivelled her head to separate the sound from all others. A voice sang, a lad's voice, high but not shrill. Sweet and true, it rang the word. 'Tintaglia, Tintaglia! Blue queen of winds and sky! Tintaglia, glorious one, terrible in your beauty, lovely in your wrath! Tintaglia, Tintaglia!'

Her keen eyes found the small figure. He stood alone, atop a mound of rubble, heedless that his silhouetted body made a perfect arrow target. He stood straight, joyous, his arms lifted, and he sang to her with the tongue of an Elderling. His flattery spelled her, and he wove her name into his song, uttering it with ineffable sweetness.

Her wings gathered the wind beneath them. She banked and turned in graceful spirals, leaning against the air currents. His song spiralled with her, wrapping her in ensorcelling praise. She could not resist him. She dropped lower and lower to hear his adoring words. Battered ships fled the harbour. She no longer cared. Let them go.

This city was poorly built to welcome a dragon. Nonetheless, not too far from her charming suitor there was a plaza that would suffice for a landing spot. As she beat her wings to slow her descent, many humans scuttled away, taking flimsy shelter behind ruined buildings. She paid them no mind. Once on the ground, she shook out her great wings and then folded them. Her head swayed with the rhythm of her minstrel's words.

'Tintaglia, Tintaglia, who outshines both moon and sun. Tintaglia, bluer than a rainbow's arc, gleaming brighter than silver. Tintaglia, swift-winged, sharp-clawed, breathing death to the unworthy. Tintaglia, Tintaglia.'

Her eyes spun with pleasure. How long had it been since a dragon's praises had been sung? She looked on the boy, and saw he was enraptured with her. His eyes gleamed with her beauty reflected. She recalled that she had touched this one, once before. He had been with Reyn when she rescued him. That solved the mystery, then. It happened, sometimes, that a mortal was enraptured by a dragon's touch. Young ones were especially vulnerable to such a linking. She looked on the small creature fondly. Such a butterfly, doomed to a brevity of days, and yet he stood before her, fearless in his worship.

She opened wide her wings in token of her approval. It was the highest accolade a dragon could afford a mortal, though his juvenile song scarcely deserved it: sweet as his words were, he was scarcely a learned minstrel. She shivered her wings so that their blue and silver rippled in the winter sunlight. He was dazzled into silence.

With amusement, she became aware of the other humans. They hung back, peering at her from behind trees and over walls. They clutched their weapons and trembled with fear of her. She arched her long neck and preened herself to let them see the ripple of her muscle. She stretched her claws, scoring the paving stones of the street. Casually, she cocked her head and looked down on her little admirer. She deliberately spun her eyes, drawing his soul into them, until she could feel how painfully his heart leapt in his chest. As she released him, he took breath after panting breath, yet somehow remained standing. Truly, small as he was, he was yet worthy to sing a dragon's praises.

'Well, minstrel,' she purred with amusement. 'Do you seek a boon in exchange for your song?'

'I sing for the joy of your existence,' he answered boldly.

'That is well,' she replied. The other, hidden humans behind Selden ventured fractionally closer to her, weapons at the ready. Fools. She clashed her tail against the cobblestones, which sent them leaping back to shelter. She laughed aloud. Yet here came one other who refused to fear her, stepping boldly out to confront her. Reyn carried a sword, but he allowed it to hang, point down, from his hand.

'So you have returned,' Reyn spoke quietly. 'Why?'

She snorted at him. 'Why? Why not? I go where I will, human. It is not for you to question a Lord of the Three Realms. The little one has chosen a better role. You were wiser to emulate him.'

Reyn set the bloodied tip of his blade to the street. She smelled blood on him and the sweat and smoke of battle. He dared frown at her. 'You clear our harbour of a few enemy vessels and expect us to grovel with gratitude?'

'You imagine a significance to yourself that does not exist, Reyn Khuprus. I care nothing for your enemies, only my own. They challenged me with arrows. They met a fitting end, as will all who defy me.'

The dark-haired Rain Wilder drew closer. He leaned on his sword, she saw now. He was wearier than she had thought. Blood had dried in a thin line down his left arm. When he lifted his face to look up at her, the thin winter sunlight glinted across his scaled brow. She quirked her ears in amusement. He wore her mark, and did not even know it. He was hers, and yet he thought he could match wills with her. The boy's attitude was more fitting. He stood as straight and tall as he could. Although he also looked up at the dragon, his eyes were worshipful, not defiant. The boy had potential.

Unfortunately, the potential would take time to develop, time she did not have just now. If the remaining serpents were to be rescued, the humans must work swiftly. She fixed her gaze on Reyn. She had enough experience of humans to know that the others would listen to him before they would listen to a boy. She would speak through him. 'I have a task for you, Reyn Khuprus. It is of the utmost importance. You and your fellows must set aside all else to attend to it, and until it is completed, you must think of nothing else.'

He stared up at her incredulously. Other humans drifted in from the rubble. They did not come too close but stood where they could hear her speak to Reyn without attracting undue attention to themselves. They regarded her with wide eyes, as ready to flee as to cheer her. Champion or foe, they wondered. She let them wonder, concentrating her will on Reyn. But he defied her. 'Now *you* imagine a significance to yourself that does not exist,' he told her coldly. 'I have no interest in performing any task for you, dragon.'

His words did not surprise her. She shifted back onto her hindquarters, towering over him. She opened out her wings, to emphasize further her size. 'You have no interest in living, then, Reyn Khuprus,' she informed him.

He should have quailed before her. He did not. He laughed. 'There you are right, worm Tintaglia. I have no interest in living, and that is your doing already. When you allowed Malta to go to her death you killed any regard I ever held for you. And with Malta died my interest in living. So do your worst to me, dragon. But I shall never again bend my neck to your yoke. I regret that I attempted to free you.

Better you had perished in the dark before you drew my love to her death.'

His words shocked her. It was not just that he was insufferably rude to her; he truly had lost all awe of her. This pathetic little two-legs, creature of a few breaths, was willing to die this very instant, because – she turned her head and regarded him closely. Ah! Because he believed she had allowed his mate to die. Malta.

'Malta is not dead,' she exclaimed in disgust. 'You waste your emotion and grandiose words on something you have imagined. Set aside such foolishness, Reyn Khuprus. The task you must perform is vastly more important than one human's mating. I honour you with an undertaking that may well save the whole of my race.'

The dragon lied. His contempt knew no bounds. He himself had been up and down the river in the Kendry, and found not a trace of his beloved. Malta was dead, and this dragon would lie to bend him to her will. He gazed past her disdainfully. Let her strike him where he stood. He would not give her another word. He lifted his chin, set his jaw, and waited to die.

Even so, what he saw now widened his eyes. As he stared past Tintaglia, he glimpsed furtive shadows stalking through the ruins towards her. They moved, they paused, they moved, and each time they got closer to the dragon. Their leather armour, and tails of hair marked them as Chalcedeans. They had rallied, despite the shattered ships in the harbour, despite their many dead, and now, swords and pikes in hand, battleaxes at the ready, they were converging on the dragon. A grim smile twisted Reyn's lips. This turn of events suited him well. Let his enemies battle one another. When they were finished, he would take on any survivors. He watched them come and said nothing, but wished them well.

But Grag Tenira sprang forwards, crying, 'Dragon, 'ware your back! To me, Bingtown, to me!' And then the fool charged the Chalcedeans, leading no more than a bloodied handful of his householders in an attack to defend the dragon.

Swift as a striking serpent, the dragon turned to confront her attackers. She bellowed her fury and beat her great wings, heedless that she sent several of her defenders rolling. She sprang towards the Chalcedeans, her jaws gaping wide. She breathed on them. No more than that could Reyn see, and yet the results were horrifying. The hardened warriors recoiled from her, shrieking like children. In an instant, every face ran blood. A moment later, clothing and leather armour fell in tatters from their red-streaming bodies. Some tried to run, but got no more than a few steps before they stumbled. Some of the bodies fell in pieces as they collapsed. Those furthest away from the dragon managed a staggering retreat before they collapsed screaming on the ground. Even the screams did not last long. The silence that followed their fading gurgles was deafening. Grag and his men halted where they stood, fearing to approach the bloody bodies.

Reyn felt his guts heave. The Chalcedeans were enemies, lower than dogs and deserving of no mercy. But to see any creature die as those men had died was wrenching. Even now, the bodies continued to degrade, losing shape as they liquesced. A head rolled free of its spine, settling on its side as flesh flowed from the collapsing skull. Tintaglia swivelled her great head back to stare at him. Her eyes spun; was she amused at his horror? An instant ago, he had told her that he no longer valued his life. That had not changed, but he also knew that any other death was preferable to the one he had just witnessed. He braced himself, determined to die silently.

Where Grag Tenira found his courage, Reyn could not say. He strode boldly between the Rain Wilder and the dragon. He lifted his sword high, and Tintaglia bridled in affront. Then the Bingtown Trader bowed low and set the blade at her feet.

'I will serve you,' he offered Tintaglia. 'Only free our harbour

of these vermin, and I will set myself to any task you propose.'
He glanced about; his look plainly invited others to join him.
Some few crept closer, but most kept their distance. Selden
alone advanced confidently to stand beside Grag. The shining
eyes the boy turned up to the dragon made Reyn feel ill. Selden
was so young, and so deceived by the creature. He wondered if
that was how his mother and brother had seen him when he
was advocating so strongly on the dragon's behalf. He winced
at the memory. He had turned this creature loose on the world,
and his price for that folly had been Malta.

Tintaglia's eyes flashed as she considered Grag. 'Do you
think I am a servant to be bought with wages? Dragons have
not been gone that long from this world, surely? The will of
a dragon takes precedent over any feeble goals of humans.
You will cease this conflict, and turn your attention to my
wishes.'

Selden spoke before Grag could reply. 'Having seen the
marvel of your wrath, mighty one, how could we wish to
do otherwise? It is those others, the invaders, who dispute
your will. See how they sought to attack you, before they
even knew your bidding. Smite them and drive them from
our shores, wide-winged queen of the skies. Free our minds
from considering them, that we may turn willingly to your
loftier goals.'

Reyn stared at the lad. Where did he find such language?
And did he think a dragon could be so easily manoeuvred?
With amazement, he watched Tintaglia's great head dip down
until her nostrils were on a level with Selden's belt. She gave
the boy a tiny nudge that sent him staggering.

'Honey-tongue, do you think you can deceive me? Do you
think pretty words will convince me to labour like a beast
for your ends?' There was both affection and sarcasm in
her voice.

Selden's boyish voice rang out clear and true. 'No, mistress of
the wind, I do not hope to deceive you. Nor do I try to bargain

with you. I beg this boon of you, mighty one, that we might more fully concentrate on your task for us.' He took a breath. 'We are but small creatures, of short lives. We must grovel before you, for that is how we are made. And our small minds are made likewise, filled with our own brief concerns. Help us, gleaming queen, to put our fears to rest. Drive the invaders from our shore, that we may heed you with uncluttered minds.'

Tintaglia threw back her head and roared her delight. 'I see you are mine. I suppose it had to be, as young as you were, and so close to my wings' first unfurling. May the memories of a hundred Elderling minstrels be yours, small one, that you may serve me well. And now I go, not to do your bidding, but to demonstrate my might.'

She reared, taller than a building, and pivoted on her hind legs like a war stallion. Reyn saw her mighty haunches bunch, and threw himself to the ground. An instant later, a blast of air and driven dust lashed him. He remained down as the beating of her silver-blue wings lifted her skyward. He rose and gaped at the suddenly tiny figure overhead. His ears felt stuffed with cotton. As he stared, Grag suddenly gripped his arm. 'What were you thinking, to defy her like that?' the Trader demanded. He lifted his gaze in awe. 'She's magnificent. And she's our only chance.' He grinned at Selden. 'You were right, lad. Dragons change everything.'

'So I believed once, also,' Reyn said sourly. 'Push aside her glamour. She is as deceptive as she is magnificent, and her heart has room only for her own interests. If we bow to her will, she will enslave us as surely as the Chalcedeans would.'

'You are wrong.' Small and slight as Selden was, he seemed to tower with satisfaction. 'The dragons did not enslave the Elderlings, and they will not enslave us. There are many ways for different folk to live alongside each other, Reyn Khuprus.'

Reyn looked down on the boy and shook his head. 'Where do you get such ideas, boy? And such words as could charm a dragon into letting us live?'

'I dream them,' the boy said ingenuously. 'When I dream that I fly with her, I know how she speaks to herself. Queen of the sky, rider of the morning, magnificent one. I speak to her as she speaks to herself. It is the only way to converse with a dragon.' He crossed his thin arms on his narrow chest. 'It is my courtship of her. Is it so different from how you spoke to my sister?'

The sudden reminder of Malta and how he had used to flatter and cajole her was like a knife in his heart. He started to turn aside from the boy who smiled so unbearably. But Selden reached out and gripped his arm. 'Tintaglia does not lie,' he said in a low voice. His eyes met Reyn's and commanded his loyalty. 'She considers us too trivial to deceive. Trust me in this. If she says Malta is alive, then she lives. My sister will return to us. But to get this, you must let me guide you, as I let my dreams guide me.'

Screams rose from the vicinity of the harbour. All around them, men scrabbled for vantage points. Reyn had no desire to do so. Chalcedeans or not, they were his own kind that the dragon was slaying. He heard the crack of massive timbers giving way. Another ship dismasted, no doubt.

'Too late for those bastards to flee now!' A nearby warrior exulted savagely.

Close by, others took up his spirit. 'Look at her soar. Truly, she is queen of the skies!'

'She will cleanse our shores of those foul Chalcedeans!'

'Ah! She has smashed the hull with one swipe of her tail!'

Beside him, Grag suddenly lifted his sword. His weariness seemed to have left him. 'To me, Bingtown! Let us see that any who reach the beach alive do not long remain so.' He set off at a jogging run, and the men who had earlier cowered in the ruins hastened after him, until Reyn and Selden alone remained standing in the ruined plaza.

Selden sighed. 'You should go quickly, to gather folk from

all of Bingtown's groups. It is best that when we treat with the dragon, we speak with one voice.'

'I imagine you are right,' Reyn replied distractedly. He was remembering the strange dreams of his own youth. He had dreamed the buried city, alive with light and music and folk, and the dragon had spoken to him. Such dreams came, sometimes, to those who spent too much time down there. But surely, such dreams were the province of the Rain Wild Traders only.

Wistfully, Reyn reached down to rub a thumb across the boy's dust-smeared cheek. Then he stared, wordless, at the fan of silver scaling he had revealed on Selden's cheekbone.

SEVENTEEN

Bingtown Negotiations

T<small>HE ROOF ON</small> the Traders' Concourse was gone. The Chalcedeans had finished what the New Traders had begun. Ronica picked her way past the sooty remains of the roof that had collapsed on the Concourse floor. It had continued to burn after it fell, streaking the stone walls with soot and smoke. Tapestries and banners that had once decorated the hall hung in charred fragments. Above, a few beams remained, burned to black points. The afternoon sky threatened rain as it looked greyly down on the gathering inside the roofless building, yet the Bingtown Traders had stubbornly insisted on meeting in a structure that could no longer shelter them. That, Ronica thought, spoke volumes about the legendary tenacity of the Traders.

The fallen timbers had been pushed to one side. Folk stepped over and through the rest of the rubble. Cinders crunched underfoot and the smell of damp ash rose as the crowd milled. The fire that had taken the roof had claimed most of the tables and benches as well. Some scorched chairs remained, but Ronica did not trust any of them enough to sit on them.

And there was a strange equality to standing shoulder to shoulder with the others gathered here. Bingtown Traders, New Traders, tattooed slaves and brawny fisherfolk, tradesmen, and servants all stood with their friends and kin.

They filled the hall. Outside, the overflow sat on the steps and clustered in groups on the grounds. Despite their differing origins, there was an odd sameness to the folk. All faces bore the shock and grief of the Chalcedean invasion and the havoc it had wrought. Battle and fire had treated them equally, from wealthy Bingtown Trader to humble kitchen slave. Their clothes were stained with soot or blood and sometimes both. Most looked unkempt. Children huddled near parents or neighbours. Weapons were carried openly. The talk was muttered and low, and most had to do with the dragon.

'She breathed on them, and they just melted away like candles in a flame.'

'Smashed the whole hull with one blow of her tail.'

'Not even Chalcedeans deserve to die like that.'

'Don't they? They deserve to die however we can manage it.'

'The dragon is a blessing from Sa, sent to save us. We should prepare thanksgiving offerings.'

Many folk stood silent, eyes fixed on the raised stone dais that had survived to elevate the chosen leaders from each group.

Serilla was there, representing Jamaillia, with Roed Caern glowering beside her. The sight of him on the dais made Ronica clench her teeth but she forced herself not to stare at him. She had hoped that Serilla had broken off with Roed following his ill-advised attack upon the New Traders. How could she be so foolish? The Companion stood, eyes cast down as if in deep thought. She was dressed far more elegantly than anyone else on the dais, in a long, soft, white robe, decorated with crossing ropes of cloth-of-gold. Ashes and soot had marred the hem of it. Despite the garment's long sleeves and the thick woollen cloak she wore, the Companion stood with her arms crossed as if chilled.

Sparse Kelter was also on the dais, and the blood on his rough fisherman's smock was not fish blood today. A heavy-boned woman with tattoos sprawling across her cheek and onto her neck flanked him. Dujia, leader of the Tattooed, wore ragged trousers and a patched tunic. Her bare feet were dirty. A rough bandage around her upper arm showed that she had been in the thick of the fighting.

Traders Devouchet, Conry and Drur represented the Bingtown Council. Ronica did not know if they were the only surviving Council heads, or the only ones bold enough to dare displeasing Caern and his cohorts. They stood well away from Serilla and Roed. At least that separation had been established.

Mingsley was there for the New Traders. His richly-embroidered vest showed several days of hard wear. He stood at the opposite side of the dais from the slave woman and avoided her gaze. Ronica had heard that Dujia had not led an easy life as his slave, and that he had good reason to fear her.

Sitting on the edge of the dais, feet dangling, oddly calm, was her grandson, Selden. His eyes wandered over the crowd below him with an air of preoccupation. Only Mingsley had dared question his right to be there. Selden had met his gaze squarely.

'I will speak for us all when the dragon comes,' he had assured the man. 'And, if needed, I will speak for the dragon to you. I must be here so she can see me above the crowd.'

'What makes you think she will come here?' Mingsley had demanded.

Selden had smiled an otherworldly smile. 'Oh, she will come. Never fear,' he had replied. He blinked his eyes slowly. 'She sleeps now. Her belly is full.' When her grandson smiled, the silvery scaling across his cheeks rippled and shone. Mingsley had stared, and then stepped back from the boy. Ronica feared that she could already detect a blue shimmer to Selden's lips beneath the chapping. How could he have changed so much, so swiftly? As baffling, perhaps, was the inordinate pleasure he took in the changes. Jani Khuprus, representing the Rain

Wilds, stood protectively behind Selden. Ronica was glad she was there, but wondered at her intent. Would she claim the last heir to the Vestrit family and carry him off to Trehaug? Yet, if she did not, what place would there be for him in Bingtown?

Keffria stood so close to the dais that she could have reached out and touched her boy. But she didn't. Ronica's daughter had been silent since Reyn had brought Selden to them. She had looked at the silvery path of scales across the tops of her son's cheeks, but she had not touched them. Selden had joyously told her that Malta was alive, for the dragon said so. When Keffria had said nothing in response to his news, he had seized her arm, as if to waken her from sleep. 'Mother. Put your grief aside. Tintaglia can bring Malta back to us. I know she can.'

'I will wait for that,' Keffria had said faintly. No more than that. Now she looked up at her son as if he were a ghost, as if a tracery of scales had removed him from her world.

Just beyond Keffria stood Reyn Khuprus. He, like Jani, went unveiled now. From time to time, Ronica saw folk turn their heads and stare at the Rain Wilders, but both were too pre-occupied to be offended. Reyn was in deep conversation with Grag Tenira. There seemed to be a difference of opinion, one that was civil but intense. She hoped it would not cause discord between them tonight. Bingtown needed every semblance of unity it could muster.

Ronica's eyes travelled across the assembled folk in all their variety. She smiled grimly to herself. Selden was still her grandson; despite his scales, he was still a Vestrit. Perhaps the changes on Selden's face would be no more of a stigma than the tattoos that others would wear unashamedly in the new Bingtown. One of the ships that the dragon had dismasted had been filled with Bingtown captives. Many had already been forcibly tattooed, their faces marked with the sigils of their captors so that each raider would receive his profit when they were sold in Chalced. The Chalcedeans had abandoned the dismasted ship and attempted to escape in galleys, but Ronica did not think any had been successful. Bingtown folk had poled out on a makeshift raft to the listing vessel to rescue their kin, while the dragon pursued Chalcedean prey. Many who had never expected to wear a slave tattoo now did, including some New Traders. She suspected they might shift their politics in response.

Anxiety shifted the gathered folk endlessly. When the dragon had returned from hunting Chalcedeans, she had ordered their leaders to assemble, saying that she would treat with them soon. The sun had been high then. Now night threatened and still she had not returned. Ronica returned her gaze to the dais. It would be interesting to see who would try to call this gathering to order, and whom the crowd would follow.

Ronica was expecting Serilla to use her claim of the Satrap's authority, but Trader Devouchet stepped to the front of the dais. He lifted his arms high and the crowd hushed.

'We have gathered here in the Bingtown Traders' Concourse. Since Trader Dwicker has been murdered, I step up to the position of head of the Bingtown Traders' Council. I claim the right to speak first.' He looked over the assembled folk expecting some dissent, but for now, all was silent.

Devouchet proceeded to state the obvious. 'We are gathered here, all the folk of Bingtown, to discuss what we will do about the dragon that has descended upon us.'

That, Ronica thought to herself, was inspired. Devouchet mentioned nothing of the differences that had set the town to battling in the first place. He focused all of them, as a single entity, on the problem of the dragon. Devouchet spoke on.

'She has driven the Chalcedean fleet from our harbour and hunted down several roving bands of raiders. For now, she has disappeared from our skies, but she said she would soon return. Before she does, we must decide how to deal with her. She has freed our harbour. What are we prepared to offer her in exchange?'

He paused for breath. That was his mistake, for a hundred voices filled in, with a hundred different answers.

'Nothing. We owe her nothing!' one man bellowed angrily, while another made heard his comment, 'Trader Tenira's son has already struck our deal. Grag told her that if she drove the Chalcedeans away, we would help her with a task she named. That seems fair enough. Does a Bingtown Trader go back on his word, even to a dragon?'

'We should prepare offerings for it. The dragon has liberated us. We should offer thanksgiving to Sa for sending us this champion!'

'I'm not a Trader! Neither is my brother, and we won't be bound by another man's word!'

'Kill it. All the legends of dragons warn of their treachery and cruelty. We should be readying our defences, not standing about talking.'

'Quiet!' Mingsley roared, stepping forwards to stand at Devouchet's shoulder. He was a stout man, but the power of his voice still surprised Ronica. As he looked about over the crowd, the whites showed all around his eyes. The man, Ronica realized, was deeply frightened. 'We have no time for squabbling. We must move swiftly to an accord. When the dragon returns, we must meet her as a united folk. Resistance would be a mistake. You saw what she did to those ships and men. We must placate her, if we hope to avoid the same fate.'

'Perhaps some here deserve the same fate as the Chalcedeans,' Roed Caern observed callously. He pushed forwards to stand threateningly close to the stout merchant. Mingsley stepped back from him as Roed turned to the crowd. 'I heard it spoken clearly, earlier. A Trader has already struck an accord with the dragon. The dragon is ours! She belongs to the Bingtown Traders. We should honour our bargain, Bingtown Traders, without recourse to any of the foreigners who have sought to claim our town as their own. With the dragon on our side,

Bingtown can not only drive the dirty Chalcedeans back to their own land, we can force out the New Traders and their thieving slaves with them. We have all heard the news. The Satrap is dead. We cannot rely on Jamaillia to aid us. Bingtown Traders, look around you. We stand in our ruined hall in a ravaged town. How have we come to this pass? By tolerating the greedy New Traders in our midst, folk who came here in violation of our Charter, to plunder our land and beggar us!' A sneer of hatred curled his lip as he stared at Mingsley. With narrowed eyes, he suggested, 'How can we pay our dragon? With meat. Let the dragon rid us of *all* outsiders.'

What happened next shocked everyone. Even as the mutter of outrage at his words became a roar, Companion Serilla stepped forwards resolutely. As Roed turned, surprised, she set her small hand to the centre of his chest. Baring her teeth in sudden effort, she shoved him backwards off the dais. The fall was a short one; it would have been an easy jump if he had been prepared, but he was not. He went over with a yell, arms flailing. Ronica heard the sharp crack of his head against the floor, and then his howl of pain. Men closed in around him. There was a brief flurry of struggle.

'Stand clear of him!' Serilla shouted, and for one confusing instant, Ronica thought she defended the man. 'Disperse, or share his fate!' Like trickling water vanishing in sand, those few who had attempted to help Roed fell back and merged suddenly into the crowd. Roed alone remained, held immobile by his captors, one arm twisted up behind him. He gritted his teeth against the pain, but managed to spit a curse at Serilla. Traders, both Old and New, were the ones who held him. At a nod from Serilla, they wrestled him away from the gathering. Ronica wondered, as she watched him taken away, what they would do with him.

Companion Serilla suddenly flung her head up and looked out over the crowd. For the first time, Ronica saw the woman's face alight as if a true spirit resided in her. She did not even look after the man she had overthrown. She stood, whole and temporarily in command.

'We cannot tolerate Roed Caern, or those who think like him,' she declared loudly. 'He seeks to sow discord when what we need is unity. He speaks against the authority of the Satrapy, as if it perished with Satrap Cosgo. You know it has not! Heed me, folk of Bingtown. Whether or not the Satrap is alive does not matter at this time. What does matter is that he left me in authority, to take on the weight of his rule if he should perish. I shall not fail him, nor his subjects. Whatever else you may be, one and all, you are subjects of the Satrap, and the Satrapy rules you. In that, at least, you can be equal and united.' She paused and let her gaze travel over the others who shared the dais with her. 'None of you are needed here. I am capable of speaking for all of you. Moreover, whatever treaty I work out with the dragon will bind all of you equally. Is not that best? To let someone with no personal ties to Bingtown speak for all of you, impersonally?'

She almost succeeded. After Roed, she sounded reasonable. Ronica Vestrit watched folk exchanging glances. Then Dujia spoke from the other end of the dais. 'I speak for the Tattooed when I say that we have had enough of the "equality" the Satrap bestowed upon us. Now we will make our own equality, as residents of Bingtown, not Jamaillian subjects. We will have a voice in what is promised to this dragon. For too long, others have disposed of our labour and our lives. We can tolerate it no longer.'

'I feared this,' Mingsley broke in. He pointed a shaking finger at the tattooed woman. 'You slaves will spoil everything. You care only for revenge. No doubt you will do all in your power to defy the dragon, for the sake of bringing her wrath down on your masters. But when all is done, even if all your New Trader masters die, you will be the same folk you are today. You are not fit to govern yourselves. You have forgotten what it is to be responsible. The proof of it is in how you have behaved since you betrayed your rightful masters and abandoned their discipline. You have reverted to what you were before your masters took control of you. Look at yourself, Dujia. You became a thief first, and a slave afterwards. You deserved your fate. You chose your life. You should have accepted it. But master after master found you a thief and a liar, until the map of those you have served stretches across your face to your neck. You should not even be up here, asserting the right to speak. Good people of Bingtown, the slaves are not a separate folk, save that they are marked for their crimes. As well give the whores a right to speak in this, or the pickpockets. Let us listen to Serilla. We are all Jamaillian, Old Trader and New, and all should be content to be bound by the Satrap's word. I speak for the New Traders when I say I accept Companion Serilla to negotiate for us with the dragon.'

Serilla stood straight and tall. She smiled, and it seemed genuine. She looked past Mingsley to include Dujia in the smile. 'As the Satrap's representative, of course I shall negotiate for you. For all of you. New Trader Mingsley has not well considered his words. Has he forgotten that some in Bingtown now wear the tattoos of slavery, when their only crime was to be captured by the Chalcedeans? For Bingtown to survive and prosper, it must go back to its oldest roots. By its charter, it was a place where ambitious outcasts could forge new homes and lives for themselves.' She gave a small, disarming laugh. 'Left here to wield the Satrap's power, I, too, am an exile of sorts. Never again will I return to Jamaillia. Like you, I must become a citizen of Bingtown, and build a new life for myself here. Look at me. Consider that I embody all that Bingtown is. Come,' she urged them softly. She looked all around at the crowd. 'Accept me. Let me speak for all of you, and bind us into one accord.'

Jani Khuprus shook her head regretfully as she stepped forwards to claim the right to speak. 'There are those of us who are not content to be bound by the Satrap's word, or any man's word, save our own. I speak for the Rain Wilds. What has Jamaillia ever done for us, save restrict our trade and steal half our profits? No, Companion Serilla. You are no companion of mine. Bind Jamaillia as you will, but the Rain Wilds will bear that yoke no more. We know more of this dragon than you do. We will not let you bargain our lives away to placate her. My people have said that I speak for them, and I shall. I have no right to let their voices be muffled in yours.' Jani glanced down to exchange a look with Reyn.

Ronica sensed that Jani and Reyn had prepared for this moment.

Reyn spoke up from the floor. 'Listen to her. The dragon is not to be trusted. You must guard your senses against her glamour, and your hearts against her clever words. I speak as one who was long deceived by her, and paid for that deception with a deep and painful loss. It is tempting to look on her beauty and believe her a wondrous wise creature, sprung from legend to save us. Do not be so gullible. She would have us believe she is superior to us, our conqueror and ruler simply by virtue of what she is. She is no better than we are, and in my heart I believe she is truly no more than a beast with the cunning to shape words.' He raised his voice to be heard by all. 'We have been told that she is sleeping off a full belly. Dare any of us ask, full of what? On what meat has she fed?' As his words settled on his listeners, he added, 'Many of us would rather die than be slaves any more. Well, I would rather die than be either her slave or her food.'

The world dimmed suddenly. An instant later, a blast of cold air, noisome with the stench of snakes, swept over the crowd. There were shrieks of terror and angry shouts as the gathered folk cowered in the shadow of the dragon. Some instinctively sought shelter near the walls while others tried to hide themselves in the centre of the crowd. Then, as the shadow swept past and the fading light of day returned, Ronica felt the creature land in the Concourse grounds. The impact of her weight travelled through the paving stones and made the walls of the Concourse shudder. Although the doors were too small to admit her, Ronica wondered if even the stout stone walls would withstand a determined assault by the dragon. An instant later, the creature reared up; her front clawed feet came to rest on the top of the wall. Her cart-sized head on her serpentine neck looked down on them all. She snorted, and Reyn Khuprus was staggered by the blast of air from her nostrils.

'So, I am a beast cunning enough to speak, am I? And what title do you give yourself then, human? With your paltry years and truncated memory, how can you claim to be my equal?'

Everyone pressed back against their fellows to clear a space around the object of Tintaglia's displeasure. Even the diplomats on the dais raised their arms to shield their faces as if they feared to share Reyn's punishment. All waited to see him die.

In a move that made Ronica gasp, Selden jumped lightly from the edge of the dais. He placed himself in the dragon's sight, then boldly inserted his small body between Reyn and the dragon's angry gaze. To the dragon, he swept a courtly bow. 'Welcome, gleaming one!' Every eye, every ear was focused only on him. 'We have gathered here, as you bid us. We have awaited your return, sky-ruler, that we might learn exactly what task you wish us to perform.'

'Ah. I see.' The dragon lifted her head, the better to observe all the folk. There was a general cowering, an unintended genuflection before her. 'You did not, then, gather to plot against me?'

'No one has seriously considered such a thing!' Selden lied valiantly. 'Perhaps we are merely humans, but we are not stupid. Who among us could think to defy your scaled mightiness? Many tales have we told one another of your valiant deeds today. All have heard of your fearsome breath, of the wind of your wings and the strength of your tail. All recognize that without your glorious might, our enemies would have overrun us. Think how sorrowful this day could have been for us, for they would have had the honour of serving you instead of us.'

Who, Ronica wondered, did Selden address? Did he flatter the dragon, or were his words to remind the gathered folk that other humans could serve her just as well. The people of Bingtown could be replaced. Perhaps the only way to survive was to claim to serve her willingly.

Tintaglia's great silver eyes spun warmly at Selden's flattery. Ronica gazed into their swirling depths and felt herself drawn to the creature. She was truly magnificent. The lapping of the scales on her face reminded Ronica of the flexible links of a fine jewellery chain. As Tintaglia considered the gathered folk, her head swayed gently from side to side. Ronica felt caught in that motion, unable to tear her attention away. The dragon was both silver and blue; every movement called forth both colours from her scales. The grace of her bent neck was like a swan's. Ronica was seized with a desire to touch the dragon, to discover for herself if the smoothly undulating hide were warm or cool. All around her, people edged towards the dragon, entranced with her loveliness. Ronica felt the tension ebb away from her. She felt weary still, but it was a good weariness, like the soft ache of muscles at the end of a useful day.

'What I require of you is simple,' the dragon said softly. 'Humans have always been builders and diggers. It is in your nature to shape nature to your own ends. This time, you will shape the world to my needs. There is a place in the Rain River where the waters flow shallow. I wish you to go there and make it deeper, deep enough for a sea serpent to pass. That is all. Do you understand?'

The asking of the question seemed to loosen their silence. People murmured amongst themselves in gentle surprise. This was all she asked, this simple thing?

Then far back in the crowd a man shouted a question.

'Why? Why do you want serpents to be able to go up the Rain Wild River?'

'They are the young of dragons,' Tintaglia told him calmly. 'They must go up the river, to a special place, to cocoon so that they may become full dragons. Once, there was a hauling out place near the Rain Wild city of Trehaug, but the swamps have swallowed those warm and sandy banks. Upriver, there is still a site that may serve. If the serpents can reach it.' Her eyes spun pensively for a moment. 'They will require guards while they are cocooned. You will have to protect them from predators during the winter months while they are changing. This was a task, long ago, that dragons and Elderlings shared. The Elderlings built their cities not far from our hatching grounds, the better to be able to guard our cocoons until spring brought the bright sunlight needed for us to hatch. If not for the Elderling city near the lower hatching ground, I would not have been saved. You can build where the Elderlings once lived.'

'In the Rain Wilds?' someone asked in incredulous horror. 'The water is acid; only the rain is drinkable. The land trembles constantly. Folk who live in the Rain Wilds for too long go mad. Their children are born dead or deformed, and as they age, their bodies become monstrous. All know that.'

The dragon made an odd sound in her throat. Every muscle in Ronica's body tightened, until she realized what it was. Laughter. 'Folk can live by the Rain Wild River. Trehaug is proof of that. But before Trehaug, long before, there were wondrous cities on the banks of the Rain River. There can be again. I will show you how the water may be made drinkable. The land has subsided; you must live in the trees, as they do in Trehaug; there is no help for that.'

Ronica felt an odd prickling sensation in her mind. She blinked her eyes rapidly. Something . . . ah. That was what had changed. The dragon had shifted her gaze to a different part of the gathering. Ronica felt more alert again. She resolved to be more wary of the dragon's spinning glance.

Jani Khuprus spoke from the dais. Her voice shook as she dared to address the dragon, but iron determination ran through her words. 'Indeed, folk can live in the Rain Wilds. But not without cost and not without skill. We are proof of that. The Rain Wilds are the province of the Rain Wild Traders. We will not allow them to be taken from us.' She paused, and took a shaky breath. 'No others know how to subsist beside the river, how to build in the trees, or how to withstand the madness seasons. The buried city we once mined for trade goods is lost to us now. We must find other ways to survive there. Nevertheless, the Rain Wilds are our home. We will not surrender them.'

'Then you must be the one to do the winter guarding,' the dragon told her smoothly. She cocked her head. 'You are more suited to this task than you know.'

Jani visibly gathered her determination. 'That, perhaps, we can do. If certain conditions are met.' She glanced out over the gathered people. With fresh confidence she directed, 'Let torches be kindled. The settling of the details may take some time.'

'But surely not long,' the dragon intoned warningly.

Jani was not daunted. 'This is not a task for a handful of men with shovels. Engineers and workers from Bingtown will have to help us deepen the river channel for you. It will take planning and many workers. The population of Trehaug may not be great enough to support such a venture on its own.' Jani's voice became more certain, and took on the cadence of a bargainer. This was something she knew how to do well. 'There will be difficulties to surmount, of course, but the Rain Wild Traders are accustomed to the hardships of the Rain Wild. Workers will have to be fed and sheltered. Food supplies would have to be brought in, and that requires our liveships, such as the Kendry, who was taken from us. You will, of course, aid us in recovering him? And in keeping the river mouth free of Chalcedeans, so that supplies can flow freely?'

The dragon's eyes narrowed slightly. 'Of course,' she said a bit stiffly. 'Surely that will content you.'

Throughout the roofless Concourse, torches were being kindled. Their brightness seemed only to make the night sky darker. Cold was settling over the gathered folk. Breath showed in the light of the torches and people moved closer to one another, taking comfort in body warmth. The night sky began to draw the warmth of the brief day away, but no one thought of leaving. Bargaining was the blood of Bingtown, and this was far too important a deal not to witness its birth. Outside, a man's raised voice was conveying the negotiations to the folk waiting there.

Jani knit her scaled brows. 'We shall have to build a second city, near this "upper hatching ground" you speak of. That will take time.'

'Time we do not have,' the dragon declared impatiently. 'It is of the essence that this work begin as soon as possible, before other serpents perish.'

Jani shrugged helplessly. 'If haste is necessary, then even more workers will be needed. We may need to bring them from as far as Jamaillia. They must be paid. Where is the money to come from?'

'Money? Paid?' the dragon demanded, becoming incensed.

Dujia suddenly claimed the floor. She stepped to the edge of the dais, to stand beside Jani. 'There is no need to go to Jamaillia for workers. My people are here. The Tattooed were brought here to work, and paid nothing at all. Some of us will be willing to go up the river and do this work, not for money, but for a chance. A chance for homes and futures of our own. Give us, to begin with, food and shelter. We will work to make our own fortunes.'

Jani turned to confront her. A terrible hope gleamed in the Rain Wild woman's face. She spoke clearly and slowly, laying out the terms of a bargain. 'To come to the Rain Wild, you must become of the Rain Wild. You cannot hold yourselves back from us.' She stared deep into Dujia's eyes, but the Tattooed woman did not glance away from Jani's Rain Wild scales and gently glowing eyes. Jani smiled at her. Then her eyes suddenly roved over the assembled people. She seemed to see the Tattooed in a new way. 'Your children would have to take husbands and wives among us. Your grandchildren would be Rain Wilders. There is no leaving, once you have come to the Rain Wilds. You cannot remain a separate people, with separate ways. It is not an easy life. Many will die. Do you understand what you are offering?'

Dujia cleared her throat. When Jani glanced back at her, she met her look squarely. 'You say we must become of the Rain Wild. Rain Wild Traders are what you call yourselves. That is what we would become? Traders? With the rights of Traders?'

'Those who marry Rain Wild Traders always become Rain Wild Traders. Mingle your families with ours, and yours become ours.'

'Our homes would be our own? Whatever we acquired, it would be ours?'

'Of course.'

Dujia looked out over the assembled folk. Her eyes sought out the Tattooed groups. 'This is what you told me you wanted. Homes and possessions that you could pass on to your children. To be on an equal footing with your neighbours. The Rain Wilders offer us this. They warn us fairly of hardships to come. I have spoken for you, but each of you must decide.'

From somewhere amongst the Tattooed, a voice called a question. 'And if we don't want to go to the Rain Wilds? What then?'

Serilla stepped forwards.

'I speak with the authority of the Satrapy. Henceforth, there shall be no slaves in Bingtown. Tattooed are Tattooed; no more nor less than that. It would violate the original charter of the Bingtown Traders for me to elevate the Tattooed to an equal standing with the Traders. I cannot do that. But I can decree that henceforth, in conformity with the original laws of Bingtown, the Satrapy of Jamaillia will not recognize slavery or the claims of slave-owners in Bingtown.' She let her voice drop dramatically. 'Tattooed ones, you are free.'

'We always were!' someone called out from the crowd, spoiling the moment for the Companion.

Mingsley made a final bid to save his people's labour force. 'But indentured servants, surely, are another matter?'

He was shouted down, not just by the crowd but by a roar from the dragon. 'Enough. Solve these petty issues on your own time. I care not how you colour your skins or name yourselves, so long as the work is done.' She looked at Jani Khuprus. 'You can draw on Bingtown for engineers and planners. You have a labour force. I myself will soar forth tomorrow, to free the Kendry and find the other liveships and send them to you. I pledge I will keep the waters between Trehaug and Bingtown cleared of enemy ships while you do this work. Surely, all is now in agreement.'

The sky was black. The dragon was a gleaming entity of silver and blue. Her head swayed gently over them as she awaited their assent. The flickering torchlight caressed her wondrous form. Ronica felt as if she were in a tale of enchantment, witness to a great miracle. The petty problems that remained suddenly seemed unworthy of discussion. Had not Tintaglia pointed out that they were creatures of brief life? Surely, it could matter little what happened in such a tiny flicker of time as they occupied. Serving Tintaglia in restoring dragons to the world would be a way to ensure their lives had some impact on the greater world.

A sigh of agreement ran through the crowd. Ronica moved her own head in a slow nod.

'Malta,' Keffria said quietly beside her. The word disturbed

Ronica. It had grown so quiet within the Concourse that the sound was like a pebble dropped in a still pool. A few heads turned towards them. Her daughter took a deep breath and spoke the name louder. 'Malta.'

The dragon turned to regard them, and her eyes were not pleased. 'What is it?' she demanded.

Keffria stepped towards the dragon, aggression in her stride. 'Malta!' she shouted the name. 'Malta was my daughter. I am told you lured her to her death. And now, by some wicked magery, my son, my last child, stands before you and praises you. All my people murmur and smile at sight of you, like babies entranced with a shiny dangle.'

As Keffria spoke, Ronica felt a strange agitation. How dare she speak so to this glorious and benevolent creature, the creature who had rescued all of Bingtown – the creature responsible for Malta's death. Ronica felt an instant of disorientation as if she woke from a deep sleep.

'But Mother –' Selden began pleadingly, taking her arm. Keffria set her son firmly aside, out of harm's way, and spoke on. Her rising anger at how the dragon manipulated the crowd had cracked her frozen heart. Fury poured out with her pain.

'I do not succumb to your glamour. I do contemplate how I could take revenge on you. If it is so unthinkable that I will not worship the one who let my daughter die, then you had best slay me now. Breathe on me and melt the flesh from my bones. It will be worth it if it opens my son's eyes to you, and the eyes of those others willing to grovel before you.' She spat her final words. Her eyes swept the gathered folk. 'You refused to heed the words of Reyn Khuprus. Watch now, and see what this creature truly is.'

The dragon drew back her head. The faint luminescence of the creature's silver eyes made them pale stars. Her great jaws opened wide, but Keffria had finally found her courage.

Selden stood, stricken by horror, eyes darting from his mother to the dragon. It cut her that he seemed unable to choose, but she stood her ground. All the other folk crowded back and away from Keffria as the dragon drew breath. Then, pushing her way forwards, her mother stepped to her side. Ronica took her arm. Together they stared defiantly up at the creature that had taken Malta's life and Selden's heart. Keffria found her voice again. 'Give me back my children! Or give me my death!' From somewhere, Reyn Khuprus hurtled into them, jostling them all aside. Keffria staggered to her knees and Ronica went down beside her. She heard Jani Khuprus' cry of horror from the dais. The young Rain Wilder stood alone where they had been. 'Run!' he ordered them, then spun to face the dragon, his scaled face contorted with fury. 'Tintaglia!' he roared. 'Stop!' A sword was bared in his hand.

For a wonder, the dragon froze. Her jaws still gaped. A single drop of liquid formed on one of her myriad teeth. When it dripped to the stone floor of the Concourse, the stone sizzled and gave way to it.

But Reyn had not stopped her. Selden had. He had stepped quietly forwards, to crane his neck up at Tintaglia. His words and manner healed Keffria's heart. 'Please, don't hurt them!' the boy begged shrilly, his courtier's manners fled. 'Please, dragon, they are my family, as dear to me as yours are to you. All we want is to have my sister back. Mighty as you are, can't you give that to us? Can't you bring her back?'

Reyn seized Selden by his shoulders, thrust him towards his mother. Keffria caught hold of him in numbed silence. Her son, truly hers still, no matter how scales lined his face. She held him tight to her, and felt her mother's grip on her arm tighten. The Vestrits stood together, no matter what else might come.

'No one can bring back the dead, Selden,' Reyn said flatly. 'It is useless to ask that of her. Malta is dead.' As he flung back his head to confront the dragon, a trick of the torches sent light dancing along his scaled face, making Reyn appear as dragon-like as Tintaglia. 'Keffria is right. I will not be seduced. No matter what you can do for Bingtown, you should be revealed for what you are, to keep others from falling to your wiles.' He turned to the gathered folk and opened wide his arms. 'Hear me, people of Bingtown! She has entranced you with her glamour. You cannot believe or trust this creature. She will not keep her word. When the time suits her, she will throw aside all bargains, and claim one so great as herself cannot be bound in agreement by beings as insignificant as we are. Aid her, and you restore to life a race of tyrants! Oppose her now, while there is only one to fight.'

Tintaglia flung her head back and gave a roar of frustration that surely must have shaken the stars in their sockets. Keffria shrank back, but they did not run. The dragon lifted her front feet from the wall's edge and slammed them down again. A great jagged crack raced through the stone wall at the impact. 'You tire me!' she hissed at Reyn. 'I lie, you say. You poison minds against me with your venomous words. I lie? I break my word? You lie! Look into my eyes, human, and know the truth.'

She thrust her great head at him, but Reyn held his ground. Ronica, gripping Keffria's shoulders, tried to drag her back, but she would not budge. She grasped Selden as he strained towards the dragon. Their tableau held, a frozen statue of fear and longing. Then Keffria heard Reyn gasp out his breath, and not take another. He was transfixed by the swift silver spinning of the dragon's eyes. The creature did not touch Reyn, but the Rain Wilder leaned towards her, his muscles standing out as if he resisted a great force. Keffria reached to restrain him, but beneath her hand, his flesh was set like stone. Reyn's lips moved, but he uttered no sound.

Abruptly, the dragon's eyes stopped their silver swirling. Reyn dropped at their feet like a puppet with severed strings. He sprawled motionless on the cold stone floor.

*   *   *

Reyn had not known she could reach out and touch his mind so effortlessly. As he stared into her eyes, he felt and heard her within his thoughts. 'Faithless little man,' she said scathingly. 'You measure me by your own actions. I have not betrayed you. You blame me because you could not find your female, but I had already kept my word to you. I could not rescue your Malta. I did all I could and then I left you to solve your problem. You failed. That was not my fault, and I do not deserve to be reviled for it. The failure is yours, little male. Nor did I lie. Open yourself. Touch me and know that I spoke true. Malta lives.'

Twice before, he had touched souls with Malta. In the mystic intimacy of the dream-box, in the joining made possible by finely powdered wizardwood, their thoughts had mingled. They had dreamed well together. The memory of it still stirred his blood to heat. In the dream-box unity, he had known her in a way he could never mistake for another. Beyond scent or touch or even the taste of her lips was another sensation that was the essence of Malta in his mind.

The dragon seized his mind: He was held, whether he would or not. He struggled, until he sensed in the dragon another reaching. Faint as perfume on the wind, a rare yet familiar sensation touched his mind. Malta. Through the dragon he sensed her but could not touch her. It was as taunting as seeing her silhouette on a blowing curtain, or smelling her scent and feeling the warmth of her cheek on a recently vacated pillow. He leaned towards it, yearning, but could find no substance. He felt Tintaglia's efforts, as if she sorted Malta's thread from a tangled skein of sensations. Here it was strong and clean, and then it vanished into memories of wind and rain and saltwater. *Where is she?* his mind frantically demanded of Tintaglia's. *How is she?*

I cannot know such things by this sense! the dragon replied disdainfully. *As well sniff for a sound, or taste sunlight! This is the bonding sense, not meant to flow between human and dragon. You*

*have not the ability to reciprocate, and so she is unaware of your
yearning. I can only tell you that she lives, somewhere, somehow.
Now do you believe me?*

'I believe. Malta is alive. I believe she lives. She lives.' Reyn
hoarsely whispered the words. Agony or rapture could have
been his emotion; it was hard to tell.

Jani had clambered from the dais and forced her way
through the crowd to kneel beside her son. Now she looked
across Reyn's body at Selden. 'What did she do to him?'
she cried.

Keffria watched them both. Did Jani know how much she
resembled the dragon? The fine scaling on her lips and brow
and the faint glow of her eyes in the torchlight all contributed
to the effect. Jani knelt by Reyn's body and stared down at him
just as Tintaglia looked down on them. How could one who
looked so like the dragon ask her son such a question? Selden
knelt beside them, but he gazed raptly up at the dragon that
loomed over them. His lips moved as if he prayed, but his eyes
were on Tintaglia.

'I don't know,' Keffria replied for her son. She looked down
at Malta's stirring betrothed. He looked half a dragon himself,
but he had been willing to risk his life to save hers. His heart
was as human as hers. She glanced at her own son, regarding
the dragon so intently. Light ran across Selden's light scaling.
He, too, had stood before the dragon and begged for his family.
He was still hers. In an odd way, so was Reyn. Keffria set her
hand gently on Reyn's chest. 'Lie still,' she bade him. 'You'll
be all right. Just lie still.'

Above them, the dragon threw back her head and trumpeted
triumphantly. 'He believes me! You see, folk of Bingtown. I
do not lie! Come. Let us seal this bargain we have made, and
tomorrow begin a new life for all of us.'

Jani swept suddenly to her feet. 'I will not agree. There

will be no bargain here until I know what you have done to my son!'

Tintaglia gave Reyn a careless glance. 'I have enlightened him, Trader Khuprus. That is all. He will not doubt me again.'

Reyn abruptly clutched Keffria's wrist in his scaly hand. His eyes bored into hers. 'She lives,' he promised her wildly. 'Malta truly lives. I have touched minds with her, through the dragon.'

Beside her, Ronica gave a broken sob. Keffria still could not find hope. Was this true, or a dragon's deception?

The whites of Reyn's copper eyes glowed as he struggled to a sitting position. He drew an uneven breath. 'Strike what bargain you will with Bingtown, Tintaglia,' he said in a low voice. 'But before you do, we will make our own agreement.' Now his voice dropped. 'For you have handed me the final piece of a puzzle.' He lifted his eyes to stare at her boldly as he offered, 'Others, dragons like yourself, may still survive.'

At this last sentence, Tintaglia froze, looking down on Reyn. She twisted her head speculatively. 'Where?' she demanded.

Before Reyn could reply, Mingsley had clambered down from the dais to push between the dragon and Reyn. 'This is not fair!' he proclaimed. 'People of Bingtown, listen to me! Do the Rain Wilds speak for all of us? No! Should this one man be able to halt our bargaining over a matter of the heart? Of course not!'

Selden stepped up to him. 'A matter of the heart? A matter of my sister's life!' He switched his gaze to the dragon. 'She is as dear to me as any serpent is to you, Tintaglia. Keep faith with me on this. Show them all that you see my family's need for her is as pressing as your drive to save your own kind.'

'Silence!' The dragon's head shot down. A tiny nudge sent Mingsley sprawling to one side. Her eyes fixed on Reyn. 'Other dragons? You have seen them?'

'Not yet. But I could find them,' Reyn replied. A faint smile played about his mouth but his eyes were grave and hard. 'Provided you do as Selden suggests. Prove that you understand our kin matter as much to us as yours do to you.'

The dragon flung her head up suddenly. Her nostrils flared and her eyes spun wildly. She spoke as if to herself. 'Find them? Where?'

Reyn smiled. 'I do not fear to tell you. It will take man's work to unearth them for you. If the Elderkind took cocooned dragons into shelter in one city, perhaps they did in another as well. It is a fair trade, is it not? Restore my love to me, and I shall endeavour to rescue any of your kin who may have survived.'

The dragon's nostrils flared wide. The glow of her eyes brightened. Her tail lashed with excitement and from outside the walls, Keffria heard the fearful cries of watching folk. But within the walls, Reyn stood still, teetering on the edge of triumph. All around him, folk were frozen into a listening silence.

'Done!' roared the dragon. Her wings twitched, shivering and rustling as if she longed to spring into flight immediately. They stirred the cold night air and sent it whispering past the huddled folk in the roofless building. 'These others will make plans for the dredging of the river. You and I will leave at first light, to begin the search for the ancient ruins –'

'No.' Reyn's reply was quiet but the dragon's outraged roar rang against the night sky. People cried out in terror and cowered where they stood, but not Reyn. He stood tall and still as the dragon vented her fury.

'Malta first,' Reyn dictated calmly as she drew breath.

'Seek for your female, while my kind lies trapped in the cold and dark? No!' This time the blast of anger from the dragon vibrated the floor beneath Keffria's feet. Her ears rang with it.

*   *   *

437

'Listen to me, dragon,' Reyn resumed calmly. 'High summer is the time to explore and dig, when the river runs low. Now is the time for us to seek Malta.' As the dragon threw back her head, jaws wide, he shouted up at her, 'For this to work, we must negotiate as equals, without threats. Will you be calm, or must we both live with loss?'

Tintaglia lowered her head. Her eyes spun angrily, but her voice was almost civil. 'Speak on,' she bade him.

Reyn took a breath. 'You will aid me to save Malta. And I will then devote myself to unearthing the Elderling city, not for treasure, but for dragons. That is our agreement. Your bargain with Bingtown is more complicated. The dredging of a river for the protection of their coast, with other stipulations. Would you have it set down in writing, and the agreement acknowledged as binding?' Reyn looked away from the dragon to Devouchet. 'I am willing to be bound by my spoken word in this. Will the Council of Bingtown deal likewise?'

Up on the dais, Devouchet glanced about indecisively. Keffria supposed he was rattled to have control put back into his hands. Slowly the Trader drew himself up. To her surprise, he shook his head slowly. 'No. What has been proposed tonight will change the life of every person who lives in Bingtown.' The Trader's eyes travelled gravely over the hushed crowd. 'An agreement of this magnitude must be written and signed.' He took a breath. 'Moreover, I propose that it must be signed, not just by our leaders, but as we did of old in Bingtown, when every Trader and every member of the Trader's family set hand to the document. But this time, marks must be made by every person, young and old, who wishes to remain in Bingtown. All who sign will bind themselves, not just to an agreement with the dragon, but to each other.'

A mutter ran through the crowd, but Devouchet spoke on. 'Every one who makes a mark agrees to be bound by the rules of old Bingtown. In turn, each head of a family will gain a vote on the Bingtown Council, as it was of old.' He looked around, including the leaders on the dais. 'All must agree that the Bingtown Council's judgements upon their disputes will be final.' He took a deep breath. 'And then, I think, there must be a vote to choose new members of the new Bingtown Council. To assure that every group gains a voice.'

Devouchet's eyes went back to the dragon. 'You, too, must make a mark to signify your agreement. Then the Kendry must be returned to us, and the other liveships summoned back, for without them no workers or materials can be carried upriver. Then you must look at our charts with us, and help us mark out the stretches of the river that we do not know, and show us where this deepening of the river must occur.'

People were nodding, but the dragon gave a loud snort of disgust. 'I have no time for this writing and marking! Regard it as done, and let us begin tonight!'

Reyn spoke before any one else could. 'Swift is better; on that you and I agree. Let them set their words to paper. Between you and I, I offer you my word, and I am willing to take yours.'

Reyn took a breath. When he spoke again, he made his tone formal. 'Dragon Tintaglia, do we have a bargain?'

'We do,' the dragon replied heavily. Tintaglia looked at Devouchet and the others on the dais. 'Set your pen to paper, and do it swiftly. I am bound by my name and not by a mark. Tomorrow, Tintaglia begins to do what she has promised. See that you are as quick to keep your word.'

EIGHTEEN

Loyalties

KENNIT LOOKED DOWN at the scroll in his hand. The pieces of wax seal on his desk had borne the sigil of Sincure Faldin. That worthy merchant had adapted to the loss of his wife and one daughter. His sons and his ship had survived the slavers' raid on Divvytown unscathed, for they had been out trading at the time. As Kennit had predicted to Sorcor, Sincure Faldin had accepted Sorcor's marriage to Alyssum, for the Durjan merchant had always been swift to see where power resided. This urgent message was but one more effort by him to curry goodwill with Kennit. As such, he regarded it suspiciously.

The writing on the scroll was laboriously elaborate, and the wording stilted. A full third of the page was an opulent greeting and wish for Kennit's good health. How like the over-dressed Durjan merchant, to waste his ink and his time so painstakingly before unfolding his dire news. Despite the hammering of his heart, Kennit forced himself to reread the scroll with an impassive face. He sifted facts from the merchant's flowery prose. Faldin had mistrusted the strangers who came to Divvytown, and had been among the first to suspect the ship was a liveship. He had had his son lure the captain and his woman into his shop and ply them with tales to get them to divulge some of their own history, but to little avail. Their abrupt departure in the middle of the night was as strange as their arrival had been, and tales told the next day by men who had deserted the ship bore out his suspicions. On board was one Althea Vestrit, who claimed ownership of the Vivacia. The crew of the liveship had been oddly mixed, men and women, but the captain had been that Brashen fellow, lately of the *Springeve*, and before that, Bingtown born and bred, or so rumour had it. If one could believe deserters, the ship's true mission was to reclaim the liveship Vivacia. Hence, due to his vast respect for the pirate Kennit and his great loyalty to his king, and with another long string of flowery compliments, Sincure Faldin was sending Kennit this warning by the swiftest ship in the Divvytown harbour. The ship had been a liveship, the figurehead badly damaged, and by name Paragon.

The inked name seemed to burn into his eyes. It was hard to concentrate on the meandering section that followed and quoted gossip and bird-borne rumours that Jamaillia City was raising a fleet to sail northward and inflict punishment on Bingtown for the kidnapping of the Satrap and the destruction of his tariff dock there. It was Faldin's studied opinion that the nobles of Jamaillia had long been seeking an excuse to plunder Bingtown. They seemed to have found it.

Kennit raised incredulous eyebrows at that tale. The Satrap had left Jamaillia, gone to Bingtown and been kidnapped there? The whole narrative seemed far-fetched. The meat of the rumour, of course, was that Jamaillia City was raising a retaliatory fleet. Purposeful warships passing through Pirate Isle waters were to be avoided. When they returned with the spoils of their war-making, however, they would be fat prey. His serpents would make such piracy near effortless.

The missive closed with another string of earnest compliments and good wishes, and rather unsubtle reminders that Kennit should be grateful to Sincure Faldin for sending him these tidings. At the bottom was an intricate signature done in two colours of ink, followed by a tasteless postscript exulting over how ripely Alyssum was swelling with Sorcor's seed.

Kennit set the scroll down on his desk and let the cursed thing roll itself up. Sorcor and the others gathered in his cabin stolidly waited to hear the news. The messenger had followed Faldin's explicit orders to deliver the message to Sorcor so that he could take it immediately to Captain Kennit, probably so Sorcor could admire his father-in-law's cleverness and loyalty.

Or was there more? Could either Sorcor or Sincure Faldin suspect what this news meant to Kennit? Had there been another message, for Sorcor's eyes only, in which Faldin bid him watch how his captain reacted? For an instant, doubt and suspicion gnawed at Kennit, but for an instant only. Sorcor could not read. If Faldin had wanted to rope his son-in-law into a plot against Kennit, he had chosen the wrong medium.

The first time Kennit had read the liveship's name and description, his heart had lurched in his chest. He had forced himself to continue breathing evenly, and maintained his calm expression. A second slow perusal of the page had allowed him time to compose his voice and manner. There were many questions to answer. Did Faldin suspect the connection? If so, how? He did not mention it, unless the words about the sailors who had jumped ship from the Paragon were a hint. Did those sailors know and had they talked? Did this Althea Vestrit know, and if she did, did she intend to use Paragon somehow as a weapon against him? If it was known, how widely was it known? Was it beyond the control of killing a few men and sinking a ship again?

Would his past never stay submerged?

For one wild instant, Kennit offered himself escape. He did not have to go back to Divvytown. He had a liveship under him and a fleet of serpents at his disposal. He could abandon all and go anywhere, anywhere there was water, and still make his fortune. He would have to begin all over, of course, to establish his reputation, but the serpents would assure that that happened swiftly. He lifted his eyes briefly and scanned the people in his room. They would all have to die, unfortunately. Even Wintrow, he thought with a pang. And he'd have to get rid of his entire crew and replace them somehow. And still the ship would know who he had been . . .

'Captain?' Sorcor prodded him gently.

The daydream popped like a bubble. It wasn't feasible. Far more pragmatic to go back to Divvytown, tidy away whoever suspected, and go on as before. There was the ship himself, of course, but he had dealt with Paragon once. He'd just have to do it again. He pushed that thought aside. He could not face it yet.

'Bad news, Cap'n?' Sorcor dared to ask.

Kennit managed a sardonic smile. He would parcel out the tidings and see if anyone flinched. 'News is news, Captain Sorcor. It is up to the recipient to make good or bad of it. But these tidings are . . . interesting. I am sure we are all pleased to know that your Alyssum grows ever rounder. Sincure Faldin also reports that a strange ship has visited Divvytown, professing a desire to join us in our crusade to rid the Inside Passage of slaveships. But our good friend Faldin was not convinced of their sincerity. The ship arrived rather mysteriously, negotiating the passage to the harbour in the dark of night, and leaving the same way.' He glanced back at the scroll negligently. 'And there is a rumour that Jamaillia City raises a fleet to plunder Bingtown, in revenge for some affront to the Satrap.'

Kennit leaned back casually in his chair to have more faces in view. Etta was there with Wintrow at her side. He always seemed to be at her side lately, he reflected briefly. Sorcor, his broad, scarred face beaming loyalty and devotion to Kennit and pride in his woman's fecundity, stood next to Jola, Kennit's current first mate.

All were resplendent in the rich yields of their most recent piracies. Etta had coaxed even Wintrow into a wide-sleeved shirt of dark blue silk embroidered with ravens, by Etta's own needle. Staunch Sorcor wore emeralds in his ears now, and a broad belt of leather worked with silver held two matching swords. The richness of the fabrics Etta wore was only heightened by her remarkable cut of them. Had cloth-of-gold ever been worn to climb a mast before? In the hold were other harvests from the sea: rare medicines and exotic perfume oils, gold and silver stamped with the likenesses of many different Satraps, jewels both raw and wrought into jewellery, and fabulous pelts and glowing tapestries. The wealth in his hold now easily equalled last year's full gathering.

Hunting had been bountiful lately; piracy had never been so effortless. Flanked by his flotilla of serpents, he need do no more than sight an interesting sail. He and Bolt selected their targets and she sent the serpents forth. An hour or two of harassment by the serpents, and the prey surrendered. At first, he had then closed on the demoralized ships and demanded surrender of all their valuables. The crews had always been subservient and willing. Without even a sword drawn, Kennit fleeced the vessels and then sent them on their way, with a stern reminder that these waters were now the province of King Kennit of the Pirate Isles. He suggested that if their rulers were interested in establishing generous tariffs to pass through his territory, he might be willing to treat with them.

The last two ships, he had ordered the serpents to 'fetch' for him. The Vivacia anchored until the serpents herded her victims to her. The last captain had surrendered on his knees while Kennit sat enthroned on a comfortable chair on the Vivacia's foredeck. Bolt delighted in the captive captain's ill-concealed terror of her. After Kennit had made his selections from the ship's manifests, the captured crew had seen to the cargo transfer. Kennit's only concern would be to keep his own crew from becoming bored or complacent. From time to time, he planned to stop a slaver, to let the crew indulge their need for bloodshed and feed the serpents to increase their loyalty to him.

Faldin's message had arrived on a swift little ship named *Sprite*. Although Jola had recognized the ship and she had been flying Kennit's raven flag, neither Kennit nor Bolt had been able to resist flaunting their power. The serpents had been sent forth to surround the small ship and escort it to Kennit. The captain had made a brave show of greeting Kennit but no amount of bravado could quite banish the quaver from his voice. The messenger had been pale and silent when he reached the deck of the *Vivacia*, for he had made the crossing in a tiny boat through the gleaming backs of serpents.

Kennit had taken the missive and dismissed the messenger to a 'well-deserved ration of brandy'. Every man aboard the *Sprite* would carry word to Divvytown of Kennit's new allies. It was well to impress one's enemies with a show of strength. It was even better to be sure one's friends remembered it as well. Kennit kept that in mind as he slowly surveyed the faces around him.

Sorcor's brow furrowed as he endeavoured to think. 'Did Faldin know the skipper? He should. He knows damn near everyone in Divvytown, and it takes an experienced man to bring a ship up the slough, even in daylight.'

'He did,' Kennit confirmed easily. 'One Brashen Trell, of Bingtown. I gather he did business in Divvytown last season on the *Springeve* with old Finney.' Kennit feigned glancing at the missive again. 'Perhaps this Trell is an extraordinary navigator with an excellent memory, but Faldin suspects it was more the ship he used than the man. A liveship. With a chopped face. By name, Paragon.'

Wintrow's face betrayed him. His cheeks had flushed at the name of Trell. Now he stood, tongue-tied and sweating. Interesting. Impossible that the lad was in league with Sincure Faldin; he simply had not had enough free time in Divvytown. So this was something else. As if by accident, he let his eyes meet the boy's. He smiled mildly at him. And waited.

Wintrow looked stricken. Twice his lips parted and closed again before he cleared his throat faintly. 'Sir?' he managed in a whisper.

'Wintrow?' Kennit put warm query into his voice.

Wintrow crossed his arms on his chest. What secret, Kennit wondered, did he seek to hold inside? When Wintrow spoke, his voice was small. 'You should heed Faldin's warning. Brashen Trell was first mate to my grandfather, Captain Ephron Vestrit. Perhaps he truly seeks to join you, but I doubt it. He served aboard the Vivacia for years, and may still feel great loyalty to the Vestrits. To my family.'

At these final words, the boy's fingers tightened on his arms. So there it was. Wintrow chose to be loyal to Kennit but still felt it as a betrayal of his family. Interesting. Almost touching. Kennit steepled his fingers on the table before him. 'I see.' A vague shivering had passed throughout the ship at the mention of her old captain's name. That was even more interesting than Wintrow's divided loyalty. Bolt claimed that there was nothing left of the old Vivacia. Why, then, would she tremble at Captain Vestrit's name?

Silence reigned. Wintrow stared down at the edge of the table. His face was very still, his jaw set. Kennit tossed up his last bit of information. He gave a small, resigned sigh. 'Ah. That would explain the presence of Althea Vestrit among the crew. Deserters from the Paragon say that she intends to take Vivacia away from me.'

A second shivering ran through the ship. Wintrow froze, his face paling. 'Althea Vestrit is my aunt,' he said faintly. 'She was closely bonded to the ship, even before she awakened. She had expected to inherit Vivacia.' The boy swallowed. 'Kennit, I know her. Not well, not in all things, but where this ship is concerned, she will not be dissuaded. She will try to take the Vivacia. That is as certain as sunrise.'

Kennit smiled faintly. 'Through a wall of serpents? If she survives them, she will discover that Vivacia is no longer who she once was. I do not think I need to fear.'

'No longer who she once was,' Wintrow repeated in a whisper. His look had become distant. 'Are any of us?' he asked, and lowered his face into his hands.

Malta was sick of ships. She hated the smells, the motion, the appalling food, the coarse men, and most of all she hated the Satrap. No, she corrected herself. Worst of all she hated that she could not show the Satrap how much she loathed and despised him.

The Chalcedean mother ship had taken them up days ago. Kekki's body had been hastily abandoned with the badly leaking galley. As Malta and the others had been hauled to safety aboard the three-masted ship, their rescuers hooted and pointed at the sinking galley. She suspected the captain of the galley had suffered a great loss of status by losing his ship that included forfeiting his rights to his 'guests' for they had not seen the man since they had come aboard. The single chamber she now shared with the Satrap was larger, with real walls of solid wood and a door that latched securely. It was warmer and drier than the makeshift tent cabin on the deck of the galley, but just as bare. It had no window. It offered little more than the absolute necessities for life. Food was brought to them, and the dishes taken away afterwards. Once every two days, a boy came to carry away their waste bucket. The air of the cabin was close and stuffy; the sole lantern that swung from an overhead beam smoked incessantly, contributing to the thick atmosphere. Fastened to the wall were a small table that folded down for use and a narrow bunk with a flattened mattress and two blankets. The Satrap ate while seated on his bunk; Malta stood. The chamberpot was under the bunk, with a small railing to keep it from sliding about. A jug for water and a single mug rested on a small, railed shelf by the door. That was it. As Malta disdained to share the bunk with the Satrap, the floor was her bed. After he was asleep, she could sometimes filch one of the blankets from under his slack grip.

When she and the Satrap had first been shown to the room and the door shut securely behind them, he had stared slowly around himself. His pinched lips white with fury, he had demanded, 'This is the best you could do for us?'

She had still been sodden with shock. Her near-rape, the death of Kekki and the sudden change in ships had left her reeling. 'I could do for us?' she asked stupidly.

'Go now! Tell them I will not tolerate this. Right now!'

Her temper snapped. She hated the tears that brimmed her eyes and spilled down her cheeks as she demanded, 'Just how am I to do that? I don't speak Chalcedean, I don't know who to complain to if I did. Nor would these animals listen to me. In case you haven't noticed, Chalcedeans don't exactly respect women.'

He gave a snort of contempt. 'Not women like you, they don't. If Kekki were here, she would soon set things right. You should have been the one to die. At least Kekki knew how to manage things!'

Going to the door, he had flung it open. He stood in the doorframe and yelled for attention until a deckhand came, then shrieked at the man in Chalcedean. The deckhand had looked from the Satrap to Malta and back again, in obvious puzzlement. Then he had bowed sketchily and disappeared. 'It's your fault if he doesn't even come back!' the Satrap had spat at her, flinging himself down on the bunk. He pulled the blankets over himself and ignored her. Malta had sat down in the corner on the floor and sulked. The deckhand had not returned.

The corner had become her part of the room. She sat there now, her back braced against the wall contemplating her grubby feet. She longed to get out on the deck, to get one breath of clean, cold air, to see the sky and above all to discover in which direction they sailed. The galley had been carrying them northward, towards Chalced. The Chalcedean ship that had picked them up had been travelling south. But she had no way of knowing if it had continued on its course, or had turned back to Chalced. To be so confined, and have no idea of when their voyage would end was yet another torture. Enforced idleness and tedium had become the fabric of her days.

Nor could she wring any information from the Satrap. The wallowing of this round-hulled ship made him queasy. When he was not vomiting, he was complaining of hunger and thirst. When food and drink were brought to him, he immediately gorged himself, only to disgorge it a few hours later. With each of his meals came a small quantity of coarse smoking herbs. He would thicken the air of the small cabin until Malta was dizzy with them, all the while complaining that the poor quality of the herb left his throat raw and his head unsoothed. In vain had Malta entreated him to take a bit of air; all he would do was lie on the bed and groan, or demand that she rub his feet, or his neck.

As long as the Satrap confined himself to the cabin, Malta was effectively jailed there as well. She dared not venture out without him.

She rubbed at her burning eyes. The smoke from the lantern inflamed them. Their noonday repast had already been cleared away. The long hours until dinner stretched endlessly before her. The Satrap, against her gentle counselling, had once more stuffed himself. He now puffed at a short black pipe. He took it from his mouth, glared at it, and then drew on it again. The dissatisfied look on his face spoke of trouble brewing for Malta. He shifted uncomfortably on the bed, and then belched loudly.

'A stroll about the deck might aid your digestion,' Malta suggested quietly.

'Oh, do be quiet. The mere thought of the effort of walking makes my poor belly heave.' He suddenly snatched the pipe from his mouth and flung it at her. Without even waiting for her reaction, he rolled to face the wall, ending the conversation.

Malta leaned her head back against the wall. The pipe had not hit her, but the implied threat of his temper had rattled her nerves. She tried to think of what she should do next. Tears threatened. She set her jaw and clenched her fists against her eyes. She would not cry. She was a tough descendant of a determined folk, she reminded herself, a Bingtown Trader's daughter. What, she wondered, would her grandmother have done? Or Althea? They were strong and smart. They would have discovered a way out of this.

Malta realized she was absently fingering the scar on her forehead and pulled her hand away. The injury had closed again, but the healed flesh had an unpleasant gristly texture. The ridged scar extended back into her hairline a full fingerlength. Malta wondered what it looked like and swallowed sickly.

She pulled her knees in tightly to her chest and hugged them. She closed her eyes, but kept sleep at bay. Sleep brought dreams, terrible dreams of all she refused to face by day. Dreams of Selden buried in the city, dreams of her mother and grandmother reviling her for luring him to his death. She dreamed of Delo, recoiling in horror from Malta's ruined face. She dreamed of her father, turning away, face set, from his disgraced daughter. Worst were the dreams of Reyn; always, they were dancing, the music sweet, the torches glowing. First her slippers fell away, showing her scabby, dirty feet. Then her dress tattered suddenly into filthy rags. Finally, as her hair tumbled lankly to her shoulders and her scar oozed fluid down her face, Reyn thrust her from him. She fell sprawling to the floor, and all the dancers surrounded her, pointing in horror. 'A moment of beauty, ruined forever,' they taunted, pointing. A few nights ago, the dream had been different. It had been so real, almost like the shared visions of the dream-box. He had outstretched his hands to grasp hers. 'Malta, reach for me!' he had begged. 'Help me come to you.' But, even in the dream, she had known it was useless. She had clasped her hands behind her, and hidden her shame from him. Better never to touch him again than to see pity or revulsion on his face. She had awakened sobbing, stabbed by the sweetness of his voice. That dream had been worst of all.

When she thought of Reyn, her heart ached. She touched her lips, remembering a stolen kiss, the fabric of his veil a soft barrier between their mouths. But every sweet memory was edged with a hundred sharp regrets. Too late, she told herself. Forever too late.

With a sigh, she lifted her head and opened her eyes. So. Here she was, on a ship, bound Sa knows where, dressed in rags, scar-faced, stripped of her rights and rank as a Trader's daughter and in the company of an insufferable prig of a boy. She certainly couldn't depend on him to do anything to better their circumstances. All he did was to lie on the bunk and whimper that this was no way to treat the Satrap of all Jamaillia. Clearly, he had not yet grasped that they were the prisoners of the Chalcedeans.

She looked at Cosgo and tried to see him impartially. He had grown pale and bony. Now that she thought of it, he had not even complained much the last day or so. He no longer tried to groom himself. When they had first come aboard, he had tried to keep up his appearance. With no combs or brushes, he had directed Malta to groom his unbound hair with her fingers. She had done so, but had scarcely managed to conceal her distaste. He had enjoyed her touch too obviously, leaning his body back against her as she sat on the edge of his bed. In grotesque flirtation, he had mocked her, foretelling that someday she would brag to others of how she had attended the Satrap in his hardship. But he would tell all how miserably she had failed as both a dutiful subject and a woman. Unless . . .

And then he had seized her wrist and tried to guide it where she would not let it go. She had jerked free of him and retreated. But all of that had been before the seasickness mastered him. Since he had become sick, he had grown quieter every day. A sudden worry shook her. If he died, what would become of her? Dimly, she recalled something Kekki had said, back on the galley . . . She knit her brow, and the words came back to her. 'His status will protect us, if we protect it.' Abruptly she sat up straight and stared at him. She did not need to be a Bingtown Trader here to survive on this ship, she must think like a woman of Chalced.

Malta went to the bunk and stood over the Satrap. His closed eyelids were dark; he clutched feebly at the blanket with thin hands. As much as she disliked him, she found she pitied him. What had she been thinking, to even imagine that he could do anything for them? If anyone was to better their situation, it would have to be her. It was what the Satrap expected, that his Companions would care for his needs. More, she realized, it was what the Chalcedeans had expected. She had cowered in their room while she should have angrily demanded good treatment for her man. Chalcedeans would not respect a man whose own woman doubted his power. The Satrap had been right. She, not he, had condemned them to this miserable treatment. She only hoped it was not too late to salvage his status.

She dragged the blanket away from him despite his mumbled protest. As she had seen her mother do when Selden was sick, she set her hand to the Satrap's brow, and then felt under his arms, but found no fever or swellings. Very gently, she tapped his cheek until his eyes cracked open. The whites were yellowish, and when he spoke, his breath was foul. 'Leave me alone,' he moaned, groping for the blankets.

'If I do, I fear you will die, illustrious one.' She tried for the tone that Kekki had always used with him. 'It grieves me beyond words to see you misused this way. I shall risk myself and go to the captain to protest this.' The thought of venturing out alone terrified her, yet she knew it was their only chance. She rehearsed the words that she hoped she'd be brave enough to say to the man's face. 'He is a fool, to treat the Satrap of all Jamaillia so shamefully. He deserves to die, and his honour and name with him.'

The Satrap's eyes opened wider and he stared at her in dull surprise. He blinked and sparks of righteous anger began to burn in his eyes. Good. If she played her role well enough, he would have to live up to it with disdain of his own. She took a breath.

'Even on this tub of a ship, they should be able to provide better for you! Does the captain reside in a bare room, with no comfort or beauty? I doubt it. Does he eat coarse food, does he smoke stable straw? Whatever balm for the soul he enjoys should have been offered you when you boarded. Day after cruel day, you have waited with patience for them to treat you as you deserve. If the wrath of all Jamaillia falls upon them now, they have only themselves to blame. You have practised the very patience of Sa himself. Now I shall demand that they right this disgrace.' She crossed her arms on her chest. 'What is the Chalcedean word for "Captain"?'

Consternation touched his face. He took a breath. '*Leu-fay.*'

'*Leu-fay,*' she repeated. She paused and looked more closely at the Satrap. Tears of either self-pity or amazement had welled to his eyes. She covered him, snuggling the blankets around him as if he were Selden. A strange resolve had wakened in her. 'Rest now, lordly one. I shall prepare myself, and then I shall see that you are treated as the Satrap of Jamaillia deserves, or die trying.' That last, she feared, was true.

When his eyes sagged shut again, she stood and went to work. The robe she wore was the same one she had worn since the night she had left Trehaug. She had managed to rinse it out once on board the galley. The hem hung in tatters, and it was stained with hard use. She took it off, and with fingers and

453

teeth she tore the dangling pieces away. She shook it well, and rubbed the worst of the dirt from it before putting it back on. It left her legs bared from the knees down, but that could not be helped. She used the scraps from her robe to fashion a long braid of material. She combed her hair as best she could with her fingers, and then fashioned the braided fabric into a head wrap for herself. Covering her hair, she hoped, would make her appear older, as well as concealing most of her scar. There was some water in the pitcher. She used a scrap of material as a washing cloth to cleanse her face and hands, and then her feet and legs.

With a bitter smile, she recalled how carefully she had prepared herself for her Presentation Ball, and how she had fretted over her made-over gown and slippers. 'Attitude and bearing,' Rache had counselled her then. 'Believe you are beautiful, and so will everyone else.' She had not been able to believe the slave woman. Now her words were Malta's only hope.

When she had done her best, she composed herself. Stand straight, head up. Imagine little brocade slippers on her feet, rings on her fingers, a crown of blossoms on her head. She fixed her eyes angrily on the door and addressed it firmly. '*Leu-fay!*' she demanded of it. She took a deep breath, then another. On the third she walked to the door, lifted the latch, and went out.

She ventured down a long walkway lit only by a swaying lantern at the other end. The shadows shifted with the light, making it difficult to keep her regal bearing. She walked between stowed cargo. The variety of it aroused her suspicions. Honest merchant ships did not carry such a wide spectrum of goods, nor would they stow it so haphazardly. Pirates or raiders, she told herself, though perhaps they thought otherwise of themselves. Was the Satrap no more to them than plunder to be sold to the highest bidder? The thought nearly sent her back to the room. Then she told herself that she would still demand that he be treated well. Surely, such a trade-good would command a better price if it were in the best possible condition.

She went up a short ladder, and found herself in a room full of men. It stank of sweat and smoke. Hammocks swung nearby, some with snoring occupants. One man mended canvas trousers in the corner. Three others were seated around a crate, with a game of pegs scattered across the top of it. As she entered, they all turned to stare. One, a blond man of about her age, dared to grin. His grimy striped shirt was opened halfway down his chest. She lifted her chin, and reminded herself once more of her glittering rings and blossom crown. She neither smiled nor looked away from him. Instead she reached for her mother's disapproving stare when she encountered idle servants. '*Leu-fay.*'

'*Leufay?*' a grizzled old man at the game table asked incredulously. His eyebrows leapt towards his balding pate in astonishment. The other man at the table chuckled.

Malta did not allow her face to change expression. Only her eyes became colder. '*Leufay!*' she insisted.

With a shrug and a sigh, the blond man stood. As he advanced towards her, she forced herself to stand her ground. She had to look up at him to meet his eyes. It was hard to keep her bearing. When he reached for her arm, she slapped his hand away contemptuously. Eyes blazing, she touched two fingers to her breast. 'Satrap's,' she told him coldly. '*Leufay. Right now!*' she snapped, not caring if they understood her words or not. The blond man glanced back at his companions and shrugged, but he did not try to touch her again. Instead, he pointed past her. A flip of her hand indicated that he should lead the way. She did not think she could stand to have anyone behind her.

He led her swiftly through the ship. A ladder took them up through a hatch onto a wind-washed deck. Her senses were dazzled by the fresh cold air and the smell of salt water and the sun sinking to its rest behind a bank of rosy clouds. Her heart leapt. South. The ship was taking them south, towards Jamaillia, not north to Chalced. Was there any chance a Bingtown ship might see them and try to stop them? She slowed her steps, hoping to catch sight of land, but the sea merged with clouds at the horizon. She could not even guess where they were. She lengthened her stride to catch up with her guide.

He took her to a tall, brawny man who was directing several crewmembers splicing lines. The sailor bobbed his head to the man, indicated Malta, and rattled off something, in which Malta caught the word '*leufay*'. The man ran his eyes up and down her in a familiar way, but she returned his look with a haughty stare. 'What you want?' he asked her.

It took every grain of her courage. 'I will speak to your captain.' She guessed that the sailor had taken her to the mate.

'Tell me what you want.' His accent was heavy, but the words were clear.

Malta folded her hands on her chest. 'I will speak to your captain.' She spoke slowly and distinctly as if he might be merely stupid.

'Tell *me*,' he insisted.

It was her turn to gaze him up and down. 'Certainly not!' she snapped. She tossed her head, turned with a motion that she and Delo had practised since they were nine years old (it would have flounced the skirts on a proper gown) then walked away from them all, keeping her head high and trying to breathe past her hammering heart. She was trying to remember which hatch they had come up when he called out 'Wait!'

She halted. Slowly she turned her head to look back at him over her shoulder. She raised one brow questioningly.

'Come back. I take you Captain Deiari.' He made small hand motions to be sure she understood.

She let him flap his hand at her several times before returning, at a dignified pace.

The captain's quarters in the stern were resplendent compared to the chamber she shared with the Satrap. There was a large bay window, a thick rug on the floor and several comfortable chairs and the chamber smelled sweetly of tobacco smoke and other herbs. In one corner, the captain's bed boasted a fat feather mattress as well as thick coverlets and even a throw of thick white fur. Books leaned against one another on a shelf, and several glass decanters held liquors of various colours.

The captain himself was seated in one of the comfortable chairs, his legs stretched out before him and a book in his hands. He wore a shirt of soft grey wool over heavy trousers. Thick socks shielded his feet from the cold; his sturdy wet boots were by the door. Malta longed for such warm, dry, clean clothing. He looked up in annoyance as they entered. At the sight of her, he barked a rough question at the mate. Before the man could reply, Malta cut in smoothly.

'Deiari Leufay. At the merciful Satrap Cosgo's pleasure, I have come to offer you the chance to correct your mistakes before they become irredeemable.' She met his eyes, her gaze cold, and waited.

He let her wait. A chilling certainty grew in her; she had miscalculated. He was going to have her killed and thrown overboard. She let only the coldness show on her face. Jewels on her fingers, a crown of blossoms, no, of thick gold on her brow. It was heavy; she lifted her chin to bear the weight and watched the man's pale eyes.

'The merciful Satrap Cosgo,' the man finally said colourlessly. His words were clear, unaccented.

Malta gave a tiny nod of acknowledgement. 'He is a more patient man than many. When first we came aboard, he excused your lack of courtesy towards him. Surely, he told me, the captain is busy with all the men he has taken aboard. He has reports to hear, and decisions to consider. The Satrap knows what it is to command, you see. He said to me, "Contain your impatience at this insult to me.

When he has had time to prepare a proper reception, then the *leufay* will send an envoy to this poor cabin, little better than a kennel, that he has provided for me." Then, as day after day passed, he found excuse after excuse for you. Perhaps you have been ill; perhaps you did not wish to disturb him while he was recovering his own strength. Perhaps you were ignorant as to the full honour that should be accorded him. As a man, he makes little of personal discomfort. What is a bare floor or poor food compared to the hardships he endured in the Rain Wilds? Yet as his loyal servant, I am offended for him. Charitably, he supposes that what you have offered him is your best.' She paused, and looked about the chamber slowly. 'Such a tale this will make in Jamaillia,' she observed quietly, as if to herself.

The captain came to his feet. He rubbed the side of his nose nervously, then made a dismissive wave to the mate who still stood at the door. The man whisked himself out of sight immediately, and the door shut solidly behind him. Malta could smell the tang of sudden sweat, but the captain appeared outwardly calm.

'It was such a wild tale, I scarcely gave it credit. This man is truly the Satrap of all Jamaillia?'

She gambled. All pleasantness faded from her face as she lowered her voice to an accusation. 'You *know* that he is. To profess ignorance of his rank is a poor excuse, sir.'

'And I suppose you are a lady of his court, then?'

She met his sarcasm squarely. 'Of course not. My accent is Bingtown, as I am sure you know. I am the humblest of his servants, honoured to serve him in his hour of need. I am acutely aware of my unworthiness.' She gambled again. 'The demise of his Companion Kekki on board a Chalcedean galley has grieved him greatly. Not that he blames the captain of the galley. But surely if first his Companion, and then the Satrap himself dies in Chalcedean hands, it will speak poorly of your hospitality.' Very softly, she added, 'It may even be seen as political intent, in some circles.'

'If any were to hear of it,' the captain pointed out heavily. Malta wondered if she had overplayed her game. But his next question re-armed her. 'What, exactly, were you doing up that river anyway?'

She smiled enigmatically. 'The secrets of the Rain Wilds are not for me to divulge. If you wish to know more perhaps the Satrap might choose to enlighten you.' Cosgo did not know enough about the Rain Wilds to betray anything of significance. She breathed out. 'Or not. Why should he share such secrets with one who has treated him so shamefully? For one who is nominally his ally, you have shown yourself a poor host. Or are we your captives in fact as well as in circumstance? Do you hold us with no thought but to ransom us, as if you were a common pirate?'

The directness of her question jolted the man. 'I . . . of course not, not captives.' His chin came up. 'If he were a captive, would I be bearing him with all haste to Jamaillia?'

'Where he will be sold to the highest bidder?' Malta asked dryly. The captain took a sudden angry breath, but she went on before he could speak. 'There must, of course, be that temptation. Only a fool would not see that possibility, in the midst of the current unrest. Yet a wise man would know of the legendary generosity of the Satrap to his friends. Whereas the largesse of a man who pays you blood-money brings his disdain and shame with it.' She cocked her head slightly. 'Will you be instrumental in cementing the friendship of Chalced and Jamaillia? Or will you forever tarnish the reputation of Chalcedeans, as turncoats who sell their allies?'

A long silence followed her words. 'You speak like a Bingtown Trader. Yet the Traders have never been fond of Chalced. What is your interest in this?'

My life, you idiot. Malta feigned scandalized surprise. 'You wish to know the interest of a *woman*, sir? Then I tell you: My father is of Chalced, sir. But *my* interest, of course, does not factor into this. The only interest I consider is the Satrap's.' She bowed her head reverently.

Those last words lay like ashes on her tongue. In the silence that followed them, she watched the careful working of the man's mind. He had nothing to lose by treating the Satrap well. A healthy, living hostage would undoubtedly bring more than one on the point of death. And the gratitude of the Satrap might be worth more than what could be wrung out of his nobles for his return.

'You may go,' the man dismissed her abruptly.

'As you wish, I am sure,' Malta murmured, her submission tinged with sarcasm. It would not do for the Satrap's woman to be too humble. Kekki had shown her that. She inclined her head gravely, but then turned her back on him rather than reversing from the room. Let him make what he would of that.

When she stepped out into the chill evening wind, a wave of vertigo spun her, yet she forced herself to remain upright. She was exhausted. She once more lifted her head beneath the weight of her imaginary crown. She did not hasten. She found the right hatch, and descended into the noisome depths of the ship. As she passed through the crew quarters, she pretended not to notice any of the men; for their part, they ceased all conversation, and stared after her.

She regained the cabin, shut the door behind her, crossed to the bed and sank shakily to her knees before it. It was as well that this collapse fit with the role she must continue to play. 'Exalted one, I have returned,' she said quietly. 'Are you well?'

'Well? I am half-starved and nattered at by a woman,' the Satrap retorted.

'Ah. I see. Well, lordly one, I have hopes that I have bettered our situation.'

'You? I doubt it.'

Malta bowed her forehead to her knees and sat trembling for a time. Just as she decided she had failed, there was a knock at the door. That would be the ship's boy with their dinner. She forced herself to stand and open the door rather than simply bid him enter.

Three brawny sailors stood outside behind the mate. The mate bowed stiffly. 'You come to *Leufay's* table tonight. You, for you, wash, dress.' This message seemed to strain his vocabulary, but a gesture indicated the men bearing buckets of steaming water and armloads of clothing. Some, she noted, was woman's garb. She had convinced him of her own status as well. She fought to keep delight and triumph from her face.

'If it pleases the Satrap,' she replied coolly, and with a gesture bade them bring it all inside.

'What will you do?' Wintrow dared to ask the ship. The chill night wind blew past them. He stood on the foredeck, arms wrapped around himself against the cold. They were making good time back to Divvytown. If Wintrow could have done so, he would have stilled the wind, slowed the ship, anything to gain time to think.

The sea was not dark. The tips of the waves caught the moonlight and carried it with them. Starlight snagged and rippled on the backs of the serpents that hummocked through the water beside them. Their eyes shone in lambent colours, copper, silver and warm gold, eerie pink and blue, like night-blooming sea flowers. Wintrow felt they were always watching him whenever he came to the foredeck. Perhaps they were. Coinciding with the thought, a head lifted from the water. He could not be sure in the gloom, but he thought that it was the green-gold serpent from the Others' beach. For the space of three breaths, she held her place beside the ship, watching him. *Two-legs, I know you* whispered through his mind, but he could not decide if she spoke to him or if he only recalled her voice from the beach.

'What will I do?' the ship taunted him lazily.

She could smash him at will. Wintrow pushed the useless fear aside. 'You know what I mean. Althea and Brashen are seeking us. They may be lying in wait for us near Divvytown, or they may simply confront us in the harbour. What will you do, you and your serpents?'

'Ah. About that. Well.' The figurehead leaned back towards him. Her dark locks writhed like a nest of snakes. She put a hand to one side of her mouth, as if to share a secret with him. But her whisper was loud, a stage-whisper intended for Kennit as he came step-tapping onto the deck. 'I will do whatever I please about that.' She smiled past him at the pirate. 'Good evening, my dear.'

'Good evening, and good wind, lovely one,' Kennit responded. He leaned over the railing and touched the large hand the ship held up to him in greeting. Then he smiled at Wintrow, his teeth white as a serpent's in the moonlight. 'Good evening, Wintrow. I trust you are well. When you left my cabin earlier, you looked a bit peaked.'

'I am not well,' Wintrow replied flatly. He looked at Kennit, and his heart came up in his throat. 'I am torn, and I cannot sleep for the fears that roil through me.' He turned his gaze back to the ship. 'Please, do not be so flippant with me. We are speaking of our family. Althea is my aunt, and your long-time companion. Think, ship! She set the peg in you, and welcomed you as you awoke. Don't you remember that?'

'I well remember that she left me not long after that. And allowed Kyle to turn me into a slaver.' Bolt arched one eyebrow at him. 'If those were your final memories of her, what reaction would *you* have to her name?'

Wintrow clenched his fists at his side. He would not be distracted from his question. 'But what are we to do? She is still our family!'

'Our? What is this "our"? Are you confusing me with Vivacia again? Dear boy, between us there is no "we", no "our". There is you and there is me. When I say "we" or "our", I am not referring to you.' She ran her eyes over Kennit caressingly.

Wintrow was stubborn. 'I refuse to believe there is nothing of Vivacia in you. Otherwise how could you be so bitter at the memories you do recall?'

'Oh, dear,' the ship muttered, and sighed. 'Are we back to that again?'

'I'm afraid we are,' Kennit answered her consolingly. 'Come, Wintrow, don't glare like that. Be honest with me, lad. What do you expect us to do? Surrender Bolt back to Althea to prevent your feelings from being hurt? Where is your loyalty to me in that?'

Wintrow came slowly to stand beside Kennit at the railing. Eventually, he spoke. 'My loyalty is yours, Kennit. You know that. I think you knew it even before I admitted it to myself. If you did not have my loyalty, I would not be in such pain now.'

The pirate seemed genuinely moved by this confession. He set his hand on Wintrow's shoulder. For a time, they shared silence. 'You, my dear boy, are so very young. You must speak aloud what you want.' Kennit's voice was no more than a whisper.

Wintrow turned to him in surprise. Kennit gazed ahead through the night as if he had not spoken. Wintrow took a breath and forced his thoughts into order. 'What I would ask of you both is that Althea not be harmed. She is my mother's sister, blood of my blood, and true family to the ship. Bolt may deny it, but I cannot believe that she could see Althea die and not be harmed by it.' In a lower voice he added, 'I know I could not.'

'Blood of your blood, and true family to the ship,' Kennit repeated to himself. He squeezed Wintrow's shoulder. 'For myself, I promise not to harm a hair of her head. Ship?'

The figurehead shrugged her great shoulders. 'Whatever Kennit says. I feel nothing, you see. I have no desire to kill her, or to let her live.'

Wintrow heaved a sigh of relief. He did not believe that Bolt felt nothing. There was too much tension thrumming through him; not all of it could be his own. 'And her crew?' he ventured.

Kennit laughed, and gave his shoulder a friendly shake. 'Come, Wintrow, we can scarcely guarantee how they will fare. If a man chooses to fight to the death, how am I to stop him? But as you have seen, of late we shed blood only when forced to it. Consider all the ships we have set free to continue on their way. Slavers, of course, are another matter. When it comes to slavers, I must keep faith with all the people in my kingdom. To the bottom they must go. You cannot save everyone, Wintrow. Some folk have made up their minds to be killed by me long before I encounter them. When we encounter Captain Trell and Paragon, then we will act as befits the situation. Surely you can ask no more of us than that.'

'I suppose not.' It was the best he could do tonight. He wondered, if he had been alone with the ship, could he have forced her to admit she still had a bond with Althea? *Althea*, he thought fiercely at the ship. *I know you remember her. She woke you from your long sleep, she greeted your return to life. She loved you. Can you turn your back on that kind of love?*

A shudder of agitation ran through the ship, and beside her, a loud splashing announced the return of the green-gold serpent. The figurehead, eyes narrowed and nostrils flared, turned to glare at Wintrow. He braced himself, expecting her to fling pain at him. Instead, Kennit gave him a shake. 'Enough of that!' he told Wintrow sternly. 'Do you think I cannot feel what you are doing to her? She has said she feels nothing. Accept it.' Then he gave Wintrow's shoulder a sympathetic push. 'Feelings end, lad. Bolt is not who she was to you. Why don't you go find Etta? She always seems to cheer you.'

As Kennit watched Wintrow cross the main deck, the charm spoke. It did not whisper, or try to conceal itself from the ship at all. 'Feelings end,' it mocked. 'Bolt is not who she was. Oh, yes. Convince yourself of that, dear heart, and you'll be able to deal with Paragon again.' It suddenly dropped its voice to a confiding undertone. 'You always knew you'd have to deal with him again, didn't you? When first the rumour reached you of a blinded liveship returned to Bingtown, you knew that eventually your paths must cross again.'

'Shut up!' Fear tinged Kennit's flash of fury. The hair on the back of his neck prickled against his collar.

'I know Paragon,' the ship said suddenly. 'That is, I have Althea's memories of him. And her father's. Ephron Vestrit did not like that ship. He didn't want his daughter to play near him. Paragon is mad, you know. Quite mad.'

'Oh, quite mad,' the charm agreed affably. 'But then, who wouldn't be, given all the memories that are soaked into his planks? It's a wonder he can speak at all. Don't you agree, Kennit? Wasn't it enough to strike a boy dumb? No need to cut his tongue out, when he hardly spoke a word for three years. Oh, Igrot believed his secrets were quite safe. All his secrets. But secrets do have a way of leaking out.'

'Be silent!' Kennit raged in a hoarse whisper.

'Silent,' the carved wizardwood on his wrist breathed. 'Silent as a blinded ship, floating hull up in the sea. Silent as a scream underwater.'

NINETEEN

Strategies

THE FOG AND mists were relentless. Even on days when it did not rain, everything dripped with the constant condensation. Garments hung in the galley to dry merely became steamy. The clothes in in her duffel bag were as damp as the wool blanket she took from her bunk. Everything smelled green and sour. She half-expected to comb moss from her hair in the mornings. Well, at least they would all have a bit more room now. She'd cleared Lavoy's things from the first mate's cabin and was moving her gear in today. The promotion was traditional and hers by right. Brashen had moved Haff up to second. He seemed very pleased with his new rank; an even better sign was that the crew in general approved of his promotion.

'Do the rain and the fogs never cease in these wretched islands?' Amber demanded as she came into the tiny cabin. Moisture had beaded on her hair and eyelashes. Water dripped from the cuffs of her shirt.

'In summer,' Althea offered her. 'But for now, this is the weather. Unless it rains hard enough to clear the air.'

'That would almost be preferable to this constant dripping. I climbed the mast to see what I could see. I'd have been as wise to stuff my head in my duffel bag. How do the pirates move about on days like these? There's neither sun nor star to steer by.'

'Let's hope they don't. I'd hate to have one run us down in the fog. Try to think of it as concealing us from hostile eyes.'

'But it conceals them from us just as effectively. How will we know when Kennit returns to Divvytown if we can't even see the island?'

They had been anchored for the last day and a night in a small, sheltered inlet. Althea knew what others did not. They anchored here, not in wait for Kennit, but to try to salvage some sort of plan. Last night, sequestered together in Brashen's cabin, they had considered options. Brashen had not been optimistic. 'It's all gone down to the bottom,' he said bleakly. He stared up at the ceiling above his bunk. 'I should have foreseen that Lavoy would do something like that. He's destroyed any hope of surprise that we ever had. Someone will send word to Kennit and at first sight of us, he'll surely attack. Damn Lavoy. When I first suspected him of talking mutiny, I should have keel-hauled him.'

'That would have been good for morale,' Althea had murmured from the shelter of his arm. She lay in his bunk beside him. The length of his naked body was warm against hers and her head was pillowed on his shoulder. The mellow lantern light made shifting shadows on the wall, tempting her to simply clasp Brashen close and fall asleep beside him. Her fingers idly walked the long seam down his ribs that was the track of the pirate's sword.

'Don't,' he had muttered irritably, twitching away from her. 'Stop distracting me and help me think.'

She had breathed out a long sigh. 'You should have said that before you bedded me. I know I should be putting all my wits to regaining Vivacia from Kennit, but somehow, here with you . . .' She had smoothed a hand down his chest to his belly, and let his thoughts follow it.

He had rolled towards her. 'So. Do you just want to give it all up? Go back to Bingtown, and leave things as they are?'

'I've thought about it,' she had admitted. 'But I can't. I'd always thought that Vivacia would be our major ally in reclaiming her from Kennit. I'd counted on the ship defying him to turn battle in our favour. Now that we know that Wintrow is alive and well aboard her, and that they both seem content with Kennit, I don't know what to think. But I can't just walk away from her, Brash. They're my family. Vivacia is my ship, in a way she can never belong to anyone else. To give her up to Kennit would be like giving up a child to him. She may be satisfied with Kennit now, but in the end, she'll want to come home to Bingtown. So will Wintrow. Then where will they be? Outcasts and pirates. Their lives will be ruined.'

'How can you know that?' Brashen had protested. A smile curved his lips and he raised his brows as he asked her, 'Would Keffria say this was where you belonged? Wouldn't she say the same things, that eventually you will want to come home and that I'm ruining you? Would you welcome her trying to rescue you from me?'

She had kissed the corner of his mouth. 'Perhaps I'm the one ruining you. I don't intend to let you go, even when we do go back home. But we are both adults, aware of what this decision may cost us.' In a lower voice she added, 'We are both prepared to pay that cost, and count it still a good bargain. But Wintrow is scarcely more than a boy, and the ship had barely wakened to life before she left Bingtown. I can't let them go. I have to at least see them, speak to them, know how they are.'

'Yes, I'm sure Captain Kennit would find time for us to visit them,' Brashen had replied dryly. 'Perhaps we should return to Divvytown and leave calling cards, asking when he is at home.'

'I know it sounds ridiculous.'

'What if we did return to Bingtown?' Brashen had asked, suddenly serious. 'We have Paragon, and he's a fine ship. The Vestrits would still have a liveship, one that is paid for. You and I would stand shoulder to shoulder and refuse to be parted. We'd be married, with a proper wedding, in the Traders' Concourse. And if the Traders wouldn't allow that, well, to the bottom with them, and we'd sail up to the Six Duchies and make our promises to one of their black rocks.'

She had to smile. He kissed her and went on, 'We'd sail Paragon together, everywhere, up the Rain Wild River and down past Jamaillia to the islands your father knew so well, and trade where he did. We'd trade well, make lots of money, and pay off your family's debt to the Rain Wilds. Malta wouldn't have to marry anyone she didn't want to. Kyle's dead, we know that, so we can't rescue him. Wintrow and Vivacia don't seem to want to be rescued. Don't you see, Althea? You and I could just take our lives and live them. We don't need much, and we've already got it. A good ship and a good crew. You beside me. That's all I'm asking of life. Fate has handed it all to me, and damn it, I want to keep it.' His arms suddenly closed around her. 'Just say yes to me,' he had urged her sweetly, his soft breath warm on her ear and neck. 'Just say yes and I'll never let you go.'

Broken glass in her heart. 'No,' she had said quietly. 'I have to try, Brashen. I have to.'

'I knew you'd say that,' he had groaned. He loosened his arms and fell back from her. He gave her a weary smile. 'So, my love, what do you propose we do? Approach Kennit under a truce flag? Creep up on him by night? Challenge him on the open sea? Or just sail back into Divvytown and wait for him there?'

'I don't know,' she had admitted. 'All of those sound suicidal.' She paused. 'All save the truce flag. No, don't stare at me like that. I'm not crazy. Listen. Brashen, think of all we heard in Divvytown. The folk there don't speak of him as a tyrant they fear. He is a beloved ruler, who has put the best interests of his people first. He frees slaves that he could just as easily sell. He is open-handed in sharing the booty he takes. He sounds like an intelligent, rational man. If we went to him under a truce flag, he'd know the most sensible course was to hear us out. What could he gain by attacking us before he'd talked to us? We could offer him ransom money, but more than that, we could offer him the good-will of at least one Bingtown Trader family. If he genuinely wants to make a kingdom of the Pirate Isles, eventually he will have to seek legitimate trade. Why not with Bingtown? Why not with the Vestrits?'

Brashen had leaned back on his pillow. 'To make it convincing, you'd have to have it all written out. Not some verbal agreement, but a binding contract. What little ransom we offer him now would be just the opening. The trade agreements would be the real bait.' He rolled his head on the pillow to meet her eyes. 'You know that some folk in Bingtown will call you a traitor. Can you bind your family to an agreement with outlaws like these?'

She had been silent for a time. 'I'm trying to think as my father would,' she said quietly at last. 'He said the mark of a good Trader was the ability to see ahead. To lay the groundwork for the trading of tomorrow with the deals one struck today. It was short-sighted, he said, to squeeze the last bit of profit out of a trade. A wise Trader never let the other man walk away feeling sour. I think this Kennit is going to succeed. And when he does, the Pirate Isles will either become a barrier between Bingtown and all the trade to the south, or it will become one more trading stop. I think Bingtown and Jamaillia are close to parting ways. Kennit could be a powerful ally for Bingtown, as well as a valuable trading partner.' She sighed, not with sadness but finality. 'I think I'd like to chance it. I'll make an overture, but I'll be clear that I'm not speaking for all of Bingtown. However, I'll let him know that where one Trader comes, others soon follow. I'm going to tell him I speak for the Vestrit family. I need to decide exactly what I can honestly offer him. I can make this work, Brashen. I know I can.' She gave a short, rueful laugh. 'Mother and Keffria are going to be furious when I tell them. At first. But I have to do what I think best.'

Brashen's fingers had traced a lazy circle around one of her breasts, his weathered hand dark against her pale skin. He bent his head to kiss her and then asked gravely, 'Mind if I stay busy while you're thinking?'

'Brashen, I'm serious,' she had protested.

'So am I,' he had assured her. His hands had moved purposefully down her body. 'Very serious.'

'What are you smiling about?' Amber broke into her reverie. She grinned at Althea mischievously.

Althea started guiltily. 'Nothing.'

'Nothing,' Jek agreed sourly from her bunk. Her arm had been flung across her face and Althea had assumed she was sleeping. Now she straightened. 'Nothing except a bit more than the rest of us are getting.'

Amber's face had gone grave. Althea bit her tongue to hold it silent. Best to let this discussion die right here. She met Jek's gaze squarely.

Jek didn't agree. 'Well, at least you don't deny it,' she observed bitterly, sitting up. 'Of course, it would be rather hard to do so, when you come in here late, purring like a kitten that's been into the cream, or sit smiling to yourself, your cheeks as pink as a new bride's.' She looked at Althea and cocked her head. 'You should make him shave, so his whiskers don't rash the side of your neck like that.'

Althea lifted a guilty hand before she could stop herself. She let it drop to her side and considered Jek's flat gaze. There would be no avoiding this. 'What's it to you?' she asked quietly.

'Other than that it's completely unfair?' Jek asked her. 'Other than that you're stepping up to the mate's position at the same time you're falling into the captain's bed?' Jek rose from her bunk to stand before Althea. She looked down at her. 'Some people might think you don't deserve either.'

The tall woman's mouth was a flat line. Althea took a deep breath and readied herself. Jek was Six Duchies. On a Six Duchies boat, fists out on deck was how a dispute over a promotion would be settled. Did Jek expect that here? That if she could beat Althea on the deck, she could step up to the mate's position?

Then Jek's face broke into her customary grin. She gave Althea a congratulatory punch in the shoulder. 'But I think you deserve the both, and wish you the best.' With a quirk of an eyebrow and a widening grin, she demanded, 'So. He any good?'

Relief numbed her. The look on Amber's face consoled Althea that she was not the only one that Jek had duped. 'He's good enough,' she muttered abashedly.

'Well. I'm glad for you then. But don't let him know that. Best to keep a man thinking there's still something you wish he were doing. It keeps them imaginative. I get the top bunk now.' Jek looked at Amber as if expecting her to challenge this.

'Help yourself,' Amber replied. 'I'll get my tools and dismantle the other bunk. Which do you think we want, Jek? A fold-down table, or room to turn around?'

'Isn't Haff moving into the empty bunk?' Jek suggested innocently. 'He is taking Althea's position as second. He should have the bunk to go with it.'

'Sorry to disappoint you,' Althea grinned. 'He's staying in the forecastle with the rest of the crew. He thinks they need a bit of settling out. Lavoy and his deserters have rattled the order of things. Haff feels that the men who left with him did so because they were frightened; Lavoy had convinced them that they should side with him against Brashen, because going up against Kennit was suicidal.'

Jek gave a shout of laughter. 'As if that was something we didn't all know.' At the look on Althea's face, she sobered slightly. 'Sorry. But if they didn't know from the beginning that the odds were against us, then they were idiots and we're well rid of them.' She levered herself up easily onto the bunk Althea had just stripped and shouldered herself into it. 'Snug. But it's up higher. I prefer to sleep high.' She gave a sigh of contentment. 'So. Just what secret is Brashen keeping?'

'About what?' Althea asked.

'About Kennit and what he plans to do to him? I'll wager it's a good one.'

'Oh. That. Yes. It is indeed.' Althea slung her duffel to her shoulder. She tried not to wonder what judgement Sa reserved for those who led others to their deaths.

Mingsley pursed his lips and set the chipped cup carefully back on its odd saucer. It held a thin tea of wintermint from the kitchen garden. The good black Jamaillian tea had gone up in flames with everything else that the Chalcedeans had hoarded in the warehouses. He cleared his throat. 'So. What have you managed for us?'

Serilla gazed at him levelly. She had already made up her mind to one thing. Now that she was rid of Roed Caern, no man was ever going to intimidate her again. Especially one who thought he had her under his finger. Had yesterday taught him nothing?

True to her word, Tintaglia had set out in search of the Kendry and any other liveships she might find. In her absence, the humans had sat down together to try and craft a binding agreement. Early in the proceedings, speaking on her behalf but without consulting her, Mingsley had insisted that Serilla be given the final word on the document. 'She represents Jamaillia,' he had intoned loudly. 'We are all subjects of the Satrapy. We should be willing not only to have her negotiate with the dragon for us, but to assign us our correct roles in the new Bingtown.'

The fisherman, Sparse Kelter had stood and spoken. 'With no disrespect to this lady, I refuse her authority. She is welcome to sit in with us and speak as a representative of Jamaillia, if she wishes. But this is Bingtown business for Bingtown folk to sort out.'

'If you will not cede her the authority due her, then I see no reason for the New Traders to remain here,' Mingsley had blustered. 'It is well known that the Old Traders have no intention of conceding our right to our lands and . . .'

'Oh, do just leave,' the Tattooed woman had sighed. 'Or shut up and be a witness. But there is not enough daylight for us to discuss the things we must cover, let alone deal with your posturing.'

The others had stared at him, agreement in their silence. Mingsley had stood threateningly. 'I know things!' he had intoned. 'Things you will wish I had stayed and shared with you. Things that will render useless all you agree to here. Things that . . .'

But all the rest of his 'things' had been lost as two brawny young Three Ships men literally picked him up and set him outside the Council chamber. His final astonished glare at Serilla had said plainly that he had expected her to take his part. She had not. Nor had she tried to claim authority over the meeting, but had been, as suggested, a witness for Jamaillia. And, incidentally, one who was very clear on the original terms of the Bingtown Charter. On many of the provisions, her knowledge was clearer than that of the Traders, gaining the Bingtown Traders' surprised respect for her erudition. Perhaps they were beginning to see that her precise knowledge of the legal relationship between Bingtown and Jamaillia could benefit them after all. The New Traders had not been as pleased. Now she stared at their spokesman, daring him to take the confrontation further.

Mingsley mistook her long silence for abashment. 'I will tell you this. You have failed us twice, and badly. You must remember who your friends are. You can't seriously intend to support the old Charter. It offers us nothing. Surely you can do better for us than that.' He moved the cup on the saucer. 'After all we've done for you,' he reminded her slyly.

Serilla took a slow sip of tea. They were in the drawing room of Davad's house. The Chalcedean raiders had burned the east wing, but this end of the house was still habitable. She smiled small to herself. Her cup was not cracked. A small thing, but a satisfying one. She had stopped fearing to offend him. She looked at Mingsley levelly. It was time to draw a line. 'I do intend to enforce the old Charter. More, I intend to suggest it as a basic foundation for the new Bingtown.' She smiled brightly at him as if a brilliant idea had just occurred to her. 'Perhaps, if you were willing to go upriver, the Rain Wild Traders might offer you the same status as they have offered the Tattooed. Of course, it would have the same requirements. You'd have to bring your true-born daughters and sons with you. When they married into Rain Wild families, they'd become Traders.'

He recoiled from the table, and snatched a kerchief from his pocket. He patted hastily at his lips. 'The very idea is abhorrent. Companion, are you mocking me?'

'Not at all. I am merely saying that the so-called New Traders had best come to the bargaining table with everyone else. And they must understand that, like everyone else, they will have to meet certain terms to be accepted here.'

His eyes flashed. 'Accepted here! We have every right to be here. We have charters granted by Satrap Cosgo himself, ceding us land and . . .'

'Charters you bought from him, for outrageous bribes and gifts. Because you knew that bribing him was the only way you could get such a charter. What he could not legitimately grant you, you bought from him. Those charters were founded on dishonesty and broken promises.' She took another sip of tea. 'If they hadn't been, you never would have consented to pay so much for them. You bought lies, "New Trader" Mingsley. Now the truth has come to Bingtown. The truth is that the

Three Ships immigrants have a true right to be here. They negotiated it with the Bingtown Traders when they first came here. Last night, they negotiated further. They will be given grants of lands, and votes in the Council, in recognition of all they have done against the Chalcedean invasion. Oh, they will never be Bingtown Traders, of course. Not unless they marry into the families. However, I imagine the Bingtown Traders will become a ceremonial aristocracy of sorts, rather than a true ruling class any more. Moreover, Three Ships families seem to cherish the distinction of being Three Ships. Those of the Tattooed who choose to remain in Bingtown rather than go to the Rain Wilds will have the opportunity to earn land of their own, by assisting in the rebuilding of Bingtown. Those that do will receive voting privileges with the land, and stand on an equal footing with every other landowner.'

'Ah, well, then.' Mingsley leaned back in his chair and rested his hands contentedly on his belly. 'That is what you should have told me first. If voting and control of the town are to be based on land ownership, then we New Traders have nothing to fear.'

'Certainly, that is true. Once you legally acquire some land, you, too, will be allowed to vote on the Council.'

He went red, and then his face darkened until she feared he would collapse. When he spoke, the words burst from him like steam from a kettle. 'You have betrayed us!'

'And how did you expect to be served? You betrayed the Satrapy once, luring Cosgo to issue grants to you that you knew were illegal. Then you came here, and further betrayed Bingtown, by dirtying its shores with slavery and undercutting its economy and way of life. But that was not enough for you. You and your cohorts wanted it all, not just the lands of Bingtown, but the secret trade of Bingtown.'

She paused for a sip of tea, and to smile at him. 'And for that you were willing to betray the Satrap into death. You would have used his slaughter as an excuse to let the Chalcedeans kill the Bingtown Traders, so long as you could keep their wealth for yourselves. Well, you were betrayed once, by the Chalcedeans. How that astonished you! But you did not learn. Instead you sought to bend me as you bent the Satrap, not with wealth but threats. Well. Now you are betrayed again, by me. If betrayal you would call it, that I stand up for what I have always believed in.'

In a very reasonable voice, she continued, 'New Traders who labour alongside the Three Ships folk and the slaves in helping to rebuild Bingtown will be granted land. That the Bingtowners themselves decreed, with no prodding from me. It is the best offer you will get. But you will not take it, for your heart is not here. It never was. Your wives and your heirs are not here. Bingtown, to you, was a place to plunder, never home, never a new chance.'

'And when the Jamaillian fleet arrives here, what then?' he demanded. 'The birds that were sent out to Jamaillia primed them to expect Old Trader treachery against the Satrap. Lo and behold, we were more right than we knew! Your Bingtown Trader friends were the ones who sent the Satrap to his death.'

Her voice was cold. 'You are so bold, you admit your part in the plot against Satrap Cosgo, and then threaten me with the consequences?' She shook her head in patrician disbelief. 'If Jamaillia were going to muster a fleet against us, it would have done so by now. Unless I am much mistaken, those who hoped to sail north and plunder Bingtown have found they must stay at home to protect what they have. If this threatened Jamaillian fleet ever arrives, I doubt there will be much to it. I assure you, I am all too familiar with the financial state of the Jamaillian treasury. The death of a Satrap and the threat of civil war will prompt most nobles to keep their wealth and their strength close to home. I know what the conspiracy hoped. You believed your Jamaillian partners would arrive with ships and turn Bingtown over to you. Doubtless you thought it wise to have this fall-back defence against the Chalcedeans in case they became too greedy. As they did, and far sooner than you expected.'

She gave a small sigh and poured herself more tea. With a social smile, she waved the pot questioningly towards Mingsley's cup, then interpreted his outraged silence as a refusal. She took up her lecture again. 'If this fleet ever arrives here, they will be greeted with diplomacy, a cordial welcome and a well-fortified harbour. They will find a city rebuilding itself after an unjustified Chalcedean attack. I suggest you consider the New Traders' position in Bingtown from an entirely different angle. Whatever will you do if the Satrap is not dead? For if the dragon speaks truth when she says that Malta Vestrit lives, then perhaps the Satrap has survived alongside her. How uncomfortable could that be for you? Especially as I have it, in your own hand, that there was a New Trader plot against him. Not that you were personally involved, of course.' She idly stirred a bit of honey into the mint tea. 'In any case, if the fleet is met, not with a show of force, nor a scene of civil disorder, but with a courteous and diplomatic welcome . . . well.' She cocked her head at him and smiled winningly. 'We shall see. Oh. Did I caution you to remember that this Jamaillian fleet must first come here through not only the Pirate Isles, but through the Chalcedean "patrol" vessels? It will, I think, be rather like coming past an enraged hive of bees. If and when the fleet reaches us, they may be glad of a peaceful harbour and a dragon guardian.' She stirred her tea again as she idly asked, 'Or had you forgotten about Tintaglia?'

'You will regret this!' Mingsley told her. He stood with a fine crash of china and cutlery. 'You would have been carried alongside us to power! You could have returned to Jamaillia a wealthy woman, and lived out your days in civilization and culture. Instead you have doomed yourself to this backwater town and its rustic folk. They have no respect for the Satrapy here. Here you will be nothing more than just another woman on her own!'

He stormed from the room, slamming the door behind him. *Just another woman on her own.* Mingsley was not to know that he had flung a blessing at Serilla in the tones of a curse.

Kendry came back to harbour under sail, a diminished crew working his decks, but making good time nonetheless. Reyn Khuprus sat on the skeletal rooftop of a half-destroyed warehouse and watched him come. Overhead, Tintaglia circled once, flashing silver. The dragon touched Reyn's mind briefly as she passed overhead. 'Ophelia is your name for her. She comes, also.'

He watched Kendry as the men brought him alongside one of the shattered docks and tied him off. The liveship had changed. The affable boyish figurehead did not wave his arms in greeting, or clap and whoop with joy at his safe return. Instead his arms were crossed on his chest and his face was closed. Reyn could guess what had happened. Tintaglia had told Kendry who and what he truly was. The last few times he'd sailed on the Kendry, he had been uncomfortably aware of the dragon lurking below the ship's surface personality. Now those memories would have bloomed in full.

A slow and terrible knowledge rose in Reyn. He was doomed to see this change in every liveship. With each stricken or closed face, he would have to confront what his ancestors had done. Knowingly or not, they had taken the dragons' lives from them, and then condemned their spirits to a sexless, wingless eternity as ships. He should have been happy to know that the liveship Ophelia had prevailed in her encounters with the Chalcedeans. Instead, he did not want to be there when Grag Tenira went down to greet the ship he had loved all his life, and encountered a glowering dragon instead. It was not only dragonkind he had injured; soon he would see in

479

his friend's eyes the damage done to Bingtown's liveship families.

Too many changes, too many chances, he told himself. He could not sort out what he felt any more. He should have been joyous. Malta was alive. Bingtown had formed a solid alliance and had a treaty ready for the dragon's mark. The Chalcedeans were vanquished, at least for now. And sometime in the future, if all went well, there was another Elderling city for him to explore and learn. This time, he would be in charge, with no plundering or hasty robbing of treasure. He would have Malta at his side. All would be well. All would be healed.

Somehow, he could not trust it to be real. The brief sensing of Malta that he had received through Tintaglia was like the aroma of hot food to a starving man. The possibility of her was not enough to satisfy the longing in his heart.

At a noise in the building below him, he glanced down, expecting to see a stray dog or cat. Instead, he saw Selden picking his way through the rubble below. 'Get out of there,' he called down in annoyance. 'Can't you see this whole roof could fall on you?'

'Which is why you're sitting on it, obviously,' Selden called up to him, unimpressed.

'I just needed a place where I could look out over the harbour and watch for Tintaglia to return. I'm coming down now.'

'Good. Tintaglia's gone to groom, but soon she'll return to make her mark on the scroll the Council has drawn up.' He took a breath. 'She wants the Kendry immediately loaded with supplies and engineers and sent up the river so her work can be begun.'

'Supplies from where?' Reyn asked sarcastically.

'She doesn't much care. I've suggested that she should begin with the Kendry just taking builders up there, stopping in Trehaug to pick up folk who know the ways of the river, and then going to the place she wants dredged. They must see what needs to be done before they plan how to do it.'

Reyn did not ask him how he knew so much. Instead, he came to his feet, and picked his way back to the eaves of the building. The winter sun woke the glints of scaling on Selden's brows and lips. 'She sent you to fetch me, didn't she?' Reyn asked as he made the final jump down. 'To make sure I'd be there?'

'If she wanted you there, she could have told you herself. No. I came myself to make sure you would be there. So you can hold her to her promise. Left to herself, she will worry first about her serpents and the possibility of other cocooned dragons surviving. If we leave it up to her, it will be months instead of days before she sets out to look for Malta.'

'Months!' Reyn felt a surge of rage. 'We should be departing today!' A sick certainty came over him. It would be days. Just signing the contract would probably take a day in itself. And then the selection of folk to go upriver, and the supplying of the Kendry. 'After all Malta did to free her, you would think she would have at least a scrap of gratitude for her.'

The boy frowned to himself. 'It isn't that she dislikes Malta. Or you. She doesn't think that way at all. Dragons and serpents are so much more important to her than people, to ask her to choose between rescuing her own kind and saving Malta is like asking you to choose between Malta and a pigeon.'

Selden paused. 'To Tintaglia, most humans seem very similar, and our concerns seem trivial matters indeed. It is up to us to make such things important to her. If she succeeds in her plans, there will be other dragons sharing our world with us. Only they will see it as us sharing their world. My grandfather used to say, "Start out dealing with a man the way you intend to go on dealing with him." I think the same may be true of dragons. I think we need to establish now what we expect of her and her kind.'

'But, to wait days until we depart –'

'To wait a few days is better than to wait forever,' Selden

pointed out to him. 'We know Malta is alive. Did her life feel threatened to you?'

Reyn sighed. 'I could not tell,' he was forced to admit. 'I could sense Malta. But it was as if she refused to pay attention to me.'

They both fell silent. The winter day was cold but still under a clear blue sky. Voices carried, and hammers rang throughout the city. As they walked together through the Bingtown streets, Reyn could already feel the change in the air. Everywhere, the bustle of activity clearly spoke of hopes for and belief in tomorrows. Tattooed and Three Ships people worked alongside Traders both Old and New. Few of the businesses had reopened, but there were already youngsters on street corners hawking shellfish and wild greens. There seemed to be more folk in town as well. He suspected the flood of refugees had reversed, and that those who had fled Bingtown to outlying areas were returning. The tide had turned. Bingtown would rise from the ashes.

'You seem to know a great deal about dragons,' Reyn observed to Selden. 'Whence comes all this sudden knowledge?'

Instead of replying, Selden asked a question of his own. 'I'm turning into a Rain Wilder, aren't I?'

Reyn didn't look at him. He wasn't sure Selden would want to consider his face just now. The changes in Reyn's own appearance seemed to be accelerating. Even his fingernails were growing thicker and hornier. Usually such changes did not come to a Rain Wilder until he reached middle age. 'It certainly looks that way. Does it distress you?'

'Not much. I don't think my mother likes it.' Before Reyn could react to that, he went on, 'I have the dreams of a Rain Wilder now. They started the night I fell asleep in the city. You woke me from one, when you found me. I couldn't hear the music then, like Malta did, but I think that if I went back now, I would. The knowledge grows in me, and I don't know where it comes from.' He knit his scaled brows. 'It belonged to someone else, but somehow it's coming down to me now. Is that what is called "drowning in memories", Reyn? A stream of memories flow through me. Am I going to go crazy?'

He set his hand to the boy's shoulder and gripped it. Such a thin and narrow shoulder to take on such a burden. 'Not necessarily. Not all of us go crazy. Some of us learn to swim with the flow.'

TWENTY

Prisoners

'ARE YOU SURE you'll be warm enough?' Jani Khuprus asked him again.

Selden rolled his eyes at Reyn in sympathy, and the Rain Wilder found himself smiling. 'I don't know,' Reyn replied honestly. 'But if I put on any more layers of clothing, I'm afraid I'll slip out of them when the dragon is carrying me.'

That silenced her. 'I'll be fine, Mother,' he assured her. 'It won't be any worse than sailing in foul weather.'

They stood in a hastily cleared area behind the Traders' Concourse. Tintaglia had demanded that henceforth every city in the Traders' control must have an open space sufficiently large for a dragon to land comfortably. And whenever a dragon chose to land in a city, the inhabitants must guarantee the creature a warm welcome and an adequate meal. Negotiating what an 'adequate meal' was had taken several hours. The meat had to be alive, and equal at least the size of a 'well-fleshed bull calf at the end of his first year.' When told she was more likely to get poultry, as Bingtown lacked grazing lands for cattle, she had sulked until someone had offered her warmed oil and assistance in grooming her scales whenever she visited. That had seemed to mollify her.

Days had been taken up with such quibbling, until Reyn had thought he would go mad. The dozen or so surviving pigeons that served Bingtown and Trehaug had been flown into a state of exhaustion. The terse missives sent and received had seemed incapable of explaining all that was going on in both cities. Reyn had been relieved when a single line informed them that his stepfather and half-sister had returned to the city in good health. Bendir had left Trehaug to venture upriver to locate the place Tintaglia had indicated on the tiny river chart they'd sent. He would begin both to ponder a method of deepening the river, and to survey for signs of a buried city. Content that her goals were being advanced, Tintaglia had finally agreed to depart to search for Malta. Reyn was surprised at how many folk had gathered to watch his departure, probably more from curiosity than any deep concern for his mission. Malta's life or death would little affect them.

'Are you ready?' Tintaglia asked him irritably. Through their bond, she spoke in his mind, so that he could *feel* her annoyance.

Resolutely, he set her emotions aside from his own. Unfortunately, that left him with little more than nervousness and dread. He stepped up to the dragon. 'I am ready.'

'Very well then,' she replied. She swept her gaze over those assembled to bid them farewell. 'When I return, I expect to see progress. Great progress.'

Selden broke suddenly from his mother's side and thrust a small cloth bag into Reyn's hands. It rattled. 'Take these. They were Malta's. They might help you get through.'

Gravely Reyn poked the mouth of the small bag open, expecting some token of jewellery. Instead, he found a handful of tinted honey drops. He looked up from the candy in puzzlement. Selden shrugged.

'I was at our old house yesterday, seeing what was left there. Almost everything had been stolen or destroyed. So I looked in some of the less obvious places.' Selden grinned, abruptly a small brother. 'I always knew where Malta hid her candy.' The smile softened at the edges. 'She loves honey drops. But they might keep you going in the cold. I don't think she'd mind if you ate them.'

It was so Malta. Hoarded sweetness against an uncertain tomorrow. Reyn tucked the bag into the top of his pouch. 'Thank you,' he replied gravely. He pulled a wool veil down over his face and tucked it into the throat of his jacket. It would keep his face warm, but limited his vision.

'That's wise,' Selden observed encouragingly. 'You've been changing a lot, you know. When I first saw you, I didn't think Malta would mind much. But you're a lot more lumpy now.' The boy lifted an unselfconscious hand to his face, and ran his fingers over his eyebrows. 'She's going to have fits when she sees me,' he predicted merrily.

The dragon reared back onto her hind legs. 'Hurry up,' she ordered Reyn tersely. To Selden, she spoke more gently. 'Move to the side, small minstrel, and turn your eyes away. I would not blind you with dust blasted by my wings.'

'I thank you, Great One. Though to be blinded might not be so great a loss, if my last sight were of you, gleaming silver and blue as you rose. Such a memory might sustain me to the end of my days.'

'Flatterer!' the dragon dismissed his words, but she did not hide her pleasure. As soon as Selden was clear, she snatched Reyn up from the ground as if he were a toy. She held him around his chest, his legs and feet dangling.

She shook out her wings and crouched on her powerful hind legs. Once, twice, she flapped her wings in a measuring way. He tried to call a farewell, but could not summon enough breath. She sprang upward with a suddenness that snapped his head back. The shouted farewells were lost in the steady thunder of her wings. He closed his eyes against the cold wind. When he forced them open again, he looked down on a glittering carpet of blue and grey, a pattern rippling slowly across it. The sea, he realized, was very, very far below him. Nothing was below him except deep, cold water. He swallowed against a rising fear.

'Well. Where did you want to go?'

'Where do I want to go? To wherever Malta is, of course.'

'I told you before, I can sense she is alive. That doesn't mean I know where she is.'

Desolation swallowed Reyn. The dragon took sudden pity on him. 'See what you can do,' she suggested. Through her, he again shared her awareness of Malta. He closed his eyes and slipped into that sensing that was not hearing nor sight nor scent, but an eerie shadow of all three. He found himself opening his mouth and breathing deep as if he could taste her scent on the cold air. Something of himself, he was sure, flowed out to meet her.

They merged in a warm sleepy lassitude. As they had when they shared the dream-box, he experienced her perceptions of her world. Warm. A slow rocking motion. He breathed deep with her, and tasted the unmistakable smell of a ship. He loosened his awareness of his own body and reached more boldly for her. He felt warm bedding around her. He caught the deep rhythm of her breathing and then shared it. She slept with her cheek on her hand. He became that hand, cradling the warm softness of her cheek. He caressed it. She smiled in her sleep. 'Reyn,' she acknowledged him, without recognizing his true presence.

'Malta, my love,' he returned her greeting gently. 'Where are you?'

'In bed,' she sighed. There was warm interest in her voice.

'Where?' he persisted, regretfully ignoring that invitation.

'On a ship. Chalcedean ship.'

'Where are you bound?' he asked her desperately. He could feel his contact with her fading as his irritating questions clashed with her dream. He clung to her, but her mind pulled away from sleep, disturbed by his insistence that she answer. 'Where?' he demanded. 'WHERE?'

*   *   *

'Jamaillia bound!' Malta found herself sitting bolt upright in her bedding. 'Jamaillia bound,' she repeated, but could not recall what prompted the words. She had the tantalizing feeling that she had just left a very interesting dream, but now could not remember even a scrap of it. It was almost a relief, really. By day, she could control her thoughts. Nights were when her treacherous mind brought her dreams of Reyn, achingly sweet with loss. Better to awake and remember nothing than to awake with tears on her face. She lifted her hands to her face and touched her cheeks. One tingled strangely. She stretched, then conceded she was irrevocably awake. She threw back the coverlet and stood up, yawning.

She was almost accustomed to the opulence of the chamber now. That had not dulled her pleasure in it. The captain had allotted her two deckhands and permission to search the hold for whatever might make the Satrap more comfortable. She had cast aside all moderation. A thick rug of soft wool on the floor and brightly-figured hangings warmed the room. Candelabra had replaced the smoky lantern. Stacked blankets and furs made up her pallet. The Satrap's bed was lined with thick bearskins and sheepskins. An elaborate hookah squatted next to it, and a damask drapery around it curtained him from draughts.

From behind the drapery came his fitful snore. Good. She had time to dress herself before he woke. Moving quietly, she crossed the room to a large trunk, opened it and dug through the layers of garments within. Fabrics of every hue and texture met her questing hands. She selected something warm, soft and blue and pulled it out. She held the robe against her. It was too large, but she would make it do. She glanced uncomfortably at the Satrap's bed hangings, then pulled the blue robe over her head. Beneath it, she let her nightgown fall, then thrust her arms through the long blue sleeves. A faint perfume clung to it, the scent last worn by its owner. She would not wonder how the trunk of lovely clothing had come to the Chalcedeans. Going in rags herself would not restore life to the rightful owner. It would only make her own survival more precarious.

There was a mirror in the lid of the trunk, but Malta avoided looking in it. The first time she had gleefully opened the trunk, her own reflection had been the first thing she saw. The scar was far worse than she had imagined. It stood up, a double ridge of pale, rippling flesh that reached almost to her nose and disappeared in her hair. She had touched the lumpy cicatrix in disbelief, and then scrabbled back from the trunk in horror.

The Satrap had laughed.

'You see,' he mocked her. 'I told you so. Your brief moment of beauty is gone, Malta. You would be wise to learn to be useful and accommodating. That is all that is left to you now. Any pride you retain is self-delusion.'

She could not respond to his hateful words. Her voice was stilled, her gaze trapped in her own image. For a time she had stared in silence, unable to move, unable to think.

The Satrap had broken the spell by nudging her with his foot. 'Get up and busy yourself. I am to dine with the captain tonight, and you have not yet set out my clothes. And Sa's name, cover that split in your head. It is humiliating enough to me that the whole crew knows you are disfigured without your flaunting it.'

In numbed silence, she had obeyed him. That night, she had sat on the floor beside his chair like a dog. She had reminded herself of Kekki, subservient but alert. But for a few words of Chalcedean, the table conversation was out of her reach. From time to time, he passed food down to her. After a time, she realized it was when he had sampled a dish and disliked it. She kept silent behind a stiff little smile, even when he had casually wiped his fingers on her gown. Once the men at the table spoke of her. The Satrap said something, the captain replied, and then there was general laughter. The Satrap had given her a disparaging nudge with his foot, as if she sat distastefully close to him.

She was astonished at how hurt she felt at that. She had fixed the small smile on her face as she stared at nothing. They feasted on rich foods and valuable wines pirated from other ships. After dining, they shared rare pleasure herbs from Captain Deiari's own lacquer-boxed cache. Later, the Satrap would disdainfully tell her this ship was not a pirate vessel, but one of his patrol ships, and that all the loot was cargo confiscated from smugglers and real pirates. In point of fact, he'd gone on loftily, one of his favourite nobles in Jamaillia had contributed heavily in commissioning this ship, and had an interest in her spoils.

She had managed to keep her mask in place all evening. Even when she had dutifully followed the Satrap back to their cabin and assisted him in disrobing for bed and resisted his lackadaisical advances, she had kept her aplomb. Only after she was sure he was asleep had the tears come. Accommodating and useful. Was that truly all that was left to her life? With creeping dismay, she realized it sounded like her mother. Accommodating and useful to her Chalcedean father. What would he think if he could see her now? Would he be horrified, or would he think that she had finally learned to be graciously female? It hurt to wonder such things about someone she loved. She had always believed that he loved her best of all his children. But how did he love her? As an independent young woman, a Trader's daughter? Would he more approve the role she played now?

The same thought haunted her as she tightened the bodice laces on the blue robe and belted it securely so she would not tread on the hem. She coiled her hair and pinned it at the back of her neck. She concealed her scar with a scarf. When she was finished, she considered her face in the mirror. Shipboard life did not agree with her skin. She was far too pale, save for her eyes and lips, which were wind chafed. 'I look coarse,' she said quietly to herself. 'Like a hard-used servant.'

Resolutely, she shut the lid of the trunk. Attitude, not

appearance, had won her the captain and crew's deference. If she lost that now, she would lose her ability to deal with them. She had small faith that Cosgo could continue this farce without her. Only her continued obsequiousness to him enabled him to act like a Satrap at all. It was disgusting that she spent so much of her strength bolstering his belief in his superiority. Worse: the more she flattered him, the more attractive he found her, but she was stronger than he was. His few efforts at physical advances she had easily defeated, setting his pawing hands aside and reminding him that she was not worthy of his attentions.

Soft leather slippers covered her feet, and then she was ready. She crossed to the Satrap's bed, cleared her throat loudly, and drew back his curtain. She did not wish to surprise him in any sort of nastiness. 'Lordly one, I hesitate to disturb your rest, but I ask your permission to fetch your breakfast.'

He opened one eye. 'You may. See that it comes hot to me, not lukewarm like yesterday.'

'I shall, my lord,' she promised humbly. She could not remind him that he had lain abed smoking long after she had brought his tray yesterday. Nothing was ever his fault. She settled a cloak about her shoulders, and left quietly.

This was her stolen time. Out of the Satrap's sight, moving purposefully, she could enjoy a measure of freedom, unchallenged by anyone. When she encountered any of the sailors, they stared at her bound brow, and made comments behind her back, but they gave way.

The cook-stove was in a deckhouse located amidships. When she reached it, the sliding door stood open. The cook, a pale, mournful man, nodded a greeting to her. He set out a tray and two bowls and some utensils, then took up a ladle and stirred the thick porridge that was morning ration for everyone. Some things not even the complaints of a Satrap could change. A sudden outcry from the lookout sent the cook hastening to the door. An instant later, a wild clamour

491

of voices broke out on deck. The relative peace of the swiftly-moving ship was broken by thundering feet and shouted orders. She did not need her limited Chalcedean to know that a great number of curses were mixed with the shouted words. At the door, the cook added a few choice phrases of his own, flung his ladle aside, and sternly ordered Malta to do something. Then he left, slamming the door behind him. Malta immediately opened it a crack to peer out.

The deck swarmed with purposeful activity. Was a storm coming? She watched in awe as ropes were loosened, sails unfurled and ropes fastened off again. As she watched, more canvas blossomed on masts already white with sail. She felt the deck tilt under her feet as the ship's speed increased.

Lookouts at the tops of the masts shouted reports down. Malta ventured two steps outside the deckhouse and craned her neck. She caught a glimpse of an outstretched hand and her eyes followed the pointing finger.

Sails. Another ship coming up fast. A second shout from above made her duck back into the deckhouse and peer out the opposite window. Still another ship, sails full of wind, was likewise swiftly gaining on them. Both ships flew odd patchwork flags showing a spread-winged raven. Her mind worked frantically. The Chalcedean ship fled from those two others. Did that mean they were from Bingtown? Or were they pirates? Did pirates prey on other pirates? She did not know whether to hope the Chalcedean ship outran them or was captured. If they were captured, and the other ships were pirates, what would become of her and the Satrap? A hasty plan formed in her mind.

She waited for an opportune moment, then dashed from the deckhouse to dart down the hatch like a mouse down a hole. The hatch cover dropped down behind her, plunging her into darkness. She scurried through the ship and found the crew's quarters deserted. By the fading light of a lantern, she helped herself to an assortment of garments before hastening to the

Satrap's cabin. When she burst into it, he opened one lazy eye and regarded her irritably.

'Your behaviour is unseemly,' he told her. 'Where is my breakfast?'

Even in this crisis, she must play her role. 'Your forgiveness, lordly one, I pray you. Our ship flees from two others. If they catch us, there will be battle. If there is battle, I fear we will be overwhelmed. I fear they are pirates from the Pirate Isles with little love or respect for the Satrap of Jamaillia. So I have borrowed clothing for you to disguise yourself. As a simple sailor, you may escape their notice. And I, also.'

As she spoke, she began to sort the clothing hastily. She chose a rough shirt and trousers for herself, and a sailor's cap to conceal her brow. A heavy sweater, far too large for her, might help her pass herself off as a boy. For the Satrap, she had chosen the cleaner garments. With these over her hands, she advanced to the bed. He scowled at her and clutched the edge of his blanket tighter.

'Rise, glorious one, and I will help you dress first,' she offered. She wanted to bark it like a command to a recalcitrant child, but knew that would only make him more stubborn.

'No. Put those disgusting rags aside and lay out proper garb for me. If I must rise and dress before I've had any breakfast, I will dress as befits me. You do a great injustice to our Chalcedean sailors to imagine they shall be captured and beaten so easily. There is no need for me to hide myself behind a churlish disguise.' He sat up in his bedding, but crossed his arms resolutely on his chest. 'Bring me decent clothes and shoes. I shall go out on the deck, and watch my patrol vessel disperse these common pirates.'

Malta sighed, defeated. Well, if he would not hide himself, then she would make his ransom value obvious. Might not pirates be more gentle with valuable captives?

She bowed low. 'You are right, of course, gracious one. Pardon the foolishness of a simple woman, I beg you.' She threw the rejected sailor garb out into the companionway. Back in their chamber, she selected the most resplendent robes she could find and took them to the Satrap.

A sudden shock sent her crashing against the bed. She caught her breath and then held it, listening. The sounds on the deck above had changed. The tread of feet and angry shouts and wild cries. Had they been rammed? Were they being boarded even now? She snatched a breath. 'Lordly one, I think we would be wise to hurry.'

'Very well.' With a martyred sigh, he pushed his blankets aside. He held his arms out from his side. 'You may garb me.'

Tintaglia shook him. Reyn opened his eyes, and saw the wrinkled shimmer of dark water far below him. He cried out in terror and clutched wildly at the claws that held him.

'That's better,' the dragon proclaimed mercilessly. 'I thought you were dead. I had forgotten that humans are not so well attached to their bodies as dragons are. When you venture too far from them, you can lose your way back.'

Reyn clung sickly to her claws. He felt dizzy and cold and small, but he did not think it was the effect of the flight. He suspected he had been unconscious. He tried to reach back to the last thing he could remember. It eluded him. He stared down, and suddenly made sense of what he was seeing. 'Are those galleys down there Chalcedean? What are they doing, where are they bound?' There were seven of them, moving southward in formation like a V of geese.

'How can you expect me to know such things? Or care about such things?' She glanced down almost idly. 'I have seen many such ships moving southward through these waters. I chased them away from Bingtown, as I agreed to do. But there are far too many for one dragon to disperse them all.' She seemed offended that he had forced her to admit this. She diverted the topic. 'I thought all your concerns were for Malta?'

'They are,' he said faintly. 'But those ships . . .' He let his words trail away. He grasped what he should have seen all along. Chalced's move was not just against the Rain Wilds and Bingtown. Chalced had been heavily involved with the New Traders against the Satrap. That they had turned on the New Traders meant only that Chalced was treating allies as it always did. Now Chalced was moving against Jamaillia, in force. Bingtown was but a stop along the way, a place to cripple and occupy so that Chalced would not have an enemy at its back while it went after bigger prey. He stared down at the ships. Many like those, Tintaglia had said. Jamaillia's sea power had been declining for almost a decade. He did not know if Jamaillia could wage war against Chalced, let alone win such a struggle. Could Bingtown survive the disruption to trade that such a war would wreak? His mind spun with the implications of all he saw.

Tintaglia was annoyed. 'Well. Did you find your mate? Could you tell where she was?'

He swallowed. 'Somewhat.' He sensed her impatience with his answer. 'A moment,' he begged her. He took deep breaths of the cold air, hoping it would restore him while he tried to make sense of the fragmented dream-memory. 'She was on a ship,' he told the dragon. 'A deep-hulled ship, from the motion, not a galley. Yet she said it was Chalcedean.' He knit his brows. 'Did not you sense that also?'

'I was not that attentive,' she replied carelessly. 'So. A Chalcedean ship. A large one. There are many like that to choose from. Where?'

'Bound for Jamaillia.'

'Oh, that's helpful.'

'South. Fly south over the Inside Passage.'

'And when we fly over the ship she is in, you will simply know it,' the dragon continued sceptically. 'And what then?'

He stared down at the water below his toes. 'Then, somehow, you will help me rescue her. And take her home with us.'

The dragon made a rumble of displeasure. 'A foolish and impossible errand. We waste time, Reyn. We should go back now.'

'No. Not without Malta,' he replied adamantly. To her silently simmering anger, he retorted, 'What you ask of me is just as foolish and impossible. You demand that I slog through the Rain Wild swamps and somehow locate a city engulfed Sa alone knows how many years ago, and that I then somehow rescue any cocooned dragons buried deep within it.'

'Are you saying now that you can't do that?' The dragon was outraged.

He gave a snort of laughter. 'One impossible quest at a time. You first.'

'I will keep my word,' she promised sulkily.

He regretted having offended her. That was not the way to win her best effort. 'I know you will keep your word,' he assured her. He took a breath. 'I have touched souls with you, Tintaglia. You are too great-hearted to go back on your promise.'

She did not reply, but he sensed her mollification. Why she found such gratification in praise, he had no idea, but it was a small price to pay. She bore him on, her wide wings beating steadily. He became aware of the working of a mighty heart inside her chest. Where she clasped him against her, he was warm. He felt a surge of confidence in both of them. They would find Malta, and they would bring her safely home. He gripped her claws in his hands, and ignored the ache of his swinging legs.

Malta's hands shook as she twitched his jacket straight. A deep-voiced cry of agony resounded through the deck. She clenched her teeth against it and tried to believe the Chalcedeans were winning. She had suddenly discovered that she preferred the known danger to the unknown. Gently, she tugged the Satrap's collar straight. There. The Satrap of all Jamaillia, heir to the Pearl Throne, Magnadon Satrap Cosgo was now presentable. The Satrap regarded himself in the small mirror she lifted. Unruffled by the smothered sounds of fighting, he smoothed the thin line of his moustache. Something fell heavily to the deck above them. 'I will go up now,' he announced.

'I don't think that's wise. It's battle up there, can't you hear it?' She had spoken too hastily. He set his jaw stubbornly.

'I am not a coward!' he declared.

No. Only an idiot. 'Lordly one, you must not risk yourself!' she begged him. 'I know you do not fear for yourself, but consider Jamaillia, bereft and lost as a rudderless ship if aught should befall you.'

'You are a fool,' the Satrap told her tolerantly. 'What man would dare to physically assault the Satrap of Jamaillia? Those pirate dogs may dispute my rule, but only from a safe distance. When they look me in the face, they will cower in shame.'

He actually believed it. Malta gawked in stunned silence as he walked to the door. He paused, waiting for her to open it for him. Perhaps that was the solution. Maybe if she didn't open the door for him, he would simply stay in the room. But after a long frozen moment, he scowled at her and announced, 'I suppose I must do everything for myself,' and opened it. She trailed after him in sick fascination.

As she stood at the foot of the ladder that led to the deck, she reflected that the hatch cover might save him. It was always hard to lift and slide; perhaps it would defeat him. But when he was halfway up the ladder, the hatch opened, and a square of sunlight fell down onto them. A bare-chested man glared down at them. The spread-winged raven tattooed on his chest was spattered with fresh blood, seemingly not his own. Slave tattoos sprawled across his face and down one side of his neck. The knife he held dripped red. Then his wide-eyed stare changed to a whoop of delight.

'Hey, Cap! Come see what pretty birds I've found caged

below!' To the Satrap and Malta, he barked, 'Come on up here and don't be slow!'

As the Satrap emerged from the hatch, the pirate seized him by the arm and hauled him onto the deck. The Satrap cursed and struck out at the man, who sent him sprawling with a careless shove. As he grabbed Malta, she set her teeth and refused to cry out. She glared at him as he lifted her by one arm and swung her onto the deck. She landed on her feet beside the Satrap. Without taking her eyes from the gloating pirate, she stooped down, seized the Satrap by his upper arm and helped him to his feet.

Around them, the deck was a shambles. A huddle of disarmed Chalcedeans were corralled at one end, guarded by three mocking invaders. Just past the base of the mast, Malta could see a man's sprawled legs. They did not move. Other pirates were dropping down into the hold to see what cargo they had won. Malta heard a splash and turned in time to see some men throw a body overboard. It might have been the mate.

'You will die for this! You will die!' the Satrap was puffing with fury. Two red spots stood out on his pale cheeks and his hair was dishevelled. He glowered at all of them. 'Where is the captain? I demand to see the captain!'

'Please be quiet,' Malta begged him in an undertone.

He did not listen. He pushed at her, as if his fall were her fault. 'Silence!' he spat at her. 'Stupid woman. Do not presume to tell me what to do!' His eyes sparked with anger but his voice betrayed him with its shrillness. He set his fists to his hips. 'I demand that the captain be brought to me.'

'What have you found, Rusk?' A short, brawny man asked their captor with a grin. Curly red hair spilled out from under a head kerchief marked with a raven. He gripped a sword in his left hand. With the tip of the blade, he lifted the embroidered edge of the Satrap's jacket. 'This is a finely-feathered bird. Rich merchant or noble blood, I'd say.'

Cosgo swelled his chest in affront. 'I am the Magnadon Satrap Cosgo, ruler of all Jamaillia and heir to the Pearl Throne! And I demand to speak to the captain.'

Malta's hopes died within her.

A smile split the man's freckled face. 'You *are* speaking to the captain. Captain Red.' He swept a low bow and added purringly, 'At your service, great Satrap, I'm sure.'

The man who had first discovered them laughed so hard he choked.

Cosgo's face went scarlet with fury. 'I mean the real captain. Captain Deiari.'

Captain Red's grin went wider. He dared a wink at Malta. 'I'm so sorry, Magnadon Satrap Cosgo. Captain Deiari is presently entertaining the fish.' In a stage-whisper, he explained to Malta, 'That's what happens to men who don't know when to put their swords down. Or men who lie to me.' He waited.

Behind him, two sailors seized the fallen man behind the mast and dragged him away. Malta stared in fascinated horror. His lifeless body left a swathe of blood behind it. His dead eyes looked at her as they lifted him and his mouth fell open in a joyless smile as he flopped over the railing. She felt she could not breathe.

'I tell you, I am the Magnadon Satrap Cosgo, ruler of all Jamaillia.'

The freckled captain spread wide his arms, sword still in hand, and grinned. 'And here are gathered all your loyal retainers and grand nobles, to attend you on this remarkable voyage from . . . where? Chalced? The Satrap journeys from Chalced to Jamaillia?'

Cosgo's nostrils were pinched white with outrage. 'Not that it is the affair of a thieving, murdering cutthroat, but I am returning from Bingtown. I went there to resolve a dispute between the Old and New Traders, but then I was kidnapped by the Bingtown Traders and taken up the Rain River. The Rain Wild Traders, a race of folk so horribly deformed that they must constantly wear veils, held me captive in an underground city. I escaped during an earthquake and journeyed down the Rain Wild River until I was rescued by a . . .'

As the Satrap spoke, the Captain looked from one to another of his men, all the while pulling faces that feigned his wonder and astonishment at the Satrap's tale. As his men guffawed in delight, the captain suddenly leaned forwards to set the tip of his blade at Cosgo's throat. The Satrap's eyes bulged and his flow of words ceased. All colour drained from his face.

'Stop it now, do, stop!' the captain pleaded merrily. 'We have work to do here, my men and I. Stop your jesting and tell the truth. The sooner you tell us your name and family, the sooner you can be ransomed back to them. You do want to go home, don't you? Or do you fancy you'd make a good addition to my crew?'

Cosgo looked wildly about at the circle of captors. When at last his eyes met Malta's, tears suddenly brimmed in them.

'Stop it,' she said in a low voice. 'Leave him alone. He *is* the Magnadon Satrap Cosgo, and he is far more valuable to you as a hostage if he does not have a cut throat.'

The blade's tip lifted from the Satrap's throat. An instant later, it pressed between her breasts. She looked down on it, paralysed. Someone else's blood was still on it. Captain Red slid the tip under the lacing that secured her bodice. 'And you, of course, are the lovely and learned Companion of his Heart. Also on your way back to Jamaillia.' His gaze travelled over her slowly.

His mockery broke her fear. She met his gaze furiously and spat a single word at a time. 'Don't. Be. Stupid.' She lifted her chin. 'I am Malta Vestrit, a Bingtown Trader's daughter. As wild as his tale sounds, he truly is Magnadon Satrap Cosgo.' She took a breath. 'Kill him, and you will henceforth be known as the stupidest captain ever to discard a Satrap's ransom.'

The captain roared out his delight, and his crew echoed him. Malta felt her cheeks grow red, but she dared not move while the blade pressed her breast. Behind her, the Satrap whispered angrily, 'Don't anger him, wench.'

'Cap'n Red. The ship's secured.' This from a sailor, little more than a boy, wearing an embroidered vest, far too large for him. Malta remembered seeing it on Captain Deiari. A dead man's clothes were the ship's boy's plunder.

'Very good, Oti. How many prisoners?'

''Sides these two? Only five.'

'Condition of the ship?'

'Fit to sail, sir. And full holds as well. She's loaded with good stuff.'

'Is she indeed? Marvellous. I think a prize this fat is enough to take us straight back to port, don't you? We've ranged a bit this time, and Divvytown will look good to us, hey?'

'Very good, sir,' the boy replied enthusiastically. There were assenting noises from the rest of the crew.

The captain looked around. 'Secure the five belowdecks. Get names, find out if they've got families that will ransom them. They fought well. If any express an interest in turning pirate, have him brought to me. Carn! Pick yourself a prize crew. You'll be bringing this one home for us.'

Carn, the man who had first found them, grinned broadly. 'That I will, sir. All right, you two, right back down where you came from!'

The captain shook his head. 'No. Not these two. I'll be taking them back to the *Motley* with me. Even if he's not the Satrap of all Jamaillia, I'll wager he brings a rich ransom from someone.' A deft lift of his blade tip cut Malta's laces. She caught at the loose bodice of her dress and held it to her, gasping in outrage. The captain only grinned. 'As for the lady, she shall have dinner with Captain Stupid and tell me whatever tales she pleases. Bring her along.'

TWENTY-ONE

Paragon of the Ludlucks

ALTHEA WAS AT the top of the mast, watching, when Vivacia's sails first appeared, white against the threatening overcast. Paragon was lurking in an inlet with a clear view of a channel just outside Divvytown, but Vivacia had not yet passed the mouth of the inlet. Brashen had studied his scraps of charts, and gambled that this was the approach Vivacia would use to return to Divvytown, assuming Kennit would be returning from the direction of the Others' Island. Brashen had guessed correctly. Even before Althea could see her hull or her figurehead, she recognized her mast and sails. For a moment, the long-awaited sight left Althea speechless. Several times over the last seven days, she had spotted ships she thought might be Vivacia. Twice she had even called Brashen to the top of the mast to confer. Each time, she had been wrong.

Now, as she watched the familiar rigging come into sight, she was certain: this was her ship, and she knew it as she knew her mother's face. She did not cry out the news to all, but came spidering down the mast and hit the deck running. Without knocking, she barged into Brashen's cabin. He was in bed; he had taken the night watch. 'It's her. To the southeast, whence you thought she would come. No mistake this time, Brashen. It's Vivacia.'

He was instantly awake and on his feet. 'Then it's time.

Let's hope that Kennit is truly as intelligent and rational as you believe he is. Otherwise, we're offering our throats to a butcher.'

For a moment, she could only stare at him, wordless. 'Sorry,' he offered huskily. 'I didn't need to say that. We both decided on this plan. We've both convinced the crew it will work. Don't feel I'm putting it all on you.'

She shook her head. 'You only spoke aloud what I've been thinking for too many days. One way or another, Brashen, it *is* all upon me. But for me, this ship and this crew would not even be out here, let alone considering this mad plan.'

He caught her in his arms for a rough hug. For an instant, the scent of his bare skin was in her nostrils and his loosened hair against her cheek. She rubbed her face against the warmth of his chest. Why, she wondered, was she willing to gamble this man's life and her own on such a wild venture? Then he turned her loose and caught up his shirt from a chair. As he put it on, he became the captain again.

'Go shake out our truce flag and run it up. Tell the crew to have weapons ready, but none in hand. We're offering to talk first to Kennit; we're not inviting him to board us. At the first sign of aggression from him, we respond in kind.'

She bit her tongue to keep from telling him that the crew needed no reminders. They had drilled it into them rigorously. Without Lavoy's subversion to deal with, she felt far more confident of the men. They would obey. Perhaps, in a few hours, she'd stand on the Vivacia's deck again. She jumped to carry out his orders.

'There, sir. See it now?' Gankis pointed and squinted as if that would aid his captain's vision. 'The ship is holding anchor just off the beach. He's probably trusting to the shoreline and the trees to make him hard to see, but I spotted –'

'I see him,' Kennit cut the man off tersely. 'Go about your

duties!' He stared at the masts and riggings. A strange certainty filled his soul. The old lookout left Kennit's side, chastened by his captain's tone. The chill wind blew past Kennit and his ship plunged on through the waves, but he was suddenly separate from it all. Paragon. The other half of his soul rode at anchor in the inlet.

'Can I know him from this far away?' he asked himself softly. 'How? Is it a feeling in the air? A scent on the wind?'

'Blood calls to blood,' whispered the charm at his wrist. 'You know it's him. After all these years, he has come back.'

Kennit tried to breathe, but his lungs felt heavy and sodden. Dread and anticipation warred in him. To speak to the ship again, to tread once more his decks would be to come full circle. All the past defeats and pain would be drowned in that triumph. The ship would take joy in how he had prospered and grown and . . . No. It would not be like that; it would be confrontation and accusation, humiliation and shame. It would open the door to all past sorrows and let them pour out to poison the present. It would be looking into the face of your betrayed beloved. It would be admitting what he had done to ensure his own selfish survival.

Worse, it would be public. Every man on his ship would know who he had been and what had been done to him. The crew of the Paragon would know. Etta and Wintrow would know, Bolt would know. None of them would ever respect him again. Everything he had built so painstakingly, all his years of work would come undone.

He could not allow it. Despite the screaming in the back of his mind, he could not allow it. The beaten, begging boy would have to be silenced once more. One last time, he would have to erase the grovelling, craven lad from the world's memory.

Jola came running down the deck to him. 'Sir, that ship the lookout spotted? They've unfurled a truce flag. They're taking up their anchor and coming towards us.' His words died away at a baleful look from Kennit. 'What do you want us to do?' he asked quietly.

'I suspect treachery,' he told Jola. 'Faldin's message warned us. I will not be lulled by their actions. If necessary, I shall make an example of this ship and its crew. If this is perfidy, the ship goes to the bottom with all hands.' He made his eyes meet Jola's. 'Prepare yourself to hear many lies today, Jola. This particular captain is a very clever man. He tries to use a liveship to take a liveship. We will not allow that to happen.'

Abruptly, his throat closed with pain. Terror rose in him, that Jola might turn towards him just now and see his eyes brim with sudden tears. *Feelings change*, he reminded himself savagely. *This is the choking of a boy, the tears of a boy who no longer exists. I stopped feeling this long ago.*

He coughed to cover his moment of weakness. 'Ready the men. Bring us about and drop anchor. Run up a truce flag of our own to chum them in closer. We'll pretend to be gulled by his ruse. I shall have the ship send forth the serpents.' He showed his teeth in mockery of a smile. 'Let Trell negotiate his truce with them.'

'Sir,' Jola acknowledged him and was swiftly gone.

Kennit made his way forwards. The tapping of his peg sounded loud to him. Men hurried past and around him, each intent on getting to his post. None of them really paused to look at him. None of them could really see him any more. They saw only Kennit, King of the Pirate Isles. Wasn't that what he always wanted? To be seen as the man he had made of himself? Yet still he could imagine how Paragon would bellow in dismay at the sight of his missing leg, or exclaim in delight over the fine cut of his brocade jacket. Triumph was not as keen, he suddenly saw, when it was shared only with those who had always expected you to succeed. On all the seas in all the world, there was only one who truly knew all Kennit had gone through to reach these heights, only one who could understand how keen the triumph was and how deep the pits of misfortune had been. Only one who could betray his past so completely. Paragon had to die. There was no other way. And this time, Kennit must be sure of it.

As he climbed the short ladder to the foredeck, he saw with dismay that Etta and Wintrow were already there. Wintrow leaned on the railing, deep in conversation with the figurehead. Etta stared across the water at Paragon, a strange expression on her face. Her dark hair teased the rising wind. Kennit shaded his eyes to follow her gaze. The Paragon was drawing steadily closer. His heart turned over at the sight of the cruelly chopped face. Shame burned him, followed by a rush of fury. It could not be blamed on him. No one, not even Paragon could blame him. Igrot's fault, it was all Igrot's fault. The cold horror of it reached across the water and burned him. Dread dizzied him, and he lifted a shaking hand to his face.

'You let him take all the pain for you,' the charm breathed by his ear. 'He said he would, and you let him.' The charm smiled. 'It's all there, waiting for you. With him.'

'Shut up,' Kennit grated. With trembling fingers, he tried to unknot the damnable thing from his wrist. He would throw it overboard, it would sink and be gone forever with all it knew. But his fingers were oddly clumsy, almost numb. He could not undo the tight leather knots. He tugged at the charm itself, but the cords held.

'Kennit, Kennit! Are you well?'

Stupid whore, always asking the wrong questions at the wrong time. He wrenched his emotions under control. He took out his handkerchief and patted sweat from his chilled brow. He found his voice.

'I am quite well, of course. And you?'

'You looked so . . . for an instant, I feared you would faint.' Etta's eyes roved over his face, trying to read it. She tried to take his hands in hers.

That would never do. He smiled his small smile at her.

Distract her. 'The boy,' he asked in a low voice. 'This may be hard for Wintrow. How is he?'

'Torn,' Etta immediately confided. A lesser man might have been offended at how easily he had turned her concern from himself to Wintrow. But Etta was, after all, only a whore. She sighed. 'He strives to wring some response from the ship. He demands that she react to him as Vivacia. Of course, she does not. Just now, he seeks some reaction to Althea's presence from her. She gives him nothing. When he reminded her that you had promised him Althea would not be harmed, she laughed and said that was your promise, not hers. It struck him to the heart when she said that an agreement with you was not a promise to him.' She lowered her voice. 'Could you reassure him that you will keep your word?'

Kennit lifted one shoulder in a shrug. 'As much as I can, I will. It is as I told him before. Sometimes folk are determined to fight to the death, and then what can I do? Surely he does not expect me to allow her to kill me in order to keep my word to him?'

For a moment, Etta just looked at him. Twice she seemed on the verge of saying something, but made no sound. Finally she asked quietly, 'I suppose the truce flag could be a deception. But . . . but you will try to keep your promise?'

He cocked his head at her. 'Such an odd question. Of course I shall.' He made his smile warmer. He offered her his arm, and she took it and walked beside him to the railing. 'If things begin to go badly – use your judgement in this – but if you suspect that things may not turn out as Wintrow would wish, take him below,' he said quietly. 'Find an excuse, a distraction of any kind. Any kind at all.'

Etta flickered a glance at him. 'He is scarcely a child, to forget one toy when another is waved at him.'

'Do not misunderstand me. I only say what we both know is true. You are a woman well capable of distracting any man. Whatever you must do, I would not hold it against you.

Anything. I do not expect you can make him forget his family is involved in this, but he need not witness it.' There. He could not make the hint any broader without actually commanding her to seduce him. Sa knew the woman had enough appetite for two men. Of late, she had been insatiable. She should be able to keep Wintrow busy for as long as it took Kennit to deal with this problem. She seemed to be thinking deeply as they approached Wintrow.

Wintrow spoke softly, earnestly. 'Althea practically grew up on your deck. If the choice had been hers, she would never have left you. When she stands on this deck again, your feelings for her will return. Vivacia, she will bring you back to yourself, and I know you will welcome her. Let go the anger you feel over something she was forced to do.'

Bolt's arms were crossed on her breast. All around her, the water seethed with serpents. 'I am not angry, Wintrow. I am bored. Bored with your whole recitation. I have often heard of priests that they will argue until a man agrees with them simply to still their tongues. So I ask you this. If I pretend to feel something for her, will you shut up and go away?'

For an instant, Wintrow bowed his head. Kennit thought she had defeated him. Then he lifted it to stare at the advancing Paragon. 'No,' he said in a low voice. 'I won't go away. I'm staying right here, beside you. When she comes aboard, there should be someone here to explain to her what has happened to you.'

That would never do. Kennit made a swift decision. 'Actually, Wintrow, I have a small task for you. Take Etta with you. As soon as we are anchored, I wish you to take the ship's boat over to the *Marietta*. Some of Sorcor's men are a bit hot-headed. Tell Sorcor, diplomatically, that I alone will approach this ship. I wish him to hold the *Marietta* well back; it would suit me best if his crew did not even crowd the railings. This ship comes to us under a truce flag; I don't wish them to

feel outnumbered and threatened. That could lead to violence
where none is needed.'

'Sir, could not you send . . .' Wintrow began pleadingly.

Kennit patted Etta's hand heavily. She took the hint.

'Don't whine, Wintrow,' she rebuked him. 'It will do you
no good to remain here and let Bolt torment you. She toys
with you like a cat with a mouse, and you have not the sense
to remove yourself. So Kennit is doing it for you. Come. You
have a gift for smooth words, and will be able to pass this order
on to Sorcor in such a way that he does not feel slighted.'

Kennit listened in admiration. She was so adept at making
Wintrow seem both foolish and selfish for trying to oppose him.
It must be a female talent. So his mother had often spoken to
him, letting the edge of impatience show to convince him of
his error. He thrust the memory aside. The sooner Paragon was
gone, the better. Not for years had so many buried recollections
stirred so uncomfortably in him.

Wintrow glanced uncertainly from one to the other. 'But I
had hoped to be here when Kennit met –'

'It would look as if we flaunted you as hostage. I wish them
to see you are a willing member of my crew. Unless . . .' Kennit
paused, and gave Wintrow an odd look. 'Did you wish to leave
the ship? Are you hoping to go with them? For if that is your
desire, you but have to speak it. They could take you back to
Bingtown, or your monastery . . .'

'No.' Even Etta looked surprised at how swiftly Wintrow
replied. 'My place is here. I know that now. I have no desire
to leave. Sir, I would remain at your side, and be witness to
the creation of the Pirate Isles as a recognized kingdom. I feel
– I feel this is where Sa intended me to be.' He looked down
at the deck silently for an instant. Then he met Kennit's gaze
again. 'I'll go to Sorcor, sir. Right now?'

'Yes. I'd like him to hold off where he is. Be sure he is clear
on that. No matter what he sees he is to let me resolve it.'

As they hastened away, he took Wintrow's place at the

railing. 'Why do you take such delight in tormenting the boy?' he asked the ship in amused tolerance.

'Why does he insist on bothering me with his fixation on Vivacia?' the ship growled in return. 'What, exactly, was so marvellous about her? Why cannot he accept me in her stead?'

Jealousy? If he had had more time, it would have been an interesting possibility to explore. He rolled her questions aside with, 'Boys always strive to keep things as they always have been. Given time, he'll come around.' Then he asked a question he had never dared before: 'Can serpents sink a vessel? I don't mean just batter it so it can't sail; I mean send it down to the bottom?' He took a breath. 'Preferably, in pieces.'

'I don't know,' she replied. Glancing at him from the corner of her eye, she asked him, 'Would you like us to try?'

For a moment, his mouth could not find the shape of the word. Then, 'Yes,' he admitted. 'If it becomes necessary,' he added feebly.

Her voice dropped throatily. 'Consider what you ask me. Paragon is a liveship, like myself.' She stared across the water at the oncoming ship. 'A dragon, kin to me, sleeps within those wooden bones. You are asking me to turn on my own kind, for your sake. Do you think I would do that?'

This sudden gaping hole in his plans nearly unmanned him. They were bringing the Paragon about and dropping anchor, just out of arrow range. They were not complete fools. He had to win her over, and swiftly.

'With me, you come before all others. Should you ask a similar sacrifice from me, I would not hesitate,' he promised her heartily.

'Really?' she queried him callously. 'Even if it were Etta?'

'Without a pause,' he promised, refusing to let himself think.

'Or Wintrow?' Her voice had gone soft and knowing.

A knife twisted in him. How much did she truly read of his

heart? He took a deep breath. 'If you demanded it.' Would she? Could she insist he give him up? He pushed the thought aside. 'I hope I hold as dear a place with you.' He tried to think of other fine words for her. Failing, he asked her instead, 'Will you do it?'

'I think it's time you knew the price,' she countered.

The *Marietta* had taken up Wintrow's small boat. Sorcor's ship was veering off. Soon they would drop anchor at a discreet distance. He watched the routine of Sorcor's crew and waited.

'When we are finished here,' she told him, 'you will muster all your ships, every one that flies a raven flag. You and they will serve as escort for us. The serpents must travel north to a river mouth they scarcely remember, but one I have entered many times in my life as Vivacia. As we move north, we will seek to gather up other serpents. You will protect them from humans. When we reach the river, I will guide them up it, while your other ships keep guard behind us. No ordinary wooden ship can accompany them on that migration. You will give to me, Kennit Ludluck, all that remains of this winter, all of spring, all your days until high summer and the sun's full heat, as we aid the serpents in what they must do, and guard them through their helpless time. That is the price. Are you willing to pay it?'

In the naming of his name, she bound him. How had she known? Had she guessed? Then he glanced down at the small grinning charm on his wrist. Looking into features twin to his own, he knew his betrayer. The charm winked up at him.

'I, too, was once a dragon,' it said quietly.

There was so little time to think. For him to vanish with the serpents now for all those months might undo all he had built. Yet, he dared not refuse her this. Perhaps, he thought grimly, it would only add to his legend. The Paragon was lowering a small boat into the water. Althea Vestrit would be in it. 'If I do as you ask, you will sink Paragon?' It was harder to ask now, for he knew that she knew all the reasons he desired Paragon to end.

'Tell me why you want him to be gone. Say the words.'

He took a breath and met her gaze. 'My motives are the same as yours,' he said coldly. 'You do not wish Althea to come aboard, for you fear she would "bring you back to yourself".' He lifted his eyes and stared at the Paragon. 'There floats a piece of myself I could do without.'

'Then it seems wisest, for both of us,' she agreed. 'He is mad. I cannot count on him to aid us; worse, as a liveship, he could follow us up the river and oppose us. He can never fly again as a dragon. So let us put him out of his misery. And end your misery as well, while binding you to me. Only me.'

Jealousy. This time it was unmistakable. She would tolerate no rivals for his attention, let alone so potent a competitor as Paragon. In this also, they were alike. She tucked her chin to her chest and summoned the serpents. The sound she made was something Kennit more felt than heard. Their serpent escort had lagged behind them to hunt and feed, but at her call, they came swiftly. Soon a forest of attentive heads sprouted around them. The green-gold serpent from Others' Island came to the front of the throng. When Bolt paused, the serpent opened her jaws and roared something back at her. Bolt threw back her head and sang. Her voice battled against a wind that promised a storm to come. There were several exchanges of moans, bellows and high, thin cries between the two. Two other serpents added their voices as well. Kennit grew restless. This had to be a discussion of Bolt's orders. That had not happened before. It was not auspicious, but he dared not interrupt her with a question. His own crew was watching curiously. He glanced down to his hands gripping the railing, and saw the small face at his wrist staring up at him. He brought the charm close to his face.

'Do they oppose her?' he asked.

'They question the necessity. She Who Remembers thinks

Paragon might be useful to them alive. Bolt counters that he is both mad and a servile tool of the humans aboard him. Maulkin asks if they may eat him for his memories. Bolt opposes this. She Who Remembers demands to know why. Now Maulkin asks if the ship holds knowledge she wishes to keep from the serpents.'

Bolt was visibly angry now. Behind him, Kennit was aware of his gawking crew. Without turning his head, he warned Jola, 'The men to their posts.' The mate obeyed, sending them running.

'What do they say?' he demanded of the charm again.

'Use your eyes,' was the whispered retort. 'They obey her.'

Brashen had remained on board Paragon. It did not seem wise for both of them to leave the ship, and Althea could not bear to be so close to Vivacia and not speak to her. In the boat with her, Haff and Jek bent to their oars. Lop, clutching a mooring line, sat in the bow and stared grimly ahead. Althea sat stiffly in the stern seat. She was freshly washed and attired in the clothes she had worn when the Paragon had left Bingtown. She resented the weight of the split skirt, but the occasion called for formality, and these were the best clothes she possessed. Indeed, of all her garments, these were the only ones still remotely presentable. The rising winter wind tugged hopefully at her plaited and pinned hair. She hoped Kennit would not see her attempt at formality as hiding behind feminine garb. He had to take her seriously.

She clutched the scroll in her hands and stared at their destination. On the foredeck of her beloved Vivacia, a single figure stood. His dark blue cloak flapped in the wind and he stood hip-shot, all his weight on one leg. It had to be Kennit. Before she had left Paragon's deck, there had been others with him. She had thought that one young man might be Wintrow. She could not claim to recognize him, but the figure's dark hair and stance put her in mind of her father. Could it have been him? If it was, where had he gone? Why did Kennit alone await her?

Reflexively, she glanced back at Paragon. Brashen stood anxiously on the foredeck. Clef stood beside him, hands on his hips in unconscious mimicry of his captain. Amber's hair blew like silk strands in the wind, and her set face made her a second figurehead. Paragon, arms crossed and jaw set, stared sightlessly towards Vivacia. There was a terrible finality in the brace of his muscles. He had not spoken a word to anyone since Vivacia was sighted. When Althea had dared to reach out and touch his muscular shoulder, she had found it set and hard as wood. It was like touching the tensed back of a snarling dog.

'Don't be afraid,' she had told him softly, but he had made no reply.

A composed Amber, sitting on the railing beside her had shaken her head. 'He's not afraid,' she had said in a low voice. 'The anger that burns in him destroys every other emotion.' Amber's hair lifted slightly in the rising wind and she had spoken in a distant voice. 'Danger cups us under its hand, and we can do nothing but stand witness to the turning of the world. Here we walk on the balancing line between futures. Humanity always believes it decides the fate of the whole world, and so it does, but never in the moment that it thinks it does. The future of thousands ripples like a serpent through the water, and the destiny of a ship becomes the destination of the world.' She turned to look at Althea with eyes the colour of brandy in firelight. 'Can't you feel it?' she asked in a whisper. 'We are on the cusp. We are a coin spinning in the toss, a card fluttering in the flip, a rune chip floating in stirred water. Possibilities swarm like bees. In this day, in a moment, in a breath, the future of the world will shift course by a notch. One way or another, the coin will land ringing, the card will settle to the table, the chip will bob to the surface. The face that shows uppermost will set our days, and children to come will say, "That is just the way it has always been."'

Her voice dwindled away, but Althea had a sense of the wind carrying the words around the world. Her scalp prickled. 'Amber? You're frightening me.'

Amber had turned a slow and beatific smile on her. 'Am I? Then you grow wise.'

Althea did not think she could bear the steady gaze of those eyes. Then Amber blinked and saw her again. She had hopped from the railing to the deck, dusting her bare hands on the seat of her pants before drawing on her gloves. 'It's time for you to go,' she announced. 'Come. I'll help you with your hair.'

'Watch over Paragon for me,' Althea had said quietly. 'Don't leave him alone.'

'I would like to.' Amber's long-fingered hand caressed the railing. 'But today is a day he must face alone.'

Now, Althea looked back from the ship's boat and wished Amber had come with her. She tightened her grip on the scroll and prayed Kennit would be swayed by the carefully-penned offer. He had to be! Everything she had heard of this man spoke of a resolute intelligence coupled with great foresight. He had hung out a truce flag of his own, so he was open to negotiation. He would at least hear her out. Even if he loved Vivacia, perhaps especially if he loved Vivacia, he would see that returning her to the Vestrits in exchange for trade agreements was in everyone's best interest. Suddenly, Amber lifted a finger and pointed ahead of Althea. At the same instant, Lop gave a wild cry, echoed by Haff who dropped his oar and came halfway to his feet. Althea swivelled her head to see where Amber pointed and froze.

The sea around Vivacia bristled with serpents. Head after glittering head lifted from the depths until a forest of serpents stood between Althea and her ship. In the boat, Haff cowered and babbled, while Jek demanded, 'Do we go back?' Lop crawled through the boat and took up Haff's oar hopefully.

Stricken, Althea watched the horde of serpents menace her ship. Yet what happened next was even worse.

Vivacia threw back her head and sang to the creatures. Her throat swelled and she opened her mouth wide. Inhuman moans and roars and trills came from her mouth. The serpents' heads swayed, captivated by her song. After a time, they sang back as if ensorcelled by her. Althea realized she stood in a half-crouch, staring at the figurehead. Uneasiness squirmed through her. Vivacia spoke to them, that was plain, and they spoke back to her. The face of the ship as she stretched her features to make the serpent sounds was alien, as was the unnatural lifting and writhing of her hair. It reminded Althea of a serpent's mane unfolding just before she shook venom from it. Was Vivacia miming the actions of a serpent to convince them not to harm her?

As Althea stared up at her, a terrible chilling knowledge moved deep inside her. She pushed it aside as one flings off the lingering terror of a nightmare. Mine, she insisted, Vivacia is mine, my family, my blood. Yet she gave the low-voiced command, 'Lop, Jek, get us out of here. Haff, shut up if you can't be useful.' She did not have to speak again. Lop and Jek bent eagerly to their oars.

Vivacia lifted a great hand and pointed commandingly at Paragon. From her throat issued a high *qui-ii-ii* like the cry of a striking hawk. Like a wheeling flock of birds, every serpent head turned towards the blind liveship. In the next instant a wave of serpents moved towards him in a purposeful rippling of scintillant colours. Their heads split the water and their gleaming backs wove through the sparkling surface of the waves as they arrowed towards Paragon. Althea had never seen anything so lovely or so terrifying. As she watched, their jaws gaped wide, displaying scarlet maws and white teeth. Like flowers turning to the sun, their multi-hued manes began to open around their throats, standing out like deadly petals.

On Paragon's deck, Brashen bellowed for them to return to

the ship now, as if his command could somehow make the small craft move faster. Althea stared back at the oncoming serpents and knew it was too late. Lop and Jek rowed hard, long deep stokes that sent the boat shooting forwards, but a small boat and two rowers could never outdistance these creatures of the sea. Poor Haff, victim to his memory of his last encounter with a serpent, huddled in the bottom of the boat. Althea did not blame him. She watched the serpents gain on them, transfixed by danger. Then a towering blue serpent rose over the boat, his erect mane an immense parasol of tentacles.

All in the boat cried out, but the huge creature merely shouldered them out of its way. The little boat rocked wildly in the serpent's wake, only to be struck and spun about by yet another passing snake. The brush of the passing serpent snatched the oar from Jek's grip and tore the oarlock loose. Althea clung to the seat with a white-knuckled grip and hoped they would not capsize. As the wild rocking of the boat settled, she watched with horror as the serpents surrounded Paragon. There was nothing she could do for the ship or the crew on board him. She forced herself to think only of what measures she could take.

The first mate made her decision. 'Use that oar as a scull and make for the Vivacia. She's our only hope now. We'll never get back to Paragon through all those serpents.'

Brashen watched helplessly as Althea's small boat wallowed and swung in the wakes of the serpent horde. His mind rapidly sorted and discarded possibilities. Launching another ship's boat could not aid them; it would only put more crew at risk. He looked away from her and took a deep breath. When his eyes found her again, he regarded her as her captain. If he believed in her at all, he'd trust her to take care of her boat and her crew. She'd expect him to do the same. The ship had to be his first responsibility.

Not that there was much he could do. He issued orders anyway. 'Get our anchor up. I want to be able to manoeuvre if we have to.' He wondered if he only said it to give the men something to do so they wouldn't stare at the oncoming wave of serpents. He glanced at Amber. She held tight to the railing, leaning forwards and speaking low to Paragon, telling him all she could see.

He cast his mind back over his other encounters with serpents. Recalling Haff's serpent, he commanded his best bowmen to the rails. 'Don't shoot until I tell you,' he told them harshly. 'And when you do, take your shot only if you can strike the brightly coloured spots just back of the angle of their jaws. No other target! If you can't hit it, hold fire until you can. Every shot has to count.' He looked back to Amber and suggested, 'Arm the ship?'

'He doesn't want it,' she replied in a low voice.

'Nor do I want your archers.' Paragon's voice was hoarse. 'Listen to me, Brashen Trell. Tell your men to set their bows and other weapons down. Keep them to hand, but do not brandish them about. I want no killing of these creatures. I suspect they are no danger to me. If you have any respect for me at all . . .' Paragon let the thought die away. He lifted his arms wide and suddenly shouted, 'I know you. I KNOW YOU!' The deep timbre of his bellow vibrated through the whole ship. Slowly he lowered his arms to his sides. 'And you know me.'

Brashen stared at him in confusion, but motioned for his bowmen to obey. What did the ship mean? But as Paragon threw back his head and filled his chest with air, Brashen suddenly knew that the ship spoke to the oncoming serpents, not the crew.

Paragon dropped his jaw open wide. The sound that came from him vibrated the planks under Brashen's feet, and then rose until it became a high ululation. Another deep breath, and then he cried out again, in a voice more like sea-pipes than a man speaking.

In the silence that followed, Brashen heard Amber's breathless whisper. 'They hear you. They slow and look at one another. Now, they come on, but cautiously, and every one of them looks to you. They halt and fan out in a great circle around you. Now one comes forwards. He is green but gold flashes from his scales when he turns in the sun –'

'She,' Paragon corrected her quietly. 'She Who Remembers. I taste her in the wind, my planks feel her presence in the water. Does she look at me?'

'She does. They all do.'

'Good.' The figurehead drew breath again, and once more the cavernous language of the sea serpents issued from his jaws.

Shreever followed Maulkin with heavy hearts. Her loyalty to him was unshaken; she would have followed him under ice. Shreever had accepted his decision when he surrendered his dominance to She Who Remembers. She had instinctively trusted the crippled serpent with a faith that went beyond her unique scent. The serpent herself inspired her confidence. Shreever felt certain that those two serpents together could save their race.

But of late it seemed to her that these two leaders had given authority over to the silver ship called Bolt. Shreever could find no trust for her. Although the silver one smelled like One Who Remembered, she had neither the shape nor the ways of a serpent. Her commands to the tangle made no sense, and her promises to lead them safely to a cocooning place always began with 'soon'. 'Soon' and 'tomorrow' were concepts that the serpents could ill afford. The cold of winter was chilling the waters, and the runs of migratory fish were disappearing. Already the serpents were losing flesh. If they did not cocoon soon, they would not have the body reserves to last the winter, let alone enough to metamorphose.

But She Who Remembers heeded Bolt, and Maulkin heeded her. So Shreever followed, as did Sessurea and the rest of the tangle. Even though this last command from the ship made no sense at all. Destroy the other silver ship. Why, she wanted to know. The ship had not threatened them in any way. He smelled of serpent, in the same confusing, muted way as Bolt did. So why destroy him? Especially, why destroy him but leave his carcass undevoured? Why not bear him down and share out his flesh amongst themselves? From the scent of him, it would be rich with memories. The other silver they had pulled down had willingly surrendered both flesh and memories to them. Why should this one be any different?

But Bolt had given them their strategy. They were to spray the ship with venom to weaken its structure. Then the longer males were to fling themselves against the ship to turn it on its side. Once its wings were in the water, the smaller serpents could add their weight and strength to drag it down. There they must batter it to pieces, and leave the pieces to sink to the bottom. Only the two-legs could they eat. A foolish, deliberate waste of energy, life and food. Was there something about the ship that Bolt feared? A memory hidden in the silver ship that she did not wish them to share?

Then the silver ship spoke. His voice was deep and powerful, shimmering through the water. It brushed along Shreever's scales commandingly. She slowed, her mane slackening in wonder. 'Why do you attack me?' he demanded. In a harsher voice, he added, 'Does *he* bid you do this? Does he fear to face me then, but sends others to do this task in his stead? He was not once so guileful about treachery. I thought I knew you. I thought to name you the heirs to the Three Realms. But they were a folk who served their own ends. They did not scurry and slither to a human's bidding.' His voice dripped disdain like venom.

Abruptly the serpents were milling in confusion. They had not expected their victim to speak to them, let alone question and disparage them. She Who Remembers spoke for them all as she demanded, 'Who are you? What are you?'

'Who am I? What am I? Those questions have so many answers they are meaningless. And why do I owe you an answer, when you have not replied to my question. Why do you attack me? Do you serve Kennit?'

No one replied to his question, but no serpent attacked either. Shreever spared a glance for the silent two-legs that clustered along the ship's flanks and clung to his wing tips. They were unmoving, silently watching what transpired. They knew they had no say in this: it was business for the Lords of the Three Realms. What did his accusations mean? A slow suspicion grew in Shreever's mind. Had the command to kill this ship truly come from Bolt, or from the humans aboard her? Shreever watched avidly as both She Who Remembers and Maulkin waited for the other to reply.

But it was the white serpent, Carrion, who spoke. He had remained an outsider to the tangle, always on the edges, listening and mocking. 'They will kill you, not at the command of a man, but because the other ship has promised to guide them home if they do so. Being noble and high-minded creatures, they immediately agreed to murder as a small price for saving themselves. Even the murder of one of their own.'

The creature that was part of the ship spread wide his limbs. 'One of your own? Do you truly claim me, then? How strange. For though with one touch I knew you, I still do not know myself. Even I do not claim myself. How is it that you do?'

'He is mad,' a scarred scarlet serpent trumpeted. His copper eyes spun with impatience. 'Let us do what we must do. Kill him. Then she will lead us north. Long enough have we delayed.'

'Oh, yes!' the white serpent chortled throatily. 'Kill him, kill him quickly, before he forces us to face what we have become. Kill him before he makes us question what Bolt is, and why we should give credence to her.' He twined himself through an insulting knot, as if he courted his own tail. 'Perhaps this is a thing she has learned from her time infested with humans. As we all recall, they kill one another with relish. Have not we been assisting them in that task, all at Bolt's behest? If, indeed, those commands come from Bolt at all. Perhaps she has become the willing pupil of a human. Let us show her what apt students we are. Kill him.'

She Who Remembers spoke slowly. 'There will be no killing. This is not right, and we all know it. To kill this creature, not for food nor to protect ourselves, but simply because we are commanded to do so is not worthy of us. We are the heirs of the Three Realms. When we kill, we kill for ourselves. Not like this.'

Relief surged through Shreever. Then Tellur, the slender green minstrel, spoke suddenly. 'What then of our bargain with Bolt? She was to guide us home, if we did this for her. Shall we now be left as we were before?'

'Better to be as we were before we encountered her than as she nearly made us,' Maulkin replied heavily.

She Who Remembers spoke again. 'I do not know what kinship we owe this ship. From all we have heard, we converse with death when we speak to these beings. Yet once they were of us, and for that we owe them some small respect. This one, we shall not kill. I shall return to Bolt, and see what she says. If this command comes from the humans aboard her, then let them fight their own petty battles. We are not servants. If she refuses to guide us home, then I will leave. Those who wish to can follow me. Perhaps what I recall will be enough to guide us. Perhaps not. But we will remain the heirs of the Three Realms. Together, we shall make this last migration. If it does not lead to rebirth for us, it will lead to death. Better that than to become like humans, slaughtering our own for the sake of personal survival.'

'Easily said!' trumpeted an orange serpent angrily. 'But harder to live. Winter is here, prophet, perhaps the last winter we shall ever know. You cannot guide us; the world is too much changed. Without a sure guide, to go north yet again is to die. What real choice have we but to flee to the warm lands? When next we return, there will be far fewer of us. And what will we remember?' The orange swivelled her head to stare at the ship coldly. 'Let us kill him. It is a small price for our salvation.'

'A small price!' A long scarlet serpent agreed with the orange. 'This ship who gives us no answers, not even his name, is a sacrifice for the survival of our kind. She Who Remembers has said it herself. When we kill, we kill because we choose to do so. We kill for ourselves. This will indeed be for ourselves, to buy survival for us all.'

'Do we buy our lives from humans, paying with the blood of our own? I think not!' The mottled saffron serpent who challenged these words did so with mane erect. 'What will come next? Will humans command us to turn on one another?' In a display of disdain, the challenger shook fish-stun toxins from his mane onto the red.

The long red serpent retaliated, shaking his head and spattering venom wildly on his neighbours. Almost instantly, the two serpents locked in combat, wrapping one another and releasing spray after spray of venom. Others darted into the conflict. A drift of toxin hit one of the giant blues, who reacted reflexively with a stinging spray of his own. Furious with pain, a green closed with him and wrapped him. Their struggle thrashed the water to white foam, driving lesser serpents to collide with others, who sprayed or snapped in response. The chaos spread.

Over it all, Shreever heard the bellowing of the silver ship. 'Stop! You injure one another! Kill me if you must, but do not end yourselves in this useless wrangling!'

Did one of the serpents take him at his word? Was the drift of venom that brought hoarse screams from him an accident? Too late to wonder, useless to know. The silver ship bellowed his agony in a human voice, flailing uselessly at the burning mist. The cries of humans were mixed with his, a wild pitiful screaming. Then from the deck of the ship, a winging arrow skipped over Shreever's hide and bounced harmlessly off Maulkin. The futile attack on their leader enraged the agitated serpents. A score of them closed on the hapless ship. One immense cobalt rammed it as if it were an orca, while several lesser ones spattered venom at him. They were not accustomed to fighting above the Plenty. The fickle winds of the upper world carried most of their spray back into their own faces. It only increased the frenzy of the attack.

'Stop them!' Maulkin was roaring, and She Who Remembers lent her voice as well. 'Cease this madness! We battle ourselves, to no good end.'

Carrion's voice rang out over all of them. 'If Bolt wants this ship killed, let her do it herself! Let her prove herself worthy of being followed. Challenge her to the kill!'

It was his words, rather than those of the leaders, that damped the frenzy. Sessurea wrapped two struggling serpents and carried them down and away from the ship. Shreever and others followed his example, dragging the combatants down and away into the calming depths until they could master themselves.

As abruptly as the attack had begun, it ceased. 'I don't understand.' Brashen staggered to the railing and stared incredulously at the serpents as they flowed away from his ship. 'What does it mean?'

Clef stared up at him in white-faced relief. He clutched at his scalded forearm but still managed a grin. 'Means we don't gotter die yet?'

The length of the ship, men were screaming and staggering. Only two archers had been hit with a direct spray of the stuff, but the drift had debilitated many. Those who had been affected writhed on the deck, pawing uselessly at the corrosive slime. 'Don't rub your injuries! You'll only spread the stuff. Seawater!' Brashen bellowed through the confusion. 'Get the deck pumps going! Every man who can manage a bucket! Wash down the figurehead, your mates and the deck. Dilute the stuff. Scramble!'

Brashen quickly scanned the water, hoping for a glimpse of Althea's boat. He had seen her regain command of it. While the serpents surrounded Paragon, she had turned back towards Vivacia. The dazzle of sunlight on the waves and the moving, flashing backs of the serpents surrounding the other ship dazzled his eyes. Where was she? Had she reached safety? It was a physical wrench to turn his back on the water. He could do nothing for her; his immediate duties were closer to hand.

In several places, the railing and the deck smoked with the cold burning of the serpent's venom. Brashen seized a bucket of seawater from a passing hand and took it forwards to the figurehead. Amber was there before him. She dashed a bucket of water over Paragon's steaming shoulder. As the seawater carried away a gelatinous mist of serpent venom, the whole ship shuddered in relief. Paragon's keening dropped to panting moans. Amber turned to Brashen and tried to take the bucket he held. His breath seized in his chest. 'Stand still,' he ordered her gruffly, and upended the bucket over her head.

Great hanks of her hair flowed away with the running water. On the left side of her body, her clothing hung in steaming tatters. That side of her face was rippled with blisters. 'Strip off those clothes, and wash your skin thoroughly,' he ordered her.

She swayed where she stood. 'Paragon needs me,' she said faintly. 'All others have turned on him. Every family, every kin he has ever claimed have turned on him. He has only us, Brashen. Only us.'

Paragon suddenly turned a pocked and steaming face towards

them. 'I do need you,' he admitted hoarsely. 'I do. So get below and strip off those clothes before the venom eats you through.'

There was a sudden shout of horror from Clef. He was pointing with a shaking hand. 'Ship's boat, ser! A serpent's tail struck it, en they all went flyin' like dolls! Right into the middle o'em serpents. En now I ken't see'm atall.'

In an instant, Brashen stood beside him. 'Where?' he demanded, shaking the boy's shoulder, but all Clef could do was point at nothing. Where the boat had been there was now only the colourful rippling of serpent backs and glittering waves. He doubted Althea could swim; few sailors bothered to learn, claiming that if one went overboard, there was small sense in prolonging the agony. The weight of her clothes would pull her under; he groaned aloud. He could not let her go like that, yet to put out another ship's boat into that sea of serpents would simply murder the men he sent.

'Up anchor!' he shouted. He would take the Paragon in closer to Vivacia and search the stretch of water where Clef had last seen them. There was a tiny chance they remained alive, clinging to the capsized boat. Pirates and serpents notwithstanding, he'd find her. He had to.

Kennit watched the oncoming wave of heads and gaping maws and tried to keep his aplomb. The distant screaming of his ship crawled up his nerves and grated against his soul, waking memories of a dark and smoky night years ago. He pushed them away. 'Why do they return? They have not finished him.' He dragged in a breath. 'I thought they could do this swiftly. I would have a quick end to this.'

'I do not know,' Bolt replied angrily. She threw back her head and trumpeted at the oncoming serpents. Several of them replied, a confusing blast of sound.

'I think you will have to vanquish your own nightmares,'

the charm informed him quietly. 'Behold. Paragon comes for you.'

In a moment of great clarity, Kennit watched the ship ponderously swing in the wind, and then start towards him. So. It was to be battle after all. Perhaps it was better that way. When the battle was over, he would tread Paragon's decks once more. There would be a final farewell, of sorts. 'Jola!' He was pleased that his voice rang clear and strong despite how his heart shook inside him. 'The serpents have done their task. They have weakened and demoralized our enemy. Prepare the men for battle. I will lead the boarding party.'

Brashen should have noticed that despite all the roaring and thrashing, the serpents were not attacking Vivacia. He should have noticed the pirates massed along the railings as Paragon came alongside. His eyes should have stayed on Kennit's ship instead of searching the water for Althea. He should have known that a truce flag was no more than a white rag to the pirate king . . .

The first grapples hit his deck when he thought he was still out of their range. Even as he angrily ordered them cleared away, a line of archers stepped precisely to Kennit's railing. As Brashen shouted that they searched for survivors, arrows flew, and his men went down. Men who had survived the serpents' venom died shocked deaths as Brashen reeled in horror at his own incompetence. More grapples followed the first, the ships were pulled closer together, and then a wave of boarders swung from their rigging into his. Pirates were suddenly everywhere, pouring over his railings and onto his decks in a seemingly endless wave. The defenders were pushed back, and then their line broke and became small knots of men struggling against all odds to survive.

Paragon bellowed and thrust and parried with a staff that found only air. From the moment the first grapples were thrown, victory was an undreamt dream. Paragon's decks soaked up the blood of the dying and the ship roared with the impact of the losses. Worse was the sound that reached Brashen's ears with the relentless whistling of a wind in the rigging. Vivacia cried out in words both human and alien as she urged the pirates on. Almost he was glad Althea had perished before she had heard her own ship turn against them.

His crew fought bravely and uselessly. They were outnumbered, inexperienced, and some were injured. Young Clef remained at his side, a short blade in his good hand, throughout the heartbreakingly brief struggle. As the wave of boarders engulfed them, Brashen killed a man, and then another, and Clef took out a third by hamstringing him but got a nasty slash down his ribs for his bravery. More pirates simply stepped over the bodies of their comrades, blades at the ready. Brashen grabbed the boy's collar with his free hand, and jerked him back behind him. Together they retreated through the disorder, fighting only to stay alive, and managed to gain the foredeck. Brashen looked down at a deck fouled with downed men. The pirates were in clear command of the carnage; his own men were reduced to defending themselves or scurrying like chased rats through the rigging as laughing freebooters hunted them down. Brashen had thought to call out commands to re-form his fighters, but a single glance showed him no strategy could save them now. It was not battle, but slaughter.

'I'm sorry,' he said to the bleeding boy at his side. 'I should never have let you come with me.' He raised his voice. 'And I'm sorry, Paragon. To bring you so far and raise such hopes in us both, only to end like this. I've failed you both. I've failed us all.'

He took a deep breath and bellowed out the hated words. 'I yield! And I beg quarter for my crew. Captain Brashen Trell of the Liveship Paragon yields and surrenders his ship to you.'

It took a moment for his words to penetrate the din. The clatter of swords gradually stilled, but the moaning of the wounded went on. Walking through the mayhem towards Brashen, his moustache elegantly curled, unsullied by blood or sweat, came a one-legged man who could only be Captain Kennit. 'Already?' he asked dryly. He gestured at his sheathed weapon. 'But good sir, I've only just come aboard. Are you certain you wish to yield?' He glanced about at the scattered huddles of survivors. Their weapons lay at their feet, while circles of blades menaced them. The pirate's smile was white, his voice charming as he offered, 'I'm sure my lads would be willing to let them pick up their blades for one more try at this. It seems a pity to fail on your very first effort. This was your first effort, wasn't it?'

The laughter that greeted each of his sallies washed against Brashen like licking flames. He looked down to avoid the despairing eyes of his crew, but found Clef looking up at him. His brimming eyes were full of anguish as he protested, 'I wouldena given up, sir. I'd a died f'you.'

Brashen let his own weapon fall. He set a hand on the boy's fair head. 'I know. That was what I feared.'

And so, a tidy ending after all. Far tidier than he had expected, given all the hitches his original plan had encountered. Kennit did not even bother to step forwards to accept the captain's weapon. The churl had let it fall to the deck anyway. Had he no concept of the proper way to do things? It was not that Kennit feared to step on the foredeck.

The crew had been too long without a real battle. This one had barely whetted their appetite before it was over. He would have to hunt down a slaver or two and let them indulge themselves. For now, he commanded that the survivors be secured under the hatches. They went docilely enough, expecting that he would soon summon their captain and negotiate terms for ransom. Once they were out of sight, he had his men throw the bodies overboard. The serpents, he noted with disdain, were quick enough to come for this easy meat that they had refused to kill for themselves. Well, let it be, let them think it was bounty from Bolt. Perhaps stopping a slaver or two and feeding the serpents fat again would restore their tractability.

The Althea matter was settled easily enough. There were no women aboard, amongst the living or dead. To Captain Trell's anguished questions as to whether the Vivacia had taken up any survivors from his ship's boat, he had only shrugged. If she had been in the ill-fated rowing boat, then it had not managed to return to the ship. He gave a small sigh that might have been relief. He did so hate to lie to Wintrow. He could have an easy conscience when he said that whatever had befallen her was none of his doing.

Trell's eyes had narrowed as Kennit ordered him below, but he had gone. He had little choice, with three blades hemming him in. The hatch cover had cut off his angry shouts.

Kennit ordered all his men back to his ship, detaining only three with a quiet order that they return with casks of lamp oil. They looked puzzled, but they did not question him. While they were gone, he walked a quiet turn about the decks. His own ship buzzed with victory, but this one muttered with anxious voices from below. Some of the men they had put down the hatches were badly injured. Well, they would not suffer for long.

On the deck were the bloody silhouettes of fallen bodies. The blood marred the well-scrubbed decks. A shame. Captain Trell had run a tight ship; Paragon was as clean as Kennit had ever seen him. Igrot had run a strict ship, but had not been much for spit and polish. When Kennit's father commanded, the ship had been as cluttered as his home. Kennit walked to the door of the captain's chamber and paused there. A strange fluttering seized his heart. For a mercy, the charm on his wrist was silent. He walked another turn about the decks. The men below the hatches were quieting. That was good. His three deckhands returned, each bearing a cask of oil.

'Splash it about, lads, rigging and house and deck. Then get back to our own decks.' He looked at them gravely, making sure that each knew the seriousness of his words. 'I'll be the last man to leave this ship. Do your work and get off him. Cast him loose save for a stern line, and then I want everyone on our ship to go below as well. Understand me? Everyone. I've a final errand of my own.'

Ducking and bobbing their obedience, they left him. Kennit stood clear and let them perform their duty. When the last empty cask was rolling on the deck, he motioned for them to leave. Finally alone, he made his way forwards through the buffeting wind and stood on the deck looking down on Paragon's bowed head.

If the ship looked up at him, if he had had to meet eyes that were angry or defiant or sad or overjoyed to see him, he could not have spoken. But, foolish thought, that! Paragon could not look up at him with any sort of eyes. Igrot had seen to that years ago. Kennit had wielded the hatchet, standing on Paragon's great hands to reach his ship's face. Together, they had endured that, because Igrot had promised them both that if they did not, Kennit would die. Igrot had stood on this deck, where Kennit stood now, and watched and laughed while Kennit did the dirty task. Paragon had already killed two good hands that Igrot had sent to blind him. But he would not hurt the boy, oh, no. He would stand the pain, and even hold the boy close enough to reach his face so he could do the job, as long as Igrot promised not to kill Kennit. And as Kennit had looked deep into his dark eyes one final time and then ruined them with the rising and falling of his hatchet, he had known that no one should love anyone or anything that deeply. No one should have a heart that true. He had known then that never, never, never would he love anyone or anything as Paragon loved him. He had promised it to himself, and then he had lifted the shining hatchet and chopped into the dark eyes so full of love for him. Beneath them he found nothing, not blood, not flesh, only silvery grey wood that splintered easily away under his small hatchet. Wizardwood, he had been told, was among the hardest woods a ship could be built from, but he chopped it away like cottonwood, falling in chips and chunks into the deep cold sea beneath his bare feet. Little cold feet, so callused against his warm palm.

The double strength of the mutually relived memory seared him. Kennit could recall vision falling from him in pieces, not at all as a man would have lost his sight. Rather it was like someone cut away pieces of a picture before his eyes, leaving him in blackness. He trembled suddenly and vertigo took him. When he came back to himself, he was clutching the forerail. A mistake. He had not intended to touch any part of the ship with his bare hands, yet here he was. Linked again. Bound by blood and memories.

'Paragon.' He said the name quietly.

The ship flinched, but did not lift his head. A long silence wrapped them. Then: 'Kennit. Kennit, my boy.' His deep gentle voice was choked. Incredulous recognition overwhelmed all other emotions. 'I was so angry with you,' the ship apologized in wonder. 'How could I ever be angry with you?'

Kennit cleared his throat. It was a little time before he could speak. 'I never thought to stand here again, nor speak to you once more.' Love was rising from the ship like a flood tide, threatening to engulf him. Kennit fought to hold himself apart from Paragon. He forced out the rebuke. 'This is not what we planned, ship. This is not what we agreed upon at all.'

'I know.' Paragon spoke into his hands, cupped over his face. Shame swept through him and touched Kennit as well. 'I know. I tried. I did try.'

'What happened?' Despite himself, Kennit spoke gently. He did not really want to know. Paragon's rich deep voice reminded him of thick treacle over morning cakes, of warm summer days running on his decks barefoot while his mother begged his father to make the boy be more cautious. Memories, all those memories had soaked into the wood of this ship and were bleeding up into him.

'I went down to the bottom and stayed there. I did. Or I tried. No matter how much water I let in, I could not sink all the way. But I stayed under and I stayed hidden. Fish and crabs came. They picked clean the bones. I felt purified. All was silent and cold and wet.

'But then serpents came. They talked to me. I knew I could not understand them, but they insisted I did. They tormented me, asking me questions, demanding things of me. They wanted memories, they begged for memories, but I kept my word to you. I kept our secrets. It made them angry. They cursed me, and they taunted me and mocked me and . . . I had to, don't you see? I knew I had to be dead and forgotten by all but they would not let me be dead and forgotten. They kept making me remember. I had to get away from them. And . . . then somehow I was in Bingtown again, and they righted me and I feared they would sail me but they dragged me up on shore and chained me there. So I could not be dead. But I did my best to forget. And to be forgotten.'

The ship drew a ragged breath.

'Yet you are here,' Kennit pointed out. 'And not only here, but carrying folk who would kill me. Why, ship? Why did you betray me like that?' True agony choked him. 'Why do you make us both face this all over again?'

Paragon reached up to seize handfuls of his hair and drag at it. 'I'm sorry, I'm sorry,' he cried. The penitent boy's voice came oddly from those bearded lips. 'I did not mean to. They did not come to kill you. They only wanted Althea's ship back. They were going to offer to buy Vivacia back from you. I knew they did not have enough coin for that, but at one point I hoped that when you saw me, clean and well-rigged and riding level in the water, you would want me back. That perhaps you would take me in trade.' The voice was rising to an edge of anger now. Paragon's first shock at his presence was wearing off. 'I thought a Ludluck might want his rightful liveship instead of one he had stolen! I had heard from the lips of a pirate that you had said you had always wanted a liveship like her. But you'd had one. Me.

'Remember that night? The night you said that you had to kill yourself because you could not go on with such memories? And it was I who thought of it, I who said I would take all the memories, the pain memories, the bad memories, even the good memories of times that could never come again, and I would take them and die so that you could live and be free of them. I thought of how we could end them all. I took them all with me, everyone who knew what had been done to you. Remember? I purified your life for you, so you could go on living. And you said you would never love another ship as you had loved me, that you would never want to love another ship as we had loved. Don't you remember that?'

The abandoned memory burned up from Kennit's clutching hands to his shaking soul and settled there. Every detail, every emotion came with it. He had forgotten how painful true remembering was.

'You promised,' Paragon went on in a shaking voice. 'You promised and you broke that promise, just as I broke mine. So we are even.'

Even. A boy's concept. But the soul of Paragon had always been a boy's soul, abandoned and forsaken. Perhaps only another boy could have won his love as Kennit had. Perhaps only a boy who had been as abused and neglected as Paragon could have stood by Kennit's side through the long days of Igrot's reign. But Paragon had remained a boy, with a boy's logic, while Kennit had grown to be a man. A man could face hard truths, and know that life was seldom even or fair. And another hard truth: the shortest distance between a man and his goal was often a lie.

'You think I love her?' Kennit was incredulous. 'How could I? Paragon, she is not blood of my blood. What could we share? Memories? I cannot. I have already entrusted them all to you. You hold my heart, ship, as you always have. I love you, Paragon. Only you. Ship, I *am* you, and you are me. Everything I am, or was, is locked within you. Safe and secret still . . . unless you have divulged it to others?' Kennit asked the question cautiously.

'Never,' the ship declared devoutly.

'Well. That is good. For now. But we both know there is only one way they can be truly safe forever. Only one way to keep our secrets hidden.'

A silence followed his words. Kennit let it be. A quietness was growing in him, a certainty. He should never have doubted Paragon. His ship was true to him, as it always had been. He seized that thought and let it grow in his heart. He basked in the warmth of it, and shared that security with Paragon. For this time only, he let himself love the ship as he once had. He loved him with the complete faith that Paragon would decide to do what was best for Kennit.

'What about my crew?' Paragon asked wearily.

'Take them with you.' Kennit made the suggestion gently. 'They served you as best they could. Keep them safe forever inside you. Never be parted from them.'

Paragon took a breath. 'They will not like dying. None of them want to die.'

'Well. But you and I know that dying only takes a little time for humans. They will get over it.'

Paragon's hesitation this time was longer. 'I don't know if I really can die, you know.' A space of a breath. 'Last time, I couldn't even stay down there. Wood wants to float.' A longer pause. 'And Brashen is locked below, too. I made a little promise to him, Kennit. I promised him I wouldn't kill him.'

Kennit knit his brows thoughtfully and let Paragon feel his studied consideration of the matter. At last he offered kindly, 'Do you want me to help you? Then you wouldn't be breaking your promise. None of it would be your fault.'

At last the ship swivelled his great head towards Kennit. The chopped place that had been his eyes seemed to regard him. The pirate studied the features he knew as well as his own. The shaggy head, the lofty brow, the strong nose above the fine mouth and bearded chin. Paragon, his Paragon, best of all possible ships. His heart swelled painfully with love of his ship. Tears for both of them stung his eyes. 'Could you?' Paragon pleaded quietly.

'Of course I could. Of course,' Kennit comforted him.

After Kennit left his decks, silence flowed in and filled him. It was a silence not of the ears but of the heart. There were other noises in the world: the questioning cries of the crew inside his battened-down holds, the trumpeting of the departing serpents, the rising winds, the small sound of a stern line being released, the crackling of flames. He swung free suddenly in a gust of wind. No one was on the wheel to check his motion as the building storm pushed against his venom-tattered sails. There was a sudden whoosh and a blast of heat as the fire ran his rigging. More sure-footed than any sailor, the flames fanned out, devouring canvas and licking wood.

It would take time to spread. Wizardwood did not kindle easily, but once it took flame, it was near unquenchable. The other wood of his house and his rigging would burn first, but eventually the wizardwood would ignite. He had learned patience well. He could wait. The only distraction from his patience was his crew, hammering on the hatch covers now. No doubt, they felt him drifting; perhaps they smelled the smoke.

Resolutely he distracted himself. His boy was a man now. He was tall, from the direction of his voice. And strong. The grip on his railing had been a man's firm grip. Paragon shook his head in loving pride. He had succeeded. The sacrifice had not been in vain. Kennit had grown to be the man they had always dreamed he would be. Amazing, how the sound of his voice and the touch of his hand, even his scent on the breeze had brought it all back. The sound of his voice saying 'Paragon' had erased all the imagined slights and hoarded transgressions that had allowed the ship to be angry with him. The very thought now seemed foolish. Angry with the only one who had ever loved him whole-heartedly? Yes, Paragon had sacrificed for him, but what else could he have done? Someone had to set Kennit free. And he had. Now his boy would reign as King of the Pirate Isles, and someday, just as they had planned, he would have a son and name him Paragon. Some day there would be a Paragon Ludluck that was loved and cherished. Perhaps there already was! Paragon wished desperately now that he had thought to ask Kennit if he had a son yet. It would have been comforting to know that the child they had imagined was real.

Down inside him, the crew had torn something loose and were using it for a battering ram against his hatchcover. They did not seem to be doing it with much energy. Perhaps his hold was filling up with smoke. That would be good; they could all just go to sleep and die.

Paragon sighed and let himself list, just a little, as he always did if he wasn't thinking about it. It wasn't his fault. It was a flaw in his construction, the sort of thing that was bound to happen when a ship was built from two different logs of wizardwood. One dragon would always try to dominate the other. Fight, fight, fight, that was all they ever did, until he was sick of trying to make sense of those other selves. He had pushed them down deep and decided to be just Paragon. Paragon Ludluck. He said the name aloud, but softly. He closed his mouth. He stopped breathing. He didn't really need to breathe, that was just a part of the shape they had given him. It was a shape he could change, if he thought about it carefully. Each carefully-fitted plank of wizardwood could shift, just a tiny bit. For a time, he felt nothing. Then he knew the slow chill of water sheening down the inside of his planking. Slowly, ever so slowly he began to grow heavier. He let himself list more. Inside him, the crew began to be aware of it. There were shouts, and the thunder of feet as men ran to try to find where the water was coming in. Every seam oozed water. The only question that remained now was whether the fire or the sea would take him first. Whichever won, it would not be his fault. He crossed his arms on his chest, faced into the rising storm and composed himself for death.

'I thought you'd want to make the decision yourself, sir.' Jola stood very stiff. He knew he ventured onto dangerous ground, but he was sage enough to realize that not to defer this to Kennit would have been even more dangerous. Still, Kennit rather wished the mate had just let them drown. It would have been so much tidier.

He leaned over the railing and looked down at the woman in the water. She was obviously strong, but the cold water was taking its toll on her, as was the rising chop of the waves. Soon it would all be over. Even as he watched, a wave washed over her. Surprisingly, her head reappeared. She was treading water doggedly. She could have lasted longer if she had let go of her companion. The sailor in her arms looked dead anyway. The blonde woman in the water rolled her head back and coughed. 'Please.' She was too weak to shout, but he read it formed on her lips. Please. Kennit scratched the side of his beard thoughtfully. 'She's from the Paragon,' he observed to Jola.

'Doubtless,' the mate agreed through gritted teeth. Whoever would have suspected that Jola would be so distressed by watching a woman drown? Kennit never ceased to marvel at the strange weaknesses that could hole a man's character.

'Do you think we should take her up?' Kennit's tone made it clear he was not offering the decision to the mate, only seeking his opinion. 'We are pressed for time, you know. The serpents have already left.' In reality, Bolt had commanded them to

leave. Kennit had been relieved to see that she s̶
much control over them. Their failure to sink Para̶
rattled him badly. Only the white serpent had defied .
orders. It continued to circle the ship, its red eyes oddly
accusing. Kennit did not like it. It irritated him that it had
not eaten the two survivors in the water and saved him all
this trouble. But no, it just hung there in the water, watching
them curiously. Why didn't it obey the ship?

He looked away from it, forcing his mind to the problem
at hand. Bolt herself had indicated that she did not wish to
witness the burning of the liveship. Kennit glanced up at the
gathering storm. Leaving this place suited Kennit as well.

'Is that what you wish?' the mate weaselled. Kennit's esti-
mation of the man dropped. Sorcor, dumb as he was, would
have been brave enough to express his opinion. Jola had not
even that to his credit. The pirate captain glanced aft once
more. Paragon was burning merrily now. A gust of shifting
wind carried the smoke and stench to him. Time to go. It
was not just that he expected the figurehead to do some
screaming before the end; there was a real danger that the
wind might carry burning scraps of canvas from Paragon's
rigging to Vivacia's. 'A shame we are so pressed for time just
now,' he observed to Jola, and then his command to set sail
died in his throat.

The blonde woman had leaned back in the water, revealing
the features of the lad whose head she supported just out of
the waves. 'Wintrow!' he exclaimed incredulously. By what
misfortune had Wintrow fallen into the sea, and how had she
come to rescue him? 'Take them up immediately!' he ordered
Jola. Then, as the mate sprang to his command, a wave lifted
the two floaters fractionally higher. It was not Wintrow. It
was not even a man. Yet the compelling resemblance gripped
Kennit, and he did not rescind his command. Jola shouted for
a line to be flung.

'You know it has to be her,' his charm whispered at his wrist.

'Althea Vestrit. Who else could look so like him? Bolt will not like this. You serve your end, but not hers. You bring aboard the one person you should have been most sure to kill.'

Kennit clapped his other hand over the charm, and ignored the writhing of the small face under his hand. He watched in mounting curiosity. The blonde woman caught the rope, but her hands were so numbed with cold that she could not hold it. A sailor had to go over the side into the cold water with them. He lapped the line about them both and worked a hasty knot. 'Haul away,' he shouted, and up they all came, the women limp as seaweed. Kennit stood by until they were deposited on the deck. The resemblance was uncanny. His eyes walked over her features greedily. A woman with Wintrow's face.

He realized he was staring, recognized too the puzzled silence of the crewmen gathered around the sprawled woman. 'Well, get them below! Must I command you to the obvious? Jola, set a course for Divvytown. Signal the *Marietta* to follow. A squall is coming up. Let's be on our way before it hits.'

'Sir. Shall we wait for Wintrow and Etta to rejoin us before we sail?'

He glanced at the dark-haired woman who was beginning to cough and stir. 'No,' he replied. 'Leave them where they are for now.'

TWENTY-TWO

Family Reunion

WINTROW BLINKED AWAY the pouring rain and stared. 'I don't understand,' he said again quietly. He thought he spoke to himself and was startled when Etta replied. He had not heard her soft tread through the downpour pelting the deck.

'Stop trying to guess at what happened. Kennit will explain it all when next we see him.'

'I just want to know what happened,' he said stubbornly. He stared disconsolately at the faint smear of flame that had been the Paragon. He had watched the battle, but still could not grasp what had occurred. Why had Paragon so foolishly challenged both the serpents and the Vivacia? How had the fire broken out and why had Kennit abandoned such a valuable prize? Had he taken any prisoners? The emptiness of not knowing threatened to devour him.

The storm that had threatened all day had finally broken. The heavy rain was a billowing grey drapery between them and the blazing Paragon. Cold and drenched, he stood on the deck and stared at the foundering ship his family had sent. It would take their hopes of ransom and rescue to the bottom. The rain was a relief. He had not been able to find tears of his own.

'Come inside,' Etta suggested, her hand warm on his arm. He turned to look at her. If there was any comfort left for him at this miserable point in his life, it was Etta. She had put on Sorcor's oilskin; it hung huge on her slender form. She peered at him from the depths of the hood. A few drops of rain had found her face and jewelled her lashes. She blinked and the drops ran down her face, mock tears. He stared at her, dumb with desire and with the necessity of never acknowledging that desire. She tugged at his arm again, and he allowed her to lead him away.

Sorcor had surrendered his stateroom to her. The steaming pot of tea on the table, and the two waiting cups touched him. She had prepared this and brought him to share it. She indicated a chair and he sat, his clothes dripping, while she hung the oilskin on its peg. Once this chamber had been Kennit's and some of his furnishings remained. Elsewhere, Sorcor's taste for the bright and showy overpowered Kennit's more simple choices. The embroidered and tasselled cloth obscured the elegantly simple lines of the table beneath it. Etta shook some drops of rain from her hair and took the other chair. 'You look as woeful as a stray dog,' she commented as she poured the tea. Pushing his cup towards him, she added rebukingly, 'I do not understand why I must remind you to have faith in Kennit. Whatever happened, we should trust his judgement. Long ago, you told me he was Chosen of Sa. Do you no longer believe that?'

He sipped the tea and tasted the warmth of cinnamon. Despite his deep melancholy, it gave him pleasure. Etta seemed to know well that the small delights of the flesh were sometimes the most potent medicine against the deep pains of the spirit. 'I don't know what I believe any more,' he admitted wearily. 'I've seen the good he has done everywhere. He is a powerful force for freedom and the bettering of people's lives. He could build himself a majestic house full of riches and servants, and folk would still lionize him, but he continues to sail, to do battle with the slavers, and to free the imprisoned. Given all that, how can I doubt the greatness of his soul?'

'But you do, don't you?'

Wintrow sighed. 'Yes. I do. Sometimes, at night, when I try to meditate, when I try to find my place in his world, I cannot make it all fit together.' He pushed his wet hair away from his face and looked at her frankly. 'There is something missing in Kennit. I feel it but I cannot name it.'

A shadow of anger crossed her face. 'Perhaps what is missing is not from him, but from you. Perhaps you lose faith whenever Sa's path for you carries you where you do not wish to go.'

Her words numbed him. He had never expected to hear such a rebuke from her, let alone to have it ring so true. She spoke on. 'Kennit has his faults. But we should look at what he achieves in spite of all his own doubts and pains.' Her eyes swept up to his accusingly. 'Or do you think that a man must first become perfect before he can do good?'

'Sa's hand can fit around any tool,' he muttered. Then, an instant later, he burst out, 'But why must he take my ship from me? Not just take her, but change her to a creature I don't even recognize? Why must he kill those who came only to take us home? I don't understand that, Etta, and I never shall!'

'Perhaps, because you have already determined that you will not understand it?' She met his gaze steadily. 'I read, in a book you gave me, that our words shape our reality. Look at what your words have just done to what is. You have reshaped it to make it a grievance against yourself. Your ship, you say. Is she? Was she ever anyone's ship? Or was she a living creature, imprisoned in an unfamiliar body and then claimed as a possession? Has Kennit changed her, or has he simply freed her to become who she truly was? How do you know he has killed those who came to free you, if that indeed was what they intended? As yet, we know nothing. Yet you have already decided it is a wrong done you, so that you can nurture your anger and feel justified. That's no better than wallowing in self-pity.' Her voice had grown angrier and angrier. Now she folded her lips tight and turned aside from him. 'I wanted to share something with you, something that must remain secret between us. Now I wonder if I dare, or if you will somehow twist it to be something it is not.'

All he could do was look at her. Although he had had a hand in her transformation, the changes in her could still astonish him. She no longer flew at him with blows when he crossed her will. She did not need to; the edge of her tongue was as cutting as any blade. He had recognized her intelligence and respected her cunning and her courage from the first day he had met her. Now there was schooling behind the intellect, and an ethic behind the courage. It amplified her beauty. He turned his hand on the table, palm up, to indicate his surrender. To his surprise, she leaned over and put her hand in his.

As his fingers closed on her hand, she smiled. He had not thought she could be more beautiful, but a sudden light shone in her face. She leaned closer to breathe her next words.

'I'm pregnant. I carry Kennit's child.'

Those words shut the door between them, closing him off from her life and her light. She was Kennit's, she had always been Kennit's, and she would always be Kennit's. Wintrow himself would always be alone.

'I wasn't sure, at first. Yet, ever since a certain night, I have had a feeling it was so. And today, when he sent me away, as he has never done before, I thought perhaps there might be a reason. So I sat here and I tested myself with a needle on a thread held over my palm. It swung so violently there can be no doubt. All indications are that I carry a son, a man to follow after him.' She took her hand from his and proudly set it upon her flat belly.

Misery numbed Wintrow. 'You must be very happy.' He forced the words past his choking pain.

Her smile dimmed a fraction. 'And that is all you have to say to me?' she asked.

It was all he dared to say. Every other thought was better

left unuttered. He bit his tongue and looked at her in helpless silence.

She gave a small sigh and looked aside. 'I had hoped for more. Foolish, I suppose. But Kennit has so often called you his prophet that I – now do not laugh – I had fancied that when I told you I carried the King of the Pirates' son, you would, oh, I don't know, say some words that foretold his greatness, or that . . .' Her voice dwindled away. A faint flush rose to her cheeks.

'Like in the old tales,' Wintrow managed to say. 'A sooth-saying of wonders to come.'

She turned aside from him, suddenly embarrassed to have dreamed such large dreams for her child. Wintrow made a valiant effort, to set aside the hurt boy in himself and speak as both a man and a priest to her. 'I have no prophecies for you, Etta. No Sa-sent foretelling, no inspired prognostication. I believe that if this child is pledged to greatness, his heritage will come just as much from you as from his father. I see this in you, right now: that regardless of what other folk do or do not see in your child, he will always reign in your heart. You will see the value of him long before others do, and know that the greatest trait he will carry is simply that he is himself. A child takes root in his parents' acceptance. Your baby already has that gift from you.'

His words moved her as if he had spoken a prophecy. She glowed. 'I cannot wait to see Kennit's face when I tell him.'

Wintrow took a deep breath. Sureness filled him, and if Sa inspired him to speak, he knew it was then. 'I counsel you to keep these tidings secret for a time yet. His mind is so full of concerns just now. Wait for a time when he truly needs to hear it.'

'Perhaps you are right in this,' she said regretfully.

Wintrow doubted she would heed him.

* * *

The squall that had threatened all day had found them. Paragon turned his face up, and tasted the last rain he would ever know. The chop of the waves jolted against him, but could do little to rock him as his heavy bulk settled ever deeper. The pounding on the hatch cover had weakened. The oil-fed fires that Kennit had kindled smoked and stank in the rain, but burned still. Occasionally there was a crash as scorched rigging gave way and fell to his deck. He ignored it all. He was sinking inside himself to a place deeper than any ocean floor.

Inside him, Amber wept. That was hard to bear. He had not realized how much he had come to cherish her. And Clef. And Brashen, so proud to be his captain. Resolutely, he forced such thoughts away. He must not give in to them now. The carpenter had crawled as far forwards in his bow as she could get under the deck. Despite the pain of her scalds, she had dragged herself through the cold water flooding his holds. He wished she had succumbed to the numbing water; it would be a kinder end. But she lived, and clung to his mainstem and spoke faintly. He held himself back from her.

A serpent butted against him. 'Hey. Stupid. Are you just going to let them do this to you?' The creature's tone was disdainful. 'Wake up. You've as much a right to live as she does.'

'I've as much a right to die, also,' Paragon retorted. Then he wished he had not roused himself to speak, for now he was aware of Amber's agonized words as well.

'Paragon. Paragon, I don't want to die. Not like this. Not with all my work unfinished. Please, ship. Please don't do this.' She was weeping, and her tears scalded him as sharply as serpent venom.

'No one has the right to die uselessly,' the serpent proclaimed. Paragon recognized his voice now. He was the one who had shouted mockingly at the other serpents as they attacked him. He butted Paragon again. It was annoying.

'Dying is the most useful thing I can do for Kennit,' Paragon reminded himself. He struggled to compose himself once more.

The serpent pressed his head against Paragon's listing hull and pushed hard. 'I do not speak of "Kennit". I speak of being useful to your own kind. Bolt brags that she alone can lead us home and protect us. I don't believe her. The memories I have recall many guides and protectors. Surely what one can do well, two can do better. Why is she so eager to kill you to please this "Kennit"? Why do either of you care about him at all?'

'She wishes me to be dead, to please Kennit?' The words came slowly to Paragon. He could not attach sense to them. Surely this was Kennit's sorrowful will for him. It had nothing to do with Vivacia, or Bolt as she now styled herself?

Unless she wanted Kennit for herself. Unless she wished to do away with Paragon so she would have no rivals. Perhaps Kennit had deceived him. Perhaps Kennit wished him dead so he could be with Vivacia.

The traitor thought shocked him. 'Go away! This is my decision.'

'And who are you to decide?' the serpent pressed him.

'Paragon. I am Paragon of the Ludlucks!' The name was a talisman to hold other identities at bay.

The serpent rubbed against him, a long caress, skin to hull. 'And who else are you?' he demanded.

Inside him, he felt the sudden press of Amber's bare hands against him. 'No!' he screamed at both of them. 'No! I am Paragon of the Ludlucks. Only that.'

But within him, from a darkness deeper than any human soul, other voices spoke, and Amber listened to them.

Althea opened her eyes and waited for the bad dream to dispel. It seemed she was on board Vivacia, inside her old stateroom. The look of the room was right, but the feel of it was subtly wrong. A memory from the *Reaper* stirred. That ship had felt

547

this way. Dead wood. She received no sense of the liveship at all. She reached out, but felt only the motion of the vessel. Had they taken the ship? Was Brashen on the wheel, taking them home?

She sat up too suddenly. A violent fit of coughing shook her. A stray memory surfaced as from a dream: sprawling on Vivacia's deck, very cold, coughing up seawater. The taste of brine was still in her mouth and stinging her nose. That had been real. The deck under her had been very hard, and not just in the way of wood. She had felt refusal in the planks under her hands. Jek had been with her, but was not here now. Her hair was still damp, so not too much time had passed. The dusk of an early winter evening was in the window, darkened more by a spitting storm. A lantern, wick turned low, hung from a hook.

She sat still, trying to piece time together. The serpents had swamped the little boat, and then one had hit it broadside. Boat and all, they had bounced down the serpent's humped spine. She remembered the slap of the water as she hit it. She had struggled under water, kicking off her boots, but the cold sea had dragged at the heavy fabric of her clothing, each successive wave ducking her under for a longer time. She did not remember Jek seizing her, but she was sure the tall woman had come to her aid. They had been fished out of the water and onto the deck of Vivacia.

And now she was here. Someone had dressed her in a man's nightshirt of very fine linen, and warm woollen blankets covered her legs. Someone had cared for her with kindness. She seized on that as a sign; the truce negotiations had gone well. Brashen was probably on board right now, talking with Captain Kennit. That would explain why she had not been returned to the Paragon. She'd dress and go to find them, right after she went forwards to see the figurehead. She had been parted from her ship for far too long. Once she had words with the Vivacia, surely she could resolve whatever barrier divided them.

She glanced about the room but saw no sign of her own clothing. There were shirts and trousers hung on pegs, however, and they looked about her size. This was no time to be shy; later she would thank whoever had surrendered his room and clothes to her. Probably the mate. The books on the shelf showed him to be a man of some education. Her respect for Kennit increased. The quality of a crew said a great deal about the captain. She suspected she would get along well with the pirate. In a habitual motion that dated back to her childhood aboard the ship, she reached up and put her palms flat to the exposed beam of wizardwood overhead. 'Vivacia,' she greeted her warmly. 'I'm back. I've come to take you home.'

The impact slammed her back against the mattress. Dazed, she lay flat, looking up at the ceiling overhead. Had she struck her head somehow? It made no sense. Nothing had hit her, but the sensation was as stunning. She looked at her palms, half-expecting them to be reddened. 'Vivacia?' she queried cautiously. She tried again to sense her ship, but felt nothing.

She gathered her courage and again reached up to the beam. A finger's length short of touching, she stopped. Antagonism radiated from the wood like heat from a fire. She pressed against it. It was like pushing her hand into packed snow. Cold and burning both engulfed her fingers, followed by a spreading numbness. She set her teeth and pressed on. 'Vivacia,' she grated. 'Ship, it's me. Althea Vestrit. I've come for you.' The opposition to her touch only grew stronger.

She heard a key turn in a lock and the door was flung open. She spared a glance for the man framed in the entry. A tall man, he was handsome and well-dressed. The scent of sandalwood came with him. He carried a tray with a steaming bowl on it. His gleaming black hair shone, and his moustache was precisely curled. There was white lace at his throat and cuffs and a diamond that any dandy would envy sparkled in one ear, but the wide shoulders of his well-cut blue coat proclaimed him far from effete. He leaned on a crutch of brass and polished wood, a carefully chosen accoutrement rather than a tool for a cripple. He had to be Kennit.

'Don't!' he warned her. He shut the door behind him, set the tray on her table and crossed the room in two sloping strides. 'Don't, I said. She'll only hurt you.' He seized her wrists in his strong hands and pulled them away from the beam. She felt suddenly dizzied from both the effort and the numbing rejection. She knew what Vivacia had done to her. The ship had subtly stirred every self-doubt Althea had ever harboured and awakened in her mind every memory of bad judgement, selfishness, or stupidity that the ship had ever witnessed. She burned with shame at how inferior a person she was, even as logic tried to assert itself.

'She'll only hurt you,' Kennit repeated. He kept possession of her wrists. After one attempt to pull free of him, Althea subsided. He was strong. Better to behave with dignity than react like a thwarted child.

She met his pale blue eyes. He smiled at her reassuringly and waited. 'Why?' she demanded. 'Why should she try to hurt me? She's my ship.'

His smile widened. 'And I'm pleased to meet you also, Althea Vestrit. I trust you feel better.' His eyes roved over her frankly. 'You look much better than when I first fished you out. You vomited quite a quantity of seawater onto my clean deck.'

It was precisely the right mixture of wryly-polished comments to remind her of manners, situation, and her debt to him. She let her hands relax, and as soon as she did, he released her wrists, giving her hands a reassuring pat in passing. Her cheeks burned. 'I beg your pardon,' she said very sincerely. 'I presume you are Captain Kennit. I am sure you saved my life, and I do thank you. But to have my own ship so reject me is –' she sought for a word. 'Beyond distressing,' she finished lamely.

'Oh, I am sure it is devastating.' Casually he reached up and set his palm gently to the silvery grey wood overhead. 'To both of you. You must give one another time. I am sure you are not who you were the last time you were aboard this ship. And the ship is certainly not.' He added quietly as he lowered his hand, 'No creature of any sensitivity could endure what she has and be unchanged by it.' He leaned closer to add in a whisper, 'Give her time. Take time to meet her and accept her as she is. And be tolerant of her anger. It is well rooted, and justified.' His warm breath was scented with cloves. Without ceremony, he seated himself on the bed beside her. 'For now, tell me this. Are you feeling better?'

'Much better, thank you. Where is Jek, the woman who was with me? Is Brashen aboard? Did the serpents damage Paragon much? How did you run them off? My nephew Wintrow, is he alive and well?' With each question she asked, another formed behind it, until Kennit leaned forwards to set two fingers to her lips. She bridled at the touch, then endured it, forcing herself to realize he probably meant nothing by it.

'Hush,' he said gently. 'Hush. One at a time, though you should not be fussing yourself with such things. You have been through quite enough for one day. Jek is sleeping very soundly. A serpent must have brushed her; one leg and her ribs were scalded, but I am confident she will heal well. I gave her some poppy syrup for the pain. For now, I suggest we do not disturb her.'

A sudden disturbing question rose in her. 'Then who took care of me? Put me to bed here?' Her hand reached reflexively to the buttoned collar of the nightshirt.

'I did,' he spoke quietly without looking at her. A smile teased at the corner of his mouth, but he kept it at bay. 'It was scarcely a duty I would entrust to my deckhands, and there are no women on board.'

Althea's face burned.

'I brought you something.' He rose as he spoke, and tucked

his crutch back under his arm. He crossed the room to the table, took up the tray he had brought, and carried it back to her bedside. Despite his missing leg, he moved with the rolling grace of a true seaman. She moved her legs to make a place for the tray. He set it down and then took a place next to it. 'This is wine and brandy, mulled with spices. It's an old Divvytown recipe, very warming, very restoring, and excellent for pain. Do try some, while I talk. It is best when it is warmest.'

She lifted the bowl in both hands. The rising fumes were themselves a comfort. Dark spices swirled in the bottom of the amber liquid. She lifted it to her mouth and sipped. Warmth spread through her, unknotting tension and a sudden shiver raced up her, bringing gooseflesh to her arms. It was as if her body had trapped the cold of the sea inside it and was only now letting it go.

'That's better,' Kennit said encouragingly. 'Let me see. Wintrow is not on board the ship at the moment. He is serving on the *Marietta* under Sorcor, my second in command. I have discovered that moving a promising man from ship to ship and giving him shifting responsibilities encourages him to develop his seamanship and his ability to think for himself. You have realized, no doubt, that you occupy his room and his bed just now. Don't trouble yourself about that. He is perfectly comfortable where he is, and I know he would begrudge you nothing.'

'Thank you,' she said carefully. She tried to compose her thoughts. Kennit obviously thought of Wintrow as his, someone to train up for heavier responsibility, like a son in a family business. She had never envisioned this situation, and she could not decide how to react to it. 'It is kind of you to afford him such opportunities,' she heard herself say. A part of her was shocked at the words. Kind of him to afford Wintrow the opportunity to become a better pirate? She tried to force order on her thoughts. 'I must ask this. How does Vivacia react to

Wintrow being gone? It is not good for a liveship to be left long without a family member aboard her.'

'Please. Drink that while it is warm,' he encouraged her. As she obeyed, he glanced down at the bed between them, as if he feared his next words would displease her. 'Vivacia has been fine. The ship does not miss Wintrow that much. You see, she has me.' He reached up again to caress the silver grey beams. 'What I have discovered is that "family" is not so important to a ship as a kindred spirit. Vivacia and I share many of the same qualities: a love for adventure, a hatred for the slave trade, a desire to –'

'I think I know my own ship,' Althea broke in but Kennit's mild blue glance gently reproved her. She lifted the bowl and drank from it to cover her discomfiture. The warmth of the liquor was spreading through her now, relaxing her. A wave of vertigo swept her. She felt Kennit's hands steady the bowl she held.

'You are more weary than you know,' he said sympathetically. 'You were quite a long time in very cold water. And now my careless words have distressed you as well. I am sure this is difficult for you to face. Perhaps you thought you were coming to rescue the ship and your nephew. Instead you have discovered you would be tearing them away from a world they love. Please. Rest for a time before we talk more. Your exhaustion is making you see the worst side of everything. Wintrow is strong and happy and convinced that he has discovered Sa's will for him. The ship is avid in her pursuit of slavers, and enjoys the adventure of the life we lead. You should rejoice for them. And you are safely aboard your family ship. From this moment, things can only get better for you.'

She drank until the spices at the bottom bumped against her lips. He took the bowl from her hands and caught her as she swayed. He smelled nice. Sandalwood. Cloves. She leaned her head against the shoulder of the fine blue jacket. The lace at his neck tickled against her face. Lace would do well on

Brashen. And a jacket such as this. 'I like lace on a man,' she observed. Kennit cleared his throat. She felt her face flush. 'I'm dizzy,' she apologized, trying to straighten herself. 'I should not have drunk that so fast. It's gone right to my head.'

'No, no, that's all right. You're expecting too much of yourself. Here. Lie back.' A gentleman to the bone, he evaded her embarrassment.

He hopped from the bunk to stand on his leg while he straightened her pillow for her. Obediently she lay back. The cabin rocked around her. 'Is the storm building?' she asked anxiously.

'Here in the Pirate Isles, we consider this only a squall. We'll be out of it soon. We'll anchor in a sheltered cove and let this pass. Don't be concerned. Vivacia can handle a much harder blow than this.'

'I know. I remember.' She expected him to leave. Instead, he came back to her bedside. Memories swirled through her mind, of another tall dark-haired man standing by her bunk. Her father had taken Vivacia through many a storm with Althea on board. When she was small, this ship had been the safest place in the world. The Vivacia had been her father's world, where he controlled everything and never let her come to harm. All would be safe, all would be well. There was a strong man in command of the ship, and a steady hand on the wheel. She closed her heavy eyes. It had been a long time since she had felt so safe.

Kennit looked down on her. Her hair, curling with damp, tangled on the pillow. The eyelashes on her cheeks were not so long as Wintrow's, but even up close, the resemblance was uncanny. He pulled the blankets up and tucked them securely around her. She did not stir. He wasn't surprised. He'd already tested the mixture of poppy and mandrake in brandy on Jek. She would sleep deeply, and he would have time to ponder his role and how to deal with her questions.

Paragon had perished with all hands. So sad. The serpents had attacked in response to Brashen's arrows. That might work, as long as she never spoke to any of the crew. Could he keep her that isolated without rousing her suspicions? It was going to be difficult to concoct the right lies, but something would come to him.

He stood a time longer looking down on her. She was Wintrow, in female form. With his forefinger, he traced the curve of her cheek, the arch of her brow, the flare of her nostrils. Bingtown Trader stock, well born and raised well. There was no mistaking one's own kind. When he bent over and kissed her, her lax lips were warm. Her unresponsive mouth teased his with the taste of the spices and brandy. He could take her right now if he wanted to. No one else would know; she herself might not even realize he had done it. Such an amusing idea curved his lips in a true smile. His fingers started on the top button of the nightshirt. His own nightshirt, he thought, and it was as if he undressed himself. She breathed deeply and steadily.

'You only want her because she resembles the boy,' the charm said snidely. The nasty little voice shattered the peace in the room.

Kennit froze. He glared down at the noxious thing. Its small eyes glittered up at him. Were there truly blue sparks in the carved wood, or did he imagine them? The etched mouth turned down in disgust at him.

'And you only want the boy because he so reminds you of yourself at that age. Only, in reality, you were much younger when Igrot dragged you to his bed.'

'Shut up!' Kennit hissed. Those memories were forbidden. They had all gone to the bottom with Paragon. What else had all this been for, if not to destroy those memories? For the charm to speak such words endangered everything.

Everything. He knew now he would have to destroy the thing.

'It won't help,' it mocked him. 'Destroy me, and Bolt will know why. But I tell you this. Take this woman against her will, and the whole ship will know why you wanted her. I will see to it. And I will see that Wintrow is the first to know.'

'Why? What do you want of me?' Kennit's question was an infuriated whisper.

'I want Etta back on this ship. And Wintrow. For my own reasons. I warn you. Both Bolt and I would find rape extremely distasteful. Among dragons, it is not done.'

'A scrap of a charm, no bigger than a walnut, claims to be a dragon!'

'One does not need the size of a dragon to have the soul of a dragon. Take your hands off her.'

Kennit slowly complied. As he stood and took up his crutch, he observed, 'I'm not afraid of you. As for Althea, I will have her. Of her own free will. You will see.' He breathed out a long, slow breath. 'Ship, woman, and boy. All will be mine.'

How had she known, Paragon wondered miserably? How had Amber known just where to put her hands to reach each of them, both of them, all of him at once? Her bare fingers pressed his wood, and she was open to him now. If he had wanted, he could have reached into her and plumbed all of her secrets. But he did not wish to know any more of her than he already did. He only wanted her to give up and die peacefully. Why would not she do that for him? He had always been a friend to her. But she ignored him now, reaching past him to speak to the others that shared his wood. She spoke to him, but they listened, and their listening echoed through him, vibrating his soul.

'I need to live,' she begged. 'Only you can help me. There is still so much I must do in my life. Please. If there is any bargain we can strike, tell me. Ask of me anything, and if it is in my power, it is yours. But help us live. Close up your seams, and stop the cold water flowing. Let me live.'

'Amber. Amber.' Against all wisdom, he spoke to her. 'Please. Just let go. Be still. Be silent. We will die together.'

'Ship. Paragon. Why? Why do we have to die? What changed, why are you doing this? Why can't we live?'

She would never understand. He knew it was foolish, but he tried anyway. 'The memories have to die. If no one remembers them any more, then he can live as if they never happened. So Kennit gave the memories to me, and I was to die with them. So that one of us could live free.'

They were listening still, both of them. The Greater spoke suddenly, his thoughts ringing through his half of the hull. 'It doesn't work that way. Silencing memories does not make them stop existing. Events cannot be undone by forgetting them.'

He felt Amber's shock. Valiantly she tried to overcome it. She spoke to him as if she had not felt the Greater. 'Why does Kennit do this to you? How can he? What is Kennit to you?'

'He is my family.' Paragon could not conceal his love for the pirate. 'He is a Ludluck, like me. The last of his line, born in the Pirate Isles. A Bingtown Trader's son took a Pirate Isle bride. Kennit was their child, his son, his prince. And my playmate. The one who finally loved me for myself.'

'You are not a Ludluck,' the Greater interrupted him. 'We are dragons.'

'Yes, we are dragons, and we wish to live.' It was the Lesser, managing to insert a thought of his own.

'Silence!' the Greater one quashed him. Paragon's list became more marked as the Greater asserted his control.

'Who are you?' Amber asked in confusion. 'Paragon, why are there dragons in you?'

The Greater laughed. Paragon knew better than to try to reply.

'Please,' Amber begged of them now. 'Please, help us live.'

'Do you deserve to live?' the Greater demanded of her. He

spoke with Paragon's mouth in Paragon's voice, taking control of the figurehead and booming his voice into the wind. It did not matter to him that Amber heard his thought through her hands. He spoke as he did, Paragon knew, to prove to the ship how strong he had grown. 'If you did, you would see it is right now within your power to save all of us. But if you are too stupid to see how, I think we should all die here together.'

'Tell her how,' pleaded the Lesser. 'It is our time, come again, and you will let us die because a human is stupid? No! Tell her. Let her save us so we can go on and –'

'Silence, weakling! You have kept company with humans too long. The strong survive. Trapped as we are in this body, we are better off dead if the humans aboard us are stupid. So let her show us that she can make our life worth the living. If she can fathom how to live, we will let her give us eyes again. A Paragon we shall be, but not Paragon of the Ludlucks. Paragon of the Dragons. Two made into one.'

'What of me?' Paragon cried out wildly. Rain cascaded down his blind face and his chest. He gripped his beard and dragged at it fiercely. 'But what of me?'

'Be with us,' the Greater said. 'Or do not be. That is the only choice that remains to you. The serpent spoke true. There remains to us a duty to our own, and no other dragon or dragon-made-ship has the right to deny it to us. We can be only one. Be one with us, or do not be.'

'We're dying!' Amber cried. Her voice was weak, hoarse from the smoke she breathed. 'Fire burns above us, and water fills the hold. How can I save you, or myself?'

'Think,' the Greater one commanded her. 'Prove yourself worthy.'

For an instant, Amber rallied. She reached strongly after the Greater, as if she would steal from him what she must know. Then, a fit of coughing shook her. Every spasm of it set her scalded flesh to screaming. As the coughing passed, Amber faded from Paragon's awareness. He felt her pass to transparency, and then nothingness. As she died, he felt both grief and relief. The heaviness of the cold water in him dragged him down. The waves were getting taller. Soon they would wash over his deck. The fires would go out as the waves took him down, but that was all right. The fire and smoke had accomplished their work.

Then, like an arrow striking home to a target, Amber was suddenly within him. She gasped as she plunged deep into the memories of dragonkind. Paragon felt her floundering, overwhelmed by the unending chain of memories, going from dragon to serpent to dragon to serpent, back beyond to the very first egg. She could not hold it all. He felt her drowning in the memories. She fought valiantly, searching for what the Greater withheld from her as he allowed his memories to flood her.

'It is not in my memory, but in your own, little fool,' he told her. He witnessed her struggling as one watches tree sap flow over a trapped ant.

She wrenched clear of him as if she tore her own hands from the ends of her arms. Paragon felt her fall, and knew that she dragged in breath after smoky breath, striving for fresh air that was not there. She began to fade again, slipping below consciousness. Then, slowly, she lifted her head.

'I know what it is,' she announced. 'I know how to save us. But I will not buy my life at Paragon's expense. I will save us if you promise me this. You will be, not two made one, but three. Paragon must be preserved in you.'

He could feel her fear. It ran from her with her sweat, she expelled it with every breath. He was struck dumb by the idea that someone would be willing to die rather than betray him.

'Done!' the Greater announced. A faint thread of admiration shimmered through his words. 'This one has a heart worthy of being partnered with a dragon-ship. Now let her prove she has a mind as well.'

Paragon felt Amber strive to rise, but she had spent the last of her strength. She fell back against him. For her, he tried to close up his seams. He could not. The dragons would not let him. So he fed her such strength as he could, pouring it from his wood into the frail body that rested against him. She lifted her head in the smoky darkness.

'Clef!' she called. Her great exertion produced such a weak call. 'Clef!'

'Put your backs into it, damn you!' Brashen bellowed. Then he went off into a fit of coughing. He let the makeshift ram come to a rest on the deck. The men who had been helping him pound on the underside of the hatch sank down around him. The hatch above was not surrendering and time was fleeting. He pushed his panic away. Wizardwood was hard to kindle. There was still a little time, still a chance for survival, but only if he kept trying.

'Don't slack off on that pump! Drowning's no better than burning.' At his shouted command, he heard the pump crew go back to work, but the tempo was half-hearted. Too many of the men had been killed, too many injured. The ship was alive with ominous sounds: the working of the bilge pumps, the moaning of the injured, and from above the faint crackling of flames. The bilges were rising, bringing their stink with them. The more water Paragon shipped, the more pronounced the tilt of the deck became. The smoke filtering down into the hold was getting denser, also. Time was running out for them.

'Everybody on the ram again.' Three of the men staggered to their feet and took a grip on the beam they wielded.

At that moment, Brashen was distracted by a tug at his sleeve. He looked down, to find Clef. The boy cradled his injured arm across his belly. 'It's Amber, sir.' His face was pale with pain and fear in the uneasy lamplight.

Brashen shook his head. He rubbed at his stinging, streaming eyes. 'Do the best you can for her, boy. I can't come now. I've got to keep working on this.'

'No, it's a message, sir. She said to tell you, try the other hatch. The one in your cabin.'

It took a moment for the boy's words to penetrate. Then Brashen shouted, 'Come on! Bring the ram!' He snatched down a lantern and staggered off without waiting to see if anyone followed. He cursed his own stupidity. When Amber had lived aboard the beached Paragon, she had used the captain's quarters as her bedroom, but stored her woodworking supplies below in the hold. For her convenience, she had cut a trapdoor in the floor of the room. Both Althea and Brashen had been horrified when they discovered it. Amber had repaired the floor, bracing it from below and pegging it together well. But all the bracing for it was below and accessible from this level. Paragon's hatch covers had been designed to withstand the pounding of the sea, but the trapdoor inside his stateroom had been nailed and braced shut only.

Brashen's confidence ebbed when he looked up at the patched deck above him. Amber was a good carpenter and thorough in her work. The list of the ship made it difficult to work here. He was shoving vainly at a crate when his crew caught up with him. With their aid he stacked crates and barrels and then climbed up them to examine the patched floor above him. Clef passed up the tools.

With hammer and crowbar, Brashen pulled away the bracing. This close to the ceiling, the smoke was thicker. In the lantern light, he saw the drifting grey tendrils reaching down through the seams of the deck. If they broke through, they might find fire above them. He didn't hesitate. 'Use the ram, boys,' he directed them, scrabbling out of the way.

There was no strength behind their swing, but on the fourth attempt, Brashen saw the boards give way a bit. He waved the men aside and they fell back, coughing and wheezing. Brashen climbed his platform again and hammered at the wood blocking him from life. When they suddenly gave way, the planks of the patch cascaded bruisingly down around him. Yellow firelight illuminated the grimy faces below him.

He jumped, caught the edge of the hole, and hauled himself up. The wall of the room was burning, but the fire had not spread within yet. 'Get up here!' Brashen shouted with as much force as he could muster. 'Get out while you can!'

Clef was already at the lip of the hole. Brashen seized him by his good arm and hauled him up. The boy followed him as he made his way out onto the deck. Cold rain drenched him. A quick glance about showed him that Paragon was alone in the water. A single white serpent circled curiously. The pouring rain was an ally in putting out the fire, but by itself, it would not be enough. Flames still licked up the main mast and ran furtively along the sides of the house. Fallen rigging sheltered small pockets of burning wood and canvas. Brashen dragged smouldering debris off the top of the main hatch, undogged it, and flung it open. 'Get up here!' he shouted again. 'Get everyone up on deck, except for the pump crew. Clear this –' He had to stop to cough his lungs clear. Men began dragging themselves up onto the deck. The whites of their eyes showed shockingly in their sooty faces. Groans and coughing came from below. 'Clear away the burning stuff. Help the injured up on deck where they can breathe.' He turned and made his way forwards through a litter of charred debris. He threw overboard a tangle of rope and a piece of spar that still burned merrily. The cold downpour was as blinding as the smoke had been, but at least the air was breathable. Every breath he drew helped to clear his lungs.

He reached the foredeck. 'Paragon, close up your seams. Why are you trying to kill us? Why?'

The figurehead did not reply. The uneven light of flames danced illumination over the figurehead. Paragon stared straight ahead into the storm. His arms hugged his chest. The knotted muscles of his back showed the tension of his posture. As Brashen watched, the white serpent rose before them. It cocked its maned head and stared with gleaming red eyes up at the figurehead. It vocalized at the ship, but received no answer.

Clef spoke suddenly behind him. 'I went back for Amber. She's safe now.'

No one was safe yet. 'Paragon! Close up your seams!' Brashen bellowed again.

Clef tugged at Brashen's sleeve. He looked down at the boy's puzzled, upturned face. 'He awready did. Din't you feel it?'

'No. I didn't.' Brashen seized hold of the railing, trying to will contact with the figurehead. There was nothing. 'I don't feel him at all.'

'I do. I feel 'em both,' Clef said cryptically. An instant later, he warned, 'Hang tight, ser!'

With a startling suddenness, the ship levelled itself. The sloshing of the bilge left the deck rocking. As it subsided, Brashen heard wild oaths of amazement from the deck behind him, but he grinned into the darkness. They were riding low in the water, but they were level. If the ship had closed up its seams, if they could keep the bilge pumps going, if the storm grew no more violent, they would live. 'Ship, my ship, I knew you wouldn't let us die.'

'It warn't him. Least, not exactly.' The boy's voice was dropping to a mumble. 'It's them and him. The dragons.' Brashen caught the boy as he sagged to the deck. 'I bin dreamin' 'em for awhile now. Thought they was jes a dream.'

'Take them up,' Kennit barked at Jola. He watched in annoyance as Wintrow and Etta were brought aboard. Frustration threatened to consume him. He had anchored in this cove to wait out the squall and decide what he wished to do. His initial plans to return to Divvytown might have to be changed. He had hoped to have more time alone with Althea, not to mention Bolt.

'I did not send for you,' he greeted Etta coldly as she came aboard. She seemed undaunted by his rebuke.

'I know. I thought to take advantage of the lull in the storm to return.'

'Whether I commanded it or not,' Kennit observed sourly.

She halted without touching him, plainly puzzled. There was hurt in her voice as she complained, 'It didn't occur to me that you might not want me to return.'

Jola looked at him oddly. Kennit was well aware that the crew liked Etta and romanticized his relationship to the whore. With things as unsettled as they were now, there was no sense in upsetting them, or her.

'Regardless of the risk to yourself?' he amended sharply. 'Get to the cabin. You are drenched. Wintrow, you also. I have news to share with you.'

Kennit turned and preceded them. Damn them both for hauling him out on deck in this chilling rain. His stump began to ache with nagging intensity. When he reached his cabin, he dropped into his chair and let his crutch fall to the deck. Etta, dripping rain, picked it up reflexively and set it in its place in the corner. He watched in disapproving silence as they shed their soaked outer garments.

'Well. So you are here. Why?' he challenged them before either could speak. He gave them almost time enough to gather their thoughts, then as Wintrow drew breath, he cut him off. 'Don't bother replying. I see it in your faces. After all we have been through, you still don't trust me.'

'Kennit!' Etta cried out in unfeigned dismay. He ignored it.

'What is it about me you find so doubtful? My judgement? My honour?' He set his face in lines of bitter remorse. 'I fear you are justified. I showed poor judgement in my promise to Wintrow, and little honour to my crew in risking them attempting to keep that promise.' He gave Wintrow a piercing look. 'Your aunt is alive and aboard. In fact, she sleeps in your room.

Stop!' he ordered as Wintrow rose hastily. 'You cannot go to her just now. She was cold and battered from her time in the sea. She's taken poppy to ease her. Not disturbing her rest is simple courtesy. Despite the hostility of our reception by the Paragon, I, at least, will hold to what a truce flag means.' He swung his gaze to Etta. 'And you, lady, are to stay well away from both Althea Vestrit and the Six Duchies warrior who accompanied her. I fear a danger to your person from them. The Vestrit woman speaks fair words, but who knows what her true intentions are?'

'They approached under truce, and then attacked?' Wintrow asked incredulously.

'Ah. You were watching, then? They provoked our serpents into attacking by firing arrows at them. They mistook the serpents' retreat for flight. Emboldened by that, they brought in their ship to challenge us directly. In the final battle, we prevailed. Unfortunately, a valuable prize was lost in the process.' He shook his head. 'The ship was determined to perish.' That was a vague enough telling that he could later shift details as needed, if Wintrow doubted any of it. For now, it left the lad white-faced and stiff.

'I had no idea,' Wintrow began awkwardly, but with a sharp wave of his hand, Kennit cut him off.

'Of course you did not. Because you have not learned a thing, despite all my efforts to teach you. I deferred to my feelings for you, and made costly promises. Well, I kept them. The ship is not pleased, the crew has been risked, and a rare prize has been lost. But I kept my word to you, Wintrow. As Etta begged me to. I fear it will bring neither of you joy,' he finished wearily. He looked from one to the other and shook his head in disgust at his own stupidity. 'I suppose I am a fool to hope that either of you will obey my wishes regarding Althea Vestrit. Until I determine if she is a threat to us, I would like to keep her isolated. Comfortable, but isolated from both ship and crew. I have no desire to kill her, Wintrow. But neither can I risk her discovering the secret ways into Divvytown, or undermining my authority with the ship. Her mere presence in these waters appears to have been enough to turn you against me.' He shook his head again wearily. 'I never dreamed you would be so quick to doubt me. Never.' He went so far as to lower his face into his hands. His elbows rested on his knee as he curled forwards in mimed misery. He heard Etta's light footstep on the deck but still pretended to startle as her hands came to rest on his shoulders.

'Kennit, I have never doubted you. Never. And if you judge it best, I will return to the *Marietta* until you send for me. Though I hate to be parted from you . . .'

'No, no.' He forced himself to reach up and pat one of her hands. 'Now that you are here, you may as well stay. As long as you keep well clear of Althea and her companion.'

'If this is your will, I shall not question it. In all other things as regard me, you have always been right.' She paused. 'And I am sure that Wintrow agrees with me,' she prompted the hapless boy.

'I would like to see Althea,' Wintrow replied miserably. Kennit knew the effort it cost him, and in a tiny way he admired the boy's tenacity. Etta did not.

'But you will do as Kennit says,' she told him.

Wintrow bowed his head in defeat. 'I am sure he has good reasons for wishing me to do this,' he conceded at last.

Etta's hands were kneading Kennit's neck and shoulders. He relaxed to her touch, and let the last of his worries lift. It was done. Paragon was gone and Althea Vestrit was his. 'We make for Divvytown,' he said quietly. There, he would find a good excuse why Etta must be put ashore and remain there. He glanced at the morose Wintrow. With deep regret, he wondered if he would have to give the boy up as well. He would have to offer Bolt something by way of reconciliation. It might have to be Wintrow, sent off to be a priest.

TWENTY-THREE

Flights

Reyn had not believed he could fall asleep in the dragon's clutches, but he had. He twitched awake, then gave a half-yell at the sight of his feet dangling over nothing. He felt a chuckle from the dragon in response, but she said nothing.

They were getting to know one another well. He could feel her weariness in the rhythm of her wingbeats. She needed to rest soon. But for his presence, she had told him, she could have plunged down into shallows near an island, allowing the water to absorb her impact. Because he occupied her forepaws, she sought a beach that was open enough to permit a ponderously flapping landing. In the Pirate Isles, that was not easy to find.

The little islands below them were steep-sided and pointed, like mountaintops poking up out of the sea. A few had gentle, sandy beaches. Each rest period, she would select a site and descend in sickening circles. Then, as she got closer to the ground, she would beat her great leathery wings so fiercely that their motion snatched the breath from Reyn's lungs while filling the air with dust and sand. Once down, she would casually dump him on the sand and bid him get out of her way. Whether he did or not, she leapt into flight again. The turbulence of her passage was enough to fling him to the ground. She would be gone for a few hours or half a day, to hunt, feed, sleep, and sometimes feed again.

Reyn used these solitary hours to kindle a fire, eat from his dwindling supplies, and then roll himself up in his cloak to sleep; if he could not sleep, he tormented himself with thoughts of Malta, or with wondering what would become of him if the dragon failed to return.

In the fading light of the winter afternoon, Reyn sighted a beach of black sand amid out-thrusts of black rock. Tintaglia banked her wings and swung towards it. As they circled, several of the black boulders littering the beach stirred. Napping marine mammals lifted their ponderous heads. The sight of the dragon sent them to galloping heavily into the waves. Tintaglia cursed, finishing with, 'But for carrying you, I'd have a fine, fat meal in my talons right now. It's rare to find sea bullocks so far north this time of year. I won't have another chance like that again!'

The layer of black sand over the black bedrock proved to be shallower than it looked. Tintaglia landed, but without dignity, as her great talons scrabbled on the beach like a dog's claws on a flagged floor. Lashing her tail wildly to keep her balance, she nearly fell on top of him before she managed to stop.

Once she dropped him on the beach, he scuttled hastily away from her, but she did not take off immediately. She was still muttering disconsolately to herself about fine, fat sea bullocks. 'Lean, dark red meat and layers of blubber and, oh, the richness of the liver, nothing compares to it, soft and hot in the mouth,' she mourned.

He glanced back at the thickly-forested island. 'I've no doubt you'll find other game here,' he assured her.

But she was not consoled. 'Oh, certainly I will. Lean bony rabbits by the score, or a doe going to ribs already. That is not what I crave, Reyn. Such meat will keep me, but my body clamours to grow. If I had emerged in spring, as I should have, I would have had the whole summer to hunt. I would have grown strong, and then fat, and then strong again, and fatter still, until by the time winter threatened, I would have had the reserves to subsist easily on such lean and bony creatures. But I did not.' She shook out her wings and surveyed herself dolefully. 'I am hungry all the time, Reyn. And when I briefly sate that hunger, my body demands sleep, so it can build itself up. But I know I cannot sleep, nor hunt and eat as much as I should. Because I must keep my promise to you, if I am to save the last of my kind.'

He stood without words, seeing an entirely different creature than he had but a few minutes before. She was young and growing, despite having lived a hundred lifetimes. How would it feel, to step forth into life after endless waiting, only to be seized by the necessity for selflessness? He suddenly felt pity for her.

She must have sensed his emotion, but her eyes spun coldly. She tucked her wings back to her body. 'Get out of my way,' she warned him, but did not give him enough time to move. The wind of her wings sent a stinging cloud of sand against his abused flesh.

When he dared to open his eyes again, she was a flash of blue, iridescent as a humming bird, still rising into the sky. For an instant, his heart sang with the pure beauty of such a creature. What right had he to delay her in her quest to perpetuate her species? Then he thought of Malta and his resolution firmed. Once she was safe, he would be willing to devote all his efforts to aiding Tintaglia.

He chose a sheltered place in the lee of some boulders. The winter day was clear, and the thin sunlight almost warm. He ate sparingly of his dried food and drank water from his bag. He tried to sleep, but the bruises from her claws ached and the sun was too bright against his eyelids. He watched the sky for her return, but saw only wheeling gulls. Resigned to a substantial wait, he ventured into the forest to look for fresh water.

It was odd to walk beneath trees on solid ground. The lush Rain Wild growth towering over swamp was the only forest he had ever known. Here the branches of trees swooped lower, and the undergrowth was thicker. Dead leaves were thick underfoot. He heard birds, but he saw few signs of small game, and none at all of deer or pig. Perhaps this island boasted no large animals. If so, Tintaglia might return as empty as she had left. The terrain became steeper and he soon doubted he would find a stream. Reluctantly, he turned back towards the beach.

As he drew close to where the darkness of the forest was shot through with the light from the open beach beyond, he heard an odd sound. Deep and reverberating, it reminded him of a large skin drum struck with a soft object. He slowed his pace and peered from the brush before venturing out into the open.

The sea bullocks had returned. Half a dozen of them basked on the sand. One lifted his muzzle; his thick throat worked like a bellows to produce the sound. Reyn stared, fascinated. He had never seen such immense creatures at close range. The creature lowered his massive head and snuffed loudly at the sand, apparently puzzled by the unfamiliar scent of dragon. He bared thick yellow tusks in distaste, shook his head, then sprawled down in the sand once more. The other dozing creatures ignored him. One turned over on its back and waved its flippers lazily before its face. It turned its head towards Reyn, and widened its nostrils. He thought it would immediately roll to its feet and wallow towards the sea, but it closed its eyes and went back to sleep.

A plan unfolded in Reyn's head. Silently, he retreated from the beach. Sticks were plentiful under the trees; he selected one that was straight, stout, and long, then lashed his knife firmly to the end of it. He had never hunted before, let alone killed for meat, but he was not daunted. How hard could it be to creep up on one of the fat, docile creatures and make an end of it? A single spear thrust through the neck would provide fresh meat for both of them. When his makeshift spear was to his satisfaction, he sharpened another stake to back it up, then circled through the woods to the far end of the beach. When he emerged from the trees onto the sand, he bent low and raced up the beach to put himself between the creatures and their retreat to the water.

He had expected some alarm at the sight of him. One or two turned their heads to regard him, but the bulk of the herd went on dozing and sunbathing. Even the nervous fellow who had earlier bellowed at the dragon's scent ignored him. Emboldened, he chose a target on the outskirts of the scattered herd: a fine, fat one, scarred by a long life. It would not be tender, but there would be lots of it, and he surmised that would be more important to Tintaglia.

His crouching stalk was a foolish waste of time. The sea bullock did not so much as open an eye until Reyn was within a spear's length of him. Feeling almost ashamed for killing such dull prey, Reyn drew back his arm. The creature's wrinkled hide looked thick. He wanted to give him a swift death. He took a deep breath and put all his weight behind his thrust as he stabbed.

A moment before the point touched flesh, the sea bullock rolled to its feet with a roar. Reyn knew instantly that he had misjudged the creatures' temperaments. The spear that he had aimed at the animal's neck plunged deeply in behind its shoulder. Blood sprayed from the sea bullock's nostrils. He'd pierced his prey's lung. He clung doggedly to his spear and tried to thrust it deeper as the entire herd stirred to sudden activity.

With a roar, the animal spun to confront him. Reyn was carried along on his spear, his feet dragging in the sand. He barely managed to keep a grip on his sharpened stake. It now looked as effective as a handful of daisies, but it was the only weapon he had. For a stride, he managed to get his feet under him. He used his thrust to push the spear deeper. The animal bellowed again, blood starting from its mouth now as well as flying from its nostrils. He would win.

Through the shaft of the spear, he could feel its strength waning.

Then another sea bullock seized a great mouthful of his cloak and jerked him off his feet. He lost his grip on the spear, and as he went down, the wounded animal turned on him. Its big dull tusks suddenly looked sharp and powerful as it lunged at Reyn, jaws wide. He rolled clear of the attack, but that wrapped his cloak around him. He fought his sharpened stick clear of the entrapping fabric, and then jerked his foot away from the snapping jaws. He tried to stand up, but the other animal still gripped a corner of his cloak. It threw its head from side to side, jerking Reyn to his knees. Other sea bullocks were closing in swiftly. Reyn tried to tear free of his cloak and flee, but the knots defied him. Somehow he had lost his sharpened stake. Another animal butted him, slamming him into the bullock that still gripped his cloak. He had a brief glimpse of his prey sprawling dead on the sand. Much good that did him now.

Tintaglia's shrill *ki-i-i* split the winter sky. Without releasing his cloak, the animal that held it twisted its head to stare up at the sky. An instant later, the entire herd was in a humping gallop towards the water. Reyn was dragged along, his cloak snagged on the sea bullock's tusks.

When the dragon hit the bullock, Reyn thought his neck would snap. They skidded through the sand together, the sea bullock squealing with amazing shrillness as Tintaglia's jaws closed on its neck. With a single bite, she half-severed its head from its thick shoulders. The head, Reyn's cloak still clutched in its jaws, sagged to one side of the twitching body under Tintaglia's hind feet. Dazed, he crawled towards it and unsnagged his cloak from its tusks.

'Mine!' roared Tintaglia, darting her head at him menacingly. 'My kill! My food! Get away from it.'

As he stumbled hastily away, she lowered her jaws over the animal's belly. A single bite and she lifted her head, to snap up and gulp down the dangling entrails. A waft of gut stench drifted over Reyn. She swallowed. 'My meat!' she warned him again, and lowered her head for another bite.

'There's another one over there. You can eat him, too,' Reyn told her. He waved a hand at the sea bullock with the spear in it. He collapsed onto the sand, and finally succeeded in undoing the ties of his cloak. Snatching it off, he threw it down in disgust. What ever had made him think he could hunt? He was a digger, a thinker, an explorer. Not a hunter.

Tintaglia had frozen, a dripping mouthful of entrails dangling from her jaws. She stared at him, the silver of her eyes glistening. Then she threw her head back, snapped down her mouthful and demanded, 'I can eat your kill? That is what you said?'

'I killed it for you. You don't think I could eat an animal that size, do you?'

She turned her head as if he were something she had never seen before. 'Frankly, I was amazed that you could kill one. I thought you must have been very hungry to try.'

'No. It's for you. You said you were hungry. Though maybe I could take some of the meat with me for tomorrow.' Perhaps by then the sight of her feeding and the smell of blood would not seem so disgusting.

She turned her head sideways to shear off most of the sea bullock's neck hump. She chewed twice, and swallowed. 'You meant it for me? When you killed it?'

'Yes.'

'And what do you want from me in return?' she asked guardedly.

'Nothing more than what we've already agreed upon: help me find Malta. I saw that you wouldn't find much game here. We'd travel better if you were well fed. That is all I was thinking.'

'Indeed.'

He could not read her odd inflection. He limped over to the animal he had killed and managed on his third effort, to pull out the spear. He recovered his knife, cleaned it off and put it back in its sheath.

Tintaglia ate her kill down to a collapse of bones before she began on his. Reyn watched in a sort of awe. He had not dreamed her belly could hold that much. Halfway through his kill, she slowed her famished devouring. Jaws and claws, she seized what remained of the carcass and dragged it up the beach out of reach of the incoming tide and adjacent to his fire. Without a word, she curled herself protectively around the carcass and fell into a deep sleep.

Reyn awoke shivering in full dark. The chill and damp of the night had penetrated his misused cloak and his fire had died to coals. He replenished it and found himself suddenly hungry. He tiptoed past the curl of Tintaglia's tail and hunched over the chewed carcass in the darkness. While he was still trying to find some meat that was unmarred by the dragon's teeth and saliva, she opened one huge eye. She regarded him without surprise. 'I left you both front flippers,' she told him, and then closed her eyes again.

He suspected she had portioned him the least appetizing part of the animal, but he cut off both platter-sized limbs. The fat, pink, hairless flippers with their dulled black claws did little to tempt his appetite, but he speared one on a stick and propped the meat over his fire. In a short time, the savoury smell of fat meat cooking filled the night. By the time it was cooked, his stomach was rumbling his hunger. The fat was crisp and dripping, and the meat of the reduced digits was as flavourful as anything he'd ever eaten. He put the other flipper to cook before he'd finished eating the first one.

Tintaglia woke, snuffing, just as he took the second fin from the fire. 'Do you want some?' he asked reluctantly.

'Scarcely!' she replied with some humour. As he ate the second flipper, she finished off the rest of the animal. She ate in a more leisurely manner now and her enjoyment was obvious. Reyn nibbled the last meat from the bones and tossed them into the embers of the fire. He washed the grease from his hands in the icy lap of the waves. When he returned, he built up the fire against the deepening chill of the night. Tintaglia sighed contentedly and stretched out, her belly towards the fire. Reyn, seated between the dragon and the fire, found himself cradled in stupefying warmth. He lay on top of his cloak and closed his eyes.

'You are different to what I expected humans to be,' Tintaglia observed.

'You are not what I thought a dragon would be,' he replied. He heaved a sigh of satiation. 'We'll fly at first light?'

'Of course. Though if I had my choice, I'd stay here and pick off a few more of those sea bullocks.'

'You can't still be hungry.'

'Not now. But one should always have a care for the morrow.'

For a time, silence hovered between them. Then Reyn had to ask, 'Will you grow even larger than you are now?'

'Of course. Why wouldn't I?'

'I just thought . . . well, you seem very large now. How big do dragons get?'

'While we live, we grow. So it depends on how long one lives.'

'How long do you expect to live?'

She gave a snort of amusement. 'As long as I can. How long do you expect to live?'

'Well . . . eighty years would be a good, long life. But few Rain Wilders last that long.' He tried to confront his own mortality. 'My father died when he was 43. If I am fortunate, I hope to have another score of years. Enough to have children and see them past their childhood.'

'A mere sneeze of time.' Tintaglia stretched negligently. 'I suspect that your years will stretch far longer than that, now that you have journeyed with a dragon.'

'Do you mean it will just seem that way?' Reyn asked, attempting levity at her confusing words.

'No. Not at all. Do you know nothing? Do you think a few scales or bronze eyes are all a dragon can share with her companion? As you take on more of my characteristics, your years will stretch out as well. I would not be surprised to see you pass the century mark, and still keep the use of your limbs. At least, so it was with the Elderlings. Some of them reached three and four centuries. But of course, those ones had generations of dragon-touch to draw on. You may not live so long, but your children likely will.'

Reyn sat up, suddenly wide awake. 'Are you teasing me?'

'Of course not. Why would I?'

'Nothing. I just . . . I am not sure I wish to live that long.' He was silent for a time. He imagined watching his mother and older brother die. That was tolerable; one expected to see one's parents die. But what if he had to watch Malta grow old and die? What if they had children, and he had to see them, too, become feeble and fade while he himself remained able and alert? An extended lifetime seemed a dubious reward for the doubtful honour of being a dragon's companion. He spoke his next thought aloud. 'I'd give all the years I hope to see for a single one assured with Malta.'

The speaking of her name was like a magical summoning. He saw her in his mind's eye, the lustre of her black hair, and how her eyes had shone as she looked up at him. His traitor memory took him back to the harvest ball, and holding her in his arms as they swept around the dance floor. Her Presentation Ball, and he had given her but one dance before he had rushed off to save the world. Instead of which he had lost everything, including Malta.

His hand remembered the smallness of her fingers in his. Her head came only to his chin. He pushed away savagely the thought of Malta on a Chalcedean galley. The ways of Chalcedean men and unprotected women were well known.

Terrible fear and seething anger rocketed through him. In their wake, he felt weak and negligent. It was all his fault, that she had been so endangered. She could not forgive him. He would not even dare ask it. Even if he rescued her and took her safely home, he doubted that she would ever endure his presence again. Despair roiled in him.

'Such a storm of emotions as humans can evoke, all on the basis of imagination,' the dragon observed condescendingly. In a more reflective voice she asked, 'Do you do this because you live such short lives? Tell yourselves wild tales of what might happen tomorrow, and feel all the feelings of events that will never happen? Perhaps to make up for the pasts you cannot recall, you invent futures that will not exist.'

'Perhaps,' Reyn agreed grudgingly. Her amusement stung him. 'I suppose dragons never need imagine futures, being so rich with pasts to recall.'

She made an odd sound in her throat. He was not sure if she was amused or annoyed at his jab. 'I do not need to imagine a future. I know the future that will be. Dragons will be restored to their rightful place as Lord of the Three Realms. We will once more rule the sky, the sea and the land.' She closed her eyes.

Reyn mulled what she had said. 'And where is this Land of the Dragons? Up river from Trehaug, past the Rain Wilds?'

One eye opened halfway. This time he was sure he saw amusement in the silver glints. 'Land of the Dragons? As if there were only one, a space defined by boundaries? Now there is a future only a human could imagine. We rule the sky. We rule the sea. And we rule the land. All land, everywhere.' The eye started to close again.

'But what about us? What about our cities, our farms, our fields and vineyards?'

The eye slid open again. 'What about them? Humans will continue to squabble with other humans about who can harvest plants where, and what cow belongs to whom. That is the way of humanity. Dragons know better. What there is on the earth belongs to the one who eats it first. My kill is my food. Your kill is your food. It is all very simple.'

Earlier in the day, he had almost felt love for her. He had marvelled at her blue sparkle as she glinted across the sky. She had come to his rescue when the sea bullocks would have killed him and freed her from her promise. Even now he rested in the shelter she made with her body and the fire. But whenever they approached true companionship, she would say something so arrogant and alien that all he could feel for her was wariness. He closed his eyes but could not sleep for pondering what he had turned loose on the world. If she kept her word and rescued Malta, then he must keep his. He imagined serpents hatching into dragons, and other dragons emerging from the buried city. Was he selling humanity into slavery for the sake of one woman?

Try as he would, he could not make it seem too high a price.

Malta tapped on the door, then hurried in without waiting for a reply. She exclaimed in annoyance at the darkness. Two strides carried her across the room. She tugged open the window curtain. 'You shouldn't lie about in the dark and pity yourself,' she told Cosgo sternly.

He looked up at her from his pallet. His eyes were squinted nearly shut. 'I'm dying,' he complained hoarsely. 'And no one cares. He deliberately makes the ship pitch, I know he does. Just so he can mock me before the crew.'

'No, he does not. The *Motley* just moves like that. He showed me, last night at dinner. It has to do with her hull design. If you would come up on deck, breathe some cool air and look at the water, the motion would not bother you so much.'

'You only say that. I know what would help me. Smoke. It is a sure cure for seasickness.'

'No, listen to me. I was sick my first two days aboard. Captain Red told me to try that, and I was so desperate that I did. It works. He said it is something about seeing the ship move in relation to the water. When you sit in here and watch the walls, or huddle in the dark, your belly can't make sense of what your head feels.'

'Perhaps my belly can't make sense of what my head knows,' Cosgo retorted. 'I am the Magnadon Satrap of all Jamaillia. Yet a rag-tag gang of pirates holds me prisoner in appalling conditions. I hold the Pearl Throne: I am Beloved of Sa. I am descended of a thousand wise rulers dating back to the beginning of the world. Yet you speak to me as if I were a child, and do not even grant me the courtesy of formal address.' He turned his face to the wall. 'Death is better. Let me die and then the world will rise up in wrath and punish all of you for what you have done.'

Every shred of sympathy that Malta had for him vanished beneath his wave of self-pity. Appalling conditions indeed. He meant that his room was small, and that no one but herself would wait on him. It irked him most that she had been given her own chamber. The *Motley* was not a capacious ship, but these particular pirates assigned a high priority to comfort. She had intended to coax him to the captain's table. She abandoned the idea but made a final effort. 'You would do better to show a bit of spirit rather than sulking like a child and imagining some future revenge on behalf of your dead body. Right now, the name you carry is the only thing that makes you valuable to them. Stand up and show them there is a man behind that title. Then they may respect you.'

'The respect of pirates, murderers and thieves! Now there is a lofty goal for me.' He rolled to face her. His face was pale and thin. His eyes roved up and down her disgustedly. 'And do they respect you for how quickly you have turned on me? Do they respect how swiftly you whored yourself to them for the sake of your life?'

The old Malta would have slapped his insolent staring face. But the new Malta could ignore insults, swallow affront and adapt to any situation. This Malta would survive. She shook out the bright skirts she wore, red layered upon yellow over blue. Her stockings were red and white stripes, very warm. Her shirt was white, but the vest that buttoned snugly over it was both yellow and red. She had pieced it together herself last night. The scraps of the garments she had cannibalized to make it now formed her new headwear.

'I will be late,' she told him coolly. 'I will bring you something to eat later.'

'I shall have small appetite for your scraps and leavings,' he told her sourly. As she reached the door he added, 'Your "hat" doesn't fit well. It doesn't cover your scar.'

'It wasn't intended to.' She did not look back at him.

'Bring me some smoking herbs instead!' he suddenly yelled. 'I know that they have some on board. They must! You lie when you say that they have none. They are the only thing that can settle my belly, and you deliberately keep them from me. You witless whore! You stupid female!'

Outside, the door shut firmly behind her, she leaned against the wall and took a long breath. Then, she lifted her skirts and ran. Captain Red disliked folk coming late to his table.

At the door, she paused to catch her breath. In a habit from another world, she pinched up her cheeks to rosy them and patted her hair into place. She hastily smoothed her skirts, and then entered. They were all seated at table already. Captain Red fixed her with a grave stare. She dropped a low curtsey. 'Your pardon, sirs. I was detained.'

'Indeed.' The captain's single word was his only reply. She hastened to take her place at his left hand. The first mate, a man intricately tattooed from brow to throat, sat to his right. Captain Red's own small tattoo was subtler, done in yellow ink that scarcely showed unless one knew to look for it. While slave actors and musicians were prized as possessions, their owners usually refrained from obvious ownership tattoos that might detract from their performances. The *Motley*'s crew was largely composed of an acting troupe that had been freed by Captain Kennit.

At a sign from the captain, the ship's boy sprang to life, serving the table. The snowy cloth, heavy china and glittering crystal belied the plainness of the fare. Ship's food, Malta had decided, changed little from vessel to vessel. Bread was hard, meat was salt and vegetables were roots. At least on the *Motley*, her food was not someone else's leavings and she ate at a table with cutlery. The wine, recent loot from the Chalcedean vessel, far surpassed the food it accompanied.

There was table conversation, too, and if it was not always elevated, at least it was mannered and stylish due to the composition of the crew. Neither slavery nor piracy had eroded their intelligence nor their braggadocio. Bereft of a theatre, the table became the stage for their performances, and Malta their audience. They vied to make her laugh or gasp with shock. Lively wit was expected at the table, as were excellent manners. Had not Malta known, she would never have guessed these same men who jested and jousted with words were also bloody-handed pirates capable of slaughtering every soul on a ship. She felt she walked a tightrope when she dined amongst them. They had extended to her the courtesy of their company, yet she never allowed herself to forget that she was their captive as well. Malta had never expected that the social graces she had learned as a Bingtown Trader's daughter would serve her in such good stead. Yet whilst they conversed with razor wit on the true meaning of the widow's son in Redoief's comedies or debated Saldon's command of language versus his deplorable lack of dramatic pacing, she longed to turn the talk in more informative directions. Her opportunity did not come until the end of the meal. As the others were excused and pushed away from the table, the captain turned his attention to Malta.

'So. Our Magnadon Satrap Cosgo again saw fit not to join us at table?'

Malta patted her lips and took her time answering. 'Captain, I'm afraid he is still indisposed. His upbringing did not school him to the rigours of sea travel, I fear.'

'His upbringing did not school him to any rigours. Say rather that he disdains our company.'

'His health is delicate, and his circumstances distress him,' Malta replied easily, determined not to speak critically of the Satrap. If she turned on him, she would no longer be seen as his loyal, and perhaps valuable, attendant. She cleared her throat slightly. 'He again requested smoking herbs, to ease his sea-sickness.'

'Pah. They do nothing for sea-sickness, save make a man too dazed to be bothered by it. I have told you we allow none aboard. It was debt for smoking herbs and other similar amusements that brought our company to the tattooist's stocks.'

'I have told him that, Captain. I fear he does not believe me.'

'He longs for them so that he cannot imagine we do without them,' the captain scoffed. He cleared his own throat. His demeanour changed. 'He would do well to join us tomorrow. We should like to discuss with him, genteelly, the terms of his ransom. Do urge him to be here tomorrow.'

'I shall,' Malta replied earnestly. 'But I fear I cannot convince him that this would better the circumstances of his captivity. Perhaps you would allow me to act as a go-between with your terms. I am accustomed to his temperament.'

'Bah. Better say that you are accustomed to his temper, to his sulks, his arrogance, his childish spite. As to confiding my intentions, well, all have agreed that the Satrap of all Jamaillia will make a fine gift for Kennit, King of the Pirate Isles. Many of us would find it amusing if our boy-Satrap finished his days wearing a raven tattooed beside his nose and shackles on his feet. Perhaps he could be taught to wait at table for Kennit's meals.

'But Kennit tends towards greater pragmatism. I suspect that King Kennit will ransom the Lord High Spoiled One back to whoever will have him. It would behove Cosgo to think of who that might be. It would please me to present him to Kennit with a list of names to be invited to bid for this prize.'

Kennit. The name of the man who had taken her father and his ship. What could this mean? Could she herself eventually stand before the man and somehow negotiate her father's release? The Satrap Cosgo suddenly took on new value in her eyes. She took a breath and found a smile.

'I shall persuade him to draw up such a list of names,' Malta assured the captain. Her eyes followed the mate; he was the last of the company to leave the room. 'If you will excuse me, I will see if I cannot begin tonight.' The door shut firmly behind the man. She cursed the increased beat of her heart, for she knew that the blood rose betrayingly to her face as well. She smiled as she edged towards the door.

'Are you in such a hurry to leave me?' Captain Red asked with mock sorrow. He stood and walked around the table towards her.

'I hasten to do your bidding,' Malta replied. She smiled and let a glint of flirtation come into her eyes. She walked a difficult line with this man. He thought very well of himself, and that was to her advantage. It pleased him to suppose that she desired him, and he enjoyed his pursuit and the dramatic opportunities it afforded him. He flaunted his courtship of her to his own crew. Nor did her scar daunt him. Perhaps, she thought, once a man's own face had been marked against his will, he made less of the marks on others' faces.

'Could not you stay here and do my bidding as well?' he asked her with a warm smile. He was a very handsome man, with handsome ways. A cold, hard part of herself speculated that if she made herself mistress of this man, she could use

him against Kennit. But no. It was not the sudden memory of
Reyn's wide shoulders or her hand resting in his strong one as
they danced. Not at all. She had set all thoughts of the Rain
Wilder aside as a future she would never see. She was ruined
forever for marriage to such a man. But it was just possible, if
she was ruthless enough, that she still could save her father.
Despite all that had befallen her, he would love her still, with
a father's true love.

She had been too distracted. Captain Red captured her
hands and stood looking down on her with amusement. 'I
really *must* go,' she murmured, feigning reluctance. 'I've taken
the Satrap no dinner yet. If I am late, it will put him in a foul
temper, and getting those names for you may prove –'

'Let him starve,' Captain Red suggested brusquely, his glance
roving over her face. 'I'll wager it's a tactic no one has ever tried
on him before: it might be exactly what he needs to make him
more reasonable.'

She managed gently to disengage one hand. 'Were not his
health so delicate, I would surely be tempted to try such a
tactic. But he is the Satrap, and lord of all Jamaillia. Such
an important man must be kept healthy. Do not you agree?'

In reply, his free hand suddenly swooped around her waist.
He pulled her close and bent to kiss her. She closed her eyes
and held her breath. She tried to make her mouth move as
if she welcomed this, but all she could imagine was how it
would end. Suddenly he was the Chalcedean sailor, on one
knee between her legs. She wrenched free of him, gasping,
'No. Please, please, no!'

He stopped immediately. There was, perhaps, a trace of pity
in his amusement. 'I suspected as much. You're a fine little
actress. Were we both in Jamaillia, and I a free man and you
unscarred, we might make much of you. But we are here, my
dear, aboard the *Motley*. Such a crew as held you must have
misused you. Was it very bad?'

She could not grasp that a man could ask her such a question.

'I was threatened, but only threatened,' she managed to say. She looked away from him.

He did not believe her. 'I will not force you. Never fear that. I have no need to force any woman. But I would not mind helping you unlearn your fear. Nor would I hurry you.' He reached out a hand and traced the line of her jaw. 'Your demeanour and manners show that you were gently raised. But both of us are what life has made us. There is no going back to an innocent past. This may seem harsh advice, but it is given from my own experience. You are no longer your father's virgin daughter saving herself for a well-negotiated marriage. That is gone. So accept this new life whole-heartedly. Enjoy the pleasures and freedom it offers you in place of your old dreams of a proper marriage and a place in a staid society. Malta the Bingtown Trader's daughter is gone. Become Malta of the Pirate Isles. You might find it a sweeter life than your old one.' His fingers moved lightly from the line of her jaw to the hollow of her throat.

She forced herself to stand quietly as she revealed her last weapon. 'The cook told me that you have a wife and three children in Bull Creek. I fear folk would talk. Your wife might be hurt.'

'Folk always talk,' he assured her. His fingers toyed with her collar. 'My wife pays no mind to it. She says it is the price she pays for having a handsome, clever husband. Put them from your mind, as I do. They have nothing to do with what happens on this ship.'

'Don't they?' she asked him quietly. 'And if your daughter was taken by Chalcedean slave raiders, would you approve the same advice for her? To become whole-heartedly what they made her? Would you tell her that her father would never accept her back because she was no longer his "virgin daughter"? Would it no longer matter to you how often she was taken, or by whom?' She lifted her chin.

'Damn you,' he cursed her, but with admiration. Frustration

glittered in his eyes but he released her. She stepped back from him with relief. 'I will get the names from the Satrap,' she offered him in compensation. 'I will be sure he understands that his life depends on how much he can wring from his nobles. He sets great store on his own life. I am sure he will be generous with their coin.'

'He had better be.' Captain Red had recovered some of his aplomb. 'To make up for how stingy you are with woman's coin.'

Malta smiled at him, a genuine smile, and allowed a swagger to her walk as she left his chamber.

TWENTY-FOUR

Trader for the Vestrit Family

A FIRE OF BEACHWOOD burned in the hearth, almost warming the emptied room. It would take time to drive the chill of winter from the big house. It had stood uninhabited for weeks; it was amazing how swiftly cold and disuse changed a house.

Housework was comforting. In cleaning and restoring a room, one could assert control. One could even pretend, briefly, that life could be tidied the same way. Keffria stood slowly, and dropped her scrubbing rag back into the bucket. There. She looked around her bedchamber as she massaged her aching hand. The walls had been wiped down with herbwater and the floor scrubbed. The damp dust and musty smell were gone . . . So was every trace of her former life here. When she had returned to her home, she had found that the bed she had shared with Kyle, their clothing chests, and her wardrobe were gone. Drapes and hangings were missing, or slashed to ribbons. She had closed the door and put off worrying about it until the main areas of the house were habitable. Then she had come here alone to attack it. She had no idea how she would re-furnish it. Other, deeper considerations had occupied her mind as she did the monotonous drudgery of scrubbing.

She sat down on the floor before the fire and looked around the room. Empty, clean, and still slightly cold. Rather like her life. She leaned back on the mortared stone that defined the hearth. Refilling and restoring either the room or her life suddenly seemed like a waste of time. Perhaps it was best to keep both as they were now. Uncluttered. Simple.

Her mother ducked her head into Keffria's room. 'There you are!' Ronica exclaimed. 'Do you know what Selden is doing?'

'Packing,' Keffria answered. 'It won't take him long. He hasn't much to pack.'

Ronica frowned. 'You're letting him go? Just like that?'

'It's what he wants to do,' she replied simply. 'And Jani Khuprus has said he would be welcome, and that he can stay with her family.'

'What about staying with his own family?' Ronica asked tartly.

Keffria rolled her eyes wearily at her mother. 'Have you talked to him? I did. I'm sure you heard the same things. He is more Rain Wild than Bingtown now, and changing more every day. He has to go to Trehaug. His heart calls him to help the dragon in her quest to save the serpents.'

Ronica came into the room, lifting her hems clear of the still-damp floor. It was an old reflex. Her worn gown didn't merit such care. 'Keffria, he's still a child. He's far too young to be making these sort of decisions for himself.'

'Mother, don't. I'm letting him go. It has been hard enough to reach this decision, without your questioning it,' Keffria repeated softly.

'Because you think it's the best thing for him to do?' Ronica was incredulous.

'Because I don't have anything better to offer him.' Keffria stood with a weary sigh. 'What remains in Bingtown to keep him here?' She looked around the empty room. 'Let's go down to the kitchen,' she offered. 'It's warmer there.'

'But not as private,' her mother countered. 'Ekke is down there, cleaning the day's catch. Fish for dinner.'

'What a surprise,' Keffria feigned. She was glad to shift the topic.

'Monotonous, but far better than nothing for dinner,' her mother countered. She shook her head. 'I'd rather talk here. As big as the house is, I still feel crowded at the thought of strangers sharing it with us. I never thought to see the day when we must take in boarders for the sake of the food they share with us.'

'I'm sure that they feel just as uncomfortable,' Keffria said. 'The Bingtown Council needs to move swiftly at assigning land to the Three Ships families. Ekke and Sparse would start building tomorrow if they were granted a piece of land to call their own.'

'It's the New Traders, still,' Ronica replied, shaking her head. 'They slow down all healing. Without slave labour, they cannot possibly work those huge grants of land, but they persist in claiming them.'

'I think they merely try to make it the starting place for their bartering,' Keffria replied thoughtfully. 'No one else recognizes their claims. Companion Serilla has shown them that the language of the Bingtown Charter forbids such grants as Satrap Cosgo gave them. Now they clamour that Jamaillia must pay them back for the land they have lost, but as the grants were written as "gifts", Companion Serilla says they are owed nothing. Devouchet lost his temper when they tried to debate that; he shouted at them that if they think Jamaillia owes them money, they should go back to Jamaillia, and argue it there. Still, at every meeting of the Council, the New Traders complain and insist. They will soon have to come to their senses. Spring comes eventually. Without slaves, they cannot plough and plant. Much of the land they took is useless for crops now. They are discovering what we told them all along. The land around Bingtown cannot be cultivated as they farm in Jamaillia or Chalced. For a year or two, it bears well, but once you have broken the clay layer with ploughs, it just gets swampier year after year. You can't grow grain in a bog.'

Ronica nodded in agreement. 'Some of the New Traders understand that. I've heard talk that many of them plan to return to Jamaillia, once travel is less dangerous. I think it would be best for them. They never really put their hearts into Bingtown. Their homes, their titles and ancestral lands, their wives and their legitimate children are all back in Jamaillia. Wealth was what lured them here. Now that they've discovered they aren't going to find it here, they'll go home. I think they only persist in their claims in the hopes of having something to sell before they depart.'

'And leave us the mess to clean up,' Keffria observed sourly. 'I feel sorry for the New Traders' mistresses and bastards. They'll probably have to stay in Bingtown. Or go north. I have heard that some of the Tattooed are talking of taking ship to the Six Duchies. It's a harsh land, almost barbaric, but they feel they could begin anew there, without having to sign agreements. They feel that becoming Rain Wild Traders under Jani's terms would be too restrictive.'

'When all who choose to leave have left, then those who remain will be closer in spirit to the original Bingtown Traders,' Ronica observed. She walked to the naked window and looked out into the evening. 'I'll be glad when it is all settled. When those who remain here are those who chose to be part of Bingtown, then I think we shall heal. But that may take a time. Travel is not safe, either to north or south.' Then she cocked her head at Keffria. 'You seem very well-informed about the rumours and news of Bingtown.'

Keffria took that as an unvoiced but deserved rebuke. Once, her interests had centred only on her own home and children. 'The gossip at the Council meetings is endless. I am out and about more than I used to be. There is less at home to claim my time. Also, Ekke and I talk, when we are cooking dinner. It is the only time she seems completely comfortable with me.'

Keffria paused. Her voice was puzzled as she asked, 'Did you know that she is sweet on Grag Tenira? She seems to think he is interested in her as well. I didn't know what to say to that.'

Her mother smiled almost indulgently. 'If Grag is interested in her, I wish them the best. He is a good man, and deserves a good partner. Ekke could be that for him. She is a solid person, blunt but good-hearted, and knowledgeable about the sea and those who sail. Grag could do worse than Ekke Kelter.'

'Personally, I had hoped he would do better.' Keffria poked at the fire. 'I hoped that Althea would come home, come to her senses and marry him.'

Ronica's face went grave. 'At this point, my sole hope for Althea is that she does come home.' She came over to the fire, then sat down suddenly on the hearthstones. 'It is my prayer for all of them. Come home, however you can. Just come home.'

For a long time, there was a silence in the room. Then Keffria asked in a low voice, 'Even Kyle, Mother? Are you hoping he will come home?'

Ronica turned her head slightly and met her daughter's eyes consideringly. Then, in a heartfelt voice, she said, 'If that is what you are hoping, then I hope it for you also.'

Keffria closed her eyes for a time. She spoke from that private darkness. 'But you think I should declare myself a sea widow, mourn him, and then go on.'

'You could, if you chose,' Ronica said without inflection. 'He has been missing long enough. No one would fault you for it.'

Keffria fought the rising misery that threatened to engulf her. She dared not give in to it, or she would go mad. 'I don't know what I hope, Mother. I just wish I knew something. Are they alive or dead, any of them? It would almost be a relief to hear Kyle was dead. Then I could mourn for the good things we had, and let go of the bad things. If he comes home . . . then I don't know what. I feel too much.

'When I married him, it was because he was so commanding.

I was so sure he would take care of me. I'd seen how hard you had to work while Father was gone at sea. I didn't want that sort of life for myself.' She looked at her mother and shook her head. 'I'm sorry if that hurts your feelings.'

'It doesn't,' Ronica said shortly, but Keffria knew she lied.

'But, when Father died, and everything changed, somehow I found myself living your life anyway.' Keffria smiled grimly. 'So many details, so many tasks to be done, until I felt there was no time left for myself at all. The odd part is, now that I've taken up the reins, I don't think I can put them down again. Even if Kyle appeared on the doorstep tomorrow and said, "Don't worry, dear, I'll take care of it all," I don't think I could let him. Because I know too much now.' She shook her head. 'One of the things I know now is that I'm better at these things than he would be. I began to discover that when I had to deal with our creditors myself. I could see why you had set things up as you had, and it made sense to me. But I also knew that Kyle would not like patiently working the family out of this a bit at a time. And . . .' She swung her eyes to her mother. 'Do you hear how I am now? I don't want to have these burdens. But I can't bear to turn them over to anyone else, either. Because, despite all the work, I like being in control of my own life.'

'With the right man, you can share that control,' Ronica offered.

Keffria felt her smile go crooked. 'But Kyle isn't the right man for that. And we both know that now.' She drew a deep breath. 'If he came back now, I wouldn't let him have the family vote on the Traders' Council. Because I know more about Bingtown and can vote it more wisely. But Kyle would hate that. I think that, alone, would be enough to drive him away.'

'Kyle would hate that you had to control your own vote? That you had to be able to take care of yourself while he was gone?'

Keffria paused a moment before she answered. She forced the truth out. 'He would hate that I was good at it, Mother. But I am. And I like being good at it. It's one reason I feel I should let Selden go. Because, in his short years, he has shown me that he is better at taking care of himself than I am. I could keep him here, safe by me. But it would be a lot like Kyle keeping me in hand.'

A light tap at the door made both of them startle. Rache peered around the corner.

'Jani Khuprus is here. She says she has come for Selden.'

Rache had changed in small ways since the upheavals in Bingtown. She still lived with them, and took on the duties of a house servant. But she also spoke openly of where she hoped she would get her piece of land, and what type of a house she would build when the final agreement was settled. Now, when she spoke of Jani coming for Selden, her disapproval was more obvious in her voice than it would have been months ago. Keffria didn't resent it. The woman had cared for her children, and in doing so, had come to genuinely care about them. Rache had been overjoyed at Selden's return from the Rain Wilds. She hated to give him up again.

'I'll come down,' Keffria replied immediately. 'You should come, too, if you wish to say good-bye to him.'

Jani studied the room as she waited nervously for Keffria. It had changed from the happy days when Reyn had been here courting Malta. The room was clean but the furniture had obviously been scavenged from throughout the house. There were chairs to sit on and a somewhat wobbly table. But there were no books, no tapestries, no rugs, nor any of the small domestic touches that finished a room. Her heart bled for the Vestrits. Their home had been taken from them; only the walls remained.

True, she herself had seen the collapse of the buried city that was the source of the Rain Wilds and, indirectly, Bingtown's wealth. Trehaug faced lean times ahead. But her home had weathered the storm. She had resources to draw on. Her pictures, her embroidered linens, her jewellery, her wardrobe of clothing awaited her safely at home. She had not been left near-destitute as the Vestrits had. It made her feel all the more selfish that she had come to take away the final vestige of the family's true wealth. Their last son would go with her tonight. It had not been put into words between them, but the truth was writ large on Selden's scaled face. He was Rain Wild now. It was not Jani's doing; she would never have sought to steal a son, let alone the last of their line. It did not make her feel any less greedy that she cherished the thought of taking the boy with her. Another child for her household was a treasure beyond compare. She wished she did not have to gain it at her friends' loss.

The whisper of their sandals preceded them. First Keffria, then Ronica and finally Rache entered the room. Selden was not with them. That was as well. Jani preferred to make her proposal to Keffria before she had to say goodbye to her son. It would not seem so much like a trade. As she exchanged greetings with them, she noted that Ronica's hand seemed frailer in hers, and that Keffria was more grave and reserved. Well, that was natural enough.

'Would you care for a cup of tea?' Keffria asked in the courtesy of a bygone day. Then, with a nervous laugh, she turned to Rache, 'That is, if we have any tea, or anything close to it?'

The serving woman smiled. 'I am sure I can find some sort of leaves to steep.'

'I would love a cup of anything warm,' Jani replied. 'The cold outside bites to my bones. Why must so harsh a winter descend in our most difficult time?'

They commiserated on that for a bit. Then Ronica rescued them from pointless pleasantries as Rache reappeared with the tea. 'Well, let us stop being as nervous as if we do not well know why Jani is here. She has come to take Selden to the Rain Wilds when the Kendry sails tonight. I know Keffria has agreed to this, and it is what Selden wants. But . . .'

And there Ronica's courage failed her. Her voice went tight on her closing words, 'But I do hate to lose Selden . . .'

'I wish you did not feel that way,' Jani offered. 'That you are losing him, I mean. He comes with me now, for a time, because he genuinely believes he has a duty to help us in our preliminary work. Certainly, the Rain Wilds have marked him as their own. But that does not mean he is no longer a Vestrit. And in days to come, I hope for a time when Rain Wild and Bingtown will mingle freely and often.'

That brought little response. 'Selden is not the only reason I am here,' she added abruptly. 'I also bring two offers. One from the Rain Wild Council. One from myself.'

Before she could go on, Selden opened the door. 'I'm ready,' he announced with undisguised satisfaction. He came into the room dragging a lumpy canvas sack behind him and looked around at the gathered women. 'Why is everyone so quiet?' he demanded. Firelight danced on his scaled cheekbones.

No one replied.

Jani settled herself in her chair and accepted the cup of tea that Rache poured for her. She sipped at it, seizing the moment to organize her thoughts. It tasted of wintermint, with a tang of niproot in it. 'This is actually quite delicious,' she complimented them sincerely as she set the cup down. Her eyes travelled over the waiting faces. Keffria held her tea but had not sipped it. Ronica had not even picked her cup up. Jani suddenly knew what was missing. She cleared her throat.

'I, Jani Khuprus, of the Khuprus family of the Rain Wild Traders, accept your hospitality of home and table. I recall all our most ancient pledges to one another, Rain Wilds to Bingtown.' As she spoke the old, formal words, she was surprised to feel tears brim in her eyes. Yes. This was right.

She saw an answering sentiment in the faces of the Bingtown women.

As if it were a thing rehearsed, Ronica and Keffria spoke together. 'We, Ronica and Keffria Vestrit, of the Vestrit family of the Bingtown Traders, make you welcome to our table and our home. We recall all our most ancient pledges to one another, Bingtown to Rain Wilds.'

Keffria surprised them all when she spoke on alone. 'And also our private agreement regarding the liveship Vivacia, the product of both our families, and our hope that our families shall be joined in the marriage of Malta Vestrit and Reyn Khuprus.' She took a deep breath. Her voice shook only slightly. 'In sign of the link between our families, I offer to you my youngest son, Selden Vestrit, to be fostered with the Khuprus family of the Rain Wilds. I charge you to teach him well the ways of our folk.'

Yes. This was right. Let it all be formalized. Selden suddenly stood taller. He let go of his sack and came forwards. He took his mother's hand and looked up at her. 'Do I say anything?' he asked gravely.

Jani held out her hand. 'I, Jani Khuprus of the Khuprus family of the Rain Wilds, do welcome Selden Vestrit to be fostered with our family, and taught the ways of our folk. He will be cherished as one of our own. If he so wills it.'

Selden did not let go of his mother's hand. How wise the boy already was! He instead set his free hand into Jani's. He cleared his throat. 'I, Selden Vestrit of the Vestrit family, do will that I be fostered with the Khuprus family of the Rain Wilds.' He looked at his mother as he added, 'I will do my best to learn all that is taught me.

'There. That's done,' he added.

'That's done,' his mother agreed softly. Jani glanced down at the rough little hand she held. It had already begun to scale around the nail beds. He would change swiftly. It was truly for the best that he go to the Rain Wilds where such things were accepted. For an instant, she wondered what her young daughter Kys would think of him. He was only a few years older than she was. Such a match would not be unthinkable. Then she set aside the selfish thought. She lifted her eyes to meet Keffria's bleak stare.

'You can come also, if you wish. And you, Ronica. That is my offer to you. Come up the river to Trehaug. I do not promise you that times are easier there, but you would be welcome in my home. I know you wait for news of Malta. I, too, await the dragon's return. We could wait together.'

Keffria shook her head slowly. 'I have spent too much of my life waiting, Jani. I won't do that any more. The Bingtown Council must be pushed into action, and I am one of those who must push. I can't wait for "them" to settle Bingtown's unrest. I have to insist, daily, that all complaints be considered.' She looked at her son. 'I'm sorry, Selden.'

He gave her a puzzled look. 'Sorry that you will do what you must do? Mother, it is your own example I follow. I go to Trehaug for the same reason.' He managed a smile for her. 'You let me go. And I let you go. Because we are Traders.'

There was a sudden loosening in Keffria's face, as if an unforgivable sin had been expunged from her soul. She heaved a great sigh. 'Thank you, Selden.'

'I, too, must stay,' Ronica said into the quiet. 'For while Keffria is being the Trader for the Vestrit family, I must look after the rest of our interests. It is not just our home that was raided and vandalized. We have other holdings as well, similarly troubled. If we are not to lose them all, then I must act now, to hire workers who will labour for a share of next year's crop. Spring will come again. Vineyards and orchards will put forth new leaves. Despite all our other troubles, those things must be anticipated.'

Jani shook her head with a small smile. 'So I expected you to answer. Indeed, so the Rain Wild Council told me you would, when I told them of my plans.'

Keffria frowned. 'Why would the Rain Wild Council have an interest in how we answered?'

Jani would keep it to herself that the Council had been as anxious as she to lay claim to Selden Vestrit. Instead, she told the rest of the truth. 'They were anxious to avail themselves of your services, Keffria Vestrit. But for you to be effective, you would have to remain here in Bingtown.'

'My services?' Keffria was obviously astounded. 'What services can I perform for them?'

'You may have forgotten or dismissed the last time you spoke to the Rain Wild Council. They have not. You were quite inspiring, in your offer to risk yourself in the service of the Traders. As it was, the situation changed so swiftly that your sacrifice was not necessary. But the fact that you were willing to offer, as well as your clear grasp of the situation, left a deep impression on the Council. With all the changes now in the wind, the Rain Wild Council needs an official voice in Bingtown. When Traders such as Pols, Kewin and Lorek can all agree that you are the best choice to represent us, you must realize that you left a very favourable impression.'

A faint pink rose in Keffria's cheeks. 'But the Rain Wild Traders have always been free to speak in the Bingtown Council, just as any Bingtown Trader can claim the right to speak in the Rain Wilds. You do not need me as a representative.'

'We disagree. Changes are raining down swiftly; our communities will need to cooperate even more closely than we have in the past. Message-birds can only fly so swiftly. Liveship traffic on the Rain Wild River has been reduced in these dangerous times, as all our ships patrol against Chalcedean vessels. Yet more than ever, we need a voice sympathetic to Rain Wild concerns here in Bingtown. We see you as the ideal choice. Your family is already strongly linked to the Rain Wilds. While we would ask you to seek our advice when you could, we would also trust you to speak out when an immediate voice was needed.'

'But why not one of your own, here in Bingtown?' Keffria hesitated.

'Because, just as you and your mother have told me, they need to remain close to their homes in this troubled time. Besides, in many ways, *you* are now one of our own.'

'It would be perfect, Mother,' Selden suddenly interjected. 'For the dragon will need your voice here as well. You could help to make Bingtown see the necessity of aiding her, beyond any "agreement" we have signed.'

Jani looked at him in surprise. Even in the well-lit room, she could see Selden's eyes literally glowing with his enthusiasm. 'But Selden, there may be times when the dragon's interests are different from the Rain Wilds' or Bingtown's,' she cautioned him gently.

'Oh, no,' he assured her. 'I know it is hard for you to believe that I know these things. But what I know goes beyond who I am, and back to another time. I have dreamed the city that Tintaglia spoke of, and it is grand beyond imagination. Compared to Cassarick, Frengong was humble.'

'Cassarick? Frengong?' Jani asked in confusion.

'Frengong is the Elderling name for the city buried beneath Trehaug. Cassarick is the city you will excavate for Tintaglia. There, you will find halls built to a dragon's scale of grandeur. In the Star Chamber, you will discover a floor set with what you call flame-jewels, in a mirror of the night sky on Springeve. There is a labyrinth with crystal walls, tuned to mirror the dreams of the ones who dare it; to walk its maze is to confront your own soul. Time's Rainbow, they called it amongst themselves, for each person who completed it seemed to do so by a different route. Wonders are buried there and may be brought back to light . . .' Selden's voice trailed away in rapture. He stood breathing deeply in silence, his eyes looking afar. The adults exchanged looks over his head. Then he spoke again, suddenly. 'The wealth the dragons will bring to us all will surpass mere coin. It will be a reawakening of the world. Humanity has become a lonely race, and dangerously arrogant in our solitude. The return of the dragons will restore balance to our intellect and to our ambitions.' He laughed aloud suddenly. 'Not that they are perfect beings, oh, no. That is our value to one another. Each race presents to the other a mirror of presumption and vanity. In seeing another creature's rash posturing of control and superiority in the world, we will realize how ridiculous our own claims are.'

Silence followed his words. The thoughts he had thrown out so casually echoed through Jani's mind. His voice, his words were not the cadence or vocabulary of a child. Was this the dragon's doing? What had they released back into the world?

'You have doubts now,' Selden spoke to her silent qualms. 'But you will see. The welfare of the dragon is in the best interests of the Rain Wilds, as well.'

'Well,' Jani replied at last. 'In that, perhaps, we shall have to trust to your mother's judgement, as she represents us.'

'This is a weighty responsibility,' Keffria wavered.

'We are well aware of that,' Jani replied smoothly. 'And such a task should not be undertaken without recompense.' She hesitated. 'At the beginning, we would be hard pressed to pay you in coin. Until trade with the outside world is restored, I fear we must go back to bartering.' She glanced about the room. 'Household goods we have in plenty. Do you think we could work out a suitable exchange?'

A spark of hope kindled in Ronica's eyes. 'I am sure we could,' Keffria replied almost immediately. With a rueful laugh she added, 'I can think of no household goods that we could not find a use for.'

Jani smiled, well pleased with herself. She had feared it would seem too much as if she were buying Selden from his family. In truth, she felt she had struck that best of all bargains, the one in which each Trader felt she had won the best of the trade. 'Let us make a list of what you need most,' she suggested. She set a hand on Selden's shoulder, taking care that it did not seem too possessive. 'When we reach Trehaug, Selden can help me select what he thinks will suit you best.'

TWENTY-FIVE

Refitting

'So. Back on the beach again,' Paragon observed.

'Not for long,' Amber assured him. She set her gloved hand briefly to his deck. It was a gesture of kindness, but a gesture only. She had slept deeply for a long time and he had looked forward to her awakening, to the sense of connection they had briefly shared. But that was not to be. He could not reach her, and could scarcely feel her. He was as alone as ever.

Brashen no longer trusted him. Paragon had tried to tell him that there was no damage below the water line, but Brashen had insisted on beaching him. The captain had apologized stiffly, but said he would do the same with any ship as damaged as he was. Then he had run Paragon's scorched body up onto a sandy beach. The tide had retreated, stranding him there with most of his hull bared. At least he was out of reach of the serpent and his endless circling. The creature's nagging him towards revenge was maddening.

Brashen had tersely told what remained of the crew to make repairs. He stalked the deck, commanding with his presence, but speaking scarcely a word and the work proceeded, even if the men moved without spirit. The spare mast had been brought out and stepped. Shackles and fittings had been salvaged, sound bits of line spliced together and spare canvas and other supplies dragged out onto the deck. Ruined food stores were dumped over the side. The broken windows in the captain's quarters were planked over. A crew had been sent ashore to cut timber for spars. The green lumber would be miserable to work with, but they had no alternative. There was no chatter, no chantey, no jesting. Even Clef was withdrawn and silent. No one had attempted to scrub the bloodstains from his deck. They walked around them, or stepped over them. The serpent venom had left pits and indentations in his wizardwood. It had stippled his face and left streaks down his chest. More scars for him to bear.

Amber, clothed in a loose garment made from a sheet, had toiled alongside the others, until Brashen had brusquely ordered her to take some rest. For a time, she had lain silently in her bunk. Then she had arisen, as if she could not bear to be still. Now she sat on the foredeck, laying out tools for her next task. She moved awkwardly, favouring the burned side of her body. He had become accustomed to her verbally sharing all she was doing, but today she was quiet. Paragon felt her preoccupation, but could not fathom it.

Kennit and the Vivacia were gone as if they had never been there. Only one serpent remained of the horde that had attacked him. The mild days since the storm's passing made it all seem like a dream. But it was not. The dragons lurked in him, just below the surface. New blood marked his deck. Some of the crew were angry with him still. Or frightened. Sometimes, with humans, it was hard to tell the difference. It stung most that Amber was distant with him.

'I couldn't help it,' he complained again.

'Couldn't you?' Amber asked him unemotionally.

She had been like that all afternoon. Not accusing him, but not accepting anything he said either. His temper snapped. 'No. I could not! And since you've pawed through my memories, you should understand that. Kennit is family to me. You know that now. You know everything now. All the secrets I vowed I would keep safe for him, you have stolen.'

He fell silent, guilt roiling through him again. He could not be true. If he was true to Kennit, he was disloyal to both Amber and his dragon selves. Kennit was family to him, yet he had once again failed in his promise to him. He was disloyal and wicked. Worse, he was relieved. His feelings spun like a weathervane. He had not truly wanted to die, nor to kill all his people. Amber should know that. She knew everything now. There was shameful comfort in sharing the terrible knowledge, for he was glad that someone else finally knew it all. A childish part of him hoped that now she would tell him what he should do. For too long he had wrestled with these secrets, not knowing what to do with such frightening and shameful memories. Hiding them for so long should have made them go away, should have made them not matter. Instead they had festered like a boil, and just when he had a new life, the old wound had burst open and poisoned everything. It had nearly killed them all.

'You should have told us.' Her words came out stiffly, as if she wished to hold them back. 'All this time, you knew so much that could have helped us, and you kept it to yourself. Why, Paragon? Why?'

He was silent for a time. He could feel what she was doing. She was securing a line to a cleat. She tested her weight against it. Then she came to the railing and climbed stiffly over it. She dropped over the bow, swung across in front of him and without warning, landed light-footedly against his chest. His hands came up reflexively to catch her. She froze in his grip, then spoke resignedly. 'I know. You could kill me right now, if you chose. But from the beginning, we've had no choice but to trust our lives to you. I had hoped that trust went both ways, but obviously, it didn't. You've shown you're capable of killing us all. That being so, I see no sense in fearing you any more. Either you'll kill us or you won't. You've shown me I've no control over that. All I can do is keep my own life in order, and do what I am meant to do.'

'Perhaps that is all I can do as well,' he retorted. He made his hands a platform for her to stand on, just as he had done for the boy Kennit so many years ago.

She seemed to ignore his words. Her gloved hands moved lightly over his face, not just fingering his new scars, but touching his cheeks, his nose, and his beard.

He could not leave the silence alone. 'That night, you loved me. You were willing to lose your life to save mine. How can you be so angry at me now?'

'I am not angry,' she denied. 'I cannot help but think that it all could have turned out differently. I am . . . hurt. No. Stricken. By all you did not do when we did all we could for you. At all you held back from us. And probably the depth of that feeling has much to do with how much I do love you. Why couldn't you have trusted us, Paragon? If you had shared your secrets, it all could have come out differently.'

He considered her words for a time while she poked at his neck and jaw-line. 'You are full of your own secrets,' he suddenly accused her. 'Things you have never shared with the rest of us. How can you despise me for doing the same?'

Her tone was suddenly formal. 'The secrets I hold are mine. My keeping them does no harm to anyone.'

He picked up her doubts. 'You are not sure of that. My secrets were as dangerous to share as they were to hold. But, as you said, my secrets were mine. Perhaps the only thing in the world that were truly mine.'

She was silent a long time. Then, 'Where are the dragons? What are the dragons and why are there dragons in you? Are you why I have dreamed of serpents and dragons? Were my callings actually bringing me to you?'

He pondered a moment. 'What will you trade me for an answer? A secret of your own? To show you are trusting me as much as I am trusting you.'

'I do not know if I can,' Amber replied slowly. She had stopped touching his face. 'My secrets are my armour. Without them, I am very vulnerable to all sorts of hurts. Even hurt that folk do not intend.'

'See. You do understand,' he replied quickly. He felt that barb score.

She took a breath, and spoke quickly, as if plunging into cold water. 'It is hard to explain. When I was much younger, and I spoke of it, people thought that I was too full of myself. They tried to tell me that I could not be what I knew I was. Finally, I ran away from them. And when I did, I promised myself that I would no longer fear what other folk thought of me. I would keep to myself the future I knew lay ahead of me. I have shared my dreams and ambitions with very few others.'

'You are telling me nothing with many words,' Paragon pointed out impatiently. 'What, exactly, are you?'

She gave a small laugh that had no joy in it. 'In a word, I do not know how to tell you. I have been called a fool as often as I have been called a prophet. I always have known that there were things I must do for the world, things no one else could do. Well. The same is true of every man, I do not doubt. Yet I follow a path I cannot see clearly. There are guides along the way, but I cannot always find them. I set out seeking a slave-boy with nine fingers.' She shook her head. He felt it. 'I found Althea instead, and though she was not a boy nor a slave and had all ten fingers, I felt a connection through her. So I helped her. May the gods forgive me, I helped her seek her death. Then I encountered Malta, and wondered if she were the one I should have been aiding. I reach forwards, Paragon, through mists of time to symbols that become people and people who teeter on the verge of legend. There is a task I must do here, but what it is remains cloaked from me. All I can do is push towards it, and hope that when the time comes, I will recognize it and perform the right actions. Although there is little hope of that now.' She took a breath. 'Why are there dragons in you?' she demanded.

He felt that she changed the subject, deliberately. He

answered her anyway. 'Because I was meant to be dragons. What you call wizardwood is actually a protective casing that sea-serpents weave about themselves before they begin their change into dragons. The Rain Wild Traders came upon encased dragons in the ruins of an ancient city. They killed them, but used the casings, rich with dragon memories, to build ships. Liveships they call us, but we are truly dead. Yet while memory lives, we are doomed to a half-life, trapped in an awkward body that cannot be moved without the aid of humans. I am more unfortunate than most, for two cocoons were used in my construction. From the time I was created, the dragons within me have warred for dominance over each other.' He shook his great head. 'I woke too soon, you see. I had not absorbed enough human memories to be strongly centred in them. From the time I first opened my eyes, I have been torn.'

'I do not understand. Why are you Paragon then, and not a dragon?'

He laughed bitterly. 'What else do you think Paragon is, save a human veneer of memories over battling dragons? In quarrelling with one another for mastery, they allowed me ascendance. When I say "I", I scarcely know what I mean.' He sighed suddenly. 'That was what Kennit gave me, and what I shall miss most. A sense of self. A sense of kinship. When he was aboard me, I had no doubts as to my identity. You see him as blood-shedding pirate. I recall him first as a wild and lively boy, full of joy in the wind and waves. He laughed aloud and swung in the rigging and would not leave me alone. He refused to fear me. He was born aboard me. Can you imagine that? The only birth I have ever known was able to obliterate all the deaths that had gone before it. His father offered him to me, his birth-blood still on his skin. "You've never been my ship, Paragon. Not in your heart. But perhaps you can be his as he is yours." And he was. He kept the dragons at bay. You, you have loosed them, and now we must all bear the consequences.'

'They seem quiet. Dormant,' Amber ventured. 'You seem very much yourself, only more – open.'

'Exactly. Cracked open and leaking my secrets. What are you doing?' He had thought she was inspecting for fire damage. He had expected her to spider along his hull, not walk all over his body.

'Keeping my word, to you and to the dragons. I'm going to carve some eyes for you. I'm trying to decide where to begin to repair this.'

'Don't.'

'Are you sure?' Amber asked him quietly. He sensed her dismay. She had promised this to the dragons. What would she do if Paragon forbade it now?

'No. I mean, don't repair my face. Give me a new one. One that is all of me.'

For a mercy, she did not ask him what he meant by that. She only asked, 'Are you sure?'

He pondered a moment. 'I think . . . I do not want to be a dragon. That is, I do, but I wish to be both of them, if I must. And yet to be Paragon as well. To be, as you said, three merged into one. I want . . .' He hesitated. If he said it and she laughed, it would be worse than death, as life was always sharper and harder than death. 'Give me a face you could love,' he quietly beseeched her.

She went still and soft in his hands. The tension he had sensed thrumming through her muscles went away. He felt her do something, and then her bared hands danced lightly over his face. By her touch, she both measured him, and opened herself. Skin to skin, she hid from him no longer. He touched enough to know it was the bravest thing she had ever done. He stifled his curiosity and tried to reciprocate her trust. He did not reach into her and plunder her of her secrets. He would wait, and take only what she offered him.

He felt her hands walk his face, measuring off proportions. Then she touched his cheek flat-handed. 'I could do that. It

608

would, in fact, be easy.' She cleared her throat again. 'It will be a lot of work, but by the time we sail into Bingtown again, you will wear a new face.'

'Bingtown?' He was astonished. 'We're going home?'

'Where else? What point is there in challenging Kennit again? Vivacia seems content to be in his hands. And even if she were not, what could we do?'

'But what about Althea?' he objected.

Amber stopped what she was doing. She leaned her forehead against his cheek and shared the full depth of her misery. 'All of this was about Althea, ship. Without her, whatever task I was to perform becomes meaningless. Brashen has no heart to continue, nor has this crew the mettle for vengeance. Althea is dead and I have failed.'

'Althea? Althea is not dead. Kennit took her up.'

'What?' Amber stiffened. She set her hands flat to his face.

Paragon was amazed. How could she not know that? 'Kennit took her up. The serpent told me so. I think he was trying to make me angry. He said Kennit had stolen two of my humans, both females.' He halted. He felt something radiating from her. It was as if a shell around her cracked open; warmth and joy poured from her.

'Jek, too!' She took a deep shuddering breath, as if she had not been able to find air for a long time. She spoke to herself. 'Always, always, I lose faith too easily. By now, I should know better. Death does not conquer. It threatens, but it cannot subdue the future. What must be, will be.' She kissed his cheek, striking him dumb with astonishment, then tugged at his beard. 'Up! Up! Get me up on the deck! Brashen! Clef! Althea is not dead. Kennit took her up. Paragon says so! Brashen! Brashen!'

He came running to Amber's wild call, fearing that Paragon had injured her. Instead, Brashen saw the figurehead set her gently on his scorched foredeck. She took a stumbling step towards him, babbling something about Althea, and then collapsed to her knees. 'I told you to take some rest!' he rebuked her angrily. Her damage from the serpent venom was appallingly apparent. Her tawny hair hung in hanks from a peeling red scalp. The left side of her face and neck were scarlet. How far the damage extended down her body, he was not sure. She walked with a pronounced limp and kept her left arm close to her body. Every time he saw her, he was shocked that she was out of bed at all.

He hastened to her side, seizing her right arm to steady her. She leaned against him. 'What is it? Are you all right?'

'Althea is alive. A serpent told Paragon that Kennit took up both the women from our ship. He has Althea and Jek. We can get them back.' The words tumbled from her lips as he held her. Clef hurried up, his brow wrinkled with confusion. Brashen tried to wring sense from words. Althea was alive. No. That could not be what she meant. His grief and loss had penetrated to his bones. This offer of joy cut too sharply. He could not trust it. He said the harsh words. 'I don't believe it.'

'I do,' Amber contradicted him. 'The way in which he told me leaves me no doubt. The white serpent told him. It saw Kennit take up two women from our ship. Althea and Jek.'

'The words of a serpent, passed on through a mad ship,' Brashen scoffed. But regardless of his words, hope flared painfully in him. 'Can we be sure the serpent knows what it speaks of? Were they alive when Kennit took them up, do they still live? And even if they do, what hopes do we have of rescuing them?'

Amber laughed. She seized his shoulder in her good hand and tried to shake him. 'Brashen, they are alive! Give yourself a moment to savour that! Once you take a breath and say, "Althea lives" all the other obstacles are reduced to annoyances. Say it.'

Her gold-brown eyes were compelling. Somehow he could not refuse her. 'Althea lives,' he tried the words aloud. Amber grinned at him, and Clef cut an uneven caper about the deck. 'Althea is alive!' the boy repeated.

'Believe it,' Paragon encouraged. 'The serpent has no reason to lie.'

Something dead inside him stirred to life. Perhaps, despite his defeat, she still lived. He had accepted the burden of her death due to his failures. Trying to live with that dereliction had baffled him. This reprieve unmanned him. Something very like a sob shook him, and despite Clef's astonished look, the weeping he had refused at her death suddenly clawed its way out of him. He dashed tears from his eyes, but could not control the shaking that overtook him.

Clef was bold enough to seize his wrist and tug at him. 'Cap'n, don't yer unnerstan? She's alive. Ya don' need ter cry now.'

He laughed suddenly, the sound as painful as a sob. 'I know. I know. It's just –' His words abandoned him. How could he explain to a boy the rush of feelings that accompanied the restoration of his world?

Amber filled in other thoughts for him. 'Kennit would not bother taking her up only to kill her. He has to intend to ransom her. That's the only logical answer. We may not have enough to ransom the *Vivacia* back, nor the power and skill to take her by force, but we have enough to make a respectable offer for Althea and Jek.'

'We'll have to go to Divvytown.' Brashen's mind was racing. 'Kennit believes he sank *Paragon*. If we reappear . . .' He shook his head. 'There's no telling what kind of reception we'd get.'

'He's ne'r seen Amber 'n me. We could take the ship's boat up the slough on a high tide, an' make the offer an' –'

Brashen shook his head as he smiled down on Clef's valiant offer. 'That's a brave thought, but it wouldn't work, lad. There would be nothing to stop them taking the ransom and keeping you both as well. No. I fear there will have to be a fight.'

'You cannot win her back by fighting.' Paragon suddenly broke in. 'Nor will you buy her back with ransom. He cared nothing for your gold when you last encountered him. No. He will not sell her.' The figurehead twisted his scarred visage towards them.

'How do you know?' Brashen demanded.

Paragon looked away from them and his voice went deeper. 'Because I know what I would do. I would fear that she knew my secrets. Such knowledge is too dangerous for Kennit to let her go alive. He will kill her before he allows her to be taken from him. Yet I do not understand why he took her up at all. It would have been far safer for him to let her drown. So there is a piece of the puzzle I do not hold.'

Brashen held his breath. The ship had never before been so open with him. It was almost as if a stranger spoke with Paragon's voice.

Paragon mused on. 'If he keeps her, he will keep her for himself alone, a treasure beyond gold's power to ransom. And there is only one place where Kennit keeps such treasures. Eventually, he will cache her there. Only one place is safe enough to hide that which is too precious even to kill.'

'Could you take us there? Could we lie in wait for him?' Brashen asked.

The ship turned away from them. He hunched his head down on his chest. The muscles stood out suddenly on his back, as if he waged some terrible battle with himself.

'Ser?' Clef began, but Brashen motioned the boy to silence. They all waited.

'We sail on the next tide,' Paragon announced suddenly in his man's voice. 'I will do it. What gold cannot buy, blood may. I will take you to the Key to Kennit's heart.'

TWENTY-SIX

Courtship

'I WANT TO BE let out of here.'

Kennit shut the door behind him and set down the tray. With elaborate calm, he turned back to Althea. 'Is there something you need that you don't have here?' he asked with studied politeness.

'Fresh air and free movement,' she replied immediately. She was sitting on the edge of her bunk. As she stood, she had to catch her balance against the gentle roll of the ship. She kept one hand on the bulkhead to steady herself.

He knit his brow. 'You feel ill treated? Is that it?'

'Not exactly. I feel I am a prisoner, and –'

'Oh, never that. You are my most honoured guest. That you would think otherwise wounds me. Come. Be honest with me. Is there something about me that offends you? Is my appearance frightening? If so, I assure you it is without my intent.'

'No, no.' He watched her struggle to formulate an answer. 'You are a gentleman, and not at all frightening. You have shown me only courtesy and graciousness. But the door was locked when I tried it and –'

'Come. Sit down and eat something, and let us discuss it.' He smiled at her and managed to keep his eyes from roving over her. She was dressed in Wintrow's clothing, and with her hair tied back, the resemblance between the two was even more marked. She had his dark eyes and his cheekbones, but her face had never been marred with a tattoo. She had probably put on Wintrow's clothing believing them less provocative than his nightshirt. Exactly the opposite was true. The rise of her breasts inside Wintrow's shirt stirred his blood to pounding. Her cheeks were tinged pink with her earnestness, yet an unnatural glitter in her eyes showed that she had not completely cast off the soporific he had been giving her. He uncovered her food and set it out for her, just as the ship's boy Kennit had once waited on the pirate Igrot. Strange parallels abounded, he thought to himself. He pushed down the thought and forced himself to keep his voice conversational.

'I've explained my concerns to you. My crewmen are not the genteel society you were reared in, I fear. To allow you the freedom of the ship would be to invite an affront, or even an attack of some kind. Many of my crew are former slaves; some were slaves here on this ship. They spent time in her holds, shackled, cold and filthy. Your family put them there. They do not bear Kyle Haven's kin much fondness. You say you were not responsible for his treatment of them, nor for his treatment of your family ship. But I fear it is difficult to make the crew accept that. Or the ship herself.

'I know that Vivacia is truly what draws you.' He smiled indulgently. 'If you were free to leave this chamber, you would rush straight to the figurehead. For I know you can't believe me when I tell you that Vivacia is gone.' From the corner of his eye, he watched her fold her lips and set her jaw, just as Wintrow did when he was crossed. It almost made him smile, but he kept his demeanour. He shook his head at her gravely. 'But she is, and Bolt would not be kind to you. Would she go so far as to threaten you with physical violence? In all honesty, I do not know. And I would prefer not to find out by experiment.'

He met her flinty stare with his warmest smile. Such black eyes she had. 'Come. Eat something. You'll feel more rational.'

A shadow of uncertainty passed over her face. He recalled that feeling. Igrot, the epitome of coarseness, would, after days of harshness and cruelty, suddenly pendulum back to contrived gentility. For a week, Igrot would speak to him with gentleness, instruct him in etiquette, and bestow on him looks of fatherly tenderness. He would praise him for hard work well done, and predict a bright future for him. And then, without warning, there would come the sudden, harsh grip on his wrist, jerking him close, and the roughness of the man's whiskered cheek sanding Kennit's face as he struggled in his embrace.

He felt suddenly vulnerable. Had he put himself in danger with the woman? He tried to find his open smile again, but could only gaze at her measuringly. She returned the look.

'I don't want to eat anything,' she said flatly. 'You've put something in my food that makes me sleep. I don't like it. I don't like the vivid dreams, nor the way I feel when I try to wake up and I can't.'

He managed to look shocked. 'Lady, I fear you were much more wearied than you knew. I think you have been sleeping off not just the effects of near-drowning in icy water, but months of doubt and fear. It is natural that now you are aboard your family ship, your body relaxes and lets you rest. But . . . wait. Let me reassure you.'

He carefully seated himself on her chair. With fastidious precision, he ate one bite of everything on her plate, and mimed a sip of the wine to wash it down. He patted his lips thoughtfully with her napkin, then turned to smile at her. 'There. Satisfied? No poison.' He cocked his head at her and lifted one eyebrow. 'But why do you suppose I would want to poison you? What sort of a monster do you think I am? Do you fear and hate me so much?'

'No. No, that is . . . I know you have been kind to me. But . . .' She drew in a breath, and he could see that she regretted her foolish accusation. 'I didn't say poison. I just know that I sleep too deeply, and awake still groggy. My head is always heavy; I never feel alert.' Her head swayed a tiny pattern of unsteadiness although her feet remained planted in one spot.

He knit his brows in grave concern. 'Did you strike your head when you fell overboard? Is there a tender spot?'

'No, that is, I don't think so . . .' She set her hands to her head and pressed gravely.

'Allow me,' he insisted, and pushing the chair back, gestured that she should take his place. She moved stiffly and sat very straight as he set his hands to her head. He stood in front of her so she could see his face as his fingertips gently explored her head. With feigned casualness, he loosed her hair, and searched her skull. He frowned to himself. 'Sometimes a blow to the back of the neck or on the spine . . .' he muttered thoughtfully.

Then he stepped behind her and pushed aside the sleek black flow of her hair. He leaned close to her and traced the line of her spine down her neck to her collar. She stood, submissive before him, her head bowed, yet he could feel the thrumming of tension in her muscles. Fear? Apprehension? Perhaps, anticipation? Her hair held a trace of some fragrance, but the shirt smelled of Wintrow. The combination was intoxicating. He let his fingers slowly trail down her spine. 'Any pain?' he asked concernedly. He halted his fingers at the waistband of her trousers but did not remove his hand.

'A little,' she admitted, making him smile at his good fortune. 'In the middle of my back.'

'Here?' He walked his fingers gently up her spine until she nodded. 'Well, then. That might be your problem. Have you been dizzy at all? Fuzzy vision?'

'A bit,' she conceded reluctantly. She lifted her head. 'But I still think that there is more to my sleepiness.'

'I think not,' he contradicted her gently. His hand still rested on her back. 'Unless . . .' he paused until he was certain she hung on his words. 'I am so sorry to suggest this. I am sure you know what I speak of when I mention a bond with the

616

liveship. She senses my moods, and shares her own with me. Perchance, if the ship is angry at you, or hostile towards you, if she wishes you ill – there, I am sorry I even suggested such a thing.'

He had intentionally reinforced her apprehension, but her face had paled beyond his expectations. He would have to be more careful; he did not want to take all the fight out of her. A little struggle might add piquancy to the conquest. He smiled reassuringly. 'Eat something. Regain your strength.'

'Perhaps you are right,' she conceded huskily. He gestured at the food and she turned back to the table. As she took a bite of food from the spoon that had recently been in his own mouth, he felt a sharp jab of lust such as he had never experienced before. The intensity amazed him and it was all he could do to keep from gasping.

The food was excellent, but the pirate watched her eat so intently that she could not relax. Neither, however, could she wake up all the way. She sipped at the wine, and almost immediately her vision doubled. It went away when she blinked, but she was suddenly too tired to eat any more. She set her spoon down. It was so difficult to hold her thoughts still. A word from Kennit could send them drifting away. But there was something important, something she was missing –

'Please,' he said solicitously. 'Try to finish your meal. I know you are feeling unwell, but food is what you need to recover.'

She managed a polite smile. 'I cannot.' She cleared her throat and tried to focus her thoughts. His words kept carrying her ideas away. When he had first come in, there was something very important she had wanted to ask him . . . as important as wanting to get out of the room and speak with her ship. Brashen! Pulling him back into her mind seemed to steady her thoughts. 'Brashen,' she said aloud, and felt she gained strength from just saying his name. 'Captain Trell. Why has he not called on me, or taken me back on board the Paragon?'

'Well. I am not sure what I should say to that.' There was deep concern in Kennit's voice. She had to turn her head to see him, and it made the cabin rock. The dizziness was back. Her tongue felt thick in her mouth.

'What do you mean?'

He took a deep breath and let it out slowly. 'I thought you would have seen it from the water. I am so sorry to tell you this, my dear. The serpents did great damage to the Paragon. I'm afraid the ship went down. We tried to save those we could, but the serpents are so voracious . . . Captain Trell went down with his ship. There was nothing we could do. It was a miracle we were able to save you.' He patted her shoulder gravely. 'I am afraid this ship must become your home again. Now, have no fears. I will take care of you.'

The words swept past her in a flood. Their meaning reached her mind after the sounds of them came to her ears. When she understood what he had said, she shot to her feet. At least, she thought she had. Then she was standing, her hands braced on the tabletop to keep from falling. She hated the dizziness because it was distracting her from a pain so great it could only be death. She could not comprehend its source and then she knew that her world had ended. She had gone on alone without it, or it had somehow left her behind. Brashen. Amber. Clef. Haff. Poor old Lop. Paragon, dear mad Paragon. All dead, on her foolish errand. She'd brought them all to their deaths. She opened her mouth but the agony was such she could not even weep.

'Here, here now,' Kennit was saying, trying to help her to her bunk. She had forgotten how to make her knees bend, and then they suddenly buckled. She half-fell, banging her ribs on the edge of the bunk, and then scrabbled into the bed that had so often been her refuge. 'Brashen. Brashen. Brashen.'

She could not stop saying his name, but her throat was so tight that no sound was coming out. The room swayed around her and she was choking on the word. Perhaps she could die with his name caught in her throat.

Kennit suddenly sat down beside her. He hauled her to a sitting position. She leaned on his chest and he put his arms around her. 'Here. I am here. There, there, there. A terrible shock, I know. How clumsy of me to have told you this way. How alone you must feel. But I am here. Here. Take some wine.'

She sipped at the cup he held to her mouth. She did not want as much as she took, but the cup would not go away and she seemed to have no determination left. Kennit spoke gently to her all the while he tipped the cup against her mouth. When the wine was gone, he set the cup aside and held her. Her face was against the fine lace of his shirtfront. He stroked her hair and rocked her as if she were a child and said nonsense about taking care of her now, and that she would be fine, fine in time, all she had to do was trust him and let him make her feel better. He gently kissed her brow.

He was doing something to her throat. She reached up and discovered he was unbuttoning her shirt for her. She pushed at his hands to stop him, knowing dimly that something was amiss. He set her hands gently aside and smiled sympathetically. 'I know, I know. But you have no need to fear me. Be sensible. You cannot go to sleep dressed. Think how uncomfortable that would be.'

As before, his words pushed her own thoughts away. He undid the little buttons carefully and opened her shirt. 'Lie back,' he whispered, and she obeyed without thinking. He lowered his face to her breasts and kissed them gently. His mouth was warm, and his tongue skilled. For an instant, the dark head bent over her was Brashen's, and it was Brashen's hands unfastening her trousers. But no, Brashen was gone, drowned in the cold dark sea, and this was not right, she could take no comfort here. As warm and gentle as his mouth was, this was not something she wanted. 'No!' she wailed suddenly, and pushed Kennit away. She managed to sit up. The lantern light behind him was dazzling. She squinted at his doubled face.

'It's just a dream,' he told her reassuringly. 'It's all just a bad dream. Don't worry. It's just a dream. Nothing that happens now matters. No one else will know.' For a moment she could see the man. His pale blue eyes were foreign to her. She could not read them. His words washed away her certainty. A dream? She was dreaming this? She closed her eyes against the too-bright light.

Something nudged her shoulder and she fell back limply. Somewhere, someone tugged at her body. She felt the rasp of cloth past her legs. No. She dragged her eyelids up and tried to find sight. His face was inches from her own but she could not make her eyes resolve his features. Then she felt his hand slide up her thigh. She cried out in protest as fingers probed her, and the hand went away. 'Just a dream,' the voice told her again. He pulled up the blanket and snuggled it around her. 'You're safe now.'

'Thank you,' she said in confusion.

But then he bent and kissed her, his mouth going hard on hers, his body pinning hers. When he let her go, she found she was crying. Crying for who? Brashen? Everything was so confusing. 'Please,' she begged him, but he was gone.

It was dark suddenly. Had he blown out the light? Was he really gone? She waited but all was still and silent. It had been a dream . . . She was awake now and safe on her ship. She felt the gentle rolling as Vivacia cut her sure way through the waves. She moved like a waltz, as comforting as the rocking of a cradle and Althea had never even danced with Brashen, and now he was gone. Sobbing shook her, but it was not release. She only grew dizzier and woozier with her crying. Everything was so wrong, and she was too sick to make sense of any of it.

Brashen had needed her to be strong, but she had failed him. He was dead. Dead and gone forever, just as her father was dead and gone forever. She knelt again by her father's body on the deck, and once more felt her whole world taken away from her. 'Why?' she asked of the silence. 'Why?'

The sudden weight on top of her drove the breath from her lungs. A hand clapped over her mouth. 'Quiet, now. Quiet,' the dark voice in her ear warned her roughly. 'Best you be quiet and no one else ever needs to know. Not ever, if you're wise.'

The old nightmare was strong and she was sick. She tried to push him off, she thought she had, but when she rolled over to crawl away, she heard a quiet laugh. Then he was on her back, pushing the blanket aside. She was naked. When had she undressed? Her muscles had no strength. The more she tried to flee, the more her body collapsed. She made a sound, and the hand clapped over her mouth covered her nose as well and pulled her head back. It hurt. She could not breathe, and she was no longer certain where she was or what was happening. Needing to breathe took precedent over all else. She seized the wrist of that hand and wrestled it feebly. Sparks danced behind her eyes as he kneed her legs apart. He was hurting her, her head pulled back so far on her neck, but the pain was not as important as needing to breathe. His hand slipped until it covered only her mouth. She dragged in breath after breath through her nose, and then he thrust suddenly deep into her. She screamed without sound and bucked under him but could not evade him.

Devon had held her so, pressing her down so hard she couldn't breathe. The unwanted memory of that first time rushed back at her. The nightmares merged, and she struggled alone, afraid to cry out for fear someone else would see what was happening to her. She'd be disgraced, her father would know, and it was all her own fault. It was always her fault. She stood before Keffria, crying, and begged her sister to understand, saying, 'I was frightened, I thought I wanted him to do it and then I knew I didn't, but I didn't know how to make him stop.' 'Your own fault,' Keffria hissed at her, too horrified to feel sorry for her wayward sister. 'You led him to it, and that makes it your fault.' The words forced the deed on Althea, made it her own action rather than something done to her, and it all came back to her, sharp as blood, the stabbing impacts of the man's rough body and the panicky need for air, and the desperation of keeping it secret. No one must know. She gritted her teeth and ignored the rough clutch of his hand on her breast. She tried to wake herself up from the nightmare, she tried to crawl away from him, but he rode her and there was no escape. She butted her head hard against wood, half-stunning herself. She began to cry again, defeated. *Brashen*, she tried to say, *Brashen*, because she had promised herself there would never again be any other man, but a hand was still pressed tight on her mouth, and the brutal thrusting went on and on. It was so hard to breathe. The pain was not as frightening as the lack of air. Before it was over, a blackness reached up to drag her down, but she plunged into it willingly, diving down, hoping it was death come to take her.

Kennit turned back and carefully locked the door behind him. His hands trembled. His breath was still quick and he could not seem to calm it. It had been so intense. He had never imagined that any pleasure could be that fierce. He dared not dwell on it, or he would have to go back into the room again.

He tried to think where he would go. He could not go back to his own chamber. The whore would be there, and possibly Wintrow as well. They might see something about him and wonder. He needed to be alone. He wanted to contemplate what he had done, yes, to savour it. And to make sense of it. He could not quite believe he had given in to himself like that. He could not go to the foredeck. Not yet. Bolt would be there, and she might know what he had done.

Linked as she was to him and to Althea, she might have shared it.

That thought put a whole new layer onto the experience. Had she shared it? Had she wanted him to do it? Was that why he had been unable to stop? Was that why it had been so powerful?

He found his foot and crutch had carried him aft. The man on the wheel looked up at him curiously, then went on with his task. It was a fine, clear winter night. The skies were littered with stars. The ship rose to meet each wave and plunged on smoothly. Their escort of serpents flanked them, an undulating carpet of movement and colour in the starlight. He leaned on the railing and looked out over the ship's widening wake.

'You've crossed the line,' a tiny voice at his wrist observed coldly. 'What made you do it, Kennit? Was that the only way to banish the memories finally, by giving them to someone else?'

The whispered questions hung in the night and for a time Kennit didn't answer them. He didn't know the answers. He only knew it had brought him release, even more than sending Paragon and the memories to the bottom. He was free. Then: 'I did it because I could do it,' he said coldly. 'I can do what I want to do now.'

'Is that because you're the King of the Pirates? Igrot used to call himself that sometimes, didn't he? While he did what he wanted to do?'

A rough hand clapped over his mouth. Pain. Humiliation. Kennit pushed the memory aside angrily. It should not exist. Paragon was supposed to have taken it with him. 'It's different,' he said, hearing the defensiveness in his own voice. 'I didn't do anything like that. She likes me. She's a woman.'

'And that makes it permissible?'

'Of course it does. It's natural. It's completely different from what happened to me!'

'Sir?' the man on the wheel queried.

623

Kennit turned to him in irritation. 'What is it?'

'Beg pardon, sir. I thought you spoke to me, sir.' The whites of the man's eyes caught starlight. He looked frightened.

'Well, I didn't. Attend to your task and leave me in peace.' How much had the dolt overheard? It didn't matter. If he became a problem, Kennit could make him disappear. Send him to the side on some premise. A blow to the head, a tip over the railing, and no one would ever be the wiser. Kennit had no one to fear and would fear no one. Tonight, the last of his demons had been banished.

The charm on his wrist was silent, and the lengthening silence became more accusing than words.

Kennit finally whispered. 'She's a woman. That happens to women all the time. They're accustomed to it.'

'You raped her.'

He laughed aloud. 'Scarcely. She likes me. She said I was courteous and a gentleman.' He took a breath. 'She only resisted because she's not a whore.'

'Why did you really do it, Kennit?'

The question was relentless. Did the charm know that the same query rattled endlessly in his own mind? He had thought he was going to stop. He had stopped, until she began crying in the dark. If she had not done that, he would have been able to leave. So it was as much her fault as his. Perhaps. Kennit fumbled towards an answer. He spoke very softly. 'Perhaps so I could finally understand why he did it to me. How he could do that to me, how he could pendulum between kindness and cruelty, between lessons in etiquette and seizures of rage –' Kennit's voice fell away.

'You poor, pathetic bastard,' the charm ground out the slow accusing words. 'You've become Igrot. Do you know that? To defeat the monster, you became the monster.' The tiny voice became even fainter. 'You have only yourself to fear now.'

*　　*　　*

Etta flung down her embroidery. Wintrow looked up from his book, then, with a private sigh, set it upon the table and waited.

'I'm in love with him. But that doesn't mean I'm stupid about him.' Her dark eyes stabbed Wintrow. 'He's with her again, isn't he?'

'He took her a tray of food,' Wintrow suggested. Over the last four days since they had returned to Vivacia, Etta's temper had become ever more uncertain. He supposed it might be her pregnancy, but during his mother's times with child, she had become as content as a fat purring cat. As far as he could remember. This, he supposed, was not much. Maybe it was not her pregnancy. Maybe it was Kennit's odd, distracted behaviour. Maybe it was plain jealousy over the amount of time Kennit was devoting to Althea. He regarded Etta warily, wondering if she were going to throw anything else.

'I suggested she might dine with us. He said she still felt weak. But when I offered to take her tray to her, he said he feared she would do me harm. Does that make sense to you?'

'It seems a contradiction,' Wintrow admitted warily. Conversations like this were dangerous. While she could criticize and even accuse Kennit, any word of disparagement from him was usually met with a tirade of abuse.

'Have you spoken to her?' Etta demanded.

'No. I have not.' He would not admit he had tried. The door had been locked, from the outside. There had been no such lock on his door before. Kennit must have had it put there as soon as he cached Althea. There had been no response to his quiet call.

She stared at him quietly, but he would volunteer no information. He hated to see her like this, so agitated and yet so hurt. Against his better judgement, he asked, 'Have you told Kennit yet?'

She stared at him as if he had said something obscene. She

folded her arms, almost protectively, over her belly. 'The time has not been right,' she said stiffly.

Did that mean Kennit was no longer sharing her bed? If so, where was he sleeping? Wintrow himself was making shift wherever he could. Kennit was not at all concerned that he had given Wintrow's space to Althea. Wintrow had had to ask him twice before he remembered to bring him any of his clothing. The captain was not himself lately. Even the crew noticed, though no one was brave enough to gossip about it yet.

'And that Jek woman?' Etta asked acidly.

He debated lying, but she probably already knew he'd been down there. 'She won't talk to me.'

Kennit had ordered Jek to be held in one of the chain lockers. Wintrow had managed one visit with her. She had met him with a peppering of questions about Althea. When he could not answer any of them, she had spat at him and then refused to respond to any of his queries. She was shackled, but not cruelly. She could sit and stand and move about. Wintrow did not really blame Kennit for that. She was a large and powerful woman. She had a blanket and regular food, and her serpent burns seemed to be healing. Her lot, he reflected, was not much worse than his had been when he was first brought aboard the ship. It was even the same chain locker. It frustrated him that she would not speak to him. He wanted her telling of what had befallen the Paragon; what he had heard from the crew did not quite match what Kennit had told him. The ship would not speak of it to him at all. Bolt only mocked him when he tried to talk to her.

'I tried to talk to the figurehead about her,' he ventured. Etta looked disapproving, but also curious. 'Bolt was even less courteous to me than she usually is. She bluntly says she wants Althea off her decks. She speaks wildly of her, with curses and threats, as if she were . . .' He stopped his thoughts and shook his head, hoping Etta would not demand that he continue. The ship spoke of Althea as if she were a hated rival. Not for Wintrow's attentions, of course. She no longer had any interest in Wintrow.

He sighed.

'You're mooning about the ship again,' Etta accused him.

'I am,' he admitted easily. 'I miss her. Talking to Bolt is more a task than a pleasure. And you have preoccupations of your own these days. I am often lonely.'

'My own preoccupations? *You* are the one who stopped talking to me.'

He had thought her anger was reserved for Kennit. Now he had found his share of it. 'I did not mean to,' he offered cautiously. 'I didn't want to intrude. I thought you would be, uh . . .' He halted. Everything he had assumed about her suddenly seemed silly.

'You thought I would be so busy being pregnant I couldn't think or talk any more,' Etta finished for him. She stuck out her belly and patted it with a fatuous, simpering smile. Then she scowled at him.

'Something like that,' Wintrow admitted. He rubbed his chin ruefully and braced himself for her fury.

She laughed aloud instead. 'Oh, Wintrow, you are such a lad,' she exclaimed. She said the words with such fondness that he looked up in surprise. 'Yes, you,' she went on at his glance. 'You've been fair green with jealousy since I told you, almost as if I were your mother about to forsake you for a new baby.' She shook her head. He suddenly wondered if his jealousy pleased her. 'Sometimes, between you and Kennit, you span the foolishness of all men. Him, with his stiffness and coldness and manly reluctance to admit any need, and you with your great puppy eyes begging for any moment of attention I can spare you. I didn't realize how flattered I was by it until you stopped.' She canted her head at him. 'Talk to me as you used to. I haven't changed, really. There is a child growing inside me. It's not a disease or a madness. Why does it trouble you so?'

He let the words come almost before he knew what he was going to say. 'Kennit is going to have everything: the ship, you, a son. And I will have nothing. You will all be together, and I will always be on the outside.'

She looked stunned. 'And you want those things? The ship. A son. Me?'

Something in her voice set his heart hammering. Did she want him to desire her? Was there in her the slightest warmth for him? He would speak and be damned. If he had to lose everything, then at least let it be said. Even if she banned him from her presence, she would know. 'Yes. I want those things. The ship because she was mine. And you and a son because . . .' His courage failed him. 'Because I do,' he finished lamely and looked at her. Probably with puppy eyes, he cursed himself.

'Oh, Wintrow.' She shook her head and looked away from him. 'You are so very young.'

'I'm closer to your age than he is!' he replied, stung.

'Not in the ways that matter,' she answered inexorably.

'I'm only young because Kennit insists that I am,' he retorted. 'And you persist in believing it as well. I'm not a child, Etta, nor a sheltered acolyte. Not any more. A year on this ship would make any boy a man. Yet how am I supposed to be a man if no one allows me to be one?'

'Manhood is not something that someone allows you,' Etta lectured him. 'Manhood is something a man takes for himself. Then it is recognized by others.' She leaned down to pick up her sewing.

Wintrow stood up. His desperation was but one breath away from anger. Why did she dismiss him with platitudes? 'Manhood is to be taken. I see.' As she straightened in her chair, he put two fingers under her chin and turned her startled face up to his. He would not think. He was tired of thinking. He leaned down and kissed her, desperately hoping that he was doing it well. Then, as he felt her mouth under his, he forgot everything but this daring sensation.

She pulled away from him, her hand flying to cover her mouth. She took a quick breath. Her eyes were very wide. An instant later, sparks of anger kindled in them. 'Is this how you would begin asserting you are a man? By betraying Kennit, a man who has befriended you?'

'That was not about betrayal, Etta. That had nothing to do with Kennit. That was all about what I wished was between us, but is not.' He took a breath. 'I should go.'

'Yes,' she replied in a shaky voice. 'You should.'

He stopped at the door. 'If it were my son you were carrying,' he said huskily, 'I would have been the first to know of it. You would not have had to share such confidences with another man. You would have been sure of my joy and acceptance. I would have –'

'Go!' she commanded him harshly, and he went.

Althea. A faint echo from a beloved past. *You've come to me.*

'No.' She knew her lips moved to form the word but she did not hear her own voice speak. She did not want to awaken. There was nothing good left in wakefulness. She willed herself deeper, past sleep, past unconsciousness, reaching for a place where she was no longer connected to her dirtied body. She reached for a dream in which Brashen was alive and they were in love and free. She reached back in time to the best of times, when she had loved him and not even known it, when they had both worked the deck of a beautiful ship and her father had watched over her with approval. And back again, even further back, to a little girl monkeying barefoot up the rigging, or sprawling on the sun-drenched foredeck to nap and dream with a dreaming figurehead.

Althea! The voice rang with joy. *You have found me. I never should have doubted you.*

Vivacia? Her presence was all around Althea, stronger than a scent, more pervasive than warmth, her reality sweeter than any memory. The being of her ship embraced her. Homecoming and farewell mingled; now, she could die in peace. Althea willed herself to let go but instead Vivacia enveloped her with love and need. Althea could not bear such tenderness. It beckoned her like a light and threatened her resolve. She turned away from it. *Let me go, my dear. I want to die.*

And I with you. For I am made of death, a travesty, an abomination, and I am so weary of being held down here in the dark. Have not you come to free me, come so deep to take me to death?

Vivacia's wonder and welcome horrified Althea. To flee her own life was one thing; to end simultaneously the life of her ship was quite another. Decisions so clear a moment ago wavered. She pushed feebly at the ship, trying to disentangle her awareness from Vivacia's. Coldness crept through her from her abused body, but the more she retreated from life, the deeper she went into her ship.

I am pressed so far down, it is almost like death, the ship confirmed. *Did I know how to let go, I would. She has taken all from me, Althea. No sea, no sky, no wind on my face. If I reach for Wintrow, she threatens to kill him. Kennit cannot hear me at all. She keeps all awareness from me, and mocks me that I long for my humans. I try to die, but I do not know how. Save me. Take me with you when you die.*

No. Althea forbade it firmly. *This, I must do alone. You must go on.* She turned from her ship, but not without pain. She let go.

So this is how it is done. The heart slows, the breath comes shallower and shallower. A poison creeps through your flesh; it will bear you away. But I have no such reprieve from her. I have no true heart of my own, nor will a lack of breath still me. She keeps me here, for she needs what I know. I cannot elude her. Don't leave me here, alone in the dark. Take me with you.

Althea felt her ship tendril through her and cling to her. It reminded her of a child clinging to its mother's skirts. She endeavoured to set the link aside. Vivacia resisted but Althea was firm. The effort of moving away from the ship stirred the embers of her life. Somewhere, her body coughed. A bitter taste rose in her throat. She gasped air past it, and felt her heart labour more doggedly. No. That was not what she wanted. She wanted to let go, not to struggle. Vivacia was making this so hard. *Just let me die. Let me die and become part of you, with my father and those who went before him. Let me continue only in you. There is no joy left in life for me.*

No. You do not want to join me. What I am now is not worth sharing. If you are going to leave life, you must leave it completely, not be trapped here in the dark with me. Please. Let us go together.

Cold closed around her. The ship's resolve was stone: she desired death. Althea was horrified. Despite herself, she clutched at her own life and awareness. Air sighed in and out of her lungs. She could not let Vivacia follow her into death. She must be dissuaded. *Ship, my beautiful Vivacia, why?*

Why? You know why. Because life is ruined for me. There can be no good in any tomorrow.

In a wave, the ship's torment washed over her. The knowledge of her origin and the torment of her doubts plucked at Althea and near tore her loose from her body. Stubbornly she clung to her life now. She would not let her ship end this way. Vivacia clutched at Althea's will and tried to drag them both under. *I am made of death!* she wailed in Althea's soul.

No! No, you are not! Althea asserted it fiercely. She fought the ship's plunge to nothingness, even though to do so thwarted her own desire for oblivion. *You are made of life and beauty, and the dreams of my family for a hundred years. You are made of wind and water and wide blue days. My beauty, my pride, you must not die. If all else fails, if darkness devours all I was, you, at least, must go on.* She opened both heart and mind to her ship, and flooded her with memories: Her father's deep booming laugh, and the proud moment when she had first taken the wheel into her own hands. A sun-swept vista from the crow's nest, the horrific poetry of looking up at waves in a storm. *You cannot end with me,* Althea insisted fiercely. *For if you do, all this dies with you. All this beauty, all this life. How can you claim to be made of death? It was not his death my father poured into you, but the summation of his life. How can you be made of death, when it was inheriting his life that quickened you?*

A stillness beyond silence encompassed them both. Somewhere, Althea was aware, her body failed. Cold and dark clutched at her thoughts, but she clung to awareness, waiting for her ship to surrender and promise to go on.

And you? Vivacia asked her suddenly.

I die, my dear. It is too late for me. My body is poisoned, and so is my spirit. Nothing good is left to me.

Not even me?

Oh, my heart, you are always good in my life. Althea found a truth she had not suspected. *If by living I could restore you, I would. But I fear it is too late to change my mind.* When Althea reached towards her own flesh, she found only lethargy and cold.

Then you condemn to this darkness. For without you, I have not the strength nor the will to fight my way past her and take back my life. Will you leave me here, forever alone in the dark?

All thoughts were stilled for a time.

You have the courage to follow me into death, ship?

I do.

The profound wrongness of that gripped Althea. It was not courage to surrender to that oblivion, conceding the world to those who had wronged them. Sudden shame swept her at her cowardly flight from life. Death could make things stop, but it could not make things right. She abruptly despised herself for surrendering to death while the one who had destroyed her life went on living, for embracing death if it meant leaving her ship in darkness.

Then pick up your true courage, ship, and follow me back into life. She reached for her body, but was suddenly reminded of her time under water. How she had struggled then, trying to claw her way up through icy water. This was worse. The tides of death offered no purchase for her desperate effort. Her own body denied her presence.

Breath was stopped. Her erratic heartbeat felt like an interruption. In the timeless dark, she reached for consciousness, but could not find it. Her sense of her body became ever more tentative as her self came uncentred, and her will to live frayed. Her awareness spread wide and began to vanish in the same limitless dark that trapped Vivacia. Althea searched for more strength to draw on, but found nothing within herself. *Vivacia,* she pleaded. *Ship, help me!*

Silence. Then, *Take all I have left. I hope it will be enough.*

Ship, no, wait!

Althea! Hit the deck now!

Her father's familiar command boomed through her mind. In reflexive response, her body jerked, and she was falling. The wooden deck slammed against her, plank against flesh. Eyes and mouth jolted open with the impact. Tiny lights. Stars caught in a circle of porthole. She lay on her back, gasping like a fish. She rolled onto her side and vomited. The stuff was bitter and choking, clotting in her mouth and spewing from her nose. Reflex took over. She sneezed and then gasped.

Breathe. Breathe. Breathe. Wood to flesh, a distant voice counted the rhythm for her, Vivacia steadied the beating of her heart. The ship was joined to her, but the connection was tenuous and fading fast. Even so, it was not just Althea's body she laboured to heal, but her heart. *Oh, my dear, my dear. I never thought he would do something like this to you. I misjudged him. I misjudged you. I even misjudged myself.* The thought died away.

Althea blinked. She felt terrible. Bile had scoured her throat and mouth and the inside of her mouth. There was a deep ache inside her. She sneezed again. Her body went on working. She voluntarily took a deep breath, then pressed her palms flat to the deck. Pain. It was so wonderful to feel pain again, to feel anything again.

'So, Vivacia,' she croaked. 'We're going to live?'

There was no reply, and only wood beneath her palms.

TWENTY-SEVEN

Key Island

TRUE TO HIS own command, Paragon had sailed with the tide. Not elegantly, not smoothly, but when the rising water lifted him off the sands, the spliced lines raised his patched sails on his raw timber rigging. Half of his depleted crew bore injuries, great or small, and many were disheartened, but they sailed.

Paragon navigated. Amber had not carved his new face yet, let alone his eyes. In a flurry of work, she had roughed out her ambitions, making marks and taking measures. At the ship's urging, she had set that work aside until more essential tasks were finished. The ship sailed blind, and yet not blind, for Amber's eyes were his.

She leaned on the railing, her hair streaming in the wind, and spoke of all she saw. Through her bare hands, she conveyed to him the feel of the islands they passed. It was not sight, but it was her sense of the ocean and the scattered islands that she shared with him. In return, he shared with her. The white serpent paced them, and urged the ship on in his own mad way. Paragon suspected that he sought to awaken the dragons in him, but they were already awake and stirring more strongly every day. Their thoughts mingled with his. The dragons reached through him to Amber, changing him as they did so. They were becoming him, and he was becoming them.

'We fly,' Amber murmured. A stinging rain spattered against her face and soaked her patchy hair. Eyes wide, she stared ahead and with him dreamed these islands as once he had seen them.

'Once, I flew. But these were not islands then, but mountaintops. The Great Inner Wall we called the first range. Beyond it were the Lowlands, and then the Sea Mountains, a restless and rumbling place. Some of the mountains smoked and spat and vomited liquid stone, turning summer to winter and day to dusk. But now they are drowned. The tops of the Sea Mountains are what you call The Shield Wall and Old Woman Island and the like. These islands we thread are the sunken heights of the Great Inner Wall.'

'When you speak of them that way, I can see them in my mind.'

'Mm. But now we need to see them as Igrot saw them, and as Lucto Ludluck saw them. He was Sedge Ludluck's son. Everyone in the Pirate Isles called him Lucky Ludluck. And Kennit was Lucky's son. He seized on that name.' Paragon was silent for a time, his mind roving the years. 'Luck. It was always so important to him.'

Amber spoke cautiously. 'When Althea told me your history, she told me you left Bingtown with Sedge Ludluck.'

'Lucto was Sedge's eldest son. He sailed with his father, but the tension between them was constant. Sedge had the imagination of a rock. He bought cheap and sold dear. That was his sole ethic in life, the Ludluck ethic. He paid his men as little as he could, and changed crew often because he was so callous to them. Their lives were always worth less to him than his cargoes. He never stopped to wonder if life could be different. He didn't fear me because he lacked the imagination to know what I could do.

'Lucto, his son, was different. He was a dreamer, a young man who savoured the pleasures of life. Bingtown customs and manners and traditions stifled him. Lucto was the one who talked Sedge into a little side trade in the Pirate Isles. Lucto had a gift with the lawless folk. He relaxed among them, and in turn, they liked him. He helped the family fortune prosper again. That pleased his father. To reward him, he arranged a good match for the boy with the younger daughter of a very proper Trader. But Lucto had a heart and that heart already belonged to a girl from the Pirate Isles. He was about twenty-two the day his father dropped dead at the bargaining table in Divvytown. Lucto mourned him, but not enough to return to Bingtown and take up the dreary life planned for him. He buried his father ashore, and never went home. The crew was glad enough to follow him, for he liked whisky as much as they did, and dispensed it with an open hand. He was a generous lad, but not as wary as he might have been. He married his Pirate Isles girl and vowed he would live like a king in his own little world.'

Paragon shook his head to himself. 'He traded well and lived large. He built up a secret refuge for himself and his men. He trusted to the good will of his crew to keep his world safe. But there are always hungry men, men for whom a share of good fortune is not enough. And one brought Igrot into Lucky's world. Igrot already had a reputation as the pirate who would do what other men did not even imagine. He came to Lucky with the fable that they would be partners in trade and piracy. Lucto believed him. But in the midst of celebrating their alliance, Igrot turned on him. He imprisoned my father to subdue me, and took Kennit hostage to control me, and we all had to obey him for fear he would hurt the others. He cut out my mother's tongue –'

'Paragon, Paragon.' Amber's voice was gentle but urgent. 'Not your father. Kennit's. Not your mother. Kennit's.'

The ship smiled bitterly into the rain. 'You draw lines that do not exist. It is what you do not understand, Amber. When you speak to Paragon, you speak to the human memories stored in me. When Kennit and I killed myself, it was our suicide.'

'That is a thing I will never understand,' Amber observed in a low voice. 'How can one hate oneself so much that one is willing to murder that self?'

The ship shook his head and rain flew from his locks. 'That is your mistake. No one wants the self to die. I only wanted to make all the rest of it stop. The only way to achieve that was to put death between the world and myself.'

He suddenly turned his blinded face towards an island. 'There. That one.'

'That's Key Island?' Her voice was incredulous. 'Paragon, there's nowhere to land. The island comes straight up out of the water, like a fortress with trees.'

'No, that's not the Key. That is Keyhole Island. From this main channel, it looks like any other island. But if you leave the main channel and circle the island, you'll find an opening in that wall. The island is shaped like a crescent, nearly closed. Until you enter the crescent, it looks like an unpromising inlet. But Keyhole Island cups a bay. Inside Keyhole Island, in the bay is a smaller island. The Key in the Keyhole. On the back side of Key Island, there is a cove with good anchorage. There used to be a wharf and a pier, but I suppose it is long gone. That is where we are bound.'

Brashen was on the wheel. He saw the wide wave of Amber's arm, and nodded that he saw the indicated island. This area of the Pirate Isles was pocked with little islands jutting sharply up from the waves; this one looked no different. Paragon had been very closed-mouthed about what made this one so special. The cynical part of Brashen's soul laughed at him, yet he shouted his command to the crew, and as they shifted the wet sails, turned the wheel to bring the ship around. The steady wind had been favouring them before. Now it would be a long series of wearying tacks to take Paragon where Amber indicated.

The reduced crew was running on the ragged edge. When

the holds had flooded, much of the food had been ruined. Painful injuries, a reduced and monotonous diet, and the strenuous tasks of running the ship with too few men would have been demoralizing enough. But they knew that it was Brashen's intent that they once more face Kennit in battle and they had no interest in rushing to their doom. Their seamanship had grown both grudging and sloppy. Were the ship himself not so eager to sail, the task would have been hopeless.

Clef hastened up to the captain, blue eyes squinted against the rain. The boy seemed mostly recovered from his injuries though he still favoured his scalded arm. 'Sir! Amber says the ship says we're t' watch for an opening on the lee o' the island. It opens t' a bay inside the island, and an island in the bay. That island in turn will hev good anchorage on its windwar' side. Paragon says t' anchor up there.'

'I see. And what then?' The question was rhetorical. He didn't expect Clef to answer.

'He says that if we are lucky, the old woman who lived there will still be alive. We hev t' take her hostage, sir. She's the key t' Kennit himself. He'll trade anything t' get her back. Even Althea.' The boy took a long breath, then blurted out, 'She's Kennit's mother. So the ship says.'

Brashen raised an eyebrow to that. In a moment, he recovered. 'And that is something best kept to yourself, lad. Go tell Cypros to take the wheel for a bit. I'll hear for myself all Amber has to tell me now.'

The rain eased just as Brashen discovered Key Island's anchorage, but even the sun breaking through the day's overcast did little to cheer him. As Paragon had predicted, a sagging pier ran out into the inlet, but time had swayed its pilings and gapped its planks. The rattling of the dropping anchor seemed to shatter the winter peace of the island. But as Brashen looked at the silent forested hillside above the dock, he reflected that such precautions had probably been unnecessary. If people had once lived here, the ramshackle wharf was the only sign that remained of them. He saw no houses. At the end of the wharf, the mouth of an overgrown path vanished beneath the trees.

'Don't look like much.' Clef gave voice to his captain's thoughts.

'No, it doesn't. Still, we're here, so we'll take a look around. We'll go ashore in the ship's boat; I don't trust that pier.'

'We?' Clef asked with a grin.

'We. I'm leaving Amber aboard with Paragon and a handful of men. I'm taking the rest of the crew with me. It will do them good to get off the ship for a time. We may be able to find some game and take on fresh water here. If people once lived here, the island must have provided some of their needs.' He didn't tell Clef that he was taking most of the crew off so they couldn't abscond with the ship while he was gone.

The crew assembled dispiritedly, but brightened at the prospect of going ashore. He had them draw lots for who would remain aboard, and then ordered the rest of them to the boats. Some would hunt and forage, and a picked handful would follow the path with him. While the men readied the boat, he sauntered forwards to Paragon with feigned nonchalance. 'Want to tell me what I should expect?'

'A bit of a hike, to begin with. Lucto did not want his little kingdom to be easily visible from the water. I've Kennit's memories of the way. You'll go uphill, but when you crest the hill and start to go down, be alert. The path goes through an orchard first, and then to the compound. There was a big house, and a row of smaller cottages. Lucto took good care of his crewmen; their wives and children lived here in happier times, until Igrot slaughtered most of them. The rest he carried off as slaves.'

Paragon paused. He stared blindly at the island. Brashen waited. 'The last time I sailed from here, Mother was still

alive. Lucto had perished. Igrot had taken his games too far
and Father died. When we departed, Mother was marooned
alone. That amused Igrot, I think. But Kennit swore he would
come back to her. I believe he would have kept that oath. She
was a doughty woman. Even as battered as she was, she would
have chosen to live. She may still be alive here. If you find
her . . . when you find her, tell her your tale. Be honest with
her. She deserves that much. Tell her why you have come to
take her.' The ship's boyish voice choked suddenly. 'Don't
terrorize or hurt her. She has had enough of that in her life.
Ask her to come with us. I think she may come willingly.'

Brashen took a deep breath and confronted the villainous
aspect of the ship's plan. It shamed him. 'I'll do the best I can,'
he promised Paragon. The best he could. Could the word 'best'
be applied at all to this task, the kidnapping and bartering of
an elderly woman? He did not think so, yet he would do it to
regain Althea safely. He tried to console himself. He would
see that she came to no harm. Surely Kennit's own mother
had nothing to fear from the pirate.

He voiced the largest hole in the plan. 'And if Kennit's
mother is . . . no longer here?'

'Then we wait,' the ship proposed. 'Sooner or later, he will
come here.'

Now there was a comforting thought.

Brashen led his force of armed men up the overgrown trail.
Fallen leaves were thick underfoot. Overhead, branches both
bare and leafy dripped the morning's rain. A sword weighted
one side of his belt, and two of his men carried bows at the
ready. The precaution was more against pigs, whose hoof-tracks
and droppings were plentiful, than against any imagined resistance. From what Paragon said, if the woman still lived, she
likely lived here alone. He wondered if she would be mad. How
long could a person live in complete isolation and remain sane?

They crested the hill and started down the other side. The trees were as thick, though sizeable stumps showed that once this hillside had been logged for timber. The forest had taken it back since then. At the bottom of the hill, they emerged into an orchard. Tall wet grass soaked Brashen to the thighs as he pushed his way through it. His men followed him through the bare-branched fruit trees. Some of the trees sprawled where they had fallen. Others reached to intertwine wet black branches overhead.

But halfway through the orchard, the wide-reaching branches of the trees showed the signs of seasonal pruning. The grass had been trampled down, and Brashen caught a faint whiff of wood-smoke on the air. He saw now what the tangled trees had hidden. A whitewashed great-house dominated the valley, flanked by a row of cottages along the edges of the cultivated lands. He halted and his men stopped with him, muttering in surprise. A barn suggested livestock; he lifted his eyes to isolated sheep and goats grazing on the opposite hillside. This was too much to be the work of one set of hands. There were people here. There would be confrontation.

He glanced back at the men following him. 'Follow my lead. I want to talk my way through this if we can. The ship said she would be willing to go with us. Let's hope that is so.'

As he spoke, a woman carrying a child fled towards one of the cottages and slammed the door behind her. An instant later, it opened again. A large man stepped out onto the doorstep, spotted them, and ducked back inside the cottage. When he reappeared, he carried a woodsman's axe. He hefted it purposefully as he looked up at them. One of Brashen's archers lifted his bow.

'Down,' Brashen commanded in a low voice. He lifted his own arms wide to show his peaceful intent. The man by the cottage did not look impressed. Nor did the woman who emerged behind him. She carried a large knife now instead of the baby.

Brashen reached a hard decision. 'Keep your bows lowered. Follow me, but twenty paces behind me. Unless I order it, no man shoots an arrow. Am I clear?'

'Clear, sir,' one man answered, and the rest muttered doubtful responses. His last effort at peaceful negotiating was still fresh in their minds.

Brashen lifted his arms wide of his sheathed sword and called out to the people by the cottage. 'I'm coming down. I mean no harm. I just want to talk to you.' He began to walk forwards.

'Stop where you are!' the woman shouted back. 'Talk to us from there!'

Brashen took a few more steps to see what they would do. The man came to meet him, axe ready. He was a large man, his wide cheeks tattooed all the way to his ears. Brashen recognized his type from brawls: He would not fight especially well, but he'd be hard to kill. With a sinking certainty, he knew he had no heart for this. He wasn't going to kill anyone while their untended baby wailed inside the cottage. Althea herself would not ask that of him. There had to be another way.

'The Ludluck woman!' he shouted. He wished Paragon had told him the mother's name. 'Lucky's widow. I want to talk to her. That's why we've come.'

The man halted uncertainly. He looked back at the woman. She lifted her chin. 'We're the only ones here. Go away and forget you ever came.'

So she knew the odds were against them. If his men fanned out, they could trap them in the cottage. He decided to push his advantage.

'I'm coming down. I just want to see that you are telling the truth. If she isn't here, we'll go away. We want no bloodshed. I just want to speak to the Ludluck woman.'

The man glanced back at his woman. Brashen read uncertainty in her stance and hoped he was correct. Arms held well away from his sword, Brashen walked slowly towards the house. The closer he came, the more he doubted that they were the only people on the island. At least one other cottage had a well-trodden path to the door and a shimmer of smoke rising from its chimney. A very slight movement of the woman's head warned him. He turned just as a slender young woman launched herself from a tree. She was barefoot and unarmed but her fury was her weapon.

'Raiders. Raiders. Filthy raiders!' she yowled as she attacked with her fists and nails. He lifted his arm to shield his face from her nails.

'Ankle! No! No, stop, run away!' the other woman screamed. She came towards them at a lumbering run, her knife held high, the man only a step behind her.

'We're not slavers!' he told her, but Ankle only came at him more fiercely. He hunched away from her, then spun back to seize her around the waist. He managed to catch one of her wrists. She clawed and pulled hair with the other hand until he captured that, too. It was like hugging an angry cat. Her bare feet thudded against his shins while she bit his shoulder. His vest was thick, but it did not dull the savagery of her attack. 'Stop it!' he shouted at her. 'We're not slavers. I just need to talk to Kennit Ludluck's mother. That is all.'

At the name Kennit, the girl in his arms went limp. He took advantage of the moment to heave her towards the woman with the knife. The woman caught her with one arm and then put her behind her. She held up a hand to halt Axe-man's headlong charge.

'Kennit?' she demanded. 'Kennit sent you here?'

It didn't seem a good time to correct her. 'I've a message for his mother.'

'Liar. Liar. Liar!' The girl hopped up and down with rage, baring her teeth at him. 'Kill him, Saylah. Kill him. Kill him.' For the first time, Brashen realized all was not right with her mind. The man with the axe absently put a hand on her shoulder to calm her. There was something fatherly in the gesture. She stilled, but continued to pull faces at him.

There was no exchange of glances; the woman was obviously thinking, and he now knew who was in charge here.

'Come on,' Saylah said at length, gesturing at the cottage. 'Ankle, you run fetch Mother. Now don't you alarm her, you just say a man is here with a message from Kennit. Go on.' She turned back to Brashen. 'My man Dedge is going to stand here and watch your men. If one of them moves, we'll kill you. Understand?'

'Of course.' He turned back to the men. 'Stay there. Do nothing. I'll be back.'

A few heads bobbed agreement. None of them looked happy about it.

Ankle took off running. Her feet kicked up clods of dirt as she crossed a harvested garden. Dedge crossed his arms on his chest and fixed a glowering stare on Brashen's men. Brashen went with the woman.

The crowing of a rooster broke the grey afternoon, making him jump. He wondered suddenly if he had completely miscalculated. Tilled earth, chickens, sheep, goats, pigs . . . this island could support a substantial settlement. 'Hurry up,' Saylah snapped.

At the door of the cottage, she got in front of him. Once inside, she swooped up a lustily bawling baby and hugged the child to her, still keeping her knife at the ready. 'Sit down,' she ordered him.

He sat, looking curiously around the room. The furnishings spoke of folk with more time than skill. The table, the chairs, the bed in the corner looked like the work of their own hands. Everything was sturdy if not elegant. It was, in its own way, a cosy room. A small fire burned on the hearth and he found himself grateful for the warmth after the chill day. The baby quieted in his mother's arm. The woman began the universal rocking sway of women holding children.

'You have a nice home,' he said inanely.

Her eyes widened in confusion. 'It's good enough,' she said grudgingly.

'And better than many another place we've both been, I'm sure.'

'That's true,' she conceded.

He put on his best Bingtown manners. Small talk while they waited for the lady of the house. He tried to sit as if he had confidence in her hospitality. 'It's a good place to raise a boy. Plenty of room to run free, lots to explore. Healthy as he looks, it won't be long before he's ranging the whole island.'

'Probably,' she conceded, looking down for an instant at the baby's face.

'He's, what, about a year old?' Brashen hazarded a wild guess.

It brought a smile to her face. 'Scarcely.' Saylah gave the baby an affectionate bump. 'But I think he is big for his age.'

A sound outside the door brought her back to alertness, but Brashen dared to hope he had disarmed some of her distrust. He tried to maintain a relaxed posture as Ankle thrust her head into the room. She glared at him and pointed. 'Raider. Liar,' she asserted furiously.

'Ankle, go outside,' Saylah ordered her. The younger woman stepped back, and Brashen heard an odd muttering from outside the door. When an older woman entered, a glance told him that she was the one he sought. Kennit had his mother's eyes. She tipped her head inquiringly at him. She carried a basket on one arm; wide-capped brown mushrooms glistened inside it.

She made an inquiring noise at Saylah, who stabbed towards Brashen with her knife. 'He showed up, coming from the cove, with six men. He says he has a message for you from Kennit. But he asked for you as Lucky's widow, the Ludluck woman.'

The older woman turned an incredulous gaze on Brashen. She raised her brows in an exaggerated gesture of surprise, and muttered something. Her lack of a tongue was not going to make any of this easier. He glanced at Saylah, wondering how best to proceed. Paragon had told him to be honest, but did that mean in front of witnesses?

He took a breath. 'Paragon brought me here,' he said quietly.

He should have been prepared for her shock. Kennit's mother staggered where she stood, then gripped the edge of the table. Saylah uttered an exclamation and stepped forwards to steady the old woman.

'We need your help. Paragon wants you to come with us, to see Kennit.'

'You can't take her off the island! Not alone!' Saylah cried angrily.

'She can bring whoever she wants to bring,' Brashen said recklessly. 'We mean no harm to her. I keep telling you that. I am here to take her to Kennit.'

Kennit's mother lifted her face and stared at Brashen. Her mild blue eyes pierced him with their acuity. She knew that no one who mentioned Paragon came from Kennit. She knew that whether or not he intended harm to her, he would be taking her into danger. Her eyes were the ancient eyes of a martyr, but they met his steadily in a long look. She nodded.

'She says she will go with you,' Saylah needlessly informed him.

Kennit's mother made another sign to the woman. The tattooed woman looked stunned. 'Him? You can't take him with you.'

Kennit's mother drew herself up straight and stamped her foot for emphasis. She made the odd sign again, a turning motion of her hand. Saylah looked hard at Brashen. 'Are you sure she is to bring whoever she wants? That was part of the message?'

Brashen nodded, wondering what he was getting into. It was too dangerous to contradict himself now. He met the older woman's eyes. 'Paragon said to trust you,' he told her.

Kennit's mother closed her eyes for an instant. When she

opened them, they swam with tears. She shook her head fiercely, then turned away from him to the other woman. She gabbled away at her, punctuating her noises with hand signs. The other woman frowned as she translated. 'There are a few things she has to gather. She says you should go back to the cove, and we will come there.'

Could it be this easy? He met the pale blue eyes once more and the woman nodded at him emphatically. She wanted to do this her own way. Very well.

'I'll wait there for you,' he told her gravely. He stood, and bowed formally.

'Hold a moment,' Saylah warned him. She stuck her head out the door. 'Ankle! You put that down! Mother says we are to let him go back to the cove. If you hit him with that, I'll take a belt to you. Now, I mean it!'

Just outside the door, a heavy stick of kindling was flung disdainfully to the earth.

The tattooed woman issued more orders. 'You run tell Dedge that Mother said to let him pass. Tell him all is well. Go on, now.'

Brashen watched the girl run away. If he had stepped out the door, she would have brained him. He felt a cold rush up his spine at the thought.

'She's never been right since they chained her, but she's getting better. She can't help it!' The woman spoke the last words defensively, as if Brashen had criticized her.

'I don't blame her,' he said quietly, and found that he did not. Brashen watched the girl run. She could not have been more than sixteen. Her limp was very pronounced as she hurried up to Dedge. He listened, then acknowledged the message with a nod to Saylah.

Brashen left the cottage with another bow. Ankle made faces at him as he passed them and gesticulated wildly and obscenely. Dedge spoke not a word. His eyes never left Brashen. Brashen gave him a solemn nod as he passed, but the man's face remained impassive. He wondered what Dedge would say or do when he was told Kennit's mother planned to take him with him.

'So. How long do we wait?' Amber asked him.

Brashen shrugged. He had returned immediately to the ship and told her all. He had found his men jubilantly gutting two hairy pigs they had taken with spears. They had wanted to hunt longer, but he had insisted that the entire crew re-board. He would take no chances on any possible trickery.

Paragon had remained silent through his accounting. Amber had looked thoughtful. Now the ship spoke. 'Never fear. She will come.' He turned his face away, as if shamed to let them read his features. 'She loves Kennit as much as I did.'

As if his words had summoned her, Brashen spotted movement on the shaded trail. An instant later, Kennit's mother emerged onto the beach. She looked up at Paragon and her hands flew to her tongueless mouth. She stared at him. Dedge came behind her. He carried a sack over his shoulder; in his free hand he held the end of the chain. At the end of it shambled a wreck of a man, long-haired and pale, thin as a bundle of sticks. The chained man turned his eyes from the light, wincing as if it pained him.

'What is that?' Amber demanded in horror.

'I guess we'll soon find out,' Brashen replied.

Behind them came Saylah, pushing a barrow of potatoes and turnips. A few trussed roosters squawked loudly atop the vegetables. Amber instantly grasped what that was about. She jumped to her feet. 'I'll see what we can spare in the way of trade goods. Are we generous or sparing?'

Brashen shrugged his shoulders. 'Use your judgement. I doubt we have much, but anything they can't make for themselves will probably please them.'

In the end, the entire exchange went easily. Kennit's mother was brought aboard and immediately went to the foredeck. With her, she carried a canvas packet. It was more difficult to get the chained man aboard. He could not manage to climb the ladder; in the end, he had to be hoisted aboard like cargo. Once on deck, he huddled in a heap, moaning softly. His scarred forearms sheltered his head as if he expected a blow at any moment. Brashen guessed it had taken all his strength to get that far. Amber was generous to a fault in her trading, giving them needles and such tools and fasteners as she decided she could spare from the ship's tool chest, as well as clothing and fabric from the sea-chests of their dead crewmen. Brashen tried not to think about buying food for the living with the possessions of the dead, but the crew did not seem troubled by it, and Saylah was delighted. Amber's generosity went far to disarm her hostility and suspicion.

'You'll take good care of Mother?' she asked as they were taking leave.

'Excellent care,' Brashen promised sincerely.

Saylah and Dedge watched from the shore as they departed. Brashen stood on the foredeck by Kennit's mother as the anchor was lifted. He wondered to himself how Kennit would treat those on the island when he discovered how easily they had surrendered his mother. Then he glanced at the old woman. She seemed calm and clear of conscience. Perhaps he could be, as well. He turned to Amber. 'Shift Althea's things from the first mate's cabin into my stateroom. We'll put Mother there. And cut the chains off that poor devil and feed him. Sa only knows why she dragged him along, but I'm sure she had a reason.'

'I'm sure she did,' Amber replied in such a strange tone that Brashen was glad when she hurried off to her tasks.

As the anchor was taken up and Brashen called his commands, Kennit's mother kept her place on the foredeck. The turning of her head, and her nods of approval as the crew moved to their tasks, showed her familiarity with the ways of a ship. As Paragon began to move, she lifted her head and her veined hands ran along his forerail in the little pats of a proud mother on her son's shoulders.

As the wind took Paragon, and he began to slice the waves on his way out of the cove, the old woman unwrapped her package. Brashen rejoined her on the foredeck. Three fat worn books emerged from the yellowed canvas. Brashen knit his brow. 'Ship's logs,' he exclaimed. '"The logs of the Paragon, a Liveship Trader Vessel of Bingtown on the Cursed Shores". Paragon, they're your logs!'

'I know,' the ship replied gravely. 'I know.'

A hoarse voice creaked from behind him. 'Trell. Brashen Trell.'

Brashen turned in consternation. Amber supported the skeletal prisoner from Key Island. 'He insisted he had to speak to you,' the carpenter began in a low voice.

The prisoner spoke over her words. His blue eyes watered as he fixed Brashen with a doleful stare. His head nodded restlessly in an aimless circle. His hands palsied as well. 'I'm Kyle Haven,' he rasped. 'And I want to go home. I just want to go home.'

TWENTY-EIGHT

Dragon Dreams

TINTAGLIA'S WINGS BEAT frantically. Reyn clenched his eyes as the beach rushed up towards him. The wind was gusting horribly; this was going to be bad. As her clawed hind feet came down on the beach in a scrabbling run, her body pitched forwards. She kept hold of him this time, her clenching claws deepening the permanent bruises that rounded his chest. He managed to land on his feet as she released him, and staggered clear as she caught her weight on her front legs. He lurched a few steps further and then sank onto the damp sand, pathetically relieved to be on the ground again.

'Dragons were never meant to land like that,' Tintaglia complained.

'Humans were never meant to be dropped that way,' Reyn responded wearily. Even breathing hurt.

'As I tried to tell you before we began this foolishness.'

'Go hunt,' Reyn responded. There was no hope in conversing with her when she was hungry. No matter what they discussed, it was always his fault.

'I'm not likely to find anything in this light,' she snorted. But as she gathered herself to take flight again, she added, 'I'll try to bring you some fresh meat.'

She always said that. Sometimes she actually remembered to do it.

He didn't try to stand up until he had felt the wind of her wings pass over him. Then he forced himself to his feet and staggered up the beach to the edge of a wood. He followed what had become a weary ritual for him. Wood. Fire. Fresh water if any was to hand, water from his skins if there was not. A sparing meal from his supplies, now woefully low. Then he bundled himself up near the fire and took whatever sleep he could get. Tintaglia was right about her hunting. The short winter day had passed swiftly, and the stars were already starting to show in the sky. It was going to be clear and cold. At least he would not be rained on tonight. Only frozen.

He wondered idly how his people were getting on with the work Tintaglia had outlined for them. Dredging the Rain Wild River was hazardous, not just for the unpredictable winter flow of the waters, but for the acidity of it. Those Tattooed who bought their Rain Wild Trader status with labour would have paid fairly for it.

He wondered if Bingtown had managed to remain united, and if the Chalcedeans had made any other attacks since he had left. Tintaglia had been ruthless in her destruction of their vessels. Perhaps just the threat of a dragon might keep them at bay. In their flight over the Inland Passage, they had seen many Chalcedean vessels, both oared and sailing ships. The number of them convinced him that their plans included something more significant than overwhelming Bingtown. The ships were all moving south. They travelled as Chalcedean war clans did, with one great sailing ship for supplies and several galleys for raiding and fighting. Once, they had flown over a smoking village, possibly a pirate settlement, raided by Chalcedeans on their way south.

Tintaglia often menaced the ships and galleys they passed, taking obvious joy in the panic she created. The steady beat of oars faltered and failed as her shadow passed over their decks. Men on the decks cowered while those in the rigging fled their lofty perches. Once Reyn saw a man plummet from a mast to disappear into the sea.

Every vessel they overflew left him in an agony of doubt. Was Malta held prisoner on board that ship? Tintaglia had loftily assured him that if she had come that close to where Malta was held, she would have sensed her.

'It is a sense you do not possess, and hence I cannot explain it to you,' she added condescendingly. 'Imagine trying to explain a sense of smell to someone who had none. What sounds like an arbitrary, almost mystic ability is no different from smelling apple blossoms in the dark.'

Hope filled Reyn's heart to breaking, and anxiety clawed him daily. Each day that passed was another day of separation from her, but worse, it was another day of Malta in Chalcedean captivity. He cursed his imagination for how it tormented him with images of her in coarse hands. As he bedded down near the fire, he hoped he would not dream tonight. Too often, his dreams of Malta turned to nightmares. Yet trying not to think of her as he was dozing off was like trying not to breathe. He recalled the last time he had beheld her. Heedless of all propriety, they had been alone together, and he had held her in his arms. She had asked to see his face, but he had refused her that. 'You can see me when you say you'll marry me,' he had told her. Sometimes, in his dreams, when he finally held her safe in his arms, he foolishly allowed her to lift his veil. Always, she recoiled in horror and struggled from his embrace.

This would not do. He would never fall asleep with such thoughts.

He recalled instead Malta at a window, looking out over Trehaug while he drew a brush through her thick, black hair. It was like heavy silk in his gloved fingers, and the fragrance of it rose to his nostrils. They had been together, and she had been safe. He slipped one of her honey drops into his mouth and smiled at the sweetness.

He was skimming sleep when Tintaglia returned. She woke

him, as she always did, by adding too much fuel to his fire. In what had become a habit, she lay down beside him, between his body and the night. The curve of her body trapped the warmth of the fire around him. As the logs she had dropped on the fire warmed and then kindled, Reyn dropped deeply into slumber.

In his dream, he once more drew a brush down the shining length of her hair, but this time she stared out over the bow of a ship as he did so. The night was clear and cold. Stars shone sharply above her, piercing the winter night. He heard the snap of canvas in the wind. On the horizon, the black shapes of islands blotted out the stars, glittering stars that swam as she looked up at them, and he knew that tears stood in her eyes. 'How did I ever come to be so alone?' she asked the night. She lowered her head and he felt the warm drip of tears down her cheeks. His heart smote him. Yet, in the next instant his chest swelled with pride in her as she lifted her head once more, her jaw set in determination. He felt her draw a deep breath, and stood with her as she squared her shoulders and refused to surrender to despair.

He knew in that instant that he desired nothing more than to stand at her side. She was no cooing dove of a woman to be sheltered and protected. She was a tigress, as strong as the wind that swept her, a partner a Rain Wild man could depend on. The strength of his emotion rushed out and wrapped her like a blanket. 'Malta, my dear, my strength to you,' he whispered. 'For you are my strength and my hope.'

She turned her head sharply to his words. 'Reyn?' she asked the night. 'Reyn?'

The hope in her voice jolted him awake. Behind him, sand and stone rasped against Tintaglia's scaled body as she stirred.

'Well, well,' she said in a sleepy voice. 'I am surprised. I thought only an Elderling could dream-walk on his own.'

He drew a deep breath. 'It was like sharing the dream-box

with her. It was real, wasn't it? I was with her, as she stood there.'

'It was definitely a sharing with her, and real. But I do not know what you mean by a dream-box.'

'It is a device of my people, something lovers occasionally use when they must be apart.' His words trickled to a halt. He would not mention that such boxes worked because they contained a minute amount of powdered wizardwood mixed in with potent dream-herbs. 'Usually, when lovers meet in such dreams, they share what they imagine. But tonight I felt as if Malta were awake but I was with her, in her mind.'

'You were,' the dragon observed smugly. 'A pity you are not more adept at such dream-travel. For if you were, you could have made her aware of yourself, and she would have told you where to find her.'

Reyn grinned. 'I saw the stars. I know the heading her ship is on. And I know that she was not in pain, nor confined in any way. Dragon, you cannot know how heartening that is to me.'

'Can't I?' She laughed softly. 'Reyn, the longer we are in proximity, the thinner the barriers between us will grow. The Elderlings who could dream-walk were all dragon-friends. I suspect your new-found ability has the same source. Look at yourself. Daily you take on more of my aspects. Were you born with copper eyes? I doubt it, and I doubt even more that they ever glowed as they do now. Your back aches with your growth. Look at your hands, at the thickening of the nails that mimics my claws. Even now, the firelight dances on the sheen of scales on your brow. Even encapsulated in our cocoons, my kind left its marks on yours. Now that dragons are awake and walking in the world once more, those who claim friendship with us will wear the badges of that association. Reyn, if you find a mate, and if you can father children, you will get the next generation of Elderlings.'

Her words took his breath away. He sat up, gaping at her.

She stretched her fearsome jaws wide with amusement and spoke in his mind. *Open your thoughts to me. Let me see the stars and islands that you glimpsed. Perhaps I may recognize something. Tomorrow, we resume our search for a woman worthy to be mother to Elderlings.*

Malta took a few hesitant steps into the darkness. 'Reyn?' she whispered again, her heart hammering. Foolishness, she knew. But it had seemed so real. She had felt his touch on her hair, she had tasted his scent on the air . . . It could not be. It was only her childish heart, yearning after a lost past. Even if she could return to Bingtown, she could never be who she had been. The ridged scar down her forehead was stigma enough, but to it would be added rumours and gossip. Reyn himself might still want her, but his family could not permit their marriage. She was a ruined woman. The only socially acceptable end for her in Bingtown was to live simply and out of sight. She set her jaw and let anger be her strength. She would never go back to that. She would churn her way forwards against a tide of misfortune, and build a new life for herself. Dreaming of the past could only cripple her with longing. Resolutely she set thoughts of Reyn aside. Coldly she assessed the only tools that remained to her. Her body and her wits were hers; she would use them.

She had crept out on the night deck to be alone, away from the two men who currently plagued her life. Each continued his obstinate efforts to possess her body. Captain Red fancied himself as her instructor in carnal pleasure; the Satrap saw her body as an infant might see a sugar-sop, as a physical consolation for times of duress. The avid gallantries of the one and the pawing pleas of the other left her feeling grimy and jaded. Each must be discouraged, but not completely denied all possibility. Men, she had discovered, were ruled by their imaginations in that regard. As long as Captain

Red and the Satrap fancied that she might give in, they would both keep striving to impress her. From Captain Red she was able to extract the small liberties that made life tolerable: she could walk the deck alone, dine at his table, and speak her mind almost freely. From the Satrap, she gleaned information from his bragging tales of his glories at court. It was information that she hoped to use to buy their freedom from Kennit.

For she was determined to ransom Cosgo as well as herself. Somehow, during her captivity with the Satrap, he had come to be her possession. As annoying as he was, she felt a proprietary sense towards him. She had kept him alive and intact. If anyone was going to profit from his value as a hostage, it would be Malta Vestrit. Satrap Cosgo would be the key to her survival in Jamaillia. When the Satrap was released to his Jamaillian ransomers, she would go with him. By then, she would be indispensable to him.

She summoned her courage once more. She dreaded these sessions with Cosgo. She left her hair, her last aspect of beauty, long and loose as if she were a girl still, went to his small chamber and tapped.

'Why bother?' he called out bitterly. 'You will enter whether I wish your company or not.'

'That is true, lordly one,' she conceded as she entered. The room was dark, save for a guttering lamp. She turned up the wick and sat down on the foot of his bed. The Satrap sat hunched, his knees drawn up to his chin, on the pillow. She had known he would be awake. He slept by day, and brooded by night. As far as she could determine, he had not left his cabin since they had come aboard. He looked very young. And very sulky. She mustered a smile. 'How are you this evening, Magnadon Satrap?'

'Just as I was last night. Just as I shall be tomorrow night. Miserable. Sick. Bored. Betrayed.' This last he uttered while staring at her accusingly.

She did not react to it. 'Actually, you appear to be much better. But it is stuffy in this little room. There is a cool breeze outside. I thought you might wish to join me in a turn around the deck.'

The Satrap's seasickness had finally passed. In the last two days, his appetite had increased. The plain ship's fare she brought to him had not changed, but he had given up complaining about it. Tonight, his eyes were clear for the first time since she had known him.

'Why should I?'

'For variety, if nothing else,' she suggested. 'Perhaps the Lordly One would enjoy –'

'Stop it,' he growled in a voice she had never before heard him use.

'Magnadon Satrap?'

'Stop mocking me. Lordly this and Mighty that. I am nothing of that, not any more. And you despise me. So stop pretending otherwise. It demeans us both.'

'You sound like a man,' she exclaimed before she could stop herself.

He gave her a baleful glance. 'What else should I sound like?'

'I spoke without thinking, my lord,' she lied.

'You do that frequently. So do I. It is one of the few things I enjoy about you,' he retorted.

She was able to continue smiling by reminding herself that he belonged to her. He shifted about on his bed, then lowered his feet to the floor. He stood uncertainly. 'Very well, then,' he announced abruptly. 'I will go out.'

She covered her surprise by stiffening her smile. She found a cloak and put it around him. The garment hung on his diminished body. She opened the door and he preceded her, keeping one hand on the wall, and surprised her by taking her arm. He walked like an invalid, with small hesitant steps, but she resisted her impulse to hurry him. She opened the outer door for him, and the crisp winter wind blew past them. He gasped, and halted.

She thought he would go back then, but he went doggedly on. On the open deck, he hugged his cloak tightly to himself as if it were far colder than it was. He looked all around and up as well before stepping away from the ship's house. In his old man's shuffle, he toddled towards the railing, to stare out over the wide water and up at the night sky as if it were a foreign landscape. Malta stood beside him and said nothing. He was puffing as if he had just run a race. After a time, he observed aloud, 'The world is a wide and savage place. I never fully realized that until I left Jamaillia.'

'Magnadon Satrap, I am sure your nobles and your father felt the need to protect the heir to the Pearl Throne.'

'There was a time,' he began hesitantly. A line furrowed his brow. 'It is like recalling another life. When I was a boy, I used to ride and hawk. One year, when I was eight, I caused a stir by entering the Summer Races. I raced against other boys and young men of Jamaillia. I did not win. My father praised me, all the same. But I was devastated. You see, I had not known I might lose . . .' His voice trailed away but Malta could almost see the intentness of his thought. 'They neglected to teach me that, you see. I could have learned it, when I was younger. But they took away the things I did not succeed at, and praised my every success as if it were a wonder. All my tutors and advisors assured me I was a marvel, and I believed them. Except that I began to see the disappointment in my father's eyes. When I was eleven, I began to learn the pleasures of men. Fine wines, cunningly-mixed smokes and skilled women were gifts to me from nobles and foreign dignitaries, and I sampled them all. And, oh how I succeeded with them. The right smoke, the right wine, the right woman can make any man brilliant. Did you know that? I didn't. I thought it was all me. Shining like the high jewel of all Jamaillia.' He turned abruptly away from the sea. 'Take me back in. You were wrong. It is cold and wretched out here.'

'Of course, Magnadon Satrap,' Malta murmured. She offered him her arm and he took it, shaking with chill, and leaned on her all the way back to his chamber.

Once inside the room, he let the cloak fall to the floor. He climbed into his bed and drew his blankets closely around himself. 'I wish Kekki were here,' he shivered. 'She could always warm me. When no other woman could stir me, she could.'

'I shall leave you to rest, Magnadon Satrap,' Malta hastily excused herself.

His voice stopped her at the door. 'What is to become of me, Malta? Do you know?'

The plaintive question stopped her. 'My lord, I do not know,' she admitted humbly.

'You know more than I. For the first time since I became Satrap, I think I understand what Companions of the Heart are supposed to do . . . not that many of mine did it. They are to know the details of that which I have no time or opportunity to learn. And they are to be truthful. Not flattering, not tactful. Truthful. So. Tell me. What is my situation? And what do you advise?'

'I am not the Companion of your Heart, Satrap Cosgo.'

'Absolutely true. And you never will be. Nonetheless, you will have to serve as one for now. Tell me. What is my situation?'

Malta took a deep breath. 'You are to be a gift to King Kennit of the Pirate Isles. Captain Red thinks that Kennit will ransom you to the highest bidder, but even that is not assured. If Kennit does, and coin is all that you can bring him, then it will not matter to him if the buyer is your enemy or your ally. Captain Red has urged me to discover who among your nobles would offer the most for you.'

The Satrap smiled bitterly. 'I suppose that means they already know which of my enemies will bid for me.'

'I do not know.' Malta thought hard. 'I think that you should consider which of your allies might offer a fat reward for your life. When the time comes, you should write a letter asking them to ransom you.'

'Foolish child. That is not how it will be done. I will negotiate my own ransom with Kennit, issue him letters of credit, and insist that he provide me passage back to Jamaillia. I am the Satrap, you know.'

'My Lord Satrap,' she began hesitantly. She firmed her voice. Truthfulness he had asked for. She would see what he did with it. 'Others see your situation differently. Kennit will not accept letters of credit from you or anyone else. He will want your ransom in cold coin, and he will see it before he releases you. And he will not care who it comes from: nobles loyal to you, or those who do not wish you to return to Jamaillia, New Traders, Chalcedeans who might use you as a hostage – he will not care. That is why you must think, and think well for yourself. Whose fidelity is unquestionable? Who has both loyalty to you, and wealth enough to buy your freedom?'

The Satrap laughed. 'The answer to that is frightfully simple. No one. There is no noble whose loyalty is unquestionable. As to wealth, why, those who are wealthiest have the most to gain by my being lost. If I perish, someone must become Satrap. Why use your wealth to buy the occupant of a throne when the throne itself could be yours?'

Malta was silent. 'Then no one will ransom you?' she asked quietly.

He laughed again, and it was even more brittle. 'Oh, assuredly, I shall be ransomed, and you alongside me. We will be ransomed by those who most need me to disappear, without witnesses.' His rolled to face the wall. 'We will be ransomed by those who cheered most loudly as my ship departed from Jamaillia. By those who conspired to send me off on this ill-fated adventure. I am not stupid, Malta. The Bingtown Traders were correct: there was a conspiracy,

662

and it must have involved nobles and Chalcedean diplomats and even New Traders. They bit the hand that fed them, for each thought that once that hand was removed, each could claim the lion's share of the meat.'

'Then they will be squabbling over that division even now,' Malta hazarded. 'It all comes down to a bargain. Grandmother always said, "Look to see who benefits the most."' She knit her brows, ignoring the tugging of skin around her scar. 'She told me that when you want to cut your way into a bargain that others are striking, you must look for the one who is benefiting the least. Shore up his interest, and he will take you as a partner. So. Who benefits the least by your being removed from the throne?'

'Oh, come!' He sounded disgusted as he rolled back to face her. 'This is degrading! You would reduce my life and the fate of the throne to the squabbling of merchants.' He snorted in disdain. 'But what else should I expect from a Trader's daughter? Your whole life has been buying and selling. No doubt your mother and grandmother saw your brief beauty as a thing to be bartered away. Trader Restart certainly did.'

Malta stood taller. She did not speak until she was sure she had control of herself. Her armour, she decided, was to be impervious to such taunts. 'Merchants broker trade goods. Satraps and nobles broker power. You, noble Magnadon, deceive yourself if you believe there is a great difference in the machinations.'

He seemed unimpressed, but he did not challenge her conclusion. 'Well, then, to answer your question, all benefit from my absence. All the nobles with money or influence, anyway.'

'Then that is the answer. Consider those without money or influence. There are your allies.'

'Ah, such wonderful allies. With what will they buy my freedom? Sticks and stones? Dung and dust?'

'Before you consider how they will buy your freedom, you

must consider why it would profit them. Make them see it is to their advantage to free you, and they will find the means.' She loosened her cloak and sat down on the end of his bed again. The Satrap sat up to face her. 'So, think now.'

The Satrap of all Jamaillia leaned his head back against the wall. His pallid skin and the dark circles under his eyes made him look more like a grievously ill child than a troubled ruler. 'It's no use,' he said hopelessly. 'It is all too far away. No one in Jamaillia will rouse to my cause. My enemies are too many. I will be sold and slaughtered like a feast-day lamb.' He rolled his eyes to stare at her. 'You see, Malta, not everything can be solved with your Trader's ethic of buying and selling.'

An idea suddenly blossomed in her mind. 'But what if it could, Magnadon Satrap?' She leaned forwards tensely. 'If, with my Trader's ethic, I can save you and your throne, what would it be worth to me?'

'You cannot, so why even speculate?' He waved a lax hand at her. 'Go away. Your idiotic idea of a stroll on a freezing deck has wearied me. I will sleep now.'

'You will not,' she retorted. 'You will lie awake and pity yourself. So, instead of that, rouse yourself to my challenge. You say I cannot save you. I think I can. I propose a wager.' She lifted her chin. 'If I save you, I am saved alongside you. You will give me an appointment to . . .'

'Oh, do not ask to be a Companion of my Heart. That would be too humiliating. As well ask me to wed you.'

A spark of anger flashed in her. 'I assure you, I would not so humble myself. No. You will appoint me and my family as your representatives in Bingtown and the Rain Wilds. You will recognize Bingtown and the Traders there as an independent entity. To my family, to the Vestrits will go the exclusive right to represent Jamaillian interests there.' A slow smile dawned on her face as the full brilliance of her idea shone in her mind. With such an accomplishment, she could return to Bingtown. No scar or shame would be remembered next to such a coup.

It would be the ultimate bargain, the best trade that any dealer had ever struck. Even her grandmother would have to be proud of her. Even Reyn's family might . . .

'That is a ridiculous wager! You want all of Bingtown for yourself!'

'Is it? I'm offering you both your throne and your life in exchange for it.' She cocked her head. 'Bingtown's independence is virtually a reality anyway. You would only be recognizing what already exists, and making it possible for Jamaillia and Bingtown to continue on friendly terms. Losing this wager would only mean that you had to take what is a wise course of action in any case.'

He stared at her. 'So I have heard it argued before. I am not sure I agree with it. But how will you regain my freedom and my throne for me?'

'Show me my profit, and *I* will find the means.' She smiled. 'Agreed?'

'Oh, agreed,' the Satrap snapped impatiently. 'It is a ridiculous wager anyway, one that you cannot possibly win. I may as well agree to it.'

'And you will cooperate with me to help me win it,' she pressed.

He scowled. 'And how must I do that?'

'By striving to present yourself to our captors as I direct you to, and by agreeing with what I shall tell them.' Excitement was building in her. The fatalistic defeat she had felt earlier in the evening had evaporated. So all she had left to her fortune was her wits. Perhaps that was all she had ever needed.

'What do you intend to tell them?'

'I am not sure of that just yet. But you started me thinking when you said there was no one in Jamaillia who would profit by returning you to power.' She chewed her lip thoughtfully. 'I think we must discover a way by which the pirates themselves will profit most by returning you to power.'

TWENTY-NINE

Kennit's Women

SHE WHO REMEMBERS and Maulkin did not argue. Shreever almost wished they would. That would have meant that at least one of them had reached a decision. Instead, they discussed endlessly what had happened, what might happen and what it might mean. In the tides since Maulkin's tangle had refused to kill the other ship, the serpents had trailed after Bolt and waited to see what would happen next. Bolt herself had barely spoken to them, despite the nagging queries of She Who Remembers. The silver creature seemed caught in some dilemma of her own. Chafing under the indecisiveness, Shreever's temper frayed like an outgrown skin. With every changing tide, she felt a sense of loss. Time flowed, leaving the serpents behind. She was losing strength and body weight. Worse, she could not keep her thoughts straight.

'I am dwindling,' she said to Sessurea as she swayed with the sea. They were anchored beside one another for the night. There was a nasty bit of current here; it stirred the silt constantly, making the water murky. 'Tide after tide, we follow this ship. To what end? Maulkin and She Who Remembers swim always in her shadow, and speak only to one another. The toxins they waste on the ship's hull taste strange, and bring us no prey. Repeatedly, they say we must be patient. I have patience, but what I have lost is endurance.

By the time a decision is reached, I will be too weak to travel with the tangle. What does Maulkin wait for?'

Sessurea was silent for a time. When the blue serpent finally spoke, there was more wonder than rebuke in his tone. 'I never thought to hear you criticize Maulkin.'

'We have followed him long, and I have never questioned his wisdom,' she replied. She lidded her eyes briefly against the wash of silt. 'I wish he would lead us again. Him I would follow until my flesh could no longer hold my bones together. Now, however, he defers, both to She Who Remembers, and to the silver ship. I accept the wisdom of She Who Remembers. But who is the silver creature that we should tarry to do her bidding while our cocooning season escapes us?'

'Not who is the silver creature. What?' Maulkin materialized suddenly alongside them. His false-eyes gleamed faintly in the murky water. He anchored himself, then wrapped a lap of coil around them both. Gratefully, Shreever eased her grip on the rock. With Maulkin holding her, she would rest more fully.

'I am tired,' she apologized. 'I do not doubt you, Maulkin.'

Their leader spoke gently to her. 'You have not doubted me, even when I have vacillated. You have paid a price for that loyalty, I know. I fear that the price we all pay for my indecision is too high. She Who Remembers has already pointed this out to me. Our tangle is mostly male. It will do little good for us to cocoon and hatch if we have delayed so long that no queens rise.'

'Delayed?' Shreever asked quietly.

'That is what we debate. Every tide of lingering weakens us. Yet, without a guide, there is no sense in forging on, for this world does not match our memories. Not even She Who Remembers is sure of the way. We need Bolt's guidance, so we must wait for her. As weak as we have become, we will need her protection as well.'

'Why does she make us wait?' Sessurea, blunt as always, bit to the spine of it.

Maulkin made a disgusted sound, and a waft of toxin drifted from his mane. 'To that, she has given us a score of answers, and none. She Who Remembers thinks the silver ship is more dependent on the fickle aid of humans than she will admit. As I told you, it comes down to what she is. She insists she is a dragon. We know she is not.'

'She is not?' Sessurea thundered in dismay. 'What is she, then?'

'Why does that matter?' Shreever moaned. 'Why cannot she simply help us, as she said she would?'

Maulkin spoke soothingly, but his words were alarming. 'To help us, she will have to beg help of the humans. While she insists she is all dragon, I do not think she can humble herself to do that.' He spoke slowly. 'Before she can help us, she must accept what she is. She Who Remembers has been urging her to do that. She Who Remembers knows much of one two-legs aboard the ship. The wintrow aided her to escape the Others. In touching him, she knew him. He was full of knowledge of a ship, thoughts that She Who Remembers did not grasp fully at the time. Now she begins to piece it all together. We seek to awaken the other portion of the ship, to give her strength to emerge again. It is a slow process, stinging such a creature awake. She has been both weak and reluctant. But of late, she has begun to stir. We may yet prevail.'

Kennit balanced the tray in one hand and turned the key in the lock with the other. It was not easy, for a fine trembling was ruining his dexterity. A night and a day had passed since he had last entered this room. Since then, he had not slept and barely eaten. He had avoided the foredeck and the figurehead, avoided Etta and Wintrow. He could not completely recall how he had spent those hours. For some of them, he had been aloft. Sorcor had recently presented him with a leg-peg that had a groove cut in the bottom of it. This was the first time he had completely tested it, and he had been delighted. From the crow's nest, he could look out over his entire domain. The serpents frolicked in the crested waves about his ship and the wind sped him on. With the wind in his face, he had dreamed, savouring repeatedly his time alone with Althea Vestrit. It had not been discipline and forbearance alone that kept him away from her. Anticipation was a pleasure in itself. He had waited until his passion was once more at full tide before coming here again. Now he stood outside her door, shivering with longing.

Would he take her again? He had not yet decided. If she was wakeful enough to accuse him, he intended to deny everything. He would be so gracious, so concerned for her fears. There was such power in controlling another's reality. Never before had he realized that. 'Such a terrible nightmare,' he whispered in sham sympathy, and felt the creeping grin that threatened to overpower his face. He straightened his features and tried to calm himself. Several deep breaths later, he opened the door and stepped into the dimness.

The fading winter afternoon dimly lit the room. She huddled under the covers on the bunk, deeply asleep. The acid stink of vomit was thick in the small room. He leaned on his crutch as he shut the door, wrinkling his nose against the stench. That would never do; such a smell was very unappealing. It ruined everything. He would have to give her an extra dose of the poppy and mandrake sedative, and send in the ship's boy to give the room a good scrubbing while she slept. Bitterly disappointed, he set the tray down on the table. Her full weight hit him between the shoulders. He went down, tray, crutch, food, all falling with him in a clattering mess. His head struck the table edge as he fell. Her hands clutched his throat. He twisted around, tucking his chin tight to his chest to keep her from getting a good strangle. She had a knee in the small of his back, but as he rolled she fell with him. Her reflexes were slow, dulled by the drugs. If he had still had two legs, she would not have had a chance against him. As it was, he managed to grip her wrist for an instant before she jerked away from him. She scrabbled to her feet, panting and swaying and backed away from him in the small room as he came to his hands and knee. Her eyes were wide and black. His crutch had fallen out of reach. He edged towards it.

'You bastard,' she panted raggedly. 'You heartless beast!'

He feigned bewilderment. 'Althea, what has come over you?'

'You raped me!' she grated hoarsely. Then, her words rising to a shout, uncaring of who heard, 'You raped me. You killed my crew and burned my ship. You killed Brashen! You imprisoned Vivacia! It's all your doing!'

'You make no sense. My dear, your mind is unsettled. Calm down! You don't want to shame yourself before the whole crew, do you?'

He saw her glance about for a weapon. He had misjudged how dangerous she was. Despite the residue of drug that she fought, her muscles knotted convulsively. He knew the look of murder; he had seen it often enough in his own mirror. He lunged for his crutch, but in the next instant, she sprang not towards him, but to the door. She worked the latch clumsily, then jerked the door open, colliding with the jamb as she reeled out. He saw her strike the opposite wall, catch herself, and then stagger up the companionway.

The figurehead. She was trying to get to the figurehead. He got his crutch under his arm, caught at the table's edge and pulled himself to his feet. She would get a surprise if she got as far as the foredeck. There would be no Vivacia to beseech for aid. He was tempted to let her go, but he could not have her ranting and raving to his crew. What if Wintrow or Etta heard her?

He reached the door and looked out. Althea had slowed. She clung to the wall, stumbling doggedly on. Her dark hair hung in a lank curtain about her face. She was dressed in Wintrow's clothing, soiled now with spilled food and vomit. She must have awakened, dressed, and then huddled there, waiting for him. Quite a plan, for as much poppy as he had given her. He almost admired her. He'd have to increase the dosage.

The silhouette of a crewman appeared in the doorway at the end of the hall. Kennit raised his voice in a command. 'Detain her. Bring her back to her room. She is not well. She attacked me.'

The figure took two steps into the darkened companion-way, and Kennit suddenly saw his error. The crewman was Wintrow. 'Aunt Althea?' he asked incredulously. He offered her a steadying arm, but she disdained him. He doubted that she recognized Wintrow. Instead, she lifted her arm to point a shaking hand at Kennit.

'He raped me!' She flung back her head to peer at the lad through her draggled hair. 'And my ship is locked down deep in the dark. I'm drugged. I'm sick. Help me. Help her.' Her words ran down with her strength. She sagged against the wall and slid down it while Wintrow stood transfixed in horror. Her head swayed like a poisoned cat's. To Kennit's dismay, another crewman had arrived. Then, worst of all, he heard Etta's voice behind him.

'What did that bitch say?' she demanded furiously.

Kennit turned quickly to face her. 'She's ill. She makes no sense. She attacked me.' He shook his head. 'The loss of her companions seems to have driven her mad.'

Etta's eyes went very wide. 'Kennit, you're bleeding!' she exclaimed in horror.

He lifted a hand to his brow and his fingers came away scarlet. He had struck his head harder than he thought. 'It's nothing. I'll be fine.' He composed himself and spoke in a voice of both command and concern. 'Wintrow. Be cautious but gentle with her. She doesn't know what she's saying. Watching Paragon burn has turned her mind.'

'I'm sane enough, you raping, murdering bastard!' Althea

671

snarled. Her words ran together. She thrashed about, trying to stand.

'Aunt Althea!' Wintrow was shocked. Kennit could see the horror in the boy's face. He crouched down and helped the woman to stand. 'You need to rest,' he offered her sympathetically. 'You've had quite a shock.'

She held onto his shoulders and looked across at Wintrow as if he were an insect. He stared back at her in consternation. But for their expressions, they looked very alike. It reminded Kennit of the old depictions of Sa, male and female face to face on the ancient coins. Then Althea turned her look of disgust on Kennit. He saw her decide, and he was ready for her shambling charge. He thought he could avoid her dazed attack, but he did not have to try. With a furious screech, Etta sprang out in front of him.

The whore was larger than Althea, physically alert and more experienced in fighting. She knocked the Bingtown woman down effortlessly and then straddled her, pinioning her. Althea gave a full-throated roar of fury and struggled, but Etta held her easily. 'Shut up!' the whore shrieked at her. 'Shut your lying mouth! I don't know why Kennit bothered saving your useless life. Shut up or I'll break your teeth.'

Kennit stared in horrified fascination. He had seen women fight before; in Divvytown, it was so common a sight as to be unremarkable, but he had always considered it a tawdry spectacle. Somehow, this humiliated him. 'Etta. Get up. Wintrow. Put Althea back in her room,' he commanded.

Althea gasped her words from beneath Etta's weight. 'I'm a stupid bitch? He raped me. Here, on my own family ship! And you, a woman, defend him?' She rolled her head and stared up wildly at Wintrow. 'He's buried our ship! How can you look at him and not know what he is? How can you be so stupid?'

'Shut up! Shut up!' Etta's voice slid up the scale, cracking on hysteria. She slapped Althea, an open-handed blow that rang in the confined companionway.

'Etta! Stop that, I said!' Kennit cried in horror. He seized the whore's upraised hand by the wrist and tried to drag her off Althea. Instead, Etta only struck her with her other hand, and then, to Kennit's complete mystification, burst into tears. Kennit lifted his eyes to find half a dozen sailors crowding the end of the hall, staring in open-mouthed wonder at the spectacle. 'Separate them,' he snapped. Finally, several men moved forwards to do his bidding. Wintrow took Etta by the arm and pulled her from Althea. For a wonder, she did not fight him, but allowed him to hold her back. 'Put Etta in my chamber until she calms herself,' he directed Wintrow. 'You others, put Althea back in her room and fasten the lock. I will deal with her later.'

Althea's brief struggle with Etta had consumed her resistance. Her eyes were open, but her head lolled on her neck as two men dragged her to her feet. 'I'll ... kill ... you,' she promised him gaspingly as they hauled her past him. She meant it.

He drew his handkerchief from his pocket and dabbed at his brow. The blood on the cloth was darker; the cut was clotting. He probably looked a sight. The prospect of confronting Etta did not appeal to him, but it could not be avoided. He would not walk about with blood dribbling down his face and spattered food on his clothing. He drew himself up straight. As the crewmen returned from locking Althea up, he managed a wry smile for them. He shook his head conspiratorially. 'Women. They simply do not belong aboard a ship.' One crewman returned him a grin, but the others looked uneasy. That was not good. Was Etta that great a favourite with the crew? He'd have to do something about that. He'd have to do something about this whole situation. How had it become so untidy? He straightened his rumpled jacket and brushed food from the sleeve.

'Captain Kennit, sir?'

He looked up in annoyance at yet another rattled deckhand. 'What is it now?' he snapped.

The man licked his lips. 'It's the ship, sir. The figurehead. She says she wants to see you, sir.' The sailor swallowed, and then went on, 'She said, "Tell him right now. Now!" No disrespect intended, sir, but that was how she spoke, sir.'

'Did she?' Kennit managed to keep his voice coolly amused. 'Well, you may tell her, with no disrespect intended, that the captain has another matter to tend to, but that he will be with her presently. At his earliest convenience.'

'Sir!' The man fumbled for a way to begin a desperate protest. Kennit speared him with a cold gaze. 'Yes, sir,' he conceded. His step dragged as he departed.

Kennit did not envy him his errand, but he could scarcely let the ship see him like this, let alone have a common seaman see him dash to obey the ship's summons. He lifted a hand to smooth his moustache. 'Slow. Calm. Steady. Take control of it again,' he counselled himself.

But a tiny voice spoke from his wrist in mocking counterpoint. 'Swiftly. Messily. It all falls to pieces. In the end, dear sir, you will not even have control of yourself. No more than Igrot did when he met his fate at your hands. For when you became the beast, little Kennit, you doomed yourself to share the beast's end.'

'Etta. Etta, please,' Wintrow begged her, helplessly torn. He should be seeing to Althea. She had appeared both sick and deranged, but how could he leave Etta like this? She paid no attention. She wept on, sobbing into the pillows as if she could not stop. He had never seen anyone weep this way. There was a terrible violence to her gasping sobs, as if her body sought to purge herself of sorrow, but the misery went too deep for tears to assuage.

'Etta, please, Etta,' he tried again. She did not even seem to hear him. Timidly, he patted her on the back. He had dim memories of his mother patting his little sister so, when Malta was so immersed in a tantrum that she could not calm herself. 'There, there,' he said comfortingly. 'It's all over now. It's all over.' He moved his hand in a small, comforting circle.

She took a deep breath. 'It's all over,' she confirmed, and broke into fresh mourning. It was so unlike Etta that it was like trying to comfort a stranger. Her behaviour was as incomprehensible as Althea's.

The scene with Althea had been horrible; something was deeply wrong with his aunt, and he had to speak with her, regardless of what Kennit commanded. Her wild accusations of rape and strange talk of a buried ship stirred deep fears for her sanity. He should never have let Kennit prevent him from seeing her. The isolation had not rested her, but had left her alone with her grief. How could he have been so stupid?

But Etta wept on, and he could not leave her. Why had Althea's crazed words affected Etta like this? Then the answer came to him: She was pregnant. Women always behaved strangely when they were pregnant. He felt almost giddy with relief. He put his arm around her and spoke by her ear.

'It's all right, Etta. Just cry it out. These emotional storms are to be expected, in your condition.'

She sat up on the bed abruptly, her face mottled red and white, her cheeks shining with smeared tears. Then she swung. He saw her clenched fist coming, and almost managed to evade the punch. It clipped the point of his chin, clacking his teeth together and jolting stars into his eyes. He recoiled, his hand going to his jaw as he stood. 'What was that for?' he demanded, shocked.

'For being stupid. For being blind, as they say only women are blind. You are an idiot, Wintrow Vestrit! I don't know why I ever wasted my time on you. You know so much, but you learn nothing at all. Nothing!' Her face suddenly crumpled again. She dropped her face to her knees and rocked back and forth like a disconsolate child. 'How could I have ever been so stupid?' she moaned. Sitting up, she reached for him.

Hesitantly, he sat down on the bed beside her. When he tried to pat her on the shoulder, she came into his arms instead. She put her face against his shoulder and sobbed, her shoulders shaking. He held her, gingerly at first, and then more firmly. He had never held a woman in his arms before. 'Etta,' he said softly. 'Etta, my dear.' He dared to stroke her shining hair.

The door opened. Wintrow startled, but did not release her. He had nothing to be ashamed of, nothing to be guilty about. 'Etta is not herself,' he told Kennit hastily.

'Indeed. That may be a relief, if whoever she is can behave better than the real Etta,' he returned churlishly. 'Brawling in the corridor like a common guttersnipe.' When Etta did not lift her head from Wintrow's shoulder, he went on sarcastically, 'I do hope I'm not interrupting you two. A small matter like my face bleeding or my clothes being filthy should not distress either of you.'

To Wintrow's amazement, Etta slowly lifted her head. She looked at Kennit as if she had never seen him before. Something passed between them in that look, something Wintrow was not privy to. It seemed to break the woman, but she wept no more. 'I'm finished,' she said brokenly. 'I'll get up and find . . .'

'Don't bother,' Kennit snarled as she stood. 'I can see to my own needs. Go to Jola instead. Tell him to signal Captain Sorcor to send a boat for you. I think it will be better if you stay aboard the *Marietta* for a time.'

Wintrow expected an outburst at those words, but Etta stood silent. She looked different. Slowly he realized the change in her. Usually, when she looked at Kennit, her eyes shone and a glow of love suffused her. Now she stared at him, and it was as if her life were draining out of her. When she spoke, her capitulation was complete. 'You are right. Yes. That would be best.' She lifted her hands and rubbed her face as if awakening from the long dream. Then, without another word or glance, she left the room.

Wintrow stared after her. This could not be happening. None of it made sense to him. Then, 'Well?' Kennit demanded icily. His cold blue stare swept Wintrow head to foot.

Wintrow came to his feet. His mouth was dry. 'Sir, I don't think you should send Etta away, not even for her own safety. Instead, as soon as possible, we should remove Althea from the ship. Her mind is turned. Please sir, take pity on the poor woman and let me send her home. We are only a few days from Divvytown. I can pay her passage home on one of the trading vessels that comes to Divvytown now. The sooner she is gone, the better for all of us.'

'Really?' Kennit asked dryly. 'And what makes you think you have any say at all in what I do with Althea?'

Wintrow stood silent, numbed by Kennit's words.

'She is mine, Wintrow. To do with as I will.' Kennit turned away from him and began to disrobe. 'Now. Fetch me a shirt. That is all I require of you just now. Not thinking, not deciding, not even begging. Fetch me a clean shirt and lay out trousers for me. And get me something to clean this cut.' As Kennit spoke, he was unbuttoning his soiled shirt. His jacket already lay on the floor. Without thinking about it, Wintrow moved to obey him. The anger coursing through him obliterated all thought. He set out the clean clothing, and then found a cloth and cool water for Kennit. The cut was small, and already closed. Kennit wiped the blood from his brow and tossed the wet cloth disdainfully to the floor. Wintrow retrieved it silently. As he returned it to the washbasin, he found the control to speak again.

'Sir. This is not a good time for you to send Etta away. She should be here. With you.'

'I think not,' Kennit observed lazily. He held out his wrists for Wintrow to button his cuffs. 'I prefer Althea. I intend to keep her, Wintrow. You had best get used to the idea.' Wintrow was aghast.

'Will you hold Althea here, against her will, while you banish Etta to Sorcor's ship?'

'It will not be against her will, if that is what upsets you. Your aunt has already indicated that she finds me a comely man. In time, she will come to accept her role beside me. Today's little . . . incident was an aberration. She merely needs more time to rest and adapt to the changes in her life. You need not be troubled on her behalf.'

'I will see her. I will speak – What was that?' Wintrow lifted his head.

'I heard nothing,' Kennit replied disdainfully. 'Perhaps you should join Etta on board the *Marietta* until –' It was his turn to stop in mid-sentence. His eyes widened.

'You felt it, too,' Wintrow said accusingly. 'A struggle. Inside the ship herself.'

'I felt no such thing!' Kennit replied hotly.

'Something is happening,' Wintrow declared. Bolt had taught him to dread his connection to the ship. He felt his link to her roiling with turmoil, yet he feared to reach towards her.

'I feel nothing,' the pirate declared disdainfully. 'You imagine it.'

'Kennit! Kennit!' It was a long, drawn-out call, threatening in its intensity. Wintrow felt the hair stand up on the back of his neck.

Kennit shrugged hastily into his fresh jacket and straightened his collar and cuffs. 'I suppose I should go and see what that is about,' he said, but Wintrow could see his nonchalance was feigned. 'I imagine the little fracas in the corridor has upset the ship.'

Wintrow made no reply, except to open the door for Kennit. The pirate hastened past him. Wintrow followed him more slowly. As he passed Althea's door, he heard the low murmur of a voice. He stopped to listen, his ear close to the jamb. The poor woman was talking to herself, her voice so low and rapid that he could not make out any words. 'Althea?' He tried the door, but the lock on it was stout. He stood a moment in indecision, then hastened after Kennit.

He had nearly reached the door when Etta entered the companionway. She walked very straight and tall, and her face was impassive. He lifted his eyes to meet hers. 'Are you all right?' he asked.

'Of course not.' Her voice was soft and flat. 'Sorcor has a boat on its way. I must gather a few things.'

'Etta, I spoke to Kennit. I asked him not to send you away.'

She seemed to vanish in stillness. Her voice came from far away. 'I suppose you meant well by that.'

'Etta, you should tell him you're with child. It might change everything.'

'Change everything?' Her smile was brittle. 'Oh, Kennit has already changed everything, Wintrow. There is no need for me to add to it.'

She started to walk away. He dared to reach out and take her arm to restrain her. 'Etta, please. Tell him.' He clenched his jaws to keep from saying more. Perhaps if Kennit knew that she was pregnant, he would not set her aside to claim Althea. Surely, it would change his heart. What man could remain unmoved by such news?

Etta shook her head slowly, almost as if she could hear his thoughts. 'Wintrow, Wintrow. You still don't understand, do you? Why do you think I was so shaken? Because I'm pregnant? Because she struck Kennit and made him bleed?'

Wintrow shrugged in helpless silence. Etta leaned her head closer to his. 'I wanted to kill her. I wanted to do whatever I had to do to her to make her be silent. Because she was speaking the truth, and I couldn't stand to hear it. Your aunt is not mad, Wintrow. At least, no more mad than any woman becomes after rape. She spoke the truth.'

'You can't know that.' His mouth was so dry he could scarcely form the words.

Etta closed her eyes for an instant. 'For women, there is an outrage that cannot be provoked in any other way. I looked at Althea Vestrit, and I recognized it. I have seen it too often. I have felt it myself.'

Wintrow glanced at the locked door. The betrayal numbed him. Believing her hurt too much. He clung to doubt. 'But why didn't you confront him?'

She looked deeply into his eyes, turning her head as if she were trying to see how he could be so foolish. 'Wintrow. I have told you. Hearing the truth was bad enough. I don't want to live it. Kennit is right. It is best that I stay on the *Marietta* for a time.'

'Until what?' Wintrow demanded.

She shrugged one shoulder stiffly. The gleam of tears sprang into her eyes again. Her voice was tight as she said very quietly, 'He may weary of her. He may want me back.' She turned away. 'I have to gather my things,' she whispered hoarsely.

This time, when she stepped away from him, he let her go.

They were all looking at him. Kennit could feel the eyes of every crewman tracking his progress as he made his way forwards. He dared not hurry. The spat between the two women had been bad enough. They would not witness him racing to the ship's summons, no matter how urgent.

'Kennit!' The figurehead threw back her head and bellowed the word. In the twilit waters beside the ship, the serpents arched into sight and dove again with lashing tails. The sea around the ship seethed with the ship's agitation. He gritted his teeth to keep his expression bland and limped on. Althea had left several bruises that were starting to ache. The ladder to the foredeck was annoying, as always, and all the while he struggled, the ship shouted his name. By the time he reached her, sweat coated him.

He took a breath to steady his voice. 'Ship. I'm here. What do you want?'

The figurehead swivelled to look at him and he gasped. Her eyes had gone green, not a serpent green, but a human green, and her features had lost the reptilian cast they had assumed of late. She did not entirely look as Vivacia had, but this was definitely not Bolt. He almost stepped back from her.

'I'm here, too. What do I want? I want Althea Vestrit out here on the foredeck. I want her companion, Jek, as well. And I want them here *now*.'

His mind raced. 'I'm afraid that isn't feasible, Bolt,' he ventured. He used the name deliberately, and waited for her response.

The ship gave him the most disdainful look he had ever endured from a feminine face. 'You know I am not Bolt,' she replied.

'Are you Vivacia, then?' he asked soberly.

'I am myself, in my entirety,' she replied. 'If you must name me by a name, then address me as Vivacia, for that part of me is as integral as the plank I was built from. But I did not call you to discuss my name or identity. I want Althea and Jek brought here. *Now*.'

'Why?' he countered, his voice as controlled as hers.

'To see them for myself. To know that they are not being ill-treated.'

'Neither of them have been ill-treated!' he declared indignantly.

The lines of the ship's mouth went flat. 'I know what you did,' she said bluntly.

For a moment, Kennit stood in the centre of a great stillness. In all directions, it led to disaster. Had his luck finally deserted him? Had he finally made the one error that was not correctable? He took a breath. 'Are you so swift to believe such evil of me?'

Vivacia glared at him. 'How can you ask me something like that?'

She was not absolutely certain. He read it in her response. Once, she had cared for him, in a gentler way than Bolt had. Could he rouse that in her again? He ran his hand soothingly along the railing. 'Because you see, not with your eyes, but with your heart. Althea believes she experienced something horrible. And so you believe her.' He paused dramatically. He let his voice drop. 'Ship, you know me. You have been inside my mind. You know me as no one else can.' He took a chance. 'Can you believe that I am capable of such a thing?'

She did not answer him directly. 'It is the greatest wrong that can be done to a female, human or dragon. It affronts and disgusts me on all levels. If you have done this, Kennit, it is irreparable. Not even your death could atone for it.' There was more than human fury repressed in her voice: there was a cold reptilian implacability. It went beyond revenge and retaliation to annihilation. It sent a chill up his spine. He gripped her railing to steady himself. His voice was tight with self-justification when he spoke.

'I assure you, I intend no harm at all to Althea Vestrit. Hurting her, offending her would run counter to all my hopes for her.' He took a great breath and confided in her, 'Truth be told, in the few days since she came aboard, I have conceived a great fondness for her. My feelings for her bewilder and confuse me. I am not sure how to deal with them.' Those words, at least, rang with honesty.

A long silence followed his words. Then she asked quietly, 'And what of Etta?'

Who was stronger in the ship, Bolt or Vivacia? Bolt had seemed to like Etta: Vivacia had never disguised her jealousy of her. 'I am torn,' Kennit admitted. 'Etta has been at my side a long time. I have seen her grow far beyond the common whore I rescued from Bettel's bagnio. She has bettered herself in many ways, but she must suffer in comparison to Althea.' He paused, and sighed lightly. 'Althea is altogether a different sort of woman. Her birth and her breeding show in every movement she makes. Yet there is a competency to her that I find very attractive. She is more like . . . you. And I confess, part of the attraction is that she is so much a part of you. The same family that shaped you created her. To be with her is, in a sense, to be with you.' He hoped she would find that flattering. He held his breath, waiting.

Around them the night deepened. The serpents became disembodied sounds, their odd singing mingled with the random splashes of their passage. As the darkness became complete, the brief flashes of their gleaming, scaled bodies lit the waters around the ship.

'You killed Paragon,' she said quietly. 'I know that. Bolt saw it. I have her memories.'

He shook his head. 'I helped Paragon die. It was what he wanted. It was what he had tried to do for himself so many times. I only made it easier for him.'

'Brashen was dear to me.' The ship's voice was choked.

'I am sorry. I did not realize that. In any case, the man was a true captain to the end. He would not leave his ship.' There was regretful admiration in his voice. He went on more quietly, 'You have Bolt's memories. Then you will remember she wanted Althea dead. I refused that. What does she remember of Althea's "rape"?' His lips scarce touched the word.

'Nothing,' the ship admitted. 'She refused to touch minds with Althea. But I know what Althea recalls.'

Relief fuelled his voice with kindness. 'And Althea recalls a nightmare, a poppy dream, not a reality. Such dreams are especially vivid. I do not blame her, or you, for believing her nightmare was real. I blame myself. I should not have given her poppy syrup. I meant no harm, only to help her rest and give her time to absorb the tragedy that had changed her life.'

'Kennit, Kennit,' the ship burst out in an anguished voice. 'You have become precious to me. It gives me pain even to

683

try to believe such things of you. For me to admit such a horrendous act by you means I must admit I have been duped and deceived as to all you are. If it is true, it will make lies of all truths there have ever been between us.' Her voice dropped to a whisper. 'Please, please, tell me she is mistaken. Tell me you could not have done such an odious thing.'

What one wants to believe badly enough becomes real. 'I will show you my proof. I will have Althea and Jek brought to you. You will see for yourself that they have taken no harm while in my care. Althea may have a few bruises, but,' he chuckled deprecatingly, 'probably fewer than she gave me. She is not a large woman, but she is spirited.'

A faint smile came to the ship's face. 'She is that. She has always been that. You will bring her here?'

'Immediately,' he promised. He turned his head as Wintrow came up onto the foredeck. Kennit watched his face as he got his first look at the transfigured figurehead. His dark eyes, so troubled an instant before, kindled. Life came back to Wintrow's face, flowing into it as if he were a carved statue awakening. He started forwards eagerly. Kennit lurched to stand between them. That would not do. The ship was his; he could not let Wintrow reassert a claim to her.

Swiftly, he took a ring of keys from his pocket. 'Here, lad!' he exclaimed and tossed it. The keys flashed in the ship's lantern light before Wintrow caught them. As their eyes met, the light of his joy in Vivacia dimmed. He gave Kennit an oddly measuring look. Kennit read it plainly. Wintrow wondered whom to believe. The pirate shrugged it off. To wonder was not to know. His luck was holding. He considered the boy through the darkness. With a wrench, he wondered if he could part with Wintrow if he had to. The idea dismayed him. But if Wintrow forced him to it, then it must be done in a way that did not compromise his luck, nor alienate the crew. Perhaps he could die in selfless service to Kennit. That might, perhaps, be arranged. The crew might find it inspiring to witness such dedication. He looked at him, mourning him already, then steeled himself to the harshness of life.

'Wintrow,' he exclaimed heartily. 'As you can see, Vivacia has rejoined us. She desires to see your Aunt Althea. Escort her and Jek to the foredeck, please. Make them comfortable for the time being. I myself will see that Althea's old room is made more fitting for them to share.' He turned back to the ship, but his words were for Wintrow as well. 'I will do all I can for their comfort. You will see, in the days to come, that they are my honoured guests, not prisoners.'

It was cowardly, he supposed, but he freed Jek from her chains first. 'Vivacia wants both you and Althea on the foredeck,' he began, but before he could explain any further, the blonde woman had snatched the keys from his hands and was working on the lock. Once free, she surged to her feet and looked down on him with cold blue eyes. Serpent venom had eaten through her clothing and bared her scalded skin. Despite her injuries, she was a formidable and powerful woman. 'Where's Althea?' she demanded.

She followed him through the ship, and jostled him aside at the door. She worked the lock and opened the door, only to have Althea charge into her. His aunt's shoulder caught the tall woman in the sternum. 'Althea!' Jek exclaimed, and wrapped the smaller woman in her arms, containing her wildly flailing arms. 'It's me, it's Jek, calm down!'

After a moment, Althea stopped struggling. She threw her head back to look up at Jek. Her hair was wild, her eyes dilated to black pits. She breathed the stench of vomit. 'I have to kill him,' Althea grated. Her head swayed on her neck. She clutched at her friend's shoulder. 'Promise me you'll help me kill him.'

'Althea, what's wrong with you?' Jek turned a furious gaze on Wintrow. 'What has been done to her?'

'He raped me,' Althea gasped. 'Kennit raped me. He kept coming into my room, pretending kindness and kissing me, and then . . . And my ship, he's been holding my ship down under where she couldn't see or feel the wind . . .'

Jek looked at Wintrow over Althea's bent head, horrified at her friend's rambling state. 'You'll be all right now,' she said faintly. Her eyes were uncertain.

'Vivacia is asking for you, right now,' Wintrow told her hastily. It was the most comforting thing he could think to say. 'She wants you to come to her right away.'

'My ship,' Althea half-sobbed. She staggered free of Jek's embrace and careened down the hallway.

'What's wrong with her?' Jek demanded of Wintrow. Cold fury was in her eyes.

'It's too much poppy,' he explained, and then found he was talking to empty air. She had hastened after Althea.

The foredeck had never been so far away. Althea moved in a dream. The air was gelid against her, but if she leaned on it, it gave way all too easily. She forced her way down the companionway, one shoulder braced against the wall. When she reached the open deck, it stretched leagues before her. She dared herself to brave it. Then Jek was at her side, taking her arm. Without a word, she leaned on her and began to step away the distance.

Tears stung her eyes. She felt she walked through time as much as distance. She was finally walking away from her foolish decisions and towards the place she was meant to be. She had lost Brashen, and poor Paragon, and all the hands who had come so far with them. Kennit had brutalized her body and her ship was still in his hands, but somehow if she could just reach the foredeck and once more look into Vivacia's eyes, she could deal with it all. It would not hurt less, the grief would not be eased, but there would still be something in her life worth the effort of living.

That dog's son Kennit still stood on the foredeck. He had the nerve to look down on her and smile welcomingly. He moved back from the ladder as she approached it. He probably knew that if he stood too close, she'd try to pull him down and break his neck.

'Move your other foot now,' Jek said quietly. 'Lift it to the next rung.'

'What?' What was she talking about?

'Here,' she offered, and abruptly Althea felt herself lifted and shoved up the ladder. She scrabbled at it faintly, got a grip, and then Jek unceremoniously shoved her the rest of the way up it. She crawled onto the foredeck on her hands and knees, knowing that something was wrong with that, but unable to think of a different way to manage it. Then Jek was beside her, hauling her onto her feet.

'Let me go,' Althea told her plainly. 'I want to go alone.'

'You're not well,' Kennit said sympathetically. 'I hold none of this against you.'

'Bastard,' she spat at him, and she thought he had moved closer. She swung at him, and then suddenly he was where he had been standing all along, the coward. 'I'm still going to kill you,' she promised him, 'but not where you'll bleed on my deck.'

'Althea!'

The beloved voice was shocked with worry for her, but there was something else there too, something she couldn't name. She turned and after a blurry moment found Vivacia looking back at her. She should have looked joyful, not anxious. 'It will be all right,' she assured her. 'I'm here now.' She tried to run to her, but it became a stagger. Jek was suddenly at her side again, helping her to the railing. 'I'm here, now, ship,' she told her, finally, after all the months. Then, 'What has he done to you? What has he done to you?'

It was Vivacia and it was not. All her features had subtly changed. Her eyes were too green, and the arch of her brows too pronounced. Her hair was like a mane, wild around her face. Yet for all that, the difference was what she felt as she clutched the railing. Once they had fit together like complementary parts of a puzzle box and completed one another. Now it was as if she gripped Jek's hands, or Paragon's railing. It was Vivacia, but she was complete without Althea.

Yet Althea was not complete without her. The places she had expected the ship to fill were still empty and ached more horribly than ever.

'I am one now,' the ship confirmed softly to her. 'The memories of your family have merged with the dragon. It had to be, Althea. There was no going back to denying her, any more than she could truly go on without me. You don't begrudge me that, do you? That I am whole now?'

'But I need you!' The words broke from her before she could consider what they meant. Terrible to blurt out to all a truth you had never recognized yourself. 'How can I be myself without you?'

'Just as you have been,' the ship replied, and she heard her father's wisdom in the words, and an elder sapience as well.

'But I'm hurt,' she heard herself say. Words were welling from her like blood from a wound.

'You will heal,' Vivacia assured her.

'You don't need me . . .' The knowledge of that sent her reeling. To have come all this way, striven so hard and lost so much, only to discover this.

'Love can exist without need,' she pointed out gently. In the seas beyond the bow, several serpents had risen to regard them gravely. Either her eyes were still tricking her, or the yellow-green one was deformed.

From somewhere, Wintrow had come to grip the railing beside her. 'Oh, ship, you feel beautiful,' he exclaimed. Althea felt an odd tension run out of him. 'You . . . you make sense now. You are complete.'

'Go away,' Althea told him distinctly.

'You need to rest,' he told her gently. Mealy-mouthed, empty courtesy, just like Kennit's.

She swung at him, but he jerked his head back. 'Go away!' she shouted at him. Tears, useless tears, started down her face. Where had her strength gone? She lurched with the realization that the ship did not reach out to her and supplement her in her need.

Vivacia spoke quietly. 'You must do that for yourself now, Althea. Each of us must.'

It was as if her own mother had pushed her aside. 'But you were with me. You know what he did to me, how he hurt me . . .'

'Not exactly,' the ship replied gently, and in those words, the separation was complete. The ship was a separate creature from her now, and just as capable of misunderstanding her as any human. Just as capable of disbelieving her.

'I know how real your pain is, and was,' Vivacia offered her. 'It is just that . . . perhaps I know you too well, Althea. All the years you lived aboard me, all the dreams you dreamed with me before I awoke. I shared them, you know. And this is not the first time such a nightmare has plagued you.' There was an awkward silence, then she added, 'Devon did you great wrong, Althea. And it was not your fault. It was never your fault. And neither was Brashen's death.' She lowered her voice to a whisper. 'You don't deserve to be punished.'

Vivacia had got too close to a truth Althea didn't want to hear. It was a truth she could not bear just now. All the connections between pain and fault, between Althea's wicked wilfulness and the deaths of those she loved and the bad things that happened to her because she deserved bad things – cause and effect suddenly spun dizzyingly around her. If she hadn't defied her mother to go on the ship with her father, her mother would have loved her more and not given the ship to Keffria, and if Devon hadn't taken her maidenhead, she wouldn't have told Keffria, and Keffria wouldn't have despised her all these years, and none of it would even have begun, and Paragon wouldn't be sunk and Brashen dead, and Amber, and young Clef, how could she even think of him –

'I need to go back to my room,' she begged huskily.

'I'll take you,' Jek said.

Wintrow tapped at the door of his room cautiously then jumped when Jek jerked it open. For an instant, he stood mutely looking up at the northern woman. Then he found his tongue. 'Kennit thought you might want some women's clothing.'

She scowled as if he had already offended her, but stepped back and waved him in. Althea sat on the bunk, her knees drawn up to her chest. A pallet had been made up on the floor for Jek. She looked better, in a haggard but alert way. The tension in the room suggested he had walked in on an argument. His aunt glanced disdainfully at his burden of slithering fabric. 'Take them away. I accept nothing from him.'

'Wait,' Jek intervened. She gave Althea an apologetic look. 'I've been in these clothes since we went overboard. I'm tired of smelling myself.' She winced, then added reluctantly, 'And you. Those clothes you're in smell like vomit.'

'Don't you see what those dresses are?' Althea flared. 'They're a bribe. And if I wear one of them, I'd be seen as a whore, bought with clothes. No one would ever believe what he did to me.'

'I don't think he intends it that way,' Wintrow said quietly. He suspected the gift was more to gain the ship's approval than Althea's, but the look she shot him silenced him. He did not know how to begin to talk to her. Give her time, he told himself. Let her be the one to begin talking. He shut the door behind him before placing the armload of clothing on the foot of the bunk. He also unburdened himself of a chest of jewellery and several bottles of scent.

Jek raised an eyebrow at the trove, then glanced back at Althea. 'Would you mind if I looked through it?'

'I don't care,' Althea lied. 'You've already made it obvious you doubt my story.'

Jek flipped open the lid of the jewellery chest. She spoke as she considered the glittering contents. 'You don't lie, Althea.' She took a deep breath and added reluctantly, 'It's the circumstances that make me . . . have doubts. The whole thing just doesn't make sense. Why would he rape you? He has a woman of his own, he's forbidden rape on this ship, and his reputation is that of a gentleman. Back in Divvytown, no one spoke ill of him. He saw me twice every day, and treated me with courtesy, despite the chains. Even the ship herself is shocked at the idea that he might do such a thing.' She rummaged through the garments, and held a soft blue skirt up against herself. 'I won't be running the rigging in this,' she observed in an aside. Althea wasn't distracted by her humour.

'So you believe the whole thing was a poppy dream?' Althea demanded fiercely.

Jek shrugged. 'He gave me poppy syrup in brandy for my burns. It helped. But it did give me vivid dreams.' She knit her brow. 'I hate the man, Althea. But for him, my friends would be alive still. Despite that, he displays a sense of honour that –'

'It wasn't a dream.' Althea turned her accusing gaze on Wintrow. 'You don't believe me, do you? You've become his meek little follower, haven't you? You gave our family ship over to him without a fight.'

Before Wintrow could defend himself, Jek spoke. 'Put yourself in my place, Althea. What if I'd told you that Brashen had attacked me? Think how difficult that would be for you to accept. Althea. You've been through a horrible experience. Near drowned, and recovered only to find your ship and all hands and Brashen drowned. You're grieving. It is natural for you to hate Kennit and believe him capable of any evil. It could turn anyone's mind.'

'It didn't turn your mind.'

Jek was silent for a moment. In a quieter voice, she went on, 'I'm grieving in my own way. Amber wasn't some chance-met acquaintance. I've cut a lock of hair to mourn her, not that I expect you to understand that. But I lost a friend, not my lover. You lost Brashen. It's bound to affect you more strongly.'

The sense of Jek's words settled onto Wintrow and stunned him. He stared at his aunt, unable to imagine such a thing. She glared at his scandalized expression. 'Yes, I was sleeping with Trell. I suppose that you share your mother's opinion of that. Can't rape a whore, right, Wintrow?'

The injustice of her words stirred his own anger. He stood his ground. Enduring Etta's temper had taught him some courage at least. 'I didn't condemn you,' he defended himself. 'I was just surprised. I've a right to be shocked. It's not what one expects of a Trader's daughter. But that doesn't mean I . . .'

'Fuck you, Wintrow,' she retaliated savagely. 'Because you're exactly what I'd expect of Kyle Haven's son.'

Those words stung him more than they had a right to. He struggled to keep his voice level. 'That wasn't fair. You want to be angry with everyone, so you're putting meanings to my words that I don't intend. You haven't given me a chance to speak at all. I haven't said I don't believe you.'

'You don't have to say it. Your standing with Kennit proves what you believe. Get out. And take that with you.' She extended a leg to kick the chest disdainfully to the floor.

He walked to the door. 'Maybe I'm not standing with Kennit. Maybe I'm standing with my ship.'

'Shut up!' she roared. 'I don't want to hear your excuses. I've heard enough.'

'If you carry on like a mad woman, people will treat you like one,' he warned her harshly. He shut the door firmly behind himself. He heard the crash and tinkle of a bottle of scent shattering against it. In the dim companionway, he shut his eyes for a moment. Some of her accusations had been fair, he forced himself to admit. He wouldn't have believed her. Her story was illogical and implausible. He doubted that anyone on board believed what she said about Kennit. Except for him. And it wasn't her word that had forced him to believe her. It was Etta's.

THIRTY

Convergence

'IT'S FINISHED. I'LL have to bore a hole through your ear. Will you mind?'

'After everything else you've done, I shan't even notice. May I touch it first?'

Amber put the large earring into Paragon's open hand. 'Here. You know, you could just open your eyes and look. You needn't do everything by touch any more.'

'Not yet,' Paragon told her. He wished she would not speak of that. He could not explain to her just why he could not open his eyes yet. He would know when the time was right. He weighted the earring in his hand and smiled, savouring the newness of the facial sensation. 'It's like a net carved of wood links. With a lump trapped in the middle.'

'Your description is *so* flattering,' Amber observed wryly. 'It's to be a silver net with a blue gemstone caught in it. It matches an earring I wear. I'm on the railing. Hold me so I can reach your earlobe.'

When he offered her his palm as a platform, she climbed on without hesitation. He held her to his ear, and did not wince as she set a drill to his earlobe. The reconstruction of his face had not been painful as humans understood pain. Amber leaned against his cheek as she worked, bracing herself against the impacts as he breasted each wave. The bit passing through his earlobe tingled strangely. Wizardwood chips fell in a fine shower that she caught in a canvas apron. He ingested them at the end of each day. None of his memories had been lost.

He no longer hid from his memories. Mother spent part of each day on the foredeck with his log books. On wet days, she sheltered herself and her books under a flap of canvas. He could not understand the gabbling of her truncated tongue, but that did not matter. She sat on his deck and leaned against his railing as she read. Through her, the ancient memories came trickling back to him. Recorded in those books were the sparse observations of his captains through the years. It did not matter. The notations were touchstones for memories of his own.

The tool passed completely through his lobe. Amber drew it back, and after a moment of fumbling, hung the earring from his ear. She fastened a catch at the back of his earlobe. Then she stood clear as he accepted the wood back to himself. He gave an experimental tug on it, then shook his head to accustom himself to the dangling weight. 'I like it. Did I get it right?'

'Oh, so do I.' Amber sighed with satisfaction. 'And you got it exactly right. It went from grey to rosy, and now it shines so brilliantly silver that I can barely look at it. The gemstone winks out from among the links and flashes blue and silver, just like the sea on a sunny day. I wish you would look at it.'

'In time.'

'Well, you're complete, save for final touch-ups. I'll take my time on the finish work.'

She ran her bared hands over his face again. It was an odd gesture, partly affectionate and partly a search for small flaws in her carving. Immediately after they left Key Island, Amber had come to the foredeck. She clattered down her carrier of tools. Then, without more ado, she had roped herself to the railing and climbed over the side. She had measured his face, marking it with charcoal and humming as she did so. Mother had come to the railing, gabbling questioningly.

'I'm repairing his eyes. And changing his face, at his own request. There's a sketch there, under the mallet. Take a look, if you like.' Amber had spidered across his chest as she spoke. She favoured the scalded side of her body. He spread his hands protectively beneath her.

When Mother returned to the railing, she made approving sounds. Since then, she had watched most of the work. It took dedication, for Amber had worked nearly day and night on him. She had begun with saw and chisel, removing great slabs of his face, not just his beard, but from his brow and even his nose. Then she attacked his chest and upper arms, 'To keep you proportional,' she had explained. His groping hands had found only the rough suggestion of features. That swiftly changed, for she worked on him with a fervour such as Paragon had never known. Neither rain nor wind deterred her. When daylight failed her, she hung lanterns and worked on, more by touch than sight he thought. Once, when Brashen cautioned her against keeping such hours, she had replied that this work was better than sleep for restoring her soul. Her healing injuries did not slow her. Not only her tools flew over his countenance, but she had a trick of using her fingers as well. He had never felt a touch like hers. A press of her fingertips could smooth a line while a brushing touch erased a jagged spot. Even now, as she encountered a rough bit, she dabbed at the grain of his face and it aligned under her tingling touch. 'You loved him, didn't you?'

'Of course I did. Now stop asking about it.'

Sometimes, when she worked on his face, he could feel her affection for the countenance she carved. His face was beardless now, and youthful. It was more in keeping with his voice and with whom he felt himself to be, and yet it made him squirmingly curious to know he wore the face of someone Amber loved. She would not speak of him, but sometimes in the brushing touch of her fingers, he glimpsed the man she saw in her mind.

'Now I am layer upon layer upon layer,' he observed as he held her up to the railing. 'Dragon and dragon, under Paragon Ludluck, under ... whoever this is. Will you give me his name, also?'

'Paragon suits you better than any other name could.' She asked quietly, 'Dragon and dragon?'

'Quite well, thank you, and how are you today?' He grinned as he said it. His polite nothing conveyed his intent. His dragons were his business, just as the identity of the man whose face he wore was hers.

Brashen had come to the foredeck. Now, as Amber climbed down from the railing, he sternly reminded her, 'I don't like you out there without a line on you. At the clip we're going, by the time we discovered you were gone, it would be too late.'

'Do you still fear I would let her fall unnoticed, Brashen?' Paragon asked gravely.

Brashen looked at the ship's closed eyes. His boyish brow was unlined, serene as he waited for Brashen's reply. After a short but very uncomfortable silence, Brashen found words. 'A captain's duty is to worry about all possibilities, ship.' He changed the subject, addressing Amber. 'So. Nice earring. Are you nearly finished then?'

'I am finished. Save for a bit of smoothing on his face.' She pursed her lips thoughtfully. 'And I may do some ornamentation on his accoutrements.'

Brashen leaned out on the fore-rail. He swept his eyes critically over the whole figurehead. She had accomplished an amazing amount of work in a very short time. From her myriad sketches, he surmised she had been planning this since they left Bingtown. In addition to the earring, the extra bits of wood Amber had carved away to reshape his face had been fashioned into a wide copper bracelet for his wrist and a leather battle harness pegged to his chest. A short-handled battleaxe hung from it.

'Handsome,' Brashen observed. In a quieter voice, he asked Amber, 'Are you going to fix his nose?'

'There is nothing wrong with his nose,' Amber asserted warningly.

'Mm.' Brashen considered the crooked line of it. 'Well, I suppose a sailor should have a scar or two to his face. And a broken nose gives him a very determined look. Why the axe?'

'I had wood to use up,' Amber replied, almost evasively. 'It's only ornamental. He has given it the colours of a real weapon, but it remains wizardwood.'

Mother made an assenting sound. She sat cross-legged on the deck, a logbook open in her lap. She seemed always to be there, mumbling through the words. She read the logbooks as devoutly as some folk read Sa's Edicts.

'It completes him,' Amber agreed with great satisfaction. She drew her discarded gloves back on and began gathering her tools. 'And I'm suddenly tired.'

'Doesn't surprise me. Get some sleep, then come to my quarters. We draw closer to Divvytown with every breath of this wind. I want to discuss strategy.'

Amber smiled wryly. 'I thought we had agreed we didn't have any, except go to Divvytown and let the word out that we want to trade Kennit's mother for Althea.'

Mother's bright eyes followed the conversation. She nodded assent.

'And you see no flaws in that plan? Such as, perhaps, the whole town rising against us and taking Mother to gain favour with Kennit?'

Mother shook her head; her gestures indicated she would oppose such an act.

'Oh, that. Well, the whole plan is so riddled with flaws that

one of that magnitude seemed too obvious to mention,' Amber
replied lightly.

Brashen frowned. 'We gamble for Althea's life. This isn't a
jest to me, Amber.'

'Nor to me,' the carpenter swiftly replied. 'I know you are
worried to the bone and justly so. But for me to dwell on that
anxiety with you will not lessen it. Instead, we must focus
on our hopes. If we cannot anchor ourselves in a belief that
we will succeed, we have already been defeated.' She stood,
hefting her tools to her shoulder, then cocked her head and
looked at him sympathetically. 'I don't know if it will draw
any water with you, Brashen, but there is something I know,
right down to my bones. I will see Althea again. There will
come a time when we will all stand together again. Beyond
that moment, I cannot see. But, of that, at least, I am sure.'

The carpenter's odd eyes had taken on a dreaming quality.
Their colour seemed to shift between dark gold and pale brown.
It sent a chill up his back, yet he was oddly comforted by it.
He could not share her equanimity, but he could not doubt
her, either.

'There. You see. Your faith is stronger than your doubts.'
Amber smiled at him. In a less mystical voice she asked, 'Has
Kyle told you anything useful?'

Brashen shook his head sourly. 'To listen to him wearies
me. A hundred times, he has detailed how both Vivacia
and Wintrow betrayed him. It is the only thing he willingly
discusses. I think he must have lived it repeatedly the whole
time he was chained in that cellar. He speaks only evil of
them both. It is harder to control my temper when he says
Althea brought all her troubles on herself and should be left
to face them the same way. He urges us to return immediately
to Bingtown, to forget Althea, his son, the family ship, all of it.
And when I say I will not, he curses me. The last time I spoke
to him, he slyly asked if Althea and I had not been in league
with Wintrow from the beginning. He hints that he knows we

have all plotted against him.' Brashen shook his head bitterly. 'You have heard his tale of how Wintrow seized the ship from him, only to give it to Kennit. Does any of that sound possible to you?'

Amber gave a tiny shrug. 'I do not know Wintrow. But this I do know. When circumstances are right, unlikely people do extraordinary things. When the weight of the world is behind them, the push of events and time itself will align to make incredible things happen. Look around you, Brashen. You skirt the centre of the vortex, so close you do not see how wondrous are the circumstances surrounding us. We are being swept towards a climax in time, a critical choice-point where all the future must go one way, or another.

'Liveships are wakening to their true pasts. Serpents, reputed to be myths when you were a boy, are now accepted as natural. The serpents speak, Brashen, to Paragon, and Paragon speaks to us. When last did humanity concede intelligence to another race of creatures? What will it mean to your children and your grandchildren? You are caught up in a grand sweep of events, culminating in the changing of the course of the world.' She lowered her voice and a smile touched her mouth. 'Yet all you can perceive is that you are separated from Althea. A man's loss of his mate may be the essential trigger that determines all events from henceforth. Do you not see how strange and wonderful that is? That all history balances on an affair of the human heart?'

He looked at the odd woman and shook his head. 'That isn't how I see it, Amber. That isn't how I see it at all. It's just my life, and now that I have finally discovered what I must have to be happy, I'm willing to lay down my life for it. That's all.'

She smiled. 'That is *all*. You are right. And that is all that *All* ever is.'

Brashen drew a shuddering breath. Her words were edged with mystery and fraught with import. He shook his head. 'I'm just a simple sailor.'

Mother had been watching the interchange intently. Now she smiled, a smile at once beatific in its peacefulness and terrifying in its acceptance. The expression was like a confirmation of all Amber had said. Brashen felt suddenly cornered by the two women, compelled towards he knew not what. He fixed his gaze on Mother. 'You know your son. Do you think there is any chance we will succeed?'

She smiled, but sorrow edged it. She lifted her shoulders in an old woman's shrug.

Paragon spoke. 'She thinks you will succeed. But whether you will know you have succeeded, or if the success will be the one you would have chosen for yourself, well, those are things no one can say now. But she knows you will succeed at whatever you are meant to do.'

For a moment, he tried to unknot the ship's words. Then Brashen sighed. 'Now don't you start with me, too,' he warned the ship.

Malta sat at the captain's table, her fingers steepled before her. 'This is a fair offer, one that benefits all. I cannot see any reason why you would refuse it.' She smiled charmingly over her hands at Captain Red. The Satrap, impassively silent, sat beside her.

Captain Red looked shocked. The others at the table were equally stunned. Malta had chosen her time well. The most difficult part had been persuading the Satrap to do it her way. She had dressed and groomed him carefully, and by dint of badgering and begging, convinced him to come to dinner at the captain's table. She had dictated his manner to him as well, and he had complied, being courteous but not affable, and more silent than talkative. It was only when the meal was nearly over that he had cleared his throat and addressed the captain.

'Captain Red, please attend Malta Vestrit as she presents a negotiation on my behalf.'

Captain Red, too startled to do otherwise, had nodded.

Then, in a speech she had practised endlessly before the little looking-glass in her chamber, she had presented the Satrap's offer. She pointed out that monetary wealth was not the essence of the Satrapy; power was. The Satrap would not offer coin for his release, nor would he petition his nobles to do so. Instead, he would negotiate the terms himself. Speaking concisely, she outlined his offer: recognition of Kennit as King of the Pirate Isles, an end to slave raids in the Isles and the removal of the Chalcedean patrol vessels. The finer points of this would, of course, have to be negotiated more thoroughly with King Kennit. Perhaps they might include trade agreements; perhaps they might include pardons for those in exile who wished to return to Jamaillia. Malta had deliberately presented the offer while many still lingered at the table. In her conversations with the crew, she had gleaned the concerns dearest to them. She had gathered their fears that they might return to Divvytown or Bull Creek and find their homes burned, alongside their longing to see friends and family in Jamaillia City, to perform once again in the grand theatres of the capital.

She had distilled their desires into this offer. His silence was eloquent. He rubbed his chin, and swept a glance around the table. Then he leaned towards the Satrap. 'You're right. I thought only of coin. But this –' He stared at him almost suspiciously. 'You're truly ready to offer us these sorts of terms?'

The Satrap spoke with quiet dignity. 'I'd be a fool to let Malta say such things if I had not well considered them.'

'Why? Why now?'

That was not a question Malta had prepared him for. She held her smile on her lips. They had agreed he would defer such queries to her. Yet, she was not surprised as he calmly ignored their agreement.

'Because I am a man who can learn from his errors,' he announced. Those words alone would have stunned her to silence, but what followed nearly made her gape. 'Coming away from Jamaillia City and travelling through my domain has opened my eyes and my ears to facts that my advisors either hid from me, or were ignorant of themselves. My bold journey has borne fruit. My "foolishness" in leaving the capital will now shine forth as true wisdom.' He smiled graciously round the table. 'My advisors and nobles often underestimated my intelligence. It was a grave error on their part.'

He had them in the palm of his hand. Everyone at the table waited for his next words. The Satrap leaned forwards slightly. He tapped his finger on the table as he made each point. Malta was entranced. She had never seen this man.

'I find myself in the company of pirates, of men and women tattooed with the shame of slavery. Yet you are not what I was told you were. I do not find ignorance or stupidity amongst you, nor yet barbarism and savagery.

'I have seen the patrol vessels negotiated by treaty with Chalced. Yet I see far too many of them in my waters. They wallow with the wealth they have taken. Clearly, I have put my trust in the wrong allies. Jamaillia City stands vulnerable to attack by the ships of Chalced. I would be wise to seek truer allies. Who better than those who already have learned to do battle with Chalcedeans?'

'Who better indeed?' Captain Red asked those at his table. He grinned broadly, but then brought his smile under control as he added, 'Of course, King Kennit will make all final decisions. But I suspect we are bringing him a prize far weightier than all the gold we have ever shared with him. We are only a few days out of Divvytown. A bird shall be sent at once to alert Kennit to what we bring.' He lifted his glass in a toast. 'Here's to ransoms paid in more than coin or blood!'

As all lifted their glasses and joined in, Malta heard the lookout's cry of 'Sail!'

The men at the table exchanged wary looks. Chalcedean ships were to be avoided, now that the *Motley* was fully loaded. There was a rap at the door. 'Enter!' Captain Red conceded, annoyance in his voice. The man detested anything that disrupted his meals, let alone a dramatic moment.

The door opened. The ship's boy stood there, his cheeks pink with excitement. With a broad grin he announced, 'Sir, we've sighted the Vivacia, and the *Marietta*.'

Kennit watched the approach of the small boat from the *Motley* with mixed feelings. Sorcor had come over from the *Marietta* for the occasion. He was attired in several acres of scarlet fabric. He stood just behind his captain's right shoulder. Captain Red, at his other side in his own garish garments, was too caught up in his own triumph to be aware of his leader's personal reservations. He was delivering to King Kennit a prize that no other of his captains would ever match. For a man with his theatrical background, it was the ultimate achievement. Ever after, he would be known as the pirate captain who gave the Satrap of all Jamaillia to King Kennit as a gift.

Captain Red had come first to the Vivacia to share the news. Now, dramatically poised, he hovered by Kennit's side as they watched the loot delivered. Kennit was both elated, and annoyed. The capture of the Satrap was remarkable, and the potential for gain from his ransom was vast. But this windfall also came at a time when his mind had another focus. He gave a sideways glance to where Althea Vestrit also stood at the railing watching the small boat approach. Jek was at her side. Jek was always at her side. The winter wind blew their hair and Jek's bright skirts, and brought colour to their faces. Jek was a stunning woman, tall, fair, and bold. But Althea captivated Kennit as no other woman could.

In the days since she had emerged from her cabin and been given the freedom of the ship, he had walked a careful line with her. He maintained to everyone that her terrible dream had been the result of poppy syrup, given her for the pain of a damaged back. For that, he had publicly apologized to her, while gently reminding her that she had complained of a painful back. Didn't she recall taking the syrup? At her snarling denial, he had shrugged helplessly. 'It was when you said you liked lace on a man,' he had delicately prompted her, even as his hand toyed with the lace at his throat. He had smiled fondly at her.

'Don't try to make that mean something,' she threatened him.

He composed his face to injured resignation. 'Doubtless you are far more susceptible to the poppy than you knew,' he courteously suggested.

His luck had given him the power to adorn her as he saw fit. Her lack of garments had forced her to accept the clothing he selected from his plunder and sent to her stateroom. Jewellery, perfume, and bright scarves he sent as well. Jek availed herself of this feminine bounty unashamedly, but Althea had resisted them for days. Even now, she kept herself as plain as one could be in silk trousers and damask vest. It pleased him that he chose the colours she wore, that he had touched the garments that now clung to her. How long could she remain proof against such largesse? Like a caged bird, she must eventually come fluttering to his hand.

She avoided him as much as she could, but Vivacia was not a large ship. From threats of murder and foul names, she had simmered to seething hatred and murderous looks. He had met all her stares with grieved concern and solicitous courtesy. Deep inside him, a bizarre merriment bubbled at her predicament. He had a power over her that he never could have foreseen, even if he had deliberately created this situation. She believed herself a wronged victim, but was treated as the hysterical accuser of an innocent man. If she spoke of the rape, her words were received with pity rather than shared outrage. Even Jek, who bore him an impersonal hate for the sinking of the Paragon, had reservations about Althea's accusations. A lack of support for her cause was undoubtedly very daunting to her desire to kill him.

Most of the crew were disinterested in what he had or had not done to her. He was, after all, the captain and the pirates of his crew had never been overly afflicted with morality. Some, those fondest of Etta, were more concerned by her absence than by Althea's presence. A few seemed to think he had wronged Etta somehow. He suspected that this was what troubled Wintrow most. He never spoke of it directly but from time to time, Kennit would catch Wintrow looking at him speculatively. Fortunately for Wintrow, he did not do this often. Instead, the boy spent most of his time in a futile effort to establish some sort of bond with his aunt.

Althea resolutely ignored her nephew. Wintrow bore her rebuffs mildly, but managed to spend most of his free time in her vicinity. He obviously hoped for reconciliation. To busy him, Kennit had passed most of the day to day tasks of the ship's command on to him. His wits were far sharper than Jola's. If the circumstances had been different, Kennit would have moved him up to mate. He had the instinct for command. What grated on Kennit was that he had not had even a moment alone with Althea. As far as the pirate could determine, when Althea was not in the stateroom she shared with Jek, she was on the foredeck with the figurehead. It amused Kennit, for he knew the ship spent much time trying to convince her that Kennit would not have mistreated her as she claimed. More than any other influence, Vivacia's attitude seemed to undermine the experience of Althea's own senses. When he himself came to the foredeck each evening to converse with Vivacia, Althea no longer stormed away with Jek in her wake, but retreated a little way and then eavesdropped on them. She watched his every move, trying to see the monster she would make of him. His façade defied her.

As the little boat drew nearer, Kennit saw that it held not only the Satrap, theatrically resplendent in borrowed garb, but also his young Companion. The Satrap stared straight ahead, ignoring their rippling serpent escort, but the young woman stared up at the ship, white-faced. Even at this distance, her dark eyes seemed immense. The oddly fashioned turban atop her head was doubtless some new Jamaillian fashion. He found himself wondering how Althea would look in such head-garb.

Althea glanced over at Wintrow. He stared down at the *Motley*'s boat as it battled towards them. He had matured since he had left Bingtown Harbour. It was uncanny to look at him in profile; they shared so many features, it was like looking at herself made male. That he looked so like her somehow made his betrayal all the more intolerable. She would never be able to forgive him.

A trickle of rebuke rose through her from the railing she grasped. 'I know, I know. Set it aside,' she murmured in response. Repeatedly, the ship had urged her to let go of her anger. But if she let go of her anger, all that would remain was grief and pain. Anger was easier. Anger could be focused outward. Grief corroded from within.

She could not let the matter go. The rape made no sense, served no logic. She could not argue with that. It was the act of a mad man, but civil and shrewd Captain Kennit was certainly not mad. So what had happened? Images of Devon and Keffria were mixed with her memories of the attack. Could it have been what he said, a twisted poppy-induced dream? The ship had tried to placate her by suggesting that perhaps it had been some other crewman. Althea refused that. She clung to the truth as she clung to her sanity, for to let the one go was to deny the other. In some ways, she thought savagely, it did not matter whether Kennit had raped her or not. He had killed Brashen and sunk Paragon. Those were reasons enough to hate him. Even her beloved Vivacia had been stolen from her, and changed so deeply that some of her thoughts and ideas were completely foreign to Althea. All her judgements were based on her deeper dragon nature. At one time, Althea had been sure she knew the ship to her core. Now she frequently glimpsed the stranger within. The values and concerns of a personage that did not share her humanity often baffled her. Vivacia agonized over the plight of the serpents. The commitment that once belonged to the Vestrit family now went to those scaled beasts.

As clearly as if the figurehead had spoken, Althea sensed her thought through their renewed bond. *Do you begrudge me that I am who I truly am? Should I pretend otherwise for the sake of pleasing you? If I did, it would be a lie. Would you rather love a lie than know me as I truly am?*

Of course not. Of course not.

All the same, her ship's distraction left her adrift and alone. She clung to an ugly reality that others believed was a dream. How could she leave it behind, when over and over it recurred as a nightmare? She had lost count of how many times Jek had shaken her from the confinement of that dream. Her traitor mind carried her from false memories of drowning with Brashen to a frightening struggle for breath in a dark bunk. The lack of sleep told on her judgement. She felt brittle and insecure. She longed for Vivacia as she had once been, a mirror and a reinforcement of Althea's self. She longed for Brashen, a man who had known her to her bones. She drifted in her identity with no kindred spirit to anchor her.

'There is something about that young woman in the boat,' Vivacia murmured. 'Do not you feel it also?'

'I feel nothing,' Althea replied, and wished it were so.

Heart in mouth, Malta stared up at the ship's railing. The snatching waves, the chilling spray, the wind that pushed at the tiny boat and most of all the recklessly surging serpents all threatened her. The white-faced men pulling on the oars shared her fear of the serpents. She saw it in their set stares and straining muscles. As the creatures rose out of the water beside the boat, they stared at her with eyes of gold or silver or bronze. One after another, they threw back their heads as they passed the boat, trumpeting deep cries from their toothy scarlet maws. Not since she had dealt with Tintaglia had she felt such a pressure of sentience from another creature. Their gazes, fixed unwaveringly upon her, were too knowing, as if they sought to reach into her soul and claim her as their own. In terror, she fixed her gaze on the Vivacia to keep from looking at the scaled monsters.

She focused on presenting a composed face to the pirate king that awaited them. *Motley*'s entire company had poured their energy into preparing her. In their eagerness that Kennit see the true sumptuousness of their gift, they had bathed and primped and dressed the Satrap more finely than when she had first seen him at the Bingtown ball. The attention had bolstered his self-importance to a near-unbearable level. Malta had not been neglected. A burly deckhand with a pale snake tattooed beside his nose had insisted on painting her face for her. She had never seen such cosmetics and tools as he had brought to her room. Another had fashioned her turban, while one of the others had selected her jewellery, scent and robes from the plums of their plunder. Malta's heart had sung at how they aided her in her role, all with the intent of making their gift seem more extravagant. She would not let their efforts go to waste. She fixed her eyes on Vivacia, and tried not to wonder if her father was alive, or what he would think of her transformation.

Then she saw Wintrow standing at the railing. Unbelieving, she came halfway to her feet. 'Wintrow!' she called wildly to her brother. He stared at her stupidly. A glimpse of gold hair on a tall figure made her heart leap with hope, but it was not her father who looked down on her, but a woman.

The Satrap scowled at her for her lack of decorum, but she ignored him. Anxiously she scanned the waiting folk, hoping against hope that Kyle Haven would step forwards and call her name. Instead, the hand that lifted suddenly and pointed at her belonged unmistakably to her Aunt Althea.

Althea leaned forwards precariously on the railing. She gripped Jek's forearm and pointed emphatically at the girl in the boat. 'Sa's Breath! It's Malta!' she exclaimed.

'It can't be!' Wintrow joined his aunt at the railing and peered down at the girl. 'She does look very like Malta,' he faltered.

'Who is this Malta?' Kennit asked despite himself.

'My little sister,' Wintrow observed faintly as every stroke of the oars brought her closer. 'She looks very like her. But it cannot be.'

'Well, it would be an extraordinary coincidence. But we shall soon see,' Kennit replied blithely. The wind seemed to echo his words in a whisper. His stomach tightened and he lifted his hand, pretending to smooth his hair. The charm spoke close to his ear.

'There is no such thing as extraordinary coincidence. There is only destiny. So say the followers of Sa.' Soft as a breath, it added, 'This is not good fortune for you, but the delivery of your death. Sa will punish you for abandoning Etta.'

Kennit snorted, and put his hands casually behind his back. He had not abandoned the whore; he had simply put her aside for later. Sa would not punish him for that. No one would. Nor would Kennit tremble at the size of the opportunity presented to him. The biggest prizes went to the men with the boldest hands. He smiled to himself as his one hand gripped his other wrist, securely covering the charm's eyes and mouth in a smothering of lace.

Then Wintrow spoke and a shivering of dread ran down

Kennit's back. He stared at the oncoming boat and the girl's upturned face as he said almost dreamily, 'In Sa, there are no extraordinary coincidences. Only destiny.'

Malta stared up at them, frozen in shock beyond response. What could it mean? Had Althea joined Kennit's pirate crew instead of rescuing the family liveship? She could not be so false. Could she? What of Wintrow, then? When they reached the side of the ship, the Satrap was hoisted aboard first. At the encouragement of the sailors, she herself seized the rope ladder that was dropped to them. One of the *Motley's* crewmen accompanied her as she climbed the nastily swaying contraption of wet, rough rope. She tried to make a show of climbing it easily. The wet rungs bit right through the light gloves she wore to cover her roughed hands. The arduous climb was forgotten the moment she seized the railing and was assisted on board. A strange energy seemed to hum through her. She forgot to look for King Kennit as her eyes sought only for her father.

Abruptly Wintrow was there, sweeping her into a more manly hug than she would have thought her spindly brother was capable of. But he had grown and muscled, and when he cried out, 'Malta! Sa himself has brought you safely to us!' his voice was deep and sounded not unlike their father. The tears that sprang to her eyes shocked her, as did the way she clung to him, unreasonably glad of his strength and welcome. After a long moment of being held, she realized that Althea's arms were also around her. 'But how? How do you come to be here?' her aunt asked her.

But she had no desire to answer questions until the most important one had been asked. She leaned away from Wintrow, and was astonished to find how her brother had grown. 'And Papa?' she asked him breathlessly.

The deep anguish in his eyes told her all. 'He is not here,' he told her gently, and she knew better than to ask where he was. He was gone, gone forever, and she had endured all, risked all for nothing. Her father was dead.

Then the ship spoke and in Vivacia's voice was a timbre that she had heard before, when Tintaglia spoke to her through the dream-box. A terrible recognition of kinship swept through Malta as the ship hailed her. 'Well met and welcome, Dragon-Friend.'

THIRTY-ONE

Bargaining Chips

ALL EYES TURNED to the figurehead. Malta stepped free of Wintrow's embrace. No one save herself seemed to realize the ship spoke to her. Instead, their gazes travelled to the Satrap and back to the ship again. The Satrap stared at the moving, speaking figurehead in astonishment, but Malta's eyes went past him. Beside the Satrap stood a tall dark man with one peg leg. His handsome, self-possessed face showed displeasure. Beside him, the confident look was fading from Captain Red's face. He hated being upstaged. Captain Red glanced at the tall man, and Malta suddenly knew who he was. Captain Kennit, the King of the Pirate Isles. She took advantage of the distraction to appraise him. Her reaction was immediately both attraction and distrust. Like Roed Caern of Bingtown, he radiated danger. Once, she would have found him mysterious and alluring. She had grown wiser. Dangerous men were neither romantic nor exotic; they were men who could hurt you. This man would not be as easy to manipulate and convince as Captain Red had been.

'Are you too shy to speak to me?' the ship invited her warmly.

She sent the figurehead one desperate, pleading glance. She did not want the peg-legged man to see her as especially important. She must be only the Satrap's advisor. Did a flicker of understanding pass through Vivacia's eyes?

The Satrap seemed offended at the ship's coaxing words. He believed she spoke to him. 'Greetings, liveship,' he accorded her stiffly. His brief moment of wonder at her had passed. Malta supposed it reflected a lifetime of being showered with new and surprising gifts. No miracle amazed him for long. His gratitude was likewise short-lived. At least he seemed to recall her counsel: 'Do not behave as a captive, nor as a supplicant.'

He turned to Kennit. He did not bow or salute him in any way. 'Captain Kennit,' he addressed him unsmilingly. His official recognition of Kennit as King of the Pirate Isles was one of the negotiation points.

Kennit regarded him with cool amusement. 'Satrap Cosgo,' he acknowledged him familiarly, already claiming equality. The Satrap's gaze grew frostier. 'This way,' Kennit indicated. He frowned slightly at the Vestrits. 'Wintrow. Come.' To Malta, it seemed that he spoke as if her brother were a dog or a servant.

'Malta!' The Satrap's chill voice sternly reminded her of her duties.

She had a façade to maintain. She could not be Wintrow's sister, nor Althea's niece right now. She kept her voice low. 'Ask me nothing now. We must talk later. Please. Trust me. Don't interfere with what I do.' She stepped away and they let her go, but Althea's eyes were flinty. Wintrow hurried to his captain's command.

As the others left the foredeck, Althea asked aloud, 'How does she come here? What does it mean?'

'She's your niece,' Jek returned bluntly, staring wide-eyed after them.

'As if that gives me any answers. I will hold my questions

and not interfere, not because she is such a font of wise actions, but because there is nothing else I can do. I hope she realizes what a treacherous snake Kennit is.'

'Althea.' The ship cautioned her wearily.

Althea turned back to the ship. 'Why did you greet him as Dragon-Friend? The Satrap is a friend to dragons?'

'Not the Satrap,' the ship replied evasively. 'I would as soon not speak of it just now.'

'Why?' Althea demanded.

'I am troubled about other things,' Vivacia replied.

Althea sighed. 'Your serpents. Their need to be guided back to their spawning river and escorted up it. It is hard for me, still, to think of you as a dragon.' And harder still for her to accept that Vivacia had a loyalty that superseded all others. But if the serpents were first in her heart, before the Vestrits, perhaps they preceded Kennit as well. Childishly, Althea perceived a possible wedge. 'Why do you not simply demand it of Kennit?'

'Do you know anyone who reacts well to a demand?' Vivacia asked rhetorically.

'You fear he would refuse you.'

Vivacia was silent, and that quiet jolted Althea from the rut of her own concerns. It was like being lifted high on a wave and suddenly seeing to a farther horizon. She perceived Vivacia's confinement, spirit of a dragon encased in a body of wood, dependent on the men who set her sails and the winds that pushed her canvas. There were, she suddenly saw, many ways to be raped. The revelation broke her heart. Yet her next words sounded childish in her ears. 'Were you mine again, we would leave today, this minute.'

'You mean those words. I thank you for them.'

Althea had almost forgotten Jek was there until she spoke. 'You could force him. Threaten to open up your seams.'

Vivacia smiled bitterly. 'I am not mad Paragon, to recklessly menace my entire crew with wild acts of defiance. No.' Althea felt her sigh. 'Kennit will not be swayed by threats or demands. Even if I had the will, his pride would make him defy me. For this, I must hark back to your family's wisdom, Althea. I must bargain, with nothing to offer.'

Althea tried to consider it coldly. 'First, what do you want of him? Second, what can we offer him?'

'What do I want? For him to sail me back to the Rain Wild River, as swiftly as possible, and up it to the cocooning grounds. For me to remain there, near the serpents all winter, doing all we could to protect them until they hatched.' She laughed hopelessly. 'Even better would be an escort of his vessels, to guard my poor, weary serpents on their long journey. But every bit of that runs counter to Kennit's best interests.'

Althea felt stupid for not seeing it earlier. 'If he helps the serpents, he loses the use of them. They disappear to become dragons. He loses a powerful tool against Jamaillia.'

'Bolt-self was too eager to flaunt her strength to him. She did not foresee this.' She shook her head. 'As for your second question, I have nothing to offer him that he does not already possess.'

'The dragons could promise to return and aid him after they hatched,' Jek speculated.

Vivacia shook her head. 'They are not mine to bind that way. Even if I could, I would not. It is bad enough that, for as long as wizardwood endures, I must serve humans. I will not indenture the next generation.'

Jek rolled her shoulders restively. 'It's useless. There is nothing he wants that he doesn't have already.' She smiled mirthlessly. 'Save Althea.'

A terrible quiet followed her words.

Just when Etta would have been useful, she was not on board, Kennit reflected in annoyance. He had to see to everything himself, for Wintrow seemed completely addled by the presence of his sister. 'Arrange chairs and a table in the chart room. Get some food and drink as well,' he instructed him hastily.

'I'll help him,' Sorcor volunteered good-naturedly, and lumbered off after Wintrow. As well. Sorcor and his family had suffered much at the hands of the Satrap's tax collectors and his slave-masters. In their early days together, he had often drunkenly held forth on exactly what he would do if he ever got his hands on the Satrap himself. Best not to give him too much opportunity to dwell on that right now.

Kennit followed them at a leisurely pace, to give Wintrow and Sorcor time to prepare the room. He saw the young woman eyeing his stump and peg. Malta Vestrit resembled her father. Kyle Haven's arrogance was in her carefully-held mouth and narrowed eyes. He halted suddenly, and flourished his stump at her. 'A serpent bit it off,' he informed her casually. 'A hazard of life upon the seas.'

The Satrap recoiled, looking more distressed than his young Companion did. Kennit kept his smile small. Ah. He had forgotten the noble Jamaillian distaste for physical disfigurement. Could he use that? Captain Red had outlined the details of the Satrap's proposal. A dazzling offer, Kennit reflected gleefully, and only the first offer.

Kennit led them into the chart room. The preparations were adequate. Wintrow had spread a heavy cloth and added silver candlesticks. The silver tray that Wintrow held bore a collection of bottles and several glazed jugs of a Southby Island intoxicant, all recent plunder. Glasses and noggins suitable for the various drinks had been assembled as well. It was a suitable showing of wealth, without being extravagant. Kennit was pleased. He gestured at the table. 'Please, please, come in. Wintrow, do the honours with drink, there's a good fellow.'

Malta Vestrit stared round the room. Kennit could not resist. 'No doubt this chamber has changed since last you saw it,

Companion. But, please, be as at ease as if your father still occupied it.'

That provoked an unforeseen response. 'Malta Vestrit is not my Companion. You may address her as Advisor,' the Satrap informed him haughtily.

But even more interesting was how pale Malta went. She fought a look of anguish from her face.

Weakness was made to be exploited. Captain Red had warned him she was a wily negotiator. A bit of rattling might take the edge off her wits. Kennit cocked his head at her and gave a small shrug. 'A pity Captain Haven became involved in the slave trade. If he had not made that choice, this ship might still be his. I am sure you are aware of my promise to my people. I will rid the Pirate Isles of slavers. Taking Vivacia was one of my first steps.' He smiled at her.

Her mouth moved slightly, but her agonized questions went unvoiced.

'We are here to negotiate my restoration to Jamaillia City,' the Satrap observed tightly. He had already seated himself at the negotiation table. The others had chosen seats but remained standing, waiting for Kennit. This assumption of protocol did not escape the pirate.

'Of course we are,' Kennit smiled widely. He limped to the head of the table. 'Wintrow,' he said, and he obediently drew the chair out and accepted Kennit's crutch after he was seated. 'Please. Be comfortable,' Kennit invited them, and the others took their places. Sorcor was to his right, and Captain Red beyond him. Wintrow claimed the seat to his left. The Satrap and Malta were opposite Kennit. She had regained her composure. She steepled her hands on the table before her and waited.

Kennit settled himself comfortably in his chair. 'Of course, your father is still alive and in my custody. Oh, not on this ship, of course. Kyle Haven generated far too much ill-will among the crew for that. But he is quite secure where he is. If we reach a satisfactory finish today, perhaps I shall throw him in as a token to Advisor Malta Vestrit, in humble gratitude for helping us negotiate.'

The Satrap's boyish face flushed with rage. There. That had divided them. Malta had instantly suppressed it, but hope had flared bright in her eyes. She now had an interest in pleasing Kennit rather than protecting the Satrap.

She drew a sharp breath. Her voice was almost steady. 'That is most kind of you, Captain Kennit. But my interests are not those of my family today.' She tried to make eye contact with the Satrap, but he stared stonily at Kennit. 'I am here as the Satrap's most loyal subject,' she finished. She tried to put the ring of truth in her words, but Kennit heard her doubts.

'Of course, my dear. Of course,' he purred.

Now, he was ready to begin.

Brashen was catnapping on his bunk. Divvytown was little more than a day and a night away. He shifted in his bedding, trying to burrow his way to sleep. He had wrapped himself in Althea's blanket. It still smelled of her. Instead of soothing him, it made him ache with longing. He feared for her. What if their plans failed? All had gone well the last few days, he reminded himself. The crew's morale had vastly improved. A day ashore, fresh meat and vegetables, and the triumph of 'stealing' Kennit's mother had restored their faith in themselves. Mother herself seemed to have a cheering effect on them. When weather drove her from the foredeck, she went to the ship's galley, where she revealed a gift for turning hardtack into a sort of doughy pudding much favoured by the crew. Most encouraging to Brashen was that Clef had assured him that the men were putting their hearts into recovering Althea. Some felt loyalty to her; others yearned to regain pride lost at the drubbing they had received from the pirate.

A deep, recurrent sound penetrated Brashen's mind. Sleep

fled. He rolled from his bunk, rubbed his sandy eyes, and thrust his feet into his shoes. He emerged onto the deck into thin winter sunlight and a fresh breeze. Paragon knifed effortlessly through the waves. The crew took up a sudden chorus, and he looked up to see still more canvas blooming on the masts. He suddenly realized what had wakened him. Paragon's deep voice vibrated the deck with a chantey, marking time for the crew as they hoisted canvas. A shiver went up Brashen's spine, followed by a lurching lift of his heart. Familiar as he was with how a liveship's dispositions could affect their crews, he was still unprepared for this. The crew aloft was working with good-hearted energy. He hurried forwards and encountered Semoy. 'Too fine a wind to waste, sir!' the acting mate greeted his captain with a gap-toothed grin. 'I think we could see Divvytown before noon tomorrow if we can keep our canvas full!' Squinting with determination, he added, 'We'll get our Althea back, sir. You'll see.'

Brashen nodded and smiled uncertainly. When he reached the foredeck, he found Amber and Mother. Someone had secured Paragon's long dark hair in a warrior's tail. 'What goes on here?' Brashen asked in quiet disbelief.

Paragon turned his head, mouth wide as he held the final note of the chantey, then cut it off abruptly. 'Good afternoon, Captain Trell,' he boomed.

Amber laughed aloud. 'I'm not sure, but no one can resist his mood today. I don't know whether it's because Mother finished reading his logs to him, or simply that he is –'

'Decided!' Paragon declared abruptly. 'I've reached a decision, Brashen. For myself. As I never have before. I've decided to put my heart into what we do. Not for you, but for myself. I now believe that we can prevail. So does Mother. She is sure that, between the two of us, we can make Kennit see reason.'

The old woman smiled gently. The chill wind flushed her cheeks. In a strange contradiction, she seemed both frailer and more vital than she had. She nodded, approving Paragon's recital.

'The log-books were a part of it, Brashen, but not the largest piece. The largest piece is me. It has done me good to look back and see my voyages through my captains' eyes. The places I've been, Brashen, and the things I've seen, just in my life as a ship; they're all mine.' He turned away from Brashen. His eyes were still closed but he seemed to stare far over the waters. In a lowered voice he went on, 'The pain was just a part of all that. I had lives before this one, and they are just as much mine as this. I can take all my pasts, keep them, and determine my own future. I don't have to be what anyone made me, Brashen. I can be Paragon.'

Brashen lifted his hands from the railing. Did the others hear the desperation behind the ship's hopeful words? If Paragon failed at this last grasp for wholeness, he suspected the ship would spiral down into madness. 'I know you can,' Brashen told the ship warmly. A black corner of his soul felt sour and old at his lie. He dared not trust the ship's sudden elation. It seemed a mirrored distortion of his formerly bleak moods. Could not it vanish just as swiftly and arbitrarily?

'Sail!' Clef's clear tenor called down from aloft. Then, 'Sails!' he amended. 'Lots o' 'em. Jamayan ships.'

'That makes no sense,' Brashen observed.

'You want me to go aloft and take a look?' Amber offered.

'I'll do it myself,' Brashen assured her. He wanted some time alone, to think over the situation. He hadn't been up in the rigging since they'd done their reconstruction. This would be as good a time as any to see how their repairs were holding up. He started up the mast.

He was soon distracted from the repaired rigging. Clef was right. The distant ships were Jamaillian. The hodge-podge fleet flew not only the colours of Jamaillia, but the flags of the Satrapy as well. Ballista and other siege machines

cluttered the decks of several larger ships. This was no merchant fleet. The same wind that was speeding Paragon north
towards Divvytown drove them. Brashen doubted that they
were heading for the pirate town. All the same, he had no
desire to attract their attention.

Once on the deck, he ordered Semoy to slack off the speed.
'But gradually. If their lookouts are watching, I want it to
appear that we are merely falling behind due to their speed,
not slowing down to avoid them. They have no reason to be
curious about us. Let's not give them any.'

'Althea said something about rumours in Divvytown.' Amber
spoke up. 'She thought it was just a wild tale. Something about
the Bingtown Traders offending or injuring the Satrap, and
Jamaillia sending out a fleet to punish the town.'

'Like as not, the Satrap has finally tired of both the real
pirates and the pirates that masquerade as Chalcedean patrol
vessels.'

'Then they may be our allies against Kennit?' Amber speculated.

Brashen shook his head and gave a rough laugh. 'They'll be
after plunder and slaves as much as clearing the channels of
pirates. Any ship they capture, they'll keep, and the folk on
board. No. Pray Sa to keep Vivacia well out of their sight,
for if they seize her, our chances of getting Althea back are
reduced to buying her on the slave block.'

'More candles, Wintrow,' Kennit suggested merrily.

Wintrow stifled a sigh and rose to obey. The Satrap looked
like a hollow-eyed ghost and the paint showed starkly on
Malta's pale face. Even Captain Red and Sorcor had begun
to show signs of weariness. Only Kennit still possessed his
frenzied energy.

Malta had come to the table with the dignity and composure
of a Trader. Wintrow had been proud of his younger sister. She

had presented her proposal in careful phrases, and at every point, had enumerated the advantages it would bring both to Kennit and the Satrap. Recognition of Kennit as King of the Pirate Isles, a sovereign state. An end to Jamaillian slave raiders in the Pirate Isles. No more Chalcedean 'patrol' boats in the Pirate Isles. Captain Red and Sorcor had grinned with triumph. They had been more subdued as she went on to list what the Satrap wanted in exchange: his safe return to Jamaillia City, escorted by Kennit's fleet, with the assurance that the Pirate Isles recognized and supported him as the Satrap of Jamaillia. In the future, Kennit would pledge safe passage for Jamaillian-flagged ships through the Inside Passage, and would himself subdue any 'independent' pirates who ignored the agreement.

At first, Kennit had waxed enthusiastic. He had sent Wintrow for parchment, pen, and ink, and instructed him to write it up. That had been straightforward, save for the matters of the proper forms for referring to the Satrap. That alone took nearly half a page of 'His Most Glorious and Magnificent Honour' and the like. Kennit had leaped into the spirit of it, dictating that the document refer to him as 'The Daring and Undefeated Pirate Captain Kennit, King of the Pirate Isles by Virtue of his Boldness and Cunning.' Wintrow had seen the dancing merriment in Captain Red's eyes as well as the profound pride in Sorcor's as he transcribed these illustrious titles. He had thought that would bring a swift end to the negotiations, but Kennit had only begun.

Swiftly and surely, he began to tack other provisions on to the pact. The fabulously powerful Satrap of Jamaillia could not expect him, King of scattered towns of outcasts, to patrol these waters against miscreant pirates with no remuneration. Whatever agreement Jamaillia had had with the Chalcedean patrol vessels would be passed on to Kennit and his 'patrol' ships. How could the Satrap object? It would not be any more coins out of his coffers; they would simply be going to a different set of ships. And, of course, in reciprocal courtesy, ships bearing Kennit's Raven flag would pass unmolested in Jamaillian waters on their journeys to points south. As for selective pardons to criminals who had fled to the Pirate Isles, why, that was all much too confusing. A blanket pardon of every one of Kennit's subjects would be much easier to manage.

When the Satrap objected that these 'Tattooed' would be indistinguishable from the lawful slaves of Jamaillia, Kennit had appeared to take him seriously. He had gravely proposed that the Satrap, by edict, have all free folk of Jamaillia tattooed with a special mark that would proclaim them free subjects of the Satrap. Captain Red had had a coughing fit to cover his laughter, but the Satrap had flushed scarlet. Standing, he had declared himself irrevocably offended. The Satrap had stalked to the door and out of it. Malta had followed him miserably. Her humiliated stare betrayed that she realized what the Satrap did not. There was no place for him to go. This 'negotiation' was to become little more than a documented robbery. While they waited out the Satrap's temper tantrum, Kennit ordered Wintrow to pour the finest spirits for his lieutenants, and sent him to fetch samples of the cheeses and exotic preserved fruits he had captured on his most recent foray. They were relaxed and warm and comfortable when the Satrap returned followed by a defeated Malta. They resumed their seats at the table. In a chill voice, the Satrap offered Kennit one hundred signed pardons that he could distribute as he saw fit.

'A thousand,' Kennit countered as coolly. He leaned back in his chair. 'And you would give me the authorization to issue others as needed.'

'Done,' the Satrap snapped sulkily as Malta's mouth opened in angry protest. The young ruler glared at her. 'It costs me nothing. Why should not I give it to him?'

That set the tone for all that followed. Malta's efforts to give ground grudgingly were undermined by the Satrap's obvious despair and ultimately his boredom with the whole process.

Jamaillian ships that stopped for water, supplies or trade in the Pirate Isles would pay a fee to Kennit. Jamaillia would not interfere with Kennit's right to regulate trade and ships passing through the Pirate Isles. Sorcor's triumph was that persons condemned to be sold on the block for debt would be offered the option of exile to the Pirate Isles. Captain Red inserted that individual actors would no longer be responsible for the debts of a troupe. From there, the political significance of Kennit's demands dwindled to mere piracy of privilege. A suite of rooms in the Satrap's palace would be reserved exclusively for Kennit in the event that he ever chose to visit Jamaillia City. Any serpent sighted in Inside Passage waters was to be considered Kennit's property and left unmolested. Kennit was always to be referred to as the Merciful and Just King Kennit of the Pirate Isles. The negotiations flagged only when Kennit's inventiveness began to fail him.

As Wintrow rose to fetch fresh candles for the table, he reflected that soon they would not need them. The talks had consumed the night: a late winter dawn was breaking over the water. He stood beside Malta as he fitted the candles into the heavy silver holders and wished he could reach her as he did the ship, with no more than a focused thought. He wished she knew that although he sat with those who opposed her, he was proud of her. She had bargained like a true Trader. If Kennit's offer of restoring their father had weighed on her mind, she had refused to show it. Small hope that Kennit would honour that offer. How Malta had come to be in the Satrap's company was still a mystery, but the rigours of that journey showed on her face. If the negotiations went successfully, what then? Would she leave with the Satrap?

He longed for this to be over, so he could talk with her. His hunger for news from home was more powerful than his need for food and sleep. He lit the last candle and resumed his seat. Kennit surprised him by clapping him genially on the shoulder. 'Tired, son? Well, we are nearly at the end of this.

All that remains to negotiate now is the actual ransom itself. Some prefer coins, but I am more lenient in these matters. Precious gems, pearls, furs, tapestries, even . . .'

'This is outrageous!' Despite his weariness, the Satrap lurched to his feet. His mouth had gone white and pinched. His clenched hands trembled with fury. For one horrifying instant, Wintrow feared he would burst into angry tears. Malta reached a supportive hand towards him, but stopped short of touching him. She sent Kennit a killing glare. When she spoke, her voice was calm.

'Lord Magnadon Satrap, I see the logic of this. Your nobles will value you less if they have not had to pay anything to recover you. Consider this. It will give you a way to gauge who is truly loyal to you. You will reward those who are willing to contribute to your recovery later. Those who are not will feel your magnificent wrath. King Kennit is, after all, my lord, still a pirate.' She gave Kennit a tight-lipped smile, as if to be sure her barb hit home. 'All your nobles would distrust a treaty in which he did not demand some sort of reward for himself, rather than merely benefits for his people.'

It was pathetic. She saw that the Satrap was powerless to refuse Kennit. She sought to save the boy's pride for him. The Satrap's mouth worked soundlessly for a moment. He shot Malta a venomous look. Then, in a quiet voice, he hissed, 'Certainly that is so. It has nothing to do with you grovelling to regain your father, does it?' He swung his look to Kennit. 'How much?' he snapped bitterly.

'SAILS!' All heads turned to the lookout's cry, but Kennit merely looked annoyed. 'See to that, would you, Sorcor?' he requested lazily. He turned back to the Satrap and smiled, a great black tomcat toying with a mouse. But before Sorcor could reach the door, Wintrow heard running footsteps outside it. Jola did not knock, he pounded on the wood. Sorcor jerked the door open.

Jola blurted out, 'Sir, Jamaillian ships! A whole fleet of

them headed our way from the south. Lookout says he sees war machines on their decks.' He drew breath. 'We can escape them if we up anchor now.'

Hope kindled in the Satrap's eyes. 'Now we shall see!' he declared.

'Indeed we shall,' Kennit agreed affably. He turned to his mate with a rebuke. 'Jola, Jola, why would we flee, when fate has given me every advantage in this confrontation? We are in familiar waters, our serpents surround us, and we have the supreme Magnadon Satrap as our . . . guest. A small demonstration of power is in order.' He turned to the Satrap. 'Your fleet may be more prone to honour our agreement if they have first enjoyed the attentions of a few serpents. Then we shall see how well they negotiate for your release.' He gave a thin-lipped smile to the Satrap and thrust the treaty towards him. 'I am going to enjoy finalizing this. Your signature, sir. Then I shall affix mine. When they confront us, if they do, we shall see what regard they have for their Satrap's word. And for his life.' He grinned at Sorcor. 'I believe we have several Jamaillian flags among our plunder. As the Lord High Magnadon Satrap of all Jamaillia is our guest, it is only fitting that we fly them in his honour.'

Kennit rose from the table, abruptly a sea captain again. He gave his first mate a disdainful look. 'Jola. Calm yourself. See that the Satrap's flag is added to our own, then have the men prepare themselves for battle. Sorcor, Red, I recommend you return to your ships and do likewise. I must consult with my ship and the serpents. Ah, yes. Our guests. Wintrow, make them comfortable and secure in Althea's room, will you? She and Jek will join them there until this is over.'

He did not specifically command that they be locked in. Wintrow clutched that omission to himself. He would have a few moments with his sister.

THIRTY-TWO

An Ultimatum

Althea was not gracious about leaving the foredeck. She had seen the oncoming sails, and her fears for Vivacia battled with her hopes of Kennit's defeat. Wintrow's urgent pleas went unheeded until Vivacia herself turned to her. 'Althea. Please go below. This might be my chance to strike a bargain with Kennit. It will be easier for me if you are not present.' Althea had scowled, but left the foredeck, Jek trailing after her.

Wintrow made a hasty side trip to the galley, to cobble together a large tray of food and drink. By the time he reached the cabin, Althea and Malta were already facing one another across the room. The Satrap had thrown himself onto the bunk and was staring at the wall. Jek sat morosely in the corner. Malta was furious. 'I don't understand why either of you would take his part. He pirated our liveship, killed her crew and holds my father captive.'

'You are not listening,' Althea said coldly. 'I despise Kennit. All the assumptions you have made are false.'

Wintrow clashed the tray down onto the small table. 'Eat and drink something. All of you. Then talk, one at a time.'

The Satrap rolled to look at the table. His eyes were red. Wintrow wondered if he had been weeping silently. His voice was choked with an emotion, possibly outrage. 'Is this another of Kennit's humiliations for me? I am expected to eat here, in these crowded circumstances, in the company of common folk?'

'Magnadon Satrap, it is no worse than sharing a table with pirates. Or eating alone in your room. Come. You must eat if you are to keep up your strength.'

Wintrow and Althea exchanged incredulous looks at Malta's solicitous tone. Witnessing this, Wintrow felt suddenly uncomfortable. Were they lovers? His aunt's admission had made all sorts of unthinkable things possible. 'I'm going up on deck, to see what is happening. I'll try to bring back word to you.' He hastened from the room.

The Jamaillian ships drew ever closer, spreading out as they came. Their obvious strategy was to bar his way south and surround him. The ships on the wings of the formation had picked up their speed. If he was going to flee, he must turn tail soon, before the Jamaillians could close their net. This was no time for talk, but the liveship spoke anyway.

'Kennit. You cannot question my loyalty to you. But my serpents grow weary. They need food and rest. More than anything else, they need me to lead them home soon.'

'Of course they do.' Kennit heard the haste in his own voice and tried to change his tone. 'Believe me, sweet sea lady, your concerns are my own. We, you and I, shall see them safely home. I shall give you the time you have asked me to give you, that you may watch over them. Immediately after this.'

One of the smaller ships separated from the fleet and came on. No doubt, it would hail them soon. Kennit needed to be ready, not engaged in conversation. The opportunity for complete victory was as large as the danger of complete failure. If the serpents did not help him, his three ships stood small chance against such a fleet.

'What do you ask of us?' Vivacia asked wearily.

Kennit did not like the sound of that. He tried to change

it. 'We will ask them to subdue this fleet for us. It would take little effort from them. Their presence alone may be enough to persuade the ships to surrender. Once we show the Jamaillians that we have the Satrap, I suspect we'll gain their full co-operation. Then the serpents would escort us as we journey to Jamaillia City, in a show of force. Once the Satrap and his nobles have conceded to the terms of our treaty, why then, we will be free to follow our hearts. I will summon every vessel at my command. We will protect and guide the serpents on their journey home.'

Vivacia's face had grown graver as he spoke. Desperation came into her eyes as she slowly shook her head. 'Kennit. Bolt in her rashness made you offers that we cannot keep. Forgive me, but it is so. The serpents do not have that sort of time. Their lives begin to dwindle within them. We must go soon. Tomorrow, if we can.'

'Tomorrow?' Kennit suddenly felt as if the deck were falling away from him. 'Impossible. I would have to let the Satrap go, release him to his own ships, and then flee like a dog with its tail between its legs. Vivacia, it would destroy all we have worked for, just when our goal is within our grasp.'

'I could ask the serpents to help you this last time. After the fleet concedes to you, you could take the Satrap onto the *Marietta*. Have the *Motley* carry the word to Divvytown, and have it disperse from there that all your ships are to join you on your journey south. That would be as impressive as weary and dying serpents.' She stopped herself as if she heard the sarcasm that had crept into her voice. 'Let Wintrow and Althea take me north, with my serpents. They could stay with me as I keep watch over the cocoons, freeing you to firm your kingship. I vow I would return to you by high summer, Kennit.'

She spoke her treachery aloud to him. Here, at the pinnacle of his need for her, she would leave him, to return to her Bingtown family. He cursed himself silently for not heeding Bolt. He never should have brought Althea on board. He gripped his crutch and forced calmness on himself. The terrible plummet from dawning triumph to imminent disaster choked him.

'I see,' he managed to say. Behind him, the mood on the deck was jubilant. Unaware of her betrayal, his crew exchanged rough jests as they eagerly awaited the encounter. The ostentatious Captain Red had spread wide the news of Kennit's negotiations. All expected him to succeed. To fail now, so publicly, was unthinkable.

'Help me as you can today,' he suggested. He refused to think he begged. 'And tomorrow will have to take care of itself.'

A strange look passed over Vivacia's face, like anticipated pain. She closed her wide green eyes for an instant. When she opened them, her gaze was distant. 'No, Kennit,' she said softly. 'Not unless you give me your word that tomorrow we take the serpents north. That is the price for them helping you today.'

'Of course.' He did not think about the lie. She knew him too well. If he paused to consider it, she would know the falsehood. 'You have my word, Vivacia. If it is that important to you, it is important to me as well.' Tomorrow, as he had told her, would have to take care of itself. He would deal with the consequences then. He watched the single ship separate itself from the Jamaillian fleet and come towards him. Soon it would be within hailing distance.

'Can you see anything?' Jek asked.

Althea, her forehead pressed to the porthole, did not answer. This tiny, expensive window had been a major indulgence from her father. The rest of her room had changed, but she could not touch this without thinking of him. What would her father think of her now? She burned with shame. This was her family's ship, and here she was, hiding belowdecks while a pirate negotiated from her deck. 'What is going on out there?' she wondered aloud. 'What is he saying to them?'

The door opened and Wintrow entered, cheeks red from the wind. He began speaking immediately. 'The Jamaillians challenged our passage. Kennit called himself King of the Pirate Isles and demanded they give way. They refused. He returned that he had the Satrap aboard and that the Satrapy had recognized him as the legitimate King of the Pirate Isles. They scoffed at him, saying the Satrap was dead. Kennit replied that the Satrap was very much alive, and that he was taking him to Jamaillia to restore him to his throne. They demanded proof. He shouted back that the proof they would get, they would not like. Then they offered to let him leave if he first surrendered the Satrap to them. He replied he was not a fool. Now the Jamaillian negotiating ship has pulled back. Kennit has said they may have time to think, but warns them to stand where they are. All wait to see who will make the next move.'

'Waiting. More waiting,' Althea ground out the word. 'Surely he won't sit still and wait while they surround us. The only logical course is to flee.' Then she stared at the Satrap. 'This is true, what Kennit says? You have recognized him as king? How could you be so stupid?'

'It's complicated,' Malta flung back at her while the indignant Satrap glared. 'He would have been more stupid to refuse.' In a lower voice, she added, 'We took our only chance at survival. But I don't expect you to understand that.'

'How could I?' Althea retorted. 'I still don't know how you even came to be here, let alone with the Satrap of Jamaillia.' She took a breath. She evened her tone. 'As long as we are stuck here and must wait, why don't you tell me how you came to be here. How did you leave Bingtown at all?'

Malta did not want to speak first. A tiny motion of her

eyes towards the Satrap cued Wintrow to her reluctance. Althea did not notice it. Her aunt had never been one for subtleties. She scowled at Malta's reticence, and Malta was relieved when Wintrow interfered. 'I was the first to leave Bingtown. Althea knows a bit of what I've been through, but Malta knows nothing. Althea is right. As we must wait, let's use the time wisely. I'll tell my travels first.' His eyes were both sympathetic and shamed as he added, 'I know you are anxious for news of our father. I wish I had more to tell.'

He launched into an honest but brief account of all that had passed. Malta felt incredulous when he spoke of being tattooed as a slave at her father's command. What had become of the tattoo, then? She bit her tongue to keep from calling him a liar. His tale of their father's disappearance was as incredible as the story of rescuing a serpent. When he told of how the ship had cured him and erased the scar, she was sceptical but kept silent.

Althea's face betrayed that she had not heard a full accounting of Wintrow's journey. She, at least, looked perfectly willing to believe that Kyle Haven was capable of anything. When Wintrow spoke of his father's disappearance at Kennit's hands, she only shook her head. Jek, the hulking Six Duchies woman, listened attentively, as if she appreciated a good yarn. Meanwhile, beside Malta, the Satrap ate and drank, with no concern for the others. Before Wintrow had finished speaking, the Satrap had claimed the bunk and turned to face the wall.

When Wintrow finally ran out of words, Althea looked at her expectantly. But Malta suggested, 'Let us tell our stories in order. You left Bingtown next.'

Althea cleared her throat. Wintrow's simple telling had moved her more than she was willing to show. Decisions she had faulted him for were now made clear. Truly, she should have allowed him to speak of this before. She owed him an apology. Later. Given what he had gone through with Kennit, it was no wonder he had sided with the man. It was understandable, if not forgivable. She realized she was staring silently at him. His face had reddened. She looked aside and sought order for her own thoughts. There was so much she did not wish to share with these youngsters. Did she owe Malta the truth about her relationship with Brashen? She would give them, she decided, the facts, not her feelings. Those belonged only to her.

'Malta will remember the day we left Bingtown on Paragon. The ship handled well, and the sailing was good for the first few days, but –'

'Wait,' Wintrow dared interrupt his aunt. 'Go back to the last time I saw you, and tell me from there. I wish to hear it all.'

'Very well,' Althea conceded gruffly. For a time, she looked at the sky outside the porthole. Wintrow could see her deciding how much to share with him. When she spoke, she told things in a bare, bald way, her voice becoming dispassionate as she approached more recent events. Perhaps it was the only way she could speak of them. She did not look at Wintrow, but spoke directly to Malta of the sinking of Paragon with all hands, including Brashen Trell. In a cold flat voice, she spoke of her rape. Wintrow lowered his eyes, shocked by the flare of both understanding and hatred in Malta's eyes. He did not interrupt her. He kept his peace until she said, 'Of course, no one aboard believes me. Kennit has impressed them all with his gentlemanly ways. Even my own ship doubts me.'

Wintrow's throat and mouth were dry. 'Althea. I don't doubt you.' They were among the most painful words he had ever spoken.

The look she gave him near broke his heart. 'You never spoke out for me,' she accused him.

'It would have done no good.' The words sounded cowardly, even to himself. He lowered his eyes and said honestly, 'I

believe you because Etta told me she believed you. That was
why she left the ship. Because she could not live as witness to
what he had done. Sa help me, I remained, but kept silent.'

'Why?' The flat, one word question came not from his aunt
but his sister. He forced himself to meet Malta's eyes.

'I know Kennit,' he found himself saying. The truth he
acknowledged now cut him. 'He has done good things, even
great things. But one reason he could do them was because
he does not bind himself by rules.' His eyes went from Malta's
doubting face to Althea's frozen one. 'He accomplished much
good,' he said softly. 'I wanted to be part of that. So I followed
him. And I looked aside from the evil things he did. I became
very good at ignoring that which I could not countenance.
Until finally, when the evil was directed at one of my own
blood, it was still easier not to avow it aloud.' His voice had
become a whisper. 'Even now, to admit it makes me . . . part of
it. That is the most difficult part. I wanted to share in the glory
he gained for the good he did. But if I claim that, then –'

'You can't play in shit and not get some on you,' Jek observed
succinctly from her corner. She reached up to set a large hand
on Althea's knee. 'I'm sorry,' she said simply.

Shame burned in him. 'I am sorry, too, Althea. So sorry.
Not only that he did this to you, but that you suffered my
silence.'

'We have to kill him,' Jek continued when neither Althea
nor Malta spoke. 'I see no alternative.'

For an icy moment, Wintrow supposed she spoke of him.
Althea shook her head slowly. Tears stood in her eyes but did
not spill. 'I've thought about that. At first, I thought about
little else. I would do it in an instant, if I could do it without
injuring the ship. Before I take that step, she must see him for
what he is. Wintrow. Are you willing to help me with that?
To make Vivacia see him as he truly is?'

Wintrow lifted his chin. 'I must. Not for you, not for the
ship. For myself. I owe myself that honesty.'

'But what of Father?' Malta demanded in a low, agonized voice. 'Althea, I beg you, consider that. If not for his children, for Keffria, your sister. Whatever you think of Kyle, please do not endanger my father's return to us. Hold back your hand from Kennit, for at least that long –'

A long low sound suddenly travelled through the ship. Althea heard it with her ears, but her bones shook with the sound. A meaning she could almost grasp ran along her skin, leaving goosebumps in its wake. She forgot all else, reaching after it.

'It's Vivacia,' Wintrow said needlessly.

Malta got a distant look. 'She calls the serpents,' she said softly.

Althea stared at Malta, as did Wintrow. Her eyes were wide and dark.

In the silence that followed, a long snore sounded from the Satrap's bunk. Malta jerked as if awakening, then gave a small sour laugh. 'It sounds as if I may now speak freely, without interruptions, corrections and accusations of treachery.' To Althea's surprise, Malta swiped at sudden tears, smearing the paint from her face. She drew a shuddering breath. Then she tugged off her gloves, revealing hands scalded scarlet. She snatched her headwrap off and threw it down. A shocking ridge of bright red scar began high on her brow and stood up well into her hairline. 'Get the staring part over with,' she ordered them in a harsh hopeless voice. 'And then I will speak . . .' Her voice broke suddenly. 'There is so much. What happened to me is the least of it. Bingtown is destroyed; when last I saw it, fires smouldered and fighting was widespread.' Althea watched her niece as she spoke. Malta spared them nothing. Her tale was in its details, but she spoke swiftly, the words tumbling from her lips, her voice soft. Althea felt the tears run down her cheeks at news of Davad Restart's death; the strength of her reaction surprised her, but what followed left her numbed and reeling.

The rumours of unrest in Bingtown were suddenly a personal disaster. She was devastated when she realized Malta had no idea if her grandmother or Selden still lived. Malta spoke of Bingtown and Trehaug with detachment, an old woman telling quaint stories of her vanished youth. Emotionlessly, she told her brother of her arranged marriage to Reyn Khuprus, of fleeing to his family in Trehaug when Bingtown fell, of the curiosity that had drawn her into the buried city and the quake that had nearly claimed her life. Once, Malta would have made an extravagance of such a tale, but now she simply recounted it. When Malta spoke of Reyn, Althea suspected the young Rain Wilder had won her niece's heart. Personally, she felt Malta was still too young to make such decisions. Yet as Malta spoke on, her voice hushed and hurrying through her days with the Satrap, Althea realized the girl faced the world as a woman. Her experiences aboard the galley left Althea shuddering. Malta laughed, a terrible sound, at how her disfigurement had preserved her from worse treatment. By the time Malta finished, Althea loathed the Satrap, yet understood the value Malta placed on him. She doubted he would keep his promises to her, but it impressed Althea that even in her time of danger, Malta had thought of her home and family and done all she could for them. Truly, the girl had grown up. Althea recalled ashamedly that she had once felt that some hardship would improve Malta. Undoubtedly she had been improved, but the cost had been high. The skin on her hands looked as coarse as a chicken's foot. The cicatrix on her head was a monstrous thing, shocking in both colour and size. But beyond the physical scarring, she sensed a dulling of her high spirits. The girl-child's elaborate dreams of a romantic future had been replaced with a woman's determination to survive tomorrow. It felt like a loss to Althea.

'At least you are with us now,' Althea offered her when Malta finished. She had wanted to say, 'Safe with us,' but Malta was no longer a little girl to be cozened with falsehoods.

'I wonder for how long,' Malta replied miserably. 'For where he goes, I must follow, until I am sure he is safely restored to power, and that he will keep his word to me. Otherwise, all this has been for nothing. Yet, if I leave you here, will I ever see you again? Althea, at least, must find a way to get off this ship and away from Kennit.'

Althea shook her head with a sad smile. 'I cannot leave my ship with him, Malta,' she said quietly. 'No matter what.'

Malta turned aside from her. Her chin trembled for an instant, but then she spoke harshly. 'The ship. Always the ship, distorting our family, demanding every sacrifice. Have you ever imagined how different our lives would have been if great-great-grandmother had never bargained our lives away for this thing?'

'No.' Althea's voice went cold. She could not help it. 'Despite all, I do not begrudge her anything.'

'She has made a slave of you,' Malta observed bitterly. 'Blind to all else.'

'Oh, no. Never that.' Althea tried to find words to express it. 'In her lies my true freedom.' But did it? Those words had once been true, but Vivacia had changed. She and the ship no longer completed one another. A tiny traitor portion of her mind recalled her stolen day with Brashen in Divvytown. If he had lived, would she have been able to say such words? Did she cling to Vivacia because she was all that was left to her?

The whole ship suddenly reverberated with the trumpeting of serpents. 'They come,' Malta whispered.

'It would be safest for all of you if you stayed here,' Wintrow announced. 'I'll find out what is going on.'

Kennit stood on the foredeck, relief coursing through his body. The serpents were coming. He had spoken boldly to the envoy from the fleet, wondering all the while if the serpents would aid him. When he granted the Jamaillians time to confer, he was secretly stealing time for Vivacia to persuade the serpents. When first Vivacia had called them, the water about the ship had boiled with the serpents, but had dispersed suddenly, and for a time, he feared that they had forsaken him. The Jamaillian ship rejoined its fleet and boats from the other vessels converged on it. Time dragged for Kennit. There, across the water, men discussed strategy to crush him while he waited docilely on his foredeck in the biting wind.

After a time, the Jamaillian boats returned to their ships. He had not dared ask Vivacia what was happening. His crew had come to the ready and now waited. The anticipation aboard the ship was palpable. Kennit knew every pirate waited to see the serpents suddenly flash towards the fleet. At a distance, he would see a sudden turmoil of serpents and hear their muted calls. But none came near. Soon he would have to make a decision: stand and confront the Jamaillian fleet, or flee. If he fled, the fleet would certainly give chase. Even if they didn't believe he held the Satrap, the odds against him were too great for the Jamaillians to resist. His piracy and his destruction of the slave trade would rankle with all of them.

Then, with a suddenness that roused whoops of delight from his crew, a forest of serpent heads on supple necks rose suddenly around the Vivacia. They spoke to the ship, and she answered in their tongue. After a time, she glanced at him. He drew close to her to hear her soft words to him.

'They are divided,' Vivacia warned him quietly. 'Some say they are too weary. They will save their strength for themselves. Others say, this last time, they will aid you. But if we do not take them north tomorrow, all will leave without us. If I fail to keep my word –' She paused before stiffly resuming, 'Some talk of killing me before they leave. Dismembering me and devouring the wizardwood parts of me for my memories might be helpful to them.'

It had never occurred to him that the serpents might turn on Vivacia. If they did, he could not save her. He would have to flee on the *Marietta*, and hope the serpents did not pursue them.

'We'll take them north tomorrow,' he confirmed to her.

She murmured something that might have been agreement.

Kennit considered only briefly. Tomorrow, this weapon might no longer be his to control. He would wield it one last time, in a way that would become the stuff of legend. He would break Jamaillia's sea power while he had the strength to do so. 'Attack them,' he commanded flatly. 'Show no mercy until I say otherwise.'

He sensed a moment of indecision from Vivacia. Then she lifted her arms and sang in that unearthly voice to the gathered serpents. The maned heads turned towards the fleet and stared. As silence fell, the serpents surged forwards, living arrows flying towards their targets.

The serpents flashed and glittered as they streamed towards the oncoming ships. Only about a third of them went. Those that remained were impressive, he told himself, flanking his ship like an honour guard. He became aware of Wintrow behind him.

'I did not send as many this time,' Kennit hastily told him. 'No sense in risking sinking the ships, as they did with Paragon.'

'And safer for the serpents as well,' Wintrow observed. 'They will be more spread out, and harder to hit.'

This had not occurred to him. Kennit watched the phalanx of serpents. Perhaps no other human eye could have discerned that they did not move as swiftly as they once had, nor swim as powerfully. Even their colours were less jewel-like. Truly, the serpents were failing. Those who surrounded his ship still confirmed his fears. Once-gleaming eyes and scales had dulled. Rags of skin hung from a maroon serpent's neck as if it had tried to slough its skin but failed. No matter, he told himself. No matter. If they would get him through this final battle, he would have no further need of them. He had pirated well before the serpents allied with him. He could do so again.

The decks of the oncoming Jamaillian ships teemed with activity as war machines were readied against the advancing creatures. Human shouts mingled suddenly with serpent calls. The smaller ships released volleys of arrows. Rocks arced over the glittering water, finishing in silvery splashes as several large ships released their catapults. By the sheerest luck, they struck a serpent on the first volley. Harsh cheers of triumph rose from the Jamaillian ship. The injured creature, a skinny green serpent, shrilly trumpeted its pain. The other serpents flocked to its cries. Its long body wallowed on the surface, sending up sprays of silver water as it thrashed.

'Broke its back,' Wintrow harshly whispered. His eyes were narrowed in pained sympathy. The figurehead gave a low moan and dropped her face into her hands. 'My fault,' she whispered. 'He lived so long and came so far, to die this way? My fault. Oh, Tellur, I am so sorry.'

Before the green serpent sank out of sight, the rest of the serpents left Vivacia's side. The purposeful wave of creatures cut the water in a multitude of wakes as they sliced towards the oncoming ships. On board the threatened ships, crews worked frantically, rewinding and reloading the ballistae. The serpents no longer roared. The shouts of the frightened humans carried clearly across the water. Beside him, Kennit heard Wintrow draw in a deep breath. A deep mutter swelled behind him. Kennit glanced over his shoulder. His crew had halted in their tasks. They were transfixed in the anticipation of horror.

They were not to be disappointed.

The serpents encircled the ship that had fired the successful shot. The long-necked serpents reminded him of the closing tendrils of a sea anemone. Roaring and spraying venom, they engulfed the ship. The canvas melted from the masts, then masts and rigging tumbled to the deck like an armful of kindling. The shrill screams of the crew were a brief accompaniment to the serpents' roars. Then the larger serpents threw themselves across its deck like living heaving-lines. Their great weight and thrashing coils bore the ship under, where it swiftly broke apart.

From behind Kennit came hushed exclamations of awe and horror. Kennit himself could vividly imagine how Vivacia could come apart in their coils.

As the Jamaillian ships retreated from the serpents' victim, they continued a hail of stones. The serpents snatched up the drowning crewmen and devoured them, then turned their attention to the other ships. Several vessels sought to flee, but it was already too late for that. The serpents spread throughout the fleet, as yielding but capturing as a bed of kelp. The efforts of the creatures were divided now, the results not as swift. Serpents circled the ships, spraying venom. Some of the larger serpents resorted to ramming. One ship lost its sails. Another serpent was hit. It screamed furiously, and lunged at the ship before falling away lifelessly. That ship became a target for the surviving serpents' concentrated fury.

'Call them back,' Wintrow pleaded in a low voice.

'Why?' Kennit asked conversationally. 'If we were in their hands and dying, do you think they would be seized with sudden mercy for us?'

'Please, Vivacia! Call them back!' Wintrow cried out to the ship herself.

Vivacia shook her great head slowly. Kennit's heart soared to find her so loyal to him, but then in a mutter meant only for Kennit and Wintrow, she slew the pirate's dream.

'I cannot. They are beyond anyone's control now. They are in a frenzy, driven as much by despair as revenge. I fear that when they are finished, they will turn on me.'

Wintrow's face paled. 'Should we flee now? Can we out-run them?'

Kennit knew they could not. He chose to put a brave face on it. Well, at least no one would outlive him to tell any tales. He clapped Wintrow on the shoulder. 'Trust the luck, Wintrow. Trust the luck. All will be well. Sa did not bring me through all this to leave me serpent bait at the end.' A sudden thought occurred to him. 'Signal Sorcor on the *Marietta*. Tell him to send Etta back to me.'

'Now? In the midst of all this?' Wintrow was horrified.

Kennit laughed aloud. 'There's no pleasing you, is there? You told me that Etta belonged at my side. I've decided you're right. She should be beside me, especially on a day like this. Signal Sorcor.'

Tiny Chalcedean galleys flanked a sailing ship on the seas below them.

'Shall we liven up their day?' Tintaglia suggested in a low rumble.

'Please, no,' Reyn groaned. The deep bruises on his chest made even breathing painful. The last thing he wanted was to be shaken in her clutches as she swooped and darted above the ships. He felt a shudder of anticipation run through her and groaned, but she did not dive on the ship.

'Did you hear that?' she demanded.

'No. What?' he demanded, but instead of answering, her great wings stroked with a sudden energy. The ocean and the ship upon it receded beneath him. He shut his eyes as she beat her way higher still. When he dared to open them again, the ocean below them was a rippling fabric, the islands scattered toys. He could not get his breath. 'Please,' he begged dizzily.

She did not reply. Instead, she caught a cold current of air with her wings and hung there. He closed his eyes and endured miserably. 'There!' she cried out suddenly. He did not have the breath to ask her what. They tipped and went sliding down the sky. The cold wind bit to his bones. Just when he thought he could be no more miserable, Tintaglia gave vent to an ear-shattering scream. The sound rang in his ears even

743

as his small human soul was consumed by her mental shout of triumph. 'See them! There they are!'

'Something's happened!' Althea announced to the others in the room. 'The serpents cease their attack. They all turn their heads.' She stared out of the small porthole. She could see a small segment of the battle, but by it she judged the whole. Of the five ships she could see, all had taken damage. On one, sails drooped in tatters and there was little deck activity. It would never see port again. The serpents had broken the fleet's formation and scattered them, forcing each ship to battle individually. Now the serpents had suddenly ceased their attacks and stared up at the sky with their huge gleaming eyes.

'What?' Malta asked anxiously, sitting up straight.

Jek gave up her vigil at the door. 'Let me see,' she demanded, coming to the porthole. Althea ducked out of her way and stepped to the middle of the room. She reached overhead to put her hands flat to a beam. 'I wish I were more closely linked to Vivacia. I wish I could see with her eyes, as I once did.'

'What does she feel? Wait! Where are all the serpents going?' Jek demanded.

'She feels too much. Fear and anxiety and sorrow. Are the serpents leaving?'

'They're going somewhere,' Jek replied. She turned away from the porthole with an impatient snort. 'Why are we staying in here? Let's go out on the deck and see.'

'Might as well,' Althea replied grimly.

'Wintrow said we'd be safer here,' Malta reminded them. She lifted her hands suddenly to her head as if even the thought of venturing onto the deck pained her.

'I don't think he expected things to go this way,' Althea replied reassuringly. 'I think we should find out what is happening.'

'I demand that you all remain here!' the Satrap shouted suddenly. He sat up, his face creased with anger. 'I will not be abandoned! As my subjects, you owe me loyalty. Remain here, to protect me as necessary.'

A grin twisted Jek's mouth. 'Sorry, little man. I'm not your subject, and even if I were, I'd still go up to the deck. But if you want to come with us, I'll watch your back for you.'

Malta dropped her hands from her face. She drew a sudden breath through her gaping mouth, then announced, 'We have to get to the deck. Right now! Tintaglia comes! The dragon calls to the serpents.'

'What? A dragon?' Althea demanded incredulously.

'I can feel her.' Wonder was in Malta's voice. She jumped to her feet, her dark eyes growing ever larger. 'I can feel the dragon. And hear her! Just as you can know things through the ship. Don't doubt me, Althea. This is true.' Then she paled, her wonder turning to despair. 'And Reyn is with her. He comes, all this way, seeking me. Me!' She lifted a hand to cover her mouth and her face crumpled.

'Don't be frightened,' Althea said gently. Abruptly she feared for Malta's sanity. Had she dreaded her arranged marriage that much? The girl hunched on her chair. Her fingertips prodded the ridged scar on her brow. She dropped her hands away as if burned, then stared at her claw-like fingers. 'No,' she whispered. 'No, it's not fair.'

'What is the matter with her?' the Satrap demanded disdainfully. 'Is she ill? If she is ill, I wish her taken away.'

Althea knelt beside her niece. 'Malta?' What ailed the girl?

'Stop.' The word was as much command as plea. Malta pushed herself ponderously to her feet. She moved as if she were made of separate pieces, none of which fit together very well. Her eyes were flat. She picked up her headwrap from the table, looked at it, then let it fall from her fingers. 'It doesn't matter.' Her voice was distant, impartial. 'This is who

I am now. But . . .' She let her thought die away. She walked towards the door as if she were entirely alone. As she passed through it, Jek held it wide for her. The Six Duchies woman gave Althea a quizzical look. 'Are you coming?'

'Of course,' Althea murmured. She suddenly grasped what her mother must have felt down the years, wanting good things for her daughters, but so powerless to make them go well. It was a sickening feeling.

'Halt! What about me? You cannot leave me here, unattended.' The Satrap protested angrily.

'Well, hustle along then, little man, or be left behind,' Jek told him. But she did hold the door for him, Althea noted.

Kennit stared up, aware that he gaped but unable to do anything about it. He was dimly aware that Vivacia gazed upwards also, her hands clasped before her bosom as if she prayed. Beside him, Wintrow did pray, not a prayer for mercy, as Kennit might have expected, but instead a joyful flow of words that celebrated the wonder of Sa. The boy sounded as if he were chanting in a trance. 'The wonder, the glory is yours, Creator Sa . . .' He could not tell if Wintrow mouthed familiar words or if the majesty of the creature above them had spurred him to spontaneous worship.

The dragon circled again, blue scales glinting to silver as the winter sunlight ran along its flanks. Again, it gave cry. When the dragon spoke, Kennit felt Vivacia's response. A terrible deep yearning ran through the ship and infected him. She longed to move that freely through the sky, to soar, and dip, and circle at her own pleasure. It put the ship in mind of all she was not, and never would be again. Despair like poison seeped through her.

The serpents had ceased their attack on the Jamaillian ships and swarmed in the open sea. Some were near-motionless, heads raised high, great eyes spinning as they stared aloft.

Others frolicked and cavorted as if their antics could attract the dragon's attention. The Jamaillian fleet had seized this opportunity. From certain death, they grasped at survival. One smaller vessel was sinking, her decks awash. Her crew was abandoning her for another ship. On other decks, men sought to make order out of chaos and disaster. They cut fallen rigging free and threw canvas overboard. Yet even there, despite all they had endured, men shouted and pointed at the dragon as their ships retreated.

In the boat that Sorcor had dispatched, Etta crouched low. Her gaze darted from the cavorting serpents to the circling dragon. Her face was pale, her eyes fixed on Kennit. The men in the boat with her pulled savagely at the oars, their heads hunched down between their shoulders.

On every circling pass, the dragon swooped lower. Unmistakably, Vivacia was at the centre of its gyre. It clasped something in its front legs, Kennit saw. Prey, perhaps, but he could not make out what it was. Was it sizing up the ship before an attack? Would it land on the water like a gull? It swept past yet again, so close that the gust of its wings buffeted the ship's sails and set her to rocking. The sea serpents set up an ungodly ululation that rose in volume and pitch as the dragon descended. Then, as it passed right over Etta's rowing boat, the dragon let its burden drop. Whatever it was narrowly missed hitting the boat; it landed beside it in a gout of water. With a ponderous flapping of wings, the creature rose laboriously. It roared and the serpents clamoured an answer. Then it flew away, much more slowly than it had come.

The serpents followed it. Like autumn leaves caught in a gust of wind, they trailed after the dragon. The swift led the way, while others hummocked painfully through the water in the foaming wake, but all were leaving. The dragon gave a final, drawn-out cry as it flew away, taking Kennit's triumph with it.

*   *   *

It was a man, and he was alive. Etta had a single, astonishing glimpse of him as he plummeted into the water. His legs kicked wildly as he fell, then the splash of his impact swallowed him. The dragon had dropped him so near the boat that he had nearly swamped it. Etta would have sworn it was deliberate. The boat rocked wildly in the surge of his dive. Despite that, she seized the edge of the boat and leaned over the side, looking after him. Would he drown? Would he come up at all? 'Where is he?' she shouted. 'Watch for him to come up!'

But the men in the boat paid no attention to her. The serpents were flowing away with the retreating dragon. They seized the opportunity to make all speed for the Vivacia. On the main deck, amidst pointing and babbling crewmen, both Kennit and Wintrow stared after the dragon.

Only the figurehead shared Etta's concern. Vivacia gave one last, anguished look after the dragon. There her eyes, too, scanned the waters around the small boat. Etta was still the first to see a pale movement under the waves and she pointed, crying, 'There, there he is!'

But the creature that shot gasping to the surface of the water was not a man. He had the shape of a man, but his staring eyes gleamed copper. His dark wet curls, streaming water, reminded her of tangled kelp. He saw the boat, and strained towards it with a reaching hand, but Etta saw that his hand shone with more than wet. He was scaled. With a bubbling cry, he sank again. The rowers who had seen him roared with dismay and leaned into their task. Etta was left transfixed, staring at the place where he went down.

'Take him up! Please!' A girl's voice shrieked. Etta lifted her eyes to an elegantly garbed girl on the deck. Why, the Satrap's Companion looked no older than Wintrow!

Then Vivacia pointed a large and commanding finger at the water. 'There! There, you fools, he comes up again! Quickly, quickly, take him up!'

Panicked as they were, the rowers had ignored Etta's plea, but the figurehead's command was another matter. White-faced, they slacked their oars. Then, as the man bobbed up again, they dug their oars in to spin the boat towards him. He saw them and reached desperately. He tried to claw his way towards them, but went under.

'That's it for him,' one of the rowers predicted, but an instant later grasping hands broke the surface of the water. His drowning white face appeared and Etta heard him gasp for breath. A rower thrust an oar within his reach. He seized it so strongly he nearly tore it from the man's grip. They pulled him closer to the boat. In another moment, he had managed to seize the side. He could do no more than cling there. It took two men to haul him on board. When they had him in, he lay in the bottom, water streaming from his garments. He gagged. When he snorted his nose clear of seawater, blood followed it. He blinked his inhuman eyes up at Etta. At first, he did not appear to see her. Then he mouthed silent words. 'Thank you.' His head fell to one side and his eyes closed.

THIRTY-THREE

Ship of Destiny

THE CREWMEN PARTED to make way for Kennit. He stepped past them and peered down at the figure sprawled face-down on his deck. Water ran from his clothes. Dripping hair masked his features. 'Interesting bit of flotsam, Etta,' he observed sourly. Whoever he was, or, Kennit privately amended as he studied his hands, whatever he was, he represented an unwelcome complication to a situation that was already too confusing. He had no time for this.

'You fished him out. You may keep him,' Kennit announced, then staggered as the Satrap's advisor pushed past him. Kennit glared at her, but she did not notice. He started to speak, then his words died. What was that thing on her head? Althea crowded behind her, managing to brush past him while ignoring him completely. Jek stayed at the edge of the crowd with the pouting Satrap.

'Is he breathing? Is Reyn alive?' Malta demanded breathlessly. She hovered over the man but did not touch him.

Althea knelt beside her. Gingerly, she set her fingers to the side of the man's throat. Her face was still for an instant, then she smiled up at her niece. 'Reyn is alive, Malta.' Wintrow had joined them. At Althea's words, he started, then gave his sister an incredulous smile.

As Wintrow smiled at his sister, something almost like

jealousy flitted across Etta's face. In an instant, it was gone. She transferred her gaze to Kennit. Her voice was almost sulky as she said, 'You sent for me?'

'I did.' He became aware that the gathered crew closely followed this conversation. He softened his voice. 'And you came. As you always have.' He smiled at her. There. She and the crew could make whatever they wanted out of that. He gestured at the man at his feet. 'What is this?'

'The dragon dropped him,' Etta explained.

'So, of course, you picked him up,' Kennit observed wryly.

'Vivacia said we should,' one of the men of Sorcor's boat explained nervously. Was King Kennit displeased with him?

'He's Reyn Khuprus, a Rain Wilder. My sister is betrothed to him.' Wintrow uttered these amazing words quite calmly. 'Sa alone knows how he managed to find her here, but he did. Help me turn him over,' he added. He seized the man by one shoulder. As he tugged, Reyn groaned. His hands scrabbled weakly against the deck.

Althea crouched beside Wintrow. 'Wait. Give him time to clear his lungs,' she suggested as he began to cough. Reyn wheezed, lifted his head slightly from the deck, and then let it sag back. 'Malta?' he asked in a thick voice.

She gasped and sprang back from him. She threw her hands up before her face. 'No!' she cried out, then wheeled and jostled her way through the crowd. Etta stared after her in consternation.

'What was that about?' she asked of anyone.

Before anyone could answer, a lookout shouted, 'Sir! The Jamaillian ships are coming back!'

It was Kennit's turn to whirl and hasten away. He should not have let anything distract him from his enemy, no matter how damaged and scattered they had appeared. He gained the foredeck as swiftly as he could and stared in amazement at the oncoming ships. They were attempting to close around his three ships. Were they insane? Some were obviously limping, but two in good condition had come to the fore, leading the others. On their decks, he saw the telltale scrabble of men readying war machines. He appraised them thoughtfully. He had the *Marietta* and the *Motley* to back him, both with seasoned crews. The Jamaillian men would, at the least, be wearied, and they had probably spent a good amount of their shot. Technically, the Jamaillian fleet still outnumbered him, but most of their ships had taken substantial damage. Two were already going down, their crews seeking safety in small boats.

Kennit held the Satrap as a bargaining chip. It was as good a time as any to challenge the fleet of Jamaillia. 'Jola!' he commanded. 'Get the men back to their posts and have them stand ready.'

Vivacia watched the oncoming ships with him but her mind was elsewhere. 'How is the Rain Wilder?'

'Alive,' he replied briefly.

'The dragon brought him. Here, to me.'

'Wintrow seems to think the dragon dropped him off for his sister,' Kennit replied acidly.

'That would make sense,' the ship said thoughtfully. 'They belong together.'

'As much sense as anything that has happened today. What are the odds of such a thing happening, Vivacia? Out of all the ships around us, the dragon drops Malta's beloved by the correct one to find her.'

'There was nothing random about it. The dragon came seeking Malta and found her. But –' The figurehead slowly scanned the approaching ships and said in a soft voice, 'Something hovers here, Kennit. Something even more powerful than the luck you worship.' She smiled but there was sadness in her expression. 'Destiny knows no odds,' she added mysteriously.

He had no answer to that. The very idea of it annoyed him. Destiny was all very well when it meant he would succeed. But today fate seemed to be weighting the balance against him. He recognized Etta's footfalls on the foredeck behind him. He turned to her. 'Bring the Satrap up here. And Malta.'

She didn't reply. 'Well?' he asked her at last. Her expression was odd. What was wrong with her today? He'd brought her back to the ship. What more could she want from him? Why must she want it right now?

'I've something to tell you. It's important.'

'More important than our survival?' He glanced back at the oncoming ships. Would they halt and parley first, or just attack? Best not to take a chance. 'Send Jola and Wintrow to me as well,' he commanded her.

'I shall,' she promised. She took a breath and added, 'I'm pregnant. I carry your child.' Then she turned and walked away from him.

Her words froze time around him. He suddenly felt he stood, not on a deck, but encapsulated in a moment. So many paths spread out from this instant, and in so many directions. A baby. A child. The seed of a family. He could be a father, as his own father had been. No. Better. He could protect his own son. His father had tried to protect him, but his father had failed. He could be a king and his son a prince. Or he could be rid of Etta, take her somewhere and leave her there, and go on, with no one to depend on him, no one he could fail. His thoughts did not spin; they rattled in his brain like stones. Maybe she was lying. Maybe she was wrong. Did he want a child? What if it was a girl?

'Would you still name her Paragon?' the charm on his wrist whispered viciously. It gave a low laugh. 'Destiny no longer hovers. Some of it has flown off with the dragon. It decrees that the Lords of the Three Realms will fly again. The rest of today's destiny has fallen upon your head. It weighs a bit more than a crown, does it not?'

'Leave me alone,' Kennit whispered. He spoke not to the charm, but to the past that had reached forth and reclaimed him. Other memories, memories most deeply denied flooded

753

back to him. Standing within the circle of his father's arms, reaching up to rest his own small hands on the inner spokes of Paragon's wheel while his father held the ship steady. He recalled riding tall on his father's shoulders, his mother laughing up at him, a bright scarf fluttering in her dark, dark hair as they strode through Divvytown. These recollections, bright and joyful were more intolerable than any remembered pain. They were a mockery, a lie, for all fondness and safety had been erased one dark and bloody night.

Now Etta would start it all over again. Was she mad? Didn't she know what must come? Eventually, of course, he'd have to hurt the child. Not because he wanted to, but because it was inevitable. This moment marked one end of the pendulum's swing. Ride it they must, until it peaked at the other end, the place where he was Igrot and Igrot was he. Then the child must step up to play the role that had once been Kennit's.

'You poor pathetic bastard,' the charm whispered in horror. But pity would not stay destiny. Nothing could save him, or the child. Events had to follow their pattern. Nothing could disrupt the cycling of time. Things would happen again just as they always had. Just as they always would.

'Sir?' It was Jola, standing at his elbow. How long had he been there? Kennit's musings blew away like dandelion fluff blown by a child's lips. What had he been thinking? When had it begun to rain? Damn the woman! Why had she chosen to distract him just now? His first mate swallowed and spoke. 'The Jamaillian ship is hailing us.'

'Where is the Satrap?' he demanded angrily. He pulled his cloak more tightly around him, and dashed water from his face. The rain was cold.

Jola looked frightened. 'Behind you, sir.'

Kennit glanced back at him. Malta, her headwrap again in place, stood beside the Satrap. Wintrow hovered near his sister.

When had they all come up on the foredeck? How long had he stood there, dazed with Etta's news?

'Of course he is!' he kept his anger, but refocused it. 'Exactly where he should be. Return their hail. Tell them King Kennit bids them think well. Remind them that I can recall the serpents at any time. Then tell them that my intent is not to destroy them, but simply to make them heed a lawful treaty. They may send one ship forwards with representatives. We will allow them aboard. They shall hear from the Satrap himself that my claims are true.'

Jola looked relieved. 'Then the serpents haven't left us? They'd come back if you called them?'

If there had been a serpent close by, Kennit would have fed him to it.

'Relay my message!' he barked at Jola. He turned back to stare at the threatening fleet. He recognized the type of fleet it was. Each ship belonged to a noble, and each cherished the hope of returning laden with booty and crowned with glory. They would vie to be the one to treat for the Satrap's release; every noble would want to negotiate it. Would they be foolish enough to send him a hostage from every ship? He hoped so, and yet he knew that there might still be bloody fighting today.

When Malta fled, Jek and Althea had carried Reyn down to Althea's room. On her bunk, he had come to himself. 'Where's Malta?' he demanded woozily. 'Didn't I find her?' Blood leaked sluggishly from one nostril and water dripped from his hair.

'You did,' Althea assured him. 'But Captain Kennit has summoned her.'

Reyn suddenly clapped both hands to his bared face. 'Did she see me?' he demanded, horrified. A question like that, at such a time, demanded a truthful answer.

'Yes. She did,' Althea replied quietly. There was no point in lying, or trying to save his feelings. His copper eyes were hard to read but the set of his mouth was not. 'She's very young, Reyn,' Althea excused her niece. 'You knew that when you began courting her.' She tried to make her words gentle as well as firm. 'You can't expect –'

'Leave me for a time. Please,' he requested quietly.

Jek left off staring at him, and opened the door. Althea followed her out. 'Those are Wintrow's clothes on the pegs,' she said over her shoulder. 'If you want some dry things on.' Not that there was much hope any of it would fit him. Despite his scaly face and bird eyes, he was a well-made man, tall and muscled.

Jek seemed to have been following her thoughts. 'Even with the scales, he's not bad-looking,' she observed quietly.

Althea leaned against the wall outside her room, Jek beside her. 'I should be out on the foredeck, not down here,' she grumbled to her friend.

'Why? It's not like you have any control over what happens up there,' Jek pointed out maddeningly. She lowered her voice suddenly. 'Admit it, Althea,' she coaxed. 'When you look at the scales on his face, you have to wonder about the rest of him.'

'No, I don't,' Althea replied icily. She didn't want to think about it. The man was a Rain Wilder, kin to Bingtown Traders; she owed him loyalty, not idle speculation about his body. She'd seen Rain Wilders before and, she told herself, she wasn't shocked. They could not help what the Rain Wilds did to them. The Khuprus family was renowned for both their wealth and honour. Reyn Khuprus, scaled or not, was a good catch; that he had come seeking her so far, in such a way, was undeniable evidence of a brave heart. Still, she did not blame Malta for running away. She had probably fantasized a handsome face beneath his veil. To confront her scaly betrothed must have shaken her.

* * *

Reyn pulled his wet shirt off. It slapped to the floor atop his other clothes. He took a deep breath through his tight throat and stared into the room's small mirror forcing himself to see what Malta had seen. Tintaglia had not lied to him. His contact with her had accelerated the Rain Wild changes. He touched the fine dragon-scaling of his face, lidded and opened the copper reptile eyes that stared at him. The scaled planes of his bared chest glinted bronze. There was a bluish cast to the skin beneath; bruising or a colour change? He had seen Rain Wild gaffers of fifty who had not shown as much change as he already did. What would become of him as he aged? Would he grow dragon claws, would his teeth become pointed, his tongue ridged?

It scarcely mattered, he told himself. He'd grow old alone now, underground most of the time, digging for dragons. How he looked would not matter to anyone. Tintaglia had kept her end of the bargain. He would keep his. The irony did not escape him. He'd wagered the rest of his life against the hope that he could rescue Malta. He would not deny his wild fancies now. He'd dreamed that he would rescue her, unscathed despite the horrible dangers she'd endured, and that she would collapse into his arms and promise to always be at his side. He'd dreamed that when he unveiled before her, she would smile and touch his face and tell him it did not matter, that it was him she loved, not his face.

But the reality was crueller. Tintaglia had dropped him and departed with her precious serpents. After days of battering flight and sleeping cold on isolated beaches, he'd nearly drowned. Malta's kin had had to rescue him. They must think him an utter fool. His entire quest had been to no purpose, for Malta was safe already. He had no idea why the Vivacia was flying the Jamaillian flag, but obviously Althea Vestrit had managed to regain her ship and rescue her niece. They not only hadn't needed his pathetic efforts, they'd had to rescue him.

He took one of Wintrow's shirts from a peg and held it up. With a sigh, he hung it up again. He picked up his own shirt from the floor and watched the water run from it. His veil was tangled with it. For a time, he stared at it. Then he tugged it loose and wrung it out. It was the first thing he put on.

Malta stood unseeing in the pelting rain. The fine scaling of Reyn's face had been like silken mail, the warm gleam of his copper eyes like a beacon. Once, she had kissed those lips through the fine mesh of a veil. She felt her scrub-maid's fingers on her chapped lips and snatched her hand away. Unattainable, now. She lifted her face to the cold rain and welcomed its icy touch. *Numb me,* she begged of it. *Take away this pain.*

'I'm cold,' the Satrap whimpered beside her. 'And I'm tired of standing here.'

Kennit shot him a warning glance.

The Satrap had his arms wrapped tightly around himself but he still shook with the cold. 'I don't think they're coming. Why must I stand here in the wind and rain?'

'Because it pleases me,' Kennit snapped at him.

Wintrow thought to intervene. 'You can have my cloak, if you like,' he offered.

The Satrap scowled. 'It's dripping wet! What good would that do me?'

'You could be wetter,' Kennit snarled.

Malta took a long breath. The pirate and the Satrap did not seem much different from one another. If she could manage one, she could manage the other. It was not courage that motivated her to march across the deck and stand before Kennit with her arms crossed, but profound despair. He was a dangerous, violent man, but she didn't fear him. What could he do to her? Ruin her life? The thought almost made her smile.

Her low, even words were meant only for Kennit but the tall woman who stood behind his shoulder listened, too.

'Please, King Kennit, let me fetch him a heavier cloak and a chair, if you will not allow him to go inside to shelter.'

She felt his gaze on her head, searching for signs of her scar. He answered her callously. 'He's being foolish. He takes no harm from a little rain. I do not see where it is your concern.'

'You, sir, are being more foolish than he.' She spoke boldly, no longer caring if she gave offence. 'Forget my concern. Consider your own. Whatever pleasure you take from making him miserable is not worth what you will lose. If you wish the captains of that fleet to see him as valuable, then you should treat him as the Lord High Magnadon, Satrap of all Jamaillia. If you think to bargain him for riches, that is who you must be holding. Not a wet, cranky, miserable boy.'

Her eyes flickered once from Kennit's pale blue ones to those of his woman. To her surprise, she looked faintly amused, almost approving. Did Kennit sense that? He looked at Malta but spoke to his woman. 'Etta. See what you can manage for him. I wish him to be very visible.'

'I can arrange that.' The woman had a soft contralto voice, more refined than Malta had expected from a pirate's woman. There was intelligence in her glance.

Malta met her gaze frankly, and dropped her a curtsey as she said, 'My gratitude to you, lady.'

She followed Etta from the foredeck and kept up with her. The wind had stirred a nasty little chop and the wet deck was unsteady, but in her days aboard the *Motley*, she had finally found her sea legs. She amazed herself. Despite all that was wrong in her life, she took pride in being able to move well on her father's ship. Her father. Resolutely, she banished all thoughts of him. Nor would she dwell on Reyn, so close that she could feel his presence. Eventually, she must stand before him, ruined and scarred, and face the disappointment in those extraordinary copper eyes. She shook her head and clenched her teeth against the sting of tears in her eyes. Not now. She would not feel anything for herself just now. All her thoughts and efforts must go into restoring the Satrap to his throne. She tried to think clearly as she followed Etta into her father's stateroom.

The room was as Malta recalled it from her grandfather's days as captain on Vivacia. She looked in anguish at the familiar furnishings. With a flourish, Etta threw open a richly-carved cedar chest. It was layered with garments in fabrics both sumptuous and colourful. At any other time, Malta would have been seized with envy and curiosity. Now she stood and stared sightlessly across the room as Etta dug through it.

'Here. This will serve. It will be large on him, but if we seat him in a chair, no one will notice.' She dragged out a heavy scarlet cloak trimmed with jet beads. 'Kennit said it was too gaudy, but I still think he would look very fine in it.'

'Undoubtedly,' Malta agreed without expression. Personally, she felt it little mattered how a rapist dressed once you knew what he was.

Etta stood, the rich fabric draped over her arm. 'The hood is lined with fur,' she pointed out. Abruptly she asked, 'What are you thinking?'

There was no point at flinging harsh words at this woman. Wintrow had said that Etta knew what Kennit was. Somehow, she had come to terms with it. Who was she to criticize Etta's loyalty? She must find Malta as craven for serving the Satrap. 'I was wondering if Kennit has thought this through. I believe an alliance of Jamaillian nobles sought to have the Satrap die in Bingtown so they could blame the Traders for his murder and plunder our town. Are these nobles in this fleet of ships loyal to the Satrap and intent on his rescue? Or are they traitors hoping to finish what was begun in Bingtown? As well blame the Pirate Isles as Bingtown. Or both.' She knit her brows, thinking. 'They may have more interest in provoking Kennit to kill the Satrap than in saving him.'

'I am sure Kennit has considered everything,' Etta replied stiffly. 'He is not a man like other men. He sees far, and in times of great danger, he manifests great powers. I know you must doubt me, but all you need do is ask your brother. He has seen Kennit calm a storm and command serpents to serve him. Wintrow himself was cured of serpent scald at Kennit's hand, yes, and had the tattoo that his own father placed on his cheek erased by his captain.' Etta met Malta's sceptical gaze unwaveringly. 'Perhaps a man like that does not have to abide by ordinary rules,' she went on. 'Perhaps his own vision prompts him to do things forbidden to other men.'

Malta cocked her head at the pirate's woman. 'Are we still talking about negotiating to restore the Satrap to the throne?' she asked. 'Or do you seek to excuse what he did to my father?' And my aunt, she added silently to herself.

'Your father's behaviour needs more excuses than Kennit's,' Etta returned coldly. 'Ask Wintrow what it is like to wear slave-chains and a tattoo. Your father got what he deserved.'

'Perhaps we all get what we deserve,' Malta returned sharply. Her eyes swept up and down Etta, and she saw the woman flush with anger. She experienced a moment's remorse when she glimpsed sudden, unmasked pain in Etta's eyes.

'Perhaps we do,' the woman replied coldly. 'Bring that chair.'

It was, Malta thought as she hefted the heavy chair, a petty revenge. She carried it awkwardly, knocking her shins against its thick rungs as she walked.

Reyn Khuprus stood well back from the foredeck where he could observe without being seen. He watched Malta. The veil obscured his view, but he stared hungrily at her anyway. What he saw pained him, but he could not look away. She smiled at the Satrap as she set a chair in place for him. She turned to the tall woman beside her and indicated with pleasure the scarlet cloak she carried. The Satrap's face did not lose its proud cast. He lifted his chin to her. What came next was like a knife turning in Reyn. Malta unfastened his wet cloak for him, smiling warmly all the while. He could not hear the words, but her tender concern showed on her face. She cast the wet cloak carelessly aside, and then hastened to wrap the Satrap in the grand red cloak. She pulled the hood up well and fastened it warmly around him. With light touches of her hand, she gently pushed the damp locks back from the Satrap's forehead and cheeks. When the Satrap seated himself, she fussed with the fall of the cloak, even going down on one knee to adjust the folds of it.

There was fondness in her every touch. He could not blame her. The Satrap with his pale, patrician countenance and lordly ways was a far more fitting match for Malta Vestrit than a scaled and battered Rain Wilder. With a pang, he recalled that the man had shared the first dance with her at her Presentation Ball. Had her heart begun to turn to him even then? She moved to stand behind the Satrap's chair, and set her hands familiarly to the top of it. The trials they had endured together would undoubtedly have bonded them. What man could long resist Malta's charm and beauty? No doubt, the Satrap felt great gratitude as well; he could not have survived on his own.

Reyn felt as if his heart had vanished from his chest, leaving a gaping hole behind. No wonder she had fled the sight of him. He swallowed hard. She had not even had a word of greeting for him, even as a friend. Did she fear he would hold her to her promise? Did she fear he would humiliate her before the Satrap? He bathed in the pain of watching them. She would never again be his.

Althea had helped her niece hoist the heavy chair up to the

foredeck. She thought it a foolish bit of show herself, but none of this made any sense to her. They were all trapped in Kennit's ridiculous and dangerous display of strength. She watched Malta take the Satrap's wet cloak from his shoulders and wrap him warmly in the fresh one. She pulled the hood well up as if the man were Selden. When he had seated himself in his makeshift throne, she even tucked the cloak more snugly about his feet and legs. It pained her to watch Malta do such humble service. It stung her worse that Kennit watched the whole performance with a snide little smile on his face.

Hatred so hot it tinged her vision red rushed through her. She actually gasped for breath as her nails bit deep into her palms. She leaned back against the ship's rail and concentrated on letting it pass through her.

'You want to kill him that badly,' the ship observed quietly. The comment seemed intended for her alone, yet Althea saw Kennit turn slightly to the words. He raised one eyebrow in a slight, mocking query.

'Yes. I do.' She let him read the words on her lips.

Kennit gave his head a sorrowful little shake. Then he put his attention back on a small ship that was drawing steadily closer to them. It came sluggishly through the darkening afternoon. Kennit wondered if it had taken damage in the serpent attack. An array of impressively-garbed men stood on its deck staring towards them. Most of them looked portly beneath their rich cloaks. Sailors stood ready on deck to assist their betters to cross to Vivacia. A smile crooked his lips. It would be amusing if it began to sink while it was alongside. 'Perhaps I should have dressed for the occasion,' he observed aloud to Etta. 'Just as well that we have decked our Satrap so royally. Maybe clothing is all they can recognize.' He folded his arms on his chest and grinned expectantly. 'Toss some heaving lines, Jola. Let's see what catch they bring us.'

*   *   *

'There they are,' Malta went on in an undertone to the Satrap. 'Sit tall and regal. Do you recognize any of them? Do you think they are loyal to you?'

He eyed his nobles sullenly. 'I know old Lord Criath's colours. He was most enthusiastic about my journey north, yet declined to join me because sea travel pains his joints. Yet, look how easily he crosses to our deck, and how tall he stands. He scarcely needs the man who hands him across. The fifth man, he who comes now, he wears the colours of house Ferdio, but Lord Ferdio is a small, slight man. This must be a stouter, taller son of his. The others . . . I cannot tell. They are so well hooded and hatted, their collars pulled so high, I scarce can see their faces –'

Malta suspected it, an instant before anyone else did. She glanced past the men boarding the Vivacia. On the deck of the other ship, sailors assisted their leaders to cross. Many surly, glaring sailors, all cloaked against the day's cold. Too many?

''Ware treachery!' she shouted suddenly. Her cry forced them to act, perhaps sooner than they had planned. Some finely-dressed men remained on the other ship, but at Malta's cry, all flung aside their cloaks, sailors as well as counterfeit nobles. Their weapons came into view, as did the garb of common fighting men. With a roar, the sailors who had been 'assisting' their cohorts flung themselves across the gap that separated the ships. More men appeared from belowdecks, a flood of fighters leaping across, blades in hand.

Kennit's men, never trusting souls, sprang to meet them. In an instant, the main deck of the Vivacia was a mêlée of struggling men and flashing blades. Everywhere Malta turned, there was chaos. Kennit stood, sword drawn, barking orders about cutting lines and pushing off, while Etta guarded his back with both a sword and a shorter blade. Even Wintrow, her gentle brother, had drawn a knife and stood ready to repel any who tried to come up onto the foredeck. Jek and Althea, empty-handed, had moved to back him. All this, in the merest blinking of an eye.

Horror transfixed the Satrap. He shrank back in his chair, even drawing his feet up from the deck. Malta stood helplessly beside him. 'Protect me,' he cried shrilly. 'Protect me, they've come to kill me, I know they have.' He seized her wrist in a surprisingly strong grip. He sprang to his feet, stumbling on the too-long cloak, and pulled her in front of him. 'Guard me, guard me!' he pleaded. He dragged her away from the chair to the point of the bow and huddled there, clutching her wrist.

Malta struggled desperately to break free. She needed to see what was happening on the main deck. 'Let me go!' she cried but he was too frightened to heed her. More men were pouring over from the other vessel.

There was a great crash as Jek snatched up the Satrap's chair and smashed it on the deck. She seized one leg of it, and tossed another carved leg to Althea. She was grinning wildly; the woman was crazy. 'Malta!' she shouted, and Malta ducked as the woman flung a heavy rung from the chair at her. 'Use this!' Then she sprang back to the ladder, clubbing savagely at the men who had nearly gained the foredeck. Althea joined her. Wintrow had taken up a position near Kennit, who was shouting orders to his men.

Malta threw her head back and stared wildly around her. The other ships of the Jamaillian fleet were drawing near. She caught a glimpse of the *Marietta* charging down on them. She could not see the *Motley*, but she doubted it had fled. She glimpsed another ship, coming swiftly, not flying Jamaillian colours. Had another pirate ship chanced upon the fray? Then she saw the figurehead move.

'A liveship comes! A Bingtown ship comes to our aid.' Malta shouted the news, but no one paid any heed.

The Satrap had hold of her shoulder. Now he shook her

frantically. 'Get me below, take me to safety. You must protect me.'

'Let me go!' she cried desperately. 'I can't protect you if you cling to me like this.' She strained against his grip and managed to reach the rung Jek had thrown. She hefted it in her hand, but didn't feel any safer.

'We have no idea what we're charging into!' Amber shouted up to him.

'We know Althea's on that ship!' Brashen bellowed angrily as he clambered down the mast. 'We can't hold back here and do nothing while the Jamaillians take the Vivacia. I don't trust them any more than I do Kennit. She may be killed, or captured. I've no desire to see Althea with a slave tattoo across her cheek. So let's try to turn this to our advantage.' He sprang to the deck. 'Semoy! Break out the weapons!'

Semoy came on the run. 'Right away, Captain. But you ought to tell the men who we're fighting.'

Brashen grinned wild and reckless. 'Anyone that gets between us and Althea!'

A surprising bellow burst suddenly from Paragon. 'But save Kennit for me!'

The battle, confined to the main deck of the Vivacia, suddenly shifted. The sheer pressure of men pouring over from the Jamaillian ship was turning the tide. In horror, Malta saw Jek pulled down. Althea dove into the mêlée after her. As she vanished, a wave of Jamaillian warriors came up over the lip of the deck. She had one glimpse of Wintrow, Etta and Kennit, all in a tight group, fighting for their lives.

'Here he is!' roared a Jamaillian sailor as he leapt up to her. She swung her rung at him. It hit his sword arm, but he simply shifted his arm so the blow was glancing. With his free hand, he snatched the rung out of her grip as easily as taking a toy from a child. He roared with laughter and pushed her aside. His push and the Satrap clinging to her sent her sprawling. The man grabbed the Satrap by the back of his collar, shook him free of his grip on Malta. When she snatched at the Satrap, the fighter held him out of her reach and drew his sword back to plunge it into Malta, then stared in sudden disbelief at a sword tip standing out from his chest. Behind him, a tall man roared his fury. He jerked both sword and victim back and away from Malta. He shoved the dead man into his comrades, pulling the sword out as he did so.

'Get down! Be small!' Reyn shouted at her furiously, and then he turned his back to her. His copper eyes flashed through his tattered veil. She had a glimpse of his left sleeve, sodden with blood. Then three men flung themselves at him and he went down before her very eyes.

'Reyn! No!' she cried and tried to spring forwards, but the Satrap was a clinging, shrieking weight behind her. He latched onto her shoulders like a limpet, gibbering and weeping. A man seized her by the hair and flung her aside. With a wild laugh, he sprang on the Satrap as if he were a child seizing a cornered puppy. 'I have him!' he roared. 'I have him!'

Malta jerked her head aside to avoid a kick. It glanced off her skull, dazing her for an instant. It was not deliberate. Now that they had the Satrap, no one was interested in her any more. She saw him picked up like a sack of meal and flung to a man's shoulder. He bore him away, roaring his triumph. The battle parted for him and receded after him. The boarders had what they had come for and now they were leaving. She had one glimpse of the Satrap's white face, his mouth and eyes wide with terror. She could not see Reyn anywhere. She scrabbled to her knees and stared wildly about. The Satrap was toted across a deck where dead men sprawled amongst the rolling, groaning wounded. The pirates who still fought were in defensive positions, battling for their own lives, unable to spring to his rescue.

The Satrap was an annoying, useless person, but she had cared for him like a child. Day and night, she had been at his side. It smote her heart to see him being borne off to his death. 'Malta!' he cried, and his one free hand strained towards her.

'The Satrap!' she shouted uselessly. 'They have taken him! Save him, save him!' No one could answer her cry for help. As his captors bore him off, the other Jamaillian warriors fell back around him, grinning and shouting with triumph. As the focus of the battle shifted, Malta caught a glimpse of Althea. She had taken a blade from someone. She made an abortive attempt to break free of the knot of fighters that engaged her, but Jek dragged her back.

'He's not worth your life!' the tall woman shouted at her. Her blonde tail of hair dripped blood.

Then, from a tangle of bodies on the deck, Reyn reared up. Malta shrieked aloud with joy at the sight of him. When he had gone down, she had given him up for dead. 'Reyn!' she cried, and then as he snatched up a blade and staggered after the Satrap's captors, she screamed, 'No! No, come back, don't, Reyn!'

He did not get far. A wounded man clutched at him as he dashed past and Reyn fell solidly to the deck. Malta staggered to her feet. Reyn was all she could see. He grappled with the man who had dragged him down. The other man had a knife, already reddened with blood. Heedless of all else, Malta flung herself towards the struggling men.

'Let me go!' Althea tried to break Jek's grip, but her friend was relentless.

'No! Let him go. They've taken him onto their deck. Will you take the fight there, where the odds are even worse? We've lost him, Althea, at least for now!'

Althea knew she was right. The man carrying the Satrap had caught a dangling line and swung across to the other ship's deck. The Jamaillian sailors were retreating in triumph, cutting the lines that had bound the ships together during the short, fierce fighting. As swiftly as they had come, they left, taking the Satrap with them.

Althea saw Reyn's curtailed charge. She thought he would get up, but before he could scrabble to his feet, an unlikely saviour sprang to the Satrap's rescue. With a wild cry of fury, Kennit sprang from between Etta and Wintrow and into the fray. 'Don't let them take him!' he roared angrily. He had a short blade in one hand and his crutch gripped under his other arm. She did not expect him to get more than a few steps, but he swung his way across the deck, loping from foot to crutch with a grace that amazed her. 'To me!' Kennit roared as he ran. Loyal pirates closed in behind him. Etta and Wintrow sprang after him, but others had filled the gap. They were cut off from him. When Kennit came to the ship's railing, he didn't pause. His peg hit the deck, his foot the railing and he flung himself out. With a leap that would not have shamed a tiger, he sprang after the departing ship. Althea expected him to fall between the vessels but he hit the other deck and rolled. A bare handful of his men followed him. One fell short, yelling as he plummeted into the water. She could not see what became of Kennit after that. Too many men converged on the outnumbered pirate king and his men. Etta screamed in rage and gathered herself. Wintrow tackled her to keep her from flinging herself after Kennit. The gap between the ships had widened to an impossible leap. Jeering laughter and triumphant calls rose stingingly from the other ship as it pulled steadily away from the Vivacia. Two men held the pale Satrap aloft and shook him mockingly at Vivacia's crew.

Etta pushed savagely free of Wintrow. In her despair and anger, she turned on him. 'You fool! We cannot let them have him. They'll kill him. You know that.'

'I don't intend to let them keep him. But your drowning just now would not save him,' he retorted angrily. His voice deepened in command. 'Jola! They've taken Kennit! Vivacia! After them, they've taken Kennit, we must pursue!'

Vivacia took up the cry. 'Up anchor! Put on sail! We must go after them, they've taken Kennit.'

'No!' Althea groaned, low. 'Let him go, let them have him.' But she knew the ship would not. She could feel Vivacia's anxiety, pulsing up through her wood. The ship loved him and she would have him back, no matter the cost. Althea looked across the water at the Jamaillian fleet spread before them. If Vivacia challenged them, she had no chance, even if the *Marietta* and the *Motley* backed her. It would not be swift, it would be bloody with more men dying on Vivacia's decks and in the end, her ship would be in Jamaillian hands. It was a lost cause already, but she knew that the ship would pursue it. She would be borne along with her to face a savage end.

Then a voice reached her, booming across the water and setting the hair on the back of her neck on end. 'Halloo the Vivacia! Who has taken Kennit?'

She turned slowly as a chill raced over her. It was a voice from the grave. Paragon's voice reached across the water as no man's could do. She looked at him, and then looked again. It was not Paragon. The battered liveship with its makeshift rigging bore Paragon's nameplate, but the figurehead was an open-countenanced young man, beardless, with his hair bound back in a warrior's tail. Then she had a glimpse of a golden woman standing on the deck just back of the figurehead, waving both her arms in a wild greeting. For an instant, all other thoughts and fears were suspended as she watched them come on. She could not see Brashen; there was no way to be sure he was alive, too, but she suddenly felt he must be. Paragon's eyes were closed and he sailed with his hands stretched blindly before him. That wrung her heart. It was as they had feared. Amber had recarved him, but it had not restored his sight. A white serpent cut the water before his bow.

'They're alive!' Jek was suddenly beside her, jumping up and down and pounding her on the back with a bloody fist. It was unnerving yet wonderful to be snatched off her feet and whirled around by the larger woman as Jek gave a howl of joy.

'Ho, Paragon!' Vivacia cried in despair. 'There, that ship, he's on board her. They'll kill him, Paragon, they'll kill him!' She pointed frantically and uselessly across the water. Her own anchor was just rising from the muck.

Her cry carried to the *Marietta* and the *Motley* as well. Althea saw them divert in their courses towards Vivacia to pursue the one Jamaillian ship that was fleeing for the shelter of its fleet.

But Paragon was already underway and the will of a liveship propelled him as much as the wind in his sails. He gathered speed unnaturally. Even the crew of the Vivacia, familiar with the ways of liveships, cried out in wonder as he swept past. Althea had a glimpse of Brashen running down Paragon's decks with Clef at his heels. At the sight of him, her heart sprang to life in her chest. Then Paragon had swept by them, showing Vivacia his stern. She stood staring, stunned with joy.

The beleaguered crew of the Vivacia had sprung to at the news that their captain was taken. Every man who could move sprang to hoist the anchor and raise the sails. For the time being, they ignored the bodies that littered the deck. The wounded that could staggered to their feet to help run the ship. Malta, unharmed but obviously shaken, wandered, stricken, through the tangled dead. Wintrow had taken command away from the rattled Jola. Etta seemed to be everywhere, lending a hand and shouting for speed at every task.

'Althea!' Jek shouted, breaking her from her trance. 'Get moving!' Jek had already joined the men at the anchor.

'After him!' Althea joined her shouts to Wintrow's. 'Paragon must not face them alone!'

Before the anchor was completely out of the water, Vivacia was gathering momentum.

THIRTY-FOUR

Rescues

'I DON'T CARE ABOUT Kennit!' Brashen roared. 'Go back for Althea!'

'She is safe where she is for now!' Paragon shouted defiantly. 'I must have Kennit back. I need him.'

Brashen clenched his teeth. So close, for an instant, and then they had swept past. The need to see Althea and know she was safe hollowed him but the headstrong ship seemed intent on bearing them to their deaths. Every time Brashen began to trust Paragon, he dashed his hopes again. He defied both rudder and orders, arrowing after the fleeing Jamaillian ship. The white serpent leapt and dove in their bow-wave like a dolphin. On the foredeck, Mother leaned on the railing as if she could push the ship to go faster. Amber stood straight and tall, the wind whipping her hair. Her eyes were wide as if she listened to distant music.

'At least slow down,' Brashen begged. 'Let the other ships pull even with us. We don't need to face the whole Jamaillian fleet alone.'

But Paragon rushed blindly ahead. Brashen surmised that somehow the white serpent guided him. 'I can't delay. They'll kill him, Brashen. They might be killing him right now. He must not die without me.'

That had an ominous tone. Brashen suddenly felt a light

touch on his wrist. He glanced down to find Kennit's mother standing beside him. Her pale eyes locked with his dark ones and spoke all the words her tongue could no longer say. The eloquence of that appeal could not be refused. Brashen shook his head, not at her but at his own foolishness. 'Go then!' he suddenly shouted at the ship. 'Fling yourself forwards blindly. Satisfy whatever madness drives you once and for all.'

'As I must!' Paragon flung back at him.

'As must we all,' Amber agreed quietly.

Brashen rounded on her, glad of a new target. 'I suppose this is the destiny you bespoke,' he challenged Amber in frustration.

She gave him an ethereal smile. 'Oh, yes indeed,' she promised him. 'And not just Paragon's. Mine. And yours.' She flung an arm wide. 'And all the world's.'

Kennit had never been in a worse place. Crutchless, weapon-less, he sat on the deck while working sailors moved matter-of-factly past him. The few men who had boarded with him were bloody corpses. Pointless to take satisfaction in the Jamaillians they had taken with them. The Satrap was a crumpled heap behind him. He was uninjured but swooned. Kennit himself was battered, but as yet unbloodied.

He sat on the open deck near the house of the ship. He had to look up at his guards. He refused to do so. He'd had enough of their sneering faces and mocking grins. They'd taken much pleasure in snatching his crutch away and letting him fall. His ribs ached from their boots. The sudden change in his fortunes dazed him as much as his injuries. Where had his good luck vanished? How could this have happened to him, King Kennit of the Pirate Isles? But a moment ago, he'd held the Satrap of all Jamaillia captive and had the signed treaty that recognized him as King of the Pirate Isles. He had felt his destiny, had briefly touched it. Now this. He had not been so helpless and defeated since he was a boy. He pushed the thought aside. None of this would have happened if Wintrow and Etta had followed him, as they should have. Their courage and faith in his luck should have matched his own. He'd tell them so when they rescued him.

Behind him, he felt the Satrap stirring from his dead faint. He moaned faintly. Kennit elbowed him unobtrusively. 'Quiet,' he said in a low voice. 'Sit up. Try to look competent. The more weakness you admit, the more they'll hurt you. I need you in one piece.'

The Lord High Satrap of all Jamaillia sat up, sniffled and looked fearfully around. On the deck, men thundered past them, intent on wringing yet more speed out of the ship. Two men guarded them, one with a long knife, the other with a nasty short club. Kennit's left arm was near numb from his last encounter with it.

'I am lost. All is lost.' The Satrap rocked himself.

'Stop it!' Kennit hissed. In a low voice he continued, 'While you whine and moan, you are not thinking. Look around us. Now, more than ever, you must be the Satrap of all Jamaillia. Look like a king if you wish to be treated as one. Sit up. Be alert and outraged. Behave as if you have the power to kill them all.'

Kennit himself had already followed his own advice. If the Jamaillians had taken the Satrap to be rid of him, he reasoned, they would have killed him outright. That they both still lived meant that the Satrap had some living value to them. And if he did, and if the Satrap felt some small measure of gratitude to Kennit, perhaps he might preserve the pirate's life as well. Kennit gathered strength into his voice. He poured conviction into his whisper. 'They shall not emerge unscathed from this treatment of us. Even now, my ships pursue us. Look at our captors, and think only of how you will kill them.'

'Slowly,' the Satrap said in a voice that still shook slightly. 'Slowly they will die,' he said more firmly, 'with much time to

regret their stupidity.' He managed to sit up. He wrapped the
scarlet cloak more closely about himself and glared at their
guards. Anger, Kennit reflected, suited him. It drove the fear
and childishness from his face. 'My own nobles turned on me.
They will pay for their treason. They, and their families. I will
tear down their mansions, I will cut their forests, I will burn
their fields. To the tenth generation, they will suffer for this.
I know their names.'

A guard had overheard him. He gave the Satrap a disdainful
shove with his foot. 'Shut up. You'll be dead before the day is
out. I heard them say. They just want to do it where they all can
witness it. Binding by blood, they call it.' He grinned, showing
a sailor's teeth. 'You, too, "King" Kennit. Maybe they'll let me
do it. I lost two shipmates to them damn serpents of yours.'

'KENNIT!'

The roar was the voice of the wind itself, the cry of an
outraged god. The taunting guard spun around to look aft.
A terrible shiver ran over Kennit. He did not have to look.
It was the voice of his dead ship, calling him to join it. He
struggled to stand, but without his crutch, it was hard. 'Help
me up!' he commanded the Satrap. At any other time the royal
youth would probably have disdained such a command, but the
sound of the pirate's name still lingered in everyone's ears. He
stood quickly and extended a hand to the pirate. Even the men
on deck had slowed in their appointed tasks to look back. A
look of horror dawned on some faces. Kennit hauled himself to
a standing position by the Satrap's slender shoulder and stared
wildly about for the ghost ship.

He found it, coming up swift on their starboard.

Impossibly, it was Paragon, transfigured in death to a youth.
A ghostly white serpent gambolled before the ship. More swift
than the wind, unnaturally fleet, the liveship drew alongside.
Completing the nightmare, his mother stood on the foredeck,
her white hair streaming in the wind. She saw him. She
reached a beseeching hand towards him. A golden goddess

stood beside her, and a dead man commanded the crew. Kennit's tongue clove for an instant to the roof of his mouth. The ghosts of his past came on, impossibly swift, drawing abreast of the Jamaillian ship and then veering towards it. 'Kennit!' the voice thundered again. 'I come for you!' Paragon put cold fury in his voice. 'Yield Kennit to me! I command it! He is mine!'

'Yield!' Vivacia's voice cracked the sky, coming from the port side of the ship. Kennit's view of her was blocked, but he knew she was close. His heart lifted painfully in his chest. She could save him. 'Yield, Jamaillian ship, or we take you to the bottom!'

The Jamaillian ship had nowhere to go. Despite her master's frantic commands to spill wind from her sails, he could not slow her fast enough. The Paragon cut recklessly towards her bow. The Jamaillian ship veered, but it was not enough. With a terrible splintering sound followed by the groans of stressed timbers, she caromed at an angle against Paragon. His wizardwood absorbed her impact, but splinters flew from the Jamaillian ship. The Jamaillian ship slewed around, all control lost. Overhead, canvas flapped wildly. Suddenly, there was another grinding impact as the Vivacia pressed up against her other side. It was a reckless manoeuvre, one that could take all three ships down. The halted momentum of the ships swung them all in a slowly turning circle. Sailors on every deck roared in dismay. Overhead, rigging threatened to tangle. To either side, the *Marietta* and the *Motley* swept past, to hold off approaching Jamaillian vessels.

The deck under Kennit was still shuddering from the impacts when grapples from both liveships seized onto it. Boarders from both sides leapt over the railings. The clash of fighting rose around them, supplemented with the wild shouts of the liveships themselves. Even the serpent added his trumpeting. Their captors were suddenly intent on defending their own lives.

'Satrap! We must try to get to the Vivacia.' Kennit kept his firm grip on the Satrap's shoulder and shouted by his ear. 'I'll guide you there,' he asserted, lest his living crutch try to go on his own.

'Kill them!' The Jamaillian captain's roar cut through the sounds of battle. It was the furious cry of a desperate man. 'By Lord Criath's order, they must not be taken alive. Kill the Satrap and the pirate king. Don't let them escape!'

Bodies still cluttered Vivacia's deck, the blood beading and running over the sealed wood. Walking was slippery. The frantically scrambling sailors, the outstretched, pleading hands of the injured, and the increased shifting of the deck made Malta's journey to where Reyn had fallen a nightmare. She felt she moved sluggishly, alone, through chaos and insanity, to the end of the world. Pirates darted past her to Wintrow's shouted commands. She did not even hear them. Reyn had come all this way, seeking her, and she had been too cowardly to give him even a word. She had dreaded the pain of his rejection so much that she had not had the courage to thank him. Now she feared she sought for a dead man.

He lay face-down. She had to pull another body off his. The man on top of him was heavy. She tugged at him hopelessly while all around her the world went on a mad quest to save Kennit. No one, not her brother, not her aunt, came to her aid. She sobbed breathlessly, tearlessly as she worked. She heard the two liveships shouting to one another. Rushing sailors dodged around her, heedless of her toil. She fell to her knees in the blood, braced a shoulder against the dead man's bulk, and shoved him off Reyn.

The revealed carnage left her gasping. Blood soaked his garments and pooled around his body. He sprawled in it, horribly still. 'Oh, Reyn. Oh, my love.' She squeezed out the hoarse words that had lived unacknowledged in her heart since their first dream-box sharing. Heedless of the blood, she bent to embrace him. He was still warm. 'Never to be,' she moaned, rocking. 'Never to be.' It was like losing her home and her family all over again. In his arms, she suddenly knew, was the only place where she could have been Malta again. With him died her youth, her beauty, her dreams.

Tenderly, as if he could still feel pain, she turned him over. She would see his face one last time, look into his copper eyes even if he did not look back at her. It would be all she would ever have of him.

Her hands were thick with his blood as she untucked the veil from the throat of his shirt. She used both hands to lift it up and away from his face. It peeled away, leaving a latticework of blood inked on his slack face. Tenderly she wiped it away with the hem of her cloak. She bent down and kissed his still mouth, lips to lips, no dream, no veil between them. Dimly she was aware that the shouting world of sail and battle went on around them. She did not care. Her life had stopped here. She traced the scaled line of his brow, the pebbled skin like a finely-wrought chain under her fingertip. 'Reyn,' she said quietly. 'Oh, my Reyn.'

His eyes opened to slits. Copper glints shone. Transfixed, she stared, as he blinked twice, then opened his eyes. He squinted up at her. He gave a gasp of pain, his right hand going to the wet sleeve on his left arm. 'I'm hurt,' he said dazedly.

She bent closer over him. Her heart thundered in her ears. She scarcely heard her own words. 'Reyn. Lie still. You're bleeding badly. Let me see to you.' With a competence she did not feel, she began to undo his shirt. She would not dare to hope, she hoped for nothing, no, she did not even dare to pray, not that he would live, not that he would love her. Such hopes were too big. Her shaking hands could not unfasten the buttons.

She tore the shirt and spread it wide, expecting ruin within. 'You're whole!' she exclaimed. 'Praise Sa for life!' She ran a

Robin Hobb

wondering hand down his smooth bronze chest. The scaling on it rippled under her hand and glinted in the pale winter sunlight.

'Malta?' He squinted, as if finally able to see who knelt over him. In his bloody right hand he caught both of hers and held her touch away from him as his eyes fixed on her brow. His eyes widened and he dropped her hands. Shame and pain scorched Malta, but she did not look away from him. As if he could not resist the impulse, he lifted a hand. But he did not touch her cheek as she had hoped. Instead, his fingers went straight to her bulging scar and traced it through her hair. Tears burned her eyes.

'Crowned,' he murmured. 'But how can this be? Crested like the ancient Elderling queen in the old tapestries. The scaling is just beginning to show scarlet. Oh, my beauty, my lady, my queen, Tintaglia was right. You are the only one fit to mother such children as we shall make.'

His words made no sense, but she did not care. There was acceptance in his face, and awe. His eyes wandered endlessly over her face, in wonder and delight. 'Your brows, too, even your lips. You are beginning to scale. Help me up,' he demanded. 'I must see all of you. I must hold you to know this is real. I have come so far and dreamed of you so often.'

'You are hurt,' she protested. 'There is so much blood, Reyn . . .'

'Not much of it mine, I think.' He lifted a hand to the side of his head. 'I was stunned. And I took a sword thrust up my left arm. However, other than that –' He moved slowly, groaning. 'I merely hurt all over.'

He drew his feet up, got to his knees and slowly managed to stand. She rose with him, steadying him. He lifted a hand to rub his eyes. 'My veil,' he exclaimed suddenly. Then he looked down at her. She had not thought such joy could shine on a man's face. 'You will marry me, then?' he asked in delighted disbelief.

'If you'll have me, as I am.' She stood straight, chose truth. She could not let him plunge into this blindly, not knowing what others might later whisper about his bride. 'Reyn, there is much that you first need to know about me.'

At that instant, Vivacia shouted something about yielding. An instant later, a wrenching impact threw them both to the deck again. Reyn cried out with pain, but rolled to throw himself protectively over her. The ship shuddered beneath them as he gathered her into his embrace. He lay beside her, holding her tight with his good arm, bracing them both against the blows of the world. As sailors clamoured and the fresh clatter of battle rose, he shouted by her ear, 'The only thing I need to know is that I have you now.'

Wintrow knew how to command. Amidst all else, as Althea scrambled to his orders with the others, she saw the sense of them. She saw something else, something even more important than whether she approved of how he ran his deck. The crew was confident in him. Jola, the mate, did not question his competence or his authority to take over for Kennit. Neither did Etta. Vivacia put herself in his hands, without reservations. Althea was aware, jealously, of the exchange between Vivacia and Wintrow. Effortless as water, it flowed past her. Naturally, without effort, they traded encouragement and information. They did not exclude her; it simply went past her the way adult conversation went over a child's head.

The priest-boy, small and spindly as a child, had become this slight but energetic young man who roared commands with a man's voice. She knew, with a sudden guilt, that her own father had not seen that possibility in Wintrow. If he had, Ephron Vestrit would have opposed Keffria sending him off to the priesthood. Even his own father had intended to use him only as a sort of place-holder until Selden, his younger, bolder son, came of age. Only Kennit had seen this, and nurtured this in him. Kennit the rapist had somehow been also the leader that Wintrow near worshipped, and the mentor who had enabled him to take his place on this deck and command it.

The thoughts rushed through her head as swiftly as the wind that pushed the sails, trampling her emotions as the barefoot sailors trampled Vivacia's decks. She poured her angry strength into hauling on a line. She hated and loathed Kennit. Even more than she longed to kill him, she needed to expose him. She wanted to tear his followers' love and loyalty away from him the way he had torn her dignity and privacy from her body. She wanted to do to him what he had done to her: take from him something he could never regain. Leave him always crippled in a way that did not yield to logic. She did not want to hurt those two, her nephew and her ship. But no matter how much she cared for both of them, she could not walk away from what Kennit had done to her.

It hurt worse, now that she knew Brashen was alive. Every time she caught a glimpse of him on Paragon's deck, her leaping joy was stained with dread. The thought of telling him tainted her anticipation of reunion. Would even Brashen grasp the whole of it? She was not sure what she feared most: that he would be enraged by it, as if Kennit had stolen from him, that he might spurn her as dirtied, or that he might dismiss it as a bad experience that she would get over. In not knowing how he would react, she suddenly feared that she did not know him at all. The open love and trust between Brashen and her was, in some ways, still new and fresh. Could it bear the weight of this truth? Her anger roiled inside her as she wondered if that, too, would be a thing that Kennit had destroyed.

Then there was no time to think any more. They were beside the Jamaillian ship. Althea heard a terrible sound as it collided with something. Probably the Paragon, she thought with sudden agony. Her poor mad ship flung into this battle for Kennit's sake. The Jamaillian ship loomed larger, and closer and –

'Brace!' Someone shouted the word.

An instant later, she knew it had been meant as a warning, but by then, she was sliding across the deck. Anger flashed through her as she rolled and skidded. How dared Wintrow risk her ship that way? Then she felt, through her flesh against the wizardwood, how intent the ship had been on this chase and capture. Vivacia had chosen the peril. Wintrow had done all he could to minimize it. Althea fetched up against one of the bodies on the deck. With a shudder, she rolled to her feet. The side of the Jamaillian ship was as close as a pier. She saw Etta make the jump, deck to deck, a blade in her hand. Had Wintrow led the way? She could not see him anywhere. She scrabbled for the blade the dead man still clutched.

An instant later, her feet hit the Jamaillian deck. There was fighting all around her, too thick for her to make sense of any of it. Where was her nephew? A Jamaillian sailor sprang to meet her wavering blade. Althea clumsily parried his first two efforts at killing her. Then, from somewhere, another blade licked in, slashing him across the chest. He turned with a cry and staggered away from her.

Jek was at her shoulder suddenly, grinning insanely as she did for any danger. 'Think if I save the Satrap, he'll marry me? I'd fancy being a Satrapess, or whatever she's called.'

Before Althea could answer, something rocked the deck under her, sending combatants staggering. She clutched at Jek. 'What was that?' she asked, wondering if the Jamaillian fleet was using its catapults against the locked ships. Her answer came in a frenzied shout from a Jamaillian sailor. 'Cap'n, Cap'n, the damnable serpent has torn our rudder free. We're taking on water bad!'

'We'd best get what we came for and get off this tub,' Jek suggested merrily. She plunged into the battle, not singling out any opponent, but scything a way for herself through the mêlée. Althea followed on her heels, doing little more than keeping men off their backs. 'I thought I saw Etta – ah, here we are!' Jek exclaimed. Then, 'Sa's breath and El's balls!' she swore. 'They're down and bloody, both of them!'

The Jamaillian captain had taught his men to obey without question. That was a thing to admire, until it was turned on you. Their complete obedience was in their eyes as they closed on Kennit. They'd kill them both, without hesitation, on their captain's order. Evidently the Satrap either had to be in their control, or dead. Kennit's estimate of Cosgo's value soared. He'd keep him alive and in his own control. Clearly that was where he was the greatest threat to the Jamaillians, and hence most valuable. They'd come through a serpent attack and risked everything to capture him. Kennit would take him back, and then they'd pay more dearly than they had ever imagined. Vivacia was alongside; he only needed to hold them off for a few minutes until Etta and Wintrow came for him.

'Get behind me!' he commanded the Satrap, and pushed him roughly back. Kennit braced his hand on the ship's house to keep from toppling over. His body shielded the cowering Magnadon. With his free hand, Kennit tore his cloak loose. The oncoming men didn't pause. He foiled the first man's thrust by flinging his cloak around the blade as it came in and shoving it aside. He tried to grab for it, risking that he could wrench it loose from its owner's grip, but it slipped out from the folds of heavy cloak.

The second man was a big beefy fellow, more blacksmith than swordsman. Without finesse or pretence, he stepped up and thrust his heavy blade through Kennit and into the Satrap. The blade pinned them together. 'Got 'em both!' he exclaimed in satisfaction. His killer's striped shirt was stained with grease, Kennit noted in shock. The man wrenched the blade back out of them and turned to face the boarding parties. Kennit and the Satrap fell together.

Even as he fell, Kennit did not believe it. This could not

be happening, not to him. A shrill screaming, like a cornered rabbit, rose right behind him. The screaming ran down and became pain. It ruptured inside him and spread through his entire body. The pain was white, unbearably white, and so intense there was no need to scream. A long time later it seemed, the deck stopped his fall. Both his hands clutched at his middle. Blood poured out between his fingers. A moment later, he tasted blood, his own blood, salt and sweet in his mouth. He'd tasted blood before; Igrot had loved to backhand him. The taste of blood in his mouth, always the forerunner to worse pain.

'Paragon,' he heard himself call breathlessly, as he had always called when the pain was too intense to bear. 'I'm hurt, ship. I'm hurt.'

'Keep breathing, Kennit.' The tiny voice from his wrist was urgent, almost panicked. 'Hang on. They're almost here. Keep breathing.'

Stupid charm. He was breathing. Wasn't he? Unhappily he turned his eyes down. With every heavy breath, he spattered blood from his lips. His fine white shirt was ruined. Etta would make him a new one. He tasted blood, he smelled it. Where was Paragon? Why didn't he take this pain? He tried to summon him by speaking his ship's old words for him. 'Keep still, boy,' he whispered to himself, as Paragon had always done. 'Keep still. I'll take it for you. Give it all to me. Just worry about yourself.'

'He's alive!' someone cried out. He rolled his eyes up to the speaker, praying for deliverance. But the face that looked down at him was Jamaillian. 'You jerk, Flad! You didn't even kill him.' Efficiently, this man stabbed his slender blade into Kennit's chest and dragged it out. 'Got him that time!' The satisfaction in the voice followed Kennit down into the darkness.

*   *   *

They were too late. Wintrow shouted his agony and killed the man who had just killed his captain. He did it without thought, let alone remorse. The crew who had followed him from the Vivacia cut them a space on the crowded deck. Etta flung herself past Wintrow to land on her knees by Kennit. She touched his face, his breast. 'He breathes, he breathes!' she cried in stricken joy. 'Help me, Wintrow, help me! We have to get him back to Vivacia! We can still save him.'

He knew she was wrong. There was far too much blood, dark thick blood, and it still spilled from Kennit as they spoke. They couldn't save him. The best they could do was to take him home to die, and they would have to act swiftly to do that. He stooped and took his captain's arm across his shoulders. Etta got on the other side of Kennit, crooning to him all the while. That he did not cry out with pain as they lifted him proved to Wintrow that he was nearly gone. They had to hurry. The Jamaillians had been beaten back, but not for long.

The Satrap was underneath Kennit. As they lifted him off, the Satrap spasmed into life, screaming and rolling himself into a ball. 'No, no, no, don't kill me, don't kill me!' he babbled. With the voluminous red cloak, he looked like a child hiding under his blankets.

'What a nuisance,' Wintrow muttered to himself, and then bit his tongue, scarcely believing he had uttered such words. As they started back to the ship with Kennit, he shouted to his crew, 'Somebody bring the Satrap.'

Jek bounded past him from the edge of the group. Stooping, she picked the Satrap up in her arms, then shifted him over her shoulder. 'Let's go!' she proclaimed, ignoring the Satrap's cries. Althea, at her side, menaced the closing Jamaillian warriors with a sword, guarding Jek's back. Wintrow caught one flash from her dark and angry eyes. He tried not to care. He had to bring Kennit back to his own deck. He wished she could understand that despite what Kennit had done to her, there was still a bond between Kennit and him. He wished he could understand it himself. They crossed the deck at a half-run. Kennit's leg and peg dragged behind them, leaving a scrawl of his blood in their wake. Someone caught his legs up as they went over the railings and helped them. 'Cast off!' he shouted to Jola as soon as Althea and the others had regained the deck of the Vivacia. They turned to slash at Jamaillians, who sought to board them, intent on reclaiming the Satrap or at least his body. The ships began to move apart. A Jamaillian made a furious leap and fell into the widening gap. Their ship was wallowing now. Whatever the serpent had done to their rudder was flooding their holds. The same serpent watched their ship avidly, positioned just beneath the boat they were trying to get off. Wintrow tore his eyes away.

'Wintrow! Bring me Kennit!' Vivacia shouted. Then, even louder, 'Paragon, Paragon, we have him! Kennit is here!'

Wintrow exchanged a glance with Etta. The pirate hung silently between them. Blood dripped from his chest to puddle on the deck. Etta's eyes were wide and dark. 'To the foredeck,' Wintrow said quietly. Then he shouted to the crew, 'Get us clear of the Jamaillian ship. It's sinking. Jola! Get us away before the fleet can close us in.'

'We're a bit late for that!' Jek announced cheerily as she dumped the Satrap to his feet on Vivacia's deck. Althea caught his arm to keep him from falling. As he gasped in outrage, Jek took hold of his shirt and tore it open. She inspected the dark wound that welled blood sluggishly down his belly. 'I don't think it hit anything really important. Kennit took your death for you. Best get below and lie down until someone has time to see to you.' Casually, she tore a hank of his shirt free and handed it to him. 'Here. Press this on it. That will slow the blood.'

The Satrap looked at the rag she had thrust into his hand. Then he looked down at his wound. He dropped the rag nervelessly and swayed on his feet. Althea kept a firm grip on him as Jek took his other arm with a shake of her head. She rolled her eyes at Althea.

Althea stared after Wintrow. Kennit's arm was across her nephew's shoulders, Wintrow's arm around his waist as they dragged him along. She clenched her jaws. That man had raped her and Wintrow had still risked his own life for him. The Satrap took a gasp of air. Then, 'Malta!' he wailed, as a child would have cried 'Mama!' 'I'm bleeding. I'm dying. Where are you?'

A good question, Althea thought. Where was her little niece? She scanned the deck. Her eyes halted in amazement. Malta and Reyn were working together to take a wounded pirate below. Reyn's left arm was swaddled in a thick white bandage. He went unveiled and Malta's head was uncovered. In the sunlight, her scar glinted red. Althea saw her turn and speak briefly to Reyn, who nodded to her without hesitation. He put his arm around the man they had been helping and took him below while Malta hastened over to the Satrap. But she addressed her first words to Althea.

'Reyn thinks I'm beautiful. Can you believe that? Do you know what he said about my hands? That they will scale heavily as far as my elbows, most likely. He says if I rub off the dead skin, I'll see the scarlet scales working through. He thinks I'm beautiful.' Her niece's eyes shone with joy as she rattled words at Althea. And more than joy? Althea leaned forwards, incredulously. Reyn was right. Malta had a Rain Wild gleam to her eyes now. Althea lifted a hand to cover her mouth in shock.

Malta did not seem to notice. She slipped her arm around the Satrap, her face suddenly concerned. 'You are hurt!' she exclaimed, surprised. 'I thought you were just – oh, dear, well, come along, let's take you below and see to that. Reyn! Reyn, I need you!' Cozening and coaxing, Malta led the Satrap of all Jamaillia away.

Althea turned away from the spectacle of the unmasked

Rain Wilder hastening to her niece's imperious summoning. She nudged Jek out of her stare. 'Come on,' she told her. They hastened towards the foredeck, following Kennit's blood trail. The beads and puddles of blood looked odd to her. Then it struck her. The wizardwood was refusing it. Kennit's blood remained atop it, as did the other blood shed today. She tried to puzzle out what that might mean. Was Vivacia rejecting the dying pirate? She felt a sudden lift of hope.

An instant later, it turned to dismay as an immense splash showered her. 'That was close!' Jek exclaimed. The next ballast stone hit Vivacia's hull. The hard wood rang with the impact and the ship shuddered. Althea turned wildly, seeking a gap in the circle of ships that surrounded them. There wasn't one. The *Marietta* and the *Motley* were trapped as well, though they were trying to break free. Another catapult lofted an immense stone towards them as Paragon drifted around the bow of the Jamaillian ship and into full view.

'Etta, Etta.' His panting whisper barely reached her ears.

'Yes, dearest, I'm here, hush, hush.' Another splash rocked the ship. 'We'll take you to Vivacia. You'll be all right.' She tightened her hold on Kennit as they hurried him forwards. She wanted to be gentle, but she needed to get him to the foredeck. Vivacia could lend him strength; she knew it, despite the wooden despair on Wintrow's face. Kennit would be all right, he had to be all right. The danger of losing him drove all doubts from her mind and heart. What could it matter to her what he had done to anyone else? He had loved her, loved her as no one else ever had.

'I won't be all right, my dear.' His head hung forwards on his chest, his gleaming black curls curtaining his face. He coughed slightly. Blood sprayed. She did not know how he found strength to speak. His gasped whisper was desperate, urgent. 'My love. Take the wizardwood charm from my wrist.

Wear it always, until the day you pass it on to our son. To Paragon. You will name him Paragon? You will wear the charm?'

'Of course, of course, but you aren't going to die. Hush. Save your strength. Here's the ladder, this is the last hard bit, my love. Keep breathing. Vivacia! Vivacia, he's here, help him, help him!'

The crewmen and Wintrow seemed so rough as they hauled him up onto the foredeck. Etta leapt up the ladder and hurried before them. She tore off her cloak and spread it out on the deck. 'Here,' she cried to them. 'Put him here.'

'No!' Vivacia thundered. The figurehead had twisted round as far as she could, farther than a real human could have turned. She held out her arms for Kennit.

'You can help him,' Etta sought her reassurance. 'He won't die.'

Vivacia didn't answer her question. Her green eyes were deep as the ocean as they met Etta's gaze. The inevitability of the ocean was in her look. 'Give him to me,' she said again quietly.

An unuttered scream echoed through Etta's heart. Air would not come into her lungs. Her whole body tingled strangely, and then went numb. 'Give him to her,' she conceded. She could not feel her mouth move, but she heard the words. Wintrow and Jola raised Kennit's body, offering him to Vivacia. Etta kept Kennit's hand tightly in hers as the ship took him in her cradling arms. 'Oh, my love,' she mourned as Vivacia received him. Then the figurehead turned away and she had to release his dangling hand.

Vivacia lifted Kennit's limp body to her breast and held him close. Her great head bent over him. Could a liveship weep? Then she lifted her head, flinging back her raven hair. Another rock struck her bow. The whole ship rang with the impact.

'Paragon!' she cried aloud. 'Hurry, hurry. Kennit is yours. Come and take him!'

'No!' Etta wailed, uncomprehending. 'You would give him to his enemy? No, no, give him back to me!'

'Hush. This must be,' Vivacia said kindly but firmly. 'Paragon is not his enemy. I give him back to his family, Etta.' Gently, she added, 'You should go with him.'

Paragon loomed closer and closer still. His hands groped blindly towards Vivacia. 'Here, I am here,' she called, guiding him to her. It was an insane manoeuvre to bring two ships into such proximity, bow to bow, let alone in the midst of a hail of stones. One such missile crashed down, the splash wetting them both. They ignored it. Paragon's hands suddenly clasped Vivacia and fumbled their way to Kennit in her arms. For a long instant, the two liveships rocked in a strange embrace, the pirate between them. Then, silently, Vivacia placed Kennit's lax body in Paragon's waiting arms.

Etta, standing at the railing, watched the change that came over the ship's young face. He caught his lower lip between his teeth, perhaps to keep it from trembling. Then he raised Kennit's body.

Paragon's pale blue eyes opened at last. He looked a long time into the pirate's face, gazing with the hunger of years. Then, slowly, he clasped him close. Kennit looked almost doll-like in the figurehead's embrace. His lips moved, but Etta heard nothing. The blood from Kennit's injuries vanished swiftly as it touched Paragon's wood, soaking in immediately, and leaving no stain of passage. Then he bowed over Kennit and kissed the top of his head with an impossible tenderness. At last, Paragon looked up. He gazed at her with Kennit's eyes and smiled, an unbearably sad smile that yet held peace and wholeness.

An elderly woman on Paragon's deck strained towards Kennit's body. Tears ran down her face and she cried aloud but wordlessly, a terrible gabbling wail. Behind her, a tall dark-haired man stood with his arms crossed tightly on his chest. His jaw was set, his eyes narrowed, but he did not try to interfere. He even stepped forwards and helped support Kennit's body as Paragon released it into the woman's reaching arms. Gently they stretched him on the liveship's deck.

'Now you,' Vivacia said suddenly. She reached for Etta, and she stepped into the liveship's grasp.

Somewhere in the darkness, someone was beating a drum. It was an unsteady rhythm, loud-soft, loud-soft, and slowing, slowing inexorably to peace. There were other sounds, shouts and angry cries, but they no longer mattered. Closer to his ears, familiar voices spoke. Wintrow muttering to him and to someone else, 'Damn, sorry, sorry, Kennit. Be careful, can't you, support his leg as I lift –'

On the other side of him, Etta was talking. '. . . Hush. Save your strength. Here's the ladder, this is the last hard bit, my love. Keep breathing . . .' He could ignore them if he chose. If he ignored them, what could he focus on? What was important now?

He felt Vivacia take him. Oh, yes, this would be best, this would be easiest. He relaxed and tried to let go. He felt the life seeping out of his body, and he hovered, waiting to be gone. But she held him still, cupped in her hands like water, refusing to take him. 'Wait,' she whispered to him. 'Hold on, be, just for a moment or two longer. You need to go home, Kennit. You are not mine. You were never mine, and we always knew that. You need to be one once more. Wait. Just a bit longer. Wait.' Then she called loud, 'Paragon. Hurry, hurry. Kennit is yours. Come and take him!'

Paragon? Fear stabbed him. Paragon was lost to him, no more than a boyish ghost now. He had killed him. His own ship could never take him back. He could never go home. Paragon would fling him away, would leave him to sink beneath the sea just as he had –

He knew the touch of the big hands that accepted him.

He would have wept, but there were no tears left. He tried to make his mouth move, to speak aloud how sorry he was. 'There, there,' someone said comfortingly. Paragon? His father? Someone who loved him said, 'Don't fear. I have you now. I won't let you go. You will not be hurt any more.' Then he felt the kiss that absolved him without judgement. 'Come back to me,' he said. 'Come home.' The darkness was no longer black. It grew silvery and then as Paragon embraced him and took him home he faded into white.

THIRTY-FIVE

Hard Decisions

'COME BELOW SO I can bandage this,' Malta insisted.
'Lordly one, you must not take chances with yourself.' She
flinched as a rock landed in the water aft of them. She glanced
back and Reyn followed her stare. Their aim was getting better.
The Jamaillian ships were closing in.

'No. Not yet.' The Satrap clung to the railing and stared
down gloatingly. Malta was beside him, pressing a rag to his
sword-thrust. The Satrap himself refused to touch his wound.
Only Malta would do for that duty, but Reyn refused to be
jealous. The Satrap clung to her presence as if she anchored
his world, yet refused to acknowledge his dependence on her. It
amazed him that the man could not hear the falsity in Malta's
sweetness to him. The Satrap leaned forwards suddenly and
cupped his hands to his mouth so that his shouted words would
carry his gleeful satisfaction to the men on the foundering
Jamaillian ship.

'Farewell, Lord Criath. Give your good counsels to my white
serpent now. I'll be sure your family in Jamaillia City know
of your bold cries for mercy. What, Ferdio? Not a swimmer?
Don't let it trouble you. You won't be in the water long,
and there's no need to swim in the serpent's belly. I mark
you, Lord Kreio. Your sons will never see their inheritance.
They lose all, not just my Bingtown grants to you but your

Jamaillian estates as well. And you, Peaton of Broadhill, oh best of smoking partners! Your forests and orchards will smoke in memory of you! Ah, noble Vesset, will you hide your face in your hands? Do not fear, you will not be overlooked! You leave a daughter, do you not?'

The noble conspirators gazed up at him. Some pleaded, some stood stolidly, and some shouted insults back at him. They would all meet the same end. When they had balked at entering the water in the ship's boats while the serpent prowled so near, the crew had abandoned them. Their distrust of the ship's boats had been well founded. They were floating wreckage now. Reyn had not seen a single sailor survive.

It was too much for the Rain Wilder. 'You mock the dying,' he rebuked the Satrap.

'I mock the traitorous!' the Satrap corrected him savagely. 'And my vengeance will be sweet!' he called loudly across the water. Avidly, his eyes tallied the Jamaillian nobles who stood helplessly on the deck of the foundering ship. It was already awash. He muttered names, obviously committing them to memory for later retaliation on their families. Reyn exchanged an incredulous look with Malta. This savage, merciless boy was the Lord High Magnadon Satrap of all Jamaillia? Cosgo opened his mouth again, crying, 'Oh, serpent, don't leave, here's a tender – Ah!'

He gasped suddenly and bent over his wound.

Malta looked as innocent as a babe as she held the rag firmly to the injury and proclaimed, 'Oh, Lord Satrap, you must stop your shouting. Look, it has started your bleeding again. Come, we must below. Leave them to Sa's justice.'

'Bleeding again – ah, the treacherous cowards deserve to die more slowly. Kennit was right. He saved me, you know.' Without asking permission, he clutched Reyn's arm and leaned on him as they tottered him towards the ship's house. 'At the end, Kennit recognized that my survival was more important than his. Brave soul! I defied those traitors, but when they

795

came with the killing thrust, brave Kennit took my death for me. Now there is a name that will be remembered with honour. King Kennit of the Pirate Isles.'

So the Satrap sought to crown himself with Kennit's deeds and reputation. Reyn embroidered his conceited fantasy for him. 'No doubt minstrels will make wondrous songs to tell of your great adventure. To Bingtown and the Rain Wilds the bold young Satrap journeyed. To be saved at the end by the unselfish pirate king who belatedly recognized the ultimate importance of the Satrap of all Jamaillia is the only fitting end for such a song.' Reyn drawled the words, loving that Malta must fight to keep from smiling. Between them, the Satrap's face lit with delight.

'Yes, yes. An excellent concept. And a whole verse devoted to the names of those who betrayed me and how they perished, torn apart by the serpents that Kennit had commanded to guard me. That will make future traitors pause before they conspire against me.'

'Doubtless,' Malta agreed. 'But now we must go below.' Firmly, she eased him along. Her anxious eyes met Reyn's, sharing her fear that they would not survive the day. Despite the darkness of the emotion, Reyn treasured that he could sense so much of what she felt just by standing near her. He gathered his strength and radiated calmness towards her. Surely, Captain Kennit had been in worse situations. His crew would know how to get them out of this.

'I'll lay out canvas for a shroud,' Amber offered.

'Very well,' Brashen agreed numbly. He looked down on Kennit's body. The pirate that had nearly killed them all had died on his deck. His mother rocked him now, weeping silently, a tremulous smile on her lips. Paragon had gone very still since he had handed Kennit to his mother. Brashen feared to speak to him lest he did not answer. He sensed something happening within his ship. Whatever it was, Paragon guarded it closely. Brashen feared what it might be.

'We gonna get out of here?' Clef asked him pragmatically.

Brashen looked down at the boy by his side. 'Don't know,' Brashen answered him shortly. 'We're going to try.'

The boy surveyed the enemy ships critically. 'Whyer they holdin' back?'

'I suspect they fear the liveships. Why risk lives when rocks will work?'

The Jamaillian ship was going down. A few desperate souls had fled to her rigging, for the white serpent had shown them that their ship's boats would provide no escape for them. Kennit's other two ships had engaged adjacent Jamaillian vessels and were trying to force a gap in the ring of vessels that surrounded them. Another missile landed uncomfortably close. Paragon rocked slightly with it. No doubt, as soon as they were clear of the Jamaillian ship, the rest of the fleet would be bolder with their rock-throwing. 'If we could get the white serpent to help those two pirate vessels, we might be able to break out. But then we'd have to outrun the fleet, too.'

'It doesn't look good,' Clef decided.

'No,' Brashen agreed grimly. Then he smiled. 'But we aren't dead yet, either.'

A strange woman was stepping down onto the railing from Paragon's hands. She did not even glance at Brashen, but settled herself silently beside the fallen pirate. An inexpressible grief dulled her black eyes. She lifted Kennit's hand and held it to her cheek. Mother reached across Kennit to rest a wrinkled hand on her shoulder. The women's eyes met across his body. For a moment, the dark-haired woman studied Mother's face. Then she spoke quietly.

'I loved him. I believe he loved me. I carry his child.'

The woman smoothed Kennit's curls back from his still face. Brashen, feeling an intruder, looked away from them to the retreating Vivacia. Wintrow and Althea stood together on the foredeck, conferring about something. Brashen's heart leapt at the sight of her. Cursing himself for a fool, he sprang suddenly to the rail. If one woman could cross, so could another. 'Althea!' he bellowed, but the two ships had already drifted apart. Nevertheless, at his call, she spun. She sprinted wildly towards the bow. His heart choked him as he saw her spring wildly to the figurehead's shoulder. There was no mistaking the shock on Vivacia's face. She caught Althea in her headlong flight.

Her words to her ship carried clearly across the water to him. His heart flew on them. 'Please, Vivacia. You don't need me. I want to go to him.'

Vivacia glanced over at Paragon. Then her voice rang clear across the water. 'Paragon! This one I give to you as well!'

As a parent might playfully loft a child, Vivacia swung Althea high, low, and then high again, letting her fly towards the blind ship. Her body arced through the air.

'No!' Brashen roared in terror, clutching the rail.

'I've got her!' Paragon cried reassuringly, and then, miraculously, he did.

He caught her and swung her with her momentum, whirling her around before handing her off suddenly into Brashen's reaching arms. She stumbled off the railing and slid down into his embrace. He clasped her to him, folding her into his arms. He didn't even try to speak. He had no breath left. When he looked up at Paragon, the ship looked back. His pale blue eyes crinkled in a grin. Brashen was transfixed.

'Welcome aboard and le's get out of here ef we can!' Clef greeted her.

'Oh, Brashen,' Althea said shudderingly into his chest. Her voice jolted Brashen from his shock. She lifted her face to look up at him but held him as closely as ever. She took a deep breath. 'Wintrow's plan. If we can break free, run north for Divvytown. That harbour's defensible now. We can hold out there as long as we need to, until birds can bring Kennit's other ships to help us.'

She broke her flow of words suddenly. She stared at Kennit's still body. An old woman and Etta on either side of him seemed unaware of anyone else. 'He's dead,' Brashen whispered into her hair. 'He died in Paragon's arms.' Althea clung to him as she never had before. He held her, wishing there were time for them. But there was not. Death threatened all around them. 'Break free,' he muttered sceptically. 'How?'

Paragon spoke suddenly. He looked at Brashen over Althea's bowed head and spoke as if they were completely alone. 'Once I promised not to kill you. I was mad, and you knew it, and still you believed in me.' The ship looked around, scanning their situation with cold blue eyes. 'I'm whole now. Now I make you both a new promise. I'll do all I can to keep you alive.'

'Take them up!'

The command came from behind them. Malta, Reyn and the Satrap turned to it. Wintrow, his shirt crimson with Kennit's blood, pointed at the desperate nobles on the foundering ship. Jola hastened to his side. 'Launch a boat?' he asked incredulously.

'No. I won't risk any of mine for them.' He raised his voice to the Jamaillian nobles. 'We'll throw you a line! Those brave enough to cross may survive. It's your choice. Your fleet isn't giving us time to rescue you. Jola, see to it.' He strode off to the foredeck again.

Chaos broke out among the nobles. They crowded the side of the listing ship. One old man lifted his hands and begged Sa to be merciful. A dapper young man, more pragmatic, ran to the other side of the ship, where he waved his cloak and cried to their ships to cease their attack. No one heeded him. The waves lapped over the top of the railings now. Jola prepared a heaving line and threw it.

All the men snatched at it, and one immediately tried to swarm up it.

'Not like that, you fool!' the mate roared down at them. 'Secure the end to something, and come up it hand over hand.'

But some were greybeards and others gentlemen of leisure. Few could make the climb unassisted. In the end, it took several lines and some diligent but rapid hoisting to bring them aboard. By the time they arrived what remained of their finery was in tatters. 'Be grateful she's a liveship,' Jola informed them callously. 'They don't hold barnacles like regular wood. A smoother keel-hauling than most is what you got.'

They stood before the Satrap, a dozen men that he knew by name, men he had dined with, men he had trusted. Malta gave him credit for a small courage. He stood face to face with them. Some met his gaze steadily, but most stared at their feet or off to the horizon. When he spoke, it was the last word Malta had expected to hear from him.

'Why?' he asked. He looked at each in turn. Malta, still holding the rag to his belly, could feel that he trembled slightly. She glanced up at his face and saw a truth that perhaps no one else did. He was hurt by their betrayal. 'Did you hate me that much, to seek my death by treachery?'

The one he had called Lord Criath lifted grey eyes to stare at him. 'Look at you,' he growled. 'You're weak and foolish. You think of nothing except yourself. You've plundered the treasury and let the city go to ruin. What else could we do but kill you? You were never a true Satrap.'

Satrap Cosgo met the man's eyes squarely. 'You have been my trusted advisor since I was fifteen years old,' he returned gravely. 'I listened to you, Criath. Ferdio, you were Minister of the Treasury. Peaton, Kreio, did not you offer me counsels as well? Counsels I always heeded, despite what some of my Companions said, for I wanted you to think well of me.' His eyes moved over them. 'That was my mistake, I see. I measured myself by how sweetly you complimented me. I am what you taught me to be, gentlemen. Or I was.' He stuck out his jaw. 'A time out in the world among true men has been very enlightening. I am no longer the boy you manipulated and betrayed, my lords. As you will come to discover.' As if he had the authority, he instructed Jola, 'Secure them below. They need not be too comfortable.'

'No.' Wintrow had returned. He countermanded the order without apology. 'Fasten them about the ship's house, Jola. I want them visible to their fleet. They may discourage some of the arrows and boulders that will come our way when we break free of this.' He spared a look for his sister, but she scarcely recognized him. Grief had set lines in his face and chilled his eyes. He tried to soften his voice, but his words still sounded like a command. 'Malta, you are safer inside the captain's stateroom. Reyn, will you take her there? And the Satrap, of course.'

She gave a final glance to the sinking Jamaillian ship. She did not linger to watch the nobles tied up as a living shield. This was war, she told herself harshly. He did what he did to try to save them all. If the nobles died, it would be because their own men fired on them. Death was a risk they had chosen when they plotted against the Satrap.

That did not mean she took any satisfaction in it. Bitterly she reflected that scores of Bingtown folk, slaves and simple tradesmen as well as Traders, had died for their ambitions. If their plot had succeeded, Bingtown itself would have fallen and eventually the Rain Wilds as well. Perhaps it was time they felt what it was like to stand in danger they could not avoid.

From the top of Paragon's mast, Althea had a wide view of the battle. She had told Brashen she would climb the mast to try to see a way out of their situation. He had believed her, not knowing she fled Paragon's blue-eyed stare and his own possessive touch on her. The combination had suddenly filled her with unease. Brashen had not noticed. He had put Semoy to assembling Paragon's reduced crew into defence while he took Paragon's helm. It had wrung her heart to see how many of the sailors had perished, and how many of the survivors bore wounds. Amber's scalded face and burnt scalp and Clef's still-peeling burns horrified her. She felt oddly shamed that she had not shared their danger.

From her vantage, she looked down on a scene of disaster and battle. She saw crews abandoning their serpent-damaged ships, and others struggling with fallen rigging and injured men. But those of the Jamaillian fleet that could still function seemed intent on continuing the battle. As far as she could see, there was no easy escape. The *Motley* had rammed a ship that had tried to head her off. The ships were locked together now, their rigging tangled and bloody battle raging on both decks. Althea suspected that no matter who won, both ships were doomed. The *Marietta* could have slipped through and escaped, but Sorcor held her back, trying to aid the *Motley*. Flight after flight of arrows soared from her deck, picking off the Jamaillian sailors, while her own small catapult launched stones at the surrounding ships in a vain effort to keep them back.

It was a very uneven contest, growing worse. Now that Vivacia and Paragon were on the move, only their desire to keep their catapults at a useful range kept the Jamaillian ships from hemming the two liveships completely. The white serpent hummocking through the water beside Paragon kept some of the ships at bay, while the lingering effects of the earlier serpent attacks delayed others. Althea saw a mainsail on one vessel suddenly crash down, and surmised that an earlier spraying of serpent spittle had finally eaten through the sheets.

Their only hope was to break out of the circle and flee for Divvytown. Wintrow had said the town was defensible, but defensible did not mean it could withstand a prolonged siege. She suspected that as long as the Satrap lived, the Jamaillian fleet would not give up. And once he had died, they would eliminate all witnesses. Would they hold back from wiping out a whole pirate settlement? She did not think so.

Down on the deck, men were moving Kennit's body. The old woman trailed after her son's body, but Etta lingered on the foredeck, gripping the railing and staring past the figurehead's shoulder, careless of the battle around them. Perhaps she, too, sensed that more of Kennit remained with the figurehead than in the lolling body. Kennit was a part of Paragon now. He had died on Paragon's deck, and the ship had welcomed him. She still had not grasped why.

Amber suddenly spoke below her. 'Best come down. Brashen is sure a rock is going to come by and carry you off with it.'

Paragon had already taken one solid hit that had taken out part of his railing and scored his deck.

'I'd best get down, too,' Amber continued. 'It sounds like Kyle is making a fuss over Kennit's body being here.'

'Kyle?' The word burst out of Althea.

'Didn't Brashen tell you? Kennit's mother brought him on board with her. Evidently Kennit had stashed him on Key Island.'

'No. He didn't. We haven't had much time to talk.' Now there was an understatement. Mother? Key Island? Althea scooted down the mast, passing Amber to gain the deck. She had thought that nothing could further complicate this day. She had been wrong.

Kyle Haven, Keffria's missing husband, stood in the door of Paragon's house, blocking the way. Althea recognized his voice. 'Throw it over the side!' he demanded harshly. 'Murderer! Thieving c-c-cut-throat!' He stammered hoarsely in his fury. 'Deserved to die! Feed him to the serpents – as he fed my crew to the serpents.'

The two men bearing the body looked disgruntled, but the woman who must be Kennit's mother looked stricken. She still clutched her dead son's hand.

Althea dropped lightly to the deck and hurried over. 'Let her pass, Kyle. Tormenting her won't change a thing that Kennit did.' As she spoke the words, she suddenly knew the truth of them. She looked impassively at Kennit's dead face. He was beyond her vengeance now, and she would not take out her bitterness on this grieving old woman. Kyle, however, was not out of her reach. She had waited long for this confrontation. His arrogance and selfishness had nearly destroyed her life.

Nevertheless, as he turned to stare at her, her hatred melted into horror. His angry confidence had vanished the moment she challenged him. His hands jerked spasmodically as he glared at her without comprehension. 'What?' he demanded querulously. 'Who?'

'Althea Vestrit,' she said quietly. She stared at him.

He bore the marks of many beatings. Teeth were missing and scars seamed his face. Grey streaked his unkempt blond hair. Blows to his head had crazed his control of his head and hands. He moved with trembling and corrections like a very old man.

Amber stood just behind Althea. She spoke gently, in the same tones she had used when Paragon was in one of his tempers. 'Let it go, Kyle. He's dead. It doesn't matter any more. You're safe now.'

'Doesn't matter!' he sputtered, outraged. 'Does matter! Look at me. Damn mess. Your fault!' he suddenly declared, pointing at Althea with a shaky, crooked finger. His twisted hands made her feel faint to look at him. They bore the marks of systematic breaking. 'Your fault – you unnatural – want to be a man. Shamed the family. Made the ship hate me. Your fault. Your fault.'

Althea scarcely heard his words. She saw instead how he struggled to find words and force them from his mouth. Kyle took a great breath, his face mottling red with his effort. 'I curse you! Die on this mad ship! Curse you with bad luck. Dead man on board. You'll die on this deck. Mark that! I curse you! All! I curse you!' He threw wide his shaky hands and saliva flew from his lips.

Althea stared at him, unspeaking. The true curse was that he was Keffria's husband, the father of Wintrow, Malta and Selden. It was her duty to restore him to them. The thought made her blood cold. Had not Malta suffered enough? She had idealized this man. Must she return this bitter wreckage to her sister's side?

When his words did not make his wife's sister flinch, his face wrinkled with fury. He spat on the deck before her, intending insult, but the spittle dribbled from his chin and she felt only appalled. She found words and spoke them calmly. 'Kyle. Let him by, for the sake of his mother's grief. Let them pass.'

While Kyle stared at her in slow comprehension, the men slipped past him with Kennit's body. Mother followed with one reproachful glance back at him. Etta was beside her now. For an instant, her eyes met Althea's. There were no words for what passed between them. 'Thank you.' The words were stiff and resentful. Hatred still burned in Etta's eyes, but the hatred was not for Althea. It was for the shameful truth that tormented both of them. Althea turned aside from that searing knowledge. Kennit had raped her. Etta knew, and the admission was a stake in the heart of her memories of him. Neither woman could escape what he had done to them.

Althea looked away, only to have her eyes fall on Kyle. Still muttering and swinging feeble fists in a display of anger, he gestured wildly as he shuffled away from them. His left foot turned out awkwardly.

Amber spoke quietly. 'At night, in our room, you used to say you longed to meet him just one more time. Just so you could confront him with what he did.'

'He stole my ship from me. He ruined my dreams.' She spoke the old accusation. It sounded impossible now. Althea could not look away from the lurching figure. 'Sa save us all.' The encounter had taken but a few seconds but she felt years older. She dragged her gaze from Kyle to look at her friend. 'Cheated of vengeance twice in one day,' she observed in a shaky voice.

Amber gave her a surprised look. 'Is that truly how you feel?'

'No. No, it isn't at all.' Althea searched her heart and was surprised at what she felt. 'Grateful. For my life, for my intact body. For a man like Brashen in my life. Sa's breath, Amber, I have nothing to complain about.' She looked up suddenly, as if waking from a nightmare. 'We've got to survive this, Amber. We have to. I've a life to live.'

'Each of us does,' Amber replied. She looked across the water to where men fought on the decks of the locked ships. 'And a death to die as well,' she added more softly.

'What would Kennit do now?' Wintrow muttered to himself as he scanned the closing circle of ships. He had taken up the men from the Jamaillian ship because he had not the heart to leave them to drown or be eaten. Weakness, Kennit would have said. Precious time wasted when he should have been getting his ship away. Jola was dutifully chaining them up, at his command. The thought made him queasy. But there was no time for second thoughts. He was alone in this now. Kennit was dead, and Etta sent off to mourn him. Althea had crossed to the Paragon. He had taken command of Vivacia, for he could not tolerate Jola captaining her. Now that he had her, he was afraid he would lose her and all hands. His mind flew back to the last time he had seized control of the ship. Then he had been replacing his father to bring her through a storm. Now he stepped up to fill Kennit's place, in the midst of battle. Despite the time that had passed, he still felt just as uncertain. 'What would Kennit do?' he asked himself again. His mind refused to work.

'Kennit is dead.' Vivacia spoke the harsh words softly.

'You are alive. Wintrow Vestrit, it is up to you. Save us both.'

'How? I don't know how.' He looked around again. He had to act and swiftly. The crew believed in him. They had answered his every command willingly, and now he stood paralysed as death closed in on them. Kennit would have known what to do.

'Stop that.' She spoke in his heart as well as aloud. 'You are not Kennit. You cannot command as he did. You must command as Wintrow Vestrit. You say you fear to fail. What have you told Etta, so often it rings in my bones? When you fear to fail, you fear something that has not happened yet. You predict your own failure, and by inaction, lock yourself into it. Was not that what you told her?'

'A hundred times,' he returned, almost smiling. 'In the days when she would not even try to read. And other times.'

'And?'

He took a breath and centred himself. He scanned the battle again. His oldest training came suddenly to the fore. He drew another deep breath. When he let it out, he sent doubt with the spent air. He suddenly saw the battle as if it were one of Etta's gameboards. 'In conflict, there is weakness. That is where we will break through.' He pointed towards the *Marietta* and the *Motley*, already locked in a struggle with the Jamaillian ships. Several others were moving to join the battle.

'There?' Vivacia asked, suddenly doubtful.

'There. And we do our best to free them with us.' He lifted his voice in sudden command. 'Jola! Bring us about. Archers to the ready. We're leaving!'

It was not what they expected, but once he had realized he could not forsake his friends, the decision was simple. Vivacia answered the helm readily and for a blessing, the wind was with them. Paragon followed without hesitation. He had a glimpse of Trell at the liveship's helm. That simple act of confidence restored Wintrow's faith in himself. 'Do not hesitate!' he urged the ship. 'We'll make them give way before us.'

A Jamaillian ship veered in to flank her. It was a smaller vessel, fleet and nimble, her railing lined with archers. At the cries of his hostages, the bowmen faltered, but an instant later they let fly. Wintrow flung himself flat to avoid two shafts aimed at him. Another struck Vivacia's shoulder, but rebounded harmlessly. She shrieked her outrage, a cry as shrill as a serpent's. Wizardwood need fear no ordinary arrow. Pitch-pots and flames would be another matter, but Wintrow judged correctly that they would fear to use them in such crowded circumstance. The lively wind would be very ready to carry scraps of flaming canvas from one vessel to another. Vivacia's archers returned the volley, with far greater accuracy. The smaller boat veered off. Wintrow hoped the news of their hostages would spread.

Just as he thought they had escaped unscathed, a man fell from the rigging. The arrow had pierced his throat; Gankis had died soundlessly. The old man had been one of Kennit's original crew. As his body struck the deck, Vivacia screamed. It was not a woman's cry, but the rising shriek of an outraged dragon. The anger that surged up from her invaded Wintrow as well. An answering roar came from Paragon, echoed by a shrill trumpeting from the white serpent.

A large ship was moving steadily into their path. No doubt, her captain sought to force Vivacia back into the thick of the fleet. Wintrow gauged their chances. 'Cut it as fine as you can, my lady,' he bade her. 'Cry the steersman as you wish.' He gripped the forerail and hoped he was not leading them all to their deaths. Canvas full and billowing, it became a race of nerves between the two ships. At the last possible moment the other captain slacked his sails and broke away. Vivacia raced past virtually under his bow. Wintrow became aware that the white serpent had moved up to pace them when it roared and sprayed the ship in passing.

Now the embattled *Motley* was right before them. One of her brightly-coloured sails was down and drooping uselessly. The crew had cleared most of her deck of boarders, but the two ships were still both grappled and tangled. Vivacia bore down on them, screaming like a dragon, archers ready. The *Marietta* moved off to allow them room. Sorcor's supply of both arrows and shot were probably nearly spent.

'Look at that!' Wintrow exclaimed suddenly. The white serpent had surfaced by the Jamaillian ship that was locked with the *Motley*. As if it knew their plans, it roared, and then opened wide its jaws to spray the deck with venom. Men screamed. The serpent was too close for their catapult to be of any use. Their volley of arrows rattled off him harmlessly. He disappeared beneath the waves, then surfaced again off the ship's bow. He sprayed the ship again, then bent his great head to press his brow against the wood of the hull. He pushed furiously, lashing the sea to cream with his efforts. Wintrow heard the groan of wood. The great timbers, smoking with the serpent's venom, actually bent with the pressure. On board the *Motley*, men struggled to push their ship clear. Overhead, tangled rigging resisted, but sailors with axes were swarming aloft. They cut themselves free with reckless abandon. With a lurch, the ships suddenly parted.

As the pirates on the *Motley* gave an uneven cheer, the serpent rose once more to spray the other ship with venom. A lone archer, screaming with the pain of his scalds, let fly a single arrow. It struck the white serpent, just behind the angle of his jaw. The shaft plunged out of sight and the serpent screamed in agony. It whipped its head about wildly as if it sought to dislodge the arrow. In horror, Wintrow saw a sudden wound open on the serpent's neck. It ran blood and steaming white toxins. Its own venom was eating away at its flesh. Vivacia gave a cry of fury and horror.

Paragon suddenly swept past them. With complete disregard for the figurehead, the ship rammed the Jamaillian craft. As his bow caught the other vessel amidships, Paragon screamed in wordless fury. He seized the ship's railing and tore it loose.

Wintrow had never thought to gauge the strength of a liveship's figurehead. Before his eyes, an enraged Paragon used the ship's railing as a club to batter at the hapless vessel. Splinters flew at every blow. Men fled, seeking shelter from the flying pieces of wood. When the railing gave way, he snatched the war-axe from his belt. He wielded it two-handed. With every crushing stroke, Paragon roared. Deck planks gave way, and then he reached overhead to tear at canvas and rigging. With his axe and his hands, he reduced the ship to wreckage before Wintrow's disbelieving eyes. On Paragon's deck, his own crew darted for cover, shouting with terror.

The other Jamaillian ships had moved back defensively. Paragon continued to throw chunks of wreckage at them. An anchor trailing a length of chain crashed into the rigging of one ship. A ship's boat, flung with wild strength, cleared half the deck of another. In their haste to be out of his range, one Jamaillian ship rammed another. They drifted in a circle, rigging tangled. Paragon's wild attack had broken an opening for them. Small good it would do them, but Althea watched as the *Marietta* swept through it, followed by the limping *Motley*. They at least would escape.

'Paragon! Paragon!' From the helm, Brashen yelled the ship's name hoarsely. It did no good. The rage of a dragon burned in him, and with every wild blow, he roared it. Vivacia swept through the gap in the circle. 'Follow, follow!' she cried to Paragon as she escaped, but he appeared not to hear. His sails strained to push him on, but he caught hold of the Jamaillian ship with one hand and kept punishing it with the other. The two vessels groaned against one another. A stone thudded against their stern, reminding Althea that the Jamaillian ships were still attacking. Another stone hit the afterdeck and took out a piece of Paragon's railing. If they smashed his rudder, they were doomed. Another stone struck. Death reached for them.

Kyle Haven had emerged from hiding. In the midst of the chaos, he danced a madman's jig on the main deck. 'Die here, die here!' he chanted shrilly. 'Die as you all deserve, every one of you! Serves you right! You brought his body on board! We'll take it to the bottom with us.'

Etta had been closeted with Mother. Now she appeared and made a determined rush down the deck. As she ran, a small ship swept past, the same one that had harried Vivacia earlier. 'Get down!' Althea cried as the row of archers let fly.

Etta heeded her. Kyle did not.

He fell, jerking, with two arrows through his body. Etta did not give him a glance. She picked herself up and ran. When she reached the foredeck, she screamed her words with the force of a sudden cold wind. 'Faithless ship! Bear us away! Or Kennit's child will die unborn, a child he bid me name "Paragon".'

The figurehead twisted back to look at her. His wide blue eyes shone with madness. He stared at her and a sudden silence fell. In one hand, he gripped a timber from the shattered ship. He lifted it high over his head, then flung it into the rigging of an approaching Jamaillian ship. He thrust his axe back into his harness. At last, he seized the battered hulk in both hands and pushed savagely free of it. The impetus aimed them towards the closing gap and thrust the wreckage into the path of two other ships. Suddenly unimpeded, his full sails sent him shooting forwards. Swift as only a liveship was swift, he cut past the bow of a Jamaillian ship and into clear water.

Like a blessing from Sa, there was suddenly open ocean before them. Paragon poured himself into it. The wind sped them as they fled after Vivacia. On the deck, Kyle Haven's blood pooled in standing puddles.

THIRTY-SIX

Secrets

T HEIR ESCAPE HAD forced them north, the wrong direction for fleeing to Divvytown.

The day was fading as Paragon caught up with the others. Vivacia moved swiftly and surely to the fore of their little group of vessels. Wintrow had clearly taken over command of the small pirate force. Althea was proud of him. It was a shame his father had never seen his son as Kennit had, she thought.

No one who had ever loved Kyle Haven would have to look at what had been done to him. Amber had silently helped her slide his body into the sea. Althea herself had wiped from Paragon's deck the blood his wizardwood refused to absorb. She still did not know what she would tell Malta or Keffria. She knew what she would not tell them. She felt sick and bloated with ugly secrets.

Althea lifted her eyes and studied the ships critically. Vivacia led the way, sailing as only a liveship could. The *Marietta*, Sorcor's trim little vessel, strove to keep pace with her. The battered *Motley* trailed them substantially. Last came Paragon. Althea could feel that he still mourned the serpent. Kennit was part of the ship now, and yet she could not deny her bond with him. A shiver, half shudder, ran up her.

Althea made her way aft to the wheel looking for Brashen.

She was not ready to be near the figurehead yet. She excused herself that Etta stood on the foredeck, and undoubtedly wished to be alone. As she walked the deck, Amber emerged from the hatch, carrying a pannikin of stew. The smell of it sickened Althea. She could not recall when she had last eaten.

Semoy was on the wheel. He greeted her with a grin and a wink. 'Knew we'd get you back,' he claimed. She clapped him on the shoulder in passing, surprised that his welcome should move her so. Wordlessly, Amber handed him the food. He gave the wheel to her and came to stand beside Althea. Between shovelled mouthfuls, he nodded aft. 'They still aren't giving up, are they?'

Behind them the Jamaillian ships had sorted themselves out from Paragon's rampage. Some were giving chase. 'I don't think they dare,' Althea replied. 'As long as we have the Satrap and he's alive, they can't give up. If he isn't dead, all the rest of their plan falls to pieces. They lose everything.' She watched the enemy ships critically. 'We're right to flee. Some of those ships won't last the night. I've seen the effects of serpent spittle. What looks like sound canvas will soon split and shred. If we run, we can leave at least some of them behind. Then, when we must fight, we'll face a smaller force.'

'An even better hope is that we may lose them in the night.' Brashen spoke behind them. 'Even if we don't, Wintrow has hostages now.' A shadow came over his face. 'I don't think he'll hesitate to use them.'

'Hostages?' Althea asked as Brashen came to join them at the aft railing. His face was grey; he looked as if he had aged a year in a day. Still, he put his arm around Althea and pulled her close. She hooked an arm around his waist.

From his tone, she could not tell if Brashen approved or was horrified. 'At the last possible moment, Wintrow pulled a dozen or so men off the Jamaillian ship. Nobles, by their clothing. They should be worth something as hostages. But we're right to flee until we're in a position to bargain. There are many places to hide in the Isles, and we follow three ships that know these waters well. We may escape death today.'

Semoy had finished his food. He thanked Amber and traded her the dish for the wheel. It seemed strange that such an ordinary exchange could occur on such a day. Peace seemed foreign to Althea now.

Brashen spoke suddenly, addressing Amber. 'Ornamental?' he asked accusingly.

She shrugged, and there was wonder in her strange eyes. 'I pegged the axe in place. I never dreamed he'd be able to take it out and use it.' She shook her head. 'The more I know of it, the stranger stuff is wizardwood.'

'Lucky for us he could,' Semoy observed approvingly. 'Didn't the splinters fly?'

No one seemed ready to reply to that observation.

Althea leaned against Brashen and watched the distance widen between them and their pursuers. There was so much to tell him, and absolutely nothing to say that was not said better with this simple touch. Clef appeared suddenly. He stood before Althea and Brashen, and shook his head reprovingly. 'In fronter the crew an' all,' he disparaged them with a disrespectful grin. Althea assayed a playful swipe at him. To her surprise, Clef caught her flying hand and held it firmly to his cheek. 'Good yer back,' he blurted. 'So good yer ent dead.' As swiftly as he had seized her hand, he released it. 'How come yer heven't said nought to Paragon yet? He's got a new face, y'know. An' an axe. An' blue eyes like me.'

'Blue eyes?' Amber exploded incredulously. 'They're supposed to be dark brown, nearly black.' She suddenly spun about and hastened forwards.

'Wizardwood is strange stuff,' Brashen reminded her smugly.

'Bit late to change 'em,' Clef observed cheerily. ''sides, I like 'em. They're kind. Like Mother's.' He hastened after her.

They were nearly alone now, if one did not consider Semoy. The old sailor considerately kept his eyes forwards as Brashen kissed her. Only for an instant did her memory of Kennit's assault intrude. Then she seized him and kissed him firmly in defiance, refusing any comparison between this and the pirate's attack on her. She would not let that stand between them.

Yet, when she released him, there was a shadow in Brashen's eyes. He was too perceptive. He looked into her face questioningly. She gave a tiny shrug. Now was not the time to tell him. She wondered if it would ever be the time to tell him all of it.

He probably thought he was changing the subject. 'So, why don't we go forwards and assure Paragon you're aboard and well?'

'He knows that I am. But for him, I wouldn't be,' she replied. The shock of seeing his eyes as he caught her had still not left her. Kennit's eyes. She had nearly shamed herself by screaming as the ship's big hands had closed on her. She knew Paragon had sensed it. He had not paused, but had set her swiftly into Brashen's reach. To Brashen's puzzled silence now, she replied, 'I will see him and speak with him in a quiet moment, Brashen. Not just yet.' She made the beginning of an attempt. 'Kennit is part of him now. Isn't he?'

He tried to explain it to her. 'Kennit was a Ludluck. Had you worked that out?'

'No,' she said slowly. Kennit was Bingtown Trader stock? It appalled her.

Brashen gave her a few moments to absorb that before he added, 'We suspected since Divvytown that Paragon was Igrot's fabled ship. Bingtown always denied the pirate might have had a liveship. But he did: Paragon. And in Kennit he had a hostage, to keep the ship subservient to him.'

'Sa's breath.' The pieces were all fitting now. Her mind struggled to encompass it all. 'So Kennit came home to die on his deck. To be one with his ship.' A little chill of horror ran up her spine.

Brashen nodded, watching her face. 'He always has been, Althea. I don't think his death on the ship has changed Paragon, save to put him at peace. He is finally one, a complete self. The dragons, the Ludlucks, men and boy, and Kennit are all merged into one.' She turned aside at that but he put two fingers under her chin and turned her face up to his. 'And us,' he said almost fiercely. 'You and I. Amber and Jek. Clef. All we have put into him became a part of him, too. Don't turn away from him now. Please. Don't stop loving him.'

She could scarcely concentrate on his words. She had dreaded telling Brashen about the rape, but had resolved she must. Yet, how could she tell him, without compromising his feelings for his ship? The convolutions of her thoughts dizzied her.

'Althea?' Brashen asked her anxiously.

'I'll try,' she said faintly. She suddenly didn't care who was watching. She tugged his arms around her and stepped into his embrace. 'Hold me,' she told him fiercely. 'Hold me very, very close.'

She had said she would try. With difficulty, Brashen did not press her for more than that. Something had happened on board Vivacia, something that kept her apart from him now. He set his chin upon her dark head and wrapped her in his arms. He thought he knew what.

Althea seemed to sense his thoughts, for she changed the subject. 'The chop's getting worse.' She shifted slightly in his arms. He pretended not to see that she wiped tears on his shirtfront.

'That it is. I suspect we've got a bit of a squall coming up. But we've been through storms before. Paragon's a good ship for stormy weather.'

'All the better for us to hide in.'

'I think we're gaining distance from the Jamaillians.'

'They've doused their lights. They're hoping to creep up on us in the dark.'

'They'll have to find us first.'

'It will be harder for the *Marietta* and the *Motley* to keep pace with the liveships in the dark.'

'They're running dark, too.'

'*Vivacia* won't leave them behind. She'll protect them no matter the risk to herself.'

An ordinary conversation, discussing the obvious. It spoke too plainly to Brashen. She had been back on the Vivacia, and found her heart once more. He could not blame her. Vivacia was Althea's family ship. With Kennit dead, she had a much better chance of reclaiming her. And unlike Paragon, Vivacia had not embraced the anma of a murdering pirate who had done vast damage to Althea's family. When she had come back from Vivacia, he had deceived himself that she came back to him. Instead, she had come to share battle plans. Watching the distracted frown on her face, he knew where her thoughts were.

She loved him, in her way. She gave him as much as she could, without forsaking her ship and her family. He had no right to ask more than that. If he'd still had a family to claim him, perhaps he would have been just as torn. For a fleeting instant, he considered leaving Paragon to follow her. But he couldn't. No one else knew this ship as he did. No one else had endured alongside him. He could not make Paragon vulnerable to a captain that might not tolerate his uneven moods. And what of Clef? Would he tear the boy from the ship that loved him? Or leave him on Paragon, to be trained by a master who might not have his best interests at heart? And Semoy would not be first mate under any other captain. He'd go back to being a washed-up drunk, and lose whatever years he had left to a bottle. No. As much as he loved Althea, he had responsibilities here. She would not respect a man who abandoned his ship to follow her. Brashen Trell was finished with walking away from his duties. Here he must remain, and if need be, love Althea from afar and when they could.

In that acknowledgement, he suddenly knew that he did have a family again.

Etta leaned on the railing, staring forwards into the dark. Paragon could feel her there, though her presence was limited to the warm press of her forearms against his wizardwood railing. With no bond with her, he could not sense her emotions at all.

She broke the silence suddenly. 'I know a little bit of liveships. From Vivacia.'

He had nothing to say to that. He waited.

'Somehow, I don't understand how, Kennit was your family. When he died, he went into you?' Her voice tightened on the awkward words. He felt her trembling.

'In a manner of speaking.' His words sounded too cold; he sought to add something gentler. 'He was always a part of me and I of him. For many reasons, we were bound more tightly than is usual. It was very important, to both of us, that he come back at the moment of his death. I knew that. I don't think Kennit realised it until it happened.'

She took a breath. In a strangled voice she asked, 'So you are Kennit now?'

'No. I'm sorry. Kennit is a part of me. He completes me. But I am, irrevocably, Paragon.' It felt good to make that declaration. He suspected that it might be painful for her to hear. To his surprise, he felt genuine sorrow that he had to hurt her. He tried to remember the last time he had had such a feeling, and could not. Was this yet another aspect of being whole: the ability to feel sympathy? It would take time to adjust to feeling such things.

'Then he is gone,' Etta said heavily. He heard her take a struggling breath. 'But why couldn't you heal him as Vivacia healed Wintrow?'

He thought silently for a time. 'You say she healed him? I know nothing of that. I can only guess at what she did. It is what dragons can do, if they must. They burn the resources of their bodies to speed a healing. If Vivacia did that to Wintrow, he was lucky to survive it. Few humans have such reserves. Kennit certainly did not.'

Her silence lasted long. The night deepened around them. Even darkness was a pleasure to his newly restored vision. Night was not truly dark. He turned his eyes to the skies above, to clouds obscuring and then revealing the moon and stars. Phosphorescence outlined the waves. His keen vision, part of his dragon heritage, picked out the outlines of the ships he followed.

'Would you know something about him – Kennit? If I asked you something, could you tell me true?'

'Perhaps,' Paragon hedged. He glanced back at her. She had lifted her hands from the railing and was turning her bracelet restlessly.

'Did he love me?' The question burst from her, painful in its intensity. 'Did he truly love me? I need to know.'

'Kennit is part of me. But I am not Kennit.' Paragon debated furiously with himself. She carried a child, the child promised him so long ago. Paragon Ludluck. A child needed to be loved, loved without reservations.

'If you have his memories, you know the truth.' Etta insisted. 'Did he love me?'

'Yes. He loved you.' He gave her what she needed to hear, without compunction. *I have Kennit's memories, but I am not Kennit. Still, I can lie as well as he did. And for better cause.* 'He loved you as fully as his heart could love.' That was true, at least.

Thank you. As clear and brief as a drop of falling rain, the thought reached him. He groped for the source, but found nothing. The feel of the voice was oddly familiar, almost as if it came from Kennit, yet it was outside himself.

'Thank you,' Etta unconsciously echoed the sentiment. 'Thank you more than you can know. From both of us.' She walked swiftly away from the foredeck, leaving him with a mystery to ponder.

Ahead of him, on the *Motley*'s deck, a lantern flashed suddenly. It was held aloft thrice and swung once, then masked again. It was still almost a surprise to have access to Kennit's memories. The old pirate signals were his to decipher. Brashen was summoned to the Vivacia.

'This had better be important,' Brashen grumbled to Althea as they bent to the oars. Etta and Amber manned a second pair. The gusting wind blew Amber's ragged hair past her mottled face. Etta stared straight ahead.

'I'm sure it is,' Althea muttered. They worked heavily, struggling against wind, water and the darkness to catch up with the lead ship. The four ships had closed up the gap between them, but they had not stopped, even for this meeting. Vivacia led them as they picked their way through a maze of small islands. Some loomed steep and rocky, while others showed only as waves breaking and running on a jagged surface. The ships threaded a meandering path through them. Brashen guessed that at a lower tide this route would be impassable. He prayed that both Wintrow and Vivacia knew this route as well as they seemed to.

Brashen approved the choice to put as much distance between them and the Jamaillian fleet as possible, but he still had reservations about leaving his ship to go to Vivacia. Althea had assured him that Wintrow could be trusted, but he reminded himself that they knew little of the crew on the Vivacia, or the captains and crews of the other two ships. They had been thrown into an unlikely alliance with the pirates. Memories of being under the hatch in a sinking ship were still fresh in his mind.

Vivacia took them up just as a drenching rain began to fall. By the light of a dimmed lantern, they were hauled aboard. She already trailed boats from the *Marietta* and the *Motley*. They were last to arrive. Brashen's wariness rose another notch. Etta climbed up first. Althea began to follow, but he stopped her with a touch. 'I'm going next,' he growled low. 'At any sign of treachery, go back to Paragon.'

'I don't think you need fear,' Althea began but he shook his head.

'I lost you once. I won't gamble you again,' he told her.

'Wise man,' Amber observed quietly as he seized the wet ladder and began to climb. As he set his hands to the Vivacia's railing, incredible emotions raced through him. For an instant, he was unmanned. Tears stung his eyes. Warmth and welcome flowed through him. Joy at his safety. He set foot on the deck he had not trod since the day of the ship's awakening.

'Brashen Trell!' the ship called back to him a low contralto. 'Paragon has done you good. You are more sensitive to us than ever you were when you worked my decks. For the first time in my waking life, I bid you welcome aboard.'

'Thank you,' he managed. Etta was nowhere in sight. Wintrow stood on the deck in the pouring rain, offering him a hand to shake. The self-effacing lad he had met at Ephron's funeral now stood straight and met his eyes. Heavy grief had aged his face. He would never be a large man, but man he definitely was. 'You remember the way to the chart room, I'm sure,' he said and Brashen found himself answering a familiar smile with one of his own. Wintrow's resemblance to Althea was truly uncanny.

He watched Althea's face as she came aboard the ship. When she set hands to the rail, he saw how she suddenly glowed. Malta came to meet her and they immediately fell into conversation as they hurried inside. Amber seemed less affected by her first contact with the liveship. It was when she set eyes on Wintrow that her face went slack with shock. 'The nine-fingered slave boy,' she blurted out.

Wintrow lifted a hand swiftly to his cheek, then dropped it self-consciously. He gave Brashen an uneasy glance as Amber stared at him. It was only broken when Jek burst from the shadows to seize Amber in a fierce hug. 'Aow, you look worse than I do!' she greeted her as Wintrow hastily turned away. Brashen felt mixed emotions as he trod the once-familiar deck. Kennit, he observed, had run a tight ship. The man had been a good captain. Then he shook his head, incredulous that such a thought could even come to him.

The chart room was crowded. Etta was there, as was Malta's Rain Wilder. Reyn seemed to be determined to be unaware of the attention he attracted. The Satrap was dramatically aware of his own importance. Two men, one broad and stocky, the other flamboyantly clad, would be the other pirate captains. The stocky man's eyes were reddened with weeping. His red-headed comrade wore a grave demeanour. They knew of Kennit's death, then.

The captured Jamaillian nobles lined the walls, a bedraggled and weary group. Several looked on the verge of collapse. Wintrow shut the door behind him and gave them a moment to discard wet cloaks. He gestured to seats around the crowded table, while he remained standing. The heavy-set pirate captain was pouring brandy for all of them. Brashen was glad of the warming stuff. He recognised the snifter. Ephron Vestrit had reserved it for special occasions. Althea hastened to a seat beside him. She leaned close to him and whispered hurriedly, 'The best of news! When Reyn and the dragon left Bingtown, my mother and Keffria and Selden were all there and in good health.' She took a breath. 'I fear that is the only good news, however. My family is beggared, my home a vandalized shell, our holdings sacked. Now more than ever, a liveship would . . .

I'll tell you later,' she amended hastily as she realized all other conversation at the table had ceased. All turned to Wintrow at the head of the table.

Wintrow drew a breath and spoke decisively. 'I know none of you are easy at being called away from your ships. It was necessary. Kennit's death has forced a number of decisions on us. I'm going to tell you what I've decided, and let each of you plot your course accordingly.'

There it was, Brashen thought: the assumption of command and authority was in his voice. He half expected someone to challenge it, but all were silent. The other pirate captains had already deferred to him. Everyone waited respectfully. Only the Satrap's satisfied smile let everyone know he already knew what was to come.

Wintrow took a breath. 'The treaty, so painstakingly hammered out by King Kennit of the Pirate Isles and the Lord High Magnadon Satrap Cosgo of Jamaillia has been acknowledged and approved by these nobles.'

A shocked silence followed these words. Then both Captain Red and Sorcor leapt to their feet with cries of triumph. Etta lifted her eyes to Wintrow's face. 'You've done it?' she asked in wonder. 'You've finished what he promised us?'

'I've made a start on it,' Wintrow replied grimly. 'My sister Malta has been instrumental in persuading them to this wise action. But there remains much to do.'

At a look from him, his two captains resumed their seats. Sorcor's deep voice broke the silence. There was fierce satisfaction in his voice. 'When you told me Kennit was dead, I thought our dreams had died with him. I should have had more faith, Wintrow. Kennit chose well in you.'

Wintrow's voice was grave, but the hint of a smile played on his face as he spoke on. 'We know these waters well. We've left the Jamaillian fleet behind us in the dark. I recommend that as soon as Sorcor and Red return to their vessels, they separate and loop back through the islands and return to Divvytown.

Send birds to command a massing of the pirate fleet. Then lie quiet there for a time until the other ships arrive.'

'And you, sir?' Sorcor asked.

'I'll be going with you, Sorcor, on the *Marietta*. Also Etta and the Lord High Magnadon Satrap Cosgo. As well as our captives . . . noble guests,' he amended smoothly. He raised his voice to forestall questions. 'The Satrap requires our protection and support. We will mass our fleet at Divvytown. Then we will undertake to return him to Jamaillia City, where he can present to the rest of his nobles the endorsed treaty that allies him with the Kingdom of the Pirate Isles. Our guests shall remain well cared for in Divvytown until our claims are recognized. Now, Etta –' He paused, then plunged on, 'Queen Etta, chosen by Kennit to sail beside him, and the mother of his unborn son, will go with us to see that the claims of the Pirate Isles are recognized. She will reign for her child until he comes of age.'

'A child? You carry his child?' Sorcor jumped to his feet, then lunged to engulf Etta in a hug. Tears ran unabashedly down his face. 'No more swordplay until after the baby's born, now,' he cautioned her, holding her at arm's length, then looked offended when Red laughed aloud. Etta looked shaken, and then amazed. Even when Sorcor resumed a seat, he kept his big hand upon Etta's wrist as if to keep her close and safe.

'Kennit left us a son,' Wintrow confirmed when the hubbub had died down. His eyes met Etta's as he spoke. 'An heir to reign after him, when he has come of age. But until then, it is up to us to carry out Kennit's ideas and keep his word.'

Brashen felt Althea's muscles tighten every time the pirate's name was spoken. Her eyes were black as she stared at her nephew. Under the table, Brashen's hand sought hers. She gripped it hard.

The Satrap suddenly surged to his feet. 'I will keep my word,' he announced as if it were a surprising gift to them. 'These last few days, I have seen for myself why the Pirate Isles has the right to rule its own. I must count on your support to regain my own throne, but once I am returned to Jamaillia City –'

'Hey. What about Vivacia? Why is everyone coming on the *Marietta?*' Sorcor seemed unaware that he had interrupted the Lord High Magnadon Satrap of all Jamaillia. Wintrow took control back easily.

'Vivacia goes to keep one of Kennit's other promises. We all are indebted to the serpents. They have gone north, following the dragon. But Vivacia insists that they will need her help to make the journey. She feels she must follow them. Moreover, Kennit had promised this to her.' He paused, and then spoke with obvious difficulty. 'I cannot go with her. I long to, for I long to see my family again. But my duty is here, for a time longer.' He fixed his eyes, finally, on Althea. 'I ask Althea Vestrit to take Vivacia north. Jola has spoken for the crew. They'll follow her, as that was Captain Kennit's will. However, I caution you, Althea. Vivacia promised Kennit that when her service to the serpents was over, she would return. And that, too, is what the ship wishes to do. Guide the serpents home. Take news of us to Bingtown. But after that, you both must return to us.'

Wintrow held up a hand as Althea began to speak, and for a wonder she heeded it and kept silent. His gaze swung to meet Brashen's. Brashen stared at him numbly. He'd suspected it was coming, but the reality still stunned him. Wintrow had just taken Althea away from him. Once more, duty to her family and her ship claimed her. She would have her dream: she would captain Vivacia, she would sail victorious into Bingtown. Afterwards, she must return Vivacia to Divvytown. Would she then leave her ship to come back to him? He doubted it. He held her hand tightly, but knew she was already gone. It was hard for him to focus on Wintrow's next words.

'You and Paragon are free to do as you wish, Brashen Trell. But I ask that Paragon accompany Vivacia to the Rain Wild River with the serpents. Vivacia says that two liveships will guide and protect better than one. Malta and Reyn will undoubtedly wish to make that journey also.'

Reyn spoke, surprising them all. 'We will need two ships against all the Chalcedeans headed this way. One to guard, one to fight.'

'We had heard rumours,' Wintrow acknowledged in dismay. 'But only rumours.'

'Believe them,' Reyn said. He turned in his chair to address the Jamaillian nobles who lined the walls. His copper eyes walked over them. 'As Tintaglia and I flew south, we saw Chalcedean ships accompanied by galleys. That, as you know, is their configuration for serious warfare. I suspect Jamaillia City is their target. I believe they have decided that the little plunder left in Bingtown is not worth fighting a dragon for.'

Malta's words followed Reyn's. ' I see in your faces that you doubt us. But I saw their first attack on Bingtown. Reyn was present during their last one. Your Chalcedean conspirators saw no reason to wait for you. They expected to claim the cream of the plunder before you arrived. Nor do I think they ever intended to turn Bingtown over to your New Trader sons and brothers. Cheated of the easy prey you promised them in Bingtown, driven away by Tintaglia, they now come south. Those are the allies you chose. Your Satrap has been wiser. You have signed the treaty under duress. I can read your hearts. Given the chance, you will retract your agreement. That would be foolish. You should speed your Satrap's alliance with the Pirate Isles, for when the Chalcedean ships and their raiding galleys arrive, you will need every friend you can call upon.' Her eyes raked them. 'Mark my words. They are without mercy.'

A scant year ago, Malta had turned her wiles on Brashen. In her words, he heard her girlish cunning matured into genuine diplomacy. Some of the nobles exchanged looks, impressed with her words. Even the Satrap seemed pleased with her, nodding to her words as if she but spoke aloud his own thoughts.

*   *   *

Malta clapped her hands to her ears before Reyn heard the sound. When it broke into his hearing range, he flinched with her. The others looked about wildly, while one Jamaillian lord wailed, 'The serpents return!'

'No. It's Tintaglia,' Reyn replied. Anxiety clutched him. The dragon cried for help as she came. He moved towards the door, and everyone else at the table rose and followed him. Malta seized his hand as they emerged onto the deck. Together, they stared up into the downpour. Tintaglia swept over them, a pale gleaming of silver and blue against the overcast night sky. Her wings beat heavily. She swung in a wide circle, then gave cry again. To Reyn's amazement, her call was answered. The ship's deck hummed with the force of Vivacia's reply. A deeper call from Paragon echoed hers.

Malta was frozen, looking up in awe. An instant after the sound died, she met Reyn's eyes with a question. 'She asks for help?' Reyn snorted.

'No. She demands our help. Tintaglia seldom "asks" for anything.' His heart sank despite his callous words. They had grown too close for her to conceal her fear from him. He felt both her weariness and the deep grief in her soul.

'I did not understand all of it.' Malta added, 'I am shocked that I understood any of it.'

Reyn replied in a low voice. 'The longer you are around her, the more clear it comes to your mind. I think our ears have little to do with it.' The dragon's vocalisations shook the skies again. All around them, sailors either craned to look at the beast or cowered under shelter. Reyn stared up, heedless of the rain that pelted his face. He spoke loud to be heard through the answering cries of the ships.

'The dragon is exhausted. She flies too swiftly for the serpents to keep up with her. She has had to constantly circle to match her pace to theirs. She has not hunted or fed, for she has feared to leave her serpents. When they encountered a Chalcedean ship, it attacked her. She was not injured badly but the serpents rose against the ship.' He took a breath. 'They knew how to kill serpents. Archers killed six of the tangle before they sank the ship.' The outrage and sorrow of the liveship rose through them. 'The tangle rests for the night, but she has returned to ask our aid.' He turned beseechingly to the captains. 'Darkness caught her on the wing. She needs a sandy beach to land on – or any beach, with a fire to guide her in.'

Sorcor spoke suddenly. 'Would muck do? It's slippery, but softer than rock.'

'Stink Island,' Etta confirmed.

'It's not far,' Red added. 'She probably flies over it each time she circles. Bad place for a ship, though. Shallow water.'

'But you can run a boat up on it,' Etta dismissed this problem. 'And there's lots of driftwood there for a fire.'

'We need to get there. Now.' Reyn glanced up anxiously at the sky. 'If we do not hurry, the ocean will claim her. She is at the end of her strength.'

THIRTY-SEVEN

A Dragon's Will

THE WET DRIFTWOOD would not kindle. While Reyn struggled with tinder that the wind kept claiming, Malta took off her cloak and stuffed it into the tangle of wood. He looked up to the sudden crash as she smashed their lantern onto the pile. A moment later, flames licked up the edges of her cloak. He feared the fire would die there, but after a few moments, he heard the welcome crackling of wood igniting. By then, Malta had come to the shelter of his cloak. When her brother gave them an odd look, she lifted her chin and stared him down defiantly. She pressed her wet and shivering body firmly against Reyn's. In the sheltering darkness, he held her, smelling the fragrance of her hair. Boldly he kissed the top of her head. The fine scaling of her crest rasped his cheek, and Malta gave an involuntary shiver. He felt her body flush suddenly with warmth. She looked up at him, surprise intensifying the pale gleam of her Rain Wild eyes.

'Reyn,' she gasped, caught between delight and scandal. 'You should not do that,' she chided primly.

'Are you sure?' he asked by her ear.

'Not when my brother is watching,' she amended breathlessly.

The bonfire was burning well now. Reyn lifted anxious eyes to the sky. He had not heard Tintaglia pass overhead for some time, but her anxiety hung strong and infected him. She was still up there, somewhere. He glanced around at the people who had come to the beach with them. Stink Island lived up to its name. All were in muck to the knee, and Red, much to his disgust, had fallen in the stuff and was probably regretting his desire to see a dragon up close.

A second bonfire was kindled from the first. Out on the water, the ships suddenly cried out and the dragon replied from a distance. Reyn sounded the warning: 'Get out of her way!'

Tintaglia came down in a heavy battering of wings, fighting both the rain and the gusting wind. Unencumbered by a human burden, she would land gracefully, Reyn expected. But as Sorcor had predicted, the muck was slippery. The dragon's braced feet slid and mud flew up from her wildly lashing tail and flapping wings. She skittered to a halt nearly in the bonfire. Tintaglia's eyes flashed angrily over her compromised dignity. She quivered her dripping wings, spattering more mud on the humans.

'What idiot chose this beach?' she demanded furiously. In the next breath, she demanded, 'Is there no food ready?'

She complained her way through two hogsheads of salt pork. 'Nasty, sticky stuff, too small to bite properly,' she proclaimed at the end of her meal, and stalked off to a nearby spring.

'She's immense,' Sorcor exclaimed in wonder.

Reyn realized he had become accustomed to her magnificence. Malta had her memories from the dream-box, but this was the first opportunity for the others to see a dragon other than on the wing.

'She is full of beauty, in form and movement,' Amber whispered. 'I see now what Paragon meant. Only a true-born dragon is a real dragon. All others are but clumsy imitations.'

Jek gave Amber a disdainful glance. 'Six Duchies dragons suited me just fine. Would have been fine by you, too, if you'd lived with the fear of being Forged. But,' she admitted grudgingly, 'She is astounding.' Reyn turned aside from their incomprehensible conversation.

'I wonder what Vivacia would have looked like,' Althea said quietly. Firelight danced in her eyes as she stared at the dragon's shadowy shape.

'Or Paragon's dragons,' Brashen inserted loyally.

Reyn felt a grating of guilt at their words. His family had transformed dragons into ships. Would there some day be an accounting for that? He pushed the thought away.

When Tintaglia came stalking back from the spring, she had cleaned much of the muck from her wings and belly. She gave Reyn a baleful look from her spinning silver eyes. 'I said "sand",' she rebuked him. She swung her great head to regard the gathered humans. 'Good,' she acknowledged them. Smoothly she shifted from complaining to demanding. 'You will have to build another fire, farther from the waves, where the muck turns to rock. Stone does not make the best of beds, but it is preferable to mud, and I must rest tonight.' Then she caught sight of Malta. Her eyes spun more swiftly, gleaming like full moons.

'Step out into the light, little sister. Let me see you.'

Reyn feared Malta would offend the dragon by hesitating, but she came boldly to stand before her. Tintaglia's eyes travelled over her from crest to feet. In a warm voice, she announced, 'I see you have been well rewarded for your part in freeing me, young queen. A scarlet crest. You will take much pleasure from that.' At Malta's puzzled blush, the dragon chuckled warmly. 'What, not even discovered it yet? You will. And you will enjoy a long life in which to relish it.'

She swung her gaze to Reyn. 'You chose well. She is fit to be an Elderling queen, and a speaker for dragons. Selden will be delighted that she has changed as well. He has been a bit worried, you know, that she would disparage his changes.'

Reyn smiled awkwardly. He had not yet apprised the Vestrits

of Selden's changes. Tintaglia distracted them from their exchange of puzzled glances.

'I will sleep the night, and require more food before I fly in the morning. The tangle rests well north of here. For the night, at least, they are safe.' She blinked her great eyes and the silver whirled coldly. 'I have done away with those who dared to threaten them. But my serpents are wearied. Serpents, even in prime condition, cannot keep pace with a dragon a-wing. In the days of old, there would have been several of us to shepherd them along, and several serpents with the memory to guide them. They have only me, and one serpent guide.'

She lifted her head. There was determination to the motion, but Reyn sensed desperation beneath her boldness. Despite her arrogance, his heart went out to her.

'I have spoken to the liveships. Paragon will accompany my serpents north. That ship's crew will aid me in protecting the serpents, and will anchor beside them each night when I must come ashore to feed and rest.'

Wintrow spoke up boldly. 'Both liveships will go north. We have already made decisions –'

'That interests me not in the least!' The dragon cut in harshly. 'Or do you think you still "own" the liveships? Vivacia will go south, to your big city. My Elderlings will go with her, to speak for me, to arrange the shipments of grain and foodstuffs for the workers, to hire engineers as Reyn sees fit, to inform the people in that city of what dragons will henceforth require of it, to arrange –'

'Require?' Wintrow cut in coldly. Outrage had stiffened him.

The dragon rounded on Reyn in exasperation. 'Have you told them nothing? You've had the whole day!'

'Perhaps you don't recall that you dropped me in the middle of a sea battle?' Reyn asked irritably. 'We have spent most of our day trying to be alive at the end of it.'

'I recall well enough that my serpents had been endangered

for purely human ends. Humans are always squabbling and killing one another.' She glared at them all. 'It will no longer be tolerated. You will put such things aside until my ends have been served, or risk my wrath.' She threw her head high and half-lifted her wings. 'That, too, my Elderlings will establish. No ship is allowed to interfere with a serpent! No petty warfare will be tolerated if it interferes with supplies to the Rain Wilds. You will not –'

Wintrow was incensed. 'What manner of creature are you, to seek to order our lives by force? Do our dreams, our plans, our ambitions count for nothing in your greater scheme of things?'

The dragon paused and turned her head, as if considering his questions gravely. Then she leaned her great head close to him, so close that his clothing moved in the rush of her breath. 'I am a dragon, human. In the greater scheme of things, your dreams, plans and ambitions count for next to nothing. You simply do not live long enough to matter.' She paused. When she spoke again, Reyn could tell she was trying to make her voice kinder. 'Save as you assist dragons, of course. When you have completed this task, my kind will remember your service for generations. Could humans hope for a higher honour?'

'Perhaps we hope to live out our insignificant little lives as we see fit,' Wintrow retorted. He did not move back from the dragon he defied. Reyn recognized the set of his shoulders and the way he held his mouth. Her brother shared Malta's stubborn streak. The dragon's chest had started to swell.

Malta hastened to stand between her brother and the dragon. She looked fearlessly from one to the other. 'We are all weary, too weary to bargain well tonight.'

'Bargain!' the dragon snorted contemptuously. 'Oh, not again! Humans and their bargaining.'

'Far simpler to kill anyone who disagrees with you?' Wintrow suggested tartly.

Malta set a restraining hand to her brother's arm. 'All of us must sleep,' she suggested firmly. 'Even, you, Tintaglia, are in need of rest. By morning, we will be rested, and each can state what he needs. It is the only way this can be resolved.'

The dragon, Althea reflected, was the only one to get any sleep. The humans gathered once more, aboard the *Motley* this time, for Captain Red had bragged that he had coffee as well as a slightly larger chart room. She was beginning to have a grudging admiration for Malta's ability to negotiate. She had inherited some of Ronica's trading skills but much rested in Malta's inherent charm. Her first achievement was in insisting that the Jamaillian nobles be seated at the table with them. Althea heard a few words of her whispered argument with the offended Satrap: '. . . bind them to your service with their own interests. If you break them too low, they will ever after be as a treacherous cur at your heels. This will assure that they will not later disclaim the treaty,' she had insisted heatedly.

For a wonder, the Satrap acceded to her demands. Her second stroke of genius was in arranging food for all before they convened. When they finally gathered around Captain Red's table, tempers were calmed. Malta and Reyn had privately conferred as well, for she arose and announced that they could not proceed until she had informed everyone more fully of events in Bingtown. Despite her own interest in Malta's tale, Althea found herself watching the faces of the others. The Jamaillian nobles looked stricken as they finally recognized the fullness of the Chalcedean betrayal. Etta listened quietly but attentively. Amber stared obsessively at Wintrow, a look of near-tragic speculation on her face. Brashen beside her was unnaturally silent, but his hand under the table was warm in hers. The only time he spoke was when Reyn began to discuss the quake damage to Trehaug. Brashen leaned forwards to claim attention with a light slap on the table. His words were only for Reyn as he asked,

'Is Rain Wild Trader business so openly discussed before outsiders?'

Reyn did not take offence. He bowed his head gravely to Brashen's concern and replied, 'We have discovered that we must become a part of the greater world, or perish. I say nothing that has not already been openly spoken at a town meeting in Bingtown. The time has come to share our secrets or perish alongside them.'

'I see,' Brashen replied gravely, and leaned back in his chair.

When Reyn had finished speaking, Wintrow claimed attention by standing. To Althea, he looked too weary to remain upright. The note of resigned amusement in his voice surprised her. 'Considering what Reyn has told us and the nature of liveships, I believe we must follow Tintaglia's wishes.'

'If the liveships agree with her, I don't see where we have any choice,' Althea agreed.

Reyn spoke to Malta, but all overheard. 'Would you rather go straight home to Bingtown than to Jamaillia?'

Her glance flickered over her brother and her aunt. She didn't lower her voice as her eyes met his unequivocally. 'I'll go where you go.'

A small silence followed her words. She boldly disarmed it by turning to Lord Criath. 'Now. As you have heard, the dragon desires us to negotiate for foodstuffs to be shipped to the Rain Wilds. It remains to be seen which of the Satrap's loyal nobles will win the privilege of supplying us.'

Criath knit his brows in puzzlement. Malta continued to meet his eyes levelly, waiting for him to realize what she offered. Then Lord Criath cleared his throat. He nodded round to his fellows, seeking support, as he spoke. 'Magnadon Satrap Cosgo. I think I am not alone in now accepting the wisdom of your alliance. In fact,' he smiled at Malta, 'I would like to offer my assistance to the dragon's representatives. My holdings in Jamaillia include grainfields, and pastured cattle.

Mutually beneficial trade with the Rain Wild folk could go far to make up the losses I must reconcile from my renunciation of my Bingtown land grants.'

The deepest part of night passed as they haggled. Althea kept silent, stunned by the realization that she witnessed the reordering of her world. Tintaglia was wise to send 'her Elderlings' to Jamaillia to speak for her. They would not only open trade avenues between Jamaillia and the Rain Wilds. In Reyn's scaled visage the Jamaillians would confront the copper-eyed future of the world. She felt she floated on her exhaustion, disconnected from the scene around her. In a shifting of perception, she perceived a vast juncture left behind, and a swift current ahead. This new world of men and dragons would be ordered by negotiation rather than wars. Here, in this room, they set that precedent. Suddenly, she understood, and she tried to catch Amber's eye to acknowledge that, but the carpenter contemplated Wintrow ruefully.

The Jamaillian nobles scented only profit and power. They were soon fiercely competing among themselves to set grain prices and tried yet again to assert some rights to Bingtown. Both Reyn and Malta drew the line firmly. Althea was relieved that they still negotiated for their own kind as shrewdly as they did for the dragon. As the night wore on, most of the negotiating was between nobles arranging sub-agreements with other nobles, the Satrap setting the percentage of their profits that would go to the treasury, the captains backing Wintrow and Etta as they reminded the others that there would be a tariff for goods passing through the Pirate Isles.

Althea jerked awake as Brashen elbowed her. 'They're finished,' he whispered. Around the table, men were signing papers, while Wintrow offered Etta his arm. She ignored it, standing on her own and rolling her shoulders.

Althea tried to stretch unobtrusively. How long had her eyes been closed? 'Did any of it have anything to do with us?' she asked quietly.

'Never fear. Both Reyn and Malta stood up well for Bingtown, and when it came to the cutting edge, Bingtown and the Pirate Isles stood together.' He gave a short laugh. 'Wonder what your father would have thought of that? He'd have been damn proud of Malta, that I know. That woman's as sharp a Trader as I've ever seen.'

Althea felt a tickle of jealousy at his admiration for her niece.

'And now?' she asked him quietly. Everyone was standing. A sleepy ship's boy was gathering coffee mugs onto a silver tray.

'And now, we can have a few hours' sleep before we get up, bid our farewells, and set our sails again.' He didn't look at her as he spoke. She followed him out onto the deck. The chill night air was welcome after the stuffy chart room. The rain had paused.

'Think the dragon will accept our terms?'

Brashen rubbed his eyes wearily. 'We're only asking her help in what she already said we must do. Put an end to the territorial fighting on the Inside Passage. Best way to do that is chase the Chalcedeans out of here. After what they did to "her" serpents yesterday, I think she'll be happy to help us do that. All the rest of it was wrangling between the other parties.' He shook his head. 'I think it's all over save for her telling us what she wants us to do.'

'That worries me, too,' Althea agreed. 'We have struggled so hard and come so far, all in uncertainty, only to have a dragon suddenly decree, "This is how your life will go." I don't like her directing our actions, saying who will go where. And yet,' she shrugged and almost laughed, 'in an odd way it would almost be a relief to have those decisions snatched away. A lifting of a burden.'

'Some might see it that way,' Brashen replied sourly.

'Hey, Bingtown!' A hail from Sorcor distracted her. 'Watch the current,' the pirate captain warned them as he descended to his boat. 'It runs tricky here when the tide is changing. Better check your anchors, and leave a good man on watch.'

'Thank you,' Althea answered for them. From what she had seen of the burly old pirate, she liked him. She watched him now as he annoyed Etta by watching her get safely into Vivacia's boat. Malta leaned on Reyn's shoulder as they waited for Wintrow. Althea frowned at that, but something stranger claimed her attention. To Althea's surprise, Amber was also in Vivacia's boat.

'I overheard her tell Wintrow that she had something important to discuss with him. He was reluctant, but she was insistent. You know how unnerving she can be when she gets that look on her face.' These tidings were from Jek, who had appeared at Althea's shoulder.

'Then it's only we three returning to Paragon for the night?'

'Two,' Jek corrected her with a grin. 'I've been invited to stay aboard the *Motley*.'

Althea looked about and saw a handsome pirate leaning against a mast. Waiting.

'Two,' she agreed, and turned to exchange a glance with Brashen. He was gone. She looked over the side to see him fitting the oars into the oarlocks of Paragon's boat. 'Hey!' she cried in annoyance. She more slid than climbed down the ladder, and deliberately rocked the small boat as she dropped into it. 'You might have said you were ready to leave,' she informed him snippily.

He stared at her. Then he looked over at the Vivacia's boat. 'When Amber climbed down, I assumed you were both going.'

She looked after the boat, and then to where she knew Vivacia rocked at anchor. It was too dark even to see her profile. A last night aboard her ship before she bid her farewell? Perhaps she should have. She suddenly had a strange echo of memory as if she had made this decision before. The day

Vivacia had first awakened, she had quarrelled with Kyle and stormed off the ship, to spend the evening getting drunk with Brashen. She had had no last words with her ship then. She had regretted it ever since. If she had spent that first night with her, would all that followed have turned out differently? She looked back at Brashen, sitting with the oars suspended above the water. Would she go back and change that, if it meant she would not end up here with him?

That was the past, however. Vivacia was not her ship any more. They had both recognized that. What was left to tell her, save goodbye?

She cast off from the *Motley*, then clambered through the boat to sit down beside Brashen. 'Give me an oar.'

He silently surrendered one to her, and together they pulled for the Paragon. Sorcor had been right to warn them. The current was tricky, and it took every bit of Althea's remaining energy to keep the small boat on course. Brashen evidently felt similarly taxed for he did not speak a single word all the way back. A sleepy Clef caught their line, and Semoy welcomed them gruffly aboard. Brashen passed on Sorcor's warning about the current at tide change and told him to put two men on anchor watch and get some sleep.

'We're going north,' Paragon asserted immediately.

'Most likely,' Brashen agreed wearily. 'Escorting sea serpents. The last thing I ever expected to be doing. But then, little of late has turned out as I expected it to.'

Paragon burst out, 'Are you going to say nothing of the dragon? Your first close look at a dragon and you say nothing of her?'

A slow smile spread on Brashen's face. As he often did, Althea realized, he gripped the railing when he spoke to the ship. He spoke fervently, 'Ship, she is beyond words. As a liveship is beyond words, and for much the same reason.'

Pride swelled Althea's heart. Tired as Brashen was, he had the wisdom to acknowledge the link between the dragon and the liveship, but carefully said nothing that would make Paragon feel more sharply the loss of his true form.

'And you, Althea?'

Not Kennit. Not Kennit. Paragon. Paragon who she had played upon as a child, Paragon who had brought her so far and endured so much for the sake of her mad quest. She found words for that Paragon. 'She is incredibly beautiful – her scales are like rippling jewels, her eyes like the full moon reflected in the sea. Yet, in all honesty, her arrogance was intolerable. Her calm assumption that our lives are hers to order is hard to take.'

Paragon laughed. 'You are wise to school your tongue to flattery, for queens such as Tintaglia feed upon praise more than they do meat. As for her arrogance, it is time humans recalled what it is like to receive such commands as well as give them.'

Brashen almost laughed. 'That's fair, ship. That's fair. Keep an eye to your anchor tonight, will you?'

'Of course. Sleep well.'

Was there a touch of irony to that wish? Althea glanced back at him. He watched her with his pale blue eyes. He tipped her a wink. It was like Paragon to do and say such a thing, she told herself. He was not Kennit. She raised her eyebrows at finding all her gear heaped in a corner in Brashen's cabin. 'I had to put Mother in yours,' he almost apologized. There was a moment of awkwardness. Then she saw the captain's bed with its more generous mattress and thick covering of blankets and all she could think of was sleeping until someone forced her to wake up. With the arrival of the dragon, it seemed decisions were out of her hands. She might as well sleep until someone told her what would happen next.

She sat down on the bunk with a sigh and pulled off her boots. Sweat had dried on her skin and the muck on the beach had penetrated her clothes. She felt sticky. She didn't care. 'I'm not washing,' she warned him. 'I'm too tired.'

'That's understandable.' His voice had gone very deep. He sat next to her. With gentle hands, he took down the hair she had knotted out of her way. She sat still under his touch, until she realized she was clenching her teeth. She drew a breath. She could get past this. With time. She reached up to gently catch his hands.

'I'm so tired. Can I just sleep beside you tonight?'

For a moment, he looked stricken. Then he pulled his hands from hers. 'If that's what you want.' He stood up suddenly. 'Or if you prefer, you can have the bed to yourself.'

His abrupt withdrawal and brusque tone hurt her. 'No,' she snapped. 'That's not what I prefer. That's stupid.' She heard herself and tried to mend things. 'As stupid as starting a quarrel when we are both too tired to think.' She moved over on the bed. 'Brashen. Please. I'm so tired.'

For a moment, he just stared at her wordlessly. Then his shoulders sagged in defeat. He came back to the bed and sat on the edge of it. Outside, the rain returned in a sudden downpour. It rattled against the wall and came through the broken window. They'd need to fix that tomorrow. Maybe everything could be fixed tomorrow. Bury a pirate. Bid a liveship farewell. Leave it all behind.

As Brashen kicked off his boots, he observed sullenly, 'Maybe I've no pride left. If the most you'll offer me this last night is to sleep beside me, I'll take it.' He began unbuttoning his shirt. He would not look at her.

'You're not making any sense,' she complained. He had to be at least as weary as she was. 'Let's just go to sleep. Too much has happened to us today for either of us to deal with it well. Tomorrow will be better, and tomorrow night better still.' She hoped.

He gave her a look that was completely wounded. His dark eyes had never looked so vulnerable. His hands had frozen on his shirt. 'Brashen. Please.' She nudged his hands aside and undid the last three buttons herself. Then she moved over on the bed, taking the side by the wall although she hated being confined. She tugged at his shoulder, pulling him back to lie beside her. He tried to turn away from her, but she pushed him onto his back and pillowed her head on his shoulder to hold him down. 'Now go to sleep,' she growled at him.

He was silent. She could feel him staring at the darkened ceiling. She closed her eyes. He smelled good. Suddenly everything was safe and familiar, and it was good to be there. His strong body rested between her and all the rest of the world. She could relax. She sighed deeply and rested a hand on his chest.

Then he rolled towards her and put his arm around her. All her apprehensions stirred again. This was stupid. This was Brashen. She forced herself to kiss him, saying to herself, 'This is mine, this is Brashen.' He drew her closer and kissed her more deeply. But the weight of his arm upon her and the sound of his breathing was suddenly too much. He was bigger than she was, and stronger. If he wanted to, he could force her, he could hold her down. She'd be trapped again. She set her hand to his chest and pushed a little away from him.

'I'm so tired, my love.'

He was very still. Then, 'My love,' he said quietly. Slowly he turned onto his back. She moved a little apart from him. He was still, and she stared into the darkness.

She closed her eyes, but sleep would not come. She could feel the damage her secret was doing. With every passing moment, the misunderstanding loomed larger. One night, she told herself. One night is all I need. Tomorrow will be better. I'll watch Kennit slip over the side, and I'll know he's gone forever. One night, she excused it, was not too much to ask him.

It didn't work. She could feel Brashen's hurt radiating from him like warmth. With a sigh, she turned slightly away from him. Tomorrow, she would repair things between them. She could get past this, she knew she could.

*   *   *

The woman was peculiar. She was not even pretty, though Etta would admit she was fascinating in a mysterious way. Serpent scald had marred her face and left her hair hanging in uneven hanks. A faint sheen of fuzz on her skull foretold that eventually it would grow back, but for now, she was certainly no beauty. Yet Wintrow had given her sidelong looks all evening. In the midst of the most important decisions of his life, she had still had the power to distract him. No one had said who she was, or why she was included in the talks.

Etta had lain down on Kennit's bed, pillowed her head on cushions that smelled of his lavender, burrowed into his blankets. She could not sleep. The more she immersed herself in his things, the more isolated she felt. It was almost a relief to ponder Amber. Not that it mattered to her, but yes, it did. How could Wintrow be giving his attention to a woman at a time like this? Did not he realize the gravity of the tasks Kennit had left him?

Even more unsettling than the way Wintrow looked at Amber had been her whole-hearted fascination with him. The woman had studied him with her peculiar eyes. It was not honest lust, such as the blonde barbarian displayed all evening. Amber had observed Wintrow as a cat watches a bird. Or as a mother watches her child.

She had not asked if she might go back to Vivacia with them. She had merely been waiting in the boat. 'I must speak to Wintrow Vestrit. Privately.' No apology, no explanation. And Wintrow, for all his obvious exhaustion, had curtly nodded to her request.

So why did it bother her? With one man dead, did she so swiftly seek another? She had no claim upon Wintrow. She had no claim upon anyone. But, she realized uneasily, she had been counting on him. In her half-spun dreams for Kennit's child, it had always been Wintrow who taught him to read and to write, Wintrow at his side to temper Kennit's aloofness and her own uncertainties. Wintrow had named her queen tonight, and none had dared challenge him. But that did not mean he would remain at her side. Tonight, a woman had looked at him, and Etta knew that he might simply step aside from her to claim a life of his own.

Etta drew a comb through her dark hair. She caught sight of herself in Kennit's mirror, and suddenly wondered, Why? Why bother combing her hair, why bother sleeping, or breathing? Her head pounded with the pain of her thoughts. Why bother thinking? She bowed her head into her hands again. She had no tears left. Her eyes were full of sand, her throat rasped rough with her grieving, but it gave her no relief. Not tears nor screaming could ease this pain. Kennit was dead. The agony knifed through her again.

But his child is not.

As clearly as if Kennit himself had whispered the words, the thought reached her. She straightened herself and took a breath. She would walk a turn around the deck to calm herself. Then she would lie down and rest at least. She would need her wits about her tomorrow, to look out for the interests of the Pirate Isles. Kennit would have expected that of her.

'I'm sorry. You'll have to speak to me here. Currently, I don't have a room to call my own.'

'It doesn't matter where we speak, only that we do.' Amber studied him as if he were a rare book. 'And sometimes public is far more private than private can be.'

'I'm sorry?' The woman had an intricate and tricky way of speaking. Wintrow had the feeling he should be careful what he said to her, and even more careful of what she said to him. 'I'm very tired,' he excused himself.

'We all are. Far too much has happened in one day. Who would have believed so many threads could converge in one location? But so it happens, sometimes. And the end of the thread must pass through the tangle many times before all is unknotted.' She smiled at him. They stood on the afterdeck in the darkness. The only light came from the distant bonfires on the beach. He could not really see her features, only the shifting planes of her face. But he knew she smiled as she toyed with her gloves.

'I'm sorry. You wanted to speak to me?' He hoped she would get to the point.

'I did. To say to you what you've said three times to me. I'm sorry. I apologize to you, Wintrow Vestrit. I don't know how I missed you. For over two and a half years I searched for you. We must have walked the same streets in Bingtown. I could feel you, so close for a time, and then you were gone. I found your aunt instead. Later, I found your sister. But somehow, I missed you. And you were the one I was meant to find. As I stand near you now, I know that without any doubt.' She suddenly sighed and all puzzles and levity were gone from her words as she shook her head and admitted, 'I don't know if I've done what I was meant to do. I don't know if you have fulfilled your role, or only begun it. I'm so tired of not knowing, Wintrow Vestrit. So tired of guessing and hoping and doing my best. Just once, I'd like to know I did it right.'

His body hummed with weariness. Her words almost made sense to him. But he had no thoughts to offer her, only courtesy. 'I think you need sleep. I know I do. I don't have a bed to offer you, but I can find you a clean blanket or two.'

He could not see her eyes, but still felt her looking into his. Almost desperately, she asked, 'Is there nothing here for you? When you look at me, there is no spark? No sense of connection, no echo of opportunity missed? No wistfulness for a path untrod?'

He almost laughed at her twisting words. What response did she hope to wring from him? 'Just now, my only regret is for a bed unslept in,' he suggested wearily.

Once, at the monastery, he had taken shelter in a wooden hut during a thunder storm. As he watched the storm, gripping the wet doorframe, lightning had struck a tree nearby. As the blast split the oak, a sensation of power had darted through him and left him sprawled on the earth in the falling rain. A similar feeling shocked him now. The woman twitched as if he had poked her. For an instant the distant flames of the bonfires leapt in her eyes.

'A bed unslept in, and a woman unbedded. The bed is yours by right, but the woman, though she may come to you in time, never completely belongs to you. Yet the child is yours, for this child belongs not to he who makes him but to he who takes him.'

Meanings danced all around him, like the spattering rain that began to fall. Small hail was mixed with it, bouncing off the deck and Wintrow's shoulders. 'You speak of Etta's child, don't you?'

'Do I?' She cocked her head. 'You would know better than I. The words come to me, but the sense of them belongs to another. But mark how you call him. Etta's child, when all others speak of him as Kennit's.'

Her words nettled him. 'Why should I not name him hers? It takes two to make a child. His value is not solely in that Kennit fathered him. When they name him so, they discount Etta. I tell you this, stranger. In many ways, she is more fit to be the mother of a king than Kennit was to father one.'

'You should remain near him, for you will be one of the few that know that.'

'Who are you? What are you?' he demanded.

The drenching rain descended suddenly in a roar that drowned out speech, and the hailstones grew larger. 'Inside!' Wintrow shouted, and led the way at a run. He held the door open and waited for her to follow him. But the cloaked figure who hastened in from the downpour was not Amber but Etta. He looked past her, but saw no one there.

Etta pushed her hood back. Her dark hair was plastered to her skull and her eyes were huge. She caught her breath. Her voice came from the depths of her soul. 'Wintrow. I have something to tell you.' She drew another breath. Her face suddenly crumpled. Tears ran with the rain down her face. 'I don't want to raise this child alone.'

He did not take her in his arms. He knew better than that. But the words came easily. 'I promise you, you won't have to.'

He attacked her in the darkness, his weight pinning her down. Fear paralysed her. Althea gasped for air, trying to find a scream. She could not even squeak. She thrashed, trying to escape him, but only hit her head on the wall. There was no air. She could not fight him. With a spectacular effort, she freed an arm and struck him.

'Althea!'

His outraged yell woke her. She jerked to consciousness. The grey of early dawn leaked in the broken window. Brashen sat up on the bed, holding his face. She managed to get a breath in, then panted another. She hugged herself tightly, trying to still her own trembling. 'What? Why'd you wake me?' she demanded. She groped after her dream, but could find only the ragged edges of terror.

'Why'd *I* wake *you*?' Brashen was incredulous. 'You nearly broke my jaw!'

She swallowed dryly. 'I'm sorry. I think I had a nightmare.'

'I suppose so,' he agreed sarcastically. He looked at her, and she hated how his eyes softened with sympathy. She didn't want his pity. 'Are you all right now?' he asked gently. 'Whatever it was, it must have been bad.'

'It was just a dream, Brashen.' She pushed his concern aside.

He looked away, cloaking his emotion. 'Well. I suppose it's

morning, or nearly so. I may as well get dressed.' His voice was flat.

She forced a smile. 'It's another day. It has to be better than yesterday.' She sat up, stretching. Every muscle ached, her head pounded, and she felt half sick. 'I'm still tired. But I'm looking forward to getting under way.' That, at least, was true.

'Good for you,' Brashen growled at her. He turned his back on her. He went to his clothing chest and began to rummage through it. She'd be getting her ship back today. No wonder she was alert with anticipation. He was glad for her. Truly, he was. He could remember what it was like to step up to command. He found a shirt and dragged it on. She'd do well. He was proud of her. She'd been happy for him when he took over Paragon. He was happy for her now. Honestly. He turned back to her. She crouched on the floor by her duffel bag surrounded by scattered garments. The look she gave him was one of misery. She looked so worn, Brashen felt a rush of remorse. 'I'm sorry I'm so abrupt,' he said gruffly. 'I'm just very tired.'

'We both are. No need to apologize.' Then she smiled and offered him, 'You could go back to bed. There's no real reason we both have to be up this early.'

Was that supposed to make him feel better? That she was willing to just walk away, leave him sleeping in his bunk? This reminded him too much of the harsh way they'd parted in Candletown. Maybe this was just how Althea Vestrit said goodbye to her men. 'You must have slept through that part last night. Wintrow warned us that we'd all have to be up early to catch this tide to get clear of here. Semoy's a good hand, but I want to bring Paragon out of this maze myself.'

'I think I can steer a tricky passage as well as you can.' She rocked slightly back on her heels to give him an offended look.

'I know you can,' he barked back. 'But that won't do Paragon much good when you're at Vivacia's wheel,' he retorted.

She looked at him blankly. Then her face changed. Understanding dawned. 'Oh, Brashen.' She came to her feet. 'You thought I was going away today. On Vivacia.'

'Aren't you?' He hated the slight hoarseness in his voice. He looked at her sullenly, refusing to hope.

She shook her head slowly. He saw an echo of loss in her eyes. 'There's no place there for me, Brashen. I saw that yesterday. I will always love her. But she is Wintrow's ship. To take her away from him would be . . . identical to what Kyle did to me. Wrong.'

He fitted the words together. 'Then you're staying on with Paragon?'

'Yes.'

'And with me?'

'So I assumed.' She cocked her head at him. 'I thought we both wanted this. To be together.' She looked down. 'I know it's what I want. Even though I'm losing my liveship, I know I want to be with you.'

'Althea, I'm so sorry.' He tried to get his face under control. 'Really, I am. I know what the Vivacia meant to you, what she still means to you.'

Both amusement and irritation glinted in her eyes. 'You'd look more sincere, if you'd stop grinning.'

'I would if I could,' he assured her sincerely. She took three steps. Then she was in his arms. He held her. She was staying with him. She wanted to stay with him. It was going to be fine. For a time he just held her. A long moment later, he asked, 'And you're going to marry me? In Bingtown, at the Traders' Concourse?'

'That was the plan,' she agreed.

'Oh.'

She looked up into his face. His eyes and his heart were so open to her now. She saw all the uncertainty and pain she'd caused him, without intention. She had never meant to do that. He smiled at her and she managed to smile back. His hold on her tightened and she resisted the urge to gently free herself. She had to get past this. This was Brashen. She loved him.

She took a breath. She had never imagined that she'd have to force herself to endure his touch. But just this time, just this once, she would, for both of them. She could relax and tolerate it. He needed this reassurance of her love. And she needed to prove to herself that Kennit had not destroyed her. Just this once, she could pretend desire. For Brashen's sake. She turned her mouth up to his and let him kiss her.

Spring

THIRTY-EIGHT

Jamaillia City

Hᴇʀ ᴄʜᴀᴍʙᴇʀs ᴡᴇʀᴇ beyond anything Malta had imagined. No matter where she turned her eyes, she saw opulence. The frescoes of forests on the wall merged into a pale blue ceiling of birds and butterflies in flight. The deep carpets underfoot were green as moss, while the permanently flowing bath of steaming water bubbled through an immense tub framed by marble water birds and screened by a wall of potted reeds and cattails. And this was merely her dressing chamber.

The mirror beside her dressing table was larger than she was. She had no idea what half the little pots of cosmetics and unguents held. She did not need to. That was the business of the three maids who applied them artfully to her skin.

'If it pleases my lady, would she lift her brows, that I may outline her eyes more fully?' One of them requested gently.

Malta lifted a hand. 'They are fine as they are, Elise. All three of you have done wonderfully by me.' She had never thought she would get tired of being fussed over, but she was ready for some time alone. She smiled in the mirror at the women around her. Elise had shaved a part in her own dark hair. A comb, decorated with red glass, rested there in artful imitation of Malta's crest. The other two young women had plucked their eyebrows and replaced them with a glistening cosmetic made from flaked mother-of-pearl and colouring. One had chosen red in Malta's honour. The other's shimmering brows were blue. Malta wondered if this were an effort to flatter Reyn.

Another glance in the mirror assured her that no cosmetic efforts could make them look as exotic as Malta. She smiled at herself, enjoying how light moved on her scaling. She turned her head slowly from side to side. 'Wonderfully,' she repeated. 'You may all go.'

'But, lady, your stockings and slippers . . .'

'I shall put them on myself. Go on, now. Or would you have me believe there are no young men anxiously hoping you may be released a few moments early tonight?'

The smiles that met hers in the mirror told her that she had guessed true. A great ball such as this created excitement through all the levels of the Satrap's palace. There would be dancing in no less than four separate ballrooms, for every level of aristocracy, and Malta knew that the excitement and glitter would extend to celebration in the servants' hall as well. That it was the third such gala in less than a month did not seem to dim anyone's enthusiasm. No one wished to miss the chance to once more glimpse the grave and slender beauty that was the Queen of the Pirate Isles, let alone bypass an opportunity to see the Elderlings dance together. Newly influential advisors and nobles of Jamaillia would once more convene to flatter and exalt the young Satrap who had so valiantly set forth to adventure through the wild world and then return home with such lofty new allies. Tonight would be their last such opportunity. Tomorrow, she and Reyn would sail north on the Vivacia with Wintrow and Queen Etta. Tomorrow they would finally begin the journey home.

Malta drew on her stockings and then her little white satin slippers. In the midst of tying the second one, she looked down at it closely. She tried to remember how tragic it had been not to have new slippers for her first ball. Her heart went out to the girl she had been even as she shook her head over her ignorance. She took the white lace gloves from her dressing table. They came to her elbow, and were cleverly fashioned to permit hints of her gleaming scarlet scaling to show through the lace. Yesterday, one of her maids had told her that in the bazaar, they now sold gloves with glittering insets to mimic the effect.

Malta looked at herself in the mirror disbelievingly. Everyone, everyone thought she was beautiful. Her gown was a confection of white with hidden panels of scarlet fabric that would flash only when Reyn whirled her on the dance floor. The seamstress who had created it had told her it had come to her in a dream of dragons. She set her hands to the tiny waist of the dress and spun before the mirror, nearly falling as she tried to turn her head to catch the flashing of the red. Then, laughing at her own foolishness, she left her dressing chamber.

Moments later, she tapped twice at a door, and then boldly let herself in. 'Etta?' she gently asked of the dimness.

'In here,' the Queen of the Pirate Isles replied.

Malta swiftly crossed the darkened chamber and entered Etta's immense dressing chamber. Closets stood open, gowns were strewn on the chairs and the floor, and Etta sat in her undergarments before her mirror. 'Where are your dressing maids?' Malta asked carefully. Wintrow had warned her of Etta's temper. Malta herself had never seen her anger, only the black depths of her sorrow.

'I sent them away,' Etta said brusquely. 'Their chatter was maddening. "Try this scent, let us pin your hair so, will you wear the green, will you wear the blue, oh, lady, not the black, not again." Like so many shrieking gulls, all come to feed on my corpse. I sent them away.'

'I see,' Malta said gently. A second door opened, and Mother suddenly appeared bearing a tray. A steaming teapot was on it, and matching cups. It was a lovely service, white with flowers done all in blue. Mother muttered a soft greeting to Malta and set the tray down on Etta's dressing table. Her washed-blue eyes lingered on Etta fondly. She spoke to herself as she poured tea for Etta, a gentle stream of words, soothing as a cat's purr. Etta appeared to listen, though Malta could make no sense of them. Then Queen Etta sighed, took up the cup and sipped it. Despite Mother's status at court, she had refused title and chambers of her own. Instead, she shared Etta's chamber, and waited on her at every opportunity. Malta thought such constant attention would chafe her to fury, but Etta seemed to take comfort from it. The Queen of the Pirate Isles set down her cup.

'I will wear the black again,' she said, but there was only sadness in her voice now, no anger or bitterness. With a sigh, she turned back to her mirror. Malta found the black dress and shook out its simple lines. Etta wore it to mourn Kennit, just as the only jewellery she wore was the little miniature of him strapped to her wrist and the earrings he had given her. She seemed unaware that the tragic simplicity of her garb and demeanour had captured the dramatic interest of every poet in Jamaillia.

She sat before her mirror but looked down at her hands as Mother brushed her sleek black hair and pinned it up with jewelled pins. From anyone else, Etta would have protested such decoration, but Mother hummed a calming little melody as she did so. When she was finished, Etta's dark hair was the night sky for a score of glittering stars. Mother next took up a scent bottle, and dabbed her throat and wrists.

'Lavender,' Etta said quietly. Her voice broke on the word. 'Kennit always loved that scent.' She suddenly put her head down into her hands. Mother gave Malta a look. When the old woman withdrew to the other side of the chamber and busied herself rehanging garments, Malta humbly helped her.

When Etta lifted her head, there was no track of tears down her face. She looked weary, but she still managed to smile. 'I suppose I must get dressed,' she surrendered. 'I suppose I must be the queen again tonight.'

'Wintrow and Reyn will be waiting for us,' Malta agreed.

'Sometimes,' Etta confided as Malta fastened the endless row of tiny buttons up her back, 'when I am most discouraged, if I take a moment to myself, I swear I can hear him speaking to me. He bids me be strong, for the sake of the son I carry.'

Mother gabbled soft agreement as she brought Etta's slippers and stockings.

Etta spoke on softly, almost dreamily. 'At night, just before I fall asleep, I often hear his voice. He speaks to me, words of love, poetry, good counsel, and encouragement. I swear it is all that keeps me from going mad. I feel that in some way, the best part of Kennit is still with me. That he will always be with me.'

'I'm sure he is,' Malta replied easily. Privately, she wondered if she were as blind to Reyn's faults. The Kennit that Etta recalled did not match Malta's recollection at all. She had felt only a shiver of relief when she had seen Kennit's canvas-wrapped corpse leave Vivacia's deck to slip beneath the saltwater.

Etta stood. The black silk whispered around her. Her pregnancy did not show yet, but all knew of it. The queen carried the heir of King Kennit. None questioned her right to rule in his stead, just as none questioned the seeming youth of the man who commanded his fleet. In pirate tradition, Wintrow had succeeded to Kennit's position by a vote of his captains. Malta had heard that it was unanimous.

Wintrow and Reyn awaited them at the foot of the stair. Her brother suffered in comparison to the Rain Wilder. The close tailoring of his jacket did nothing to hide the slightness of his build. The formality of Wintrow's Jamaillian garb made him look even younger than he was until one noticed his eyes. Then he seemed a fitting match for Etta. As always, he wore black as she did. Malta wondered if it was truly to mourn the pirate, or if it was merely to complement Etta and mark them as a pair.

At the foot of the stairs, the pirate queen paused a moment. Malta watched her take a breath as if she steeled herself. Then she set her fingers atop Wintrow's proffered arm and lifted her chin. As she glided away on Wintrow's arm, Malta pursed her lips and frowned.

'Something troubles you?' Reyn asked. Her took her hand and set it firmly upon his forearm. The warmth of his hand secured her clasp there.

'I hope my brother grows taller,' she murmured.

'Malta!' he rebuked her, but then smiled. She had to look up at him, and she loved that she did. The Jamaillian styles suited Reyn very well indeed. His close-fitted indigo jacket only emphasized the width of his shoulders. The white of his cuffs and collar contrasted well with his weather-bronzed skin. White trousers and black knee boots completed him. He wore small gold hoops in his ears, which shone against the glossy black curl of his hair. She smiled sympathetically for whoever had worried it into order tonight. He had no patience with body servants. He turned his head, and the light ran along his scaling, breaking blue highlights from it. Dark as his eyes were, she could see the secret blue in their copper depths.

'Well?' he asked her. There was a faint flush on his face and she realized she had stood long simply looking at him.

She nodded her assent, and they crossed the floor together. The hall opened out around them, its lofty ceiling supported by marble pillars. They walked beneath an arch into the grand ballroom. At one end of the room, musicians played softly, a prelude to the dancing. At the other end, the Satrap presided over the festivities from an elevated throne. Three of his Companions sat in chairs ranged before his dais. A servant tended two censers set to either side of the Satrap. The yellow smoke from the herbs wreathed him. He smiled and nodded benignly on his guests. A separate dais held a slightly less ornate throne for Queen Etta. She was ascending the steps as if it were a gallows. A lower seat beside hers waited for Wintrow.

Seating arrangements for her and Reyn had been more politically perplexing. Satrap Cosgo had, grudgingly, granted that Queen Etta as the reigning monarch of a separate kingdom had, perhaps, stature equal to his own. Malta and Reyn, however, made no royal claims for themselves. Malta repeatedly but quietly asserted that Bingtown was an independent city-state, yet she did not claim to be its representative. Reyn also refused to acknowledge that Jamaillia had any authority over the Rain Wilds, but he was not their ambassador to the Satrap. Rather, they represented the interests of the Dragon Tintaglia and her kind. They were obviously not the King and the Queen of the Dragons nor nobles from afar and hence not entitled to thrones or elevation of any kind. That Cosgo had ensconced them on elevated chairs on a garlanded dais had as much to do with his desire to display these exotic new allies as a wish to honour them. That rankled with Reyn more than it did Malta. Her pragmatism had prevailed over his distaste for exhibition. It did not matter to her why he granted her this distinction; she cared only that in the minds of every noble who beheld them, it conveyed their elevated status. It could only increase their bargaining power.

She had used that leverage in every capacity. With the Satrap's strangling monopoly on Bingtown's exports broken, there were many merchants anxious to establish new ties with the Trader cities. The current fashion favour for their exotic appearances had even motivated a stream of inquiries about trade and settlement possibilities in the Rain Wilds. Reyn had replied conservatively to these, reminding them that he could not speak for the Rain Wild Council. A number of entrepreneurs and adventure seekers had offered to pay high prices to book passage on the Vivacia for her journey homeward. Wintrow had dealt with that, pointing out that Vivacia was the flagship of the Pirate Isles, not the Rain Wilds.

While he would be furnishing transport for the Elderlings' return, Vivacia was not available for hire. He suggested they seek out other ships that were Bingtown bound.

With the serpents no longer a threat, and the Chalcedean menace greatly reduced, they all foresaw increased shipping and travel between their cities. Malta had spent one long afternoon totting figures with Lord Ferdio. The outcome suggested to both of them that the Satrap's coffers would actually profit more from this new arrangement than he had from his throttlehold on Bingtown. The increased flow of ships through the Inside Passage, open trade with the Pirate Isles, and an increase in Jamaillian sailing ships profiting from trade with Chalced and points beyond might shock the city out of its downward spiral of stagnation. That was before Ferdio had begun reckoning the possible profits from freely marketing goods from the South Islands to the various northern markets. They had presented their findings to Cosgo, who had smiled and nodded for a brief time before succumbing to boredom.

Satrap Cosgo had changed, Malta thought to herself as they approached his throne, but not enough to impress her with his sincerity. Restored to wealth and comfort, women and intoxicants, he had resumed all the mannerisms of the effete youth she had first met at the Bingtown Traders' Concourse. Yet, she was willing to take the word of those who had known him for years that his transformation was truly remarkable. As she made her curtsey and Reyn his bow, the Satrap gravely inclined his head in acknowledgement. He spoke down to them.

'So. This is to be our last evening together, my friends.'

'One dares to hope otherwise,' Malta replied smoothly. 'Surely, in days to come, we shall return to the wonders of Jamaillia City. Perhaps the Lord High Magnadon Satrap will someday undertake another journey to Bingtown or Trehaug.'

'Ah, Sa forefend it! Still, if duty demands that I do so, I shall. Let it not be said that Satrap Cosgo feared the rigours of travel.' He leaned forward slightly. He made a slight gesture of annoyance at the servant, and the man immediately replenished the smouldering concoction on the brass holders. The tendrils of smoke flowed thick once more. 'You are determined to depart tomorrow, still.'

Reyn spoke. 'Determined? Magnadon Satrap, say rather obliged. As you well know, our wedding arrangements have been postponed once already. We can scarcely disappoint our families again.'

'They needn't be disappointed. You could be wed tomorrow, if you wished it, in the Satrap's own Temple of Sa. I shall command a hundred priests to preside, and a procession shall carry you through the streets. This I could arrange for you. Now, if you wish.'

'It is a most gracious offer, Lord High Magnadon. Yet I fear we must decline. Trader ways demand that we be wed among our own folk, with our own customs. A man of your learning, culture, and travel undoubtedly understands that such traditions are broken only at grave risk to one's stature. Of great importance also are the many messages you have charged us with for Traders in both Bingtown and Trehaug. Those must be delivered without more delay. Nor have we forgotten the message birds you have furnished, that communication between the Trader cities, the Pirate Isles and Jamaillia City may be improved.'

Malta bit the inside of her cheek to keep from smiling. It was good that the Satrap did not know Wintrow's opinion of the 'smelly befouling creatures' he had reluctantly welcomed aboard Vivacia. Jola had proposed pigeon pie as variety in their usual menu, but Malta was confident that the birds would live to serve as messengers.

A shadow of petulance crossed his face. 'You gained what you desired: independence for Bingtown and the Rain Wilds. I no sooner signed the scrolls than you made plans to leave.'

'Of course, Lord High Magnadon. For did not you also

command that the Vestrit family represent Jamaillia's interests there? It is a duty I take most seriously.'

'No doubt, you will take it most profitably as well,' he pointed out caustically. He inclined his head to inhale his smoke more deeply. 'Ah, well, if part we must, then I hope it will lead to good fortune for all of us.' The Satrap leaned back, eyes half-closed. Malta interpreted this, gratefully, as dismissal.

She and Reyn sought their own seats. She looked around the spectacle of the ballroom and realized that she would not miss it. Well, not immediately. She had finally been surfeited with parties, dancing, and elegance. She longed for the simplicity of unscheduled days and privacy. Reyn, for his part, chafed to be at the site of the Elderling city. Ophelia had recently arrived in Jamaillia City with letters for all of them. The news from Bingtown was both heartening and tantalising. The flow of foodstuffs through Bingtown and up the river was steady and sufficient. The young priest Wintrow had recommended as an engineer had an almost mystical knack for simple yet elegant solutions. As soon as the temporary locks that permitted the serpents to ladder up the river had been completed, Reyn's brother had turned his attention to searching for the remains of the city. In this, Selden had been most helpful to Bendir. As yet, they had not discovered any intact chambers, but Reyn was certain that was due only to his absence. The fervour of his ambition to begin the search amazed Malta.

He gave a small sigh in reply to her mood. 'I, too, long to be home again,' he confided to her. The music had begun to swell. The first dance would be a set piece for the Companions of the Satrap only. They danced together, in his honour, with him as their absent partner while he watched from the dais. She watched the elaborately dressed women move through the sedate measures. At intervals, the Satrap inclined his head, symbolizing his bows to his Companions. It struck Malta as a singularly foolish custom and a waste of good music. She stilled the tapping of her foot. Reyn leaned closer to be sure she heard him. 'I secured two more stone cutters. They will follow us on Ophelia. Wintrow says there are several islands in the Pirate Isles that may furnish stone for us, at a reasonable cost. If we replace the log walls of the locks with stone, the workers who must constantly maintain the wood because the river eats it will be free, and we can create a way for large ships to come to dock there. We could then transfer those workers to the excavation of the city –'

'Before or after our wedding?' she asked him gravely.

'Oh, after,' he replied fervently. He took her hand. His thumb swept the palm of her hand caressingly. 'Do you suppose our mothers would let it be any other way? I personally doubt we shall be allowed to eat or sleep until we have endured the wedding.'

'Endured?' she asked him with raised brows.

'Most definitely,' he replied with a sigh. 'My sisters have been in paroxysms of delight. They will meet the Queen of the Pirate Isles and your dashing brother Wintrow. Tintaglia has announced she will be there, to "receive" us afterwards, I am told. My sisters are insisting I be veiled for the wedding. They say that it matters not how I display myself in Jamaillia; I must be properly modest for the traditional Rain Wild ceremony.'

'Your modesty has nothing to do with the tradition,' Malta retorted. He was not telling her anything she had not already heard. When Ophelia had docked, she had brought thick letters for all of them. Keffria's letter had been likewise full of wedding plans. 'I will be veiled as well. It is our blind acceptance of one another that they celebrate.' A question tugged at her. 'You were closeted long with Grag Tenira. My mother wrote that he courts a Three Ships girl. Is that true?'

'He and Sparse Kelter's daughter are moving in that direction.'

'Oh. A shame. I suppose that means that Aunt Althea

has burned her bridges and will have to be content with Brashen Trell.'

'They looked more than content, the last time I saw them.'

'Grag Tenira would have been a more fitting match for her.'

'Perhaps. From the way she looked at me, I suspected she thought you could do better, also.'

'She looks at everyone that way.' Malta dismissed her aunt's reservations.

'More interesting to me were the changes in Ophelia. Or the lack of them, rather. She is the same ship she has always been. Grag claims she has no memories of being a dragon. That for her, life began as Ophelia. The same is true for Goldendown.'

'Do you suppose they will recall it later?'

'I do not know.' Reluctantly, he added, 'My suspicion is that some of the dragons in the wizardwood logs had perished before we used them. Ophelia and Goldendown, perhaps, have no dragon memories because the creature inside had died and taken its memories with it. They may remain as they always have been.' He paused. 'Grag, at least, is grateful. He says that Kendry has become well nigh unmanageable. He is a bitter creature and sails only at Tintaglia's behest.'

A silence fell between them. Malta made a valiant effort at distracting him. 'I had a note from Selden as well. His handwriting is awful. He loves the Rain Wilds. Cassarick is a torment to him, however. He wants to dig immediately, and your brother will not let him.'

Reyn smiled wryly. 'I remember being like that.'

His face was still too pensive to suit her.

'He spends much time with Tintaglia, "guarding" the cocoons.' She shook her head. 'Tintaglia says that only fifty-three appear to be developing. He does not say how she knows. Poor creature. She struggled so hard to lead them home, and so many perished along the way. She worries that not all fifty-three will hatch. They should have spent the whole winter cocooned and hatched in high summer.'

'Perhaps they will hatch in late summer to make up for their late start.'

'Perhaps. Oh.' She tugged at his hand. 'The Companions are finished. Now the real dancing will begin.'

'Do not you wish for the music to begin?' he teased her, feigning reluctance to rise.

She widened her eyes at him warningly. He came to his feet.

'You only want to show off your dress,' he accused her gravely.

'Worse. I wish to flaunt my elegant partner before all of these grand ladies, before I snatch him away to immure him as mine in the distant Rain Wilds.'

As always, her extravagant compliments brought a blush to his cheeks. Wordlessly, he led her to the floor. The musicians struck up, Jamaillian stone-drums setting the time until the other instruments swept in. Reyn took her hand and set his other hand to the small of her back, Jamaillian style. She had explained to Wintrow that it was the only proper way to tread this step, but she knew he would be frowning at Reyn's boldness. They stepped sedately to the sound of the drums until the wind instruments skirled in to bid them spin together. The dizziness was lovely, for Reyn caught her at the end, and again they stepped to the drum, the tempo building.

He spun her the second time, faster and closer to his body. 'Do you not regret waiting?' she asked him daringly in the privacy of the dance.

'I would regret more risking the legitimacy of my heir,' he chided her seriously.

She rolled her eyes at him, and he pretended a scowl at her prurience.

'Does a hungry man resent the preparation of the feast?' he asked her the next time they closed in a spin. They whirled so close she felt his breath on her crest. It brought the now familiar flush of warmth through her. She became aware that it had happened again. The floor was cleared in a great circle around them as other couples paused to watch the Elderlings dance. He spun her again, faster, so close that her breasts nearly brushed his chest. 'They say that hunger is what makes the meal so savoury,' he added by her ear. 'I warn you. By the time we reach Bingtown, I shall be as a starving man.'

The murmur of the crowd told her that they were spinning so fast on these steps that her gown was now flashing its scarlet insets. She closed her eyes, trusting him to hold her in his orbit, and wondered what could ever surpass this glorious moment. Then she smiled, knowing the answer.

Telling Delo about it.

'They are beautiful together,' Etta murmured.

Wintrow risked a sidelong glance at her. She watched the dancers with a strange hunger in her eyes. He supposed she was imagining herself in Kennit's arms, skimming the floor as gracefully as Reyn and Malta. But not as abandonedly, he decided. Even pirates had more decorum than his wayward sister did. 'It is good they're getting married soon,' he observed stiffly.

'Oh. Do you think that will put a stop to their dancing?' Etta asked him sarcastically.

He gave her a humbled smile. Every now and then, a spark of the old Etta showed through, like coals gleaming in a banked fire. 'Probably not,' he conceded. 'Malta was born dancing, I believe.' Watching the ecstasy on her face as Reyn spun her in the dance, he added, 'I suspect that a dozen children from now, she will still display her feelings as plainly.'

'What a shame,' Etta consoled him dryly. She was silent as the couple spun again, then asked, 'Do all in Bingtown disdain dancing as you do?'

'I do not disdain dancing,' he answered with surprise. 'I was learning the basic steps, and accounted graceful enough, before I was sent off to be a priest.' He watched Reyn and Malta a few moments. 'What they are doing is not that impressive. It is just that they are able to do it both swiftly and gracefully. And that they are a well-matched couple.' He frowned a moment, then admitted, 'And that incredible dress she's wearing.'

'Do you think you could dance like that?'

'With practice, perhaps.' A sudden thought came to him. He coupled it to the discovery of how stupid he still could be. He leaned towards her. 'Etta. Would you care to dance?'

He held his open hand out towards her. She looked at it for a moment, then looked aside. 'I do not know how,' she replied stiffly.

'I could teach you.'

'I would not be good at it. I would only humiliate myself, and my partner.'

He leaned back in his chair and spoke softly, forcing her to listen carefully. 'When you fear to fail, you fear something that has not happened yet. Dancing is far less difficult than reading, especially for a woman who can run the rigging and never miss a step.' He waited.

'I . . . not now. Not in so public a place.' She built up to admitting it, as admitting any desire was difficult for her. 'But someday, I would like to learn to dance.'

He smiled at her. 'When you are ready, I will be honoured to partner you.'

She spoke very softly as she added, 'And I will have a dress to surpass that one.'

The stars glittered cold in the black sky overhead. By contrast, the yellow lights of Jamaillia were warm and close. Their reflections snaked like serpent backs over the rippling water of the harbour. The sounds of merriment and music from the distant festivities wafted thin in the cold spring night. Across the dock from her, Ophelia shifted in the darkness. She was an old-fashioned liveship, a blowsy old cog. A moment later, she rattled a large dice-box at Vivacia. 'Do you game?' she asked invitingly.

Vivacia found herself smiling at the matronly figurehead. She had not expected to find the company of another liveship so convivial, especially one who professed to have lost all dragon memories. Ophelia was not only good company but a veritable fount of Bingtown gossip. Even more important to Vivacia were her detailed accounts of all she had seen and heard in Trehaug. The cocooning banks were far upriver, beyond the reach of a ship of her draught, but Ophelia was an adept meddler and an avid listener. She had contrived to know not only every fact but every rumour about the serpents' progress. The news she shared with Vivacia had been bad as well as good, but knowing the fate of her serpents was a kind of peace in itself. She served her kind best by remaining in Jamaillia for now, but the suspense had been difficult to endure. Ophelia had understood her thirst for information about the serpents. Since she had arrived in Jamaillia City, her detailed accounts had been a great comfort to Vivacia. Still, she shook her head at Ophelia's dice-box. 'Althea seemed to believe that you cheated when she played with you,' she observed lightly.

'Oh, well, that's Althea. Nice girl, but a bit suspicious. Not the best judgement in the world, either. After all, she chose that renegade Trell when she could have had my Grag.'

Vivacia laughed softly. 'I don't think your Grag ever had much of a chance. I rather suspect that "renegade" Trell was chosen for her by Ephron Vestrit a number of years ago.' At Ophelia's affronted expression, she added kindly, 'But Grag doesn't seem to have missed her for long.'

Ophelia nodded in satisfaction. 'Humans have to be pragmatic about these things. They don't live that many years, you know. Now his Ekke, she's a fine girl, knows how to seize life and make something of it. Reminds me of my first captain.

"Don't expect me to stay ashore and have babies for you," she told him, right here on my foredeck. "My children are going to be born on this ship," she said to him. And you know what Grag said? "Yes, dear." Meek as milk. I think he knows he'd better get to it if he's going to have a family. Humans only have so much time, you know.'

'That's why we have to cram so much living into those years.' This observation came from Jek. Her perfume wafted on the spring night. Despite the chill, she was barefoot, a long skirt swirling about her ankles. She came boldly to perch on Vivacia's railing. 'Evening, ladies,' she greeted them. She took a deep breath, sighed with contentment, and sat swinging her feet.

'You've been up at the dancing!' Ophelia enthused. 'Tell us about it. Did you see the Satrap's palace?'

'From the outside. It was all lit up like a bawdy-house lantern, golden lamplight and music spilling from every window and door. The streets were full of fine carriages, and there was a great line of folk parading in, dressed fine as kings, every one of them. Some were content to stand about and gawk at their betters, but not I. The courtyard was fine with me. The music was gay, the men were handsome, and the dancing lively. They were cooking whole pigs on spits, and keg after keg of beer did they broach. It was as good a feasting as I've ever seen in any town. Still and all, I'm ready to sail tomorrow. Jamaillia's a dirty place, for all its fine houses. I'll be glad to get out on the water again, and gladder still to see Divvytown. I knew it was my home port that first time I saw it.'

'The pirate town? Sa save us all. Does someone wait there for you, dearie?' Ophelia asked.

Jek laughed aloud. 'They all wait for me. They just don't know it yet.'

Ophelia's bawdy chuckle echoed hers. Then she noticed Vivacia's silence. 'Why so thoughtful, my dear? Do you miss your Wintrow? He'll be back soon enough.'

Vivacia stirred from her reverie. 'No. Not Wintrow. As you say, he will be back soon enough. Sometimes it is a pleasure to have no thoughts but my own. I was looking at the sky and recalling. The higher you fly, the more stars there are. There are stars up there that I will never see again. They didn't matter to me when the heavens still belonged to me, but now I feel it as a loss.'

'You're young. You're going to find a lot of things like that in your life,' the old liveship replied complacently. 'No sense dwelling on them.'

'My life,' Vivacia mused. 'My life as a liveship.' She turned to regard Ophelia with a sigh. 'I almost envy you. You recall nothing, so you miss nothing.'

'I recall a lot, my dear. Just because my memories have sails instead of wings, don't you discount them.' She sniffed. 'And my life is nothing for you to disdain, I might add. Nor your own. You could take a lesson from my Grag. Don't go mooning after the stars, when the wide sea is all around you. It's a sky of its own, you know.'

'And with just as many stars,' Jek observed. She hopped back onto the deck and stretched until her muscles crackled. 'Good night, ladies. I'm for my bunk. The day starts early for sailors.'

'And for liveships. Sweet dreams, my dear,' Ophelia wished her. As Jek padded softly away, the liveship shook her head. 'Mark my words. She'll regret it if she doesn't settle down soon.'

'Somehow I doubt it,' Vivacia replied, smiling. She looked back at the lights of the town. In the Satrap's palace, Wintrow and Etta prepared humans to accept the return of her kind. She knew a sudden surge of pride in them. Astonishingly, she felt the same for herself. She smiled at Ophelia. 'Jek is too busy living. She won't waste time on regrets. And neither shall I.'

THIRTY-NINE

Bingtown

'COMPANION SERILLA IS in the parlour.' Ronica walked into the chamber and looked around curiously.

'Are you certain?' Keffria heard the foolishness of her question as soon as she uttered it. She climbed down from the stool she had been standing on. She gave one critical look over her shoulder. 'Oh dear,' she muttered to herself. The old draperies from Selden's room, dyed and turned and pressed, still looked like the old draperies from Selden's room. No matter what she did to her bedchamber, it would still be the room she had shared with Kyle. Jani Khuprus had sent Rain Wild furniture to her but the lovely stuff was airy and pale, like the ghosts of the heavy bedstead and massive chests that had once filled the room. She wondered if she should move into Malta's room and keep this larger chamber for when Reyn and Malta visited.

But perhaps that would be cruel. Would not this room remind Malta of her father as much as it reminded Keffria of her husband? She shook her head at the cruelty of fate. Poor Kyle, to die on the decks of the Paragon, battling Jamaillian sailors. For what? A matter of a day later, those who had killed him had become their allies. Althea had brought her the tidings, and delivered them with uncharacteristic sensitivity when they were alone. She had been unable to cry. It had been hours before she had shared the news with anyone else.

871

Blessedly, her mother had said nothing, but only bowed her head. It was still hard to grasp that the long suspension of her life was over.

'Companion Serilla does not wait well,' Ronica reminded her.

Keffria startled as if from a dream. There was so little time for herself any more. When she did get involved in tasks for herself or personal thoughts, it was hard to tear herself away. 'Whatever could bring her here? And so early in the day?'

'She said she had a message for you.'

Now she saw the anxiety in her mother's eyes. Reyn, Malta and Wintrow were in Jamaillia. This was as likely to be bad news as good. Her stomach tightened inside her. 'I suppose the only way to hear it is to speak with her.'

She hurried through the hall to the parlour, her mother following more slowly. The slow mercy of time had finally brought spring to Bingtown. The season had turned in the last few days. The pounding rains of winter had changed to gentler sprinkling. Brisk breezes replaced cutting winds. Yesterday, she had even glimpsed a child's escaped kite fleeing, red against the bright blue day. Stalls in the market had reopened. People laughed and talked as they traded again.

Spring alone could not solve all Bingtown's problems. But the softer weather had speeded the departure of many disgruntled New Traders. With the Pirate Isles' increased patrols against the Chalcedean ships and the absence of serpents, travel would normalize swiftly. New wharves and piers were nearly completed. Six Duchies ships, anxious to court this new market, were braving the dangers of the Chalcedean coast to bring trade goods south to Bingtown. As trade revived, so did the town.

She glanced out at the atrium as she passed. In the righted pots, salvaged bulbs were beginning to sprout. Vines she had cut back as hopelessly dead were now putting out new leaves. Green nubs on the dry sticks of the clematis promised that the appearance of death was not death itself. Everywhere, life reasserted itself.

Spring had brought a welcome change in diet as well. There were fresh greens from the garden to waken the tongue and scallions to flavour chowders with something besides fish. The few bedraggled chickens that had survived theft, storm, and scanty feed were now scratching for insects and sprouts and laying eggs again. One jealously-guarded nest promised chicks to replenish the flock. The year was turning, and the luck of the Vestrit family with it. Perhaps.

Despite Ronica's words, Companion Serilla was sitting patiently in the parlour. She stared at nothing, her back to the brightness of the undraped window. She was sedately dressed, more warmly than the day warranted, as if Bingtown's spring were her autumn. At the sound of Keffria's footsteps, she turned her head slowly. She came to her feet as Keffria entered the room.

'Trader Vestrit,' she greeted her in a subdued tone. Without waiting for Keffria's greeting, she extended to her a tiny coil of paper. 'I've tidings to share. The bird arrived this morning.'

'Companion Serilla, good morning. I have appreciated so much your sharing the services of your messenger-birds. But this is an unprecedented honour, that you bring us the message yourself.'

Serilla smiled stiffly but said no more. Keffria took the paper from her hand and crossed to the window where the light was best. Pigeons could not carry heavy burdens in flight. Of necessity, messages were brief and tightly written. Jamaillian scribes excelled at the tiny lettering. A cramped addendum in Grag Tenira's hand was intended for Keffria as scribe of the Bingtown Council. She squinted to pick it out, then passed on the news to Ronica as she deciphered it.

'Ophelia has arrived safely. Letters delivered. All are well. Vivacia to sail soon.' She looked up at her mother with a smile.

'Just our personal concerns here. How kind of Grag to arrange to let us know.'

'The official tidings concern you as well,' Serilla informed her. 'Please. Read them.'

The tiny lettering in the scribe's hand almost defied her eyes. She read it once, then again. She looked up in puzzlement from her mother to Serilla. Then she spoke softly. 'Companion Serilla is dismissed from the Satrap's service. He has no further need of her here, since Bingtown has been recognized as an independent city-state. The Satrap also specifically retracts any authority she has claimed for herself. The language is . . . quite harsh.'

Ronica and Keffria exchanged awkward glances. The Companion stood quite straight, a tiny formal smile on her composed features. Ronica ventured to say softly, 'I do not see how the official tidings concern the Vestrit family.'

Keffria took a breath. 'Apparently Malta had negotiated with the Satrap. The Vestrit family will represent the interests of the Satrapy in Jamaillia. The annual fee for this service is substantial. Ten satrapes a month.' The sum was princely. A humble household could be managed quite well on one.

A heartbeat of silence followed her words. Then Keffria shook her head. 'I cannot accept this, however generous. I have been suggested for Head of the Bingtown Council. It is hard enough to trade honestly for the Vestrit family and still be even-handed in all Bingtown concerns. Mother?'

'My hands are full, with the smaller properties. I am not a young woman, Keffria, and the past few years have been hard on me. The money sounds wonderful. But what is the sense in devoting myself to another's interests, to earn money that must immediately be spent to rectify my neglect of our own properties?'

'Selden is far too young, and much too preoccupied with his own interests. Malta will be a wedded woman almost as soon as she returns. Besides, the dragon has already claimed her services. Wintrow has carved his own niche in the world.' Keffria quickly eliminated her children. She looked at her mother with a question. 'Althea?'

'Oh, please,' her mother sighed. 'If she cannot do it from the deck of the Paragon, it won't get done. She has not even found the time away from the ship to be properly married.'

'Trell's family is the problem.' Keffria defended her sister. 'Brashen insisted he would claim her hand in the Concourse, but they disputed his right. Disowned, he is not Trader any more. Or so they assert.' Keffria shook her head at their pig-headedness. 'It is his father. I think, given time, that his mother could bring him around. Young Cerwin was certainly willing enough to welcome him back to family and fold. There is gossip he is seeing a Tattooed girl, much to his parents' dismay. Perhaps he would welcome an ally in breaking free from his father's iron hand. Brashen and Althea had so little time in port; perhaps when they return, he can change his father's mind. If his pride will let him try again.'

'Enough,' Ronica replied quietly. They would not discuss this before the Companion.

'I am sure they will reach some solution,' Companion Serilla observed. 'I must be going, I have so much –'

'What will you do?' Keffria asked her in a low voice.

Serilla did not answer immediately. Then she shrugged. 'It will soon be public anyway. All will know what Keffria has been too kind to speak aloud. Cosgo has exiled me here.' She took a breath. 'He maintains that I was false to my vows, and perhaps involved with the conspiracy.' She clenched her jaws. Then she said with an effort, 'I know Cosgo. Someone must take the blame. I am the scapegoat. He must have one, and all others have negotiated forgiveness.'

'But you were never truly a part of it!' Keffria exclaimed, horrified.

'In politics, appearance matters far more than truth. The Satrap's authority was challenged and his life threatened.

There is substantial evidence that I challenged his authority, for my own ends.' An odd smile passed over her face. 'In truth, I defied him. He cannot make me regret it. That is hard for him to stomach. This is his revenge.'

'What will you do now?' Ronica asked.

'I have no real choice. He abandons me with neither funds nor authority. I stay on in Bingtown as a penniless exile.' A spark of the old Serilla shone in her retort.

A smile twisted Ronica's lips. 'All the best Bingtown families began just that way,' she pointed out. 'You are an educated woman. Bingtown is on the mend. If you cannot make your own way in such a situation, then you deserve to be penniless.'

'Restart's niece is turning me out of his house,' Serilla revealed abruptly.

'You should have moved out of there long ago,' Ronica replied acerbically. 'You never had the right to live there in the first place.' With an effort, she turned aside from that old battle. It no longer mattered. 'Have you found a place to live?'

It was like springing a trap. 'I came to you.' She looked from one to the other. 'I could help you in many ways.'

Ronica's eyes widened, then narrowed suspiciously. 'On what terms?' she demanded.

Serilla's stiffness fell away from her and Keffria felt she saw the real woman for the first time. The light of challenge shone in her eyes. 'An exchange of knowledge and expertise. I came here, gambling that I would hear what you have just said. That you cannot honestly represent Jamaillia's interests in Bingtown.' She looked from Keffria to Ronica. 'I can,' she asserted quietly. 'And I can do it honestly. Yet profitably.'

Keffria crossed her arms on her chest. Had she been manoeuvred? 'I'm listening,' she said quietly.

'Delegate,' Serilla said quietly. 'Pass the task to me, to

administer in your name. For years, I studied Bingtown's relationship to Jamaillia. Obviously, that knowledge encompasses Jamaillia's relationship to Bingtown. I can fairly represent Jamaillia's interests in Bingtown.' Her eyes travelled again from Keffria to Ronica and back again. Was she trying to decide where the true power resided? 'And at the money he has offered, you can well afford to hire me to do so.'

'Somehow I doubt that such an arrangement would please the Satrap.'

'And as Bingtown Traders, that has been a prime concern for you? Pleasing the Satrap?' Serilla asked acidly.

'In these changing times, maintaining cordial relations will be more important,' Keffria replied thoughtfully. Her thoughts flew. If she refused this opportunity, who else would the Satrap appoint? Was this her opportunity to retain control of the situation? At least with Serilla, they were dealing with someone they knew. And respected, however grudgingly that respect had been won. She could not deny the woman's expertise. She knew Bingtown's history better than most of Bingtown did.

'Must he know?' Serilla asked. An edge of desperation had crept into her voice. Then she suddenly stood straighter. 'No,' she announced before Keffria or Ronica would speak. 'That was a cowardly question. I will not hide from him. He has dismissed me as his Companion, abandoned me just as he did all the other women who loyally served his father as Companions. It is not a shameful distinction. That he has done so speaks of what he is, not what I am.' She took a deep breath and waited.

Keffria looked at her mother. Her mother gave a small shake of her head. 'It is not my decision,' she deferred.

'Ten satrapes a month promised is not ten satrapes in hand,' Keffria mused. 'I fear that in this I trust the Satrap as little as ever. Yet with or without his funds, I think the Bingtown Council can benefit from Serilla's continued advice regarding Jamaillia. If the Satrap does not honour this offer he sends because he is displeased with my advisor, that will say to me that he does not fully acknowledge Bingtown's right to regulate its own affairs. And I will tell him so.

'Then I will advise the Bingtown Council to hire Serilla. To advise us specifically on dealing with Jamaillia.' She gave the former Companion a level look. 'Selden's room is empty. You are welcome to it. I will warn you, however, that there are two conditions demanded for living here.'

'And those are?' Serilla prompted.

Keffria laughed. 'A high tolerance for fish. And a disregard for furniture.'

FORTY

The Rain Wild River

THE MORNING AIR was cool and soothing on her face. Paragon moved easily with the flow of the river. As she looked at the new day, Althea could tell Semoy was on the helm. It was more because he enjoyed it than because his skill was needed. This stretch of river was as placid as Paragon's deck. Many of the crew had jumped ship in Bingtown. Others had stayed on as far as Trehaug, only to find new jobs there as labourers. When they had left Trehaug with little more than a skeleton crew, neither Brashen nor Althea had seen it as a real loss. It was going to be difficult enough to scrape together wages for those who remained. Their present errand was to return to Bingtown, where a load of stone awaited them. Althea suspected it was salvaged from destroyed New Trader holdings. It would be used to reinforce the bank where the dragons would eventually hatch. The dragon was adept at finding work for the liveships, and less than capable at finding pay for their crews.

Althea shook such dismal worries from her head. Doggedly she seized onto optimism. She could believe all would go well, as long as she didn't think too hard. She crossed the main deck and bounded up to the foredeck. 'Morning!' she announced to the figurehead. She looked around, stretching. 'Every day, I think these jungles cannot be greener. Every morning, I awake and find I am wrong.'

Paragon didn't reply. But Amber spoke from over the side. 'Spring,' Amber agreed. 'An amazing season.'

Althea stepped up to the railing to look down at her. 'You fall in this river, you're going to be sorry,' she warned her. 'No matter how fast we fish you out, it's going to sting. Everywhere.'

'I won't fall,' Amber retorted. One of Paragon's hands cupped her before him. She sat on it, legs swinging, carving tool in hand.

'What are you doing?' Althea asked curiously. 'I thought he was finished.'

'He is. This is just decoration. Scroll work and things. On his axe handle and his battle harness.'

'What are you carving?'

'Charging bucks,' Amber replied diffidently. She sheathed her tools abruptly. 'Take me up, please,' she requested. Without a word, the figurehead restored her to the deck.

The river was a vast grey road flowing away from them. The thick forest of the Rain Wilds loomed close on the starboard side, while on the port side the wide waters stretched far to another green wall of plant life. Althea took a deep breath of cool air flavoured with river water and teeming plant life. Unseen birds called in the trees. Some of the vines that festooned the gigantic trees had put out fat purple buds. A tall column of dancing insects caught the sunlight on their myriad tiny wings. Althea grimaced at the sparkling sight. 'I swear, every one of those pests spent the night in our cabin.'

'At least one of them was in my room,' Amber contradicted. 'It managed to buzz near my ear most of the night.'

'I'll be glad to see saltwater again,' Althea replied. 'How about you, Paragon?'

'Soon enough,' the ship replied distractedly.

Althea raised one eyebrow at Amber. The carpenter shrugged. For the past two days, the ship had had a preoccupied air. Althea was willing to give him however much space and time he needed. This decades-delayed homecoming had to be a strange and wrenching experience for him. She was neither serpent nor dragon, yet the daily losses of the serpents as they guided them north had appalled and distressed her. That the serpents fed upon their own dead, however pragmatic that practice might be in conserving food and inherited memories, horrified her.

Tintaglia's circling presence had protected them from the Chalcedean ships. Only twice had they been directly challenged. There had been one brief battle, put to an end when Tintaglia had returned to drive the foreign ship away. The second encounter had ended when She Who Remembers had risen from the depths to spray the Chalcedean vessel with venom. Her death, Althea thought, had been the most difficult one for Paragon. The crippled serpent had gradually wasted but had gamely continued in her migration. Unlike many of the serpents, she had actually reached the mouth of the Rain Wild River. The journey up it, against the current, had proven too much for her. One morning they had found her, wrapped motionless around Paragon's anchor chain.

Many had perished in the acid flow of the river water. Battered and weary as they were, their small injuries turned to gaping wounds in the rushing wash of the grey water. Neither the ship nor Tintaglia could make that last long stretch any easier for them. One hundred and twenty-nine serpents entered the river mouth with them. By the time the tangle reached the river ladder the Rain Wilders had constructed, their numbers had dwindled to ninety-three. The rough interconnecting corrals of thick logs impeded and diverted the river's shallow rush, deepening the flow just enough for the serpents to wallow upriver.

Rain Wild engineering skills had combined with the strong backs of both Traders and Tattooed to create an artificial channel that led to the ancient mudbanks. Tintaglia had supervised the quarrying of the silver-streaked mud. The stuff was near as stiff as clay. Yet another log corral had been built, and workers had toiled long cold hours painstakingly mixing the hard stuff with river water until Tintaglia approved of the sloppy muck. As the exhausted serpents managed to haul themselves out on the low banks of the river, workers had transported barrows of the sloshing mud and laved it over the serpents.

It had tormented Paragon that he could not witness the cocooning of the serpents. A large ship such as he could not approach through the shallow waters. Althea had gone in his stead. To her had fallen the task of telling him that only seventy-nine of the serpents had managed to complete their cocoons. The others had died, their bodies too wasted to summon the special secretions that would bind the mud into long threads to layer around themselves. Tintaglia had roared her grief at each death, and then shared out the wasted bodies as food amongst the remaining serpents. Despite her extreme distaste for that behaviour, Althea thought it just as well. The dragon herself looked little better than the serpents. She refused to take time to hunt while the cocooning was going on. In a matter of days, her glittering hide hung on her in folds, despite the sympathetic workers who brought her birds and small game. Such largesse kept her alive, but not thriving.

Further work followed the cocooning. The muck-wrapped serpents had to be protected from the torrential deluges of a Rain Wild winter until the sheathing had dried hard. But eventually Tintaglia announced she was satisfied with the cocoons. Now the immense cases rested on the muddy bank of the river like giant seed pods hidden in a heaped litter of leaves, twigs and branches. Tintaglia once more gleamed since she had resumed her daily hunts. Some nights she returned to rest beside the cocoons, but increasingly she trusted the cadre of humans who watched over them from their treehouses. True to her word, the dragon now patrolled the river to its mouth, and overflew the coast of the Cursed Shores.

Tintaglia still spoke hopefully of more serpents returning. Althea suspected this was the true motive behind her coastal vigilance. She had even hinted that perhaps she would send liveships far south to seek for lost survivors. Althea considered that a measure of her anguish at their losses. From Selden, Althea had learned that not all the cocoons would hatch. There was always some mortality at this stage of a dragon's development, but these weakened creatures were dying at far higher rates than normal. Selden seemed to mourn them as much as Tintaglia, though he could not completely explain to Althea how he knew which ones had perished unhatched.

She had never known her nephew well. In the weeks she had spent in Trehaug and at the site of Cassarick, she had seen him grow more strange. It was not just the physical changes that she marked. At times, he did not seem to be a little boy any more. The cadence of his voice and his choice of words when he spoke to the dragon seemed to come from an older and foreign person. The only time when he seemed like the Selden she recalled was when he had returned dirty and weary from a day spent exploring with Bendir. They had festooned the swampy jungle behind the cocoon beach with bright strips of fabric tied to stakes or tree limbs. The colours were a code of sorts, incomprehensible to Althea, intended to guide future excavation. Over meals, Selden and Bendir discussed them earnestly and made summer plans for serious digging. She no longer knew her nephew, she reflected, but she was sure of one thing. Selden Vestrit was fired with enthusiasm for this new life he had found. In that, she rejoiced. It surprised her that Keffria had let him go. Perhaps her older sister was finally realizing that life was to be lived, rather than hoarded against an unseen tomorrow. Althea drew a deep breath of the spring air, savouring both it and her freedom.

'Where's Brashen?' Amber asked.

Althea groaned. 'Torturing Clef.'

Amber smiled. 'Someday Clef will thank Brashen for insisting that he learn his letters.'

'Perhaps, but this morning it does not seem likely. I had to leave them before I lost my temper with both of them. Clef spends more time arguing about why he cannot learn them than he does trying to learn them. Brashen gives him no ground. The boy is quick-witted on his seamanship. He should be able to learn his letters.'

'He will learn his letters,' Brashen asserted as he joined them. He pushed his hair back from his face with an ink-stained hand. He looked more like a frustrated tutor than a sea captain. 'I set him three pages to copy and left him. I warned him that good work would free him faster than messy.'

'There!' Paragon's voice boomed. His sudden shout flung a small flock of bright birds skyward from the looming forest. He lifted a big hand aloft, to point up and back into the trees. 'There. That is it.' He leaned, swaying the entire ship slightly. 'Semoy! Hard starboard!'

'You'll run aground!' Brashen cried in dismay. Semoy had not questioned the order. The ship swung in suddenly towards the looming trees.

'It's a mud bottom.' Paragon replied calmly. 'You'll get me off easily enough when you need to.'

Althea seized the railing, but instead of running aground, Paragon had found a deep if narrow channel of near-still water. Perhaps in the rainy season it was one of the many watercourses that fed the Rain Wild River. Now it was reduced to a finger of calm water winding back beneath the trees. They left the main channel of the Rain Wild River behind them. They did not get far, however, before Paragon's rigging began to tangle in the over-reaching branches. 'You're fouling your rigging,' Brashen warned him, but the ship deliberately moved deeper into the entangling mess. Althea exchanged an anxious grimace with him. He shook his head at her, and kept silent. Paragon was an independent soul. He had the right to command where his body would go. The new challenge to running this liveship was respecting his will for himself and crediting him with judgement. Even if it meant letting him run himself aground in a jungle lagoon.

There were questioning yells from several deckhands, but Semoy was steady on the wheel. Leaves and twiggy branches rained down on them. Startled birds gave cry and fled. The ship slowed and then stopped.

'We're here,' Paragon announced excitedly.

'We certainly are,' Brashen agreed sourly, staring up at the tangled mess.

'Igrot's hoard,' Amber breathed.

They both turned to look at her. Her gaze was following Paragon's pointing finger. Althea saw nothing save a dark mass high overhead in some ancient trees. The figurehead turned to regard them with a triumphant grin. 'She guessed first, and she guessed right,' he announced as if they had been playing a game.

Most of their reduced crew was on deck, staring up where Paragon had pointed. Igrot's infamous star had been branded deep in the bark of the near tree. Time had expanded the mark.

'Igrot's biggest haul,' Paragon reminisced, 'was when he took a treasure shipment meant for the Satrap of all Jamaillia. This was back in the days when the Satrapy sent a tribute ship once a year, to collect what was due him from his outlying settlements. Bingtown had put in Rain Wild goods, a rich haul of them. But en route to Jamaillia, the entire barge disappeared. None of it was ever seen again.'

'That was before my time, but I've heard of it,' Brashen said. 'Folk said it was the richest load ever to leave Trehaug. Some treasure chambers had been unearthed. All of it was lost.'

'Hidden,' Paragon corrected him. He looked again to the lofty trees. Althea peered up at the dark mass, festooned with vines and creepers, perched high. It spanned the live branches of several trees.

Paragon's voice was triumphant. 'Didn't you ever wonder why Igrot wanted a liveship? It was so he could have a place to hoard his trove, a place that no ordinary pirates could ever reach. Even if a member of his crew jabbered of where it was, robbers would need a liveship to recover it. He put in here, and his hearties travelled from my rigging to the trees. There they built a platform and hoisted the treasure up to it. He thought it would be safe forever.'

Brashen made a low sound. There was fury in his voice as he asked, 'Did he blind you before or after he selected this place?'

The figurehead didn't flinch from the question. 'After,' he said quietly. 'He never trusted me. With reason. I lost count of how many times I tried to kill him. He blinded me so that I could never find my way back without him.' He turned back to the awestruck crew on his deck and dropped Amber a slow wink. 'He never thought that anyone might recarve me. Neither did I, back then. Nevertheless, here I am. Sole survivor of that bloody crew. It's mine now. And hence, yours.' A stunned silence followed his words. No one spoke or moved.

The figurehead raised his eyebrows questioningly. 'No one wants to reclaim it for us?' he asked wryly.

Getting their first look at it was the easy part. Rigging catwalks and hoists through the trees to transport the stuff back to Paragon's deck was the time-consuming part. Despite the back-breaking labour, no one complained. 'As for Clef, you would think Paragon had planned this specifically to get him out of his lessons,' Brashen pointed out. As the ship's nimblest rigging monkey, the boy had been freed from his lessons for this task.

'If he grins any wider, the top half of his head may come off,' Althea agreed. She craned her neck to see Clef. A heavy sack bounced on his back as he made his way back to the ship. Neither snakes nor swarming insects had damped the boy's enthusiasm for his rope-walking trips back and forth between ship and platform. 'I wish he were a bit more cautious,' she worried.

She, Brashen and several crewmen stood on a layered platform of logs. The vines had reinforced the old structure with their growing strength through the years, actually incorporating it into their system of tendrils and air roots. The chests and barrels that had held Igrot's hoard had not fared as well. A good part of the day's work had been re-packing the spilled treasure into emptied food crates and casks. The variety of it astounded them. They had found Jamaillian coins and worked silver among the loot, a sure sign that Igrot had squirrelled more than just the Rain Wild hoard here. Some of his booty had not survived. There were the long-mouldered remains of tapestries and rugs, and heaps of iron rings atop the rotted leather that had once structured the battle-shirts. What had survived far outweighed what had perished. Brashen had seen jewelled cups, amazing swords that still gleamed sharp when drawn from their filigreed scabbards, necklaces and crowns, statues and vases, gameboards of ivory and marble with gleaming crystal playing pieces, and other items he could not even identify. There were humbler items as well, from serving trays and delicate teacups to carved hair combs and jewelled pins. Among the Rain Wild goods were a set of delicately-carved dragons with flakes of jewels for scales and a family of dolls with scaled faces. These last items Brashen was packing carefully into the onion basket from Paragon's galley.

'I think these are musical instruments, or what is left of them,' Althea theorized.

He turned, stretching his back, to see what she was doing.

She knelt, removing items from a big chest that had split its seams. She lifted chained crystals that tinkled and rang sweetly against one another as she freed them from their tomb and smiled as she turned to display them. She had forgotten that her hair was weighted with a net of jewelled chains. The motion caught glittering sunlight in her hair. She dazzled him. His heart swelled.

'Brashen?' she complained a moment later. He realized he was still staring at her. Without a word, he rose and went to her. He pulled her to his feet and kissed her, careless of the tolerant grins of two sailors who were scooping scattered coins into heavy canvas bags. He held her in his arms, still half-amazed that he could do this. He swept her closer. 'Don't ever go away from me,' he said thickly into her hair.

She turned her head up to grin at him. 'Why would I leave a rich man like you?' she teased. She put her hands on his chest and pushed gently free of him.

'I knew you were after my fortune,' he replied, letting her go. He held back a sigh. She always wanted to be clear of him before he was ready to let her go. It was her independent nature, he supposed. He refused to worry that she was wearying of him. Yet she had not seemed overly upset when he had been unable to arrange their wedding at the Traders' Concourse. Perhaps she did not wish to be bound to him quite that permanently. Then he chided himself for his lingering doubts and discontent. Althea was still beside him. That was more than he'd ever had in his life and it was worth more to him than this incomprehensible wealth of treasure.

He looked around the platform they stood on, then lifted his eyes to the similar structures in two adjacent trees. 'This booty will fill Paragon's hold. Igrot brought him here heavy with treasure, and so he will be when we leave. I try to imagine how this will change things for us, and I cannot. I get caught up in the wonder of the individual pieces.'

Althea nodded. 'I cannot relate it to myself. I think mostly of how it will affect others. My family. I can help Mother restore our home. Keffria need not worry so about the family finances.'

Brashen grinned. 'My plans are mostly for Paragon. New windows. New rigging. The services of a good sailmaker. Then, something for us. Let's make a trip south to the Spice Isles, a slow journey, exploring, with no schedules and no need to turn a profit. I want to revisit the ports we haven't seen since your father was master on Vivacia.' He watched her face carefully as he added, 'Maybe we could rendezvous with Wintrow and Vivacia. See how they're getting along.'

He watched her consider it. For Althea, a visit to the southernmost trade isles would be a return to the ports of her childhood travels. Maybe there she could lose some of the constant regret that overshadowed her. And perhaps seeing Wintrow and Vivacia could lay some ghosts to rest. If she saw her ship was content and in good hands, would it lift the burden from her heart? He refused to fear such an encounter. Much as it hurt him to admit, if he could not lift her melancholy soon, it might be better to let her go. It was not that she did not smile and laugh. She did. But always, her smiles and laughter faded too soon into a silence that excluded him.

'I'd like that,' she conceded, recalling him to himself. 'If Paragon could be persuaded. We could look for Tintaglia's serpents at the same time.'

'Good,' he said with false heartiness. 'That's what we'll do then.' He drew a deep breath and lifted his eyes. The brief spring day was closing. Through the interlacing tree tops, he could glimpse storm clouds. Winter might make a brief return tonight. 'Best get us all back to the ship for the night,' he decided. 'It gets dark fast, and I see no sense in risking man or treasure to move it tonight.'

Althea nodded. 'I'll want to see how they've stowed it anyway.' She turned to the others. 'Last load, men. Tomorrow is soon enough to finish this.'

*   *   *

She came out on deck into the darkness, bearing a lantern. Paragon did not turn to see who it was. He recognized Amber's light barefoot tread. She often came to him by night. They had had many night conversations. They had also shared many times without talk, content to let the sounds of the night birds and the river running remain undisturbed. Usually, her hands on his railing radiated peace to him. Tonight she hung the lantern on a hook, and set something down on his deck before she leaned on the railing.

'It's a lovely night, isn't it?'

'It is. But it won't be for long, for you. That lantern will attract every insect that flies. They are thickest immediately before a storm. Linger long and you'll be bitten all over.'

'I just need it for a short time.' She drew a breath, and he sensed an unusual excitement running through her. She sounded almost nervous. 'Paragon, earlier you offered to share your treasure with us. I've found something among it, something I desperately long to possess.'

He looked back at her. She was in her nightrobe, a long loose garment that reached to her bare feet. Her uneven hair fell loose to her shoulders. Her serpent scalds still showed, dead white against her golden skin. Time, perhaps, would erase those scars, or so he liked to think. In the lantern light, her eyes sparkled. He found himself returning her smile. 'So what is this treasure you must possess? Gold? Silver? Ancient Elderling jewellery?'

'This.' She stooped to a rough burlap sack at her feet, opened the mouth of it and reached within. From it, she pulled a carved wooden circlet. She handled it almost reverently as she turned it in her hands. Then, daringly, she crowned herself with it and then lifted her gaze to his. 'Reach into your dragon memories, if you can. For me. Do you recall this?'

He looked at her silently and she returned his gaze. She

waited. The crown was decorated with the heads of birds. No. Chickens. He quirked one eyebrow at her. Regretfully, she took off the crown and held it out to him. He took it carefully in his hands. Wood. Carved wood. He shook his head over it. Gold and silver, jewels and art. He had offered her the pick of the riches of the Cursed Shores. What did the carpenter choose? Wood.

She tried again to wake a response in him. 'It was gilded once. See. You can still see bits of gilt caught in the details of the rooster heads. And there are places for tail feathers to be set into it, but the feathers have rotted away long ago.'

'I remember it,' he said hesitantly. 'But that is all. Someone wore it.'

'Who?' she pressed him earnestly. He held it out to her and she took it back again. She shook her hair from her eyes, and then set the rooster crown on her head again. 'Someone like me?' she asked hopefully.

'Oh,' he paused, striving to recall her. 'I'm sorry,' he said, shaking his head at last. 'She wasn't an Elderling. That's all I can recollect of her.' The woman who wore it had been pale as milk. Not like Amber at all.

'That's all right,' she assured him quickly, but he sensed her disappointment. 'If you don't mind, I'd like to have this.'

'Of course. Did the others object?'

'I didn't ask them,' she replied sheepishly. 'I didn't give them the chance.' She took the crown off again. Her eyes and fingers wandered lovingly over the carving.

'It's yours,' Paragon confirmed. 'Take it with you when you go.'

'Ah. You guessed that I am leaving, then.'

'I did. You will not even stay with me until high summer? That is when I will return here, to be near when the dragons hatch.'

Her fingers tracked the details of the carved bird heads. 'I am tempted. Perhaps I will. But eventually, I think I must go north again. I have friends there. I haven't seen them in a long time.' She lowered her voice. 'A suspicion itches at me. I think I should go interfere in their lives some more.' She laughed with false lightness. 'I hope I will fare better with them than I have down here.' Her face grew troubled. She climbed suddenly to the railing, saying softly, 'Take me up.'

He reached over his shoulder to offer her his right hand. She climbed onto it and he turned back to contemplate the tangled jungle. It was easier to look away from the light and into the darkness. More restful. Carefully he shifted, until his arms were crossed on his chest. Trusting as a child, she sat on his crossed arms and leaned back against him companionably. All around them, night insects shrilled. Her bare legs dangled down.

She was always the one who dared to ask the questions others left unuttered. Tonight she had another one. 'How did they all die?'

He knew exactly what she meant. Pointless to pretend he didn't. And pointless to keep it a secret any more. It almost felt good to share it with someone. 'Wizardwood. Kennit kept a chunk from my face. One of his chores was to help with the cooking. He boiled it with the soup. Almost all of Igrot's crew died from it.' He felt her cringe.

He tried to make her understand. 'He was only finishing what Igrot had started. Men had begun to die on the ship. Igrot keel-hauled two sailors for insubordination. They both drowned. Two others went over the side during a stormy night watch. There was a stupid accident in the rigging. Three died. We decided Igrot was behind it. He probably meant to do away with anyone who knew where the treasure was hidden. Including Kennit.' He forced himself to unclench his hands. 'We had to do it, you see. To save Kennit's life.'

Amber swallowed. She asked the question anyway. 'And those that didn't die from the soup?'

Paragon took a breath. 'Kennit put them over the side anyway. Most were too poisoned to put up much of a fight.

Three, I think, managed to put out a boat and escape. I doubt they survived.'

'And Igrot?'

The jungle seemed a black and peaceful place. Things moved in it, outside the circle of the lantern light. Snakes and night birds, small tree-dwelling creatures, both furred and scaled. Many things lived and moved in the tangled dark.

'Kennit beat him to death. Belowdecks. You've seen the marks down there. The handprints of a crawling man.' He took a breath. 'It was fair, Amber. Only fair.'

She sighed. 'Vengeance for both of you. For the times when he had beaten Kennit to death.'

He nodded above her. 'Twice he did that. Once the boy died on my deck. But I couldn't let him go. I could not. He was all I had. Another time, curled up belowdecks in his hidey-hole, he died slowly. He was bleeding inside, growing so cold, so cold. He cried for his mother.' Paragon sighed. 'I kept him with me. I pushed life into him, and forced his body to mend itself as best as I could. Then I put him back in his body. Even then, I wondered if there was enough of him left to be a whole being. But I did it. It was selfish. I did not do it for Kennit. I did it for myself. So I would not be left alone again.'

'He truly was as much you as he was himself.'

Paragon almost chuckled. 'There was no such line between Kennit and me.'

'And that was why you had to have him back?'

'He couldn't die without me. Not any more than I could truly live without him. I had to take him back. Until I was whole again, I was vulnerable. I could not seal myself to others. Any blood shed on my deck was a torment to me.'

'Oh.'

For a long time, she seemed content to leave it at that. She leaned back against him. Her breathing became so deep and regular that he thought she slept. Behind him, on the deck, insects battered themselves against her lantern. He heard Semoy do a slow circuit of the deck. He paused by the lantern. 'All's well?' he asked Paragon quietly.

'All's well,' the ship replied. He had come to like Semoy. The man knew how to mind his own business. His footsteps receded again.

'Do you ever wonder,' Amber asked him quietly, 'how much you changed the world? Not just by keeping Kennit alive. By simply existing.'

'By being a ship instead of a dragon?'

'All of it.' A slight wave of her hand encompassed all his lives.

'I lived,' he said simply. 'And I've stayed alive. I suppose I had as much a right to do that as anyone.'

'Absolutely.' She shifted, then reclined in his arms to look up. He followed her gaze but saw only darkness. The clouds were thick beyond the trees. 'All of us have a right to our lives. But what if, for lack of guidance, we take the wrong paths? Take Wintrow for instance. What if he was meant to lead a different life? What if, because of something I failed to do or say, he became King of the Pirate Isles when he was meant to be a man leading a life of scholarly contemplation? A man whose destiny was to experience a cloistered, contemplative life becomes a king instead. His deep spiritual meditations never occur and are never shared with the world.'

Paragon shook his head. 'You worry too much.' His eyes tracked a moth. It fluttered earnestly by, intent on battering itself to death against the lantern. 'Humans live such short lives. I believe they have little impact on the world. So Wintrow will not be a priest. It is probably no more significant than if a man who was meant to be a king became a philosophical recluse instead.'

He felt a shiver run over her body. 'Oh, ship,' she rebuked him softly. 'Was that meant to be comforting?'

Carefully, he patted her as a father might soothe an infant.

'Take comfort in this, Amber. You are only one small, short-lived creature. You'd have to be a fool to think you could change the course of the whole world.'

She was silent until she broke out in a shaky laugh. 'Oh, Paragon, in that you are more right than you know, my friend.'

'Be content with your own life, my friend, and live it well. Let others decide for themselves what path they will follow.'

She frowned up at him. 'Even when you see, with absolute clarity, that it is wrong for them? That they hurt themselves?'

'Perhaps people have a right to their pain,' he hazarded. Reluctantly he added, 'Perhaps they even need it.'

'Perhaps,' she conceded unhappily. Then, 'Up, please. I think I shall go to bed and sleep on what you have told me. Before the rain and the mosquitoes find me.'

Althea smothered in nightmare. It did no good to know she dreamed. She could not escape it. She could not breathe, and he was on her back, bearing her down and hurting her, hurting her. She wanted to scream, and could not. If only she could scream, she could wake up, but she could not find the sound to give it vent. Her screams were trapped inside her.

The dream changed.

Paragon suddenly stood over her. He was a man, tall, dark-haired and grave. He looked at her with eyes like Kennit's. She cowered away from him. There was hurt in his voice when he spoke. 'Althea. Enough of this. Neither of us can endure it longer. Come to me,' he commanded her. 'Silently. Right now.'

'No.' She felt him plucking at her and she resisted. The knowing look in his eyes threatened her. No one should comprehend so fully what she felt.

'Yes,' he told her as she resisted. 'I know what I'm doing. Come to me.'

She could not breathe. She could not move. He was too big and too strong. But still she struggled. If she struggled and fought, how could it be her fault?

'It wasn't your fault. Come away from that memory; it isn't now. That is over and done. Let yourself be done with it. Be still, Althea, be still. If you scream, you'll wake yourself. Worse, you'll wake the whole crew.'

Then they all would know her shame.

'No, no, no. That isn't it at all. Just come to me. You have something of mine.'

The hand was gone from her mouth, the weight from her body, but she was still trapped inside herself. Then, abruptly, she floated free. She was somewhere else, somewhere cold and windy and dark. It was a very lonely place. Anyone's company was better than that isolation. 'Where are you?' she called, but it came out as a whisper.

'Here. Open your eyes.'

In a night storm, she stood on the foredeck. Rising wind shook the trees overhead, and little bits of debris fell in a dirty rain. Paragon had twisted to look back at her. She could not see his features, but she heard his voice. 'That's better,' he said reassuringly. 'I needed you to come here, to me. I waited, thinking that eventually you would come on your own. But you did not. And this has gone on far too long for all of us. I know now what I must do.' The figurehead paused. His next words came harder from him. 'You have something of mine. I want it back.'

'I have nothing of yours.' Did she speak the words, or only think them?

'Yes, you do. It's the last piece. Like it or not, I must have it, to make myself whole. To make you whole as well. You think it is yours. But you're wrong.' He glanced away from her. 'By right, that pain is mine.'

Rain had begun to fall, icy cold. She heard it first in the trees above. Then the drops found their way through the canopy. They fell gently at first. Then a rising wind whipped the treetops, and they dropped their cold burden in a deluge. Althea was already numbed to the cold. Paragon spoke on, softly. 'Give it back to me, Althea. There is no reason for you to keep it. It was never even his to give you. Do you understand that? He passed it on to you. He tried to get rid of pain by giving it away, but it was not his. It should have stayed with me. I take it back from you now. All you have to do is let it go. I leave you the memory, for that, I fear, is truly yours. But the hurt is an old hurt, passed on from one to another like a pestilence. I have decided to stop it. It comes back to me now, and with me it remains.'

For a time, she resisted, gripping it tightly. 'You can't take it from me. It was that horrible. It was that bad. No one would understand it, no one would believe it. If you take the pain away, you make a lie of what I endured.'

'No. No, my dear, I make it only a memory, instead of something that you live continuously in your mind. Leave it in the past. It cannot hurt you now. I will not let it.'

He reached a wide hand to her. Fearing him, but unable to resist, she set her small hand upon his. He sighed deeply. 'Give it back to me,' he said gently.

It was like having a deep splinter pulled. There was the dragging pain of the extraction, and then the clean sting of fresh blood flowing. Something clamped tight inside her suddenly eased. He had been right. She did not have to grip her pain. She could let it go. The memory was still there. It had not vanished, but it had changed. It was a memory, a thing from her past. This wound could close and heal. The injury done to her was over. She did not have to keep it as a part of herself. She could allow herself to heal. Her tears were diluted in the rain that ran down her face.

'Althea!'

She didn't even flinch. The continued rain was washing the

night from the sky, bleaching it to a grey dawn that barely penetrated the tree cover. Althea stood on the foredeck, hands outstretched to the dimness, as the pouring rain drenched her. It sealed her nightgown to her body. Cursing her and himself for a fool, Brashen dashed across the deck to seize her by the shoulder and shake her. 'Are you out of your mind? Come inside.'

She lifted a hand to her face, her eyes clenched shut in a grimace. Then she slammed suddenly into him, holding on to him tightly. 'Where am I?' she demanded dazedly.

'Out on deck. Sleepwalking, I think. I woke up and you were gone. Let's get inside.' Rain sluiced down his bare back and plastered his cotton trousers to his body. It made points of her fine hair and ran in streams down her face. She clung to him, making no effort to escape the deluge as she shivered.

'I had a dream,' she said disorientedly. 'It was so vivid, for just a flash, and now it is gone. I can't recall any of it.'

'Dreams are like that. They come and go. They don't mean anything.' He feared that he spoke from experience.

With a roar, the storm renewed its fury. The pelting rain made a hissing sound on the water of the open river that reached them even here.

She didn't move. She looked up at him, blinking water from her eyes. 'Brashen, I –'

'I'm drowning out here,' he announced impatiently, and swooped her suddenly into his arms. She leaned her head against his shoulder as he carried her. She made no protest even when he bumped her head in the narrow companionway. In his stateroom, he kicked the door shut and lowered her to her feet. He pushed his hair back from his face and felt a fresh trickle of water down his back. She stood blinking at him. Rain dripped from her chin and eyelashes. The wet cloth of her nightgown clung to every curve of her body, tempting him. She looked so bewildered that he wanted to take her in his arms and hold her. But she would not want that. With difficulty he turned away from her. 'It's near morning. I'm getting into some dry clothes,' he said gruffly.

He heard the wet slap of her nightgown falling to the floor and the small sounds of her rummaging through her clothing chest. He would not turn. He would not torment himself. He had learned to rein himself in.

He had just found a clean shirt in his cupboard when she embraced him from behind. Her skin was still wet where she pressed against him. 'I can't find any clean clothes,' she said by his ear. He stood stock-still. Her breath was warm. 'I'm afraid I'll have to take yours.' The kiss on the side of his neck sent a shiver down his back and put the lie to her words as she took the shirt from his hands and tossed it to the floor behind them.

He turned slowly in her arms to face her and looked down into her smile. Her playfulness astounded him. He had almost forgotten she could be like this. The boldness of her expressed desire set his heart racing. Her breasts brushed his chest. He set a hand to her cheek, and saw a shadow of uncertainty cross her face. He instantly took his hand away.

Dismay washed her smile away. Tears suddenly welled in her eyes. 'Oh, no,' she pleaded. 'Please don't give up on me.' Some decision came to her. She seized his hand and set it to her face. The words broke from her. 'He raped me, Brashen. Kennit. I've been trying to get past it. All the time that . . . I just wanted you,' she said brokenly. 'Only you. Oh, Brashen.' Some emotion suddenly stole her words. She pressed herself against him, hiding her face against his chest. 'Please tell me it can still be good between us.'

He'd known. On some level, he'd known.

'You should have told me.' That sounded like an accusation. 'I should have guessed,' he accused himself.

She shook her head. 'Can we begin again?' she asked him. 'And go slowly this time?'

He felt a thousand things. Killing fury for Kennit. Anger at himself that he had not protected her. Hurt that she had not told him earlier. How was he to deal with all of it? Then he knew what she meant. By beginning again. He took a deep breath. With an effort, he set it all aside. 'I think we have to,' he replied gravely. He resigned himself to patience. He studied her face. 'Would you like to have this room to yourself for a time? Until you feel differently about . . . everything? I know we must go slowly.'

She shook tears from her eyes. The smile she gave him seemed more genuine now. 'Oh, Brashen, not that slowly,' she disagreed. 'I meant we should begin again now. With this.' She lifted her mouth to his. He kissed her very gently. It shocked him when he felt the darting tip of her tongue. She took an uneven breath. 'You should get out of these wet trousers,' she chided him. Her rain-chilled fingers fumbled at his waist.

Paragon turned his face up to the sky. Rain ran over his closed eyes and into his mouth. The chill of winter eased from it as the sun touched the day more surely. He blinked his eyes open and smiled. As the rain suddenly pattered into cessation, a bird sang questioningly in the distance. Closer to hand, another answered it. Life was good.

A short time later, he felt Amber set one hand to his railing. Beside it, she rested a hot mug of something. 'You're up early,' he greeted her.

He glanced over his shoulder to find her studying him carefully. She was smiling. 'I awoke suffused with a singular feeling of well-being.'

'Did you?' He smiled smugly, then looked back to the day. 'I think I know the feeling. Amber, I think my luck is changing.'

'And everyone else's with it.'

'I suppose so.' He pondered briefly. 'Do you remember what we discussed last night?'

'I do.' She waited.

'I've changed my mind. You're right to want to go north again.' He looked around at the wonder of the spring world. 'It feels good to set people on the right path.' He smiled at her again. 'Go north.'

EPILOGUE

Metamorphosis

Shreever rested. There was no more striving, no more struggling. Even her pain had dulled to a nagging pulse. She hovered between, in the darkness that was neither serpent nor dragon. There was peace to this inevitability. When summer came, Tintaglia would scratch away the thick layer of leaves that sheltered them. When the hot light of summer touched her case, she would emerge as a dragon.

The tortuous journey was finally over. When Paragon and She Who Remembers had brought them to the mouth of the river, the serpents had been incredulous. Not one of them recognized this wild and milky flow as the ancient Serpent River. They had followed them with deep misgivings. Many had died. Only Tintaglia's frantic urging had given Shreever the heart to continue. When they had reached the awkward log construction the humans had flung up to aid them, she had despaired. The water was too shallow, the turns too tight to negotiate comfortably. The humans obviously knew nothing of serpents, and she could not trust them. Just when she had given up, a young Elderling had appeared. Heedless of the dangers of the rushing water and the toxic skin of the struggling serpents, he had walked out onto the structures and urged her to continue. In words sweet as the rush of wind over wings, he reminded them of all that awaited them when they emerged from their cocoons. He had focused her thoughts on the future. She had seen the others take heart as well, ignoring pain to struggle on through the maze.

Wallowing out on the bank had been torment. This was supposed to have been done in mild weather, not in the harsh chill of winter. Her skin began to dry too swiftly. She could not trust the humans who hastened towards her, and they obviously feared her mane. They dumped loads of silver-streaked mud near her. She wallowed in it, trying to coat herself. All around her, others did the same. Tintaglia walked amongst them, exhorting them. Some lacked the strength to devour the mud and regurgitate it mixed with the secretions that changed it into long strands. Shreever felt her own back would break as she strove to lift her head high enough to weave a complete cocoon around herself.

She had seen both Sessurea and Maulkin cocooned before she had managed to finish her own case. As they grew still and their cases dried to a dull grey, she felt both abandoned and grateful. She was glad to see them safe. Those two, at least, had a chance of emerging beside her. Slender Tellur the minstrel had died at the ship battle. Chalcedeans had slain scarlet Sylic, but immense Kelaro was encased not far from her. She would not dwell on those who had perished, she told herself, but would await the sun and the emergence of her friends who had survived.

She let her weary mind drift into dreams of high summer. In her dreams, the skies were filled with dragons. The Lords of the Three Realms had returned.